Luminosity

Luminosity

a novel

Frank & Gillian

RANDOM HOUSE OF CANADA

⑥

The authors would like to thank the
Ontario Arts Council for a Works-in-Progress grant,
which enabled them to finish this book.

⑥

Luminosity is a work of fiction. Certain characters should not be confused with their
real-life counterparts — most notably Ted Serios. For the real story of Ted Serios,
we refer the reader to Jule Eisenbud's *The World of Ted Serios: "Thoughtographic"*
Studies of an Extraordinary Mind (London: McFarland & Company, 1989).

Canadian Cataloguing in Publication Data

McEnaney, Frank, 1944–
Luminosity

ISBN 0-679-30923-3

I. Gillian, 1956-   . II. Title.

PS8575.E5L85 1998   C813'.54   C98-930785-9
PR9199.3.M33L85 1998

10 9 8 7 6 5 4 3 2 1

To
Tanya Trafford

God Appears & God is Light
To those poor Souls who dwell in Night,
But does a Human Form Display
To those who Dwell in Realms of day.

PHOTOGRAPHY. In the twentieth century we are surrounded and enveloped by photographs. Photographs in magazines, on billboards, in newspapers. Photographs taken by ourselves of friends and family. Moving photographs on the screen. Photographs of our very insides, our bones and our guts. Everywhere we go, everywhere we turn, we are face to face with images on celluloid. But surrounded as we are by photographs, we seldom stop to think what a mysterious thing a photo is. Light: that most insubstantial of things — not a thing, a wave; not a wave, a particle; in fact, neither a wave nor a particle, but both — a paradox, a contradiction — light somehow interacts with silver nitrate and an image is born.

This is a story about photography and so I'm going to start with the developing of a photo. In a tray there is a sheet of paper and on that sheet of paper an image is starting to form. It is an image of a girl's hair, beautiful and lustrous, each strand delineated as if illuminated from within. Standing watching the photo develop are two young men in their early twenties. One is my friend Breetz, the other is me. The year is nineteen sixty.

IN THE FALL OF NINETEEN SIXTY I was in my last year of university. Breetz had a job at Halberstam's Photography and Mr Halberstam, like everybody else, loved Breetz and gave him the run of the shop. Upstairs there was a small studio and every couple of weeks Breetz would use it for one of his shoots. Word quickly spread among aspiring models in Toronto that Breetz Mestrovic was working on a portfolio and so there was no shortage of beautiful girls willing to come up and pose for him. I assisted at these shoots. I'd hand Breetz his Leica, change the film on the other camera, arrange lights, do my best to keep the girls charmed and generally stay in the background — as I always had with Breetz. There were dozens of sessions that summer and fall, and I don't suppose there were many young men who saw as many gorgeous girls as I did. It's almost impossible to remember the beautiful ones. There were so many of them, and somehow they looked like all the other beautiful girls that one sees in magazines and newspapers. Tall and blonde, dark and languorous, short and perky, dazzling smile after dazzling smile. Beautiful shoulders and hips and legs. When I try to think of them now, so many years later, they all just blend in together. All but Katlyn.

A more inconspicuous girl you couldn't imagine. She stood there, awkward and shy, and while the two other girls twirled and posed she seemed to get more and more awkward and confused as the session went on. Breetz, of course, was his usual whirling dervish self.

"Part those luscious lips, more shoulder, let's see that hair."

He was addressing the shy one with the long strawberry-blonde hair. Katlyn. She looked at him.

At the time I didn't know what she was thinking; she just looked pained and awkward. But I know now. Katlyn was thinking about her mother.

She was thinking, "Is this what my mother paid all that money for? So I could dance around on this sheet of paper with two other girls while this maniac clicks furiously away?"

The more the other two girls responded to Breetz's *beautiful, beautiful, beautiful*s, the more she stiffened up.

Breetz sensed this session wasn't taking off because of the shy girl. He thought he knew what it was. He'd been focusing his attention on the other two. If he were to get any good pictures, he'd have to draw this one out somehow. Every girl had some feature that she was proud of and that could be played upon. This one wasn't stunningly good-looking, like the ash blonde, nor did she have the sophisticated languor of the brunette, but she had something. Hair. Beautiful lustrous hair. He would use the hair. He had an image of all that beautiful shining hair streaming out behind the girl.

"That hair, honey, beautiful hair, fantastic hair, we've just got to get it moving. I want you to toss it, swing it, swing it back and forth."

Katlyn tossed her hair.

"Good, more, give me more."

Katlyn did as he said in the hope that he'd leave her alone. But he wouldn't.

"Come on. Give me some of that hair. C'mon, Beautiful! That's it! Beautiful, now bend forward."

Katlyn bent over. The photographer's hands gathered her hair and flipped it forward so that it hung in front of her like a curtain.

"Yes, yes! That's beautiful. We're getting something here, yes. Keep it. Keep that pose."

And that's when the memory came — her mother, sitting on the edge of the bed, with the brush in her hand. "Bend over, Katlyn." Katlyn would bend forward, and her mother would take the brush and, with long, agonizingly slow strokes from the nape of her neck to the ends of her hair, brush and stroke, brush and stroke, and brush and brush and brush. One hundred times. She'd count out loud as she slowly brushed and stroked: One...two...three...and Katlyn would silently plead with her to go faster. If she said Hurry up, though, that only made things worse. That meant her mother would continue to slowly brush, but also lecture her on the importance of taking care of her beautiful hair, and then she'd lose count and have to start again: One...two...three...

"Beautiful, beautiful, stay with that pose, stay with it. Beautiful, beautiful!"

Katlyn was seething. Bent over like that, the stupid photographer oohing and aahing over her hair, she could feel her mother's hands stroking her. She could feel the bristles. She could smell her mother's perfume.

Katlyn stood up. She couldn't bear it, not a second longer. All that fuss about her hair. She stepped off the paper, away from the lights, and grabbed her bag. Then she left the studio.

Millie the model. When she was a child her mother had given her *Millie the Model* comics. At Christmas in her stocking, *Millie the Model*. At the beach in the summer, old *Millie the Model* comics, wrapped in plastic in packets of three. *Millie the Model*. Always *Millie the Model*.

On the corner of Bloor and St George there was a small drugstore. Impulsively, she turned and went in.

"Can I help you, miss?"

"Yes, I'd like those." Katlyn pointed to a pair of household scissors.

The man took them out from beneath the glass counter.

Back on the street, Katlyn took a huge hank of hair in her left hand. Then, with her right, she opened the scissors and pressed them as close to her scalp as she could. With all her might, she squeezed: the scissor blades sliced through the strawberry-blonde hair. With a sweep of her hand, Katlyn tossed the hank into the air. The wind caught it, shimmering it into strands. She grabbed another hank.

Shrinking Violet comics. Those had been Katlyn's favourites. Shrinking Violet could make herself so infinitesimally small, she seemed to disappear.

IN THE LATE NINETEEN THIRTIES the dark clouds of Nazism were gathering over Europe. Ivan Mestrovic was a jeweller in the town of Split, Yugoslavia. Although Yugoslavia was not directly threatened by Nazi Germany, Ivan took the precaution of sending his wife and infant son abroad. In 1941 Hitler was about to launch an invasion of Russia and to do so required transit for his troops through Yugoslavia. Permission was refused and, enraged, Hitler ordered Nazi troops to invade. When this happened, Ivan abandoned his business and joined Tito's partisans in the mountains. There, he died, one of many unsung heroes of that courageous resistance.

Eventually, Anna and Breetz arrived in Toronto. Anna, penniless by this time, needed work. Of course, there was a lot of work to be had in the booming wartime economy, but Anna had a problem. If she worked in a factory, who would take care of baby? Her baby, her beloved Breetz. And so this once prominent citizen of Split decided that the best way she could support her son was through housework. Something she had never done a great deal of, but something she understood. She had only one condition: baby must come.

"Certainly," said my mother. "By all means bring baby."

And that was how I met Breetz. I was sitting in my playroom full of toys. Toys that meant nothing to me. Toys that sat there waiting to come alive. Then the woman came in, and in her arms she had a little boy. A little boy with black hair and black eyes, squirming to be free of his mother's grip the second he saw the room full of toys. Anna set him down beside me.

"This is my beautiful Breetz," she said. "And your name?"

Richard, I remember thinking, but I didn't say it out loud. I just watched amazed as Breetz went wild with my toys. He made the top spin, he magically brought the pieces of the wooden puzzle together to form a star, he got into the Plasticine, the finger paints, the xylophone. And best of all, a pull-toy. A cricket that made the most wonderful clacking racket.

I was a solitary child. My parents weren't around much, especially when I was a baby. My father was one of Mackenzie King's wartime industrial advisers and my mother kept herself busy with

War Drives and the Red Cross. So when the exuberant little boy with black eyes arrived in my life, and it was clear to all that I adored him, my mother was quick to take advantage of it. Soon our house was the cleanest house in Rosedale, as my mother had Anna over Mondays *and* Wednesdays. By the time I was five years old I was spending many a Saturday afternoon with Breetz and Anna at their apartment. We would go shopping in Kensington Market and on wet rainy days Anna would take us to a movie. Then we would go back to my house on Glen Road and my mother and Anna would have tea in the south-facing conservatory — Anna's favourite room.

Our house backed onto a ravine. Breetz and I spent hours down by the creek fishing out tadpoles and building forts. When we'd come up, Anna would be finished her cleaning and she'd make tea. My mother would arrive home from one of her meetings and Breetz and I would sit up at the counter in the kitchen and tell our mothers all about our exciting discoveries.

When I was seven and my mother bought me a bike, she bought Breetz one too because she knew one bike would just lie rusting in the garage, whereas with two we would be all over the neighbourhood.

Throughout the war I hardly saw my father. He would come home occasionally with totally inappropriate gifts and then disappear again for long periods. This didn't change. Even long after the war was over, my father seemed to be always away.

When I was twelve years old my father came back from six weeks in Germany. As usual, there was a present. He handed me a small package wrapped in tissue and I knew by the attention I was getting opening it that this was something special. When I tore the last bit of tissue away I saw a camera.

"Thanks," I said.

I knew I was expected to show more excitement but I'd never been interested in cameras and for me it was just one more instance of my father not knowing what I really cared about. Like the time he'd given me a scale-model steam engine that actually worked, the little boiler powered by sterno tabs. And my first chemistry set at age eight. Although that one was never even opened, I received the advanced model on my tenth birthday.

"This is a Leica," my father said, lifting the camera out of my hands and looking at me through the lens. "Best camera in the world, son."

I felt a pang of regret. If only I could muster up the same kind of enthusiasm for this camera as I could for my books. At any rate, two weeks later, when my father asked where the Leica was, I tried to sound offhand.

"Oh," I said. "I've loaned it to Breetz for a while."

I hadn't loaned it to Breetz, of course — I'd given it to him. Because the moment Breetz had seen the Leica he'd fallen madly in love.

As soon as Breetz started taking photos, magic happened. That first year, Breetz photographed everything, and anything. Tadpoles, flowers, rocks and trees. But it wasn't long before Breetz found what he liked photographing best. Girls. At first, just girls he knew. Girls at school, girls in the neighbourhood. They'd giggle and protest, and say they didn't take a good picture, but a couple of days later when they saw the prints they would be amazed and delighted. Breetz always got something. It wasn't long before older girls started getting interested. Janet Marchand's older sister, Elly, and her friend Samantha. No doubt about it, Breetz had a knack. A knack for putting girls at ease. A knack for the best angle. A knack for making each and every girl look her best. The plain girls looked pretty. The pretty girls looked beautiful. And the beautiful girls, gorgeous.

When I was about to turn thirteen, my father was in Oslo. He wired my mother asking her to find out what I wanted for my birthday and saying anything I wanted I could have, whatever the cost. I didn't give it much thought, but my mother kept pressing me. As the day drew nearer and my mother tired of being met with shrugs, she decided that Breetz would know what I wanted if anyone would.

"A darkroom," said Breetz.

"A darkroom?"

"Yes," said Breetz. "You know — a real darkroom with an enlarger and safe light and running water."

"Running water?" my mother asked.

"Oh, yes. He'll need running water to wash the developer off."

This solved a problem for everybody. My mother was able to write my father in Norway with an answer, my father got the satisfaction of knowing that his original gift was bearing fruit, I was able to let my father give me something special, and Breetz got a darkroom.

FROM MY VANTAGE POINT NOW, that Saturday morning in 1960 stands out as a significant day. At the time it was just a Saturday morning like so many other Saturday mornings where Breetz and I disappeared into the darkroom to develop the week's prints. We'd been doing this for so many Saturdays that we had it down to more or less a routine. I'd check the negatives for dust; Breetz would check the developing fluid. I'd hang the contact prints; he'd examine them with a magnifying glass. Then he'd quickly choose the four or five shots he wanted to print out of the hundreds he'd taken. I remember he was especially excited about some shots of the buxom blonde.

"Wow," he said. "Now this is a photo. Look at the way she moves. The umbrella sequence really worked. Look at this, look at this one, Richard — it's like the umbrella is trying to seduce her — she's resisting, she's resisting, then she lets go."

As I write this now, the notion of an umbrella seducing a woman seems slightly revolting, but there was nothing salacious in the way Breetz spoke. He was a professional, and it was the image that excited him, not the implications of it. But while he got more and more excited about The Umbrella Sequence, I found myself looking over a different contact sheet, the one that Breetz figured was a waster. We'd developed it as a contact sheet only because Breetz always insisted on developing everything he'd shot. I could see why Breetz hadn't given it more than a cursory glance. None of the contacts had what he called oomph, that peculiar quality of lifting off the paper. They were either dull and lifeless, posed and awkward, or complete duds. Just black. Then about halfway through the contact sheet began the series of the girl with the strawberry-blonde hair.

I found myself drawn to these photos, especially the ones of her hair only. But then, when I started to examine these, I noticed something odd about the photos preceding them. In each one there was a kind of blotch or blur over her hair. As it was my job to check for dust, and I knew I'd done a good job, these blotches puzzled me. I made Breetz come over and examine them.

"It's a defect," he said.

"I know that," I remember saying. "But what caused it?"

"I don't know," said Breetz. "A speck of dust...a problem with the emulsion...maybe just some dud film."

"You checked the emulsion," I said. "I checked for dust. And if there's a defect in the film, why only on these few shots?"

Breetz just shrugged and went back to enlarging The Umbrella Sequence.

This little exchange pretty much sums up our relationship and explains, I'm sure, a lot of our attraction to each other as friends. Breetz was single-minded. He saw what worked and that's what interested him. He was like that inside the darkroom and out. I, on the other hand, have always been easily knocked from my path. I go off on tangents. A blob on a photo that I couldn't understand interested me more than a beautiful photo that I could. So, as Breetz was tilting the lamp housing and putting the negative in place, my fascination with the photos of The Girl with the Strawberry-Blonde Hair was growing. Particularly with the last in the series. The more I looked at that photo, the more unusual it seemed. Of course I was just looking at a one-inch-by-one-inch contact print, so I couldn't really define in my mind what it was that intrigued me.

"Develop this one, Breetz."

"Richard, I've looked at that sheet, and they're all wasters. Every one."

"Develop this print, Breetz."

From the day Anna had plunked him down in my playroom, Breetz had always been the leader in our relationship. He'd decide the day's activities and I'd follow along. But every now and then, when we were building a fort or going to a movie or riding our bikes, I'd see something that interested me and even though the roof of the fort was just about to go on, or the movie was just about to begin, everything had to stop while I explored whatever had piqued my curiosity. Breetz usually put up some token resistance, but once he saw that mule look in my eye he knew it was useless. This was clearly one of those times.

"Sure. Okay. Now or later?"

"Now," I said. "Right now."

I handed Breetz the negative and turned off the lights. Insert paper — set exposure — set timer to ten seconds — place the paper in the developer and set the timer again for one minute. We didn't talk during this minute. Breetz's hands were rocking the tray, but his mind was elsewhere. I was still puzzling over the blotches. Neither of us was watching the developing photo.

Ding.

Both Breetz and I looked in the tray at the sound of the timer. In the tray was the white paper with the merest shadow of an image.

"That's funny," Breetz said.

"Maybe it needs another half-minute," I said.

"Maybe," Breetz said. But after another thirty seconds the image was sharper though by no means fully developed.

"Is the developer tired?" I asked.

"No. It's fresh. I just changed it."

"Look — "

Breetz looked and, sure enough, the image was getting clearer. Paradoxically, clearer and brighter. Usually if a photo is overexposed it gets brighter and blurrier, but something strange was going on here. The photo kept getting brighter and brighter, but at the same time more and more distinct, as if it were illuminated from within. As if the source of the light were the hair itself. We stood there, mesmerized, watching this strange image form before our eyes. Then suddenly Breetz grabbed the tongs and pulled the photo out, dropping it into the stop bath.

"How long was that, Richard?"

"Had to be five minutes."

Breetz kept dabbing at the photo to keep it submerged. The image swimming before us was arresting. It was simply a sweep of lustrous hair, each strand delineated, and there was only a glimpse of skin — a bit of shoulder and nape — but the skin was pearly soft, a velvety contrast to the strands of hair. What was most arresting about the photo was its luminosity. "You know, Richard," Breetz said, lifting the print by the edges to place it in the fixer, "you were right to develop this. The more I look at it, the more I like it."

"WHAT-IN-GOD'S-NAME-HAVE-YOU-DONE-TO-YOUR-HAIR?"

"I cut it."

The fight with her mother lasted well into the night, until Katlyn had finally cried herself to sleep. And then her mother had woken her with a cup of tea and started in again, before Katlyn had even got out of bed.

"After all the money your father and I spent on you..."

But Katlyn stood up to her. Fought back. That hadn't happened in years. The last fight they'd had was when Katlyn was about twelve and ever since then there had been harmony in the household. All it took to maintain harmony was capitulation on Katlyn's part. So she'd done modelling school at thirteen.

She'd felt so silly with all that makeup on, especially at the graduation, with the older girls saying how cute she was. She got some work, though, because she was pretty and young. Catalogue work, standing with her hand on another girl's shoulder, staring off at nothing, grinning at no one. And, of course — the barrettes. Teen Tyme Barrettes. That was Katlyn's ponytail on the little pink cardboard insert. Her mother's proudest moment. She was upset, of course, that Katlyn was only in profile. Less than profile, really, as you couldn't see her lips, just her right ear and cheekbone and a hint of nose. But it was *her* and her mother never left the house without a Teen Tyme Barrette package in her purse.

The modelling work ended. Just dried up. Mercifully, for Katlyn, devastating for her mother. Then one day a friend of her mother's suggested acting classes and Katlyn thought, Oh, no, here we go again.

The friend had suggested it as a way of overcoming shyness and

Katlyn dreaded it. But to her surprise, her teacher was wonderful. Ruby Nielson didn't ooh and aah about Katlyn's looks; Ruby praised her without singling her out. Ruby challenged her for the first time in her life. Three hours a week, Wednesday nights, saved Katlyn from going insane. No matter how dull things got at school, no matter how tense things got at home, Katlyn had Wednesday nights. And Ruby Nielson.

But that ended too. Parents were invited to the last class before summer and the students put on a loosely structured show of exercises. Katlyn played a tree, a porcupine and, best of all, a tramp. It was while she was blowing her nose as the tramp that she caught sight of her mother. Spine stiff, nostrils flaring. Later, over cookies and cider, Katlyn prayed her mother wouldn't make a scene. She noticed Ruby coming towards them. Please, please, she silently begged. Please don't say anything, Mother.

Katlyn knew all too well what her mother would think of Ruby's frizzy salt-and-pepper hair and very lined face. She was wearing a long black skirt, ballet slippers and a man's shirt. Katlyn's mother looked her up and down slowly, but it didn't faze Ruby in the least.

"You were marvellous, Katie," Ruby said, and Katlyn's feelings were torn. She wanted to be pleased by her teacher's praise, but she was afraid her mother would spit out something about grovelling around like a beggar hardly being marvellous. Or worse, tell Ruby it was "Katlyn," not "Katie." She didn't get time to do either, as Ruby was looking right at her mother and saying something.

"You know, your daughter has talent. She has real presence on stage. I hope she continues — "

"Yes," said her mother, stroking Katlyn's hair. "Yes," she said, "Katlyn is very beautiful. Good day."

They left. And when they got home her father asked her how it had gone, but Katlyn disappeared into her room and didn't even listen at the door to hear what might be said. She disappeared into a fog that day. Back into the fog of total capitulation. She took the additional modelling classes her mother signed her up for. She went to the interviews, made the rounds. She did it all and felt nothing. Stand, turn, smile. Smile some more. She did it all in the most mechanical fashion and the beauty of it was — her mother never noticed. As long as she went through the motions of doing herself up and taking her classes, her mother never noticed the complete absence of vitality.

And Katlyn had gone on in that way for nearly three years. Three years when other girls were dating and giggling and pushing the limits of household rules. Those were, and probably always would be, the happiest years of her mother's life. Her daughter looked good, didn't talk back, stood up straight, did her hair and her exercises and her makeup every day. But Katlyn was wound tight. She was wound so tight she could be wound no further and at the height of that photo session she'd started to unwind. By the time she walked through her mother's door and heard that line, What-in-God's-name-have-you-done-to-your-hair, she spun out completely.

In the morning she packed. She packed slacks and sweaters and sneakers. No skirts or slips, no dainty high-heeled pumps with bows on the toes. She packed things she could feel comfortable in, invisible in, and she left. It hadn't occurred to her to find a place to stay in Toronto — her mother would find her somehow — or to go to a friend's house. She had no friends. So she went to Union Station and bought a ticket to Montreal. She could be anonymous in Montreal.

Sitting on the Rapido, watching the countryside whisk by, Katlyn felt only relief. She could get up now and grab a muffin and coffee from the snack bar and not a head would turn. She could sit there, her ankle on her knee, sipping coffee, feeling comfortable. Almost at home. She could be in the world without having to leave it. As a woman teetered by on high heels, lurching with the movement of the train, Katlyn smiled and made a promise to herself: never again. She raised her paper cup to the reflection in the window. The reflection had short short hair and a big grin on its face.

"Never again," it said back.

EVER SINCE THE JULY '56 *VOGUE*, which had tripled newsstand sales, Diana Vreeland had been angling to get Marilyn Monroe on the cover again. But the creature was evasive as only she could be.

She'd never said an outright no, but she'd never said yes, either. That maddening vagueness. Then one day she turned up at the office — drifting in as if she had nothing better to do. Diana knew just how to handle the situation. She invited Marilyn into her office and then went on with her day as if nothing unusual had happened. She pretended that the upcoming deadline was engrossing her, all the while chatting with Marilyn. She took calls, but stayed at her desk. The trick to handling Marilyn Monroe was to go on as though she weren't there yet somehow give her your complete attention. Marilyn kicked off her shoes and began strolling around in her bare feet.

"What are these?" she asked.

Diana looked up from her desk. Marilyn was picking over a table piled high with large manilla envelopes, each one with a *Vogue* letter attached to it.

"Those? That's our unsolicited pile."

"What do you do with them?"

"Jeannie types up a nice rejection and I sign."

"Don't you even look at them?"

"Certainly not."

Marilyn giggled, pulled out an envelope and started to flip through the photos. Diana made a few phone calls. Marilyn opened another envelope, riffled through the contents, then carefully put it back and picked up another. Diana slipped on her reading glasses and pretended to study a layout. Marilyn picked up another envelope. Diana knew that though Marilyn appeared childlike and scattered she was capable, at times, of amazing concentration, especially when it came to photographs. And so Marilyn sat for most of the afternoon looking at one shot after another of aspiring models. She never tired of this. Light, shadow, bone structure, makeup. What made one pose work and not another. She was well into the pile when she came across something that stopped her.

It was a photograph of hair, a simple sweep of lustrous hair, each strand delineated, and there was only a glimpse of skin — a bit of shoulder and nape — but the skin was pearly soft, a velvety contrast to the radiant strands. It was a Marilyn photograph, she thought. It had that same soft, velvety yet luminous quality. A Marilyn photograph.

She looked at it again, then set it aside, placing it on top of its envelope. Cursorily, she went through the rest of the pile. Then she stood, slipped back into her shoes and strolled over to Diana's desk.

"Him," she said.

Diana looked up.

"I'll do another shoot with *Vogue*, Diana — if it's with the guy who took this."

KATLYN LOVED MONTREAL. She arrived with hardly any money, knowing hardly any French, without a job or a place to stay and yet within a week she was happier than she'd ever thought possible. She got a small piale on Sherbrooke Street and the same day started looking for a job. She checked the newspapers, but she was most comfortable just walking along the crowded streets looking for RECHERCHE signs. It was on her second day that she walked into a little café on Ste-Catherine Street — Chez Madelaine. Madelaine herself was an enormous woman with jet-black hair, blood-red nails and wearing what seemed like pajamas. Madelaine didn't so much interview her as quiz her.

"Speak French?"

"A little, but I'm hoping — "

"How old?"

"I'll be eighteen in — "

"Not a runaway, I hope."

"No, well — "

"Ever washed dishes?"

"Well, at home I — "

"Ever wait tables?"

"No, but — "

"Ever worked a goddamn day in your life?"

"Not really, no, but I'm — "

"T'entends ça, Warford?" Madelaine called over her shoulder.

A thin older man was sweeping the hardwood floors. He seemed to be about to say something when Madelaine continued.

"Moins de dix-huit ans, jamais bossé de sa vie, parle pas un mot de français, assez bête pour ne pas reconnaître un boulot impossible."

"Prends la," Warford said. "Vite, avant qu'elle change d'avis."

"You can start tomorrow," Madelaine said. "What's your name?"

"Kate," Katlyn said.

"Kate," Madelaine repeated.

"Kate," said Warford.

It was only after the second repetition that she realized she had a new name. A name she'd given herself: Kate. No more explanations — Katlyn with a K, no I, A-T-L-Y-N. From now on she would be Kate. Just Kate. She liked it.

WHEN BREETZ AND I were boys and that inevitable tired old question got asked — What do you want to be when you grow up? — Breetz, from the time he turned fourteen, answered the same way: I want to go to New York and photograph beautiful women. I, on the other hand, had a different answer every time — Archaeologist, Egyptologist, Cosmologist — and each new ology so excited me I'd share it with anyone who'd listen. When I grew up, I was going to be an explorer and go to the Amazon and discover the lost temples of the Incas. When I grew up I was going to be a physicist like Einstein and come up with a new theory of the universe. I was interested in everything, but obsessed with nothing. And things weren't any better once I got to university.

I'd started out in History, a nice general subject I thought, only to find that the professors kept getting bogged down in details. One was concerned with the flow of capital from the Old World to the New. Another studied shifts in populations between cities and the countryside. Each one seemed to find his own particular area immensely more important than the general picture, which was what interested me.

I began auditing classes, and that was when I came up with the strategy that made university tolerable. I would find an engaging professor and then take his or her course. While this strategy made university possible, by the beginning of fourth year, when I started thinking about grad schools, my transcript was a hodgepodge. I had great marks, but when I thought about applying for, say, Linguistics at Cornell, it turned out I didn't have all the requirements. Since there was no question that Richard Bonnycastle Hathaway would go to Graduate School, I was forced to concentrate on one subject, so I chose Philosophy — Hume, Hobbes, Descartes, Kant. Philosophy wasn't what I wanted it to be either. It wasn't thinking, it was the Study of Thought, which was something completely different. No professor was interested in my thoughts, they were interested in my ability to regurgitate other peoples' thoughts. And I was getting so that I could hardly stomach another syllogism.

I was nearing the end of my fourth year and the problem was becoming more pressing: what to do when I grew up now that I'd grown up.

"Come on, Richard," Breetz said. "We know the deadline's passed. What's your decision?"

It was Friday and since Breetz and I had been in our early teens we had made dinner for Anna every Friday night at their apartment. These had progressed from hamburgers and fries to quite elaborate meals. I took a deep breath and poured myself another glass of wine.

"I've sent in four applications," I said. "But you know, just as I mailed the last one I had an inspiration."

Breetz and Anna exchanged glances.

"Biology."

"*Biology?*"

This was one they'd never have guessed.

"Yes. I've just read this book — *The Development of the Cell*. It's fascinating. If I were to study Biology in grad school — "

"Richard," Breetz interrupted. "You haven't taken any Biology."

"I'd have to take a make-up year of course — "

"Oh, that would be good, Richard," Breetz said. "Then you could put this decision off for at least another year."

We all laughed and clinked glasses.

In my actual life, this was really quite a serious problem. With anyone else, one of my professors, say, or an interested friend of my parents', I found this topic intensely painful. But when I was with Breetz and Anna the whole subject of my indecision was just a good-natured joke. Clearly they loved me and enjoyed my company and what I decided to *do* with my life didn't matter two hoots.

The fish had been cooked to perfection and Breetz's anchovy sauce was just delectable. I opened a second bottle of wine and refilled our glasses. I intended to propose a toast, but Anna beat me to it.

"To both my boys," she said, raising her glass. "My beautiful beautiful boys."

How was it that Anna could just say something like that? To both my beautiful boys. If I were to have stood then and proposed a toast to my second mother, the words would have caught in my throat and, worse, I'd have felt some sort of betrayal of Elizabeth.

So I didn't. Instead I helped myself to seconds and buried my feelings in food, wine and conversation. There was always plenty of all three at Breetz and Anna's.

It was while Breetz and I were sitting out on the back balcony, enjoying a cup of coffee and wondering aloud if we might be ready for Anna's mocha cake, that there was a knock at the door. Breetz and I both turned and looked inside. It was odd to have someone knock at that late hour. Anna was in the kitchen. She wiped her hands on her apron, paused in front of the mirror briefly to smooth her hair, and opened the door.

"Telegram," a young man said.

Anna went pale. Even so many years after the war, a telegram, to her mind, always meant a death.

"For a Mr Breetz Mestrovic."

"What is it, Mama?" Breetz asked.

He took the telegram from her shaking hands and opened it quickly. By this time I had joined them by the door. Breetz put an arm around Anna's shoulders.

"It's not bad news, Mama," he said. "It's from *Vogue*."

DIANA VREELAND WASN'T SURE what she was expecting — someone quiet, self-deprecating — a Canadian in a boxy suit and tie. But the smallish man entering her office was anything but quiet. He had a most charming extroverted manner, and he was dressed entirely in black. A black silk shirt, black well-pressed pants and highly polished black shoes. Casual yet expensive, she judged. He kissed her hand when she offered it for shaking. He was enchanting.

"Mr Mestro — "

"Breetz. Please."

"Breetz. That's an unusual name, is it...Hungarian?"

"Croatian. It means Little Brother."

There was a small silence while she took him in. He let her. Breetz was comfortable in the silence. Comfortable under her scrutiny. Besides, he was taking her in too. She liked him immediately. It was mutual. She turned to her assistant and suggested coffee.

"Now, young man — you are very young, aren't you?"

Breetz nodded.

"How young?"

"Twenty-two."

She sat back and looked at him. Twenty-two.

"And where did you get your training?"

"At my mother's knee."

It was a charming joke, but Breetz spoke the truth. When Breetz was a child, Anna allowed herself very few extravagances. *Vogue* magazine was one. Breetz would sit on the couch snuggling beside her and they would slowly work their way through the thick magazine. Anna loved looking at the beautiful ladies. "See here," she'd say to Breetz, "see what she is doing with her eyes?" and she would tell him.

Breetz learned so many tricks at his mother's knee that by the time he got the Leica, he had a store of knowledge most men never have. He could tell the girls to bend their elbows, because when a woman's arm is held straight, it appears broken. He could show them how to rest their chins on their hands without actually putting any weight on the hand itself, and to cross their legs the same way. He knew how to make things *seem* real in a photo without being real. So he would tell his young girlfriends to turn slightly this way or that. He would pose them on their bicycles, laughing. To be still and yet somehow to seem to move made for the best photos. This is what Breetz learned at his mother's knee, studying *Vogue,* and now he was sitting opposite the magazine's legendary editor.

Coffee arrived on a trolley. Diana took hers black. Breetz poured himself some cream and plopped two cubes of sugar into his cup with the little silver tongs. Diana watched him. He was clearly at ease and yet this had to be one of the biggest moments of his life. Perhaps the biggest. He had his portfolio, as she'd requested, but he didn't seem at all eager to hand it over to her. He was enjoying her company, enjoying the coffee, enjoying sitting in that office.

He wasn't handsome by any stretch of the imagination and yet... there was something about him. Sensuality? Yes, but not threatening. Little Brother, he'd said. Yes. Like a little brother. Someone you liked being around. Someone who could clearly take care of himself, but someone you wanted to take care of. Someone you wouldn't want to disappoint. That was a quality Diana felt was important. If the model wanted to please the photographer, that was when the magic happened. She held out her hand.

"Your portfolio."

If he was acting, he was very good, because he seemed jarred by her request, as though he'd been so charmed by her presence he'd momentarily forgotten why he was really there. She took the portfolio and opened it. She looked at the first photo. Then, without looking up at him, she quietly and carefully began going through the portfolio, nodding occasionally, while Breetz sat opposite, sipping his coffee. Other photographers would have offered some comments, observations, kept the conversational ball rolling, but Breetz sat across from her saying nothing, perfectly at ease. She was almost at the last page in his portfolio before she spoke.

"Those photos you sent us..."

She casually turned a page.

"There was one... black and white... hair... quite an extraordinary photo we thought..."

Breetz nodded.

"...perfectly in focus...luminous...and yet it had a velvety quality to it...quite lovely."

"Yes," Breetz agreed.

She looked up at him.

"How did you manage that?"

Any other neophyte confronted with this question by the most famous fashion editor of all time would have hesitated, then tried to explain. But not Breetz.

"I guess you'll just have to hire me to find out," he said.

She smiled.

"I guess we will."

ANNA LAY DOWN ON THE BED. She was feeling that awful tightening in her chest again. No wonder! So much excitement. She'd told him the moment he finished the interview he was to call, and he had. They'd hired him. *Vogue* had hired him. An impossible dream come true. She was so happy! She was so happy! There. There it was again. She was just so excited. Her boy's dream come true. She'd felt a little nauseous all morning — no wonder, waiting to hear the news — and now she could lie down. There was nothing more to be done; she could lie down until he arrived. She could get up fresh and rested. There it was again. And he was flying home tonight, and he and Richard would celebrate with her, and she'd made the meal already. There was nothing more to be done. Yes, if she just lay here, quietly, she'd be all rested and calm when he got back. Breetz mustn't know about the pains or he would worry. She'd just lie here, on top of the covers, and perhaps close her eyes, and when she heard his footsteps on the stairs, she would get up and be refreshed and ready to greet him at the door. But there it was again, only this time stronger, much stronger...so strong she suddenly cried out.

"Breetza! Breetza!"

But Breetz was still in New York City. At that very moment buying a silk dressing gown for his mother at Saks Fifth Avenue.

THE MOMENT I SAW BREETZ at the airport I knew things had gone well. We made just one stop on the way home: to buy champagne.

When we discovered Anna lying on the bed in her apartment, her body cold, her eyes staring, Breetz went berserk. He threw himself on the bed beside Anna and clasped her in his arms and wailed.

"Mama, Mama, Mama!"

I can still remember the feeling of panic. What was I to do? Anna was dead and Breetz was thrashing around like a wounded beast. For a moment or two I stood there stunned. Then I went into the kitchen, picked up the phone and dialled...not emergency, not a doctor, not the police, but my mother. Elizabeth, shocked, but firmly in control, told me to stay with Breetz, and she would handle everything. In the bedroom, Breetz held on to Anna and yelled.

"Mama, Mama, speak to me, Mama! Speak to me!"

He moaned, he screamed, he hugged her, and kissed her, and kept moaning, Mama, Mama!

And when the doctor arrived and tried to separate Breetz from Anna, Breetz turned on him savagely.

"No, no, I won't let you have her!"

I stood there feeling helpless, as helpless as I've ever felt. I tried to get him to let go of Anna, but he wouldn't. He kept hugging her and screaming.

"No, no, I won't let her go!"

To this day I remember with shame how I felt. It wasn't grief or shock or sorrow, but embarrassment. Embarrassment in front of that cool professional, who I felt was only trying to do his job.

Just when I thought things couldn't get any worse, they did. The doctor pronounced Anna dead. When the two attendants turned up from the funeral home to take Anna away, Breetz howled and batted at their cool impersonal hands and clasped Anna to him. When they carried Anna out the door, Breetz erupted again and refused to be separated until the attendants agreed to let him ride with them and Breetz wept and wept and wept.

And yet why shouldn't Breetz howl and wail his grief and cling to Anna? Anna was everything to Breetz. I felt sick with embarrassment and sick at the fact that I was embarrassed.

The reception was held at my parents' house. I remember standing on the doorstep, Breetz beside me, as my mother opened the door. She stretched forth both her hands and Breetz took them and squeezed them and then kissed her softly on one cheek and then the other.

"Thank you, Elizabeth," he said. "Thank you so much for everything."

And my mother smiled at Breetz.

"Anna was so important to us all," she said. "We shall miss her dreadfully."

And Breetz smiled. His first smile in the forty-eight hours since Anna's death. But once that first smile broke, suddenly Breetz was all smiles. My mother led us into the conservatory, Anna's favourite room, where the mourners were gathered — Anna's oldest friend, Mrs Boychuck, whose eyes were swollen and red, Olga Zonger, Nina Titschmann, Yvanna Nylasi. And, of course, the Rosedale ladies — Muriel Walmsley, Judith Bradshaw, Sheila Paton, Ruth Davidson — Elizabeth's friends, Anna's customers. An odd assortment.

I understood why, after two days of howling grief, Breetz was suddenly all smiles. This was Anna's party. Anna's last party. Anna loved fun, Anna was fun, and wherever Anna went, people had fun. And so instinctively Breetz knew that the most important thing that he could do for Anna on that day was to have fun. And so he would. Moments after he'd joined them, Breetz had Elizabeth's circle of friends laughing.

Now that Breetz was smiling and laughing, something in me changed. Now that I no longer had to be on guard for Breetz's next outrageous expression of grief, I began to thaw. I went back in my mind to that first day. There was Breetz playing with my toys — yes, but something else. A feeling. Anna. Anna had come to the room at the end of that day, knelt down and wrapped me in her arms. I could remember the warmth that flooded into me and the feeling of letting go and sinking into her soft embrace. With that memory I felt the tears start to come for the first time. And I wept.

It's not that I feel less than Breetz, it's just that the feeling lies deeper, that the feeling is more inaccessible, and that I have trouble knowing it's there or letting it out. But standing at the reception the tears did start to come. And to this very day, tears well up, often at odd and inappropriate times, whenever I think of Anna.

Breetz stood listening to the women reminisce about his mother.

"I remember the first time I noticed Anna's lovely skin," Elizabeth was saying.

"Lovely skin, lovely skin," echoed the others.

"Anna had been cleaning for me for, I don't know, it must've been eight, ten months."

"And me," said Muriel.

"And me," Sheila said.

"And I used to sit and have tea with her all the time," continued Elizabeth. "I'd come home from bridge and Anna would put on a pot of tea, and we'd sit and talk with the boys, so really it wasn't for quite a few months that I noticed...I remember it was in this very room, she was standing right there by that window. And I looked at her and I said, Anna, you have lovely skin!"

"Beautiful skin."

"Perfection."

"Ageless, really, wasn't it?"

"Even to the last."

"Yes. I remarked on it. She blushed." There was a collective soft *Oh* from the ladies. "Your mother blushed, Breetz."

Breetz smiled. He loved this story.

"Her English wasn't the best at that time, but we managed, she and I, to agree that the following week she'd bring me a little pot of her cream. I cancelled bridge. I cancelled bridge and was introduced to that miraculous cream."

"So light!"

"So soothing."

"Delicious."

"And of course, she had her secrets, didn't she? The way she stroked it on..."

"Up, up, up..."

"Yes, always pre-moistening the skin. My hairdresser was the first to notice. He asked if I was pregnant, or having an affair!"

Everyone laughed.

"You were so good to share her with us, Elizabeth."

"I was, wasn't I?"

They all laughed again.

"You know that trick she had for her hands?" Muriel asked.

"No, what was that?"

"She had the softest hands..."

"Mm."

"So soft..."

"And I remarked on them one day. 'Anna,' I said. 'How do you keep your hands so lovely?' Because she never wore rubber gloves, you know..."

"No, she didn't, did she?"

"...to do the dishes or anything, and I thought how *does* she do it? Well..."

They all leaned in just a little.

"...sugar and oil."

"White sugar or brown?"

"White."

"What kind of oil?"

"Mazola, Crisco, whatever was at hand. She'd rub the two together in her palms, then wipe it off. I do it myself now after I've been puttering in the greenhouse. It leaves them soft and lovely."

"Then you use her handcream?"

"Oh, yes, that delicious handcream. What *is* in that handcream, Breetz?"

Breetz paused just long enough.

"That was Mama's secret," he said. Then he smiled. "Now it's mine."

I smiled too. Breetz and I had often sat around Anna's kitchen while she made up her creams. The face cream and the hand lotion had the exact same ingredients — beeswax, mineral oil, glycerine and rose essence. The hand lotion simply had less wax and more oil, that was all. Yet the ladies of Rosedale couldn't get enough of Anna's homespun remedies.

But the lotions and potions weren't Anna's secret. It was the way she made the women feel. Over and over again, she'd tell them how beautiful they were and she'd give them her complete attention. She told them they were beautiful and they grew more so before her eyes. Thinking back on that scene — Breetz at the centre of those adoring women — I now know that *that* was the real secret Anna had passed on to him. The real secret of his future success.

Her legacy.

IN THE DAYS FOLLOWING ANNA'S FUNERAL Elizabeth and I helped Breetz get organized. We all agreed that the best thing for Breetz would be to get down to New York as fast as possible, to get going on his new life. Elizabeth took on the settling of Anna's affairs and the closing up of the apartment. I drove Breetz to New York in the Buick. He was subdued, but as we entered the great city I knew this was the best place, the only place, for Breetz. In New York everyone moved at his pace. In New York everyone knew what they wanted: fame, success, more success. New York would be able to handle Breetz's energy, his ambition.

I had gone to New York to help Breetz, but he didn't need any help. Within two days he'd found an apartment, an almost impossible feat in that city. He was starting a new life and I would have to return to my old one. We said goodbye and I promised I would be down to see him when I finished exams. When I got back I was brought face to face with the problem of what to do next. What to do with my life. I envied Breetz's direction and focus. He at least had something to help him through this period of mourning.

Wandering around that big perfect empty house, I was thinking a lot of my own mother too. I had enough self-knowledge to realize that my thoughts were prompted by the loss of my second mother, Anna. I tried to remember how old I'd been when I stopped calling my mother, Mother. I think I was about ten years old. She'd come in from some lecture or other and had announced that I should call her Elizabeth. It had never occurred to me to continue calling her Mother once she'd told me not to, and so from then on Elizabeth was Elizabeth to me. I find that now even in my thoughts she is Elizabeth, not my mother. I'll finish a book, for example, and think, Elizabeth should read this.

She was certainly unlike most mothers, even the other mothers on Glen Road. Most mothers talked *about* their children, but Elizabeth talked *to* me. She was always interested in what I thought about things and would ask me all the right questions about my latest interest. It wasn't the fun that I had with Anna and Breetz, but it was nice. I liked sitting across from my mother as she told me stories about the Bonnycastles. My great-grandfather had been a Speaker in the House of Commons, and my great-aunt had been a famous actress. Elizabeth was proud that there had been a Rhodes Scholar among the Bonnycastles and a female physicist. It was at that point, when talking about Aunt Cecilia, that Elizabeth usually told me about what she referred to as her own university career. She'd taken Humanities at the University of Toronto. Elizabeth had loved university — debating clubs, drama, sororities — and I'd never seen her happier than my last year of high school, when she would look through the U of T calendar with me.

Perhaps if I'd been a girl I'd have been aware of my mother's unhappiness, but, of course, I never saw it. All I saw was a vivacious, busy woman with an enormous house to run. All I saw was how beautiful she looked as she headed out the door in her Dior dresses and veiled hats. All I saw were the high heels and the handbags and the gloved hands waving. I never saw the strain around the eyes, the beginnings of a permanently downturned mouth.

Yes, a daughter would have seen her mother's unhappiness. A bundle of trapped intellect and frustrated desires, but I saw Elizabeth as having everything a woman could want. I was proud of the fact that where other mothers would discuss their children and their activities, Elizabeth would discuss politics and art. Where other mothers were harried and frumpy, mine was slim and beautiful. I never saw the brittleness that went with the slimness, the sadness that went with the beauty.

Darkness had settled around me as I'd sat in the study. I heard my father come downstairs and knew it must be time for dinner. I hoisted myself up out of the deep leather chair. As I went by the conservatory, something told me to look inside. There was Elizabeth, sitting on the yellow settee surrounded by azaleas and aspidistras, watching the sun go down just as I had been sitting in the study, letting the sun go down.

"Dinner, Elizabeth," I said. She stood and smiled.

"Thank you, Richard."

And together we walked the carpeted hall to the enormous dining room with its enormous table and three places set at one end. Father was already there, standing behind Elizabeth's chair to hold it for her. I stood while my mother was seated, then took my own chair. Usually Elizabeth and I carried the conversation but tonight neither of us seemed up to it. There was complete silence as Gertie put an enormous roast of beef in front of my father — he liked to carve — and dished out the Brussels sprouts and mashed potatoes herself. Gertie was wearing a uniform that looked a little tight for her, but which she always put on when "Mr Hathaway's in residence." There was silence as the gravy boat went round and silence as Gertie served up the crispy Yorkshire pudding. Gertie dissolved back into the kitchen and we bowed our heads while my father said his usual grace.

"Bless this food to our use, Oh Lord, and us to thy service. Amen."

"Amen."

"Amen."

I still wasn't feeling very hungry as I lifted the heavy silver knife and fork. My father looked back and forth from Elizabeth to me.

"Well, you two are pretty silent, I must say."

There was no response to that from either of us so he continued.

"Richard, will you pour the wine, please?"

I lifted the bottle of Bordeaux and filled each of our glasses.

My father held up his glass as if to propose a toast.

"What are we drinking to, Richard?"

I looked up, puzzled.

"Osgoode? Queen's? Not Dalhousie?"

Elizabeth spoke.

"Richard hasn't applied to law school, John."

"He hasn't?"

"No."

My father put his knife and fork back on his plate and looked at my mother.

"Elizabeth, I've always conceded that Richard could study what he wanted to study, *go where his mind would take him*, as you put it. Up till now I have capitulated. I have capitulated. But I thought it was understood that once Richard graduated from university, the situation was different. Law. Law gives a young man a basic understanding of how our society works, of what might be called the Rules of the Game. Law." He turned to me. "What other profession is available to you?"

I was amazed. Elizabeth and I had always talked over what I was going to do and my father had had no part in it. Occasionally, he had mentioned law school, and Elizabeth had just said, "Oh, never mind your father, just study what interests you." In fact, I'd always taken his favourite saying, "I was always a plodder" to mean, I was always a plodder, but. I was always a plodder, but you, Richard, are different. You can head off in whatever direction your interests take you. I was only that very night beginning to see that my father had had expectations.

"If not Law, Richard, what?"

"Well, I've applied to Philosophy at Cornell."

"Philosophy? Surely you're not serious."

I didn't answer.

"And what are you going to do when you graduate? Sit under a tree? Think about metaphysics? No. Your mother knows my opinion on this. A man is different from a woman. A man needs a profession. A man needs to support his loved ones. A man needs some respect in the world."

My father wiped his mouth with his napkin and placed it firmly to the left of his plate.

"I'll speak to Cam Bienenstock," he said. "I'll call him right now. He's an old yearmate of mine."

My father left the table that night feeling very good. He had a task. He had a little pull in the world and he would use it for his son, who, after all, had a fine mind and would be a credit to the profession.

Elizabeth and I looked at each other across the table. There were some moments of incredulous silence before I spoke.

"Well," I said, "I can't hand law school on to Breetz. He just won't take it."

For the first time in many weeks, we both laughed.

A few days later I arrived at the Granite Club to have lunch with Cam Bienenstock. My father arranged it all. Of course what I should have done was immediately tell my father how I felt about Law, but it was easier to simply go along. Naturally, I was quite apprehensive when I sat down opposite the stocky, balding senior partner of Lowrie, Goode and Bienenstock. We'd ordered our meal and were sipping scotch and sodas. Beneath the pleasant chit-chat I sensed a certain strain.

"How's your lovely mother?" Cam asked.

"Lovely as ever," I replied.

There was an uncomfortable silence as each of us realized there was no more putting off the reason for this lunch.

"So you want to be a lawyer, Richard."

I shifted in my chair. If I went on pretending I was interested in Law, I would only get myself in deeper and deeper, so I held my breath.

"Actually," I said after a moment, "it's my father who wants me to be a lawyer. I don't."

"You don't?"

"No. I feel foolish telling you this. You've gone to a lot of trouble."

"I haven't gone to any trouble yet, Richard, though I was prepared to. So...you're not thinking of Law?"

"No."

"What are you thinking of?"

"Well, actually, I've applied to Philosophy at Cornell but...I'm not really sure about that, either. I'm at a difficult point in my life. I have to decide what to do with the rest of it."

All tension between us dissolved. Cam Bienenstock leaned back in his chair and gave me a big smile.

"Nonsense!" he said. "You're a young man. I'd give anything to be your age and not know what I was going to do with my life. You know, my generation, everything was decided. We went to university, got a profession, got married. Then...we worked for the rest of our lives. I've spent a good many evenings wondering what I'd have done if I'd had some choice. I don't mean to make light of your problem, Richard, but I really don't think there's any rush. Why don't you take a year off? See Europe, maybe. Travel around a bit."

"Would you say this to your own son?" I asked.

"Certainly not! But that doesn't mean it's not good advice." He paused and took another sip of scotch. "Besides," he said, "fortunately, I have three daughters."

Walking home I thought about what Cam Bienenstock had said. Why shouldn't I take a year off? A year in Europe could be just what I needed. I could see all the places I'd read about, visit France and Italy. I saw myself living in Paris or Florence, walking through the great European galleries, reading and thinking. I could absorb European culture, read, and maybe over the year I could sort myself out. Decide what it was I really wanted to do. So by the time I reached my house I was really quite excited by Cam Bienenstock's proposal. My mother was home when I got in and could see that the lunch had not been as painful as we had both anticipated. She made us gin and tonics and we took them out into the garden and sat under the big elm tree.

"How did it go?" she asked. There was a mischievous look in her eye.

"Actually, it went quite well," I said. "He was a really entertaining and nice man."

"So, did you discuss Law?" my mother said.

"Briefly."

"And?"

"And I told him it wasn't for me."

"Good. What did he say?"

I then recounted my conversation with Cam. As I talked, however, an unusual thing happened. I could see my mother's eyes glazing over. She kept nodding and saying, yes, yes, but somehow she didn't seem to have the enthusiasm I'd expected. I could sense that the Europe idea didn't excite her. Finally I blurted out.

"But *you* spent a year in Europe!"

"Oh yes," she said. "But I was at school."

We all know what it feels like to rush home to our parents with an idea that excites us and to be met with an unexpected lack of enthusiasm. Suddenly, our idea seems much less exciting. After that I could never get my own excitement back to its original pitch. Instead of imagining myself drinking in European art and culture, I saw myself wandering aimlessly about, without direction or purpose. Where moments earlier I'd seen myself absorbed in the fascinating talk of Paris cafés, I now saw myself wasting time with a bunch of idlers. But this wasn't a big disappointment at the time. The idea of travel in Europe had sprung up quickly and it died just as quickly.

A couple of days later I joined my mother in the conservatory. She was reading *The Development of the Cell*.

"Richard," she said. "This is absolutely fascinating."

I felt that old surge of pleasure. I'd introduced Elizabeth to something she hadn't known about and she'd found it interesting. That meant there were some good talks in store.

"Biology," she said. "I never had any idea Biology could be so fascinating. No wonder you were thinking of that make-up year at McGill, Richard."

And though I hadn't thought of a make-up year at McGill for some time, that evening I started thinking about it again. For so many years I'd been living in my head, always thinking about abstract problems. Philosophy and History were so nebulous, but Biology was a Science and in Science there was a Method, and the Method would give me something I had never had before — a concrete discipline that would focus my energies. Unlike travelling in Europe, the more I thought about this, the more it made sense.

And that's how I ended up in Montreal.

AT FIRST, DIANA VREELAND WASN'T QUITE SURE what she was going to do with Breetz, how she was going to use him. She would rely on what she had always relied on: other people's ambitions to keep him in place. But he seemed to be composed of some unsinkable material so that whenever he was pushed under he just bobbed up somewhere else. He never considered himself an apprentice — he always considered himself a master and somehow he conveyed this to whomever he was working with. He was part of this new generation — these post-war kids who were pushing their way into the world. They didn't believe in waiting their turn. They didn't believe in putting in time. They didn't believe in anything but their own talent and Breetz had plenty of that. He had a gift. Not just a gift with the camera but a special gift for making women feel beautiful. And not just the models, but all women. The secretaries, the copy editors, the ad sales girls. Even cafeteria and cleaning staff. Women adored him and everywhere he went he was buoyed on a wave of female affection. Diana couldn't keep him under so she wouldn't try. Funny how talent surfaced. Here was a nobody from nowhere hired on a fluke, but whatever happened with Marilyn Monroe — if she didn't get back in touch, or if she reneged — it didn't matter. Diana Vreeland now knew she wouldn't regret the day she'd hired Breetz Mestrovic.

SEPTEMBER ARRIVED and classes in Biology began. I stood at the long formica-topped counter. I'd already taken two aspirin, but they weren't working yet. I squeezed my eyes shut and pressed my fingers to the bridge of my nose. If I worked my thumb right up under my left browbone it provided some sort of temporary relief. A counter-irritant. But then, when I took my thumb away, the throbbing was back. Not enough to make me lie down or go home for the day, just enough to make concentration difficult. And, occasionally, along with the almost-pain in my head, there was that sensation in my stomach. Almost nausea.

Formaldehyde. The room reeked of it and I reeked of it, even when I was back in the little coach-house I'd rented. The tips of my fingers, no matter how much I scrubbed and scrubbed, gave off that particularly sick-making sweet/heavy scent of formaldehyde. Sometimes just thinking about it would bring back that pain beneath my left browbone.

I grabbed onto the edge of the countertop and glanced up and down the rows ahead and behind me. Each station had a double sink with a thin rubber hose attached to the faucet, and on either side of each sink was a student wearing, like me, a white lab coat. And each student in their white lab coat was bent over a cork board on which, pinned and splayed, was a frog.

A frog. Of course. What had I expected? What had I expected? I could hear Breetz's voice — What do biologists do, Richard? What do they actually do? Study life, I'd like to have said. They study life, Breetz.

Dissect, Richard, I said to myself as I looked down at my specimen. Biologists dissect. I reached into my pocket and pulled out the little tin of Bayer aspirin I was never without those days. I turned on the cold tap and a little stream came out of the end of the rubber hose. I cupped my hand, filled it with water from the tiny stream and swallowed my third aspirin of the day. Then I looked around wondering if any of my nearest neighbours might have noticed. Not a chance. They were all busy, busy, busy, hunched over their frogs and tracing their innermost workings onto a blank piece of paper.

Most of the students had given their frogs names. This, I could not do. I couldn't even pith the frog but had handed it over to my lab partner, who'd taken the frog, squirming and live, held it firmly between his thumb and forefinger and then jammed a pin into its head. The frog had given a few kicks; then he was dead. And all I'd had to do was slit his green skin with the scalpel and pin him open. And I had done it. I looked down at my unnamed frog. I'd done it. I'd taken the little pins and pushed back the slit skin and pinned him to the cork board. My stomach turned. The little bluish liver, the stringy greyish pink sinew of his thighs. Frogs legs. Suddenly I had a vision of the time Elizabeth had taken Breetz and me to a French restaurant and we'd ordered frogs legs. I thought, I really thought, I was about to throw up. The smell of formaldehyde and the closeness of the tiny sinew combined to turn my stomach so violently that I had to actually push myself away from the counter and leave the room.

Once in the hall I felt I wouldn't actually vomit but I could still smell the formaldehyde. I walked the length of the building until I was outside in the cool air. I leaned against the railing, filling my lungs with fresh air. How many times had this happened to me? How many times had I entered into something with enthusiasm only to be disappointed? I'd had such high hopes. I loved Montreal. McGill was an excellent campus with lots of exciting lecturers from all over Canada and the United States. The coach-house I'd rented was my idea of heaven. What was wrong with me that I couldn't seem to stay with anything? What was wrong with me that I seemed doomed to forever go off on a tangent only to find that disappointing too? Here I was signed up for a year in Biology. What was I to do now? Drop out? What would I tell everyone? That I'd dropped out because I'd had to dissect a frog? They'd think I was ridiculous. Of course you had to dissect frogs in Biology, everyone knew that. Frogs and foetal pigs and, oh god, cats, too.

What was I thinking?

Of course, what was happening was that I was being sucked down into one of my slumps. These were different from my grieving for Anna. In those days of moping around the house on Glen Road after her death I had been down, certainly, but with good reason — the loss of someone I loved. But anyone who's ever gone through any sort of depression will understand how pointless they seem. There's nothing to be depressed *about*, really, and yet you go down, down, until finally the effort of lifting your head from the pillow one morning seems unbearable. On the face of it, I had everything. I was a young man with enormous resources behind me, seemingly capable of pursuing any avenue that interested me. None did.

I went to fewer and fewer labs until I dropped them entirely. They constituted twenty percent of my final mark. I didn't care. Initially, I kept attending lectures, convincing myself that they, at least, were interesting. But they weren't. I remember the day I decided to drop them too. I was sitting near the back in an aisle seat to make it easy to exit quickly once I saw the professor gathering up his papers. He was talking about the chi-square test — actually reviewing something I thought I had grasped completely in the last lecture — but to me he was rambling. I sat up a little straighter and tried to concentrate. I could understand each particular word and I could understand phrases but I couldn't hold them together long enough in my mind to make any sense of them. Was it me or was it him? I looked around at my fellow students, all three hundred of them, crammed into that lecture hall. Their heads were all down, their hands all jotting notes. No one had noticed that although the professor was still talking, his words no longer made sense. I leaned forward. Still nonsense.

I never went back. Not to that lecture nor to any of the others. But I didn't drop the courses, either. I was in a peculiar state where I could anticipate the results of my actions, thereby rendering myself paralysed. At the thought of dropping this course, for instance, I imagined myself in the Registrar's Office with some well-meaning secretary trying to solve my problems for me as if they were no more difficult than rearranging a timetable. And so I didn't; I simply stopped going.

This paralysis spilled over into my personal life, such as it was at the time. I had turned down two invitations so far to dinner and drinks with my landlords, Hilary and Alan Ross. Just as I didn't want to deal with the imagined questions of the secretary, I didn't want to deal with the imagined questions of Hilary Ross. What I really wanted to do was just stay in their perfect little coach-house. But I forced myself out. I had discovered, in the days of aimless walking before classes began, some wonderful used bookstores and they were still a comfort to me. Walking into a used bookstore is like walking into a different world. They're always jam-packed with books, over-flowing with books, books piled up, spines facing out, books on the floor. Boxes of books on tables sagging under their weight. Shelves of books reaching to the ceiling. Books you've read, like old friends, beckoning to you from older editions or newer ones or paperbacks with their covers ripped off.

Treasure Island was the best of the used bookstores. Four notes sounded on the door harp as I closed the door behind me. Anything I did do now, I did very deliberately and purposefully. I closed doors slowly to make sure they were really shut. I would put my shoes or shaving kit back down in the exact same place each time so I'd be able to find them again the next day. I stood there ostensibly deciding which section I should browse in but really allowing the atmosphere of the store to take over. Everything in it seemed a warm gold colour from the worn blond wood of the shelves and floor to the yellowed pages of the piled books to the light coming in from the two windows on either side of the door. I slowly, deliberately, made my way to the Classics section. I was vaguely aware of the door harp occasionally chiming and the sound of the till opening and closing, but mostly I stood for the longest time just taking a book out, holding it in my hands, then putting it back and taking out another one. I think it was a poetry anthology that I finally took to the counter. The man rang my purchase through and while he was doing so I noticed a small hand-written card taped to the register. It announced a lecture on Kirlian photography by a Professor Wesley Ames. I'd never heard of a photo-grapher by the name of Kirlian but because of Breetz photography was something that interested me. The lecture was for that afternoon in the Leacock Building on McGill campus, so I headed off.

It was bitterly cold and I was happy to get into the small over-heated lecture hall. I was the first to arrive and took a seat near the front. I didn't expect to be part of a very large audience and I was right. Over the next fifteen minutes a few more people trickled in. As a man behind me began to gather up some papers and a briefcase and move to the front of the room, I realized that this was the speaker and that, in fact, there were only five of us attending his lecture. So there I sat wondering just what this was all about. At the front of the room, the small man in brown pants and a hand-knitted cardigan began to speak.

"I suppose many of you are curious as to why a professor, with a teddibly English name — Wesley Ames — should be an expert on Slavic Studies. And even more curious, I suppose, is that this same Wesley Ames of the Slavic Studies Department should be lecturing on Kirlian photography. Perhaps I should start at the beginning, though whether I'm starting at the beginning, or merely digressing, you shall have to decide. I do have a problem with digressing and, yet, every-thing always seems to come around in the end. To tie together in some curious fashion.

I am an amateur photographer, of sorts. Actually, it was my wife, Mildred, who is a more than amateur horticulturist — Mildred's greenhouse has a most magnificent collection of fuchsia, passion-flower and, of course, orchids — Mildred encouraged me to photograph these plants and, as so often happens, what began as a duty ended up as a pleasure. Indeed, I'm fortunate enough to have had some of my photographs of Mildred's orchids published in the *Botanical Monthly*. So you can see that this avocation I have of botanical photography would naturally predispose me to be intrigued with Kirlian's work. Curious how these things turn out. Every so often, Mildred and I try to spend some time in Moscow so I can do research for my forthcoming study of the Slavic poet Lestrenkov. I spend many happy hours at the University of Moscow, where my dear friend Sergei Petrovich Mikilof is working on the definitive edition. I need not go into here how extremely indebted I am to my colleague Sergei's endeavours, and I need not digress into telling you how many wonderful evenings he and I have spent walking the streets of Moscow discussing our mutual passion — the poet, that is, not horticultural photography. But, of course, in our long and fascinating chats, my passion for horticultural photography did come up, and it was upon hearing this that Sergei Petrovich first mentioned the work of Kirlian — "

At this point, I noticed that someone was quietly slipping out the back door. This obviously unnerved the professor — he shuffled some papers and coughed slightly, then recovered himself.

"Where was I? Ah, yes. Kirlian. Semyon Kirlian was an electrician by trade — curious how so often these important discoveries are made serendipitously — like Wallace coming upon the Theory of Evolution in a malaria delirium — and Darwin behaving like such a gentleman — the sort of cooperation I always admire — my friend Sergei Petrovich and I have the same sort of relationship. We realize we are not competing but cooperating on bringing to light the important work of Lestrenkov — "

At this point, another person in the audience quietly got up and slipped out the back. The professor shuffled his papers.

"Quite right — that's neither here nor there — at any rate, my good friend Sergei's niece is married to a wonderful, simply charming, young man — Ivan Mikhailovich Stregninsky — whom I had the pleasure of meeting a few weeks later. By this time I, of course, had totally forgotten about Kirlian, as it had been only a passing mention. But my dear friend Sergei Petrovich had not. After a splendid meal and the requisite vodka, he mentioned to his niece's husband my interest in horticultural photography. At once, the name Kirlian came up. Ivan immediately began to discuss in the most excited manner the work of Kirlian and I must confess it was the young man's passion that really first aroused my own interest. Curious. He asked me if I would be interested in a demonstration of Kirlian's amazing machine and I was, naturally, intrigued and said of course — why have they all left do you think?"

I looked around. I was the only person in the room now and the professor was addressing me directly.

"Well, Professor — "

"Wesley, please."

"Well, Wesley, you haven't told us yet what Kirlian photography is."

"Oh. Curious. No, I suppose I haven't. Why are you still here?"

"My best friend is a photographer."

"How delightful. Well, this is a pity — I haven't shown any of my pictures yet. Would you be interested in seeing my pictures?"

"Yes."

"Splendid. Come on up here then and I'll show them to you."

I was expecting to see pictures of Mildred's orchids but was taken aback when I saw the first photo. It was clearly a photograph of a hand, except — curiously! — it wasn't a hand. It was the shape of the hand, but, rather like the Milky Way, the shape was filled with masses of little dots of light and from the outline of the hand sparks of light shot forth. It was unlike any photograph I'd ever seen.

"Fascinating," I said. "It appears to be a negative."

"Not exactly a negative, dear boy, it's a photograph. Kirlian's just photographing something we can't see."

"And what is he photographing?"

Wesley Ames laughed. "What a wonderful question!" he said. "Who knows? The biologists think he's photographing an electro-magnetic field — the religiously minded think he's photographing the soul — the mystics think he's photographing an aura — oriental physicians believe them to be the acupuncture points — but whatever he is photographing, it is of immense interest. Now look at this one."

The next photo he showed me was of a leaf, freshly picked he claimed, and the multicoloured streaks of light jutted out from its points just as they had from the fingers of the human hand.

"Now look at this. This is the same leaf with a section cut out of it."

I looked at the photo. Clearly there was the same Milky Way leaf and all around it was the luminous halo effect, but where the section had been cut, the light seemed to have died out.

"Curious, isn't it?" Wesley said. "Makes me very happy that I've always treated Mildred's plants with the utmost respect."

For the next fifteen minutes the professor and I looked at all sorts of Kirlian photographs. They were mainly of leaves and fingertips. What I found most fascinating was that some of the photographs of hands were much dimmer than others. These, Wesley explained, were the hands of older people. There was also a series of a leaf in which a photograph had been taken every half hour. In the first photograph the leaf was surrounded by a luminous glow but in each successive photograph the glow grew dimmer until finally, in the last photograph, there was hardly any light at all. Clearly whatever Kirlian was photographing was connected with life. I asked Wesley if there was anything I could read on Kirlian.

"Of course not," he said. "Kirlian's work is barely known in Russia. But my friend Sergei and I are going to publish a joint paper — he in Russian, myself in English. The problem, of course, is in what journal shall I publish it?" At this point the professor turned to me and said, rather abruptly, "By the way, what's your name?"

"Richard. Richard Hathaway."

"And you're a student here..."

"Yes."

"In what?"

"Biology. But I'm having some troubles."

"Oh, what might they be?"

"I can't stomach labs."

"Of course, of course. Detestable things."

It had taken only a few minutes for the professor to show me all the pictures he had, but a few minutes and a few pictures were all I ncedcd to know I was intrigued. The series of hands fascinated me. The tiny hand of a child had the most extraordinary scintillations of light coming off it, extending almost to the very edges of the photographic paper. One hand, an adult's, had such a small bluish white glow I couldn't stop staring at it.

"That's Kirlian's grandmother's hand," Wesley said, noticing my fascination. "He took that just a few days before she died, actually."

I was silent. Someone, this Kirlian, had invented a camera that could actually photograph — what? The life force.

So engrossed in talk was I that I barely noticed that Wesley and I were now strolling along one of the back streets off the main campus. Wesley was talking about Kirlian photography and how it related to the Chinese acupuncture points. From this Wesley switched to a discussion of Chinese medicine.

"Much more sensible system than ours," he said. "There you pay the doctor to keep you well, and when you get sick he pays *you*. A kind of reverse medical insurance. Extraordinary people, the Chinese."

At this point he turned and began up a small walkway to a house. I stopped. I wasn't entirely sure where I was, so intent had I been on our conversation. Wesley turned to me and said, "Well, here we are. Come on in. Mildred will be expecting us."

I immediately began to hem and haw, but then I thought, why shouldn't I go in and meet Mildred? I'd just had one of the most fascinating hours I'd had in a long time.

Wesley opened the door and called.

"Mildred! Yoo hoo! We're home. We have a guest."

A moment later Mildred appeared. She was wearing coveralls.

"Wesley, darling, how did your lecture go?"

"It was an astounding success! I've met Richard here. Richard is studying Biology — and yet he doesn't go to labs."

"Really? Hear that, Wordsworth? This young man doesn't do his labs." Then she turned to me. "Wordsworth quite agrees — 'We murder to dissect.'"

"Wordsworth's our cat," said Wesley, by way of explanation. "Shall we show you some of Mildred's orchids?"

As she led the way to her greenhouse Mildred brought the conversation back to Biology.

"That's what's so wonderful about Mr Kirlian's apparatus, is it not? He's found a machine to tell us what every normal, sane human being knows. That life is different from death and that it makes no sense studying death if you're trying to learn about life."

"Splendidly put, my dear."

I was amazed to find at the back of this small brick house a long, impressive greenhouse. Like farms where the barn is a showplace and the house is just where the family lives, Mildred's greenhouse was obviously the focal point. It took a good half hour to give me the over-all tour and then Wesley and I took our sherries into the kitchen while Mildred put on the rice to accompany an enormous potato curry. By the end of the evening I'd learned that they were vegetarians, child-less, admirers of Mahatma Ghandi, passionate about nuclear disar-mament, enraged at the presence of American advisers in a small Southeast Asian country I'd never heard of. In short, they were two of the best conversationalists I'd ever met. I understood completely how they could live happily in that little house with just their cat. Conver-sation leapt from subject to subject — politics, art, biology, religion — and yet, as Wesley had said, everything always seemed to come together in the end. As the evening wore down I realized that once again I'd found an engaging professor.

This time I was determined not to spoil it by actually signing up for one of his classes.

MY MEETING AND SUBSEQUENT FRIENDSHIP with Wesley and Mildred Ames was one of the turning points of my life. At least I realized that I wasn't interested in Slavic Poetry. This was a big improvement, as in the old days I'd have developed a temporary passion for the poet Lestrenkov. Instead, I learned something much more important. I learned that academia by its very nature is con-fining and that my real interests probably lay outside it. Up until then I'd been attempting to find something that would obsess me, the way photography obsessed Breetz. Clearly, that's what I'd been hoping for in Biology — an all-consuming passion. But after meeting Wesley I realized that my interests were too eclectic and diversified to be contained by a single discipline. So instead of taking something difficult for me, like Biology, I decided I would go the opposite route and take what came easily to me. Nothing was easier than English — I was a voracious reader anyway — so a couple of days later I dropped out of Biology and requested an interview with the Registrar. Looking over my academic record, the Registrar quite agreed that English would be a fine idea. He arranged a meeting with the head of the English department, who organized a quick make-up programme. So that winter I did my Beowulf to Virginia Woolf.

Wesley and I began collaborating on our first paper. He did the translating and I did most of the organizing and writing. It was a short paper on the work of Semyon Kirlian and was later published in *The Journal of Parapsychology*. I would have dinner with Mildred and Wesley a couple of times a week and I suppose the fact that they were childless and I was away from home was lost on none of us. I became a sort of son to them. Mildred knitted me a thick pullover which I wore almost constantly during the Montreal years. And it was Mildred who first suggested the idea of going to Russia. In July there was to be a conference in Moscow at which Wesley would be the keynote speaker. It would give the two of us a chance to visit the Kirlians. A chance to meet the man who had developed the apparatus that had taken those remarkable photos.

I didn't feel I could just pick up the phone or write a breezy letter asking Elizabeth for money for a trip to Russia, so I drove to Toronto. I experienced a strange sensation upon entering the house at Glen Road, which I'm sure has been shared by young men everywhere. Nothing had changed. I went up to my old room and put my small suitcase on the dresser. Then I showered and dressed and came down and Gertie made me a sandwich and bowl of soup which I ate in the kitchen. Around four o'clock I heard a car pull up and I greeted Elizabeth at the door. She was delighted to see me. We mixed ourselves a couple of drinks and took them into the conservatory. I must say it was good to be back in that familiar room talking with my mother. She felt my decision to go into English was a wonderful one.

"All along," she said, "English has obviously been what you should have done and yet somehow we never saw it."

I asked her how my father had reacted to the news. She smiled and shrugged.

"Predictably," she said.

By that I knew she meant he would have been disappointed by my choice of Biology and even more disappointed that once having made a choice I hadn't stayed with it. But for the first time in my twenty-two years I sensed something different in my mother's attention. I had always felt she couldn't hear enough about what was on my mind, but there was a slight restlessness in her manner that day and I finally asked her how she was.

"Fine, fine," she said.

Then she started talking about a new group she'd become involved with. The group was called the Voice of Women and it was very concerned with nuclear testing. This was something new for my mother. As I was growing up she'd been involved in many good causes, raising money for the Hospital for Sick Children, Board of Directors of the Art Gallery, founding member of the Stratford Festival Theatre, but this new group was clearly different from anything else she'd ever done. These were women, she said, with ideas and convictions and she was finding it very stimulating.

"It's a rare day that I come home without some new idea to think about, Richard."

After an hour it was exactly like old times with the two of us exchanging ideas back and forth. She was fascinated to hear about Wesley Ames and intrigued by my description of Kirlian photography. At one point I went upstairs and brought down the Kirlian photos Wesley had loaned me. It was wonderful to show them to someone who understood the implications of this. She could see that whatever Kirlian was doing, it was quite remarkable.

I told her all about Wesley and Mildred and how I'd met them and then I told her how Wesley went to Russia every so often and that he'd suggested I might go along that year and together we would visit

Kirlian. There was the slightest pause while Elizabeth took that in. Then she looked down at the photo in her hand.

"Certainly, Richard. Certainly," she said. "I think that's a wonderful idea."

And I knew what that meant. It meant that this trip would go ahead. My mother and I never talked about money directly. If I needed some money, I always just said I was thinking of such and such, or perhaps it would be a good idea if I did this or that, and she would respond with enthusiasm. A few days later I would have an infusion in my account, more than enough to cover whatever it was I had suggested. It also meant that I never had to come out and ask, and she never had to say no. I'd indirectly asked for money for the trip to Russia and I would indirectly be given it. And so that, I thought, would be that. We would sit there a while talking, and after my father got in and had his usual scotch and soda we would all have dinner together. But it turned out to be not quite so simple.

Around about seven o'clock I heard a small tinkle in the dining room, which was Gertie's way of announcing that dinner was served. We met my father as he came out of his study.

"Hello, Richard," he said. We shook hands.

The three of us walked to the dining room where my father held my mother's chair, then took his place at the head of the table. Gertie brought in the roast, baked potatoes and peas and carrots. Things were going quite smoothly and amiably. I poured the wine while my father sharpened the carving knife and he and I chatted a bit about the safest of all topics — the weather.

"Cold in Montreal I expect?" he said.

"Yes," I said. "But it's a dry cold. Not like Toronto."

"Cold. Now Baffin Island, that was cold."

I knew what was coming. His Baffin Island story. Fifty below zero when the generator shut down. Entire camp without power. No one worried, there was the back-up generator. No one except him and the operations manager, that is. They knew this *was* the back-up generator. The main one had blown two days before.

Just as he was about to launch into the story, my mother, who had been smoothing her napkin over her lap, said, quite calmly, that I was going to Russia this summer.

"Russia?" My father stopped mid-stroke in his sharpening and looked at my mother. She looked up from her place.

"Yes," she said. "Russia."

"Russia. Whatever for?"

I sensed a great deal of tension in the air so I tried to step in. I told my father that there was a Russian scientist — an electrical engineer, in fact — who had invented a machine that photographed light.

"Light," said my father. "This machine photographs light."

"Well, not just ordinary light," I stammered.

"Not ordinary light. What sort of light?"

I heard myself becoming inarticulate.

"It's a machine that photographs light that we can't see. A light emanating from living things."

"An invisible light, emanating from invisible things."

"No, no, not invisible things, invisible light."

"Invisible light. Invisible light from visible things."

I nodded. At this point my mother spoke up.

"Interesting, isn't it, Richard, how, when your father repeats back the most fascinating ideas, they appear foolish and inane?"

"Who's organizing this trip, Richard?" my father asked.

I told him as best I could about Wesley Ames.

"So, this Professor of Slavic Studies goes to Soviet Russia, in order to study...a poet."

"That's right," I said.

"Surely, Richard, you're not so naïve. No one gets into Soviet Russia without connections in the Communist Party."

"Your father is suggesting, Richard, that your friend Wesley is a Soviet spy."

I just looked at him.

"You would not be the first naïve young westerner the Soviets tried to recruit, son."

"Yes, Richard," my mother said. "In fact they've already recruited Hilda McDonald, Lucy Turnbull, Martha Jennings and Elizabeth Hathaway. We, too, are all working for a Communist front."

"The Communists are very clever, Richard. They infiltrate organizations made up of unsuspecting, naïve people such as yourself and use them for their own ends."

"Your father is looking at you, Richard, but talking to me. The Voice of Women is not a Communist front, John. We are not a bunch of silly women being manipulated by evil Communists. We believe nuclear testing is harmful and as leaders of our community we believe it is our duty to protest it. Don't be ridiculous!"

My father, who had been gripping the sharpening steel during this whole conversation, placed it and the knife calmly beside the platter. Then he turned and looked directly at my mother.

"Elizabeth, I haven't worked hard all my life in order to be called ridiculous in my own home."

"Oh? And why have you worked so very hard all your life, John?"

"Respect. A man works hard so that he can be respected by his peers, and so that he can provide for his family."

He then turned to me.

"And, Richard, I am not going to finance a trip to Soviet Russia so that you can look at a machine that supposedly photographs a mysterious light emanating from fingertips and leaves."

He then picked up the carving knife and fork and sliced off four slices of roast beef.

"I believe you like yours medium-rare, Richard?"

I nodded. My father then served my mother and took the well-done outside cut for himself. We all ate in silence.

I had never heard my parents fight before and I'm sure by a lot of family standards, I still hadn't. At the time all I could think of was my trip to Russia. Once Wesley, Mildred and I had decided I was going to Russia, it had never occurred to me that I wouldn't be able to go. I'd always been able to do whatever I'd wanted and, in fact, my desires always seemed to be much less than what my parents wanted to give me. Now, suddenly, I was faced with the prospect of being denied one of the very few things I wanted to do.

Gertie took away the platter with the roast and the vegetables and served us apple crisp with whipped cream. But when it came time for coffee, my father excused himself and took his in the study. As soon as we heard the door to the study quietly shut, my mother turned to me. There was an intensity to her voice that I'd never heard before and her hand was shaking as she stirred her coffee.

"Your father isn't financing your trip to Russia, Richard. I am."

FROM THE MOMENT SHOOTING BEGAN there had been trouble on *Something's Got to Give*. Big trouble. The producers claimed they hadn't given Marilyn Monroe script approval, which, technically, they hadn't. But Marilyn just said she couldn't speak the lines and if Marilyn couldn't speak the lines no lines got spoken. There were absences, illnesses. Time was money. She'd already cost them half a million. Every time Marilyn didn't show — and out of thirty-three days of shooting so far she'd missed twenty-one — one hundred and four people had to sit around twiddling their thumbs at the studio's expense. So there were negotiations, talks. Finally they had given Marilyn the script and told her to put an X beside anything that made her uneasy. If she absolutely hated a line, two Xs. And the script had come back to them with Xs all over it. She was impossible.

Marilyn was enraged. You didn't present Marilyn Monroe with a *fait accompli*. If Marilyn didn't like a script, Marilyn couldn't act it. But they'd gone ahead without her, tried to ride roughshod over Marilyn Monroe. Well, she wouldn't do it. She couldn't do it. So finally they'd told her, put an X beside a line if you're uneasy with it, XX beside a line you hate. So she'd gone through their lousy script — XX, XX, XX — she hated everything, there were double crosses everywhere and that's when she knew. It was a sign. They were going to double-cross her.

And they did. They gave her the sack.

They said she was impossible. Impossible? The only thing that was impossible was making a Marilyn Monroe movie without Marilyn Monroe.

She'd show them. You don't present Marilyn Monroe with a *fait accompli*. You don't ride roughshod over Marilyn Monroe. She knew what she'd do. She'd do what she always did when things got tough. She'd go back to the camera. Back to the still camera. She'd show them.

THAT SPRING there were visa applications and reapplications, trips to the embassy in Ottawa, inoculations, reservations, airline tickets,

Intourist coupons and an inconceivable number of bureaucratic foul-ups. But by July we did get everything more or less straightened out. Wesley was travelling as a delegate to a conference on Slavic poetry and I was registered as his assistant.

We flew from Montreal to Paris, Paris to Helsinki, Helsinki to Moscow. We were no sooner installed in our hotel in Moscow than our Intourist guide started to organize us. I can't imagine what a visit to Russia would have been like without Wesley. Wesley spoke Russian and he seemed quite confident that one was simply to wriggle out of all the planned ordeals that Intourist had arranged for us. Our biggest wriggle was the visit we made to the Kirlians. Again and again I was thankful for Wesley's fluency in Russian. He managed to get us on and off various modes of conveyance until finally we found ourselves in Krasnodar, near the Black Sea, standing on the porch of a small one-storeyed house. We knocked. A short bespectacled man — Semyon Kirlian — answered, and behind him stood his wife, Valentina. Wesley introduced himself and me and the Kirlians shook our hands with great warmth and vigour.

We entered a hall filled with electronic apparatus: oscilloscopes, generators, magnifying lenses and photographic plates. Then we went into a room that was larger than the hall, but equally crammed with Kirlian's inventions. Behind this room was another small room that served as the Kirlians' cramped living quarters. On the counter by the sink was a large samovar bubbling away. We sat down and Valentina served us hot Russian tea in glasses.

Wesley and the Kirlians were talking a mile a minute, but every now and then Wesley would stop and translate for me and I would nod. I soon gathered that the Kirlians were very happy about our little paper, the abstract of which they'd seen. The Kirlians had been working on their process since the nineteen forties with absolutely no state funding. In the last ten years a constant stream of visitors had come to the little house on Kirov Street — biophysicists, biochemists, doctors, criminologists, electronics experts and some of the most illustrious names in Soviet science — and yet official recognition was slow in coming. In the next couple of years the protest on behalf of the Kirlians would grow to such an extent that they would be moved out of their little house into a good-sized apartment and given a fully equipped lab. But when Wesley and I visited, their work was only just beginning to be officially acknowledged in Russia and our short paper represented one of the few accounts of their work abroad.

We sat around the table and talked for almost an hour before we even went into the lab. I was expecting to see a demonstration of the apparatus that had taken the photographs Wesley had shown me, but the Kirlians had something new to show us. They had developed a special optical instrument so that they could observe the phenomenon directly. Wesley went first. He put his right hand into the instrument and bent to look through the lens.

"Extraordinary," he said, and the Kirlians seemed pleased, despite the fact that they had shown this phenomenon to Russian scientists time and time again. Wesley stood upright, leaving his hand in the apparatus and nodded his head to indicate that I should have a look. It was one thing to see a single Kirlian photo, but what I saw when I looked through that lens was moving, pulsating, alive. The hand itself looked like the Milky Way in a starry sky. Against a background of blue and gold, something was taking place in Wesley's hand that looked like a fireworks display. Multicoloured flares lit up, then sparks, twinkles, flashes. Some lights glowed steadily like Roman candles, others flashed out, then dimmed. I was eager to see my own hand in the instrument. Quite frankly I expected, being younger than Wesley, to have an even more spectacular light show. This turned out not to be the case. There were the glittering flares and sparkling galaxies but they didn't have quite the intensity I'd seen in Wesley's hand. Valentina seemed to sense my disappointment.

"In the interests of Science," she said, "drink this."

She then handed me a glass of clear liquid. I drank it. Vodka.

"Now look," she said with a smile.

I bent back over the lens. Almost instantly there was an effect and in the next minute, as I felt the vodka warm my throat and chest, my whole hand became a luminous cloud of multicoloured sparks and flares. They pulsated and shot and changed. It was like seeing the aurora borealis in my own hand.

As I was watching this, Semyon was explaining to Wesley that attitude played a large part in just how the flares of energy discharged. Illness, emotion, states of mind, thoughts, fatigue, all made their distinctive imprint on the pattern of energy.

"Curiously, the more fatigued and over-strained a person appears, the more energy seems to pour out of the body. In the same way vodka, by releasing your inhibitions, somehow increased the intensity of the effect," Wesley translated.

We spent most of the day with the Kirlians and left their home late that afternoon. That night we stayed in a dreadful hotel in Krasnodar. A small insight into how real Russians travelled. Intourist wouldn't have approved.

Wesley's three-day conference took place at the end of the week, back in Moscow. I had two choices: I could go to the conference as a delegate and sit through interminable papers, not a word of which I would understand, or I could submit myself to Intourist. I chose the latter. So I rode the subway, toured a collective farm, walked through acres of pearls and jewels in the Kremlin and visited Lenin's tomb. It was at an art gallery that I saw Russian iconographic painting firsthand. Having just visited the Kirlians, I was struck by the representation of these luminous figures, always blue and gold, so similar to what I had experienced in observing my own and Wesley's hands. Obviously, the paintings of saints with halos were based on a convention, but what was the convention based on? It was based on something people saw. Some people, anyway. Van Gogh's famous self-portrait, again in blue and gold, shows spirals of light emanating from his own face. He must have experienced directly what the convention of halos was based upon.

The conference on Slavic poetry ended with a banquet where I consumed more alcohol in one night than I had in the previous year. I awoke with a splitting headache and Wesley and I spent much of the morning of our departure drinking black coffee and wandering about in a fog. But we managed to get onto the plane and the plane made its connections and ten days after we had left Montreal we returned to the city full of plans about a new and more comprehensive paper on the Kirlians.

"YOU'RE JUST A BOY," Milton Greene said. He was sitting at the bar of the Lion's Head. "How old are you?"

"Twenty-three," Breetz said.

"Twenty-three. I was thirty-three when I first met her. 'You're just a boy,' she said. 'You're just a girl,' I said. Right back. Didn't miss a beat. She liked that. Laughed that soft giggly girly laugh she has. Cotton candy. She was a girl, too. Twenty-nine. Kindest girl I ever knew. Wept buckets over some dead fish. Dropped me like a piece of shit when she was through with me. Tony, another double. And one for my friend. Know who this guy is, Tony? This is Breetz Mestrovic. The Milton fuckin' Greene of his day. Yeah. Know what he's gonna do tomorrow, Tony? This poor son of a bitch is gonna fly to Los Angeles and photograph you-know-who. There you go. Here's to You-Know-Who. Great plans. God, we were gonna take on the world. Make Art. Chekhov, Dostoevsky. She loves the Russians, Marilyn does. Lived with us, you know. In Connecticut. Had her very own room. Used to say we were the only family she ever had. 'Course she's always saying that about everybody. Only fuckin' family she ever had. Amy and me, the Kargers, the DiMaggios, the Strasbergs, the Millers. Only family she ever had. Has more fuckin' families than you can shake a stick at. We all love her. Know who she loves? She loves the camera. It's reciprocal. The only thing that really knows Marilyn — the camera. She flickers up for a second, the camera gets it, catches it, locks it away, then it disappears again and we're left with god-knows-what. A mess. So, *Vogue*'s sending you out to photograph Marilyn? She'll be late. You have any idea how late she'll be? No, you don't. She'll be so late she'll drive you out of your gourd. Just when you're about to jump out the window she'll float into the room, cool you out, be wonderful. You say you want advice? Olivier wanted advice, too. Called up Huston, Wilder, Logan. 'Don't order her around,' Logan begged. 'She knows more about the camera than anyone alive. Don't order her around.' What does Olivier do? Orders her around. 'Walk here.' 'Sit there.' 'Project.' 'Be sexy.' Oh, yeah, she was part of the family all right. The part that wore ermine, lived at the Waldorf, drove a Thunderbird, rode a pink elephant into Madison Square Garden. All out of my pocket. If you got Marilyn Monroe, you gotta use her, she'd say. So I used her. Great days. She was going to work with Olivier. Greatest actor of his age. Oh, god, it was embarrassing. Miller all tight-faced, miserable bastard, sucking up to the Great Actor. And Olivier so contemptuous of The Method. 'Be sexy,' he'd say and she'd stumble around, miss her lines, screw up. And Paula. Paula Strasberg. 'Just think of Frankie Sinatra and Coca-Cola.' There's Marilyn thinking 'Frankie Sinatra and Coca-Cola' and you could feel the contempt. Sir Laurence. Greatest actor of our time. Tony, can we have another? 'Course, when it came to the rushes, she blew him off the screen. Obliterated the pompous bastard. Josh Logan. Now there's the only film director who knows how to handle her. Just keep the goddamn cameras rolling and hope for the best. Of course, we all underestimate her. All of us. Keep figuring all she needs is a little direction. A little control. I'd form a company, get her some good parts. Get her some great directors. All she needed was me running the show. Ha. You're probably the same way. Out to save her. Everybody's always out to save her. I was gonna save her from Hollywood. Hollywood schlock. DiMaggio? DiMaggio was gonna save her too. Keep her in the kitchen while he watched TV. And Miller? Miller would save her by putting her in one of his plays. We all had our schemes. But she outfoxed us all — ha! Get it? Fox. We outfoxed Fox and Fox outfoxed us. Fuckin' Fox. Thanks, Tony. I used to think, If only she was a little sane. Not a lot, so we'd still get that magic, but a little. Anybody ever tell you she smells? It's true. Not always, but sometimes. You go to photograph her — she's dishevelled. She's a mess. Hasn't combed her hair in days. Hasn't bathed. She smells. But then you develop the prints, and you can't believe it. She's beautiful. So beautiful. Eve, Sam, Richard, Doug — they'll all tell you the same thing. You don't always know. The camera sees something we don't. She *does* something. She *does* something. You want advice? Point your camera at her and click it. And keep clicking. Don't scare her. Don't scare her. She's a hummingbird in flight. Scare her and she's gone. Could take hours to get her back. Days. Sometimes months. Those are the bad times. Alcohol, barbiturates, awake when she should be asleep, asleep when she should be awake. Bad, bad times. Just keep clicking. A mysterious thing, a photograph. Shutterspeed. Not a second, a fraction of a second. A millisecond. The human eye can't do it. So fast. And I swear to god, whatever she does doesn't last more than that. Then that fuckin' instant, that brief tiny minuscule moment of time, becomes an eternity. And it hangs in your head. And you can't get rid of it. She's there. She's made that instant eternal and your whole fuckin' life revolves around that instant. And getting another instant just like it. And another. And another. I love my wife. I love my kid. I spend days, weeks, years with them. But that instant... that instant never leaves my head. It's always there. Yeah, yeah, I took some beautiful photos of her. She glowed. Every photographer you ever talk to will tell you the same thing. Eve, Sam, Richard, Doug, me. She glows. Have you seen the one in the Actors Studio? Good. Then you know. That photo was taken in available light. She's standing there surrounded by people. She glows, the others don't. You're a photographer. You understand light. She glows, the others don't. Available light. Does that make sense? Whatever she does doesn't make sense. And yet we're always trying to make sense out of it. Be sensible, Marilyn. How many times did I bite my lip wanting to say that? Be sensible. But she doesn't make sense. She makes magic. So don't you go to L.A. trying to be sensible. Just be nice to her. That's what Josh Logan and I know. Be nice. Be soft. Be gentle. And keep that camera clicking. You come to me for advice. I give you advice. You might take it, you might not. It doesn't matter, see, 'cause it's not you. It's her. She does something. She does something. She's luminous. She'll break your heart. She breaks everyone's heart. 'Cause she's got something we all want. Poor girl. She has something. And we all want it. It's just like she says in *The Misfits*: Maybe if we hang around her light long enough, it'll rub off. Maybe. But it's not something we can take. It's only something she can give. And when she stops giving, you've had it. She broke my heart. She'll break yours. She just disappeared out of my life. Gone. Just left me hanging. Bitch. Know what Billy Wilder says about her? He says he's too old and too rich to ever work with Marilyn Monroe again. I spent all my money and four years of my life... give her a message for me, will you? Give her my love."

VOGUE HAD ARRANGED EVERYTHING. Breetz flew first class to Los Angeles. He was met at the airport by a chauffeur and driven to the Ambassador Hotel, where he was greeted as if he were a head of state and personally escorted by the manager to the Honeymoon Suite. The manager flung the door open. Breetz stepped in.

"This is terrible," he said.

The manager's face fell. This room was the pride of the hotel. And he'd stocked the bar specially with Dom Perignon, Marilyn's favourite champagne. There were a dozen red roses.

"Wrong, it's all wrong," Breetz said.

"Wrong? What's wrong?"

"The light."

"The light?"

"It's morning and the room is filled with light."

"I don't — "

"By afternoon this room will be in shade. Follow me."

The manager followed Breetz into the elevator, down to the lobby and out onto the street. They circled the hotel. When they got to the northwest corner Breetz stopped.

"Any one of those three," he said, pointing at corner rooms on the third, fourth and fifth floors. "Tomorrow, between five and eight in the evening, the light in those rooms will be perfect."

The perfect light. Breetz was going to photograph the world's most beautiful woman and he was determined that when he photographed her, he would photograph her in the perfect light.

An hour later a middle-aged couple from Des Moines found themselves ensconced in the Honeymoon Suite with a bottle of champagne and a dozen red roses and Breetz had their corner room on the fourth floor. He spent the rest of the day shopping.

The next morning Breetz got to work. He replaced the beige curtains with white sheers. He turned the ordinary twin beds into banquettes of white, stripping off the yellow chenille and replacing it with white-on-white bedspreads heaped with white and off-white cushions. He spread a white linen cloth over the chest of drawers and on it he placed the Leica and dozens of rolls of film. He set up his lights, hoping he wouldn't need them, then called Housekeeping and asked for an iron and ironing board to be brought to the room. When the bellboy left, Breetz lifted from a box, as carefully as if he were handling a ceremonial gown, a simple, impeccably tailored man's white shirt. He tested the iron with the tip of a wetted finger then spread the shirt over the ironing board. Breetz ironed that shirt with a ritual solemnity — preparing the robe for a goddess. And as he ironed he went over in his mind's eye his vision of Marilyn. It had started to form the very moment Diana had given him the news. Spontaneously, as if the images were out there and he was just tuning into them. Marilyn. Marilyn in a simple white shirt.

As he ironed, he could see her. Marilyn lounging on the chair, her leg up over the arm, sipping champagne. *Click.* Marilyn, her head tossed back, laughing. *Click.* Marilyn, flopped on the bed, wearing the white shirt. *Click.* It was as if Marilyn were there in the room — actually there — and he could see her in perfect detail. *Click, click, click.*

At noon, the flowers arrived. Dozens and dozens of chrysanthemums, roses and tulips — all white. The final touch to Breetz's vision — the perfect light, the perfect shirt, a flower-filled room.

Then he began to wait. He knew that although the appointment was scheduled for two he shouldn't even start thinking of her arriving before five. Between five and eight the light in that flower-filled room would be perfect. He had prepared himself for Marilyn's lateness but, as one after another of the men who had photographed her had told him, nothing can prepare you for Marilyn's lateness. She will be late and then she will be later still and still even more late. She will be so late she will drive you crazy.

MARILYN WOULDN'T COME. She'd known it from the moment she'd woken up. Three seconals and she'd only managed four hours' sleep. But she couldn't go back to sleep, couldn't let herself sink back into nothingness. There was something she had to do today. *Vogue* magazine.

She sat at her vanity. It wasn't the crusty white film on her right thigh that reminded her of yesterday, but the sound of Sinatra's voice singing "That's Life." She ran a hand through her hair and looked at her pale face in the mirror.

Those bastards. Those bastards. To them she was just a piece of meat to be handed around. She stared into the mirror and she saw a desperate, exhausted, depressed woman. She knew that somehow she had to do it. Do it once again. Marilyn. Every day she had to get up and create anew the World's Most Beautiful Woman. She could do it. She knew she could do it. She'd done it thousands and thousands of times before. She could do it. She could do it.

But first she needed a drink.

She stared at the mirror. What she saw, she mustn't see. That was the first step. She must see Beauty. She was a goddess — Aphrodite — and she — and she alone — could incarnate beauty. First she had to see it in her mind's eye.

It wouldn't come.

She needed another drink.

It was easier when she was young. Norma Jean would leave and Marilyn would be there in seconds. She used to be able to conjure her up for a fifty-dollar modelling job. Or, sometimes, just walking down the street, with no one noticing her, she'd flip into Marilyn just for fun. And almost instantaneously a crowd would gather and there'd be that feverish excitement, scary at times but, oh, so exciting.

She parted her lips and ran her tongue over them. Sometimes that worked. Sometimes just doing a little Marilyn could trigger the whole thing.

But not today. Nothing seemed to be working today.

She remembered those times...those horrible times when Marilyn wouldn't come. That day on *Some Like It Hot*. And everyone going frantic...but it wouldn't come. Marilyn wouldn't come, and if Marilyn wouldn't come there was nothing she could do about it. And so they'd cajoled and begged and pleaded for her to hurry hurry hurry. And so to please them she'd gone through the motions. Put on her makeup, done her hair, her lipstick and still Marilyn wasn't there.

So what could she do but stall and stall some more while they cajoled and pleaded and begged, hurry hurry hurry.

It wouldn't come. She could feel the desperation growing inside. It would never come again. She'd lost it. No, no, she said to herself, so many times before she'd *thought* she'd lost it, that tiny little vision of beauty inside of her that grew into Marilyn. Why did it have to take so long? Why couldn't she conjure it instantly? Why did she have to sit hour after hour before the mirror? It seemed she had to reach a point of hopelessness before the image would form in her mind. As if she had to destroy and create Marilyn Monroe every day.

She'd tried everything. She'd phoned all her friends. She'd even phoned Dr Greenson, but it was no use. People were nice. They tried to help, but it was no use. Nothing was any use.
Nembutals. Where were the nembutals?

What was that between her legs? Was she bleeding? No. She'd peed herself. Again. The warm wetness spread out under her thighs. She started to cry. She cried and cried and soon she was weeping uncontrollably.
She'd tried everything, all the old tricks, but none of them had worked. Vodka. More vodka was what she needed.

She hadn't come. She hadn't come. She'd sat there, while the room grew dark around her, but Marilyn hadn't come.

One little two little three little nembutals
Four little five little six little nembutals
Seven little eight little nine little nembutals
Ten little nembutal pills.
One for Norma Jean who never had a daddy
One for little Norma Jean whose mummy was crazy
One for each year in the orphanage. That's two.
One for every foster home. That's six.
One for the boarder who raped her when she was twelve
Time for more vodka to swish them all down

One for Jim Dougherty
Poor Jim, it wasn't your fault.
One for Tommy Zahn
Two for Freddy Karger 'cause he shoulda married me
One for Johnny Hyde
And here's to you, Joe, the Last American Hero.
One for Arthur
One for Yves
One for Frankie Sinatra who introduced me to Mr President
Happy Birthday, Mr President
Two for Mr President and
Three for his chickenshit brother.
Have I missed anybody? Lots and lots and lots.
So here's to all the rest of you.
It's curtains, fellas,
Thanks for nothin'.

KATE AND I GOT TO KNOW EACH OTHER SLOWLY. She worked at Chez Madelaine. I used to stop in there quite often and we'd chat about this and that the way you do when someone's a regular. I remember once she asked me about a book I was reading and then a few days after that I saw her in Treasure Island. Instead of her serving me coffee, I took her out for coffee. I suppose our friendship was inevitable. We both had lots of time on our hands, we both liked second-hand bookstores, especially Treasure Island, we both loved wandering the streets of Montreal and, of course, we both spoke English.

One night at Chez Madelaine, Kate was sitting with me during a lull. A man and a woman entered and sat at one of Kate's tables. There was something about the woman, Kate said. Something familiar. I looked over but the woman was facing her dinner companion and all I could see was frizzy grey hair. Kate took a yellow pad from her pocket, excused herself and approached their table. It wasn't near enough to mine for me to hear all that went on, but it was clear that Kate had recognized the woman and the woman, Kate.

It was Ruby Nielson, her old acting teacher.

Ruby's companion was the director Brian Reed. Ruby Nielson had known Brian all her life. They'd grown up in the same neighbourhood and had been involved in little theatre together. Both had gone to England and done some serious acting in their early twenties, but Brian had returned and gone the academic route. He'd become a professor of English at the University of Toronto and seemed to have drifted out of theatre, while Ruby continued to act and began doing a little directing. But Ruby always had trouble as a director because she didn't seem as interested in the production as she was in the actual acting. She kept getting bogged down in rehearsals, doing improvisations and exercises to release the actors' creativity. Everyone loved working with Ruby but the production itself was often a shambles. The actors would become so immersed in the process that the final product didn't read to an audience. Although admired throughout the theatre community, by the time she was in her early thirties Ruby got less and less directing work. But this was all right by her, as she had discovered by then that teaching was her true love. She gave classes for adults, professional actors and even children. She became somewhat of a legend in Canadian theatre circles.

Meanwhile, her friend Brian Reed didn't seem to be doing any theatre at all. He was teaching English, had gotten married, and had children. Then he directed an Ibsen at Hart House and to his amazement the play had been a huge success. It seemed that Brian's methodical academic nature was well suited to directing. Brian, who had never been a really great actor, had a feel for production values and for the play as a whole.

After he'd taught for four or five years, Brian took a sabbatical from the university. At Ruby's urging, he used this time to study directing at the Yale School of Drama. When he returned, he began to direct professionally. Brian found he preferred directing realism and naturalism. He loved Chekhov and Ibsen, Tennessee Williams and Arthur Miller.

As Brian's reputation in Canadian theatre grew, he found he relied more and more on his friend Ruby for advice. Almost every professional actor in Canada had been through at least one of her workshops and Brian never cast a play without consulting her. He always acknowledged this in interviews and never made a secret of how much he trusted her judgement. "I'm the head and she's the heart," he would say. His strength as a director was that he understood the text and the period and the dynamics of the play as a whole, but when it came to casting, he often relied on his old friend to sniff out the perfect actor for the perfect part. So when Centaur Theatre invited Brian Reed to direct *The Seagull* he brought Ruby along to the auditions. That afternoon they'd cast most of the minor parts and only one significant part remained.

After Kate and Ruby exchanged greetings that evening, and after Kate was introduced to Brian Reed and had taken both their orders and left their table, I noticed that Ruby and Brian kept looking her way and talking very intently. I now know what the conversation was about.

"Brian," Ruby was saying, "that girl is your Nina."

This didn't astound Brian Reed. He was used to actors, especially young actors, waiting on tables. But he was curious to know what the girl with the short hair had done.

"Nothing as far as I know," Ruby said. "But I've taught her. She's good. Really good. In fact, I've often wondered what became of Katie."

"Done," said Brian.

When Ruby Nielson and Brian Reed had left, Kate came back to my table. She couldn't quite believe what had happened. Brian Reed was directing *The Seagull* for Centaur Theatre and he'd offered Kate the part of Nina without even auditioning her. It was then she told me about her acting classes with Ruby Nielson. She told me how she'd loved the classes with Ruby because Ruby had challenged her in a way she'd never been challenged before.

I was quite boggled by the whole thing. Unlike Kate, I'd heard of Brian Reed and I knew enough about theatre to know that this was an Equity production and that Kate would be working with seasoned professionals.

"Equity?" Kate said.

And that boggled me even more. She didn't even know what that meant. But then Kate wasn't at all theatrical. I'd gone out with girls who had done some acting, and there had always been something exaggerated about their movements and gestures, onstage and off. It was a way of drawing attention to themselves. But Kate seemed to be almost invisible. Even within movement there was a stillness. She appeared at someone's table, took their order, disappeared and then reappeared somewhere else. I could hardly imagine what she would be like onstage. In fact, I couldn't.

Sometimes, if I was still around when Kate finished her shift, I'd walk her home to her piale on Sherbrooke. I'm not sure why Kate and I didn't become involved then, lovers I mean, but we didn't. She seemed so young to me, and it was clear that she really valued my friendship, and I hers. Always before with girls when I showed interest they would start to flirt. Once a girl started flirting with me I would become charming. And they would become even more interested. But charm for me was a way of warding people off. Of keeping them at a distance. Kate didn't flirt and I wasn't charming, so something else developed between us. Something far rarer in the Sixties than a one-night stand or a casual affair. Kate and I developed a friendship. A friendship that was to last many years.

DANIEL LLOYD ORDERED ANOTHER SCOTCH. Chandos was still his favourite pub, not far from the scene of his first triumph. He thought back to that production of *Love's Labour's Lost*.

Only twenty-one, and directing Shakespeare at the Aldwych. He was young, eager, anxious. For weeks he'd worked on it. He'd cut out little figures and a plan of the stage. He'd moved all the little figures around, blocking the play. And then, on the morning of the first rehearsal, all these people had shown up. Actors. They'd read through the play, and he'd said, Okay everyone, let's get to work. And the first actors stepped onto the taped rehearsal hall floor, and Daniel Lloyd started to block the play the way he'd worked it out with his cardboard figures. But when the actors moved in his preconceived directions they looked awkward, stiff, cardboardish. And suddenly he realized that these weren't cardboard cutouts, these were people. Human beings.

So he abandoned his plan and began telling them to go here and go there — and it was like a great huge wave of energy had engulfed him, and ideas started to come. And they kept coming. He'd tell an actor to try something and the actor, being a person, a unique individual, would do something totally unexpected, and, no longer having a plan, Daniel Lloyd would use that unexpectedness to create something unexpected in himself. And each unexpectedness created more unexpectedness and the whole process was astonishing.

As the rehearsal went on he felt a wonderful thing happening. He could feel the actors' confidence in him growing. And as it grew, they started doing more and more astonishing things. And each astonishing thing they did made him go in yet another unexplored direction. And all the problems that other directors talked about — problems of characterization, of motive, of blocking — seemed just so many inessential details. It was as if there was a play out there somewhere and Shakespeare had plugged into it. All Daniel had to do was plug into the same play, as if he and Shakespeare were drinking from the same source. He could feel the actors drinking from it too.

And when the play opened the best thing of all happened. The audience got it. The instant the first word was spoken everyone in the theatre melded into one great mind. Everyone disappeared into the vision. And at twenty-one Daniel Lloyd was hailed as the successor of Tyrone Guthrie, as one of the great new imaginations of English post-war theatre.

Of course the strain had been terrific. Daniel Lloyd had no idea how he'd done that first *Love's Labour's*. It certainly wasn't anything he thought he could repeat. It had been some sort of strange freak of nature. An accident. But then he'd directed *Titus Andronicus*. He'd picked *Titus* deliberately. Shakespeare's worst play — a bloody melodrama. Blood-soaked. Raped virgins and severed hands. But as he worked on it he plugged into something else. The whole Nazi terror. Was a virgin whose tongue was cut out and hands cut off a "melodramatic horror?" In view of the twentieth century it was just government policy. And somehow, once again, the actors picked up on this and they realized the play wasn't a stupid Senecan melodrama, but a play about all the horrors of this century. And again the huge flood of emotion swept through the cast. And again they astonished him. And again Daniel Lloyd was hailed as the brilliant new energy English theatre had been lacking.

By twenty-five he was being sought by every theatre in Britain. At thirty, he had been offered the Artistic Directorship of the Royal Shakespeare Company. But Daniel Lloyd refused. He knew his genius was for directing, not for administration. He knew that what he did best was to find that original vision and make it relevant for his place and his time. So he'd gone on being a guest director while his friends and contemporaries, one by one, took over the directorships of all the major theatres. But Lloyd knew that he himself was the greatest director of them all. Lloyd knew it, and what was best for those wonderful years of his thirties was that everyone else knew it too. So he went from the Royal Shakespeare Company, to the National, to Chichester, and he had carte blanche. He directed what he wanted to direct. He hired whom he wanted to hire.

Now he was in his forties. In the past couple of years, something had gone wrong. He couldn't quite put his finger on it, but he'd started to lose his intensity. He'd go into rehearsal without an idea — the way he'd gone so often in the past — and no idea would come. So he'd started to do something that as a young man he'd sworn never to do. He started to plan. And, of course, the plans worked. So in each successive production he found himself planning more and more. He was like an old athlete who in his youth had got along on sheer reflexes and skill but who now had to outmanoeuvre his opponents.

Daniel Lloyd sipped at his scotch. In his youth he had been all magic. But now, slowly, the magic was leaving him...who was that in Shakespeare? Antony...once he had felt like the young Mark Antony, the Antony of *Julius Caesar* — magnetic, inspiring, the leader whose soldiers would follow him anywhere...and then, gradually, the magic had started to wane. He was still Antony, but no longer the young, dynamic, inspired Antony — the take-on-the-world Antony of reckless youth. Slowly, he couldn't quite pinpoint when, but slowly, inexorably, he had become the old Antony, the Antony of *Antony and Cleopatra*...that wonderful scene...wonderful, but horrible and terrifying...when the soldiers wake in the night and hear Antony's music deserting him...Shakespeare. Shakespeare who knew everything...yes, yes. Daniel Lloyd took another slug of scotch. Daniel Lloyd's music was deserting him. And he must do something. Do something before the soldiers heard it too.

IN THE EARLY FIFTIES George Stevens used to work at his father's restaurant in the east end of Hamilton, Ontario. When he was nineteen and working the counter one day, a scene was played out that had happened several times before. But this day George was in charge and the scene was to have a different ending.

Two truckers came in and ordered a coffee and a doughnut. George poured them a coffee each, lifted the cover off the trivet on the counter and put a honey-dipped doughnut on each of their plates. One of the truckers started eating his, but his friend just poked at his with a fork. The doughnut was hard, stale.

"Goddammit to hell," he said. "Why is it no goddamn restaurant, anywhere, can serve a guy a half-decent doughnut? Is that too much to ask?"

"One minute, sir," George said, grabbing their plates and heading for the kitchen.

Once there he whipped out the back door and ran full tilt down the back alley to Gold's Bakery. The owner was George's girlfriend's father, so when George flew in, grabbed up a dozen doughnuts and flew out again, he just shook his head in amusement. Even as George ran back to the restaurant the delicious smell of fresh baked bread, chelsea buns and doughnuts was still with him. He burst through the door of the kitchen, pulled two doughnuts out of the bag and put one on each plate. He ran a hand through his hair, then calmly walked through the swinging doors and put the plates in front of the truckers.

"Sorry about that," he said, trying not to suck in as much air as he wanted to. "Try these."

A few days later the two truckers were back, with two more truckers. As soon as George saw them enter he skipped out the back door, grabbed a dozen fresh doughnuts from the bakery and ran back.

It wasn't long before word got around. Wonderful doughnuts, wonderful coffee. That summer George and Sally got married and George started thinking. What sold? Fresh coffee. Fresh doughnuts. But how to get fresh doughnuts? That was the problem. By the time they were baked, waited for a truck, delivered, they were already old, tired and stale. The only way to get fresh doughnuts was to bake them on the premises. But to do that, you couldn't really make anything else. So why bother? That was George's simple idea. Doughnuts, fresh baked on the premises. Coffee, freshly brewed. That fall he opened his first store.

Five years later George was rich.

Five years after that George was even richer and he'd moved to a posh home in London, Ontario. He became involved with the Rotary, the Chamber of Commerce, the United Way and the Business Improvement Association, but something was lacking in his life. George was known as the Donut King but he wanted to be known for more than that.

One day George got a call from a man who introduced himself as Michael Ras-something-or-other-koff. George asked him to spell it. "R-a-s-n-a-n-i-k-o-f-f."

He asked George if he'd be interested in becoming a member of the Stratford Festival Board. George was astounded. He'd heard of the Stratford Festival Theatre, everyone had. It did Shakespeare. He'd even seen a Shakespeare play there once. It had a king in it. But he knew nothing about classical theatre, except that everyone took it very, very seriously.

At first, George was intimidated by his fellow members. They were all so educated. They all spoke so well. And so many famous names. George kept a very low profile. Fortunately, George's new friend was very kind to him. They would lunch together and Michael would explain to George the politics of what was going on. George was in awe of him.

Michael's family were Russian aristocrats who had fled Russia during the revolution. They had gone to England, then Canada. Michael was born here, but educated at Oxford. Everything about Michael fascinated George: his learning, his world travel, his knowledge of the arts — not just theatre, but ballet, music, painting, literature. Michael knew everybody and everybody deferred to him. And yet he seemed to like George and they'd often get together and just talk.

After a few years on the board of directors, George felt more confident. He saw the smart professor types come and go. He found that some of the most impressive names couldn't be relied upon to get the simplest things done. Mostly it was Michael who helped build his confidence. Michael talked theatre to George, made him understand it was a business, like other businesses, not so different, when you came right down to it, from doughnuts.

"The Classics, fresh baked on the premises."

George roared with laughter. Fresh-baked Shakespeare. Not stale and imported.

Over the next few years, the brainy professors and the big family names came and went, but George remained. And the longer he remained, the more fascinated by the festival he became. And everyone started to take George more seriously. George was no longer just the Donut King, he was George Stevens, a man of culture, a man who knew and understood theatre. A man who passionately believed in the arts.

When the artistic director of Stratford announced his decision to accept an offer from the Lincoln Center in New York, George Stevens was unanimously elected as head of the search committee for a replacement. There was a good deal of pressure from the press to hire a Canadian, but the more George and his committee looked at the available candidates the more uneasy they became. Stratford had been founded by Tyrone Guthrie, one of the greatest directors of the twentieth century, and his successor was also a huge international name. Of all the directors that George's committee interviewed, they didn't find anyone they felt qualified to run such an enormous organization. Meanwhile, the pressure to hire was building.

Michael Rasnanikoff had been out of the country for some months when George got a call from him. George leapt at the chance to discuss his problem with his astute friend. Over lunch, Michael listened quietly while George fretted about his indecision and the fact that time was pressing.

"George," Michael said, "I have a suggestion. One that might not have occurred to you, but one I'd like you to consider. Consider seriously."

Of course George would consider any suggestion of Michael's most seriously.

"I've just returned from England where I had the good fortune to dine with an old Oxford friend of mine. By sheer coincidence, another friend of his was there. Daniel Lloyd."

Daniel Lloyd. George knew that Daniel Lloyd was one of the greatest names in English theatre. The man who had revolutionized post-war production of Shakespeare and made it relevant to the twentieth century.

"After dinner we were talking," Michael continued, "and I mentioned the problems you were having finding a suitable artistic director. I told Lloyd that there was a good deal of pressure on you to hire a Canadian."

At this George Stevens found his stomach tightening.

"Daniel Lloyd listened, how shall I say it, most intently, and then said to me, 'Theatre of the stature of the Stratford Festival should not be limiting itself to just Canadians. The Stratford Festival is a world-class theatre and needs a world-class director to run it.'"

At this point Michael paused and took a sip of his wine.

"George," he said, "there is only one world-class director who doesn't *have* a theatre."

Two days later the president of the Stratford Festival Theatre's search committee, George Stevens — the Donut King — was on a plane to London, England.

REHEARSALS FOR *THE SEAGULL* began on a dreary March day in an old warehouse on Rue Notre-Dame. Kate felt nervous as she climbed the wooden stairs up to the second floor. She walked down a long hall and through a door with a handwritten sign on it: Rehearsal Hall. On the far wall there was a row of windows under which were some radiators hissing steam. In front of the radiators were five cafeteria tables, each about eight feet in length with metal legs and formica tops. They were arranged in a U shape. There were a number of chairs around the tables and also along the warehouse walls.

Over in one corner was a coffee urn and around it were a number of people talking. Kate could just hear snatches of conversation but what she did hear slightly unnerved her. There was mention of Theatre New Brunswick and someone being miscast. Several of the actors were hugging each other and talking excitedly about how great it was to be working together again. Kate didn't know anyone and she didn't feel like coffee so she went over and looked out one of the big windows. The heat of the rad felt good against her legs and she pressed her knees up against it. She was staring at the falling rain when she heard a voice behind her.

"Kate Barnes?"

She turned around. An older woman was smiling at her.

"I'm Jennifer Howard," she said. "I'm playing Irina. I hear you're going to be Nina."

"Yes," Kate said.

The woman looked so nice. She was smiling at Kate and she had soft grey eyes. "Actually, I'm a little nervous," Kate said. "I've never been involved in a professional production before."

The woman smiled, reached forward and pressed Kate's arm.

"Don't you worry, love," she said. "You're in good hands. Brian's just a marvel to work with."

As soon as she said it, Kate started to feel a little better. She and Jennifer Howard talked for a few minutes. Jennifer was from Toronto and would be staying in a hotel in town for the production. She seemed fascinated to hear that Kate had moved to Montreal and learned French working in a small restaurant. She seemed so interested in Kate's life that it was only later, when Kate learned what a name Jennifer Howard was in Canadian theatre, that she fully appreciated how kind Jennifer had been to her that day.

Moments later Brian Reed walked into the rehearsal hall wearing a trench coat and carrying a briefcase. The coat was soaking wet and he gave it a shake before hanging it on a peg jutting out of one of the walls. He then walked over to the middle of the room and put his briefcase on one of the tables. As he did, the steam radiators started to clank and vibrate.

"You'll have to excuse the rads," he said. "They get a little rambunctious at times."

Everybody laughed.

"Grab yourselves a coffee, everyone, then gather round and we'll have a chat before we get down to work."

This time, Kate did get a coffee and a few minutes later she pulled up a chair at the tables along with everyone else. She counted eighteen people, including herself. Brian leaned against the middle table and began speaking.

"Those of you who've worked with me before know Nancy. We're lucky to get her — best stage manager in the business."

A blonde woman with a page-boy and glasses smiled and nodded.

"Nancy has copies of the rehearsal schedule, which we've also posted. We're going to rough block the play in the next three days, try to get an overall feel for it. The next two weeks we'll work the scenes in detail…solve any problems that arise…the third week we'll put it all back together again, see if it flies and move into the theatre." He gestured to a small model that was sitting at the end of the table. "I presume you've all had a chance to take a look at Blair's set. Once again, he's done a fabulous job. I want to remind you all that you can't look at this model enough. Study it, familiarize yourselves with it, remember that while we're working with taped lines, this," he pointed at the model, "is what we're really dealing with."

As he spoke, Kate examined the set model only a few feet down the table from where she sat. It really was remarkable. It was like a little doll's house showing both the inside and the outside of the Sorin's estate. The inside was amazing. There was an entire dining room built to scale with perfect little wooden chairs around a table and a bureau. Kate imagined little people moving inside it, eating their din-ner, speaking their lines.

"We're going to try to get you into some of your costumes by the second week," Brian continued. "Shoes and skirts for the ladies, top-coats and shoes for the men, so you'll have some time to get a feel for moving about in period dress. Joyce? Why don't you just quickly show us your sketches."

A girl in coveralls stood up and flipped through some pen and ink and watercolour sketches. Again, Kate was amazed at the amount of care and detail that had gone into the drawings. And these were just the drawings! She couldn't imagine what it would be like to make all these costumes from scratch.

Brian spoke again.

"In the next day or two, Joyce will be grabbing you when she can and getting measurements — no chocolate sundaes after she's got them." A ripple of laughter went around the tables. "Now, before we begin, I'd just like to say a few words about the play. I'm really very excited to be doing this. I was in my early twenties when I first read *The Seagull* and it was the play that sparked my interest in directing. It seems like such a slight piece, yet the more you live with it the deeper and more profound it gets. I know you'll all find working on it a really special experience because no playwright that I know of understands acting quite like Chekhov. I think what I love most about Chekhov is his feeling for nuance. He gives us a phrase...a ges-ture...and then we must plumb the depths ourselves. My only regret is that we don't have six months to work on this play." He smiled. "If we did, I'd spend at least another couple of hours rambling on about how much I love it. But as we don't, I guess we'd better get down to work!"

At this point there was some fumbling as people got their scripts out and open on the tables. Then the reading began. Kate was sur-prised to find that no one read the lines the way she thought actors would. There was no emphasis and no emotion. They just read their parts the way they'd read the Sunday newspaper. By the time they came to Nina's entrance on page four, Kate was feeling almost relaxed. But still it was strange hearing her own voice speak her first line.

"I'm not late am I? I can't be."

MONEY. Raymond Galdikas wanted money. He'd had enough of speaking the greatest lines in the English language. He was sick of articulating sweet sounds together. He was sick of Falstaff, sick of Lear, Galileo, Faust. He'd had enough of artistic integrity and critical adulation. He'd had enough of culture. He just wanted to make some money.

And why shouldn't he cash in on his reputation? He was, after all, one of the greatest actors in the English language. Had not the *New York Times* said he had a voice unmatched for control and resonance? Had not the *London Observer* talked of his magnificent presence? A presence equal to classical theatre's greatest parts. Had not the *Globe and Mail* waxed lyrical time and time again? And what had it got him? A towering reputation and a very lean bankbook.

Two summers ago he'd been winding up a season as Othello at the Lincoln Center and he got to talking to a young actor who was playing a Venetian attendant. He asked him what he was going to be doing after *Othello* closed. The young actor told him that he had already been hired for an afternoon soap opera and that his employment was assured for the next eight months. As he wiped off his makeup, Galdikas asked him what he would be earning playing in this soap opera. The young man mentioned a figure so astronomical it took Galdikas' breath away. Here he had played Othello for three weeks at one of the biggest theatres in North America and his non-speaking attendant was going to make five times what he had.

Galdikas, then and there, made up his mind that he'd had it with Art. He was forty years old and still living in apartments and hotels. Still shuffling around the continent living out of a suitcase. He wanted a house overlooking a ravine. He wanted a swimming pool and a nice car. He wanted to be able to throw lavish parties and invite his friends from Winnipeg to hobnob with the rich and famous. It was time he started to cash in on his immense reputation. He would go to Hollywood. He would make films. He would become a Star and he would get rich.

That had been the plan.

He went to Hollywood. He acquired an agent. And he gave the agent one simple instruction — no more theatre. He was through with the Classics. He would devote himself to crass commercialism.

He would do film. He would do TV. He would do anything that paid. He wouldn't even read the scripts, he would simply look at the bottom line.

He got a movie within weeks of arriving and for less than six weeks' work he made more than he had in the previous three years on stage. But the movie sank like a stone and it was another six months before his agent got him another part. This time a smaller part — a hitman in a gangster movie. This movie never even got distributed. It would show up occasionally on late-night TV. Raymond Galdikas learned that Hollywood was even tougher than baseball. Two strikes and you were out. He got a little TV work — thugs, villains or the irate neighbour in a sitcom — but nothing steady. No repeat work. Why couldn't he strike it big like his old friend Lorne Greene? In the first year his agent had kept telling him he was *too* good, his reputation *too* intimidating. Now the slimeball wouldn't even return his calls.

Television was shit, he knew that. Hell, most film was shit. He'd come to Hollywood prepared to do shit, and now he couldn't even get shit.

BRIAN STOOD BEHIND THE FORMICA-TOPPED TABLE. He had his right hand in his pocket, but with his left hand he made a sweeping, near circular gesture as he directed Jennifer Howard.

"You're at the table," his hand was out, palm facing Jennifer, "then turn," his hand turned, "and start to move, slowly," his whole arm swept in an arc, "around the table and bring yourself upstage to the foot of the stairs." At this point his hand twisted back towards his face a moment, "then you stand there." He made a fist.

"Nina," he said. His right hand came out of his pocket and floated towards Kate. When it was almost outstretched the hand cupped upward and he started to move his fingers in a subtle beckoning motion. Kate understood exactly what he wanted. She was to move across the front of the stage with tentative steps, much in the rhythm of his fingers. As she moved, she saw the fingers slow, then the hand gradually twist until his palm was facing her. She stopped. "Perfect," said Brian, his hands still in place. "Have you got that, Nancy?" he asked.

Nancy, who was sitting at the table and scribbling in the prompt copy, nodded.

"Irina, at this point, you speak your lines." Jennifer looked down at her script and quickly read her lines. "Then you turn and start up the stairs." Brian opened his fist so that his palm was parallel to the floor and then his hand fluttered upwards. There were, of course, no stairs to climb. Jennifer stepped over successive pieces of masking tape on the warehouse floor. But as she did she picked up her imaginary skirt and put a hand out to an imaginary rail.

Kate loved to watch Jennifer Howard. As Brian blocked her it was clear that Jennifer wasn't acting, but it was also clear that she was building the platform, so to speak, upon which her performance would take place. Kate noticed that once she got a move down — sweeping upstage, turning downstage, ascending the stairs — she would do it exactly the same way each time. There was a crispness and efficiency to her movements that Kate never tired of observing, though she still spoke her lines with the blandness of the reading. It was almost as if she didn't want any aspects of performance to interfere with the job at hand.

The job at hand was simply to work out all the stage movements, entrances and exits. To get a feeling of the entire flow of the play. It was as if Brian eliminated the other variables — emotion, characterization, motive — and this first week he was giving them a blueprint of their actions. As the week went on, Kate understood that whenever she had an important speech, somehow she was always the visual focal point of the scene. Then she would be moved unobtrusively in another direction and someone else would move so that all attention and focus was upon them. Brian kept saying this was mechanical work and they'd get to the interesting stuff next week. This week was devoted to what he called "chunking down." They would do a chunk of the play, then they would go back and run it quickly through. Then they would proceed to the next chunk. By day three of rehearsals they had just finished blocking the last act. Jennifer had been so right. Kate knew she was in good hands.

The middle section of rehearsals was what Kate found most satisfying. Slowly and methodically Brian led the actors to a complete understanding of their characters in the play. Having got the blocking out of the way, the actors were now free to concentrate on emotion and textual analysis. As they worked on their moves and their speeches, Brian would discuss the characters' motives for doing the smallest thing. Kate would speak some lines and Brian would discuss Nina's subtext. And then, when Kate understood the emotion that informed her text, she and Brian would start to refine it down, to make it more and more subtle, more and more believable.

As she became more comfortable with the whole process, Kate would sometimes have an impulse to do something as Nina and she would turn to Brian to see what he thought. Invariably, Brian would be able to articulate for Kate the subtext and the reasons behind her vague intuition. Towards the end of the second week they were working on the end of Act Three.

"Brian," Kate said.

"Yes?"

"I was wondering if at this point Nina might just turn for a moment and glance towards the front yard. I know it's a change and I know it's late."

Brian looked at her calmly, paused for a moment, and then he put his hand to the top of his head and scratched his forehead softly. Then he looked at Kate again.

"Yes. Yes, I see what you're getting at. Just before she makes her momentous decision, she remembers her performance of Constantine's play."

"Yes."

"And this evokes all the happy memories of her childhood with Constantine."

"Yes," said Kate.

"And so she has this tiny moment of hesitation."

"Yes."

"Hesitation and regret."

"Yes."

"That's wonderful, Kate. That's just what the moment needs. It will give a heightened poignancy to her turn towards Trigorin. Shall we give it a try?"

"Sure," said Kate.

Roger, playing Trigorin, mimed opening up the French doors. Kate looked at him, then her eyes sought out something in the distance. She hesitated, then she turned and, her body tightening, moved towards Roger.

"Mr Trigorin, I've made up my mind once and for all, I've burnt my boats and I'm going on the stage."

"How does that feel?" Brian asked.

"Good. Up here it feels good."

"Well, we're getting it out here too. In fact, why didn't we think of it before? Perfect."

And that's how it had been all week. Every moment of the play was analysed, worked and reworked. The other actors, many of whom already had a lot of stage experience, told Kate they'd never been in a performance where they'd felt so sure of what they were doing.

Just before they moved from the rehearsal hall into the theatre Brian sat the entire cast down and talked to them. He said that the next few days would be difficult. They would be solving technical problems. Brian said he knew this was a frustrating time for actors. That, just as their performances were gelling, they were suddenly asked to stop and start and do things over and over again for merely technical reasons that had nothing to do with the refining process of their art. But he wanted them to understand that all the props and all the technical details — lighting, music cues, incessant fussing with the costumes — had one purpose and one purpose only: to make them look good onstage. To make their characters as real and as believable as possible for an audience. So while he knew there would be a lot of frustrations over the next few days and people would find the process upsetting and sometimes tempers might flare, they must trust that it was all for the greater good of the play.

By the third day in the theatre they were ready to run the whole play. Brian, who had been so intensely involved in every detail up till now, sat quietly at the back saying nothing. Occasionally, he would turn to his prop mistress, stage manager, or lighting man and whisper a few comments. But for the most part he just sat there, notebook in hand, quietly observing. He was an audience of one and his immense concentration filled the entire theatre. He would make notes, page after page, and when the act was over sit the cast down and methodically go through them.

"Nina, are you having trouble with your left shoe?"

"Yes," Kate said. "I think it's a little tight."

"Joyce...anything we can do about that?"

"Sure," Joyce said. "We can have it stretched."

"Irina," Brian continued. "I think before your long speech you need a beat to find your light."

"Yes, I do."

"Stephan, that's a tricky cue, isn't it?"

Stephan nodded.

"Perhaps, Irina, you should finger the glass bowl. That will give you a beat or two if anything should ever go wrong."

"Good idea," Jennifer said, nodding.

"Masha, I think you're still having a little trouble on the stairs with the long dress." Chantal nodded. "That's just practice. Why don't you take a few moments after rehearsal tonight and we'll go through it together. Larry...is there any way we can tone down the music on that second interlude? I find it a little overpowering."

Two days later they were starting to feel less disjointed. By the time of full dress everyone was completely at ease. When cast and crew gathered around Brian after that, he glanced at his notebook and then shut it quite firmly. Then he spoke.

"I want you all to go home, have a good night's sleep, eat a good breakfast, relax, and we'll see you in the dressing room tomorrow at five."

IT WAS MILDRED who got me thinking about Kate's opening night. Left to my own devices I'd probably have bought myself a ticket, watched the performance, then slipped out, assuming Kate would be celebrating the rest of the night with family, friends and cast. My natural inclination being not to intrude.

"What are we talking about?" Wesley asked, looking up from his dinner.

"I have a friend who's going to be in a play," I said.

"You haven't mentioned it to Wesley?" Mildred asked, her eyebrows raised.

"No," I said.

This prompted one of Mildred's favourite all-inclusive expressions.

"Men," she said, shaking her head.

Another of my natural inclinations was to compartmentalize. I tended to talk to Wesley about things I thought would interest Wesley, and to Mildred about things I thought would interest Mildred. Of course everything interested Wesley.

"Richard's friend is going to be in *The Seagull* at the Centaur."

"*The Seagull?*" said Wesley. "Marvellous play, yes, I remember the first time I saw it, I mean the first time I saw it in Russian. Above me a chandelier with a thousand candles softly glowed. I was anticipating some sort of religious experience, when the curtain went up and the most curious thing occurred — the audience started to giggle. Yes, yes, you heard me correctly, giggle. Within minutes the entire audience was roaring with laughter, stamping their feet. I turned and looked at my friend Sergei and he was laughing so hard tears were streaming down his face. I couldn't fathom it. Here I was seeing what I felt was a play full of pathos and suffering and the audience just couldn't stop laughing. Well, I wondered if I'd just seen a particularly bad performance but Sergei assured me that no, no, it was a wonderful performance — it's just that the Russians find Chekhov hilarious."

"Hilarious?" I said. "Chekhov?"

"Yes, hilarious. Curiously, the playwright they find sombre and sad is Oscar Wilde — what part is your friend playing?"

"Nina."

"Nina? That's a marvellous character, the whole centre of the play — we must go!"

"I've already bought us tickets, Wesley, we're going with Richard."

"Marvellous, marvellous, I do look forward to that."

And that's when Mildred started asking me all kinds of questions I couldn't answer.

"Will Kate's family be coming?"

"I don't know."

She turned to me and jabbed in the air with her fork. "You find out if she's got family coming."

"Well," I said, "I just assumed — "

"Never assume anything," Mildred said. "She lives alone?"

"Yes."

"She's just nineteen?"

"Yes."

"Her family's in Toronto?"

"I think so, yes."

"Never assume. Find out."

"Quite right, dear," Wesley added. "Do find out, Richard."

And so I found out. And that was the first inkling I got about how estranged Kate was from her family. When I asked her if her mother and father were coming she just shuddered. She said that the last person she would ever want to see her in a play was her mother.

"How about friends from Toronto?" I said. "Is anyone coming?"

"No," she said.

When I reported all this to Mildred she could hardly believe it. "You mean this young girl's been picked up out of nowhere to play a major part in a professional theatre and no one's coming to see her?"

I nodded.

"How very curious," said Wesley.

"It's not curious, Wesley, it's outrageous. Richard, I want you to send her roses."

"Oh, yes," said Wesley. "She must have roses."

"A dozen red roses."

KATE WENT IN THE BACK DOOR of the theatre and made her way to the dressing room.

"Ma, ma, ma, ma, mo, mo, mo, mo."

Chantal/Masha was doing her vocal warmups.

Along one side of the dressing room was a built-in counter with mirrors behind it. In front of the counter there were three chairs. At Jennifer's spot along this counter there were several bouquets of flowers. Chantal had some cards tucked into the edges of her mirror and a little wrapped gift.

Kate took her chair and looked at herself in the mirror. She wondered if it was time to get another haircut. Her barber felt it looked best at about an inch long. She tugged at a lock on her forehead. Almost two inches. In front of the mirror was a wig form with Nina's hair on it. Nina was a brunette.

She picked up the tin of pancake makeup and began smoothing it over her scrubbed face with a tiny sponge. Chantal took a seat beside her and began doing her makeup too.

"Time for the old zit producer, eh?"

Kate grinned. She checked around her jawline then took the eyeshadow brush and dabbed dark brown in the crease of her eyelids and lighter brown on the lid. Then she put some pearly highlighter beneath her brows. She took the brown eyebrow pencil and filled in and extended her own brows by about a quarter of an inch. Then she drew some lower eyelashes with the same pencil. She outlined her lips with a plum-coloured lipstick and filled them in with deep pink. She applied pink blush to each of her cheekbones and a little white contouring powder between her eyebrows to the tip of her nose as Jennifer Howard had taught them to do. Finally she applied two coats of dark-brown mascara. Chantal was deepening her forehead lines with a grey eyebrow pencil. It looked ridiculous up close but to the audience it would accentuate Masha's weariness.

Behind Kate, running the length of the room, was a long pole that held all of the women's costumes. Kate checked that hers were all in the order she liked them to be. She took off her t-shirt and pulled the first dress over her head, being careful not to smudge her makeup on the white collar. She stepped out of her jeans and hung them on the empty hanger. There was a box on a shelf above her costumes with the name Nina written on it and Kate lifted it down and took out her shoes and stockings. The left shoe fit perfectly now.

In the dressing room next door Kate could hear the men thumping around and doing their vocal exercises. While she laced up her shoes she heard them laughing and talking. Moments later, Jennifer appeared at the dressing-room door.

Once Jennifer appeared on the scene there was a good deal of chatter. Kate listened to it as she sat down at her mirror again and lifted the wig off its form. She bent over slightly and pulled it on. When she looked back in the mirror the transformation was really quite remarkable. Nina's hair was long but done up in a smooth roll that encircled Kate's entire head.

There was a lull in the chatter for a moment. Kate looked up. Chantal and Jennifer were looking at the door. Standing in the doorway was a young man in uniform holding a long white box. How nice, she thought, more flowers for Jennifer.

"Kate Barnes?" the young man said.

Jennifer's arm swept up and pointed down the row of mirrors.

"That's her there," she said, "the Seagull herself."

The young man stepped in and awkwardly handed the package to Kate.

"For me?" Kate said aloud, but the delivery boy had already scurried away.

"Open it, open it," said Chantal.

Kate lifted the lid off the box and gasped along with Chantal.

"A dozen red roses," Jennifer exclaimed. "How perfectly lovely! Who are they from?"

"I have no idea," Kate said.

"Well, find out."

Kate found the little card inside the box and opened it. Inside, handwritten in black ink, was one sentence: "Break a leg." Underneath was the signature. Richard.

Kate looked at the card. Richard. Her friend Richard had sent her some roses on opening night.

Up to that moment Kate had never even thought about somebody watching this play. Somehow it was just something she was doing that was more interesting and more exciting than anything she'd ever done before. But as she looked at the card she suddenly realized that there would be an audience of people out there, watching the performance. Watching her.

"Places, everyone." It was Gail, the assistant stage manager. "Chantal?"

Chantal stood, bent to have one more look at herself in the mirror, then followed Gail out of the dressing room.

"Never fails," Jennifer said. "The second I hear those two words, I have to pee." She squeezed Kate's arm and disappeared into the bathroom.

Kate was alone.

Through the open dressing-room door she could hear the music fading and the audience go quiet. Then applause. Then the hammers began pounding — the opening cue.

Kate looked in her mirror. In moments Gail would be coming back for her. As she sat there staring into the mirror she found herself in the grip of a classic case of stage fright. How could that be? It couldn't. Brian had rehearsed and rehearsed everything so meticulously that in the last week alone they had done three perfect runthroughs. There wasn't a nuance, a gesture, a movement that Kate didn't know the motivation for.

She took a deep breath. There was time. There was time to just settle down and collect herself. She'd heard stories about famous actors stepping on stage without knowing what they were going to say and then, at their cue, the words just flowed out with no one in the audience knowing that moments before they'd been totally paralysed.

Yes. All she'd need to do was hear her first cue.

But what was it?

She picked up her copy of *The Seagull* and thumbed to page four. Yes. Of course. It was Constantine. I'M WILDLY HAPPY, he says. Kate closed the book and looked up.

"I'm wildly happy. I'm wildly happy."

What comes after I'm wildly happy?

She opened the book again and read her line. I'M NOT LATE AM I? I CAN'T BE. Then she shut the book. The line was gone. She couldn't believe it — the line was gone! Desperately she opened the

book again. I'M NOT LATE AM I? I CAN'T BE. She repeated it. I'M
NOT LATE AM I? I CAN'T BE.

"Kate," Gail whispered, beckoning.

Kate stood. As she placed her copy of the play on the makeup
table she had already forgotten her line. She couldn't even remember
her cue or who spoke it. She followed Gail. It was dark. Through a
tiny slit in the curtains she could see the brightly lit stage and there
were the actors speaking their lines as they had done so many times
before. But still, Kate could remember nothing. She couldn't even
remember the other characters' names. Paralysed with fright, Kate
closed her eyes, and as she did an image came into her mind. It was
an image of a seagull soaring out over a lake. Kate felt a small push
from behind and stepped out into the blazing light. There was a
rough stage and two people and they were looking at her, waiting,
but all she could think of was that seagull. She looked at the people
again but somehow they'd shifted. Suddenly, she realized, she was
looking at them from above. She looked down and she saw not two
people on the stage, but three. And the third one was speaking. What
had she said?

I'M NOT LATE AM I? I CAN'T BE.

DANIEL LLOYD WAS NO FOOL. He knew he was heading into a
tricky situation. He'd been hired late in the game and he wasn't a
Canadian. He had a number of problems. His first big problem was
that he didn't know the Canadian theatre scene. He knew he couldn't
audition every actor in the country and, anyway, he didn't believe in
auditions. He believed in seeing people's work. And he believed in
talking to people. So in the months before hiring for his first season
began he decided that he would quickly travel the country and see as
much theatre as he could. That way he could see the work of Canadian actors, Canadian directors and Canadian designers.

Daniel Lloyd's second problem was that Stratford was a tourist theatre. It did the classics, did all the great plays, but it wasn't exactly a place where innovative work was welcomed. The Disney Puppet Phenomenon. Daniel Lloyd had always been the brilliant young director who had gone in and blasted the Disney puppets out of existence. He'd gone in and shaken things up. He'd always relied on inspiration and creativity and a certain unexpectedness that made the plays actually live onstage. Now he was going to be an artistic director. Responsible for not just one play but a whole season. It was hard to be creative and explosive for an entire company and, yet, what was the alternative? To just settle into museum productions of the classics?

His third problem was that he had to attract major stars. Stratford, Ontario, was the kind of company that had discovered many great actors — but after five or six seasons the great ones always moved on. Stratford was a sort of jumping-off point. So he could do two things. He could lure some of the old great talent back, and Daniel Lloyd felt that with his name, his reputation, this was possible, or he could discover new talent. Discovering new talent was always trickier. That was where Daniel Lloyd would have to rely on his intuition.

And so he'd gone to Vancouver, Edmonton, Calgary, Winnipeg, Toronto — seeing every production he could. There were some surprisingly good things. He sensed a sort of raw energy in Canadian theatre that he had not seen since the early Fifties in England. And so as he travelled around he was becoming a little more hopeful. He'd arrived in Montreal with several things on his list. One was Brian Reed's *Seagull*. He'd heard a lot about Brian Reed. He was one of the best directors in Canada, people said. He kept hearing that Brian Reed had a "real feeling for authenticity." He'd even heard, as Daniel Lloyd was not slow to get the gossip, that Brian Reed had been one of the contenders for his own job. So, he thought as the curtain went up, let's just see what you can do, Mr Reed.

As the curtain rose there was an audible intake of breath from the entire audience, then a little gasp, then applause.

They're clapping the set, thought Daniel Lloyd.

And he knew. He knew that what he was about to see was going to be another perfect rendition of *The Seagull*. Perfect in every detail. Perfect set, perfect costumes, perfect down to the last perfect teacup.

Perfectly boring.

As soon as the actors started to speak he knew he was right. Boring, boring, boring. If he'd seen one perfect academic production of *The Seagull*, he'd seen a hundred. And every one the same. Boring, boring, boring. The moment the actors started to speak their opening lines Daniel Lloyd knew that Brian Reed was no contender. Brian Reed was no problem. The only problem now was how to slip out of this theatre as quietly and unobtrusively as possible.

And that's when it happened. The young girl playing Nina appeared onstage.

He knew the moment he saw her. That tingling he got in the back of his neck. It wasn't the first time he'd experienced that tingling. He'd felt it that first day directing *Love's Labour's Lost* when he'd abandoned his Plan and started to actually see actors and not pieces of cardboard. The tingling at the back of his neck was Daniel Lloyd's awareness that something astonishing was happening. Down on the stage all was dreariness, dust and fog, and yet in the midst of the dimness a light was glowing. The light of real talent. The light of an extraordinary talent. Daniel Lloyd loved it when he didn't have to make a decision. When he just *knew*.

Here was his Roxanne.

ONE DAY — VERA WIKLUND WOULD NEVER FORGET IT — a young man came into the store to buy milk. As she was ringing in his purchase, he noticed the brioche she had been nibbling with her coffee.

"Is that brioche?" he asked.

She nodded.

"How much?"

"It's not for sale," she said. But he was such a pleasant young man with such a nice smile. "Here," she said, reaching below the counter for another slice, "have some."

"This is delicious," he said. "Where do you get this?"

"My husband makes it."

"I've never tasted better."

Vera said she would pass the compliment along.

A few days later the young man was back.

"I'm having a little party," he said. "Is there any chance I could commission your husband to make me some brioche?"

Vera smiled and said, "And perhaps an almond cake?"

The young man smiled back.

"Perfect," he said.

A few days later the young man returned.

"And how was your little party?"

"Wonderful," he said, "and they raved about the almond cake."

He strolled about the store a while then returned to the cash register with some havarti, a head of lettuce, orange juice and butter.

"You know," he said as he was paying, "that's dead space by the window. You could put a small table and chairs there and serve coffee and cake." Then he left.

Over the next few days Vera thought about the young man's idea. She thought about it so much that two weeks later when he came in again there was a table by the window. He grinned when he saw it, sat in one of the chairs and she joined him. That was when she learned that he was Canadian, though born in Yugoslavia. His father had been killed in the war and his mother had died just a year before. It was maybe the mention of his mother dying that endeared Breetz to Vera Wiklund. Anyway, whatever it was, she found herself looking forward to his visits. Her young friend would show up, sit down, and Vera would present him with the specialty of the day. Breetz would take a bite, savour it a moment and then, and this never failed to impress Vera, make a discerning comment. After he'd left, she would go into the back room and tell Lars what he had said. He had noticed

the wine in the layer cake, the caraway in the danbo. And he was right
about so many other things too. The little table was never empty. And
just as Breetz had predicted, people were requesting take-homes.
One day, he arrived just as she and Lars were having lunch. They
beckoned him to join them in the back. There were several trays of
food on the table and some slices of bread. Vera put a plate out for
Breetz and he watched as she and her husband started putting things
together. They began with a thin slice of bread, light rye for Vera and
a darker rye for Lars. Vera smeared hers with sweetened butter and
Lars' with salted. Once they had the base they began helping themselves to the platter of herring.

"Sweet pickled, smoked, soused, sour pickled," Vera said, pointing out the different types for Breetz. When he had finished arrang-
ing his selections Vera placed on top of the herring concentric circles
of onion — in the centre of which she placed a radish rose. Then she
swirled on a little sour cream.

"This is artistic," said Breetz, looking at all three creations. "This
is like eating sculpture."

They laughed.

"At Oskar Davidsen's in Copenhagen," Lars said, "they had a
menu a yard long. A hundred and seventy-eight different ingredients
arranged any which way you liked."

Breetz looked at Lars.

"A menu six inches long and you'd have half the neighbourhood
eating here for lunch."

So they gave it a try and he was right. This made them even more
receptive to his next idea.

The awning. Breetz said they should have a small awning outside the shop and change the name. Lars worried that an awning
would be vandalized but Breetz said the neighbourhood was changing. So up went the smart navy-blue awning with the words Det
Kolde Bord in white letters. Soon ladies in dresses and hats were
making up their own open-faced creations, which Vera would garnish
artistically.

"Soon there'll be no room for me," Breetz had teased and he was
right. One Friday he came in and there was, in fact, no room at any
of the tables.

"There's always a place for you, Breetz," Vera said and that day she invited him to dinner. He couldn't make it that Sunday, but they settled on two Sundays hence.

BLOUSE AND SKIRT? Oh no. Ulrika knew what that meant. The white blouse Mom had made her and the grey flannel skirt. The blouse was the kind with an elastic neckline that puckered over her chest and the skirt had pleats that spread open over her hips. She looked at them lying on the bed and went to her closet. Surely there was something else. But the jumper was in the wash and, anyway, it made her look twelve years old. What was wrong with what she was wearing? All the girls wore shirts and dungarees. All the popular girls, at least, like her best friend Charlotte. If Ulrika could close her eyes and have one wish it would be to look like Charlotte. Charlotte was small, five-foot-two inches, and pert. She wore her brunette hair in a page-boy with a white headband and she had a little upturned nose. All the boys were crazy for her and if she liked them she'd smile up at them with her head on the side and if she didn't she'd say, Get serious, and they'd be too embarrassed to ever look her way again.

More than anything Ulrika wanted to have that effect on boys, but as she stood in front of her closet mirror she came close to tears realizing she never would. She pulled the blouse over her head and stepped into the skirt without looking at herself in the mirror. She clasped her nylons. She quickly smoothed her skirt down and stepped into her black wedgies. She turned sideways in front of the mirror. The blouse puckered, the pleats spread. She hated the way she looked. She grabbed the white cardigan from the bottom drawer even though it wasn't cold in the house and put it on, leaving all but the top button undone, then she turned sideways again. From the side the cardigan obliterated the spreading pleats. The doorbell rang.

Ulrika didn't move. She stood in her room with her arms crossed and listened. Her mother would be whipping off her apron and smoothing her hair. Pop was greeting the guest. There was laughter.

"Len! Eric! Ulrika!" her mother's loud voice boomed.

Her brothers' door opened and they stood there looking as miserable as Ulrika felt. Eric was pulling at the collar of his shirt and Len was scratching his thighs. He was getting too big for his good pants. They almost revealed his ankles and they itched. He kept scratching. None of them had moved beyond their doors.

"Uli! Eric! Len!" the loud voice called again and they all rolled their eyes.

"You first, Len," Ulrika said.

"Why me?"

"Because you're the youngest and the youngest always goes first, right, Eric?"

"Right. How long do we have to stay?"

"Just till after they've had coffee," Ulrika answered. "Then I'll start clearing the table and you two can help me."

"Aww…" Len started to protest but Eric gave him a shove. "You want to sit with them all evening?" Eric asked and Len shook his head. He looked like he might cry.

"We'd better go down," Ulrika whispered and they started down single file to meet Mom's Canadian.

He was already seated with a drink in his hand but he stood and turned and smiled at them all. While he shook hands with Eric and Len, Ulrika had a chance to observe him. He was young; she'd been expecting someone older. He was small for a man, shorter than her, and he was dressed all in black with no tie. He looked comfortable in his clothes and Ulrika was suddenly very aware of the boys' scratching and her father hitching his pants, to say nothing of her own awkwardness.

The evening wasn't as Ulrika had anticipated at all. Breetz was nice. And funny. He had Len and Eric laughing almost immediately. He was able to joke with the boys and keep the conversation with her mother and father going. When they moved into the dining room he loved everything — the fish, the cheese, the meats, the placement. Her fathered poured him some akvavit.

"Something for the fish to swim in," he said. They clinked glasses, then they talked and ate and laughed.

They must have sat there a couple of hours before Ulrika noticed her mother removing a few plates. Ulrika eyed the two boys but they didn't move so she got up and started to help. But as she moved between the kitchen and dining room she was still listening to the conversation at the table. Her father was talking about how well everything was going at the Kolde Bord.

"We work half as hard and earn twice as much," he said.

Then Breetz spoke.

"It's simple, really, isn't it? Don't do what everyone else does, do what only you can do."

Lars poured another shot of akvavit and skaaled Breetz.

"To Breetz — do what only you can do."

In the kitchen Ulrika heard the two glasses clink. It was Eric who next spoke.

"So what *do* you do, Breetz?"

"I'm a photographer."

"What do you photograph?" Len asked.

"Beautiful women."

Ulrika dropped a plate.

"That's all right, Uli, that's all right. We all have accidents."

As she went about picking up the pieces of broken china, then wiping the area with a moist rag, Ulrika heard more.

"You photograph beautiful women?" Len asked, amazed. "All day?"

"That's right."

"Do they have their clothes on?"

"Eric!" Lars said.

"Mostly," Breetz said. "I'm a fashion photographer. I work for *Vogue*."

A photographer from *Vogue*. It was enough to make a girl drop another plate. As Ulrika wiped up the last of the broken china she could scarcely believe her ears. Mom's Canadian was a fashion photographer from *Vogue*. What must he think of her in her stupid grey skirt and ugly cardigan? She felt like she would die. How was she going to get through dessert?

She got through dessert the way she had got through dinner, by keeping quiet and listening. Imagine, a photographer from *Vogue*! She could hardly wait to tell Charlotte. She and Charlotte spent hours pouring over the magazines, reading the beauty tips. Charlotte never went to bed without bending at the waist and brushing her hair a hundred times, so Ulrika did too. And Charlotte always matched her lipstick and her nail polish, so Ulrika did too. And Charlotte always ended up looking the same — pert and pretty and dainty — but even though Ulrika copied her hairstyle and her mannerisms she could never be pert and pretty and dainty. She was too big. Oh, how she had always wanted to be dainty and small. Small girls made boys feel protective. They'd put their arms around your shoulders and carry your books. She was thinking these things when she felt Breetz looking at her. He was more than looking at her, he was looking into her.

"Vera," he said, turning to her mother. "Your daughter is very beautiful."

Her mother naturally launched into how beautiful Ulrika would be if she just did this or that, most of which involved getting out of dungarees, but Ulrika wasn't listening to her mother. Beautiful. He'd called her beautiful. A fashion photographer, someone who saw beautiful women every day of his life, had found her beautiful and she knew he meant it. He wasn't trying to be nice for Mom's sake, Mom already adored him.

That night Ulrika looked at herself in the mirror. He thinks I'm beautiful, she thought. He thinks I'm beautiful. She kept looking at herself. Until that night, whenever she'd looked in the mirror all she could see was what was wrong. Her breasts, her hips. She was so big. Taller than all the other girls. Taller than most boys her age. So she would look at herself and try to figure out ways to make herself look smaller. More dainty. More like other girls. But that night she looked at herself differently. A photographer from *Vogue* had said she was beautiful. Beautiful. And he'd said it so calmly, calmly and intently. Suddenly all the things she had always hated about herself she saw in a new and different light. She was big. Tall. But weren't the models in *Vogue* tall? She was only big and awkward compared to her friends. Compared to the girls she knew. But if she stopped trying to be a girl, and looked at herself as if she were a woman...it was true. She was beautiful, she was. Well, not yet...but she could be. She could be beautiful. She knew she could.

Beautiful, beautiful, beautiful.

AT THE TIME OF THE OCTOBER 1962 missile crisis I never really felt in my guts that the Soviet Union and the United States would actually resort to nuclear war. I continued to go to the library, drop in at Chez Madelaine and work on my essays. There were, of course, demonstrations at McGill, but the crisis seemed abstract to me, something that was happening Out There in the world that had nothing to do with me personally. How wrong I was!

Apparently, the day after President Kennedy's speech in which he had said he would not shrink from nuclear war, the Voice of Women had organized an emergency meeting. They'd written a joint letter to Prime Minister Diefenbaker and President Kennedy. They'd put an ad in the Toronto *Globe and Mail* and they'd demonstrated outside the American consulate.

My father found this painful. He had told my mother that out of consideration for him he would appreciate it if she wouldn't publicly embarrass him. She continued. He told her that it was a disgrace and she must desist. She continued. He told her she must stop. She didn't.

The marriage had been no more than appearances for many years and once appearances were over, so was the marriage. My father moved out of the house.

When I arrived at the house at the end of the academic year things were certainly different. Gertie had been let go and my mother was doing her own cooking. We had tuna sandwiches and soup in the kitchen while we talked about all this. She looked very different too. At the time, I thought, not better. She was wearing a loose sweater over a tweed skirt and she wore flat shoes, the kind of thing she might have once gone walking in, but not the kind of thing I was used to.

Where formerly she had always been made up, now she wore just lip-stick and her hair was pulled into a bun. There was a bit of grey in her hair that I'd never noticed and it occurred to me that she had been dyeing it. Her nails were bare. She looked around the kitchen as we ate our sandwiches.

"The house is too big," she said. "But my lawyer tells me I'm to stay put until everything's settled. I've rattled around here for nearly thirty years, I suppose I can do it a while longer. But it seems so empty."

She didn't seem unhappy. On the contrary, she had more energy than ever before. We stayed up till four in the morning talking and for the first time that I could ever recall there was no mention of Bonny-castles. We discussed everything — my studies, Breetz, Wesley and Mildred — but mostly we talked about politics. Not the party politics of my father or the historical perspective Wesley and I enjoyed, but the kind of politics that was personal. Politics that affected my mother viscerally. She kept talking about the photo of the Buddhist monk. Of course, everyone who lived through those times knows which photo I mean. In order to protest Diem's savage repression of the Buddhist demonstrations, the monk had doused himself with gasoline and set himself afire.

When we took our tea into the conservatory that evening that very picture was pinned up on the wall beside my mother's chair. I went over and looked at it. An unbelievable photo. There he sat, utterly composed in his full lotus as the flames consumed him.

"Initially, I pinned that photo up so I wouldn't forget," my mother said. "And now, I can't get it out of my mind."

On that same visit I made an appointment for lunch with my father. We kept the conversation on safe topics: Montreal, McGill, the weather. My father asked what my plans were and I told him I was going to take an MA and most likely a PhD in English.

"You'll be a professor, then."

"Mm," I agreed.

If not happy, he seemed at least satisfied with this and we ate most of our dessert in silence. There was of course no mention of my mother, no mention of the separation, no mention of the events of the preceding year that had changed his life. We shook hands and parted. We would repeat this once or twice a year.

ULRIKA UNTUCKED THE TOWEL and let it fall to her feet. She looked at herself in the full-length mirror while the water ran for her bath. She thought back to a year ago today, her seventeenth birthday. Though she'd just met Breetz a few weeks before, he'd been invited and had arrived with a brightly coloured box. She'd opened her family's gifts first but that pretty box was all Ulrika could think of. When she'd finally opened it — oh, how disappointed she'd felt. And when she'd held up a dumbbell, her parents and brothers had looked completely befuddled, but Breetz wasn't fazed in the least.

"Weights," he'd said with his habitual enthusiasm. "For the Norse Goddess in our Ulrika."

At the bottom of the box there'd been a small fifteen-page pamphlet about weight-lifting that Ulrika hadn't held up for anyone else to see. Later that night in her room she'd taken it out and looked at it. There were some awful pictures — hideous photographs of men with veins snaking over their arms and thighs and silly smiles on their faces as they struck the poses that would show their muscles to advantage. But the very last page of the booklet had a picture of the wife of the man who'd written it, and one fascinating sentence: "Women, although they will never bulk up or get ripped the way a man will, can benefit from the toning effects of training with weights as you can see from this photo of my lovely wife." That was all. There was no more about women, just that sentence and a large photo of the man's wife in a swimsuit. She looked statuesque, regal. There wasn't an ounce of fat on the woman and yet you'd never have called her skinny. Her calves, her buttocks, her shoulders were all so well defined they commanded attention, yet so proportioned the effect was flattering — not grotesque as the men's photos had been.

That night Ulrika had stripped and looked at herself naked in the mirror. Straight on she thought she looked okay, but when she turned sideways, that was another story. There was a little roll under the belly button. The fronts of her thighs were firm but the backs, just below her buttocks, weren't as smooth. Little creases formed there. She'd grabbed the booklet and turned to the page that had arrows pointing to the various muscle groups. Biceps femoris. That was what those were called. Adductor magnus. Then she'd lifted her arm. She could pinch two inches of flesh just near her armpit.

Mademoiselle called that "underarm dingle-dangle." She'd faced forward again and cupped her breasts with her hands, lifting them ever so slightly. Though she was only seventeen, she'd have been happier if her breasts were just a fraction higher, say a quarter of an inch. She'd decided then and there to give the weights a try without telling anyone. At first she'd felt silly — breathing *out* with effort and *in* on release — and she'd wished there were some pictures of women in the book, but after just three weeks she'd realized that the weights that had seemed so heavy at first were lighter. She was swimming too — three afternoons a week at the YWCA.

Now, a year later, the change was remarkable. The image in the mirror was beautiful, truly beautiful. She thought of Breetz. Of how he looked at her. And of how, whenever he did look, somehow he made her feel beautiful.

Yes.

Breetz made Ulrika feel good, very good. The way boys with their awkwardness and their furtive pretend-this-isn't-happening gropes never could.

Vera Wiklund was of the school that a young woman should make an entrance. She had helped Ulrika dress and had done her hair but then she'd told her to stay in her room until she was called. At precisely six the doorbell rang.

"Breetz," Vera said as she opened the door. "Come right in."

It was to be Breetz and Ulrika's first formal date. They had spent a lot of time together but Breetz had made it clear that tonight would be different. He was taking Ulrika out. He chatted with Lars while Vera went to the bottom of the stairs.

"Ulrika, are you almost ready?"

Ulrika descended the stairs in her new pink suit with the bolero jacket. Her hair was done up in a French roll.

"I've been ready for half an hour," she said and Breetz smiled and held out his hand.

"We'll be late, Lars."

"Be as late as you like," Vera answered. "How often does a girl turn eighteen?"

Then they were on their own and Breetz was standing close, even though there was only the two of them. Ulrika felt her cheeks grow warm. Out on the street a cab was waiting.

"Bloomingdales," Breetz said to the driver as he slipped in beside Ulrika.

Bloomingdales? She'd thought they were going to dinner. Was he going to buy her a present? Was he going to let her choose? Ulrika felt very grown up in her suit with her chignon. She crossed her legs and tugged at her skirt as it rose above her knee.

"I like what you said back there," Breetz said.

"What?"

"About being ready for half an hour. I like that. There's no need for you to be coy, Ulrika. Coy isn't you."

She knew that had been the right thing and she was glad he'd mentioned it. She liked pleasing him. They rode the rest of the trip in silence. The cab pulled up outside Bloomingdales and Breetz held the door for her. She swung her legs around and got out of the car the way the magazines said you should. Breetz held doors for her, then took her hand and walked her to the escalator. They got off the escalator and, still holding hands, he led her to a fitting room.

"Breetz!" A fortyish woman said, breaking into a big smile. "What can we do for you today?"

He let go of Ulrika's hand and lifted a blouse off a rack. Then he went to another rack and chose a skirt.

"This is Ulrika," he said to the woman. "Can you help her with these, Maggie?"

"Certainly," said Maggie. "Come along, dear."

And before Ulrika could say a word Maggie was guiding her to a changeroom. She helped Ulrika out of her jacket. Was she going to stay there? Was Ulrika supposed to undress in front of this stranger? Apparently, because the woman showed no sign of leaving and was undoing the buttons on the blouse.

"My, what a lovely figure you have, dear. Now try this."

She held the blouse while Ulrika put her arms in the sleeves. Then Ulrika stepped out of her pink skirt and into the new one. Maggie zipped her up. As she tucked in her blouse Maggie fussed a bit with the shoulders and cuffs.

"Oh, say, doesn't that look nice, dear?"

"What colour is this?" Ulrika asked.

Maggie looked thoughtful.

"I'd call that taupe, wouldn't you?" Ulrika didn't answer. She'd have called it no colour at all. "Let's step out and look in the proper mirror."

Before following Maggie to the three-way mirror, Ulrika grabbed her pink clutch purse. She stood in front of the mirror, then held the purse behind her back so it wouldn't be part of the picture. The outfit that had looked dull, dull, dull to Ulrika on the rack looked positively amazing once it was on. The blouse was very simply cut and made of a delicate material that grazed her torso and gathered at the wrists so that the material hung beautifully when she raised her hands or puffed out slightly when she left them at her sides. The skirt couldn't have been simpler. Pencil slim, and of a soft comfortable material Ulrika had never seen, it fell to just above the knee. The new length.

"Is this velvet?" she asked.

"Panne velvet," Maggie answered. "It looks like it was made for you, dear. Doesn't it, Breetz?"

Ulrika hadn't noticed Breetz approaching but he stood admiring her and nodding slowly.

"Made for her," he said, holding out a pair of shoes.

Ulrika had purposely worn flats because she didn't want to be too much taller than her date. She slipped out of the flats, which Maggie quickly gathered up, and stepped into the suede high heels.

"Do you have a comb in there?" Breetz said, nodding at the purse Ulrika held behind her back.

"Yes, of course."

Before she could say anything Breetz had moved in close. He was taking out every one of the pins Vera had painstakingly arranged.

"I must say, though, it's a lovely smooth roll. Who did your hair, dear?"

"My mother."

"Lovely job, really."

Maggie kept up a steady stream of murmuring, perhaps because she could see the worried look on Ulrika's face. Finally, Breetz had every last pin out.

"Here," he said, handing over a handful of bobby-pins. "Put these in your bag and give me your comb."

She did as he asked, then handed the purse over to Maggie, who stood watching and murmuring encouragement. Because of the French roll Ulrika's hair tumbled down with a lovely wave once it was loosed.

"Beautiful hair," Breetz said. And for a moment he just stood with his hands in her hair.

Ulrika watched his reflection in the mirror. After a while he looked up and met her eyes and smiled. She smiled back. Then he did the most outrageous thing. He took the comb and, reaching over her forehead, "drew" a line from her perfectly straight nose up and through the centre of her scalp. A centre part? Her mother would have a conniption fit. Common, she'd say. As if sensing Ulrika's dismay, Maggie began her murmuring again.

"Oh, Breetz, yes. Quite. You're so lovely, dear."

"Just one last thing," Breetz said, pulling a handkerchief out of his pocket. "The lipstick." He wiped her lips. "Turn around and see how beautiful you are, Ulrika."

She turned. As she gazed at her new look in the mirror she understood. With her hair piled up and her lipstick and her suit she had tried to look twenty-one years old and had, consequently, seemed sixteen. But this new look — her hair flowing down around her shoulders, the soft odd-coloured material that hung on her figure so beautifully — with this look she might have been twenty or she might have been thirty. It was remarkable. Maggie was positively beaming.

"Such a lovely young woman. Are you a model, dear?"

"No," Ulrika laughed. And then she looked back in the mirror. She could hardly take her eyes away.

"I've never worn a centre part," she said to hide the fact that she really could stand there and look at herself forever.

"Most women shouldn't," Maggie said. "But with your bones, my dear, it's the only way. Really, isn't it, Breetz?"

Breetz just nodded. He seemed to be enjoying the fact that Ulrika was mesmerized by her image.

"Well," she said, feeling self-conscious.

"Well," Breetz said. "Maggie, would you box Ulrika's things for her?"

Maggie went back into the changeroom and Breetz stood behind Ulrika with his hands on her shoulders. He'd never stood so close to her before. She felt like leaning into him the way the women did in the movies. But somehow she couldn't do that. Not yet. He squeezed her shoulders and they looked at each other in the mirror. She felt she had to say something.

"Thank you, Breetz, for the beautiful clothes. I'm... you really shouldn't..."

He squeezed her shoulders again and leaned in closer to whisper in her ear.

"It's just the beginning, Uli."

BREETZ AND I STOOD IN THE VESTRY of The Little Church on the Corner. He was dressed in custom-tailored black silk, I in a three-piece charcoal-grey suit. I was nervously slapping at my pants pockets when Breetz reached inside my lapel and pulled out the gold wedding band from my breast pocket.

"It's right here, Richard," he said, holding the ring on the tip of his index finger, then slipping it back into place.

The day Breetz had phoned me up and told me he was engaged, I was rendered speechless. I knew that Breetz was very attractive to women and had no shortage of female admirers wherever he went, but somehow I'd never imagined him getting married. I thought his desire for success was stronger than any feeling he could have for a woman. When he told me he was engaged, I assumed it would be to some high-profile model at *Vogue* but he just laughed and said, "No, no. She's the daughter of my favourite baker."

That was the sort of enigmatic comment Breetz liked to make.

The Baker's Daughter conjured up the image of a round-faced girl who dipped her finger in the whipped cream more often than she should. My mother and I spent most of the short plane trip speculating about Ulrika. Breetz had phoned Elizabeth right after he'd phoned me and we'd decided that same night to go to New York together. Breetz hadn't seen my mother for a couple of years and I wondered how he would react. She seemed to me to have aged so much in the past year.

When we got off the plane Breetz was right there at the baggage carousel. He smiled at me, then enveloped Elizabeth in a warm hug. He pulled back from her a little and held her hands in his. He took in the Capri pants, flat shoes, and loose-fitting shirt.

"Elizabeth," he said. "Elizabeth, this is you. This is lovely. But something's not quite right."

Breetz turned Elizabeth around and unpinned her bun. Her hair fell down to her shoulders. There was even more grey in it than when I'd last seen her. Breetz's hands slipped in under her ears and then his thumbs pressed towards her scalp. He now had two hanks of hair which he crossed over, his right hand slipping out to grasp a third. Then, deftly, he repeated the action. Right there, in the middle of the airport, while people were elbowing each other to get to their luggage, Breetz braided my mother's hair.

"Now," he said, "just let it grow."

Elizabeth turned around to face him, her eyes shining. "Oh, Breetz," she said. "It's so wonderful to see you again."

The three of us had a marvellous couple of days in New York. Breetz didn't seem the least bit nervous about the step he was soon to take. Everything was under control and he gave himself over to entertaining us. We didn't go to *Camelot* or have a night at Sardi's or visit the Guggenheim. Instead, Breetz just took us here, there and everywhere — his favourite haunts in the Village, a wonderful Italian restaurant on 33rd Street, an art gallery, a poetry reading where people actually played bongos, and of course Det Kolde Bord. Everywhere we went people loved Breetz. We had fun. It was strange to see my mother having such fun. I had always had fun with Breetz and Anna, but this was a new and odd experience for me.

There was no time to be nervous until that moment together in the vestry. I kept feeling my breast pocket for Ulrika's ring.

"Relax, Richard," Breetz said. "If by some weird chance you should lose that ring in the ten feet between here and the altar, I'll mime putting it on her finger."

The minister walked in wearing white vestments and holding a bible. We all shook hands.

"All set, gentlemen?"

Breetz nodded. I felt my pocket one last time and we followed the minister out of the vestry.

The church was full. The bride's side was dressed formally, blue suits for the men, dresses and hats for the women. The groom's side ran the gamut from elegant to wacky. One woman had her hair piled so high and in so many perfect curls, like chain-links all around her head, that you couldn't see the person directly behind her. There was Diana Vreeland, the woman who had discovered Breetz. There were models so stunning I worried that the bride would be overshadowed. Breetz had only lived in New York a little over two years and yet the groom's side of the church was as full as the bride's.

I stood, waiting, as the music changed to Handel's familiar wedding march. The minister nodded and Breetz and I turned. My worries about Ulrika being overshadowed by the famous models were extinguished in that moment.

Breetz's bride was an updated version of Rider Haggard's She. Helen of Troy. Maud Gonne. Head and shoulders above the rest. Her dress was very plain and exquisitely made, falling from shoulder to ankle. The light played on the material so that with every movement, every inhalation of breath, it seemed to change shade. Now white-white, now a dove-grey, now cream. I don't know what I was expecting, but what I saw was a man's fantasy. This was no blushing bride. This was a creation.

She moved like liquid up the aisle, all eyes upon her. Her eyes never left Breetz's; nor his, hers. As she approached Breetz, he put out his hand and her long beautiful arm floated out to meet him. He took her hand, squeezed it, and folded it into his bent arm. Then he turned to face the minister.

AFTER *THE SEAGULL*, Kate didn't do any more theatre. I naturally assumed that because of her success Kate would be eager for more acting jobs, but she just went back to work at Chez Madelaine and seemed perfectly happy. Sometimes I would see a notice for auditions or hear of a production and I would always drop in and tell Kate. She would take the audition notice, look at it carefully, thank me, fold it and put it in her pocket. Then she wouldn't go.

At one point in the summer I got the brilliant idea that Kate should go to the National Theatre School. I went and talked to the director and he asked me what Kate had done. I told him about *The Seagull*. He was impressed. He said Kate would need three recommendations and two audition parts — one classical and one modern. I immediately went over to Chez Madelaine with the brochure and applications and told her what she'd have to do to get in. But when she heard that she had to audition she just said, Oh, no, I could never do that.

"Couldn't audition?" I said. "How will you ever get parts if you don't audition for them?"

"I guess I won't get any parts," she said.

This bothered me. I always felt that if I only had some artistic gift — writing, music, painting — that it would be a tremendous relief. If I had some sort of talent, surely I would have to pursue it. Now I knew someone with an obvious gift and she didn't feel compelled to pursue it at all. She'd been wonderful in *The Seagull*. Whenever Kate was onstage I couldn't take my eyes off her.

"Oh," she said. "That's just the way Brian blocked the play. He orchestrated it so that whenever one of us had a speech the audience would naturally look our way."

But I knew there was more to it than that. Even when Mrs Treplev was speaking, or Trigorin, I still found myself watching Kate. So did Mildred and Wesley. "Curious," said Wesley. "I suspect that's what they mean by star quality."

Kate liked to hear how much we enjoyed *The Seagull* but said she couldn't remember much about the performance herself. She said she'd loved the rehearsals but something strange had happened during the actual run. She was fairly evasive about it and so I finally let the subject drop.

I had a lot going on at that time too. I had started my MA — *The Concept of the Imagination in Romantic Poetry* — and Wesley and I were thinking about a longer piece on the Kirlians. And so that year went. Kennedy was assassinated, Lyndon Johnson became president and in the next few months it became clear that the troubles in Vietnam were far from over. And, of course, there were troubles closer to home.

Just down the street from me, a mailbox exploded. Once one exploded, it seemed every day there were reports of new bombings. Suddenly everywhere you went there were the initials FLQ painted on walls and over bridges. It was a time when you could feel the ground starting to rumble under your feet, literally and figuratively. Everything that had seemed so solid, like my parents' marriage, was coming apart. I remember walking down the frozen streets and when I'd see a mailbox I'd simply cross over to the other side and walk quietly and quickly to what I was now perceiving as the very English enclave of McGill University.

I started noticing more and more French being spoken. Of course people weren't speaking French more, it was just that I was more aware of it. I also noticed that Kate, who had arrived in Montreal with just her high-school French, was now perfectly fluent and would flip back and forth from English to French like une vrai Quebecoise. For my own part, I had already got my French requirements for my PhD and yet I was totally tongue-tied and barely able to follow conversations. I was feeling more and more English with each passing day.

In late January of 1964, I was sitting in Chez Madelaine one evening. I remember it was incredibly cold out and I was wondering why I wasn't doing my postgraduate work at Berkeley. Kate brought over two coffees and sat down with me. Then she pulled a piece of paper out of her pocket and pushed it across the table. I turned it around and read it. At the top of the piece of paper there was an S in the form of a swan, and the S formed the first letter of the Stratford Festival Theatre. Underneath was a very short note:

> Dear Miss Barnes,
>
> Unbeknownst to you, I had the pleasure of seeing your performance in *The Seagull*. This letter is to offer you a place in the Stratford Festival Company for the Summer of 1964. We anticipate an exciting season and I look forward to meeting and working with you.
>
> Best wishes,
Daniel Lloyd
Artistic Director

I looked up at Kate, dumbfounded. "So this is what comes of not auditioning," I said.

SHAKESPEARE WROTE FOR AN EMPTY SPACE. A bare platform. At the Globe theatre the stage thrust out into the midst of the audience. It was a stage that had grown out of the marketplace, the courtyard. Soliloquies were not spoken as interior monologues, but as speeches directed to auditors only a few feet away. Clowning took place right in the midst of the crowd. Asides could be spoken with a simple turn of the head. The audience didn't so much observe the action as collaborate in its creation.

But by the nineteenth century the shape of the stage had changed completely. Plays had retreated into a three-sided box that was separated from the audience by an invisible fourth wall. The spectators sat outside the action and observed it. This reflected the scientific thinking of the day. The universe existed outside of us and by impartial observation we could learn its laws. Chekhov's plays worked on this stage, and Ibsen's.

The twentieth century saw a paradigm shift in scientific thinking. Scientists stopped believing that the universe was made up of matter that was separated from mind. Heisenberg stated the Uncertainty Principle — the observer is part of the event. At the same time the great English director Tyrone Guthrie was becoming increasingly frustrated trying to squeeze Shakespeare's sprawling plays into the box set. He knew that in Shakespeare's theatre there had been no curtain, no sets, that space and time were organized to propel the dramatic action and were not viewed as entities in themselves. He knew that the empty space could be at one moment a battlefield and the next, a bedchamber. He knew that on Shakespeare's stage the action defined the space and not the space the action. He started to envision an open stage. Not a museum replica of the Globe, but a theatre that worked on the same principles. He tried to interest people in building such a theatre, but the task was too daunting. One day, in 1954, a call had come from Canada and Tyrone Guthrie was able to do an end-run around the British theatre establishment and build the theatre of his dreams in the small town of Stratford, Ontario. Hamlet's sterile promontory thrust into *Henry the Fifth*'s wooden O.

Beneath this world-famous Stratford Festival stage there is a room where the costumes are created. It's an immense sun-filled room with dozens of dress forms and rows of industrial sewing machines, scissors of every size, huge cones of thread in every colour, narrow cutting tables holding bolts of the most beautiful materials.

Lust. It was the only word to describe what this room evoked in Sofi Lamereau. Lust. She could sit here by the hour, feeling the cloth between her fingers and stroking the silks and furs while slowly and laboriously around her, her designs took shape.

And yet here she stood with nothing to do.

Cyrano. The most ambitious play in the classical repertoire. A play about the thing that Sofi Lamereau loved most in all this world. A play about style. A play about beauty. A play of so many costumes! Marquises, musketeers, thieves, pastry cooks, poets, musicians, nuns, sentries. Literally hundreds and hundreds of beautiful costumes. The moment it had been announced, ideas for *Cyrano* had leapt into Sofi's mind. She couldn't wait to get started. And yet whenever she approached Daniel Lloyd, he was evasive. Always, there seemed to be something more pressing on his mind. But for a play as opulent as *Cyrano*, what could be more pressing than design?

At first, Sofi had tried to see Daniel Lloyd's point of view. He had just come to the theatre and he was obviously trying to make some big changes. Once he had those problems solved surely he'd focus his formidable energies on *Cyrano*? But still he hadn't. A terrible thought occurred to Sofi. What if one of those big changes concerned her? What if Daniel Lloyd wasn't going to use her as *Cyrano*'s designer? What if — maybe — Daniel Lloyd was being evasive deliberately? Maybe Daniel Lloyd was thinking of some-one else.

As soon as this thought entered Sofi's mind she couldn't get it out. She started imagining one of the big British designers sweeping in, finished sketches in hand, taking over her department.

But that was impossible. She was Head of Design. If Lloyd was thinking of that, he would have to remove her.

Or would he? Could he not argue that this was a special instance and he needed someone with whom he'd worked in the past? Some-one he felt comfortable with?

The more she thought about it, the more she realized this had to be the case. *Cyrano* was immense. *Cyrano* was gigantic. Work would have to begin any day if they were to come anywhere close to getting the costumes made on time.

Sofi was enraged.

Then she caught herself. That, of course, was exactly what Daniel Lloyd would want. He would want her to storm into his office, make a big scene, accuse him publicly of trying to replace her, show herself to be unreliable or, worse, disloyal. Threaten to resign. That's just what he would want. That would be playing right into his hands. That way he could bring in the designer he'd already secretly chosen and no one on the Board could object.

So she wouldn't.

She wouldn't make a scene. She'd just wait him out. She at least would maintain her dignity. And if he was going to treat her in this despicable fashion, he'd have to go public and then he'd see what havoc *that* would create in the department. He'd see what loyalty *she* commanded.

Yes. She would maintain her dignity and make *him* come to *her*.

"THE GALDIKAS SYNDROME?"

George Stevens was sitting in a deep leather chair in Michael Rasnanikoff's book-lined study in Toronto.

"Yes," Michael said. "That's what I call it."

George Stevens knew who Raymond Galdikas was, of course. Though he'd left Stratford shortly before George joined the Board, for years whenever one of the big parts was being considered — Lear, Othello, Tartuffe — there would be a collective sigh and someone would speak that well-worn phrase, If only we could get Galdikas.

But they couldn't. And now no one in theatre could. Galdikas had gone to Hollywood and had vowed never to step on a stage again.

"Well, we can't compete with Hollywood," George said.

"Can't we?"

George looked up at his friend.

"In many ways that's so Canadian, George. That feeling that we can't do it here. But if Daniel Lloyd has chosen Stratford as his venue maybe we're at a turning point. Maybe now is the time."

"The time for what?" asked George. He felt again that strange tightening in his stomach he'd felt the day Michael had suggested he approach Daniel Lloyd.

"Film."

"Film? Movies?"

"Movies. This country has produced some of the greatest actors in the world. And yet each one of these actors finds the same thing. What do you do when you get to the top and find out it isn't there? You head south and find your Bonanza. So again and again we make the investment and Hollywood reaps the rewards. But why couldn't we make films here? And why wouldn't Stratford be the place to make them? It's got the space, it's near three major cities, and it's got the talent. You see, George, I don't think we can keep our actors here unless we offer them the ultimate reward. Film. The Stratford season is only half a year. We hire them in April and let them go in November. Then they have to dash around for four or five months trying to find work — usually in film or TV — and then we hire them back. Every year we lose a few. Usually a few of our best. But if we had a film studio in Stratford where we made good films, I mean films of the classics, the sort of films that wouldn't have a two-week run but would be around for years and years, I think we could lure the Galdikases back. And what's more, George, I think we could make money doing it."

As George sat there listening to his friend, a strange thing happened. He suddenly remembered that angry trucker. That moment, that simple idea. Fresh doughnuts. A simple idea that he'd had the guts to act upon. George knew that the reason he, George Stevens, had opened franchise after franchise and not someone else was simply because he'd beat everyone else to it. He'd seen that the moment was ripe and he'd acted upon it. Sitting here, talking to his friend Michael, he realized that this was an auspicious moment too. Daniel Lloyd had come to Canada and Daniel Lloyd knew more about theatre than anyone else in the world. He had come to Canada because he knew we had resources he couldn't get elsewhere. And if we had these resources for theatre, why not film? And if we could make films at Stratford, Michael was right: not only would we hold our own good actors but we'd attract great actors from all over the world. And the two, the theatre and the film, would feed each other. The theatre developing the talent, the film exploiting it. It was a concept of such simplicity and such magnificent daring. George was hooked.

THREE MORE WEEKS HAD PASSED and Sofi Lamereau had still not sought a meeting with Daniel Lloyd. She'd catch a glimpse of him on his way to his office or walking to the theatre or talking with one of the secretaries, but it was as if she were invisible. She even started to wonder if he knew who she was. Most disturbing of all, he never came to the costume department.

Directors always made a beeline for Costume. It was the one place they could relax. There was always fresh-perked coffee and while the sewers and cutters continued to work, they were able to chat at the same time. There was the comfort of constant activity in the costume department but nothing that demanded a director's attention.

But Daniel Lloyd had never set foot in there. Not once. There could be only one explanation. He was avoiding it because he was avoiding Sofi. And he was avoiding Sofi because he was planning to bring in someone else.

Sofi wasn't the only one who noticed it. Her head seamstress kept asking when they were going to get started on *Cyrano*. But she couldn't sketch *Cyrano* until Daniel Lloyd gave her the go-ahead.

But, oh, the waiting was painful. And going down to Costume was even more painful. It got so that Sofi couldn't bear it. As soon as she stepped in she could feel the unasked question hovering in the air. One day her head seamstress took her aside and asked it: Sofi, what's going on? And instead of replying, Sofi had burst into tears and run sobbing from the room.

Then the rumours really got circulating. Whenever Sofi came into a room people would go silent, just for a moment, then start talking again.

She had to confront Daniel Lloyd. Dignity be damned. She'd just walk into the bastard's office and ask him what the hell was going on. So the next day Sofi headed out her door prepared to sit in his outer office all day. She would not be put off.

But he didn't put her off. He saw her within minutes of her requesting an appointment.

"Sofi," he said, smiling. "I was just thinking of you."

"Mr Lloyd — "

"Daniel."

"...if you're going to fire me, I think you should do it now..."

Daniel Lloyd looked at her in genuine bewilderment.

"Sofi," he said. "Whatever are you talking about?"

"Cy-Cyrano," Sofi stammered. "Who have you got to design *Cyrano*?"

"Why, you, Sofi."

"Me?"

"Who else? You're Head of Design."

So it *was* hers. *Cyrano* was hers. All hers. There *was* no other designer. He'd just assumed all along that she was going to do it and she, foolishly, had got herself all tangled up with paranoid thoughts and insecurities.

Sofi felt such a wave of relief and gratitude to Daniel Lloyd that the time lost no longer mattered.

It was only after she'd left his office that it dawned on her. All that waiting, all that delay, hadn't been in vain. She'd never felt more ready to start a project. It was true what they said about Daniel Lloyd. He was a genius. He'd held her off and held her off until she was ready and he'd known that moment better than she herself.

She would create a *Cyrano* so beautiful, so ravishingly beautiful, it would take his breath away.

DANIEL LLOYD SAT BACK IN HIS CHAIR and listened to George Stevens. How many times had he heard this same pitch? Always some businessman who fancied himself a film producer. But he listened to George Stevens, and as he listened, he had to admit that George was making one of the best pitches he'd ever heard. You couldn't help but admire the man's conviction. Of course Lloyd knew that as George got deeper and deeper into the proposal and found out just what it entailed and how huge the risk was, how small the prospect of success, he would back off. They always did, these chaps. But in the meantime he could use George's conviction to get something he wanted.

"George," he said. "I've heard the film idea bandied about a lot in my day, and it always founders on the same reef. Cash. When it comes to actually putting up the cash, people get cold feet. I think if we're serious, and we want to convince our investors we're serious, you've got to take some bold action."

"Such as?"

"In the world today, there are really only three actors who could play Cyrano — Larry Olivier, Richard Burton and Ray Galdikas. I'm going to suggest we write up a contract in which we offer Galdikas a part in *Cyrano* — in *Cyrano* the play and *Cyrano*, the movie. But Ray's an old pro. He's not going to sign a contract unless he gets paid up front. So I'm going to suggest we pay him up front for the movie and that we use this signing as our way of announcing the project to the world."

"Perfect!" said George Stevens. "*Cyrano* directed by Daniel Lloyd and starring Raymond Galdikas. Who wouldn't be interested?"

"Good."

Daniel Lloyd slowly rose out of his chair and walked around to George's side of the desk.

"I'll get my secretary to make out a contract and you can sign it," he said. "Then I'll go to Los Angeles and present it to Galdikas myself."

"Done," said George.

The two men shook on it.

•

RAY GALDIKAS HADN'T HEARD FROM HIS AGENT in over six weeks when the call had come from Daniel Lloyd. Daniel Lloyd just happened to be in town and was wondering if Ray could join him for dinner. So Ray got his best suit out of the closet, a suit he hadn't worn in months, and joined Lloyd at one of L.A.'s finest restaurants. Ray knew that Lloyd was here to ask him to play Cyrano and he knew he was in no position to refuse. On the way over in the taxi he'd toyed with trying to bluff a bit — talk about the role he'd just landed — but he knew Lloyd couldn't be bluffed. Lloyd would know that Ray wasn't getting any film offers and that he had no choice but to return to the stage.

But Lloyd hadn't taken advantage of the fact that Ray was down on his luck. On the contrary, he'd treated him like the Ray Galdikas of old. He'd ordered the finest wine and the best cognac. And Ray Galdikas, for the first time in many many months, felt like he could be himself. Instead of twitty young directors who told him to "bring it down" and then never hired him for the goddamn part anyway, he was being courted by an equal. And he was touched.

By the time they'd got to double brandies and cigars — Lloyd had remembered he loved Cuban cigars — Ray knew he was going to take whatever terms he was offered. But they hadn't talked terms. They'd talked of theatre and of old friends. They'd talked of religion, politics, poetry and art. In short, they'd talked of everything but Stratford and *Cyrano*. Ray hadn't even noticed when Lloyd slipped an envelope out of his breast pocket and placed it on the table.

When he did notice the envelope, Ray stopped talking, paused, and without saying anything, opened it. He carefully read the contents. To his amazement, it was a contract for *Cyrano* the movie.

Cyrano the movie!

When he read the next item it took all of Ray Galdikas' formidable talent as an actor to conceal his joy. The contract stipulated that he would receive fifty thousand dollars up front whether the movie was made or not. He stretched out his hand and Daniel Lloyd placed a fountain pen in it. He signed. Then he drew on his cigar and released two perfect smoke rings.

"This movie isn't going to get made, is it, Daniel?"

"Most likely not," Daniel Lloyd replied. "But this time, Ray, you've got your money up front."

"I don't know how you did it, Daniel, but however you did, you're a genius."

Daniel Lloyd could have had Ray Galdikas on any terms, he knew that. But instead he'd been able to give a great actor what a great actor deserved.

And in so doing, he'd got more than just a great actor for his *Cyrano*, he'd got a great actor's unquestioned loyalty.

HOUR AFTER HOUR, day after day, Sofi's studio filled with sketches for *Cyrano*. Sketches of musketeers in their flaming red cloaks. Of Capuchins in burnt-sienna robes. Of viscounts and marquises strutting about like peacocks in turquoise and blue. The sombre greys of the Sisters of the Cross, the motley rags of poets and the polished buttons of Spanish officers. Sketch after sketch after sketch. And long after the cutters and sewers had gone home, Sofi's light burned on as she finished her sketch of Roxanne's duenna — a plump woman, as she imagined her, in yards and yards of poseidon blue.

The harder, the longer she worked, the better she seemed to get. It was almost as if exhaustion broke down the little critical voice which had so often tied her in knots in the past — no, too many buttons, the actor won't be able to undo them fast enough; or, too much material, she'll get it caught moving around the table — Sofi would simply execute her visions as they arose before her eyes. In fifteen days Sofi had accomplished what normally would have taken her months. It was midnight when she realized that she had completed every sketch of every character in every costume. There was nothing more to do but present her work to Daniel Lloyd.

Sofi watched as Daniel Lloyd studied her first sketch. A cavalier in navy blue. He seemed to take forever, looking at it quietly and thoughtfully, then he placed it to one side of his desk and picked up the next sketch.

"I arranged them in order of appearance," Sofi said.

Daniel Lloyd nodded and continued to study the sketch of the lackey. Next came the guardsman, one of Sofi's favourites, with his huge staff and breastplate of engraved silver.

"We can make the breastplate out of fibreglass and shellac. It won't be too heavy."

Daniel Lloyd nodded. Then he picked up the next sketch. The bouquet girl. Sofi had used the bouquet girl's waiflike appearance to contrast the opulence of the guardsman and the cavalier. A neat little touch of social commentary. Daniel Lloyd looked at the sketch of the bouquet girl for what seemed like an inordinate amount of time. Then he passed more quickly through the sketches of the porter, the citizens, the gambler, the cutpurse.

When he came to Christian, he stopped and studied the sketch for well over a minute. This was the handsome suitor's first and in many ways most important appearance in the play and Sofi had designed for him an outfit equal to the occasion. She could just see the handsome Christian moving across the stage, the light catching the silver-grey of his cloak.

Daniel Lloyd moved more quickly through the sketches. But when he came to the first sketch of Roxanne, he again stopped and studied it for a full minute. If Christian was the moon moving across water, Roxanne was the sun. For the first scene Sofi had designed a hooded full-length white lace cloak that covered her golden gown. As Roxanne moved, the lace would slide across the gown like clouds crossing the summer sun. It was the most beautiful thing she had ever designed.

Still without saying anything Daniel Lloyd placed the sketch on top of the others and flipped through the next four or five until he came to Cyrano. Sofi had kept Cyrano deliberately simple. Black hat, black cloak, black shoes. Black as the night sky. Simple, yet infinitely deep.

Sofi sat and watched while Daniel Lloyd continued to examine each sketch and then carefully placed it on the growing stack beside him. When he was finally finished, he leaned back in his chair and looked at her.

"Sofi, these sketches are ravishing. Simply ravishing. They're some of the most beautiful costumes I've ever seen."

The most beautiful costumes he'd ever seen!

"But Sofi," he continued, "there *is* a problem."

Problem?

"I'm new to this country and yet I assumed you understood how I work. The problem is that right here on my desk is the entire play. *Cyrano* complete and finished. If I take actors and put them in these costumes...there's really nothing more to do."

Nothing more to do? There was the whole play to rehearse!

"Take this, for example." He pulled from the stack the sketch of Roxanne in her lace cloak. "If I put an actress in this, the first time she appears onstage there will be a collective intake of breath by the entire audience. And then applause."

Yes, yes, thought Sofi. Exactly.

"The audience will gasp over the costume — once — and that will be that."

Sofi felt her cheeks growing hot. Once? They wouldn't be able to take their eyes off it!

"Audiences become acclimatized to a costume, even one as beautiful as this, and then what? Our Roxanne is trapped."

"Trapped?" Her designs didn't trap actors, they enhanced them.

Daniel Lloyd continued. "Roxanne is the soul of the play. She is beauty incarnate. And yet it has to be an inner beauty...a radiance... a luminosity that comes from within. And for us to try to embody it with cloth will destroy it. Our Roxanne will be trapped in external beauty and all chance of growth will be lost. We'll get that first burst of applause and that's all we'll get. Everything will be set."

"But I don't understand...what sort of costume do you want?"

"That's just it, Sofi. That's just it precisely. I don't know what I want. That's the whole secret to my directing. I don't know what I want and so I'm able to find what's Out There."

He didn't know what he wanted? How could she work with a director who didn't know what he wanted?

"Do you want *any* of the costumes?"

"Not yet. Not yet, Sofi. Not until the actors can give us something of what *they* see."

"But it's not the actors' job to design costumes."

"Who says?"

Sofi tried again. "We can't just go into rehearsals on a production as huge as *Cyrano* without costumes — "

"Can't we?"

"You'll have chaos."

"Perhaps. But maybe that's better than the kind of Disney puppet production we're all used to. The kind where everyone applauds at the beginning and sits bored out of their minds halfway through. You call it chaos, I call it unexpectedness."

"Then what do you want of me?"

"I want you to come to rehearsals. I want you to be there every day and see what the actors give you."

He couldn't mean what he was saying. She was supposed to go

and watch rehearsals and then design costumes? There wouldn't be time. There was hardly time now. He couldn't mean what he was saying.

"There's a play out there, Sofi, and we've got to find it together. You, me, and the actors. We can't impose our vision on them; nor they, theirs on us. We're going to find it together."

But to go into rehearsals without costumes, without even a clear idea about what you were doing...it was impossible.

"You see, Sofi, I'm interested in magic," Daniel Lloyd continued, and as he continued he began rolling up the sleeves of his shirt. "Real magic. Not phoney stage magic. In order to create real magic we've got to roll up our sleeves and show the world we have nothing to hide."

Sofi sat across from Daniel Lloyd as he held up his bared arms and gestured to the ceiling. She looked at him. All those hundreds of hours of work. All those designs, the best she had ever produced. All for nothing? Because he wanted to show the world he had nothing up his sleeves?

A thought crossed her mind. A thought which was to grow in intensity as the weeks wore on: the man was insane. Daniel Lloyd was insane.

ONCE I HAD A FRIEND in the Stratford Company, I kept seeing articles about Stratford. I'd always kept an eye on the theatre column but lately I could hardly pick up a paper or turn on the radio without one more tidbit about the goings on. *Maclean's* had just done a cover story on the return of Galdikas and the inception of an indigenous Canadian film industry.

"It's in the glove compartment," I told Kate.

She opened up the glove compartment and peered in.

"I could've put my bags in here, Richard."

It was true that everything about the Buick was big. The trunk was still half empty after Kate had thrown all of her belongings into it and the back seat was roomy enough for a small person to stretch out quite comfortably. Kate reached her arm in up to the elbow, dug under the maps I'd bought of Ontario and Quebec, and pulled out the magazine.

"Is this it?" she asked, holding up the *Maclean's*. The cover had a picture of Raymond Galdikas in street clothes with his hands on his hips, grinning.

"That's it," I said.

"Is that Daniel Lloyd?" Kate asked.

I should have been prepared for that but I wasn't.

"That's Raymond Galdikas," I said. "One of... *the* greatest actor Canada has ever produced."

Kate grinned. It was getting to be quite a joke between us now, her lack of knowledge of her chosen profession. She flipped to the beginning of the article.

"I've seen his Richard III, his Lear, and that very Falstaff," I said gesturing to one of the photos in the essay. "And now Cyrano. I can't wait."

"Cyrano..."

"Read the article, Kate. They're going to do *Cyrano* the play and *Cyrano* the movie. You've managed to get into theatre at probably the most exciting time since the Festival began in a tent."

She bent her head for a moment and started reading. Then she looked up again.

"*Cyrano*'s not Shakespeare?" I shook my head. "I thought Stratford did Shakespeare."

"Shakespeare... and other classics. *Cyrano*'s by a French playwright. Edmond Rostand."

"What's it about?"

"Well, it's about this man called Cyrano who's ugly, he's got a big nose — "

She flipped back to the cover.

"He can do that part," she said.

"Exactly, Kate. That's why everyone's so excited to get him. He's made for this part."

"Okay, okay, so Cyrano's ugly. Then what?"

"Well, Cyrano's ugly but he has a beautiful cousin — Roxanne —"

"And he's in love with her."

"Right."

"But she's not in love with him."

"Right."

"Because he's ugly."

"Right. Only it's a little more complicated than that. Cyrano's ugly on the outside but inside he's one of the most beautiful men who's ever lived."

"A beautiful soul."

"Exactly. Cyrano is a poet and a lover and a romantic and he's madly, insanely, wildly in love with Roxanne."

"Why doesn't he just tell her?"

"Because he's afraid she'll reject him because of his ugly nose."

"If she did that she'd be very shallow."

"This is classical theatre, Kate, you've got to accept the premise. She's not shallow, she's just young. Anyway, he does try to tell her, but by the time he gets up the nerve she's seen a handsome soldier."

"Their eyes locked across a crowded room."

"Exactly."

"And she falls in love with the handsome soldier."

"So she thinks."

"She doesn't know?"

"Well, the first time the handsome soldier tries to court her, she finds he's a little lacking in some of the qualities she wants in a man."

"Such as?"

"Poetry, eloquence, romance."

"All the things Cyrano has."

"Precisely. Eventually what happens is that Christian, the handsome soldier, ends up wooing Roxanne using Cyrano's words. Then they both go off to war — "

"Of course."

" …where Cyrano continues to write to Roxanne using Christian's name."

"Why?"

"Because he's in love with her and for once he's able to say the things he's always wanted to say to her without fear of rejection."

"This is getting sad."

"Just wait, it gets sadder. Roxanne arrives at the front and tells Christian that at first she was attracted to his handsome face but that now she truly loves the soul who wrote the letters. Once Christian hears this, he's honourable enough to tell Cyrano that Roxanne really loves him."

"That's not sad, that's nice."

"Then he dies."

"Christian?"

"Yes. He's killed at the front. Roxanne is heartbroken and Cyrano loves her too much to destroy her illusion that the handsome Christian was also a poetic soul."

"The end?"

"No. Roxanne goes into a convent and once a week Cyrano comes and visits her. This goes on for fourteen years."

"Fourteen years? Doesn't he ever tell her?"

"No. She discovers it herself the day he dies."

"So she loved him all along and he loved her all along but she never knew until it was too late."

"Exactly."

"Richard, you're getting a little choked up, aren't you?"

I coughed.

"I was thinking of my favourite line in the whole play."

Kate waited a moment and then asked what it was.

"Roxanne says it — 'I never loved but one man in my life, and I have lost him — twice...'"

After that we drove along for a while without saying anything. Though I found it a little odd that Kate hadn't heard of *Cyrano,* I shouldn't have, really. It was a play that never got done. I'd never seen a production myself. It was huge, ambitious, unwieldy. All those costumes, all those sets. As we neared the town of Stratford I wondered what Kate would make of it all.

We drove along Huron Street. On each side were small brick and stone houses. We crossed over the Avon, then turned left and drove along Lakeside. Kate was looking at the Avon, which still had a little bit of its winter ice, especially along the edges, when I made the final turn.

"What's *that*?" Kate asked.

Ahead of us, rising out of the hillside, was the Festival Theatre.

"That's it," I said. "That's the theatre."

I knew what was going through her mind. She had been expecting another theatre like the Centaur. Just one building among other buildings, indistinguishable from its surroundings. But the Festival Theatre was an enormous, circular structure perched on a knoll surrounded by rolling lawns with rows of walnut trees lining the walkway. There was a long silence as I drew the car right up to the front door. Then I turned to Kate, who was staring straight ahead, not really looking at anything.

"Oh, my god," she said.

Inside the theatre we picked up Kate's first paycheque and a friendly secretary gave us the name of a woman across the river who rented out rooms. Ten minutes later I was sitting in Mrs Morrison's parlour, flipping through a *National Geographic*, while she showed Kate the room. A few minutes later Kate appeared, smiled at me and said, "It's perfect."

I carried Kate's bags upstairs. The room was twice the size of her room in Montreal. It was clearly the old master bedroom with two dormer windows that looked out over the river towards the theatre. When we came downstairs again Mrs Morrison rattled off the house rules.

"I don't expect you to be my companion, you're a paying tenant here and you come and go as you please. No parties, no visitors after ten. No alcohol in your room." Once that was done, she softened up a bit. "You've both had a long drive. Would you like to join me for dinner?"

We did. Mrs Morrison was a feeder and she prepared us a delicious home-cooked meal. After coffee and pound cake I helped with the dishes, which made a good impression, and then took my leave. Kate said goodbye at the front door, then on the porch steps, then on the sidewalk, then at the car. Finally, as I rolled down the window, I said what we'd both been thinking.

"I'm going to miss you, Kate."

"Me too," she said. Then she smiled. "Thanks for the ride."

As I backed out of Mrs Morrison's driveway and drove off, Kate stood on the sidewalk and watched me go. As I rounded the corner I glanced back and the little figure was still there, staring after me.

She looked so small.

I got to the outskirts of Stratford, found a cheap motel, pulled in and took a room for the night.

IT DIDN'T SEEM RIGHT driving through Toronto without stopping to see my mother. I'd felt the pull going across the top of Toronto with Kate, a gentle tugging like an undertow, but now that I was on my own the tug was pronounced and I turned off the 401 and headed down Bayview into Rosedale. A couple of minutes later I was pulling up in front of my parents' house. The house. Elizabeth's house. My mother and father were now officially separated and as part of the agreement my mother had got the house and a large annuity. My father had written me a rather formal note explaining the situation and wishing me well in my studies. A few days later a sizable bond had arrived with a letter from Cam Bienenstock saying my father recognized his obligation to me until I had finished my education. Although I felt quite depressed for a few days afterwards, at the time I attributed it to the separation, not the note or the bond. I wrote back to my father offering my thanks and condolences and saying the next time I was in Toronto I would call him. It never occurred to me that it was he who should make the contact with me, he who should invite me out to lunch — I just felt vaguely sick and inexplicably guilty about the whole mess.

The house looked exactly the same but the moment I stepped in I could tell everything had changed. Although from my vantage point at the front door I couldn't see anything different, it felt different. And smelled different. Instead of silver polish and lemon oil it smelled faintly of cigarettes and coffee. And there was another smell I recognized but had never experienced in that house. The smell of people.

Just as I started down the hall, a young woman came out of the kitchen carrying a cup of coffee. She had long blonde hair and was dressed in black slacks and a loose-fitting sweater. She wore glasses. She seemed as surprised to see me as I was to see her.

"Excuse me," she said. "I didn't hear you knock."

"I didn't," I said. "I live here." Then I corrected myself. "Or, I should say, I used to."

"You must be Richard. Elizabeth's son."

"That's right."

"I'm Heather," said the young woman. "I'm a friend of your mum's. She and the others have gone to Ottawa." Heather nodded toward the dining room. "Go on in," she said. "I'll get you a coffee."

I stood in the doorway between the hall and dining room. Gone was the eighteenth-century oak table and twelve matching carved chairs which had been such a central part of my experience in that house. In its place were two cafeteria-style tables with metal legs. On the tables were piles and piles of leaflets and I noticed that where formerly the magnificent burl walnut sideboard had stood there was now a mimeograph machine and a table with a typewriter on it. On the north wall, in place of a portrait of my mother's grandfather as Speaker of the House, there hung a huge cork bulletin board.

Heather appeared in the doorway behind me and handed me a cup of coffee.

"Things have moved so fast," she said. "Ever since the Coup we've been getting hundreds of calls. We had a place down on St George, but it was tiny and in the last few weeks we just outgrew it."

"Who's we?"

"Good question — Students Against the War, the Quakers, some of your mum's friends, the Voice of Women — just anybody who's against this war and wants to try and do something to stop it."

I looked around somewhat stunned. I'd grown up with that oak table and got so that I hated it. And yet to walk into that room and not have it there was unsettling, like I'd just stepped off a stair I didn't know was there.

"You organize and you organize and nothing ever seems to happen and then suddenly some key event takes place and things start moving faster than you could ever imagine."

Heather was carrying on about her anti-war efforts and I was wondering how much of the house had changed. I listened to Heather for the minimum time I felt was polite and then excused myself and went upstairs. Everything seemed the same up there. I went to my old room and it was untouched. When I went to check on the darkroom, the door was open. I looked around inside but everything was exactly as it had been when I'd last seen it. I came out and closed the door behind me, then I felt along the top of the moulding. The key was right where it was supposed to be. The only two rooms that had ever felt like mine were the darkroom and my bedroom and the darkroom was really Breetz's. Whatever would go on in this house, I wanted to keep that separate, so after locking the darkroom I pocketed the key.

I walked back down into the dining room.

"Everything okay?" Heather asked.

I shrugged.

"Sure. Well," I said, "I guess I'll be on my way."

I turned to leave.

"Any message for your mum?"

I thought for a bit.

"Tell her I was by," I said. "Tell her I locked the darkroom and I've taken the key. Tell her I'll be in touch."

And then I left.

REHEARSALS FOR CYRANO began on April 5th, 1964. Instead of meeting in the rehearsal hall as was customary, Daniel Lloyd had invited by personal note each of the actors to join him in the Festival Theatre at ten o'clock. When the first few actors arrived Daniel Lloyd was sitting on the stage and he got up to greet them. June Kellegher, Cameron MacKenzie and Eric Fremont were members of the Company and had been for several years. They felt a little awkward. Although they'd all performed many times on this stage, they'd never been on it before without being told where to stand, which way to face or how to move. And none of them had ever been on the stage out of costume. It felt odd just standing on the stage and not performing.

As they stood there two more actors came in. Kevin Wood and Verna Harden. Kevin had joined the company at seventeen as a young apprentice and was now getting some of the plum young male leads. Verna, known for many years as Canada's Darling, had played Anne of Green Gables in Charlottetown all through her teens. Both Kevin and Verna knew that working with Daniel Lloyd represented a quantum leap in their careers.

Raymond Galdikas entered alone. He smiled at Lloyd and Lloyd smiled at him and then he walked around the stage — the stage of so many of his great successes. Always when he'd been on it before, his concentration had been on the part he was playing and the audience he was relating to. Now, for the first time really, he looked at the stage and realized with what human skill it had been constructed. Solid dovetailed joints, no nails or screws visible. It was well built, well crafted, a piece of work as finely wrought as a Shaker meeting hall. Raymond Galdikas loved fine craftsmanship. No wonder it always felt so good, so solid, to be on this stage.

The arthritis in Joanne Whyte's left knee was acting up. She wouldn't let on but thank god she could at least sit through the first reading. Youngsters. They were all youngsters. What was this fellow Lloyd up to? Joanne wasn't sure she was interested in working with a genius. She was getting a little old for that.

Clyde Drexler also arrived by himself. This was a chance he'd been waiting for all his life. To work with Raymond Galdikas. He saw Raymond looking at one of the supports of the upper stage and examining it in detail. Clyde examined Raymond. He would observe his every move. He would try to absorb into himself the qualities that made Raymond Galdikas the great actor he was. He would breathe as he breathed, stand as he stood, and he would go home and practise the minutest details over and over.

As ten o'clock grew nearer, more and more actors began to arrive. James Rawn, Leo Paverell, Chuck Bailey, Claudia Farrell, Wendy McIntyre, Roch Newberry, Carl Woodcock. Actors who all knew each other and who immediately took part in the familiar banter of pre-rehearsal jitters. But at the same time some actors arrived whom no one knew and who knew no one. River Tantoo, Larry Colton, Jocie Young and Kate Barnes. Daniel Lloyd made a special effort to greet each of these newcomers and to welcome them to the Company.

At precisely ten o'clock Daniel Lloyd walked to the centre of the stage. A hush came over the Company. People naturally drifted into a semicircle, some sitting in the front-row seats, some sprawled on the lower stage levels. A few perched on the rear stairs, one or two bolder ones on the balcony. This was it, everyone thought — Daniel Lloyd would talk about the play a bit and then he would assign parts, which, to the amazement of all and consternation of some, he still hadn't done. There was a good deal of tension in the auditorium.

Daniel Lloyd stood quietly until all attention was focused on him, then started to speak.

"What's the purpose of the first rehearsal? What are we really trying to do? If you ask me, the purpose of the first rehearsal is to get through to the second rehearsal." Everyone laughed. "And to get to know each other. But I don't think we really get to know each other sitting around reading a script. I think there's a better way. I know that I get to know people best over a meal. Good wine. Conversation. So I think we should begin today with a really good meal. A sumptuous feast. And I think that as we're all both hosts and guests in this endeavour, we should do it together. So. Let's meet back here this evening and everyone bring a little something. And let's not plan it. So what if we have ten desserts and fourteen potato salads? We'll have a good time anyway. So go away, make your favourite dish and bring it back here, say, around five o'clock and we'll celebrate the fact that we got through the first day. After all, the first day's the toughest and I think we'll deserve a celebration."

River Tantoo found himself standing alone on the stage. Everyone else had gone. They'd all rushed off, jabbering. They knew what to do. He didn't.

A couple of weeks ago he'd been working on a construction site when the foreman had signalled him. Instead of going over, River just stood there and made the foreman come to him. He was always a little nervous walking the high stuff, Harv was, but he made it over and said, "There's a guy down there, wants to talk to you." River looked down and saw a man with silver hair looking up. Harv gave him some time off, didn't count it as his break, so River hitched his belt to a rope and dropped down to the street.

"Ever thought of being an actor?" No introduction, nothing, just like that.

"Nope," said River.

"It pays."

"How much?"

"Enough."

So now here he was, standing alone on this stage. River figured maybe he'd made a big mistake. Figured he'd just take off. So he walked out the back of the theatre, cut across the grass, over the bridge and pretty soon found himself walking some fields, then into some woods. As soon as he got into the woods he felt better. He saw some familiar-looking shoots poking out of the damp earth. He used to gather those same greens with his grandmother. He crouched down and picked one.

There weren't ten desserts and fourteen potato salads — there was everything. Raymond Galdikas had turned up with a case of vintage wines. Eric Fremont arrived with a glazed ham on a silver platter. Kate brought two chicken pot pies that she and Mrs Morrison had made together. Wendy McIntyre and Claudia Farrell had made a huge batch of fudge brownies. There was a curried rice salad and even roast duckling à l'orange. There was a gigantic pizza that Ben Pallister concocted at his father's restaurant. There were three different kinds of pies, strawberry-rhubarb, apple and a magnificent lemon meringue that Marta Speers made. Trudy Stott had made a marble cake and Yvonne Wallace had brought some homemade ice cream. Joanne Whyte contributed four loaves of steaming herb and onion bread. Tessa Blume, the stage manager, had made sure there was cutlery, plates and goblets and when River Tantoo arrived with a shirt full of greens she found a large hand-carved wooden bowl for him and together they made up a salad. Klaus Fitzner provided a round of cheese and Mike Pilkey supplied the pickles. Carl Woodcock brought pretzels.

They ate. They drank. And they laughed. Larry Colton, whom

Daniel Lloyd had discovered on the streets of Vancouver, did his juggling act with a wine bottle, the ham bone and Clyde Drexler's shoe. Yvonne Wallace balanced a spoon on her nose while singing an aria from *Madame Butterfly*. Chuck Bailey did an imitation of the prime minister from the upper balcony in his horrible French, praising the meal and thanking everyone for their participation.

They got silly, and as the night wore on they got sillier. Roch Newberry, Mike Pilkey, Klaus Fitzner and Ben Pallister did a turn as a barbershop quartet. Raymond Galdikas recited To Be or Not To Be. Backwards. Verna Harden had everyone in stitches as a sex-crazed Anne of Green Gables and, finally, Trudy Stott led the Company in a truly inspiring rendition of the Mouseketeer Song. The actors drifted home that night feeling more relaxed than they'd ever imagined possible after a first rehearsal with the great Daniel Lloyd.

And Daniel Lloyd had accomplished what he'd set out to do. He'd begun the process of demystifying the world-famous Stratford Festival stage.

The next morning Tessa Blume did exactly as Daniel Lloyd had instructed her. She placed twenty-five chairs in a large circle in the centre of the rehearsal hall. She felt edgy. For weeks prior to rehearsal the actors had been trying to find out what parts had been assigned to whom, especially the main ones, and she'd been able to honestly say she didn't know. But the actors became more and more insistent and she'd finally gone to Daniel Lloyd and asked him.

"I don't know," he'd said. "I really don't know."

And then he told her that he thought casting a play too early was always a mistake; people would just give the standard interpretations of the parts. There would be nothing unexpected — a favourite word of his, Tessa was discovering. Then he said he was having his secretary type up a copy of the script in which casting wouldn't be an issue.

Over the past week Tessa had sat down a few times and tried to second-guess what Daniel Lloyd had in mind. It didn't take a mathematician to figure out that with twenty-five actors and more than fifty speaking parts there would have to be doubling, tripling and maybe even quadrupling. She'd worked out half a dozen doubling patterns herself but always came up against insurmountable problems. For instance, there were only fifteen men in the cast and yet at times there were twenty males onstage. She couldn't make it work no matter how she tried.

At ten o'clock Daniel Lloyd looked around and saw that everyone was present.

"I've had the script retyped," he said, "and we'll be working from that for a while."

As he said this he gestured to a pile of dark blue binders stacked on the table beside him. Tessa watched as the first few actors standing nearby picked up their scripts. As the stack of binders grew smaller and smaller, Tessa noticed something unusual — dead silence in the rehearsal hall.

In a modern translation of *Cyrano*, this is how the opening looks:

[ACT I]
A PERFORMANCE AT THE
HOTEL DE BOURGOGNE

[SCENE I]

As the curtain rises the audience for the play at the Hotel de Bourgogne is in the process of arriving. In the next few minutes the dimly lit stage will fill with an assortment of different types. CAVALIERS, MUSKE-TEERS, GENTLEMEN, BOURGEOISIE, PAGES, FOOTMEN, A PICKPOCKET, A BOUQUET GIRL, FOPS, DANDYS *and* ARISTOCRATS *and, finally,* THE MUSICIANS.

Offstage, we hear loud talk and laughter,
then a CAVALIER boldly enters.

PORTER: *following him.* Hello, there — your fifteen
  sols!
CAVALIER: I enter free!
PORTER: Why is that?
CAVALIER: King's Cavalry!

A MUSKETEER strides past.

PORTER: Sir!
MUSKETEER: Nor do I pay!
PORTER: But...
MUSKETEER: I am a Musketeer!
CAVALIER: *to the MUSKETEER* There's plenty of time
  before the play begins. And the pit is empty. Shall
  we exercise our weapons?

Facing each other, the CAVALIER and
MUSKETEER flourish their foils.
As they start to fence, a FOOTMAN enters.

FOOTMAN: *to a PAGE who is already on stage* Pst...
  Flanquin...
PAGE: Champagne?...
FOOTMAN: *pulling something from his doublet.*
  Cards. *He sits down.*
        I'll deal.
PAGE: *joining him*   You, rascal!

The FOOTMAN takes the stub of a candle
from his pocket and places it on the floor.

FOOTMAN: I pinched a little of my master's light.

As they start to play, the BOUQUET GIRL *enters. As she crosses the stage, a* WATCH-MAN *approaches her.*

WATCHMAN: How sweet of you to arrive before they put up the lights...

He clasps her waist.

MUSKETEER: *taking a hit* Touché!
PAGE: Clubs!
WATCHMAN: *following the girl*   A kiss!
BOUQUET GIRL: *wriggling free* People can see us!
WATCHMAN: *drawing her into a darkened corner*
    No fear!

but the script in the blue binder looked like this:

Hello, there — your fifteen sols! I enter free!
Why is that? King's Cavalry! Sir! Nor do I pay!
But...I am a Musketeer! There's plenty of time
before the play begins. And the pit is empty.
Shall we exercise our weapons? Pst...Flanquin...
Champagne?...Cards. I'll deal. You, rascal!
I pinched a little of my master's light. How sweet
of you to arrive before they put up the lights...
Touché! Clubs! A kiss! People can see us!
No fear!

A translation of the play is usually close to two hundred pages, but the "the blue version" was only a third that. Daniel Lloyd had eliminated all the stage directions. That wasn't terribly upsetting — other directors did that too — but what *was* disturbing to the actors was that the characters' names had also been eliminated and, worse, all spacing that would indicate a change in speaker. No one could figure out who was speaking what. What remained in the blue version was the words. That's all.

The words.

Daniel Lloyd believed that the great plays were not created but discovered. He believed that theatre was a collective art and that at certain extraordinary times in human culture somehow the human psyche channelled these archetypal myths and stories into a concrete form that was able to manifest itself on the stage. In western culture this had happened only a few times. In Greece, in Elizabethan England and in seventeenth-century France. In each of these times, great playwrights appeared. But these playwrights did not create the plays so much as record something that was revealed to them and their fellow performers. That's why the great plays only manifested themselves in the presence of a great company. Sophocles was not an individual genius nor was Shakespeare; they were men who were at the apex of a culture that was receptive to huge archetypal themes. They were men who made the invisible visible. Divinity's scribes. They were the means by which a culture spoke to itself of the themes most central to it.

These Ages were ephemeral. They were like flashes of lightning in the dark history of Humanity. And once the Age had passed, the magic vanished. What was left?

The words.

The actors with no experience — Larry Colton, Jocie Young and River Tantoo — were the least traumatized. These three found themselves reading a quite lovely poem that didn't make much sense. Those actors who had some experience saw only a jumble of words. The seasoned professionals — Ray Galdikas and Joanne Whyte — were intrigued. These two, after reading quietly for a few moments, sat on two of the chairs arranged in the middle of the rehearsal hall. The rest followed suit.

As they did, Daniel Lloyd pulled a small rubber ball out of his pocket and started tossing it casually into the air until everyone had taken their seats. Everyone watched him, waiting for him to speak. Finally he did. He tossed the ball one last time and, as he caught it, spoke the first word of the play:

Hello.

Then he tossed the ball to Ray Galdikas, who immediately knew what to do. Catching the ball in one hand, he spoke the second word of the play.

there

Then, with the instinct of a great actor, Ray threw it to the only other person in the circle who so far had intuited what Daniel Lloyd was up to: Larry Colton. As Larry caught the ball he spoke the third word of the play — Your — and tossed it to Roch Newberry.

fifteen

By the time Roch Newberry had got it, everyone got it.

June Kellegher:	sols!
Eric Fremont:	I
Clyde Drexler:	enter
Wendy McIntyre:	free!
River Tantoo:	Why
Carl Woodcock:	is
Joanne Whyte:	that?
Leo Paverell:	King's
Mike Pilkey:	Cavalry!
Claudia Farrell:	Sir!
Marta Speers:	Nor
Chuck Bailey:	do
Yvonne Wallace:	I
Trudy Stott:	pay!
Klaus Fitzner:	But...
Kate Barnes:	I
James Rawn:	am
Kevin Wood:	a
Jocie Young:	Musketeer!
Cameron MacKenzie:	There's
Verna Harden:	plenty
Chuck Bailey:	of
Ray Galdikas:	time

It wasn't easy to read the script and also pay attention to the movement of the ball. At any moment it might come to you and you had to be ready with the next word. The first few times the ball flew around the circle there were lots of misses. Then people started catching the ball and, forgetting to say a word, throwing it to someone else. Here Daniel Lloyd would intervene. He would make them go back and do it again. He made it clear that this was a game and that there were certain unbreakable rules. Catch the ball, say a word, throw the ball.

After the first hour there were fewer and fewer missed catches. After the second the ball moved a little more fluidly around the circle. When they came back after lunch Daniel Lloyd tossed them the ball again. Occasionally somebody would catch the ball and throw it without saying their word or speak a phrase instead of just a word but mostly everyone was getting more comfortable with the game. As the day wore on there were lots of glances in the direction of Daniel Lloyd, who sat watching them, saying nothing. At four-thirty he stood and held his hand up indicating that the ball was to be tossed to him.

Chuck Bailey:	You're
Jocie Young:	leaving?
Carl Woodcock:	For
Yvonne Wallace:	the
Kevin Wood:	war.
Daniel Lloyd:	Ah!

Then he pocketed the ball and said, "Thanks everyone. We'll meet back here tomorrow morning."

Next morning when the actors appeared in the rehearsal hall the chairs were again set up in a circle and again Daniel Lloyd began rehearsal by tossing the ball up in the air, catching it and repeating his last word of yesterday,

Ah!

Then he threw the ball to Leo Paverell, who was ready for him.

Leo Paverell:	This
Kate Barnes:	very
Marta Speers:	night.

By the second day they'd done the ball exercise so often that they were punching out their words or saying them in funny voices. At one point the entire group sustained twenty minutes of a Scottish accent. Then they did it as a Gregorian chant. At any point when someone would sneak a look to see how Daniel Lloyd was reacting to the latest innovation they would always see the same calm, attentive face.

And on it went. By the morning of the third day they were so good at it some of the younger actors decided they'd try to liven things up. They'd try to catch someone off guard. Usually they succeeded. The ball would roll into a corner and the reading would stop while it was retrieved. During these times Daniel Lloyd still sat quietly and watched. But in the afternoon of the third day, as people got tired, they found trying to trick or fool their fellow actors just interrupted the flow. They found that things felt better when they would throw the ball to someone who was ready for it. And in doing this they found that the words started to form certain rhythms. A long smooth sentence would go smoothly around the group, but for short exclamations and cries the ball would often be tossed across the centre of the circle. The actors discovered one of the primary rules of theatre: for an actor, listening is more important than speaking.

After three days of this they'd read the entire script not once, not twice, but again and again and again. Word by word. This was vastly different from most rehearsals, where an actor focused mainly on his own part and cues and only peripherally on the other parts of the play. And so while the cast thought they were hamming it up with all manner of tomfoolery, what they were actually doing was absorbing the entire play into the muscle memory of their bodies.

At the end of that day, as the actors were leaving the rehearsal hall, Tessa Blume turned to Daniel Lloyd.

"Same thing tomorrow?"

He shook his head.

"No," he said. "Time to rotate the crops."

Tessa Blume looked at the pile of bamboo sticks. She thought back to a couple of days earlier when she and Daniel Lloyd had been walking across the grounds. Some of the gardeners had been staking rose bushes and Daniel Lloyd had stopped and watched them. Then he had turned to her and said, "Get me some of those, will you? Twenty-five or thirty." Tessa had.

Joanne Whyte looked at the pile of sticks. Sticks and stones will break my bones...bones...funny how her knee hadn't been bothering her lately.

Kate Barnes looked at the pile of sticks. They were about four feet long and were heaped in the centre of the hall. This was just the sort of thing Ruby Nielson used to do. She had once piled a bunch of hats in the centre of the room and everyone had grabbed one and become a character based on it.

Kevin Wood looked at the pile of sticks. Another game, he thought. I wonder how long all this is going to go on before he starts assigning parts and we get down to work?

Cameron MacKenzie looked at the pile of sticks. Usually, in the first days of rehearsal, he became totally absorbed by the character he was going to play. He would highlight his part in red. He hadn't got to do that yet and by the looks of these sticks he wasn't going to get to do it today either.

Clyde Drexler looked at the pile of sticks. In the last few days he'd learned a lot. He'd learned about attention. He'd learned that you had to be aware of both the words and your fellow actors. He'd watched Galdikas and seen that he never missed a ball, never missed a word. He was watching him now.

River Tantoo looked at the pile of sticks. He'd made it through four days of this stuff; looked like he might make it through another.

Verna Harden looked at the pile of sticks. She was certainly glad that Roxanne had so few lines to be memorized. They could go on with this kind of thing for a long time as far as she was concerned.

Roch Newberry looked at the pile of sticks. He was exhausted. The ball exercise had wiped him out. Those words, all those words going round and round in his head. Still going round. He couldn't get rid of them.

Mike Pilkey looked at the pile of sticks. He needed to know his character's motivation. He needed to analyse every nuance of feeling that his character experienced. He needed to inhabit a character so thoroughly he knew what was in his dresser drawers. The colour of his socks, the feel of his underwear. But how could he do that when he still didn't know which part he was playing?

Marta Speers looked at the pile of sticks. In the past few days as they'd worked on the ball exercise she'd found images forming in her mind. Strange, eerie images provoked by the words. Cyrano's nose growing out of a pile of manure like a mushroom. Cadets swimming like dolphins. Puff pastries nesting in trees. Funny thing was, as she heard the same words over and over, the same strange images would accompany them, only stronger and more of them. She found it a little scary.

Larry Colton looked at the pile of sticks. In juggling the trick was to always keep your poise and not worry too much about catching the object. He'd found over the past few days that the same thing applied to words. Don't lurch or grab for them. Keep centred and aware and the right word will land in your mouth.

At ten o'clock Daniel Lloyd spoke.

"Everyone, go and pick up a stick."

He waited until everyone had. Then he waited some more. The cast looked at him and wondered what he wanted them to do. Then he spoke again.

"I don't want you to do anything," he said. "I want each of you to hold your stick with both hands. Not too hard and not too soft."

Five minutes passed.

"I'll tell you the kind of pressure you want," Daniel Lloyd said. "The pressure you would use to hold a small fluttery bird. You don't want to let the bird fly away, but you don't want to hurt it. So hold it firmly but with great delicacy."

Tessa Blume watched the actors as they did as Daniel Lloyd suggested. It was fascinating. Before they'd been standing all tight, gripping their sticks and awaiting further instructions, tensed like runners waiting for the starter's pistol. As they slowly released their grips and adjusted them, it was as if they started to expand, to fill out. They grew taller and wider. They were no longer poised for action, they were simply poised. Centred.

Daniel Lloyd waited for another few minutes before he spoke again. Then he said, "The sticks have an energy of their own. An energy independent of you. Don't make the sticks move, *allow* them to move."

Ten minutes passed. Then he spoke again.

"Don't make the sticks move, *allow* them to move."

Ten more minutes passed. Daniel Lloyd spoke again.

"Don't make the sticks move, *allow* them to move."

Then he waited some more.

The wait seemed to go on forever. Again and again one of the actors would have an impulse to do something with his or her stick. To twirl it like a baton or balance it on a finger, but each time they remembered Daniel Lloyd's words and resisted the impulse.

After forty-five minutes Kate thought she felt the slightest tremor in her stick. She waited. She felt it again. This time the tremor was stronger so she slowly and delicately tightened her grip. As she did the stick began to tremble even more. Marta Speers felt it too. A tremor and something else. Heat. The stick seemed to be growing warmer in her hands. Jocie Young's stick felt lighter, as if it had slowly filled with helium and she had to hold it down ever so slightly. River Tantoo recognized the feeling. It was the feeling he had had as a kid catching snakes in the early spring. Torpid but alive. Chuck Bailey felt his stick grow heavier. He wondered if the muscles in his arms were tiring. Larry Colton felt a tremor go right up through his arms into his neck and down his spine. A tremor that originated in the stick and travelled through his entire body. It was extraordinary. Something he'd had intimations of before but had never experienced. Yvonne Wallace's stick wanted to rotate. Remembering Daniel Lloyd's words she allowed it to do so. She watched, amazed, as her knuckles turned slowly towards the floor. Joanne Whyte felt her right hand moving up and her left hand moving down. She had a sudden impulse to push her right hand back down but didn't intervene. She watched in amazement as her stick moved into a horizontal position.

What Tessa Blume would never forget was that once the sticks started to move, they all started to move together. Some of them trembled, some of them jerked, some of them rose slowly up, others down. Four or five started to twist in a slow, circular motion. Daniel Lloyd spoke again.

"Don't try to control the stick. Allow it to move where it wants to move, but move with it."

As he said this, the actors started moving out of the circle. The sticks took them in every direction. Some of them were pulled towards the corners of the room. Others moved into the centre in slow spiral motions. Some meandered like rivers, others wriggled. Two of the actors ended up pinned to the wall by their sticks.

Tessa had never seen actors move like this before. How to describe it? They weren't moving, really, they were being moved. Moved by some invisible force — like thistle on the wind or mist rising off a summer lake or leaves in a brook.

On day seven, the actors returned to the ball game but this time Tessa had removed the chairs. This meant that the actors were able to move freely about the rehearsal hall. An actor would catch the ball, speak his or her word and then, like a quarterback, scan the room and intuitively know the receiver.

Day nine they went back to the sticks. This time, the sticks began to move after only ten minutes.

On the morning of day ten Daniel Lloyd instructed Tessa to collect all the blue binders. He then handed out gold binders. The gold version still consisted of just the words but now they were spaced differently. Instead of a solid page of print, the words were broken up into phrases. Occasionally, as in the duel scenes, there would be just a word or an exclamation, but for the most part the play was broken into lines, phrases and couplets. This script was almost a third longer. The game went on as before, but now the actors would repeat an entire phrase and then throw the ball.

On day eleven Daniel Lloyd took away the ball.

Daniel Lloyd gave one of his few explanations: "We've used the ball as an organizing principle but it's no longer necessary."

At first things were confused with long pauses or two or three people speaking at once, blurting out the same phrase. Daniel Lloyd told the actors not to worry about this. If the entire cast had an impulse to speak at the same time, so what? He told them that they should think of the words in the same way as the sticks.

"Don't speak the words, allow the words to speak through you."

It was a tough day and at times very discouraging. But on day thirteen strange things started to happen. There were moments when the actors felt that they were just instruments through which music was being played. That they were not making the sound so much as releasing it.

And there were certain speeches that seemed to come alive in the mouths of the whole group. Cyrano's long self-mocking speech about his nose was one of these. Normally delivered by Cyrano alone, it took on a strange incantatory quality when spoken by the entire cast.

By day eighteen Daniel Lloyd had taken away everything. Everything including the script. He told the actors that they should just go on as before and if no one in the cast could remember the next word, line or phrase — then they should call for it and Tessa would prompt them.

Incredibly, they never had to.

IT HAD BEEN YEARS since Kate had thought of Cindy and Bobbin. Now, lying on the bed in her huge room, the evening sun streaming through Mrs Morrison's lace curtains, Kate tried to remember when she'd last seen them.

She couldn't. She could remember what they looked like, how they talked, the clothes they wore, but not when she'd last seen them. Cindy had been about her own age — three, three and a half. She had black hair braided into two braids. She wore a blue dress with white socks and black polished shoes. She would sit at the end of the bed and they'd talk. Cindy loved to talk.

Katlyn had been playing in her sandbox one day when she'd looked up and seen her. Katlyn could see her underpants as she climbed over the locked gate and quickly scanned the kitchen window to see if her mother was watching. Her mother couldn't bear it when little girls showed their underpants. But her mother wasn't at the window just then.

Cindy landed on the walkway to their house, smoothed her blue dress and tossed her braids over her shoulders so they hung down her back.

"What's your name?" she asked. She was standing at the edge of the sandbox, eyeing the bright red pail.

"Katlyn."

"I'm Cindy," the girl said and then she stepped into the sandbox and started making roadways with the palm of her hand. Just then Katlyn's mother came out to hang some laundry on the line. She glanced over at Katlyn and Cindy, then put down her basket and started lifting out sheets and towels. This wasn't like her mother. Usually her mother would go up to a new friend and ask who they were and where they lived. Katlyn looked at Cindy and Cindy was grinning back. Then Cindy did the most extraordinary thing. She put two fingers in her mouth and whistled.

Her mother didn't react.

"Mum?"

"What?"

"Hear that?"

"Hear what?"

She hadn't even turned away from the laundry.

Katlyn stuck her finger in her still ringing ear and looked back at Cindy, who was grinning even more but not at her. She followed her gaze and saw, just beyond her mother, another small person climb halfway up the gate, reach over and undo the latch, climb back down and push the gate open. He walked right past her mother. He even brushed aside one of the sheets as he went by. She hadn't seen a thing.

"This is Bobbin," Cindy almost shouted and then Bobbin did the strangest thing. He bowed. He was dressed in corduroy pants, a white shirt and a vest that looked like it had been knitted by a granny. He acted like a grown-up but he looked about four years old. His hair was brown, parted at the side, and perfectly combed. His nails were clean.

Where had they gone? They'd been so omnipresent for so many years and Katlyn had spent so much energy as a child negotiating them through the world. Cindy was so bossy. She was always telling Katlyn what to do. If it wasn't for Cindy, Katlyn would never have gotten into any trouble at all. When Katlyn's mother would call her to dinner, Cindy would tell her not to go and her mother would have to call two or three times. And Cindy would get her to grab toys away from other kids. And it was Cindy who taught her how to hide when her mother wanted her to clean her room. The thing was, Cindy was so much fun that Katlyn and Bobbin always ended up doing what she said, even if it meant getting into trouble.

Imaginary friends. Of course she'd since learned that lots of kids had imaginary friends. Some parents even set places at the table for these friends and took them on summer holidays. But Katlyn always had to pretend to her parents that Cindy and Bobbin weren't there. After dinner she'd sneak them upstairs and when her mother came into her bedroom Cindy would hide under the bed and Bobbin behind the curtains. As they grew older, they came less and less. But there must have been one particular day, now forgotten, when they simply hadn't come at all.

Funny. Kate hadn't thought of them in years. Why was she thinking about them now?

IT HAD BEEN A STROKE OF GENIUS to announce the film project along with the signing of Raymond Galdikas. Within hours George Stevens had received numerous telephone calls expressing intense interest and soon the money started rolling in. Two hundred and fifty thousand dollars already available and seven hundred and fifty thousand in trust, to be released on the first day of filming. New investors requesting a copy of the prospectus every day. Things were going even better than anticipated when strange rumours about rehearsals for *Cyrano* began reaching George Stevens' ears.

Inside the rehearsal hall everyone in the cast knew something extraordinary had taken place. Each actor now had the entire play memorized and the memorization had been effortless. No one had gone home and studied lines. No one had done line readings with their friends. No one woke in the night terrified at being unable to remember their part. The play had not been memorized but absorbed.

Galdikas was especially intrigued by the process. Usually he thought about one thing and one thing only, his part — Lear, Falstaff, Othello — and each time it was a part that so dominated the play that

Galdikas saw his job as directing all focus towards himself. But in the three weeks he'd been working with Daniel Lloyd he'd discovered something extraordinary. There was more to *Cyrano* than Cyrano.

River Tantoo never thought about the words. He just moved. And as he moved, the same words kept coming out of his mouth. It was as if the movement created the words and not the other way around. It was easy.

Verna Harden found that whenever she tried to force Roxanne's lines into her mouth she was always in the wrong position. And if she was in the wrong position it was like a hockey player passing the puck to a receiver who wasn't there. The whole play was messed up and the game had to stop and start again. So Verna gave up trying to force Roxanne's words into her mouth. Strangely enough, she found that she was always in position when the words of the Comte de Guiche appeared. She resisted this initially but after a while she found a kind of thrill in playing a seventeenth-century French fop.

Larry Colton was resisting an impulse too. During the great self-mocking nose speech he found himself wanting to play Cyrano's nose. One day he did it just for fun at break and the entire cast picked up on it, reciting Cyrano's lines. The effect was astonishing. While the entire cast spoke the speech, Larry, like some character out of a Looney Tune cartoon, metamorphosed into Cyrano's nose in all its incarnations: Aggressive, Friendly, Descriptive, Inquisitive, Insolent, Cautious, Pedantic. Cyrano's nose, in every other production just an appendage, became what it truly is — a character in its own right.

That afternoon in rehearsal, the complex scene in which Cyrano defeats a hundred swordsmen worked in an entirely new way. Instead of Cyrano systematically defeating one opponent after another, his nose played a key part. The nose would taunt one, distract another, trip a third, and suddenly a scene that had been cumbersome, un-wieldy and unbelievable became hilarious, mesmerizing and simple. As Daniel Lloyd said at the end of that day, one unexpectedness had created another.

Excitement inside the rehearsal hall grew as more and more unexpectedness happened. But this same unexpectedness was creat-ing frustrations on the outside.

"Initially things were going very well but in the last two weeks I feel potential investors are becoming a little nervous, Michael. Wary."

"Why's that, George?" Michael's voice was calm on the other end of the line.

"Rumours — have you heard them?" There was no response. "Rumours keep circulating that *Cyrano* is in a state of chaos."

Still no response.

"Everything's behind schedule. There are no costumes. No set. He hasn't even cast the play. What are we going to do about investors? We have a deadline."

"I thought they were lining up to invest."

"They were. They were, Michael. But it's all stopped. The investment has stopped but the expenses haven't. We have to have everything ready for shooting by the end of August. An entire production crew has to be hired and soon. Once we've done that we'll need more money, and more money doesn't seem to be coming."

"Ebb and flow. Perfectly natural. But the project is in good hands, George, remember that. The best. Daniel Lloyd is a genius."

KATE AWOKE. She didn't know how long she'd slept but she knew she had been sleeping deeply. Now she was awake. Wide awake.

And someone was in her room.

She lay still. Mrs Morrison was visiting her sister. Kate was alone. At least she should have been alone, but this presence had awakened her. Not by any noise, she couldn't even hear breathing. How then? Her mind raced. Had she checked all the doors before going to bed that night? Yes, even though she'd been bone-tired she'd done the rounds: front door, side door, kitchen. Basement? Had she checked the basement door? She couldn't remember.

Panic. She immediately concocted a scenario. The crazed prowler prying open the basement door, making his way slowly, deliberately, through Mrs Morrison's kitchen to the staircase. The staircase leading to her room. His hand at her throat. Just as she felt she would pass out with terror she caught it.

Scent.

She inhaled. Carefully, noiselessly.

Perfume.

Whoever it was was wearing perfume.

A woman...?

Kate lay still. Had she dreamt it all? Dreamt herself to this point? No. The scent was still there, growing more distinct in the room. She forced herself to keep her eyes open. Slowly they adjusted to the darkness. She could make out the windows, the bureau, the bookcase. Vague shapes within the blackness. But still she couldn't see.

Whoever it was didn't make a move.

Kate lay there, motionless, her breathing shallow, her feet and hands falling asleep. Pins and needles. Pain. Her whole body was numb but she waited it out until faintly, ever so faintly, outside her window she could hear the first chirping of birds. Dawn. If she could just hold on a little longer, ignore the numbness, keep breathing, the room would grow light.

As the light thickened in the room Kate forced herself to look around. At first just with her eyes, then slowly turning her head. Nothing. There was no one there. No one. But still she could smell it. Sensuous. Celestial. A smell that filled the room.

A smell she had never experienced before.

IN VOODOO MYTHOLOGY there is a saying: the loa and the person cannot occupy the same body at the same time. The loa is the divine entity which is drummed across the waters from Africa and which takes possession of the body. When the loa takes possession, the ordinary everyday personality must vacate. That is why there is never a remembrance by the person of what happened during the state of possession. It is up to others to recognize what deity has entered the person's body and to name it, react to it and attire it appropriately.

Daniel Lloyd watched rehearsals. Every day more and more loas were appearing. Mysterious, mythological beings that would take possession of his actors and use their bodies to express themselves. There were a number of actors — he knew this would happen — who were resisting the process. They kept trying to create characters and *be* characters and use all the old tired methods that rendered theatre so deadly and dull.

When the loa entered the body it was truly astonishing. The day Larry Colton allowed Cyrano's nose to take possession was a day as important to Daniel Lloyd as that early rejection of the cardboard cutouts. Of *course* Cyrano's nose was one of the central deities of the play, and yet it was something he himself had never thought of. The danger was that an actor would try to take control of the loa, to nail down their performance. But with someone like Larry it was so wonderful because Larry didn't know what he was doing so he really had no choice except to let the spirit enter or do nothing at all. The worst, as Daniel Lloyd had foreseen, were those actors who had just enough experience to think they knew what they were doing. Actors such as Kevin Wood and Verna Harden.

Verna had surprised him. He had hired her simply because the pressure to hire her had been immense; but he was certain she wouldn't last two days. Then during that first rehearsal she had done the improv of the sex-crazed Anne of Green Gables and he realized he was dealing with someone much more interesting than her public persona. A person perhaps capable of emptying herself enough to let the loa enter. And it had. The Comte de Guiche had been drummed all the way across the Atlantic from France to enter the body of Canada's Darling.

Kevin Wood hadn't made it. Daniel Lloyd had watched as the young man's ambition had got the better of him. Kevin perceived himself as the Company's leading man and he couldn't bear to see the part of Christian go to someone else. But it had. It had entered River Tantoo. Daniel Lloyd knew the moment he'd seen River Tantoo standing with such poise and ease at the top of the girder that here was the perfect receptacle for the handsome, inarticulate but brave

Christian. Now he could sense River's own amazement as Christian's words kept coming out of his mouth. But River wasn't intimidated enough to block the process and so the loa had taken total possession. He was magic to watch. Like his name, the movement flowed out of him and he swirled and flowed effortlessly around the stage. Then there had been that ghastly moment when Kevin Wood had tried to impose himself onto the part, when the Company's leading man had felt he must take what was his due. River, of course, had demolished him, demolished him without even intending to. But then it hadn't been River, had it? He who opposes the gods will be destroyed by them.

Kevin had quit rehearsal and gone to the press and talked about *Cyrano* being a total catastrophe — chaos — and that he, Daniel Lloyd, was out of control. Something that had helped the entire process immensely. It had created panic, uncertainty, lack of confidence, and panic, uncertainty and lack of confidence were just what were needed. The loas loved chaos. They loved that moment when the ego lost control — that was often the moment they chose to enter. What excited Lloyd most were the transformations. To see one loa enter and another depart was absolutely hair-raising.

And his admiration for Galdikas grew with every passing day. Ray of course knew every trick in the trade and was used to dominating any stage he stood upon. Daniel Lloyd would watch Galdikas using all the old tricks to create the character of Cyrano and then, the next day, he would watch him do the far more difficult task of rejecting his own creation and going back to nothingness. Emptying himself of all preconceptions and allowing the mysterious spirit to take possession of his body. And when it did, it was truly magnificent. Truly magnificent because Galdikas' body was the perfect instrument, an instrument that had been trained for twenty years and had mellowed into greatness. A vessel worthy of Cyrano.

In the final week of rehearsal Daniel Lloyd sat, his face an impassive mask. More and more loas were appearing: Ragueneau, the Cadets, Valvert, Montfleury, the Pickpocket, the Poet, Mother Marguerite and Sister Claire. But every now and then the loa would depart and reappearing in its place would be a terrified actor desperate for direction and control. He wouldn't give it. At these moments he would give them nothing. Not so much as the flicker of an eye.

They must get nothing from him. They must get nothing from him because it must come directly to them from the invisible world. He must not become a mediator between the Seen and the Unseen. He too must be empty so that the process could fulfil itself.

And so he would give them nothing and allow their despair to grow and watch impassively while their fragile actor egos shattered. And then once again the loas would appear: Ragueneau, the Fruit Seller, Jodelet. More and more loas appeared. More and more loas appeared and yet, still, there was one who hadn't come. He knew she would, she had to. And so he waited for her.

Roxanne.

THIS IS HOW ROXANNE DESCRIBED IT TO ME LATER.

That first night she could see Kate lying in the bed, paralysed with fright. And she'd spoken to her, or tried to. She kept telling her not to be afraid, it was all right, she wouldn't hurt her, but it was no use. Kate couldn't hear.

So frustrating. She couldn't be seen and she couldn't be heard. Then, leaning over the bed, she knew. The merest indentation of nostrils. In out. In out. Kate smelled her. Contact.

She looked at Kate lying so rigidly under the thin sheet. She was small. Much smaller than she. And her hair was short like a nun's. But Roxanne knew she was the one.

Slowly the room filled with light and she watched as Kate's eyes moved. Then her head. Roxanne watched while Kate slipped out of bed and into her underwear, slacks and t-shirt. She opened up her closet door, looked inside, then closed it again. She stepped out of her room and into the hall. Roxanne followed. Kate walked along the hall stopping to throw open another door. Then she closed it again and continued on to the bathroom. In the bathroom she flung back the shower curtain. She splashed her face with water then rubbed it dry with a towel. Then she turned and walked out of the room and down some narrow stairs, into a strange sunlit room unlike any Roxanne had ever seen before. Kate opened the door and walked outside. Roxanne followed.

She followed Kate down a stone path. There were strange colourfully armoured carriages rolling along on their own without horses to pull them. Kate glanced at one as it went by, then crossed the hard path and went down to the river, along a narrow footpath, then onto a bridge. Roxanne followed slightly behind. On the other side of the bridge more of the strange carriages came rolling by. She knew she mustn't let herself be distracted by the strangeness of this other world or she might lose her again. She had to focus on Kate.

Up ahead was a big wooden structure. Roxanne had never seen it from the outside but she knew what it was. It was the building where she'd first seen her. She had looked down and there was a young woman at one side of a wooden platform. The platform had a balcony at the back of it and there were a number of people moving about. A stage. It was a stage. The stage was in a circular hall with strange, soft seats rising up all around it. Though it was different from any she had ever seen before, Roxanne knew this was a theatre. That's why she felt so at home here. The other figures seemed ghostly, almost invisible, but she could see the young woman as clear as could be. The moment Roxanne had seen her, she'd known this was the one.

Now she followed Kate along a narrow passageway and down some stairs through another passageway and up onto the stage. She could see other figures standing about, still ghostly and faint. Then the ghostly spirits started to speak. Even though she couldn't see many of them she recognized the words. Those words. She couldn't get enough of them. They were intoxicating to her. The more she listened the more alive she felt. Stronger. More powerful. She knew that when the moment came nothing would be able to stop her. She would enter unimpeded. It was only a matter of time.

But Mr de Bergerac can never take it off.
He wears it — or it him — and god help the man who laughs.
Cyrano's sword is that man's Fate!

He won't come.

Won't? I say he will, and I'll bet you a fine pullet à la Ragueneau.

Agreed.

Agreed. That was her cue. Her moment had arrived. Embodiment at last.

Roxanne stepped onto the stage.

I WAS TEACHING A SUMMER SESSION and my last class was Thursday before lunch, so I was able to take off for Stratford that afternoon. I had tickets for the first three performances. I arrived late and booked into the same motel I'd stayed in the day I'd driven Kate.

I slept well that night; in fact, I slept in. After breakfast I went for a long walk along the Avon, stopping in briefly at the art gallery. Then I did what I always do, I headed for the bookstore. After the better part of the afternoon at Fanfare Books, I returned to my motel, showered and shaved and then went out for a light dinner. As the performance time drew closer and closer I found myself getting edgier. If I felt that way, I could just imagine how Kate must be feeling.

I arrived at the Festival Theatre at seven-thirty. I noticed that there were lots of women with skirts above the knee. I had of course seen this in Montreal quite a bit, but you know something has moved from trend to style when you start seeing it at big cultural events.

And this was a big cultural event. In the next few minutes the limousines started to arrive. The lieutenant-governor, the governor-general, the premier of Ontario. There were lots of lesser celebrities too, including TV and radio and literary personalities. The crowd was becoming more and more voluble. The expression "excitement in the air" was made for an event like this. This was Stratford's season opener, but it was more than that. I don't suppose a Stratford production had been anticipated with as much excitement since Tyrone Guthrie's *Richard III* ten years earlier.

As always the trumpets caught me off guard. I was looking down the road, with the rest of the crowd, at another approaching limousine when the fanfare sounded behind us and from above. Five men with trumpets stood on the open terrace over the main doors. I knew they would blare again — Twice have the trumpets sounded — before we had to take our seats, but I joined one of the lines moving into the theatre. The lady took my ticket, directed me straight across the hall and I found myself standing at the top of the central aisle of the theatre. Here a teenaged boy met me and took me to my seat. I knew I had a good seat but I didn't realize just how good it was until I sat down. I was right over the central vomitory leading to the stage so there was no one in front of me and yet I had enough distance that I could easily take in the whole stage. I could feel my excitement growing. I looked down at the stage and it seemed different to me. I don't think I'd ever seen it completely bare. There wasn't a prop on it. There wasn't anything to indicate setting or atmosphere. And then I noticed something else. Usually the house lights are up at the beginning of a play and the stage lights down, but this time the whole auditorium was uniformly lit. It was a strange feeling, less like a church and more like a gathering place. I could sense it in the crowd. Usually at a Stratford show everyone talks in subdued tones, but this crowd was laughing and talking and the general noise level was high. I think people felt that the play was far from beginning. We were used to being cued ourselves — dimming lights, swelling music, stage lights rising — but there was none of that. It was a party atmosphere. You could look all around the theatre and see everyone with perfect clarity.

I opened the programme, eager to see what part Kate would be playing. Another surprise. On the lefthand page there were two columns: one titled The Characters, the other The Company. The Characters list had over fifty names on it and the Company list only half that. I noticed Kate's name immediately as it was the second, well above Ray Galdikas and Verna Harden. The names had been arranged alphabetically. The other page read *Cyrano de Bergerac* by Edmond Rostand. No mention of Daniel Lloyd. I glanced back to the Company list and noticed his name halfway down. I was pondering this and what it might mean when something odd happened. Some people had mistakenly wandered onto the stage. The stage not being elevated, this was easy to do. I heard one asking when the play would begin. Any moment an usher was sure to handle the problem so I went back to perusing my programme. Then I looked up again. The people onstage had caught the audience's attention and more and more of us were looking at them and wondering, as I was, when they would discover their mistake. It was only then that I realized they *were* the play. They weren't wondering when *Cyrano* would begin but when the play within *Cyrano* would begin. The play at the Hotel de Bourgogne.

I could hardly believe my ears. I started listening intently and so did others around me. I knew where I was. I was sitting in the Stratford Festival Theatre as I had sat many times before, listening to a play. But somehow the words sounded so real. Not like they were being performed but being spoken for the first time. As if the people on stage were not spouting memorized lines but were speaking their own thoughts. The actors weren't in costume, there were no special lighting effects, no props, nothing to suggest locale or to create atmosphere, and yet all of us were listening with total attention. Would Cyrano arrive? If so, what would he do? Surely he wouldn't disrupt a performance, no matter how much he hated Montfleury.

And then it happened. Roxanne entered. She was played by Kate. My friend Kate. She came up through the vomitory with her duenna beside her. She walked slowly and with perfect ease across the open stage, then up the stairs to the balcony.

Kate. Kate in a loose t-shirt, slacks and slip-on shoes. As I write these words I know how ridiculous they must seem. One would expect an audience to roar with laughter. Instead you could have heard a pin drop in that theatre. There was Kate with her cropped hair, in her everyday clothes, and she looked so beautiful. I couldn't take my eyes off her. No one could. And it wasn't anything she was doing, she hadn't done anything. She hadn't yet spoken a line. It was just that she was so beautiful. For the next twenty minutes she sat on the balcony, saying nothing, observing events below.

What we saw and what we *saw* were two different things. With the Outer eye we saw a young girl with shorn hair, t-shirt and slacks. With our Inner eye we saw the radiant, luminous Roxanne. Beauty incarnate. And the more you looked at her the more beautiful she became. And because Roxanne was so beautiful the play made perfect emotional sense. Of course Cyrano loved this woman beyond any-thing in the world. Of course Christian would die for her.

When Roxanne left the stage you could feel the audience momentarily relax. It was almost as if it was a relief not to experience the intensity of her beauty. And yet no sooner had she gone than we started anticipating her next appearance. Was she really as radiant as we remembered her? Yes. At every appearance — Ragueneau's pastry shop, her waiting room, her balcony, the front and, finally, in the con-vent of the Sisters of the Cross — at every appearance she was indeed as beautiful as we'd remembered. As the play moved relentlessly to its sad ending I, and everyone in that auditorium, hung on every word.

Then it was over.

We sat in hushed silence. Finally, we started to applaud. The applause quickly grew in intensity and with a roar of approval the audience was on its feet. Before us, standing on the stage, was a mere handful of people. A handful of people who had created this immense world of poets and cutpurses and musketeers. And in the centre, Galdikas holding one hand, the actor who'd played the handsome Christian the other, was Kate. My friend Kate.

Around me the tumult continued. People were clapping and shouting and each time the actors tried to leave the stage the noise would grow and grow. The audience remained in the auditorium, clapping. I think it was only from exhaustion that people finally stopped clapping and with reluctance made their way through the lobby and onto the grounds. Again and again I kept hearing the same words: So beautiful! So beautiful!

At the stage door there was a security guard and I worried that I'd have to convince him I actually knew the girl who'd played Roxanne. It proved to be no problem. He asked my name, checked a list he was holding and waved me through. I made my way down a narrow hall-way packed with people. I entered the rehearsal hall. Already the party was in full swing. Of course, none of the actors had to get out of costume. There was Galdikas, as huge in life as he had been on stage. And Verna Harden bouncing up and down and hugging someone. And the magnificent young man who'd played Christian. I scanned the crowd as best I could but I couldn't see Kate. There was a sharp report like a gun going off and I swung around. Someone had opened a bottle of champagne. This was followed by another pop! and then another. More and more champagne. But the crowd was already intoxicated. They were intoxicated by the sheer intensity of their shared experience. Everyone was talking at top volume. It was deafening. I looked around for Kate but I couldn't see her. I knew she wasn't crazy about crowds and so I was eager to find her and see how she was doing. I started struggling through the bodies. People would move apart and come together again without a break in their excited conversation. The only thing I can liken it to are those photos that one sees of Times Square at the end of the Second World War — sailors grabbing girls and bending them backwards, peoples' faces alive with joy and ecstasy, a whole crowd delirious with happiness.

Then suddenly the room went quiet. Suddenly is the wrong word; it went quiet slowly but my awareness of it was sudden. I turned to look where the others were looking and there she was. Kate. Standing alone and looking very small. Then Galdikas, in a magnificent gesture, raised his two hands above his head and brought them together in a slow rhythmic clap. Then the entire cast followed suit. The rest of us, aware that actors, normally self-involved and competitive, were paying tribute to one of their own, stood and watched and listened.

That was such a powerful moment for me that I can only report the rest of the evening the way I recall it, in snatches. Kate and I finding each other. Galdikas toasting Lloyd. Lloyd toasting the Company. Person after person coming up to Kate, telling her how wonderful she'd been. Kate becoming more and more quiet. Me going off to get us some food and a glass of champagne. Returning to find Kate engulfed by admirers. Kate saying she was tired. So tired. Me watching Verna Harden and River Tantoo doing the tango. Others joining in. Me turning to Kate. Not finding her. Not wanting to alarm anyone, searching for her myself. Apprehension swelling into panic. Finding her, finally, asleep on a couch in the green room. Picking her up like a child in my arms. Carrying her to the stage door. The security guard calling a cab. Arriving at Mrs Morrison's. Ringing the doorbell with my elbow, still carrying Kate.

Mrs Morrison answered. I told her Kate was exhausted and together we put her to bed. Then we went downstairs and Mrs Morrison put on a pot of tea. She couldn't stop talking about the show. She'd been expecting to see Kate in the tiniest of parts as would be customary for a newcomer and instead she had been the centre of it all. Mrs Morrison had seen hundreds of performances at Stratford but never one like this. She didn't want me to leave; she wanted to go over and over every detail of the show. Finally, around four in the morning, I excused myself and walked back to my motel. I fell onto my bed, exhausted.

I slept till noon. I arrived back at Mrs Morrison's at two o'clock. Kate was still sleeping. I had a cup of tea and a piece of pie with Mrs Morrison — my breakfast — and then I started wondering about Kate. Mrs Morrison hadn't heard a peep out of her yet. I went upstairs. She was lying on the bed just as we'd left her, sound asleep. I went back downstairs and talked with Mrs Morrison for another hour, then went back up and checked again. Still asleep. It was now well past four o'clock. She'd slept fourteen hours. I decided not to disturb her. I went back downstairs and Mrs Morrison made me a sandwich and a bowl of soup. At six o'clock I checked again. This time I decided to gently shake Kate's shoulders. Her eyes opened. She looked at me and smiled.

"You okay?" I said.

"Fine," she said. "I'm fine. What time is it?"

"Six o'clock," I said.

"Oh, good," she said, and then she rolled over onto her side.

"In the evening," I said. "Six o'clock in the evening."

She rolled back and looked at me in disbelief.

"You've got to be at the theatre in an hour," I said.

Instead of springing out of bed, showering, changing and tearing off to the theatre, Kate moved like lead. Everything seemed to be a tremendous effort for her. Twice she flopped down onto the bed and I believe if I hadn't kept talking to her with a growing sense of urgency she would have just fallen asleep again. Mrs Morrison made a pot of black coffee and we got two cups into her. Then together we walked her to the theatre. We got her to the stage door just moments before the first fanfare sounded. I headed up the hill and lined up to get in.

Waiting for the performance to begin this time was agony. As soon as I sat down I felt sick. Looking at the empty stage I realized that I'd somehow got caught up in the mystique of "the show must go on." My friend Kate was in no condition to act, no condition to perform, but instead of thinking about her all I'd thought about was getting her there, getting her on stage. I'd gone on automatic pilot, pouring in the coffee, ushering her out the door, escorting her to the theatre. Now I was racked with guilt: what if she was ill? What if there was something wrong? Anyone could see that Kate was in no condition to perform. I couldn't possibly imagine her as Roxanne.

And then she did it again.

She floated across the stage. I could hardly believe that the same girl who had stumbled through the stage door only minutes before was now performing with such ease and power. She positively glowed. But when I met her minutes after the performance she collapsed against my shoulder and by the time I got her back to Mrs Morrison's she was almost asleep. She slept all that night and well into the next afternoon. By this time both Mrs Morrison and I were worried.

I phoned the theatre and was put through to a Tessa Blume. She listened carefully to what I had to say, then said someone would get right back to me. Five minutes later Daniel Lloyd himself called. He listened to what I had to say. Then he told me the company doctor would see her immediately.

Half an hour later the doctor arrived. While Mrs Morrison made tea he went up to check Kate. About ten minutes later he joined us in the kitchen. He said that she was an extremely healthy young woman but clearly exhausted. Sleep-deprived. Rehearsals had taken a lot out of her and she was catching up. He said in his opinion she could perform but that she should rest as much as possible between shows. Then he said that other members of the cast were experiencing just the opposite. They were so stimulated by the whole process that he'd actually prescribed mild sedatives for a few of them, something he was normally reluctant to do. He said that in a few days he felt some sort of equilibrium would be regained and that, on the whole, he much preferred Kate's reaction to some of the others'. He ended up by misquoting *Macbeth*: Sleep knits up the unravelled sleeve of care.

By the time he left Mrs Morrison and I felt much better. We had the same trouble getting Kate to the theatre that night but this time I didn't feel sick about it, and once again she was astonishing.

At dawn the next morning I left for Montreal.

ULRIKA STRETCHED AND REACHED a hand out to Breetz's side — he wasn't there. She rolled over onto her back and stretched again from head to toe before sitting up. That had been one of Anna's rules, apparently. Never get up in the morning without completely stretching first. Not even if the telephone was ringing and someone was knocking on the door.

"Not even if the building's on fire?" she asked Breetz, teasing.

"Especially not if the building's on fire — you want to be properly limber before leaping out the window."

Ulrika stood admiring herself in the full-length mirror for a moment before wrapping the silk robe around her, a gift from Breetz. It was his favourite colour for her — taupe — the colour of nakedness. She leaned forward to look at herself more closely. Her skin was good, her eyes clear after her one-day juice fast. Anna again. She straightened. Ulrika carried herself like a model, though at six feet she was now a good inch taller than most of the girls Breetz worked with. And once she added the high heels he insisted she wear, she towered over everyone.

Ulrika stepped into the living room of their small apartment. She lay on the carpet and raised her arms angel fashion above her head. She pointed her toes. Stretch, hold, relax. Stretch, hold, relax. The stretching was easy enough but Breetz had told her to visualize waves receding on a beach as she did each repetition. She was easily distracted and would have to bring her mind back to the beach and the water. After the stretches came the exercises. These took her forty-five minutes and they were a series of movements for her legs that also worked her hips and buttocks. They were to be done slowly, carefully, with no jerking motions. For each exercise Breetz had devised a different visualization. Waves receding on a beach, wind blowing through a willow, water streaming around a boulder. She wasn't to listen to music because that would make her move to the music and not to the rhythms created by the visualization exercises. It was hard.

An hour after rising Ulrika was ready to get a little air. But first she would eat. Her juice fast ended, she went back to her regular breakfast — two pieces of toast and one egg. Poached. Caffeine was bad for the skin so she poured herself a glass of grapefruit juice. After breakfast she walked to the Y. This was still her favourite part of the routine. She was a good swimmer, strong arms pulling through the water, long legs fluttering minimally behind her. She quickly fell into a rhythm, turning her head only slightly to draw in air, then turning back and expelling it slowly, the bubbles streaming around her cheeks and ears up to the surface. At the end of the pool she would curl under, pushing herself off against the pool's edge in one fluid motion. She did fifty lengths.

She showered and towelled herself completely dry, then reached into her bag and pulled out a jar. This was her After Swim Cream. Breetz told her it was temporary, just to get her back from the pool to the apartment. In the apartment bathroom Breetz had built small four-inch open shelves that covered an entire wall. On these shelves in Venetian glass jars were her creams. Each one made from a special formula handed down to Breetz from Anna.

She ran a bath, making sure the water wasn't too hot. She washed her hair with a tiny dab of baby shampoo. After stepping from the bath she slathered on the rose-petal cream from the soles of her feet to her shoulders. Her neck was treated to a toning cream and on her face she smoothed the precious thyme oil cream that Breetz said was so difficult to make. She wasn't to tug at her hair or dry it with a dryer, so she combed it with a wide-toothed comb and let it dry naturally, spraying it now and then with Breetz's own lemon conditioner.

She poured herself a glass of mineral water and stretched out on the couch. On the coffee table was the book on anatomy that Breetz had given her. She flipped through it but soon grew bored. She picked up *Vogue*. Towards the back there was an eight-page spread shot in the Adirondacks by Breetz. The models were tumbling in leaves, dressed in wool sweaters and stretch pants. There was one photo of two of the girls in an old wooden rowboat, one trailing her fingers in the water while the other rowed, her head thrown back, laughing. They looked like they were having such fun. Later, Ulrika learned how Breetz got that effect. It was easy. They were. At a party Ulrika had met one of the models on that shoot and she'd gone on and on about how she'd never enjoyed an assignment so much. It had been like a holiday in the country, she said, horsing around in the leaves, rowing on the lake, ambling down mountain paths arm in arm. She knew she could relax and have fun because she knew, whatever she did, she'd come out looking beautiful in the photos. You always did in a Breetz shoot.

And the photos were beautiful. The rich colour of the autumn leaves and the browns, reds, yellows and greens of the wool sweaters harmonized in a way that made the models seem part of nature, as if they themselves were growing out of the forest. Every assignment Breetz did worked well and her husband's reputation was growing all the time. Ulrika longed for the day when Breetz would allow his photos of her to be published but he always refused.

"Not yet, Uli," he'd say. "Not yet. We're not ready yet."

Ulrika dozed. When she awoke she heard sounds in the kitchen. Breetz. He was home early and already making dinner. Avocadoes stuffed with crab, a salad, crusty rolls and a bottle of wine. He drank most of the wine himself but Ulrika had a glass mixed with mineral water. After dinner he opened another bottle of wine. Then they entered The Room.

It was an odd little room, so small the former tenants had used it as a walk-in closet. But Breetz had designated it a workroom and here they would sit by the hour poring over photos of famous beauties — Veronica Lake, Ingrid Bergman, Jean Harlow, Greta Garbo and, of course, Marilyn. Ulrika was always amazed at how long Breetz could spend studying a single photo. He'd examine a photo of Ingrid Bergman, then he'd turn it upside down, sideways. He would analyse how the photographer had used light, how he'd achieved certain effects. He would show Ulrika that Ingrid was dilating her pupils because, he said, they couldn't be that big with the amount of light used to take the photo. Breetz was fascinated by light and how it could make a woman look beautiful or not beautiful. He said all the great beauties understood light and were able to use it to make themselves glow. He said all of them knew exactly how a certain light fell across their faces and how that would look to the camera. He told one of his many Marilyn Monroe stories. Once, on a movie set, Marilyn had kept fussing about a light being out. Finally, just to get her off his back, a technician looked into it, only to find she was right. The light was burnt out. Of all those rows of all those blinding lights, Marilyn had known one was missing. And had known which one and its exact location.

"She knew, Uli," Breetz would say. "Not because she could see it, even the director and technicians couldn't see it, but because she could sense it. Sense that light missing from her face."

Breetz was fascinated with Marilyn. But even more than Marilyn, Breetz was fascinated with Norma Jean. He had collected every available photo there was of Marilyn Monroe and pinned them to the walls of that tiny room, but he was especially happy to find a new Norma Jean photo. He'd point to it and say, "See Uli? See how she's not Marilyn yet?" And he was right — it was more than just the dyed blonde hair. His favourite was the one of Norma Jean the young model, posing as a cowgirl in Daisy Mae shorts and gingham blouse tied at the midriff. She was all apple fresh cheeks and a big toothy grin.

"See? She hasn't lowered her lip yet, Uli. See?"

A photographer had told Marilyn that the short distance between her nose and her upper lip created a shadow there when she smiled. And it was true that in all her later, her *real* Marilyn pictures, the upper lip was lowered even when she was flashing her biggest smile.

"Secrets," Breetz said, sipping at his wine. "Tricks. It's all tricks, Uli. We've just got to discover them one by one. But not her tricks, your tricks. The tricks that work for you."

And then they would turn to what Ulrika loved best. The photos of her. Beginning on their wedding night Breetz had started taking photos of Ulrika. He would develop them, show them to no one, and together they would study them in The Room. He photographed her tangled in the sheets on their wedding bed. He photographed her bicycling in Central Park. He photographed her swinging on an old rope out over a river. He photographed her tossing her hair. He photographed her playing with children in the park. He photographed her eating an apple. He photographed her at the Museum of Modern Art looking at a sculpture. He photographed her in a beautiful gown outside the opera.

In July they'd flown to Maine and rented a little cottage on a deserted cove. They rose early and photographed Ulrika again and again as she walked out of the ocean onto the beach. Around her, there were huge rocks, craggy, and the sea burst in spray all about her. She could feel it all over her body, misting her in droplets, her nipples stiff and erect, the way she knew they looked best. Breetz got her to do it again and again and it was fun in a strange sort of way. They would stand together on the beach and count. Ten, the wave hits the rock, nine-eight, burst into the sky, seven-six, forming into mist, five-four, starts to settle, three-two, that would be your moment, one. *Click*. Then she would try it. She'd watch for his hand to drop and then she'd start to walk. It took them fifteen attempts but then they started to get it. Just as she stepped in front of the rock, still up to her thighs in the foamy sea, the mist would settle around her creating the most wonderful effects of light, strange refractions in the air. And her body all cold and goosebumpy. Sexy in a strange way, the goosebumps catching the droplets of water, the droplets of water reflecting the sun, her body a thousand scintillations of light and Breetz saying, "Beautiful, beautiful, Ulrika. We're going to love these photos. Beautiful, beautiful, beautiful."

And she did love them. She'd never imagined she could be so beautiful.

"Close, Uli. We're getting close."

She looked back to the photo he held. It was perfect. Her golden flesh sparkled against the ancient sea-worn rocks. She couldn't imagine a more beautiful photograph.

"Close?"

"Yes. This is the closest we've come yet."

He poured himself another glass of wine.

IN THOSE FIRST TWO WEEKS OF *CYRANO* no one saw the show more than Mrs Morrison. She had a trick. She was an early riser and she lived right across the river from the theatre. So first thing in the morning before breakfast she would walk over and stand outside the box office. There she would be at eight o'clock when the box office opened and she would buy a rush seat. There were only a few rush seats available but in that first week Mrs Morrison always got one. Then one morning she arrived at seven-thirty to find a dozen people ahead of her. She got a ticket that day but two days later she didn't. She arrived at seven and there were still people waiting, so the next day she arrived at six-thirty and even at that hour there was a crowd. Young people were camping out the whole night. By the end of the second week it was virtually impossible to get a ticket to *Cyrano*.

Mrs Morrison couldn't believe that the same slender young girl who slept by the hour in her upstairs room was the magnificent Roxanne. She'd seen many Stratford productions over the years and quite a few actors had lived in her house. She was used to seeing the same actress play different roles, sometimes extremely different roles. But underneath the makeup and the different costumes it was the same person. This was different. There was no makeup to disguise this girl and yet on stage she seemed transformed. For one thing she seemed bigger. Mrs Morrison couldn't quite figure out how she seemed bigger but she did. And she kept imagining she had long luxuriant black hair, which she didn't. Kate had hardly any hair at all and the hair she did have was fair. It was really remarkable. Each time she saw *Cyrano* she would try to see Kate in Roxanne and each night it became more and more impossible.

Meanwhile Kate slept and slept. The theatre provided a taxi for her at the end of each show and Kate would stumble out of the taxi and up to bed. Then she would sleep all night and all the next morning. Mrs Morrison began to worry about the fact that she wasn't eating. She started making up a tray with a number of tempting items on it. Kate would wake up, smile, and nibble at a few things. Mrs Morrison would try to make conversation with her but, though she was polite and friendly, Kate was very quiet. Mrs Morrison would sit there, sipping her own tea, watching her and trying to imagine her as Roxanne. She couldn't. She just couldn't.

One day Mrs Morrison was down in the kitchen taking some croissants out of the oven. It was two o'clock and she wouldn't start preparing Kate's tray for another couple of hours. When she opened the oven door she smelled something strange. Certainly not the croissants — a very familiar smell — but something strange and beautiful. A perfume. Then she heard a voice behind her.

"Hello."

Mrs Morrison turned. There was Kate looking rested and

refreshed. For the first time in almost two and a half weeks, there was some colour in her cheeks and she looked like she had some energy.

"Well, my dear, don't you look better today. Finally catching up on your sleep?"

"Yes, yes. I feel wonderful." Then she eyed the croissants. "Those look delicious," she said. "May I have one?"

EVERYBODY WAS SAYING that Daniel Lloyd was a genius, but Sofi Lamereau still thought he was insane. She'd thought he was insane during the few rehearsals she'd sat through. She'd thought he was insane at the so-called dress rehearsal. A dress rehearsal without dress. Actors just in their street clothes. She'd thought he was insane on opening night and even as the crowd stood on their feet and roared their approval she still thought he was insane. Sofi hadn't stood. They were all fools, taken in by the great man's reputation. Duped colonials. But the critics would see through this, so she couldn't wait to read them.

And then, one after another, they'd called the production a masterpiece. Walter Kerr of the *New York Times* said even in his wildest dreams he'd never believed a classic could be brought to life so vividly. Herbert Whittaker of the *Globe and Mail* said it was the result of fifty years' thinking about classical theatre come to fruition. Even Nathan Cohen, who hated everything, called it one of the three greatest productions he'd ever seen. All across the continent, critics hailed Daniel Lloyd as a genius.

The critics were insane. Daniel Lloyd was insane. The audience was insane. Anybody who liked this production was insane.

Three weeks after *Cyrano* had opened, Sofi got a message from Daniel Lloyd. He wished to see her. She ignored it. In the next week another summons came. She ignored that too.

She wouldn't see him. He could fire her; she didn't care — he was insane. She wouldn't have anything to do with him. If he wasn't going to use costumes, why have a costume department? See how long the critics raved when he did production after production without costumes. Once — maybe — it would work, but it would soon pale — *Lear* in street clothes, *Hamlet* in street clothes, *Cymbeline* in street clothes — ridiculous. He'd see.

No he wouldn't. He was insane. But they'd see. Everybody else would see. The Board would see. They'd turn on him. They'd fire him.

Sofi spent the better part of her days concocting scenarios of the downfall of the great Daniel Lloyd. She was just in the middle of a favourite — reading a review of a future production in which Lloyd was referred to as a puffed-up has-been — when the phone rang. She answered it.

"Sofi? Get down here."

"Why?"

"Daniel Lloyd was just here ..."

A few scathing words about the great man deigning to drop by Costume came to Sofi's lips, but the voice on the other end interrupted.

"... your sketches!"

"What? What about them?"

"For the film, dummy! He just put them on the table and told us to get to work!"

"ANYTHING FROM THE BAR, GENTLEMEN?"

Daniel Lloyd and Ray Galdikas were seated at a small table. They both ordered scotch, Galdikas on the rocks, Lloyd with a splash of soda. When their drinks came, Galdikas raised his glass to Lloyd.

"Tell me, Daniel," he said. "At what point did you know it was going to be so good?"

Daniel raised his glass, clinked it against Galdikas' and said, "I always knew. I always knew *Cyrano* was out there and all we had to do was find it."

"Marvellous," Galdikas said. Then he looked at Lloyd and laughed. "We found it, all right," he said. "We got it holus-bolus, bang smack, dead fuckin' on, didn't we, Daniel?"

"Dead fucking on," Lloyd said. Again they clinked glasses. "Though at times it got a little scary."

Galdikas took a swig of his scotch.

"I want to thank you, Daniel. I want to thank you for that. Because it was time I was scared. I hadn't felt any adrenalin in theatre for years. It was all too goddamn easy."

"I know that," Lloyd said. "As we get older it's so tempting to just rely on what we know, isn't it? Not to take any risks."

Galdikas looked at Lloyd. Then he said, very quietly, "Daniel, I'm going to ask you something and I want you to answer me honestly."

"I'll try."

"Do you smell her?"

"Yes," said Daniel. "I even smelled her before she appeared. I smelled her a week before, actually."

"Do you see her?"

"Vividly. She's big. She's got black hair…and she's so fucking beautiful it takes your breath away."

"Absolutely," said Galdikas.

The two men sat in silence for some time before Galdikas spoke again.

"Do *they* see her?" he asked.

"I don't know," said Daniel. "I don't know what they see, I just know they see something. And I know they're seeing it more and more clearly with every performance. That's what's so boggling. It's like the play is being transmitted through us — "

"Especially through her."

" — yes, and with each performance the picture gets stronger and stronger. Tell me, Ray. What's it like being up there?"

Ray leaned back and drained his scotch and signalled the waiter.

"It's the weirdest fuckin' thing I've ever experienced," he said. "She's so beautiful. She's radiant. I mean, she's literally radiant. She glows. At first it was faint. So faint I could hardly see it. And then, just before opening, it got stronger and you know what I did? It was so simple. It was as simple as Spencer Tracy's 'Learn your lines and don't bump into the furniture.' I saw that light and I just stepped into it."

"It's always so simple when you get it, isn't it?"

"Yes."

"And it's never what you expected."

"'Unexpectedness. And each unexpectedness generates another unexpectedness.'"

"That's brilliant...who said that?"

"A genius."

"Some say a madman."

"Madman. Genius. Whatever."

Over dinner they talked about the film. Daniel Lloyd had spent the last three days scouting sites with his locations man. Things hadn't begun well on the first day. They'd visited Old Fort Henry in Kingston, which the locations man thought would be perfect for the scenes at the front but Lloyd hadn't liked it. Too manicured. Too British. There seemed to be no shortage of forts in Ontario and Lloyd finally settled on Sainte-Marie Among the Hurons, which had the rugged seventeenth-century look he was after. The kitchen of Dundurn Castle in Hamilton would serve admirably for Ragueneau's bakery. But best, and most surprising of all for Lloyd, was Casa Loma in Toronto. Built in the early nineteen hundreds by a financial magnate hoping to entertain the Prince of Wales, its huge baronial hall would be perfect for the opening scenes.

Galdikas listened to all this, then the waiter came and removed their plates.

"So you're going to do it straight then."

"Yes."

"Sets, costumes, locations."

"Sets, costumes, locations."

"And casting. Are you going to cast it?"

"Of course I'm going to cast it."

"A fat this, a scruffy that?"

"A fat this, a scruffy that...and Ray Galdikas as Cyrano."

"I see."

Galdikas proposed a toast.

"To *Cyrano*, the film."

They clinked glasses.

"Too bad, though."

Lloyd knew exactly what he meant. He took a long sip of wine. It *was* too bad. But there it was. Stage magic wasn't film magic. In *Cyrano* the play they had done something extraordinary. So extraordinary it would be remembered by everyone who saw that play for as long as they lived. But if they simply set out to record what they had done, they would get nothing. A mere X-ray of a living body. He'd seen it before. A magnificent stage production that just looked like wood on film. Worse than wood, plastic store-bought dummies. At first he had wrestled with the problem and then he had come to a decision. He would honour his commitment; he would do *Cyrano* the movie and he would do it professionally, to the best of his ability. He would give them a *Cyrano* that worked on film. A *Cyrano* with elaborate sets, authentic locations, ravishing costumes. A *Cyrano* in which each character was played by someone who looked the part. It would be a good film, maybe even a great film, but it wouldn't be magic. He'd done his magic and that was that.

By this time they'd each had a fair amount of scotch and were well into their second bottle of wine. They had abandoned sentences entirely.

"Larry Colton. Too bad." Galdikas shook his head.

"Brilliant. One of the most."

"Yeess."

The waiter was there to refill the glasses.

"Wouldn't film."

"No," Galdikas agreed. "Wouldn't film. Long shot of Larry doing Arrogance. Close-up of me declaiming Cyrano's line. Shot of Larry zipping around the set. Close-up of me — disdainful. Shot of Larry all haughty and magnificent. Me thoughtful. Him Rodin's Thinker. Wouldn't work."

"Mishmash."

"Marvellous on stage, though."

"Bloody marvellous."

"So Larry shall be replaced."

Lloyd nodded.

"By what," he said, slowly raising his hand and placing the tip of his right index finger to the tip of his nose, "a piece of putty?"

"A rather large piece of putty."

Galdikas nodded. The two men sat in silence, drinking. Galdikas thought about how strange it would be doing the film. Sitting in his trailer hour after hour, the makeup man fussing over his nose. Coming out, saying a few lines, someone botching something — the cameraman, sound man, continuity girl — having to do it all again. And again. The lights hot. His wig itchy. His goddamn nose slipping off his face. Having to stop, go back to the trailer, get touched up, back out again to do the same shot only from a different angle this time. Adjust the mikes. Bring in the boom. Say it again, Ray. That's right. I think we have a take. Okay, Ray, see you in an hour. Back to the trailer. Drink a protein shake through a straw. Try to lie down. Get up. Makeup again. Hour after hour, day after day, shooting those glorious speeches bit by tiny bit. Never the whole meal, just mouthfuls.

"And her?" he asked.

"Won't do."

"Won't do? Why not?"

"No tits."

"Oh." Galdikas poured himself another glass of wine while he thought about this. Then he looked back at Lloyd. "Not with one of those bodices?" he said. "Squish 'em up?"

"Nothing to squish."

"Too bad. Shame."

Silence.

"In all seriousness, Ray, she's the most marvellous thing I've ever seen on stage — "

"Radiant — "

"Luminous. But ... have you ever actually looked at her? In actual fact she's quite unimpressive. She's small. She has no hair. She's waiflike. She's as wrong for Roxanne as a girl could possibly be. On stage, her very wrongness works for her. She's able to somehow conjure up an image more powerful than her physical presence. I don't know how she does it but she does. The mystery of great talent. But the camera, Ray. The camera reveals all. The camera is an instrument of — "

"Don't you say truth."

"Fact. It shows us what's there. If we photograph this girl we're not going to get Roxanne, we're going to get a pale little androgynous modern-looking dolly. No tits. And you know as well as I, Ray, the more we dress her up to look like Roxanne the more ridiculous she'll appear. And we're sure as hell not going to do *Cyrano* on film with her in t-shirt and slacks. That would be insanity."

"Or genius."

"Anyway, Ray, thought you wanted to make a million dollars. Thought you wanted to be a movie star."

"You, you son of a bitch. You got my juices flowing again. Now all I want to do is act. All I want to do is get up on that stage and hold them in the palm of my hand."

Although both Ray Galdikas and Daniel Lloyd could hold a good deal of liquor, by this time certain words were getting pretty rough treatment — ridiculous became ridiclius, palm became plom. "Why is film always so...wretched."

"All the gadgetry, I suppose. All that technology. All those technicians fussing about, every shot having to be planned, orchestrated so that the machines don't get upset, the mikes don't go into a flap and the cameras don't flip out."

"Fuckin' King of Donuts."

"Say what you will about the fucking King of Donuts, he stood by me. Staked everything he had, you know, when everyone else was jumping ship. A man appreciates that."

Galdikas pulled a couple of cigars out of his breast pocket and handed one to Lloyd. The two men lit up as the waiter placed two brandies in front of them.

"Oh, I don't want to go back to doughnuts. I don't want to go back to this much flour and that much sugar, throw it into the fat and sell it to the masses. I want to do Lear again with her as Cordelia. And Cymbeline and Prospero — "

"We'll do all that, Ray. We'll do it all. But first this. First *Cyrano* the movie."

"Yes...okay. *Cyrano* the movie."

The two men drank to it.

ULRIKA WAS SURE THAT THE SHOOT in that cove in Maine would be the start of her public career, but Breetz kept saying, "Not yet, Uli. We haven't got it yet."

It. What was he after? Whatever it was, he started taking fewer and fewer photographs of Ulrika and spending more and more time alone in The Room. He would take in a bottle of wine and a glass and he would sit, by the hour, studying photos of Marilyn. Sometimes Ulrika still joined him.

"How did he do it, Ulrika?" he asked one night.

He was looking at a head shot of Marilyn taken in 1955 by Roy Schatt. Marilyn wasn't wearing any makeup and she had a frumpy black hat pushed down on her hair. Ulrika didn't think she looked good at all. She thought she looked sloppy.

"How did he do that?" Breetz kept saying.

"Do what?"

"How did he get that velvety quality? She's luminous and yet the photo is soft. If you light a model enough to get that kind of exposure on her face, the photo shouldn't be so soft and velvety, it should be harsh. Somehow he got her both soft and luminous at the same time. And it's not just Roy. So many of her photos are like that. So many of them."

Ulrika stopped going into The Room after that. If they weren't going to look at photographs of her, what was the point? When Breetz figured out what he wanted to do, then he would start photographing her again. She knew he would. But she must leave him alone to try to sort it out himself. It was something technical. His problem, not hers.

Breetz seemed to have come to the same conclusion himself. His mood picked up. He started taking Ulrika to more parties. He started introducing her to other photographers and art directors. He seemed not quite so obsessed about whatever "it" was. Ulrika loved meeting all the exciting new people. And each time she went to a party, Breetz made sure she had a new dress to wear. He would come home with a box from Bloomingdales or Macys and say, "Tonight, Ulrika is going to stun them in black."

She was wearing the black strapless columnar gown at a party when a man with a goatee approached her. He had an English accent.

"God, you're beautiful," he said. "Why aren't you in the movies?"

Ulrika, taught by Breetz to take this kind of admiration in stride, looked back at the man and said, "I've often wondered that myself."

He talked to her for much of the evening. He was funny and sweet. He told her amusing stories about growing up in London and of the time he spent in a German prison camp during the war. He was fascinating and amusing at the same time.

Only later did she learn that the Philip she'd been talking to was Philip Shaw, the film director.

ROXANNE HAD KNOWN THE INSTANT SHE SAW HIM that this was the man of her dreams. He was tall. And so handsome. Silver hair and those pale blue eyes. He was handsome and mature. Christian was handsome but callow. Not his fault; he was young. But this man was like Cyrano. He had the soul of a poet. She knew that even before she heard him speak. She could tell it just by looking into his eyes. And he understood her. Oh, how he understood her. He understood her better than any man who had ever lived. Better than she understood herself. At night, on stage, she would see him sitting at the back of the theatre, his eyes, his pale blue eyes, watching her. But when the others stood and roared, he always slipped away, vanished. Gone. Gone until the next night.

Offstage was hard for Roxanne. Outdoors frightened her. Things were always taking her by surprise. She was just getting used to the strange carriages when one day a huge bird flew overhead with the roar of a thousand cannons. She was terrified. She was terrified but she knew she had to get used to this other world. She began forcing herself to go down to the river to feed the swans. One day she saw — standing on the little wooden bridge looking into the water — her Love. Roxanne felt dizzy. She wanted to approach him but she didn't dare. He stood, staring at the water, his silver hair blowing gently in the breeze, then he turned away from her and began walking towards the theatre. She followed.

Inside, she lost him. All those halls and corners and all those people dashing about. She lost him, but she now knew where to find him. She would stay by the bridge and wait. She loved him. And she knew he loved her. And nothing could keep them apart. Nothing. He would return to the bridge, he must; it was only a matter of time. Fate had conjoined them.

Daniel Lloyd stood on the bridge and watched as the water beneath him flowed around a small rock, swirled into an eddy, and then, catching its breath so to speak, doubled back to enter the main flow. He'd been standing there for twenty minutes. In those twenty minutes he could have made five decisions, two major ones, three minor. He picked up a twig that had fallen onto the bridge, snapped it in two and tossed a piece into the river. Missed. He tossed the other piece. This time the twig came down just beyond the rock, swirled around, got caught for a moment, then wriggled itself loose and flowed on past. Of course, the toughest decisions had been the casting decisions. He'd finally decided against River Tantoo. That hurt. Tantoo who moved more beautifully than anyone he'd ever seen on stage would be rendered lifeless and immobile by the technical exigencies of film. He'd end up looking ridiculous. River had taken it well. He'd told Lloyd that *Cyrano* had changed his life. Lloyd had told him they'd certainly work together again. They'd shaken hands and Tantoo had turned quickly and left the office, but not before Lloyd had noticed the moistness in his eyes. There was just one more difficult task to do: inform his leading lady. He was thinking of her when he heard her voice.

"Hello."

Startled, Daniel Lloyd turned.

When those pale blue eyes fell upon her, Roxanne sensed within her breast a welling of emotion she knew was betrayed by the flush of her cheek and the trembling of her hand. How many days had she waited? How many days had she come down to this bridge hoping to see him again? And then, to meet him quite by accident while making her way to the theatre, that it should seem so uncontrived, was too wonderful to bear.

She moved a little closer. She wanted to hear him speak. To speak a thousand endearments. To express the love he felt for her with the eloquence and passion she knew only he possessed. She clasped her hands together to stop their trembling. So close. So close she could feel his breath upon her forehead and the heat of his body upon her breast. In a moment, he would declare his love, take her in his arms and they would kiss as the water swirled beneath them.

Then the trumpets sounded. The trumpets! The trumpets!

Oh, she wanted to stay, to stay and hear him speak. But the trumpets, the trumpets that summoned her each night were summoning her now. She must go. She must go and no one understood that more than he. She turned, pulled towards the theatre. She let her arm linger behind for a moment in a vain attempt to minimize the distance that must grow between them.

And then she was gone.

Daniel Lloyd stood transfixed as she hurried along the path and crossed the road. Extraordinary. What he had experienced was simply extraordinary. He hadn't seen Kate, he'd seen Roxanne. Roxanne off stage. How did she do it? Extraordinary.

Daniel Lloyd returned to his office and steadied himself with a glass of scotch.

What he had seen, he mustn't see. There was a job to be done.

THE CAMERA ASSISTANT took a piece of thick chalk and made some marks on the platform. Today was the costume parade — just filming them to see how they looked. No boom, stationary camera, pretty straightforward stuff. She waited for the nod from Daniel Lloyd. He gave it. She stepped onto the chalk mark and held up the slate.

Daniel Lloyd sat watching each character hit his mark, turn slowly, face the camera again and then leave. He was a little irked with himself that he couldn't concentrate on what was going on, though he knew this was irrational. There was no need to concentrate, his presence here today was expected but not necessary. The problem was he couldn't stop thinking about Kate Barnes. He couldn't stop thinking about how he hadn't yet told her she wouldn't be playing Roxanne. She must know by now, everyone else knew, and yet he still hadn't made it official. It was ridiculous, unprofessional, not like him. Tonight he would call her into the office and tell her. The parade continued, with the assistant director cheerfully prompting the actors.

"Christian!"

"Lignière!"

She'd be relieved. They always were. Actors knew. They knew what they were right for and what they weren't. She'd be relieved. Even grateful. She was an actress, not a film star. He'd use her for Cordelia next year and then the year after, Saint Joan. The Maid of Orleans. She'd be perfect.

"Ragueneau!"

"First marquis!"

"Second marquis!"

Tonight. After this nonsense. He'd set up the appointment. Then it would be done.

"De Guiche!"

Then he could fully devote himself to this.

"Valvert!"

She'd be relieved. He'd take her out for dinner. Maybe Ray could come along.

"Cardinal!"

Over coffee they'd tell her about *Lear*.

"Le Bret!"

She was an actress, not a film star.

"Meddler!"

"Soubrette!"

"First pastry cook!"

"Second pastry cook!"

"Third pastry cook!"

"Apprentice!"

"I *am* Roxanne."

Daniel Lloyd blinked. There she was. The entire studio went silent as she slowly took in all that was going on around her. Her eyes lingered on the rows of lights for a while, then she brought her level gaze back to Daniel Lloyd, her head held high.

"I know what you're doing," she said. She articulated the words slowly, deliberately, but her soft voice bespoke an immense rage. "You're making a moving play. And you're trying to do it without me. Well, you can't. I *am* Roxanne."

And then she left.

The only sound that could be heard in that cavernous studio was the soft whirr of the camera.

No one knew where to look. The cameraman shifted his weight from one foot to the other. The camera assistant studied the thick cables snaking along the floor. The actors adjusted their costumes.

Slowly, Daniel Lloyd unfolded his elegant frame until he was standing tall in front of his chair. He waited a moment until all eyes were upon him. Then he spoke.

"Everyone...my apologies. This is entirely my fault. I haven't handled the situation with Miss Barnes at all well...my fault entirely." He took a deep breath, exhaled, then spoke. "Proceed." There was a brief lull, then the parade started up again.

"Musketeer!"

The rest of the day passed without incident. At five o'clock they started wrapping up. As the assistant slipped the cartridge of film from the camera, she was thinking about the angry girl. She heard a voice behind her.

"I'm going into Toronto tonight," said Daniel Lloyd. "Why don't I just drop those by the lab?"

"Sure. Saves us a trip. Thanks."

By midnight, Daniel Lloyd was holding in his hand the developed film. He knew the drive back to Stratford would be long and difficult, but he was wide awake. Wide, wide awake.

It was three a.m. by the time he arrived back in Stratford. There was no one on the streets. He closed the studio door behind him and made his way to the screening room. He turned on the lights. He took a moment to catch his breath and then walked into the projection booth that the carpenters had only just finished building a couple of days earlier. He scanned the projector quickly and saw that it was all set to go. He opened the steel canister and lifted out the developed film. Sitting on the swivel chair, he fitted the spool onto the projector and clicked it into place. Then he threaded the film through the various sprockets and gates onto the bottom spool. He hit the start button, then flicked off the light.

The parade began. He could see the camera assistant holding the slate out. The writing was slightly blurred. While the first actor appeared, stood on his mark, turned around and walked off, Daniel Lloyd adjusted the focus. The next time she held up the slate he could read it perfectly — Cavalier, Banquet Hall. Satisfied, he turned the light off and took a seat. The film seemed much slower than the actual events, but Daniel Lloyd decided he wouldn't fast-forward, he would just sit and wait. Dozens of characters appeared and disappeared off the screen.

Finally, they got to the pastry cooks. First pastry cook, second pastry cook, third pastry cook, apprentice. What the — ! something had fucked up! The fucking film had gone black at the very fucking moment she was about to appear! Black! *Black*...then white.

Then suddenly she was there.

She looked straight at the camera and spoke. There was no sound, but he could almost hear the words. *I am Roxanne*. On the word *am* her left eyebrow arched. The moment was soon gone yet the memory of it would last forever. Now she was looking down. Daniel Lloyd remembered this. She took in the cables, then the costumes, then the camera and finally all the paraphernalia overhead. At the time, as he remembered it, she had seemed to be expressing one thing only — rage. But as he watched it now, on film, her face registered a different emotion each time she shifted her gaze. What he had seen in reality had been somehow slowed down and magnified so that emotions invisible to the naked eye were projected onto the screen with an exquisite intensity. And she was luminous. She was radiant. He'd never noticed the planes in her face. This face was made to be photographed. She was speaking again. He could hear the words in his head. There was no sound, but she made those words come alive. "I know what you're doing. You're making a moving play. And you're trying to do it without me. Well, you can't. I *am* Roxanne..."

That face. That face that registered the subtlest emotion. The subtlest emotion was registered and yet it seemed amplified and enlarged. And then she was gone and suddenly the screen seemed to shrink into itself. He flicked on the light, stopped the projector, rewound the film halfway back, then started it again. He flicked off the light and sat down. First pastry cook. Second pastry cook. Third pastry cook. Apprentice. They were so bland, like dough on the screen. Puddings. Then the film went black. He was ready for it this time, but still it amazed him. Impossible. After all the splutter and flecks, there she was again. Luminous.

He rewound and watched the same segment a dozen times. Each time he couldn't wait until she came on screen and couldn't bear it when she left. He knew that his reaction would not be unique. He knew everyone who saw her on screen would feel this way. They would want more. And more. And more. She was radiant. She was the most beautiful thing he had ever seen on film. And, of course, he knew what he had to do.

Not *Cyrano*, but a company of actors *rehearsing Cyrano*. Yes, and he'd film it in black and white. She would be watching. There, on the side, watching. That face. He would film that face in close-up. That radiant, luminous face. And it would fill the screen. It would fill the screen with its own light. It would fill the screen and create a hunger only she could satisfy.

He must find her. He must find her this very night and tell her. But where? The moment he asked the question, he knew the answer.

The bridge. He would find her on the bridge.

Roxanne was standing on the bridge when she saw her Love. He had come. He had come in the night as she knew he would. As she knew he must. He had come. He had come. Her Love had come.

ERNIE WAS THINKING OF HIS LITTLE GUY. He always thought of the little guy when he ate at The Truck Stop, because they had those Moo Cow creamers. The first time the little guy had seen him pick up the Moo Cow by the tail and pour the cream out of its mouth, he'd gone bananas. So at the end of the meal Ernie had talked the waitress into selling him one. Now, every time he came back from a haul, the little guy was after him for a Moo Cow. Seemed he wanted a whole herd. What the hell, they were only a buck. He'd buy one off Mitzi.

He looked up. She was talking to a young girl. He heard her say, Stay here, I'll go talk to Ernie. When she got to him she said, "Ernie, young girl there's gotta get to Montreal. Think you could give her a lift?"

"How old is she?"

"I don't know."

"She a runaway?"

"No, no, she's legit."

"Okay, okay. Bring me a bill and, uh, put a Moo Cow on it, will ya?"

"Sure," said Mitzi, grinning. As she walked back to the girl she called over her shoulder. "One to go, Ernie?"

"Sure. And one for the little lady."

Mitzi poured the two coffees and put them in a paper tray.

"These two are on me," she said.

A few minutes later Ernie was holding open the door to his rig. Kate climbed in. The truck was idling, so Ernie just put on the lights, shifted into first and slowly the big eighteen-wheeler rolled off the lot onto the highway.

Kate held the coffee in both hands and took a sip. It was scalding hot. It felt good. Feeling anything felt good. What was the last thing she could remember, remember before tonight, that is. Richard. Richard leaning over her at Mrs Morrison's looking so concerned, asking her if she was okay.

"You okay?"

"Yeah, yeah, I'm fine. I just have to see my friend. He lives in Montreal. He drove me here."

"You from Montreal?"

"I grew up in Toronto, but I've lived in Montreal for the past few years."

"Great city," Ernie said. "Always spend a night there before I do my turnaround. Great food. Them Frenchies know how to cook, I'll say that for 'em."

Kate sipped at the coffee. She only knew one thing, she had to get out of there, and get out of there that night. She had to get far, far away.

"You drink that coffee, then try an' catch some sleep. We got a long haul ahead of us."

Kate looked over at Ernie.

"I don't want to sleep," she said. "In fact, if I start falling asleep... could you wake me up?"

Ernie shrugged. "Okay," he said. "But I don't figger we'll be there much before noon."

"I know. I just don't want to go to sleep."

Ernie shifted into fourth. Kate could feel the whole truck vibrate as it picked up speed.

"You like Country?" Ernie asked.

"Country music? Sure," said Kate.

Ernie turned on the radio.

Kate leaned her forehead against the window. In the long side-mirror, she could see the Welcome to Stratford sign retreating into the distance.

I WAS JUST SITTING DOWN with the *New York Times* and a second cup of coffee when there was a knock.

"Kate," I said. "What are you doing here?"

There were three more performances of *Cyrano*. I knew this because I'd been desperately trying to get tickets. And here Kate was standing on my doorstep in her t-shirt and slacks.

"Richard," she said. "You've got to take me away."

All that registered with me was that my friend Kate — who should have been in Stratford — was instead here, standing in front of me.

"Richard," she said again, "you've got to take me away."

"Sure, sure," I said.

She wanted to leave that instant. She just wanted to get into the

Buick and start driving. Kate was one of the least temperamental people I knew, but I realized the strain of the last few months had been tremendous. She needed some time, obviously. Some time alone or some time with me. Some time to settle down. So rather than argue with her I decided I would just do what she said until we'd achieved some equilibrium. She wouldn't come in, so I asked her to wait while I got my wallet and keys. When I returned she was already sitting in the passenger side of the Buick.

"Have you eaten? Do you want to go for lunch?"

"No, no," she kept saying. "I just want to go away."

"Okay," I said. "Where do you want to go?"

"Anywhere," she said. "I just want to go away."

Very well, I thought, I'll just drive around until she's able to talk about whatever it is that's upsetting her. Then we'll have lunch and I'll volunteer to drive her back to Stratford. I even thought selfishly that perhaps she'd be able to get me a ticket. The least she could do. I knew the next performance of *Cyrano* wasn't until Wednesday, two days from now. So there was plenty of time to indulge her.

There didn't seem much point in driving around the city so I immediately headed north. I've often found that one can talk best in a car anyway, and especially on the open road, but forty minutes later Kate still wasn't talking. With each passing mile the autumn colours of the trees became more spectacular. I could feel the car steadily climbing. All around us the rolling, rounded ancient hills grew larger. Kate sat beside me looking out the window, still saying nothing.

In St-Jérôme, I pulled over and got us both a coffee. Kate wasn't hungry, but I had a sandwich. Still no talk. Around St-Jovite the road narrowed from four lanes to two. On my right-hand side I could see Mont Tremblant in the distance. I had an idea. I suggested we turn off, walk around the lake, and then I'd take her to lunch at Grey Rocks Inn. Lac Tremblant, the autumn leaves, the mountain — I didn't see how anyone could resist.

But she did.

I pressed her on this, reiterating how scenic Tremblant was and how we could have a long relaxing time there before heading back to Montreal.

She insisted we go on.

With some trepidation I left the Laurentians. Once out of vacation country the road became more deserted and we drove for miles without seeing so much as a service station. She wanted to go on. At this point I tried to become a little more forceful. I was quite prepared to drive her all day if she liked, but I didn't see much point in heading further north where the roads were bad and the scenery far less pleasant than that we'd come through. I was for turning around, driving through the back roads of the Laurentians — maybe a side trip to Ottawa — but she insisted that we keep heading north. There was something about the way she insisted that made me feel I wasn't ready to confront her, or do battle with her, so I just kept heading north.

I knew once we hit Mont Laurier, there wouldn't be much between us and Noranda, mining country, so I stopped for gas. When we were on the road again I turned to Kate.

"How are you feeling?"

"Better," she said. "Better."

"Do you want to talk?"

"Not yet. Later."

I assumed later meant another hour or two. Maybe at dinner. We'd eat, talk, sort things out, then turn around and be back in Montreal just after dark. Next morning we could head off for Stratford and she'd be able to do the last three performances.

We drove through Mont Laurier and then mile after mile the scenery remained the same — rock, pine, lakes. We drove in silence through an Indian reserve and a couple of small towns when in the distance I saw two red-striped smokestacks. Noranda. I couldn't help but think of my father. My father had done some consulting work for Noranda Mines.

I was ravenous so we stopped for dinner. I ordered a hot turkey sandwich with gravy, mashed potatoes and peas, and for dessert cherry pie with ice cream. Kate ordered a bowl of soup and some toast. She left half her soup and barely nibbled at the toast. Throughout the whole meal she was restless. As I sipped my coffee I tried to bring the conversation around to the problem at hand. No luck. Clearly, Kate wasn't ready to talk. By this time I had a plan. Instead of trying to convince Kate that it was time to turn around and go back to Montreal, I would just press on. In a short while we would cross into Ontario and soon reach Kirkland Lake. There, the Trans-Canada divided and it would be easy to head south to North Bay, from North Bay to Barrie and from Barrie to Stratford. At this point a big loop made more sense than doubling back anyway and in her distracted state I was sure Kate wouldn't notice. Surely by the time we'd spent a whole day driving, Kate would feel settled enough to return.

"Richard," she said. "Can we go now?"

I finished my coffee and paid the bill.

The next hour's drive seemed unbearably long because I was so acutely aware of my plan. I was even beginning to feel a little self-righteous. She'd turned up at my door, she'd rejected my suggestion to stop at Tremblant and she'd rebuffed every attempt I'd made to talk about whatever was troubling her. I'd already driven all day and I had no intention of just continuing to drive aimlessly across the Shield. I felt thoroughly justified in taking some decisive action.

But we weren't half a mile outside Kirkland Lake when Kate noticed we were heading south.

"Where are we going?"

"To Stratford," I said.

"Oh no we're not."

Not being an artist, I took art very seriously. It was inconceivable to me that Kate should miss a performance. I told her so. She told me she was missing more than *a* performance, she was never going back. I was angry. I said I'd heard of temperamental actresses, but this was ridiculous, unprofessional, irresponsible. I went on at some length, actually, when she turned to me and stopped me cold. It wasn't what she said that chilled me to the bone; it was the terrified look in her eyes.

"Richard," she said. "Last night I woke up in Daniel Lloyd's bed."

In Kapuskasing I bought Kate a pair of overalls, a heavy plaid shirt, a windbreaker and a pair of workboots. In Long Lac we stopped for gas and then on we drove. Anyone who has ever driven north of Superior knows what a formidable drive it is. The highway snaking over tundra and rock, around lake and over muskeg, trees looming up on either side. All that separated us from the darkness was the narrow beam of our headlights.

In Nipigon, we stopped again to eat. I was more than ready to call it a night, but Kate wanted to press on. Against my better judgement we did. The highway went on and on and on and the strain of the day began to tell on me. As we approached Thunder Bay I knew I'd had it. My eyes were starting to swim and the lights of the oncoming cars and trucks were blurring. It was also starting to rain and I knew that the rain could turn to snow, or worse, sleet, very easily. Kate was for pushing on but I told her Thunder Bay was my limit. To drive any more would be dangerous. We'd covered a thousand miles! She relented and we checked into a small motel.

All I remember is flopping onto the bed, fully clothed, and allowing myself to be sucked down into a dreamless sleep. Moments later, or so it seemed, Kate was shaking me awake. I showered and changed into my day-old clothes and we ate breakfast at the motel. It never occurred to me that Kate might have stayed awake all night.

When we were shown to a booth in the little restaurant adjoining the hotel, it was surprisingly busy even at that early hour. The waitress started to clear away dishes and a newspaper left by the previous customer. I let her take the dishes, but I nabbed the paper. As Kate was still not talking, I asked her if she minded if I read and she said of course not. A few minutes later the waitress brought my scrambled eggs, bacon, homefries, toast and coffee. Kate had a muffin and tea. Before we hit the road again I filled up the gas tank and bought a map of the prairie provinces.

We drove in silence for an hour, but it was a different kind of silence from the day before. I could feel that as we got further and further from home, Kate was starting to unwind. At one point she spotted a moose and its calf in a distant swamp and we had to stop the car and get out to look. That was sort of a breakthrough. She began to relax and I could sense the old comfortable feeling we'd always had together renewing itself.

We passed into the Lake of the Woods area and then the landscape started to change again as we approached a huge sign informing us we were leaving Ontario. As we entered Manitoba, Kate leaned back in her seat and propped her feet up on the dashboard, her way of telling me she was feeling much better. The Shield was becoming more hummocky and marshy. Lots of streams, little lakes and bogs. We sped along making good time.

"Look," Kate suddenly said, "the nines are changing to zeros."

I looked. Two hundred thousand miles. The Buick was no longer new.

In Winnipeg we drove along Portage Street. In the centre of town I found a parking spot and we climbed out. I was glad to stretch my legs. We walked a bit and found a restaurant that looked decent, but not too fancy for our rumpled condition. Happily, Kate ate. She ordered a club sandwich with her tea. So did I. While we ate we talked. It was so great to have her talking freely with me that I wasn't about to jeopardize it by probing. We chatted about this and that, mostly about the territory we'd passed through. Kate had never been west of Ontario.

Across the street there was a huge Eaton's store. My mother had given me an Eaton's credit card for Christmas with instructions to use it whenever I pleased but I hadn't yet. I picked out some pants, underwear, socks, a shirt, sweater and a jacket — it was getting cold. I also insisted Kate select some shirts and a sweater and any personal items she needed. I've never liked shopping much, but we had a good time. It was like we were outfitting ourselves for an adventure. Kate found some heavy socks, a down vest, a toque and some underwear. We also grabbed toothpaste and shampoo, two combs and a razor and shaving soap for me.

At the corner of Portage and Main there was a newspaper vendor. I bought a *Globe and Mail* and tossed it into the back seat, relieved to have something to read. We opened the trunk and threw in our shopping bags. Immediately on the other side of Winnipeg we were into the prairies. People often talk about the prairie provinces being monotonous and dull, but that day we drove across Manitoba and into Saskatchewan was one of the most thrilling I'd ever experienced. The air was crisp and cold, the sky blue. And the clouds! Are there clouds like that in Ontario and Quebec? I'd never noticed. Something about the flatness of the landscape drew the eye upwards to a sky heaped with billowing white clouds racing in the wind. Beneath them, an ocean of wheat stretched as far as the eye could see and the same wind that moved the clouds undulated the wheat in amber waves. At one point, we saw a gigantic jackrabbit bounding through a field, an extraordinary sight. It would sail up over the wheat, disappear, then sail up again. The only thing I can liken it to is a dolphin in the sea, bounding from one element to another.

The rest of the day passed uneventfully. By mid-afternoon I noticed Kate fighting sleep. She would nod off, then jerk herself awake. I was for stopping in Regina but she wanted to push on to the next town, simply, I think, because of the name.

In Moose Jaw we took a room at a motel that reeked of stale smoke. There was a kettle, some little packets of Mother Parker's coffee and coffee whitener and two beds covered in chenille bedspreads that had seen better days. Kate took off her boots and windbreaker, then just flopped onto one of the beds, put her hands behind her head and looked up at the ceiling. I started to make us coffee, but by the time the kettle was boiling she was sound asleep. The room was hot, almost stifling, but I took an extra blanket from the closet and threw it over her. Then I sat down to the newspaper with my oily coffee.

I'm the sort of person who can spend an entire Sunday with the *New York Times* and I read the front section of the *Globe* thoroughly. In August, an American PT boat had been attacked by the North Vietnamese in the Gulf of Tonkin. Congress had now given President Johnson power to retaliate. There was talk of bombing the north. The little war was not so little any more. I glanced at the Business section and flipped through the Sports section, but when I came to Arts I read it thoroughly. At the end of Herbert Whittaker's review of the play at the Royal Alex there was a small blurb. Daniel Lloyd had taken ill and was recuperating quietly at home. He was expected to be back on the job in a few days.

Just before dropping off to sleep that night I looked over at Kate. She had rolled onto her side and was curled up like a baby.

I woke to the sound of the shower running. I quickly got up and dressed and a minute or two later Kate emerged wearing her new clothes. She had washed her hair. She looked good.

"Ready to hit the road?" I said.

"You bet."

It's amazing what good time you can make crossing the prairies. By ten o'clock we were out of Saskatchewan. As we continued to barrel along, I couldn't help thinking about something that had been troubling me off and on since we had started heading west at Kirkland Lake. Just where were we going? And what was the rush? Of course the answer was obvious. We weren't *going* anywhere in particular, we were getting *away* from somewhere in particular. Stratford. And whatever had happened there. But now that Kate was sleeping, eating and becoming her old self there was no need to push on at such a ridiculous pace. I broached the subject and she agreed. I made a suggestion. Why not head to Banff where we could spend a couple of days hiking and resting?

"At some point," I said, "we've got to talk."

She agreed.

"In Banff?" I asked.

"In Banff."

We stopped for lunch in Calgary. By two o'clock we were back on the Trans-Canada again, heading west. The land was low and rolling with lots of brush. The Foothills.

"How long till we get to the mountains?" said Kate.

Almost as soon as she'd said it, they appeared on the horizon, their craggy peaks blazing white in the afternoon sun.

"Oh," she said. Then, again, a moment later, "Oh."

I felt the same way.

The Trans-Canada followed the Bow river as it headed into Banff National Park, and as we approached those jagged remains of the earth's most recent upheaval the sun was slowly setting behind them. As the sun sank lower in the sky, its rays struck the silver ice of the peaks turning them to crimson. It's hard to describe how beautiful it was. I'd spent a summer in Banff when I was sixteen, but this was the first time I'd been back since then. I'd had a good summer, but I hadn't realized how deeply those mountains had lodged themselves in my memory. And there was something about driving into them with Kate, who had never seen them before, that affected me profoundly.

We drove on, the mountains getting bigger and bigger in front of us. And then, suddenly, they were no longer without; we were within. On either side, huge mountains planed upwards. Once inside them night fell, though we could still see the blazing remnants of day scattered on the peaks around us. By the time we'd reached the town of Banff it was dark. We stayed that night at the youth hostel on Tunnel Mountain, Kate in the women's wing, I in the men's.

Next morning we hiked up Mt Norquay. It was while doing this that I broached the subject of Stratford. It soon became apparent that Kate had genuine memory lapses. We started to play a game. I would mention something I remembered and see if she remembered it too.

"Opening night. Do you remember the party?"

"Vaguely."

She didn't really remember the party, she didn't remember falling asleep in the green room and she didn't remember me taking her back to Mrs Morrison's.

"Next day, do you remember me waking you up?"

"Yes."

Yes, she remembered that. She remembered me and Mrs Morrison leading her to the theatre, but she didn't remember anything after the trumpets blared.

"You were amazing, Kate," I said.

I started to tell her about how from the moment she stepped on stage no one could take their eyes off her. But as I talked I could sense her becoming more and more uneasy until finally she changed the subject.

About two thirds of the way up Norquay we met two men with chain-saws coming down the ski trails, clearing them of new growth. They told us they'd seen some mountain goats grazing over on the west ridge. They were the only people we met. We climbed and climbed. We would climb one swell of the mountain only to find it grew into another and then another. It seemed the higher we climbed the more there was left to climb. When we finally made it to the top, or at least as close to the top as we could reasonably manage, we sat and ate our lunch, looking out over the mountains. Sitting there, with the entire Bow Valley below us, Kate finally started to do what I had been trying to get her to do for the whole journey. Talk.

Once she started to talk she couldn't stop. She told me about the first day of rehearsals for *Cyrano*, the feast. She told me how Daniel Lloyd had got them playing with the ball. Then the sticks. Then how the entire cast had ended up knowing the entire play. Then about some of the amazing things that had started to happen with the other actors   Verna Harden, Larry Colton, River Tantoo. The only thing she couldn't talk about was what had happened to her. Around the time they moved into the Festival Theatre, things got vague. Then she blanked out.

Suddenly she sat straight up.

"Look," she said.

Below us, not two hundred yards away, was a herd of mountain goats. There had to be more than twenty of them and we sat as still as we could while they grazed closer and closer to us. They were magnificent with their shaggy coats and their thick spiral horns. We watched them for another half-hour or so until they lifted their heads and then pranced away from us single file along a narrow path. Clouds were starting to sweep down the valley and it was getting to be late afternoon, so I suggested that we head back down to the hostel.

Next morning I woke late and when I got to the kitchen Kate and some of the others were already making pancakes. It was cold out and there was quite a wind blowing, so we all sat around drinking coffee and chatting until the hostel had to be vacated. When Kate and I loaded our stuff into the car we realized it was no day for hiking, so I suggested we drive up to Lake Louise.

Lake Louise with the glacier rising behind was such a familiar image, but the photos are always taken on bright sunny days with the sun glinting on the glacial green lake. The day we were there was grey and the wind whipping across the lake was cold, so we only walked around for a few minutes, then climbed back into the car.

Beyond Lake Louise was all new to me too. Here we started to cross the Continental Divide. The road threaded in and around the railway line and at Kicking Horse Pass we stopped at a lookout. Beneath us we saw a train entering a tunnel. The tunnel formed a huge U within the mountain and after a couple of minutes we saw the engine emerging from the mountain in one direction while its caboose was still entering from the opposite. We got back into the car and started to descend the switchbacks down into the valley, bringing us to the same level as the tracks. Then, still switchbacking, we began to ascend again.

I was starting to enter into the spirit of our adventure. I asked Kate if she wanted to stop in Golden and double back to Banff or whether she wanted to push on. She was for pushing on. I checked the map. On the other side of Golden there was another green block — Glacier National Park — and a little circle labelled Rogers Pass. Every Canadian child learns about Rogers Pass. In the eighteen eighties the linking of the railway from coast to coast was blocked by the impassability of the Selkirk Range. Rogers breached the Selkirks through the pass which now carries his name. No attempt was made to put a highway through until the late Fifties and it had been completed in nineteen sixty-two, just two years before Kate and I were to travel it. It was just a ninety-mile stretch from Golden to Revelstoke, but I found the prospect of driving it quite exciting.

We weren't twenty minutes out of Golden before it started snowing. Of course there had been ominous dark clouds all day but it was so early in the fall I hadn't really considered the possibility of snow. But down it came in big fluffy flakes. I turned on the windshield wipers. Immediately I realized that the sensible thing to do would be to turn around and head back. As soon as I mentioned this to Kate, the sky cleared and the snow stopped. We pressed on.

I wasn't aware of it at the time but I now realize that Kate wanted to get the Rocky Mountains between her and the East, as if she felt she would be safe on the other side. She wanted to get through the mountains, but it was to be in the mountains that she would get caught.

It started snowing again. The wind had stopped and the thick fluffy flakes seemed to just float effortlessly down. I felt a little uneasy. This was the toughest stretch of highway in the Rockies and I didn't have snow tires. I was worried about going off the road. Up ahead I could see an avalanche shed. I turned on my lights.

Inside, the highway slowly curved as it skirted the edge of the mountain. As I rounded the curve, I could see the white square of light at the end of the tunnel. The moment the car passed out of the tunnel, the windshield was covered with snow. For an instant my visibility was zero. I turned on the wipers and the blades pushed the snow off the windshield, but by the time they had reached the end of their swipe, the windshield was already white again.

"Kate," I said. "Could you keep an eye on your side of the road? Tell me if I get too close to the guard-rail."

No answer. Kate was slumped over, her head at an awkward angle, sound asleep.

Sound asleep. I couldn't believe it. Kate, who for the first forty-eight hours of this trip hadn't slept at all, was now sound asleep. I reached out a hand and shook her, but as I did the car swerved. I quickly grabbed the wheel with both hands again and steered us out of the skid. My heart was pounding and I could feel the adrenalin rush down my neck into my spine.

"Kate," I said. "Kate! Wake up!"

But she didn't.

Or couldn't. What had happened? She'd been talking normally and then, in an instant, she was asleep. I'd read somewhere that seizures could be triggered by the intermittent flashing of lights. Could passing through the tunnel have triggered a seizure? Was she narcoleptic? It would explain so much — the sudden sleeping, the memory gaps. These thoughts, of course, flitted only briefly through my mind as all my concentration was required for driving. I considered stopping and turning around, but this was impossible. To do a U-turn in such weather was inviting disaster.

The snow kept coming down. Rogers Pass is famous for its snow accumulation and I could see why. In the next ten minutes the light blanket on the highway grew thicker and thicker. I could feel my tires occasionally lose their grip, a sickening sensation. Three times I tried to wake Kate, but she was clearly in a trance-like sleep. The driving was taking all my concentration and I desperately needed another pair of eyes. I had to maintain enough speed that I could make the grade but then the highway would turn and I'd be going too fast. Twice I went into a skid, and skidding at forty miles per hour on a highway with only a guard-rail between you and a sheer drop is terrifying.

When the wiper cleared the snow for an instant I'd get a glimpse of highway ahead of me. There were no sharp turns only slow curves, as a stretch of black arrows on an orange background indicated. Once I found myself heading towards the guard-rail. I considered just stopping and putting on my flashers and hoping it would clear, but I was afraid I'd get rammed from behind. The visibility was virtually nil.

The wipers were pushing the snow to either side of the windshield but so much was accumulating there that I was left with a smaller and smaller spot to see through. I leaned forward, as if that would help, trying to get a sense of where the highway was tending. The wipers would laboriously shove the snow off the small remaining clear section and in the moment before new flakes started to coat it, I would try to fix in my memory what I had glimpsed ahead — straight highway, gentle descent, guard-rail. The wiper pushed the snow again — straight highway, gentle descent, guardrail. And again — straight highway, gentle descent, guard-rail. Then something else.

I couldn't quite believe what my eyes were telling me. There, on the last completed and most desolate section of the Trans-Canada Highway, right in the middle of Rogers Pass, elevation one thousand one hundred feet, I saw a figure standing by the side of the road. Or, at least, I thought I saw a figure. The windshield cleared again. Yes. A figure flagging me down. I gently pumped the brakes, not wanting to put the car into a skid, and I must have been a hundred yards past the waving figure by the time I finally came to a stop. The figure was running towards me and I could tell by the way she ran that it was a woman. Oh my god, I thought, she's gone off the road. My mind flashed to children trapped in a car, a husband slumped forward on the wheel.

I opened the door and got out. Then I circled around behind the car. Yes, the woman was running towards me, not more than twenty-five yards up the road.

"Have you gone off the road?" I shouted.

"You've come! At last you've come."

"Your car," I said as she drew nearer. "Where is your car? Is anyone hurt?"

She was now only a few yards away. Her long dark hair was only lightly powdered with snow. She couldn't have been out in the storm long then.

"Are you hurt? Where's your car? Is anyone with you?"

"No, no, I am quite alone."

"Are you all right?"

"Yes, yes. Now that you have come."

I was tremendously relieved that she was alone — no bodies trapped in a car. I took off my jacket to wrap around her shoulders and held open the back door. She got in. I closed the door, then started clearing the back windshield, wiping off the heavy snow with my forearm. Then I went around and cleared the front windshield. This took a little more time as I clawed the accumulated snow out of the corners. As soon as I was behind the wheel again, Kate turned to me and smiled.

"You're awake," I said. "Thank god."

Then I turned to the woman in the back seat.

She wasn't there.

I looked again. She absolutely and unquestionably wasn't there. But that was impossible. I looked again. Lying across the white leather of the back seat was my jacket. Then I hadn't imagined it. Or had I? Was I hallucinating? I'd been under tremendous stress, my adrenalin pumping; had I somehow imagined the whole episode? I went over it in my mind — seeing the figure, stopping the car, getting out, helping her in — it had all felt so real. Is that what a hallucination was like? That real, that palpable?

Then I smelled it.

A perfume. A perfume so exquisitely fragrant and inviting that to this day I have never found anything remotely like it. But where was that exquisite scent coming from? I looked over at Kate and I knew. She didn't have to say a word. It was no longer Kate sitting beside me in the car.

It was Roxanne.

This was, and remains, one of the strangest experiences of my life and I have spent countless hours thinking about it. The easiest and most obvious explanation is that Kate was a split personality. A multiple. That she had two characters within her, one the Kate that I knew from Montreal and the other, Roxanne. But this does not explain what I experienced that day in Rogers Pass. I saw a figure standing by the highway. I stopped the car. I got out. The figure was a beautiful woman with black hair who in no way resembled Kate. I exchanged a few words with her, then I gave her my jacket.

To this day I can remember the feel of her body as I wrapped the jacket around her shoulders. I opened the door for her. I wiped the back windshield. I wiped the front windshield. I got back in the car. Kate was awake. I turned to look in the back seat but the dark-haired woman was gone. I smelled an exquisite perfume which I now know was also smelled by Daniel Lloyd, Ray Galdikas and a number of other people. Of course, again, the reasonable thing would be to assume I was under stress and had hallucinated this, but I know that's not true. I know I experienced these things. They happened.

When I returned to Montreal weeks later, the first thing I did was call my friends Wesley and Mildred. They didn't question me as to why I had left so abruptly, or where I had been, or why I hadn't written, but simply invited me over, fed me, and then listened quietly and attentively as I told my bizarre story. I told it over sherry in their book-lined study and, uncharacteristically, Wesley didn't interrupt or go off on one of his digressionary monologues. Instead, when I was finished, he stood, walked over to a bookcase and plucked an old hardcover book off the shelf.

The book, *Magic and Mystery in Tibet*, was written by an English woman, Alexandra David-Neel, who had gone to Tibet at the turn of the century and had spent fourteen years gathering what is still considered the most perceptive western account of mystic practice there. She writes of meditation techniques and the strange physical phenomena she witnessed among Tibetan lamas. Towards the end of her book, Alexandra David-Neel tells a story that Wesley read to me that night. And as he read it, I could feel the hair on the back of my neck begin to tingle. It was about the creation of a phantom figure. A thought form. Or, as the Tibetans term it, a *tulpa*. The *tulpa* had become so real that it had taken on an existence of its own, independent of its creator.

Wesley gave me the book and that evening I read it right through. In the years since I have re-read it many times. A book I keep going back to, perhaps because of the Tibetans' matter-of-fact approach to phenomena that we in the West either dismiss as impossible or revere as miraculous.

Alexandra David-Neel writes:

> Tibetan mystics also affirm that adepts well
> trained in concentration are capable of visualizing
> the forms imagined by them and can thus create any
> kind of phantom: men, deities, animals, inanimate
> objects, landscapes, and so forth.

> These phantoms do not always appear as
> impalpable mirages, they are tangible and endowed
> with all the faculties and qualities naturally pertain-
> ing to the beings or things of which they have the
> appearance.

> For instance, a phantom horse trots and neighs.
> The phantom rider who rides it can get off his beast,
> speak with a traveller on the road and behave in every
> way like a real person. A phantom house will shelter
> real travellers, and so on.

Fanciful as these stories of phantoms sound, what interested
Alexandra David-Neel was the Tibetan explanation of them. They
view these phantoms not as strange beings from another world but
as psychic phenomena created by known laws. I now believe that the
creation of Roxanne was a similar phenomenon. In the seventeenth
century Edmond Rostand wrote *Cyrano,* and in doing so created the
thought form Roxanne. Daniel Lloyd, in his rehearsals at Stratford,
concentrated the minds of many people on this thought form. Once
the thought form came into being, its existence was further strength-
ened by the many people who experienced it during the performance
of the play. Like the phantoms in Tibetan tales, the thought form
took on a life of its own independent of its original creators.

The passage that Wesley read to me the night of my return
gives the best explanation of what I experienced that afternoon in
Rogers Pass. What Alexandra David-Neel describes is a technique
for generating a phantom, or *tulpa,* by a powerful concentration
of thought.

...my habitual incredulity led me to make experiments
for myself, and my efforts were attended with some success. In order to avoid being influenced by the forms of
the lamaist deities, which I saw daily around me in
paintings and images, I chose for my experiment a most
insignificant character: a monk, short and fat, of an innocent and jolly type. I shut myself in *tsams* and proceeded
to perform the prescribed concentration of thought and
other rites. After a few months the phantom monk was
formed. His form grew gradually *fixed* and life-like looking. He became a kind of guest, living in my apartment.

Up to this point, there is nothing particularly strange in her story.
Many children, even in the West, have imaginary playmates and can
tell you at any time exactly where they are and what they happen to
be doing. But then Alexandra David-Neel went travelling, and the
monk followed her.

...now and then it was not necessary for me to think of
him to make him appear. The phantom performed various actions of the kind that are natural to travellers
and that I had not commanded...he walked, stopped,
looked around him.

Then to her dismay, the *tulpa* seemed to escape her control.

The features which I had imagined, when building my
phantom, gradually underwent a change. The fat,
chubby-cheeked fellow grew leaner, his face assumed a
vaguely mocking, sly, malignant look. He became more
troublesome and bold.

Other people began to see him too and questioned her about her
friend, the lama. She decided at this stage to dissolve the phantom.

I succeeded, but only after six months of hard struggle.
My mind creature was tenacious of life.

Roxanne was tenacious of life also. She had one consuming passion: to get back to Daniel Lloyd.

It was still snowing.

I started up the car and slowly eased into second gear. As I did, Roxanne spoke.

"All my life," she said. "I have been searching for a man both eloquent and handsome. Now at last I have found him."

I'm embarrassed to write this, but for a moment I thought she was speaking of me. She wasn't, of course. She went on to describe her Love's silver hair in the moonlight, his pale blue eyes, his hands, his forearms, the warmth of his skin. As she spoke I started to put things together. For days I had been working on a giant jigsaw puzzle made up of Kate's memory fragments. Now, here beside me in the car, was the missing piece. Suddenly things started to fit. It wasn't Kate who had performed on stage and later fallen in love with Daniel Lloyd — it was Roxanne.

"You will take me back?" she said. "You must."

She spoke with such longing. Of course, that's what Roxanne is: Pure Longing. She is always separated from her lover and enlisting the help of another man to find him. But this time it wasn't Cyrano's help she was enlisting, it was mine.

"There he waits ... by the bridge ... my Love."

Mercifully, I could see the sky up ahead growing lighter. We were through the toughest section of Rogers Pass and the weather was improving.

"Roxanne," I said, and though I was surprised at my use of her name it felt absolutely right, "how did you find her?"

"Her?" She looked genuinely puzzled.

"Kate."

Roxanne thought for a moment and then understood who I meant.

"The first time or this time?" she asked.

"The first time."

"Oh, that was easy," she said. "I saw her in the theatre. Everyone else was insubstantial, so I knew she was the one. I followed her home. I watched her sleeping, but I couldn't get in. Not till she went back to the theatre."

"And this time?"

"This time was more difficult. I saw her on the mountain, but I couldn't get close. Then I lost her again. Then I found myself standing in a snowstorm. I saw lights approaching and I knew it was her."

It's hard for me to recapture what I was thinking at the time. At one level I had no idea what was going on — was Kate insane? Was I insane? Were we both insane? But on another level I knew I was not alone. Others had experienced this phenomenon. No wonder Daniel Lloyd had taken ill. I was in a strange state where part of me accepted Roxanne's existence while another part of me stood outside the situation, trying to figure out how to deal with it. Up ahead, I saw a number of trucks pulled over in the parking lot of a small restaurant. They had known enough not to head into Rogers Pass in the middle of a snowstorm. I was exhausted and I thought a little break, a cup of coffee and something to eat, would settle my nerves. Instead, it was to unsettle me further.

Kate and I had stopped frequently at restaurants of this type on our trip, but always without incident. We would walk in, find a booth, wait until the waitress came, then order. But this time, the moment we entered that truckstop, I was aware of every eye upon us. Not us, her. She still had her short hair, was dressed in workboots, overalls, and a down vest, but from the reaction in that restaurant she might as well have been wearing a bikini. Any woman in that situation would either be acutely embarrassed or out there strutting her stuff, but Roxanne was neither. She was poised, calm and utterly at ease. Her level gaze swept quietly around the room, meeting every male eye. Not all at once, but one after another, making contact with each individual man.

Taking Roxanne by the arm, I led her over to a corner booth where I knew she would be blocked from the view of most of the restaurant. Almost immediately a waitress appeared with two menus. I positioned Roxanne so that all she could really see was me, but from my viewpoint I could see most of the booths and the entire counter with its ten red leather stools.

It was like watching starlings gathering on a clothesline. When we came in there were only two men seated at the counter: three stools between them. A trucker came along and took the seat at the end, then another took the seat nearest the cash register. Two more men entered the restaurant, looked around, then sat down on two of the three seats between the original men. The man on the right moved over one. Another man came in and sat on that man's left. My view of the counter was momentarily blocked while the waitress came with our food, but when she moved I noticed that the last three stools had been taken — the entire counter was full.

As I ate my sandwich and sipped my coffee, I looked at the girl opposite me. I had known Kate for a couple of years by that time, but I had never realized before that she had perfect features. Her nose, her eyes, her lips, her ears. No one feature stood out the way they often do with famous beauties — Bardot's pouty lips, Elizabeth Taylor's violet eyes — but every single feature was flawless, defined, even her nostrils had line.

And her most lovely feature was not a feature at all, but her skin. Why had I never noticed this? I'd spent countless hours sitting opposite Kate, and yet had never noticed her poreless skin or its translucent quality. It was as if Kate had worked against everything that made her the outstanding beauty she clearly was. I averted my eyes.

I finished my lunch and needed to go to the washroom but Roxanne was still eating heartily. She kept saying how marvellous the mushroom omelette was, how delicious the sausage. She liked the toast; the coffee was perfect. She finally finished and the waitress came over and asked us if that would be all. I was about to say yes, when Roxanne spoke up.

"May I have one of those," she said, "with lots of potatoes?"

The waitress followed her gaze to a faded picture of a hamburger, cola and fries, then flipped to a new bill.

"Burger with large fries," she said, then turned to me.

"Nothing for me, thanks," I said.

"Top up your coffee?"

"No," I said, standing. I couldn't put off going to the washroom forever.

I bolted the door and used the facilities. The light wasn't too good in there, but looking at myself in the small square mirror I realized I looked a wreck. I was ashen and my skin was blotchy. I splashed water on my face and then cranked the towel down two or three notches and patted myself dry.

When I came out of the washroom I was not in any way up to dealing with what I saw. Surrounding our booth were three men. Big men. Truckers. The kind of men I had no experience in dealing with. I didn't know what to do. I walked over, excused myself and tried to squeeze back into my seat, only to find two more men sitting opposite Roxanne.

"Well, here's hubby, eh?"

I was relieved at their mistake and just about to use my prerogative to get us out of there, when Roxanne spoke up.

"Oh, no, sir," she said. "You are mistaken. This is my dearest friend, not my beloved."

The damage was done. I was not her husband; I had no special claim. That was all they needed to hear. There was a subtle shifting of bodies and I found myself staring at the backs of their shirts. I didn't know what to do. I certainly didn't feel that I could just shove them aside, grab Roxanne and leave. I stepped back a foot or two and peered over their shoulders at her. She looked intently at each one, and for the moment or two she made contact it was clear that her attention was fully focused upon that particular individual. Each one of those men must have felt that he alone was the object of Roxanne's gaze. That he alone was her whole world. I knew the feeling myself; I'd felt it the moment she'd turned to me when I got back into the car. And, of course, there was her intoxicating perfume. They smelled it too. I could just tell.

Now and then I would attempt to break through the wall of backs, but as time went on more and more men started gathering around the table, ostensibly to see how much the little lady could pack in. An older waitress was wiping the counter with a damp cloth. I could see her keeping an eye on the situation. After a minute or two she put the cloth down on the counter, walked around and approached the group of men. It was clear she knew some of them. She was friendly but firm. The snowstorm was over, wasn't it time these guys headed on their way and stopped bothering the lady?

Unfortunately the lady didn't seem the least bit bothered. She was in her element. I thought of Roxanne in the play — how she was always surrounded by men jostling for her attention, and how comfortable she was with this masculine energy. On stage this was fun and romantic, but here it made me very uncomfortable. The men ignored the waitress' suggestion that they leave Roxanne alone so she returned to wiping the counter — but her eyes never left the group in the corner booth.

The waitress and I weren't the only ones in that restaurant who were uneasy. I saw a woman sitting at another booth with two children get up before the bill had arrived and put her children's coats on. They were objecting — they wanted dessert — but her mother's antenna told her to get her children out of the way.

"Later," I heard her saying. "We'll stop for dessert later." After ringing her bill through, the waitress disappeared into the back. I realized with a sinking feeling that there were now no women in the restaurant. Except Roxanne. The male energy was undiluted.

Of course I wasn't thinking of Roxanne; I was thinking of Kate. This *wasn't* Roxanne, this was my friend Kate and she was clearly trapped. Roxanne was laughing and charming the men, but it was Kate who would be in danger if the situation got out of hand. And it was getting out of hand. Not in any overt way — the men were still laughing and joking among themselves — but I knew each one of them thought that, eventually, if he could get rid of the others, Roxanne would leave with him. Somehow the spell had to be broken. And then, just like in a Hollywood movie — it was. Just at the point where I was holding my breath, the door to the restaurant opened and two men in uniform strode through. Mounties. These weren't the fat belligerent policemen with nightsticks we were beginning to see daily in the news. They were trim and fit and by the looks they exchanged with the waitress, I knew how they'd known to come.

I was so grateful — Mounties! I'd grown up with stories about the Mounties. How they had kept perfect law and order in the Klondike. How Sitting Bull and the Sioux were escorted from Wounded Knee by an entire regiment of U.S. cavalry only to be met at the Canadian border by a single Mountie. And I must say I was suitably impressed by how they proceeded to handle my own tricky situation. They first gestured to the man furthest away from Roxanne. Once they'd separated him from the group, they quietly asked for his identification. He grumbled and pulled it out. Then they asked him which rig was his and the younger Mountie started to head to the door as if he was going to check the truck over. The man headed out with him. As soon as he got to the door the Mountie simply handed him his identification and told him to be on his way. Then they started with the next man. And after him, the next. Instead of confronting the group as a whole, they quietly picked them off one by one. Each time the routine was the same. They'd single out a particular individual, get his identification, and let the others go on talking. As the group diminished those that remained hardly seemed to notice. I wasn't surprised. The fewer the men, the more attention each one got from Roxanne. The last two proved most difficult. They got a little unruly, but these were Mounties and the truckers' entire livelihoods were at stake. When they were finally gone I paid our bill, tipped the waitress generously, then went over to the table. I thanked the two officers and asked if they could do one more thing — accompany us to our car.

There were still three rigs out in the parking lot and we waited a moment as one pulled out in front of us, then we walked to the car. Just as we were getting in, Roxanne turned and said something to the younger Mountie. Immediately I could see a blush starting at his collar and moving up over his entire face. He nodded and touched his hat, then stepped back.

When we got into the car, Roxanne turned to me.

"A most polished gentleman."

I started the car and slowly manoeuvred past the trucks out onto the highway. I needed time. Time to figure out how to handle this bizarre situation. Time to think.

Clearly my notion of proceeding normally was out of the question. Kate and I could stop at motels, restaurants, go for walks, and no one would notice, but wherever I went with Roxanne, I knew, there would be a commotion. What was I to do? Just drive and drive? I drove through Revelstoke, Sicamous and Salmon Arm, still thinking.

Kate was my responsibility. She had come to me desperate to get away from Stratford. But it wasn't Stratford she was trying to get away from, it was this peculiar state into which she had now fallen. I knew that I had to get her out of this state, but how? Kate had gone into this state after sleep. She had fallen asleep and then Roxanne had appeared. I wondered if the solution wasn't to get her asleep again.

Sleep was obviously the transition between the two states. No wonder Kate had struggled to stay awake the first forty-eight hours of our journey! She knew that whenever she slept she was vulnerable. And she thought that the further away she got from Stratford, the less hold this character would have upon her. She'd been so much more relaxed in Banff. Then she'd let down her guard and Roxanne had entered. Perhaps if I could get Roxanne into a deep sleep I could wake her up as Kate.

In Kamloops the Trans-Canada veered south until it ended at the coast. I wasn't about to take Roxanne into more and more populated territory, so with some apprehension I turned onto the Caribou Highway and headed north. As I drove I realized this was an entirely new person beside me. She could probably last days without sleep. The problem was, I couldn't. If I stopped by the side of the highway and napped, some trucker or salesman would pull over and I knew Roxanne could transfer loyalties in an instant. He would become her dearest friend, not me. He would get her to Daniel Lloyd. So I drove on. It was at Williams Lake that I came up with the idea of pills. It wasn't as horribly premeditated as it sounds. I stopped at a small drugstore to get some No-Doze for myself, and right beside the No-Doze was an over-the-counter sleeping pill. Sleep-Eze. I bought a package of those too. The problem was, how to get her to take them? It proved to be no problem at all. I put the No-Doze in the inside breast pocket of my jacket and the Sleep-Eze next to them in my shirt. When I got back into the car, I took a No-Doze. Roxanne asked what that was and I told her it was what we took when driving to keep us awake.

"May I have one?"

"Sure."

I reached into my shirt pocket. I knew it would take more than one to make her sleepy, so every thirty miles or so I pretended to take another No-Doze and handed her a Sleep-Eze. By Prince George she had consumed four pills. She was still wide awake. I'd checked the package in the drugstore and the caution blurb warned no more than four pills in a twenty-four-hour period. Already she'd consumed her daily limit. I didn't want to harm Kate, but I felt that I could give Roxanne a few extra without danger. In the next couple of hours Roxanne took three more. She was still wide awake. I was hungry, too edgy to sleep and too edgy to drive, but I pressed on. I had to. The further I travelled with Roxanne the more I realized she had no concept of Time. She existed in a state of pure longing and, as long as she felt I was returning her to her beloved, Time didn't matter. This worked to my advantage.

There's no need to describe the next two days. I'd stop for gas, grab take-out burgers, keep reassuring Roxanne we were returning to Daniel Lloyd, and drive endlessly around the B.C. Interior. Often I'd find a truck and just stay a couple of hundred yards behind it. This greatly reduced my stress as the trucker made all the decisions. I'd turn when he turned, brake when he braked, speed up or slow down as he did. He knew the road; I didn't. At night this was especially helpful.

Every few hours I would feed Roxanne another Sleep-Eze, though I soon gave up the No-Doze. When I couldn't drive any farther, I would pull into a motel in an isolated spot, take a room, hand Roxanne the Gideon Bible and get her to read to me. Then I would fall asleep. Often I would wake up hours later and Roxanne would still be reading. Finally, in a small town in the Kootenays, I stopped at a doctor's. I was easily able to convince him that I was too edgy from driving to sleep properly at night and he gave me a prescription for a real sleeping pill. Seconals. I got it filled at the local pharmacy and that day I judiciously got Roxanne to ingest twice the suggested dosage. I drove again all day. My third with Roxanne. That night we turned into a small motel and I fell asleep as she was reading me the *Song of Solomon*. Next morning, when I awoke, she was asleep in the chair.

At last!

I didn't know how long she'd slept. Had she just fallen asleep moments ago or had she been sleeping soundly for most of the night? I didn't want to wake her up if she'd just nodded off because she might wake up as Roxanne. Then I had an idea. I checked the Bible open on her lap and it was only on the third page of the *Song of Solomon*. Obviously she'd conked out shortly after I had.

So now was the time to wake her.

I remembered how difficult Kate had been to rouse at Mrs Morrison's. How we'd tried repeatedly, and failed repeatedly. I decided that I would speak her name, softly at first, then louder and louder with each repetition until she woke up.

Kate...Kate...Kate...Kate...Kat e...Kate.

Her eyes opened and she looked at me.

"Richard," she said.

It was her. It was Kate.

"It happened, didn't it?"

I nodded.

"When?"

"Rogers Pass."

Kate thought for a moment, then nodded.

"Yes," she said. "The tunnel. That's the last thing I remember. How long?"

"Three days."

Kate groaned.

"Poor Richard," she said. "Was it awful?"

"Awful."

It was so good to have her back. It was so wonderful to linger in a diner, sipping on my third coffee, and not have to worry. All sorts of men came into the diner, ate and left again without so much as glancing our way. We talked. That entire day we talked about nothing but Roxanne. I mentioned the scent and her head whipped up.

"Yes!" she said.

She too had smelled her. She'd never seen her, but she'd smelled her.

Kate was grateful — and relieved — that someone understood her experience. That she was no longer struggling alone. She said that at some level she must have known I was the only person who could help her, and that's why she'd made her way to Montreal. I felt I had just done what anyone would have done in that situation. I told her this.

"You're a good person, Richard," she said. "Not many people would have done what you did. Most people would have tried to exploit the situation."

"Exploit the situation?"

"Most people wouldn't have cared about me. They'd have wanted Roxanne. They'd have tried to keep Roxanne alive, no matter what the cost to me. Roxanne is beautiful. Roxanne is a star. Roxanne is fame and money and status. But she isn't me, Richard. You helped me."

Kate wasn't an emotional person, but there was such feeling in her voice that I had to turn away and look out the window. In the years to come whenever I was feeling bad about myself, and there were lots of times that I did — I remained estranged from my father; I hurt my mother and deceived my best friend — I would remember those words of Kate's. *You're a good person, Richard. Not many people would have done what you did.*

When we finally left the diner we went for one of our long walks. Kate's concern was the same as mine. Would this happen again? We decided that we must take turns staying awake and we would keep saying, Roxanne doesn't exist, Kate exists. I think by the end of our walk that day we were both feeling optimistic. We thought she wouldn't appear again.

But we were wrong. Roxanne was tenacious of life.

That night I stayed awake and Kate slept. She slept soundly and woke up as herself. We headed out of town and agreed to continue north in order to avoid people. Just as we passed Toad River, we saw a figure standing by the highway. Reflexively, I put my foot to the brake, but Kate shouted, "No!" and I suddenly realized who it was.

We sped on by.

"I *saw* her," said Kate. "She has dark hair!"

Of course. Hadn't I told her that?

In any case that was a crucial moment — Kate experiencing Roxanne as separate from herself. She was outside her and therefore could be rejected.

We kept driving. At mile 632 on the Alaska Highway the Buick stopped. It just stopped. I managed to drift onto the shoulder. We walked a couple of miles into a place called Watson Creek where we found a garage. The owner drove us back in his tow truck but had already diagnosed the problem from my description.

"Transmission," he said.

He hoisted the car onto his truck and we drove back to his garage. Preliminary diagnosis confirmed. I asked him how long it would take to get it fixed.

"Depends," he said. "Could be three weeks for parts, could be six...could be eight."

Kate and I just looked at each other.

"You in a hurry to get out of here?"

That was a hard question. We weren't going anywhere, but going nowhere was a much more appealing prospect than six weeks in Watson Lake.

"We don't have much choice, do we?"

"Sure you do," he said. "The way I look at it, it'll cost you a coupla hundred to get this car fixed. You could pay me a coupla hundred and in a few weeks you'll have your old car back. Or I could pay you a coupla hundred, and in a few weeks I'll have a Buick."

We took the two hundred dollars and the offer of a ride to the airport. There were several small planes on the tarmac, including a twin otter that was heading even farther north to a mining camp. The only pilot who considered taking us on as passengers was heading south, to Wrangell on the Alaska Panhandle. We paid him a ridiculously small sum in cash and climbed in among packing cases and canvas sacks. He asked if we'd ever flown in a small plane before and when we said neither of us had, he said we might get a little weather and it could get bumpy.

It got bumpy as we flew over the mountains.

"Stikine Range," the pilot said, as if that explained the plane's tendency to drop suddenly.

We seemed to be hanging quite still in the sky, with the ground passing under us, until we encountered cloud. Being so close to the cloud created a sensation of speeding forward that registered in my stomach just as surely as the sudden drops. The sensation was suspended momentarily as we found ourselves completely in cloud.

"Flyin' bush," the pilot said over his shoulder, and he put the nose of the plane quite decisively down. When we finally emerged, the sensation of speed returned and landmarks below were more distinct. Not long after that the nose went down again, this time without any comment from the cockpit, and when we levelled out I could see ripples on the long lake below us. I looked over at Kate, who was watching out her side of the plane. I couldn't read her face. The plane did three drops, or bumps, in succession.

"Dease Lake," said the pilot.

The same long lake we had been looking at for some time was still below us but the ripples had become waves. The mountains were close enough now to contribute to the sensation of speed and I became even more acutely aware of the smallness of that plane caught between the clouds above and the earth below. There was nothing to do but hang on.

We bumped along, the wings cutting now through wisps of cloud that were somehow separate from the thick ceiling that had closed above us, until mercifully the pilot uttered another of his two-word sentences.

"Comin' in."

We were so low now that individual trees were discernible, their tops waving side to side in the wind. We made several passes over water, back and forth, back and forth, then the plane dropped and the nose came up and the sensation of speed was completely replaced by a sinking sensation. When we levelled out I saw, off the right wing, a dock. We sloshed towards it.

"Weather's closin' in," the pilot said. "We'll have to spend the night here."

"Where's here?" I asked.

"Telegraph Creek."

In the eighteen sixties there was a race on between two rival groups to get the first telegraph connection between New York and London. The Collins Overland Telegraph Company conceived of the idea of running a line over land from New York to San Francisco up through British Columbia to Alaska, across to Russia, down into Europe and over to London. Their rival's plan was even more improbable. They conceived of the idea of laying the cable directly to London under the Atlantic Ocean. The Collins Overland Telegraph Company had cut a thin trail as far as the Stikine River, less than a hundred and fifty miles from Alaska, when their rival's unlikely plan succeeded. On the day the news reached the crews cutting the trail the entire project was abandoned. Cable was left lying on the ground.

Crew cabins deserted. And all that remained of the futile endeavour was a small outpost on the Stikine River that carries the name
Telegraph Creek.

We walked into town. When we got there it was dark so we took
a room in the only place available, The Diamond C Cafe. There was
a sign fixed to the wall in the bathroom: Please Don't Gut Your
Salmon in the Sink. That night I slept and Kate stayed awake. She
woke me early. She'd already walked down to the river and watched
the sun come up.

"I like it here," she said. "I like it here."

We went downstairs to breakfast. The place was filled with what
I can only describe as characters. Prospectors with beards and hair
like Old Testament prophets. They acknowledged us as we came
in and then went back to talking. We ate a hearty breakfast of flap-
jacks, sausages, lots of blueberry syrup and some of the best coffee
I've ever tasted.

"Made it with eggshells," the hearty-looking waitress told us.

Kate looked up at me.

"I like it here," she said. "I could live here."

"Really?"

"Really."

Then Kate went on to say that she knew what she had to do.
She'd thought about it all night. She had to simplify her life down to
the absolute basics. She had been in the process of doing that in
Montreal and had been happier than she'd ever been in her life until
somehow she'd become involved in theatre. Theatre had led her
astray and now she just wanted to get back to the basics again.

"What are the basics?" I asked.

"Eating, sleeping, having a job that gives me enough to live on,
but no more, and lots of time. I've got to strip my life down to the
essentials, Richard, so I have time to figure out what this was all
about."

Kate was way ahead of me. I was still caught up in my male need
to find a place in the world, to make my mark, and I couldn't conceive
of a life outside the city. A life without libraries, art galleries, restaurants, universities, theatre and movies. But she was able to see that

she could be happy in a place like Telegraph Creek. A place with nothing. A place from the century before.

All morning Kate and I carefully avoided saying goodbye, but as I stepped onto the pontoon, Kate leaned forward and lightly kissed me on the cheek.

"Richard," she said. "You're not my dearest friend — you're my only friend."

I squeezed her shoulder, quickly turned, and climbed up into the cockpit.

The pilot started the engine. In front of me the propeller began to whirl, then there was a roar and the plane began to taxi across the choppy water. In moments we were in the air. We levelled out, then climbed again. When we got to about five hundred feet the pilot banked into a long graceful turn and from my side of the plane I could see Kate still standing on the dock below. She waved. I waved back. I waved and waved until she became a silhouette — then a dot — then so infinitesimally small, she disappeared.

BY EARLY 1965 young men in their late teens and twenties all across the United States were getting their draft cards. President Johnson had doubled the monthly draft call to thirty-five thousand men. And these men wouldn't simply be doing manoeuvres and flirting with German fräuleins; they would be going across the world to a small Asian nation to fight in swamps and jungles against an invisible enemy for no apparent reason. During the Second World War everyone knew who the enemy was — the Japanese had bombed Pearl

Harbor — and the nation had risen as one to retaliate. President Roosevelt convened both Houses and asked for a declaration of war — it was unanimously granted. But this time was different. President Johnson had not declared war; he had only manipulated Congress into giving him the power to wage it. And so young men were asked to go off and die to support a puppet government that was corrupt, inefficient and ruthless. To everyone's surprise, they didn't want to go. And so it was that all over the United States young men started thinking the unthinkable.

The braid was halfway down her back now and a lovely silver-grey. She dressed for comfort and movement. Ease. Slacks and sweatshirts and flat shoes. Elizabeth Hathaway had never felt better. Her house, a house which for so many years had seemed a mausoleum to her, was suddenly vibrant with life. Some days three or four would arrive, then a week would go by and there'd be none — but as LBJ kept upping the draft call, more and more young men were making their way north to Canada. Draft resisters and deserters. Marines, college students, black and white. Some with hair down to their shoulders, others shorn to navy regulation.

Elizabeth would look at these young men — some of them in a state of profound grief, others enraged at the so-called Land of the Free that had forced them to leave, others methodical and determined to make themselves a new life in this new country — she would look at them and marvel at how easily she could connect with them. At night she would stay up drinking coffee with one as he wept at the loss of his friends and loved ones. She felt his grief. She understood it. She understood them all. The grievers, the ragers, the disillusioned. She felt for these young men who had escaped one life and were beginning another. She felt for them, because she herself had done the same.

Some mornings she would wake up especially early and make her way quietly down to the kitchen. She would sit drinking her tea, marvelling at how she'd almost missed it. She had almost lived a non-life. She had become so encased in the concrete of meetings and hair appointments and the cultural expectations of a woman of her class that life had nearly passed her by.

PHILIP SHAW PICKED UP THE PHONE. It took him a while to figure out who this George Stevens was at the other end of the line.
Normally a call such as this would first go through his agent, but
Stevens was clearly too agitated to follow protocol. Of course Philip
knew about the troubles at Stratford, everyone did. Daniel Lloyd had
wowed them once again, but this time things had exploded. Daniel
always walked the thin edge of the wedge and everyone, certainly
everyone in England, knew he was not the sort of man you hired for
an administrative post. To get him to direct the film on top of all that
was just courting disaster.

As this fellow Stevens talked, Philip Shaw knew he was being
sounded out about taking over the film. This wasn't the first time
Philip had been approached about stepping into someone else's shoes
— in fact, that was how he'd got his early reputation. He'd taken over
a number of disasters and been able to salvage them. He was a good
man in the cutting room. But this film hadn't even begun shooting, a
tremendous advantage. He also rather liked the idea of stepping into
these particular shoes. This was no second-rater who'd fucked up,
this was Daniel Lloyd. So he said yes, he was interested, and would
George send him a copy of the script.

The script arrived the next day by special courier and when
Philip Shaw sat down with it he found himself favourably impressed.
Occasionally, clarity had been sacrificed for grandeur, but that could
be easily remedied. The location shots struck him as excessive. He'd
cut the scenes at the front and try to rearrange things so that there was
more studio work, where things were so much easier to control, but
all in all, it wasn't bad. It wasn't bad.

Funny, he'd been angling for the Hollywood production of
Savage Silence for months, flying back and forth to Los Angeles, talking to this film mogul and then that, one day everybody gung-ho
to see him and the next day hardly able to get an appointment. He
was just on the verge of flying back to England when the call from
Stratford had come. This had happened to him time and time again.
While trying futilely to make one project work, another landed in
his lap.

So Philip Shaw went to Stratford. He was impressed. The costumes were stunning, the sets sturdy and well conceived. He was

able to talk them out of Sainte-Marie Among the Hurons in favour of a stockade to be built in the rolling hills just outside Stratford. He liked the cast. And the issue that had precipitated the whole explosion — the fact that there was no Roxanne and the first day of shooting was imminent — didn't bother Philip Shaw one bit.

He had just the girl.

AS THE SIXTIES BECAME MORE TURBULENT it seemed I withdrew more and more into my own thoughts. It was as if the turbulence without and the turbulence within existed in two different worlds, Outer and Inner, and I couldn't relate to them both. So while around me the Quebec separatist movement was growing stronger every day and to the south resistance to the war in Vietnam was building into as close to a revolution as twentieth-century America would see, I was both sympathetic and detached. I stopped going to demonstrations and while I still supported my mother's work I didn't even drop by after my trip out west but simply called to let her know I was home. I spent quite a few evenings with Wesley and Mildred, the most significant of which I have already mentioned. And I began my work on the poet William Blake. I found that the more I studied Blake the more confused I got with his incredibly complex symbols and mythology, and yet he seemed to be speaking to me at some quite profound level. I knew that what was happening out in the World would have excited him very much. There was even a rock group, The Doors, who had named themselves after a line from one of his poems:

> If the doors of perception were cleansed every
> thing would appear to man as it is, infinite.
> For man has closed himself up, till he sees all
> things thro' narrow chinks of his cavern.

More and more I think the Sixties were a time of Innocence. A time when huge numbers of people were young enough and naïve enough that they thought they could impose the world of Desire onto the world of Reality by playing music, smoking dope and resisting the war. But of course they were living in threefold Beulah, that dreamy world of lovers and children, and instead of making the breakthrough into a life fully lived in the Imagination so many of them collapsed into Ulro. The collapse into single vision was coming, but in nineteen sixty-five no one could see it. Once again, as Blake had so forcefully written, humanity was repeating the Fall. The doors of perception would shrink up and man would find himself bound once again in his cavern. But all this was yet to come.

A couple of weeks after I returned to Montreal, I got a phone call from Breetz. He and Ulrika were coming to Canada. He had some big news, it was very exciting, he would tell me in person, they were leaving New York the next morning and would stop over in Montreal.

As soon as I knew Breetz would be arriving I found myself rehearsing all the things I had to tell him. My life, too, had been exciting and I wondered how he would respond to the story of my adventure out west. I imagined him listening with that intense focus he always had, especially when I got to the part in the Rockies. This was the most remarkable thing that had ever happened to me and I was eagerly anticipating sharing it with him.

I opened the downstairs door to the perfectly timed pop of a champagne cork. As Ulrika kissed me and handed me a glass Breetz proposed a toast.

"To Roxanne."

I once read Hillary's account of the climbing of Everest and at one point he was crossing an ice bridge. There was no wind, just silence, and as he inched his way across he heard a tiny *crack*. The ice shifting. He described that tiny sound as a charge of electricity that instantaneously went through his entire body. A gigantic surge of adrenalin that left him momentarily paralysed.

I stood there, trying to look normal, but inside my whole body had just convulsed.

Roxanne.

As we climbed the stairs the story came tumbling out. How Breetz had orchestrated it so that Ulrika would meet Philip Shaw. How there'd been trouble at Stratford and Philip Shaw had been asked to take over the movie. How he'd phoned Breetz to tell him that there was only one girl in North America beautiful enough to play this part.

Any possibility of me telling Breetz about my remarkable journey across the country vanished in that moment. I knew I could never tell Breetz about the other Roxanne. The Roxanne who had manifested herself in a snowstorm in Rogers Pass. The real Roxanne. And so I sat there, drinking champagne and listening while Ulrika praised Breetz and Breetz praised Ulrika and the story was told again, over a second bottle of champagne. This time Breetz elaborated on his future plans for Ulrika. Ulrika this, Ulrika that. Stratford, then Hollywood. She was going to be a film star.

As the whole story was told for the third time, I found myself drifting. Outwardly, their world was the height of excitement and glamour. Ulrika had made the jump from obscurity to impending stardom. Breetz was moving in the most dynamic circles of photography and film, and I seemed to be just sitting in my little coach-house as I had always sat, reading books and thinking. But I knew differently. I knew that I was the one who had experienced something so extraordinary that I couldn't possibly convey it to them. And that this experience would be something that would take me years to digest. And that the Roxanne in my head was infinitely more interesting than the Roxanne sipping champagne across from me, beautiful as Ulrika was.

That thought was the first wedge between me and Breetz. Up until then there had never been a conflict between his world and mine. They had mutually attracted and balanced each other. But somehow the charge had changed and the two worlds that had attracted each other started to repel. I had always been fascinated with Breetz and what was going on in his life and he had been interested in mine. But something had happened. As my world got more interesting, it looked less interesting. And as Breetz's world got less interesting, it looked more interesting.

The truth is often paradoxical.

GEORGE STEVENS COULDN'T PINPOINT the exact moment his greatest triumph turned into catastrophe. One night he had kissed his wife, rolled over and fallen asleep secure in the knowledge that the Stratford Festival Theatre was one of the finest classical companies in the world. And the next night all was in chaos. Actors were refusing to go on, the artistic director had suffered some sort of nervous breakdown and the film people, like an army without a general, were floundering. That night George had climbed into his car and driven to Toronto, his knuckles white on the wheel. He had burst in on his friend Michael Rasnanikoff, who had led him, shaking, into his study. Then the two men sat down and surveyed the damage. Operation Salvage, as they later termed it, was about to begin.

There were wild rumours concerning Daniel Lloyd and the young actress who had played Roxanne. Now she had mysteriously disappeared and Lloyd was unavailable for comment. Four days later, when Daniel Lloyd finally did emerge, looking haggard and shaken, he scooped George and Michael by announcing his resignation "for personal reasons." He said that he had enjoyed his tenure at Stratford, but that he felt unable to give the theatre the full commitment it deserved in the years ahead. When questioned about the film, he replied that he was going to request that he be released from his contract.

The film crew, which had been in a state of panic over Daniel Lloyd's breakdown, was jubilant at the announcement of Philip Shaw's takeover. Philip Shaw was a known quantity and on a venture as risky as this one everyone agreed he was the best possible choice. Shooting had been delayed, but only by a couple of weeks, and Shaw had quickly trimmed the script and simplified the schedule so that the time lost could be easily made up.

Those who remained after the shakeup reacted like survivors of a major trauma. No one spoke of the collapse but it was much on everyone's mind. They handled it the way people so often handle unthinkable thoughts — they worked. They set their minds on the future. The entire community was in a state of feverish activity when Breetz and Ulrika arrived from New York.

DEAR RICHARD,

I'm still at The Diamond C Cafe: "Pioneer Out-
fitters Est. 1874." The bad news is I haven't got a job
yet, but the good news is the money you gave me
seems to be lasting forever. Whenever I go to pay my
board, Nancy just hands me a broom and asks if I'd
mind sweeping out the dining hall or "peeling them
potatoes." I don't mind! I don't suppose I've ever
worked more than an hour or two in a day and the
rest is mine.

And what do I do with the rest of the day? Mostly
I look around. The country is so beautiful. I saw my
first eagle the other day. Ah Clem saw me watching
and said that was nothing. If you're ever here in the
spring when the salmon's running, he said, there'll
be thousands. Imagine — thousands of eagles! I
intend to be here in the spring. Ah Clem is the old
Chinese man who waved at us from his rocker,
the one with the green dog sled in his front yard.
You wondered if he had a dog team. He doesn't.
He has two dogs now, but in the old days in the
mining camps he used to feed more than two hundred dogs at a time. He made up a gruel of salmon,
grease and potatoes which he gave them twice a
week. He says you never heard such "snarlin' and
yappin'." His son is half Tlingit and he has two
grandchildren. The world divides into two types
up here — the ones who talk and tell you their
stories and the ones who don't. But the ones who
talk also talk about the ones who don't, so you
end up getting everybody's story!

I wandered down to that big log building
you admired. It used to be the old Hudson's Bay
warehouse, but now it's used by Alex Wrigglesworth.
He's an old guy, about sixty-five. Grizzled beard,
lined face, not an ounce of fat. Tough and wiry.

He knows more about boats and machines than anyone, they say. He can fix anything. Nancy tells me
that people bring in parts they've found in the woods
or down by the river, and there's nothing Alex can't
identify, "That's a discharge ball." It's a game the
people around here play with him and he never loses.
"Oh, that's a bail assembly" or "that's a throttle plate."
We got to talking and every now and then he'd ask
me to hand him a tool. I didn't know the name of
any of the tools but he could describe perfectly where
each one was, "Third log, four feet from the corner,
there, just below the hacksaw." He loves boats. He
talks about them like people, "Old Pinafore, here,
she's been through some rough times, but she's
gonna be okay." He takes the engines completely
apart, places the parts all over the floor, then polishes
and fixes and welds and even creates new parts
out of scrap metal, works on the hull, and then
slowly, over the winter, puts the boat back together
again. In the spring, what came into the warehouse
as a rotting wreck is transformed. He sells that one,
then starts another. Sometimes he has two or three
going at the same time, all the parts spread all over
the place, but he sure knows which belongs to which.
He never asks any questions about why I'm there or
what I'm doing. None of them do. I wander around
town and everybody nods at me as if I've been living
in Telegraph Creek all my life. Alex came to Telegraph
Creek in the Thirties looking for gold. He says most
of the people who came here came looking for gold.
Of course none of them ever hit it big. Alex still has
his pan hanging on the wall of the warehouse and
he says there's a creek he knows of where he goes
each summer for a few weeks and always finds a few
nuggets. He's not the only one in Telegraph Creek
who does a little panning, most everybody does,
and they all have their favourite creeks.

I'm going to sign off now and put this in an envelope because the plane is supposed to arrive soon. I never saw a post office in town so I didn't think there was a way to mail letters, but when the plane comes in, you just hand your stuff to the pilot. Nancy gave me the stamps. When I tried to pay for them she just shooed me away. I find whenever the subject of money comes up, people just wave their hands as if it never occurred to them. I like it here. Thanks for bringing me here.

> Your friend,
> Kate

P.S. No sign of R. The reason, I think? There's no audience in Telegraph Creek.

That wasn't the only letter I received that week. In one of those instances of synchronicity that were becoming more and more common in my life, in the same day's mail I received a letter with a gold embossed swan. I opened it. Inside there was a short handwritten note:

Dear Richard Hathaway,
> We met briefly on the opening night of *Cyrano* and subsequently had a telephone conversation about our mutual friend. I will be in Montreal on February 1st and would like very much to meet with you again. If that is agreeable to you, I will be at the Sheraton between eight and nine. If not, I understand entirely and remain,

> Yours sincerely,
> Daniel Lloyd

I didn't quite know what to do about this letter because I knew Kate didn't want anyone, least of all Daniel Lloyd, to know where she was. But I couldn't resist the opportunity to speak with the only other person besides me who had an inkling of what had happened. So I called and confirmed dinner on the first.

BREETZ SAT IN THE CROWDED SCREENING ROOM as Ulrika flickered to life on the screen. He said nothing. The room was a babble of excitement but the first dailies only confirmed for Breetz what he already knew, what he'd known since he'd developed the cove shoot. Whatever it was that Marilyn had, Ulrika didn't have it.

There was no time to waste.

The next day Breetz flew to Los Angeles where he checked into the Ambassador Hotel, corner room, fourth floor, then got to work. It had taken three years to create Ulrika. Three years to take a pudgy underconfident teenager and transform her detail by detail into a male fantasy. It had taken three years of meticulous work to create Ulrika. It took only a week to sell her.

In that week Breetz moved through the corridors of filmdom with an uncanny assurance. He knew exactly who to see and how to wheedle his way up the hierarchy of power to get to them. By the end of the week Breetz was lunching with *éminence grise* Benny Stern. Breetz pitched Ulrika to Benny as a "blue-chip growth stock." Benny liked the pitch. He was impressed by the photos of Ulrika and by Philip Shaw's selection of her for a key role. He agreed she was likely to pay big dividends. They sealed the deal over a bottle of single malt scotch and Benny's Cohiba cigars.

After leaving Benny, Breetz returned to the Ambassador. He headed for the bar.

"What'll it be?"

"Chivas. Straight up."

Breetz liked the light in bars. The pools of light on the mahogany counter, the white cloth in the bartender's hands.

He swirled the scotch in his glass before taking a sip.

He dealt with flesh. Flesh was so unpredictable. Flesh chafed and erupted. Sometimes too soft and sometimes too hard. He turned this flesh into light. Light that didn't corrupt or die. But it was tough. Flesh was always doing things it shouldn't. Sagging or inflaming. But the light in the bar didn't suffer from any of this. It was refracted through conducive material: crystal and polished wood. Burnished brass and stainless steel. Mercury and glass. All elements that light loved. Light didn't love flesh. Light revealed flesh in all its imperfections. Flesh had to be powdered and creamed. It had to be dressed and undressed, hidden and exposed, smoothed and shaved. And only then was light kind.

Except to Marilyn.

He gestured for the bartender, who came over and refilled his glass.

Only Marilyn's flesh seemed to really love light.

What did she have? Liquid skin? Skin made of pearl? No, it wasn't pearl, it was soft. It was soft and yet it radiated. Velvety yet luminous. But soft absorbs light and hers radiated. Why could he never get Ulrika's skin to do that? He could trick the light. He had come up with so many tricks, the best being the cove shoot, but it wasn't Ulrika that had shone, it was the droplets of water on her skin. Only Marilyn's photos shone. Only Marilyn was luminous. Marilyn and these bottles and glasses.

He could get a picture of this. He could get the light glinting off the Courvoisier and it would look in the picture exactly as it did in front of his eyes. It didn't have to be poked and prodded, cajoled and soothed, smoothed and creamed and powdered. The light in this bar was like the light in a great photograph. Light suspended in time. Controlled, not changing. Light that shone with a brilliance not its own. Light that didn't burn or scorch or sear.

Breetz knew that this light was the real light. He knew that the light out there in the streets of L.A. was too bright and too harsh and too unforgiving to be real. The light in this bar was soft and sparkling and easy on the eyes. It wasn't a light that showed flesh to disadvantage, a light that bred maggots and decay. It was a light that sat in soft pools on mahogany counters and glinted from the rims of inverted glasses, a light refracted through crystal and absorbed by rich amber liquids. A light that changed but changed only within certain set parameters. A light that never clouded over or blazed so bright it hurt. It would change, but only with the movement of objects, a glass replaced by the bartender, swaying softly, catching the light…it wasn't elusive. It was here today. He knew that if he came tomorrow it would be here again. He could always find it. It wouldn't elude him. It would always be here.

He signed for the drinks and headed out into the lobby. The elevator was waiting.

The doors slid shut.

The doors slid open.

He stepped out and made his way down the hall to the room.

He had chosen the room deliberately. He would come back and confront his past. It was in this very room that he had come so close to photographing her. He had come that close. He had chosen the room consciously but it was his unconscious that made him open the door and step into that room at the exact moment the light was perfect.

Perfect.

He threw himself on the bed and she was there before him. She was standing right there with a glass of champagne in her hand, wearing the white shirt he had tossed her. She turned and laughed and the shirt-tail caressed her thighs. She was so beautiful.

Breetz lay motionless and watched her. She twirled again. In the next few minutes she went through all the poses that Breetz had imagined so often. Marilyn lounging on a chair, her leg up over the arm, sipping champagne. Marilyn, her head tossed back, laughing. Marilyn, flopped on the bed, looking at the camera through half-lidded eyes. Marilyn, her tongue saucy.

She was so beautiful.

She was radiant.

She was luminous.

Breetz knew she wasn't there. He knew that this was the Marilyn he had created in his head. But her presence was so real it made his heart ache. He wanted to photograph her more than anything in the world. He would find her. He would find her. Somewhere out there was a girl who would photograph as beautiful as Marilyn Monroe — and Breetz Mestrovic would find her. He would find her.

I SAT ACROSS THE TABLE from Daniel Lloyd and thought Kate must be the only person in the world capable of resisting him. Though I had arrived at the appointed time and place somewhat anxious and unsettled, he had immediately put me at ease. He did this by listening. He may be the only truly good listener I have ever met. He was totally present, not waiting to jump in with his own observations, a quality I have tried to emulate ever since, with little success. He sat across from me taking in everything I said and asking pertinent questions and I found myself discussing quite eloquently thoughts about my thesis proposal that had me tied up in knots for weeks. Only that afternoon I had sat across from my adviser while he rubbed his hip distractedly and asked if I couldn't "nail it down" a little more, make it a little more "germane." I couldn't imagine what could be more germane than a discussion of Blake's epistemological theories. As I talked to Daniel Lloyd, I realized that I was able to say all sorts of things to him that I couldn't seem to write in my proposal. When I tried to write my theories I got all tangled up in my own convoluted thinking. But Daniel Lloyd clearly understood exactly what I was getting at. Gradually, our conversation turned to the real purpose of our dinner: Kate.

"Is she safe?" he asked.

"Yes," I said.

"You know her whereabouts?"

"Yes."

"Good. That's really all I wanted to know."

I had come to the dinner intending to get information but determined not to give any. I had promised Kate I wouldn't let anyone know where she was, especially Daniel Lloyd, but he made it clear he wasn't interested in finding her and so I was able to completely relax. He told me about the costume parade and his viewing of the film late that night. He told me that whatever it was Kate did on stage, she could also do on film. He had never seen anything like it. She was radiant. She was luminous.

"I knew that if I put that girl on film," he said, "the whole world would come to watch."

"But that girl wasn't Kate," I found myself saying. "That girl was Roxanne."

And then I picked up the story where he had left off. I told him about driving the real Kate across Canada and how Roxanne had manifested herself in the mountains. I told him about her scent and the scene in the restaurant outside Revelstoke. He'd been listening with rapt attention but at that point Daniel Lloyd held up his hands.

"Stop," he said.

I stopped. I realized that in a matter of moments I would have given him the story of Telegraph Creek and probably even told him she was staying at the Diamond C Cafe. He reached into his breast pocket and pulled out a small black cylinder about the size of a pill bottle. He held it in front of me between his thumb and forefinger.

"I can't do what should be done with this, Richard," he said. "But I suspect you can."

I looked at the object in his hands and knew exactly what it held. The footage of Roxanne at the costume parade. I reached out, took it and pocketed it.

"So what now?" I asked.

"For me?" said Daniel Lloyd.

"Yes."

"Paris. I keep a *pied-à-terre* and I have some admirers and a little family money of my own and I'm going to do something that's been in the back of my mind for some time. I'm going to take over some warehouse space and start playing with theatre."

"Playing?"

"Yes. Fascinating word, that: play — *play*wright. Like shipwright or millwright. Someone who makes play. And what is play? It has a sort of relaxed purposeless quality to it, doesn't it? When you get involved in theatre you get distracted by the non-essentials — box office, publicity, costumes, sets — but the greatest playwrights were people who simply made play. And I think I'm going to try to get back to that bedrock concept."

"Back to the bare essentials," I said.

"Precisely. I'm going to gather together perhaps eight or so of my favourite actors, I'm hoping Galdikas will be one of them, and we're going to strip theatre down to what it really is. An actor in an empty space. We're going to get rid of all the clutter, including the clutter of a big prestigious theatre, the clutter of success, and we're going to play. Eventually, I hope to find out what it is in theatre that affects us all so deeply."

I nodded.

"I used to think that I could strip it down to just the words and the words were what theatre was, but *Cyrano* taught me something more. That theatre goes even deeper than words. Theatre is an image that plays in our minds, and we have to keep stripping our lives down and opening our lives up for it to happen. It's the most fleeting and ephemeral of things and we must be always prepared to let it happen and then let it go." The last was said with a nod indicating the object in my pocket. "Kate was my last temptation, " he said. "The greatest temptation I have ever had to turn play into something else."

It was eleven o'clock and Daniel Lloyd had an early flight to France. I could have sat and listened to him all night. As we parted in the hotel lobby, I asked him if I could some day come and see his theatre in Paris.

"By all means," he replied.

And then he said something very nice. He reiterated that the experience with Kate was one of the most important in his life and that I was a part of that experience and therefore we should keep in touch. Then he smiled, shook my hand and stepped into the waiting elevator. I watched while the doors closed and then I turned and left.

I was feeling strangely emotional and I knew that the best thing for me to do would be to walk. It was a cold, clear night. There was a full moon. I went over and over in my head my conversation with Daniel Lloyd. Daniel Lloyd had begun the rehearsals at Stratford with the best of intentions. He had rolled up his sleeves and shown the world he had nothing to hide. He had stripped theatre down to just the words. But the words had acted as a magic spell and they had conjured up a tulpa.

That wasn't theatre.

In one of my modern drama courses I'd written an essay on Bertolt Brecht. I'd never really understood Brecht's theory of alienation, but now I was starting to. Hitler had held his audiences spellbound, but the Nazi rallies at Nuremburg were the demonic parody of real theatre. Hitler was a Medusa who turned his audience to stone. But if theatre is play, it shouldn't turn its audience to stone. It shouldn't mesmerize them or hold them spellbound, instead it should release the playful quality in the audience. It should make the audience *more* lively, *more* exuberant. It should put us back in touch with what makes us really human. That other kind of theatre deadens the audience because it transfixes them.

The morning that Daniel Lloyd had woken up and found Roxanne gone, he had despaired. But he confronted his despair and the despair sucked him down in its vortex until he passed through it to the other side. The gyres reversed themselves and he realized that Kate's disappearance was his deliverance. Two different concepts of theatre that had been struggling in his soul whirled asunder. The one consolidated into the error of demonic possession and the other into a vision of theatre that was light and lively and unmysterious. He had realized that he must let Kate go, and all that she represented for him.

> He who binds to himself a joy
> Does the winged life destroy
> But he who kisses the joy as it flies
> Lives in Eternity's sunrise.

I fingered the cylinder of film in my pocket. Daniel Lloyd's temptation. It was not something I felt I could simply get rid of — it had to be ritually destroyed.

I walked along rue Notre-Dame until I reached the Jacques Cartier Bridge. I stood on the bridge and looked down at the mighty St Lawrence flowing beneath. I held the cylinder at arm's length and let it drop.

ELIZABETH WAS LAUGHING. She was laughing so hard her stomach hurt. She and Breetz were sitting in what used to be the conservatory, now filled with sleeping bags, mattresses, backpacks and piles of dirty laundry. Breetz was telling her about his meeting in Los Angeles with the fabulous Benny Stern. As he told the story, Elizabeth could see the entire restaurant. She could see Benny jabbing the air with his cigar. She could see the sycophantic waiter struggling to keep in the background but at the same time show the profile of his aquiline nose and strong jaw to advantage. She could see the young starlet who kept wiggling past Benny on her way to and from the ladies' room. She could see the screenwriter loudly recounting the synopsis of his latest script. She could even see Breetz sitting there smoking his cigar and making his pitch.

He had surprised her, arriving on the doorstep with a bottle of scotch in one hand and a bouquet of red roses in the other. He told Elizabeth he just *loved* what she'd done to the place. Mattresses, graffiti and anti-war posters were all the rage in New York and she was obviously bringing a little much-needed culture to Rosedale. Elizabeth had started to laugh the moment he'd set foot in the door and hadn't stopped. Breetz continued his running commentary as he'd poured each of them a stiff scotch and then they'd settled down to chat.

He told her about his beautiful wife and how each morning she was laced into a corset so tight her breasts ballooned up over her bodice. Breetz did an absolutely devastating imitation of the poor girl grimacing and sucking in her breath as the costume mistress pulled and tugged. But his best story was the story of the hair.

"The hair?"

"The hair, Elizabeth, yes. The two thousand-dollar strand. I had it made into a pendant."

He pulled a small piece of Lucite out of his pocket and held it out by its golden chain. She took it and peered and, yes, inside, if she held it just right, she could see a single strand of hair. Breetz went on to tell the story. The stylist on the set of *Cyrano* kept trying to tame a particularly unruly strand of Ulrika's hair, delaying the shooting of the scene each time she fussed over it. Finally the director leapt out of his chair, rushed at Ulrika and yanked the offending hair out. Ulrika screamed and burst into tears. Breetz rushed to her side. The hairdresser stormed off the set. The union man called for a break. That one hair had delayed shooting for two hours.

As Breetz told the story he mimicked each person in turn, including himself, the solicitous loving spouse. He had retrieved the hair from the floor and was going to present Ulrika with the pendant at the première. Elizabeth laughed. He then told Elizabeth his plans for

Ulrika. *Cyrano* to begin with. A quiet artistic success which would sink like a stone and yet have a long life in art houses and on the university circuit. This would establish her as an Actress, then Benny Stern would put her into the kind of movies she'd be good at.

"And what kind of movies are those?"

"Ones in which her clothes come off."

"Breetz..." said Elizabeth, trying not to laugh.

"Oh, come on, Elizabeth, she loves taking off her clothes. Next there'll be the *Playboy* spread and then the pin-ups in every adolescent male's bedroom."

Elizabeth was still chuckling as Breetz replenished their glasses. He made them all seem so ridiculous, including himself. How could he sit here laughing with her about how ridiculous they all were and yet take the world they moved in so seriously?

"What next?" she asked.

"London."

"What about Ulrika?"

"Ulrika's fine. We'll stay in touch, but I want to be in London. That's where it's happening."

Where it was happening was where Breetz wanted to be. And where it was happening changed — sometimes it was happening in New York, sometimes L.A. — but wherever it was happening, he'd be there. Suddenly Elizabeth was overcome with nostalgia. She looked at the sophisticated young man before her and saw the little black-eyed boy. He had always been such fun. He was a surprise. He had come into her life and she'd had no expectations for him. She didn't care if he was brilliant or even intelligent, she didn't use him to club her husband or to impress her friends, he was just little Breetz. A little bundle of energy that had blown into her life. That energy had galvanized them all — the puppets, the bicycles, the movies, the forts, the camera, the darkroom — and she knew why he was moving in the circles he was, ridiculous as he made it all sound. It was a world that could contain his energy. There was always a deal cooking, a project afoot, a new place to travel to. That incredible energy of his could always find an outlet.

They sat and talked, and talked and laughed, and it wasn't until the others started arriving home that Elizabeth realized they had spent the whole afternoon sitting there in the conservatory. Breetz glanced at his watch, made some phone calls, and a few minutes later a taxi arrived. He stood on the front porch and held Elizabeth's hands in his. Then, kissing her on both cheeks, he said how wonderful she looked and what a wonderful, wonderful day they'd had. He said they must do it again, soon, and then he was off.

She stood on the front porch and watched as the taxi rounded the corner. Someone had put Country Joe and the Fish on the record player. She liked Country Joe and the Fish. She liked Bob Dylan and the Beatles. She liked the Rolling Stones and The Doors. She thought of her son. Here she was smack in the middle of youth culture and it seemed to be passing him by. He was living in Montreal like some sort of musty nineteenth-century scholar, surrounded by books. His closest friends were old people. She must drop him a note. She must tell him about her afternoon with Breetz and how she hadn't had such a good laugh since the three of them had been together in New York.

She was composing the note in her head when she drifted back into the conservatory, drawn to the last light fading over the valley. As she moved to the window her foot hit something, knocking it over. She bent down and picked it up. It was the bottle of scotch. Empty.

SPUTUM, AS THE BOYS CALLED HIM, couldn't keep his mind on his cards. Three of a kind and he could hardly be bothered to play out the hand. He'd got this idea...

"He's the best glaze I ever done."

"Listen to him," Queasy said. "You're not serious..."

"Naw, he's Sputum, Ted's Serios."

Sputum put up with these goofs. He'd put up with these goofs for years, these goofs with their goofy scams and two-bit cons. Always looking to make a buck however they could. Too bad he couldn't keep it to just him and Ted, but with what they'd just come up with they were going to need backers.

"I saw one of them stage hypnotists once," the new guy said. "Made this old fat guy quack like a chicken."

"Ducks quack, asshole, chickens cluck."

"Chickens cluck and dames fuck."

"An' you suck. See ya five, raise ya ten."

Sputum took a drag of his cigarette, then held it between his thumb and second finger and gave it a squeeze before butting it out in the ashtray. Goofs. Buncha goofs.

"Queasy — 'member the guy I could make one hand go hot, the other cold?"

"Yeah, yeah. I remember," said Queasy, popping a Tums.

"So what?" the new guy asked. Sputum ignored him.

"An' what about the big guy, worked in the kitchen? 'Member him? Got him to go back an' see all that stuff from his childhood — his cookie, the pattern on the ceiling, the dust on the floor — 'member that?"

"Yeah."

"Well, I got somethin' more amazin' than any of that stuff."

"Big deal," the new guy said. "So you can make some guy remember his cookies, very big deal."

Sputum pulled out a paper and tapped some tobacco into it. Took his time licking and rolling it while the new guy yakked on about did anyone ever make any money out of this and he didn't mean nickel-and-dime shit, bunch of dummies paying to see some fat ass stand on his head or something, he meant real bucks.

"Anybody figure out how to do that," he said. "I'll be interested."

Sputum had — that was the point. Sputum knew he was onto something big. Something no one else had ever figured on before. Something so simple, if he could make it work, he'd be rolling in dough. But these guys wouldn't listen.

"Me, Queasy and Sputum hit it big once, let me tell ya," Bud said. Then he was into it. Christ, Sputum thought, if he'd heard that story once, he'd heard it a thousand times. Of course in some crazy way he had the wrinkly scam to thank for it, thank for getting him into this stuff. Bud had worked for this wrinkle, cleaning out her garage, planting begonias. She used to make him lunch and sit there taking tea with him. That's what she called it, "taking tea," with her little pinky sticking out and everything. She used to blab on about her nephew, some hot-shot war ace got gunned down over Korea. Never knew whether he was alive or dead, just disappeared off the face of the earth. Bud would sit there nodding and saying how terrible it was and she'd feed him more sandwiches, even show him pictures of the kid. Sort of looked like Queasy, Bud thought, and that's how the scam got started.

By this time the new guy was all ears.

Ignorant goofs, Sputum was thinking. They always missed the point.

"So I told the wrinkle there was this guy hung out at the Sally Ann, sorta looked like her nephew — only trouble was, he didn't have no memory. He'd gone blank. Your deal."

The new guy started shuffling.

"The wrinkle wants to meet him so I brings Queasy over and she swears he looks just like her nephew, only Queasy don't remember anythin'; he's got whaddyacallit, amnesia. So then we bring in Sputum here as a fake hypnotist — "

"Sputum," Queasy said. "That's how Jack got his name. Rasputin ... Ras-Sputum ... Sputum."

"Yeah, so Sputum pretends to be this hypnotist, see, an' he's gonna help the nephew get his memory back, get it?"

"Yeah, yeah, I get it," the new guy said, flicking the cards around the table. "So what happened?"

"Sputum dangles this watch in front of Queasy's face and the Quease goes all glassy-eyed and starts spewing out this stuff the wrinkle had already told me. Stuff all about his teddy bear and the toy blocks he played with."

"She fell for it?"

"Hook, line and sinker. She started blubberin'. It was real touchin'. Next thing you know she's moved me and Queasy into the house. Started livin' like kings."

"Too bad the brother had to show," Queasy said, picking up his hand. "If he hadn't showed, she'd a left me a bundle. She didn't have no kids of her own. She was crazy for me."

Missing the point. They were always missing the point. The point was, he'd started out as a fake hypnotist and ended up interested in the real thing. Found he had a knack for putting people under. Could get them to do the weirdest things. And unlike these goofs, Sputum could read more than the racing forms, so he'd started going to the library and reading up on it. He looked up "hypnotism" and found a bunch of books on it. Old books nobody ever read any more. Weird old books full of weird old stuff. Weird beyond belief.

"You come up with a scam like that," the new guy was saying, "an' I'd be interested. Some way to make some bucks."

"Ignorant goofs," Sputum said. "Here I'm tryin' to tell ya I got an idea could make us all millions an' all you can think about is some two-bit scam."

The table went silent.

"Millions?"

"Millions. Gentlemen, do I have your attention?"

He did. He took a drag on his cigarette, let the smoke seep out through his nostrils, then proceeded.

"What's this town famous for?"

Queasy said, "Wind," but Bud whacked him with his Cubs cap and nodded for Sputum to go on.

"Gangsters. Al Capone, Machine Gun Charlie, The Borgisi Brothers..." Yeah, that got their attention all right. "And what do we know about these guys? They get rubbed out. They get rubbed out and what happens to the money they stashed all over this burg because they don't buy no government bonds or open no savings accounts — "

"Wait a minute, wait a minute," the new guy interrupted. Sputum hated being interrupted. "You're talkin' about — "

"I'm talkin' about loot, booty, *treasure*, goof. I'm talkin' about — say you're a bootlegger in the Twenties. You deal in cash an' cash only, pockets bulgin' with the stuff, that is, the stuff you haven't already got hidden underground somewhere, when you're hit. There's a raid, cops crawlin' all over your bubblin' boilin' mash and your pretty copper still. One of two things happens — you get rubbed out or you get sent up — either way, what happens to your loot?"

The goofs were all looking at him with their mouths open, like, We don't get it.

"Them guys got rubbed out on Saint Valentine's day, every last one of 'em, gonzo, finished, you think they left little notes for their wives and children sayin' where they left their stash? I think not."

"So?"

"So it's still there, goof. All them crooks — Big Time, Little Time, the town crawlin' with 'em — all died with the secret of where their loot was, an' if we find it, it's ours to keep. Legit."

He could almost see the little dollar signs popping out of Queasy and Bud's eyeballs. The new guy squinted at him over the top of his beer, a little foam sticking to his moustache.

"There's one major flaw in this plan of yours, dummy."

Queasy and Bud turned to the new guy.

"How do you find a dead guy's dough?"

Queasy and Bud were looking at Sputum now.

"That's where Ted Serios comes in."

"Serios? The little guy works the elevator at the Hilton?"

"Serios. Best glaze I ever done. He's amazing."

DEAR RICHARD,

How are things in Montreal? Strangely enough you probably have more snow than we do, at least in town. For some reason the town doesn't get as much snowfall as areas just a few miles away do, but that doesn't stop Nancy from complaining about it. Most locals don't, most are like Ah Clem, who says, "No point complainin' 'bout the weather."

I still go down almost every day to the warehouse and help Alex with the boats. Slumgullion is what he

has for lunch most days. It sounds like a real word —
the prospectors lived on wits and slumgullion as they
made their way to the Klondike — but he made it up.
Slumgullion is whatever you have on hand — fried.
Macaroni, carrots, potatoes, all piled together in the skillet with some kind of fat. He put cheese on it once and
served "slumgullion with cheese," but that's the only
time I've heard him vary the name. I've had slumgullion
that resembled macaroni, slumgullion that resembled
scrambled eggs with onion, slumgullion that resembled
wieners and beans. My all-time favourite (to think
about, anyway) was the time Nancy sent over a pumpkin pie and Alex threw it in the skillet with some
chicken wings. I amused myself while it cooked trying
to decide if it was pumpkin fried chicken or chicken
fried pie. Alex called it slumgullion.

There are Tahltan and Tlingit around here but
I mostly see Tahltan. There's a Tahltan reserve just
above town — come to think of it we must have walked
through it that first night. The reserve is two rows of tar-
paper houses painted bright colours. The people there are
curious about me. The kids stop their play and run to see
me and the parents look on, somehow attending without
really watching. The kids giggle when I say my few memorized words for them. Across the ravine is White Casca.
Log cabins with sagging sod roofs. It looks deserted but
the last time I was there I saw a curtain moving. When I
asked Nancy about it she said there are two old white
ladies living there. They come into town to collect their
old-age pensions and go to church and that's all.

Thanks for the sleeping bag and books. The
Diamond C is heated with wood and by morning it can
get awfully cold. Nancy still makes that great coffee
you liked. The real secret? Not eggshells. She gets top-
quality Columbian beans flown in from Fort Nelson!

Your friend,

Kate

"I SEE DIS GUY."

"What's he look like, Ted?"

"He's a kid...no more'n sixteen...got a black sweater on, grey pants...he's diggin'."

"Diggin'?"

"Yeah, yeah...got a shovel and he's diggin'...no, he's not...he's not takin' it out, he's puttin' it back...there, yeah, 'cause he's replacin' this piece of sod from where he dug."

"Look aroun', Ted, look real careful. Whatcha see aroun' where he is?"

"I see...cement...stone...I see some sorta curving stone... yeah, and water...lappin' up against the stone is water."

"So what is it, a bridge?"

"Yeah...could be a bridge...or a tunnel...the guy's leavin' now — no...yeah, he's leavin'...he sorta looked over his shoulder like he was lookin' right at me."

"Okay, Ted, look aroun'. What else you see?"

"I see...what's dat? At the bottom, down at the bottom I see somethin'...letters — "

"Letters, good. Ted, listen, I want you should bring those letters up close to your eyes so you can see 'em."

"Dey ain't letters, dey's numbers...yeah, carved into the stone... one, nine, oh, eight."

"All right! Yes! Nineteen oh eight. Okay, Ted, listen. You gotta tell us what it is. Is it a bridge? What is this thing?"

"I dunno."

"*See* it, Ted."

"I see it, I *see* it...there...only it's goin'...it's fadin'...Shit. That's it, brother. Curtains. It's gone."

Sputum turned his head and stared at a spot on the wall for the longest time without blinking. Then he turned back to Ted.

"Good, Ted, you've done good. And, Ted, I want you to fix that place in your head so if you see it again you'll remember it. Fix it real good. Right. Now, Ted, I'm bringin' you back out. I'm gonna count backwards from five and when I hit zero you're gonna be here with us. Five...four...three..."

When Ted came to, Sputum was slapping him on the back and

Bud opened the bottle the Syndicate had promised itself if they got anything. Everyone had a shot then started talking all at once. The Quease knew this place, a tunnel down by the harbour, him and his buddies when they were kids used to hang out, smoke cigarettes and jerk off. He was for hoofing it down there pronto. But Sputum figured they should go about it more methodical, like, maybe check stuff out at City Hall. See if they had some old book telling what structures were built in 1908. The new guy said it looked good but too bad it wasn't Al Capone they'd come up with, just some kid. Bud said, who knew, maybe this kid was a go-fer for one of the big guys. Doing leg work. Maybe this kid had loot stashed all over the city. Serios just sat there staring at the corner, drinking.

On State Street they hailed a cab. When they got to City Hall the skirt on the desk started giving them a hard time, like they had a nerve just walking off the street into her pretty building or something, but Sputum didn't take any guff. What was this? Some sort of military secret he was after? No, he just wanted to know when stuff was built and that was public info. So a thin guy with a bow-tie stepped in and took them down some stairs into the basement. Sure enough there was a book, just like Sputum figured there would be, listing everything built in Chicago and when and where. There was even some pictures and Serios was able to eliminate most just by looking.

Outside City Hall they hailed another cab. The Quease kept saying he knew this place, a tunnel, but Sputum figured the best bet was the bridge. Concrete, curving stones, water lapping at its base. So they told the cabby to take them there. They drove the whole way in silence. The moment they pulled up to the bridge, though, Serios said it was a no-go.

The Quease was thinking about his old haunt, clear across town, but Bud was yakking on about how it made sense to check out the nearest ones first, so they told the cabby the next destination. Another no-go. Two more tries and the new guy started saying they check out everything on this list by cab and the Syndicate'd be in the hole by the end of their first day. Bud agreed. The Quease was for checking out this place he knew, but Bud and the new guy turned on him. Told him to stop his whining. Sputum told them to clam up. Why not give the Quease a chance? Maybe he was onto something. When they got to the tunnel, Ted's fingers started snapping.

"This is it!" he said. "This is it. I've seen this curve before, I've *seen* this!"

No one bothered to congratulate the Quease, they just started firing questions at Ted.

"And the kid?" said Sputum. "Where was the kid?"

"I dunno...here...or there."

"Goddammit!" said Bud. "We forgot shovels."

So while Ted and Sputum and the Quease checked the place out, Bud and the new guy took the cab back up the hill and bought a couple of shovels. Fifteen minutes later they were back. Bud, Queasy, Sputum and the new guy took turns digging. It was hard work. After half an hour of digging out gravel Bud could feel his back starting to pull. He handed his shovel to the Quease. The Quease was never one to do muscle work, but he took the shovel and worked it down another foot. At this point Ted started snapping his fingers again.

"No, no, not dere, here," he said. "I'm gettin' it over here."

So they abandoned that hole and started working on a second one. This time the hole was much bigger and Ted kept saying, Yeah, yeah, this is it, we're getting there, we're hot. But after an hour of solid digging they'd found nothing. Bud and the new guy were getting pissed off. Bud was digging, but the new guy was just glaring at Ted, who seemed to be staring off into space, not even interested. The new guy climbed out of the hole, walked over to Ted and thrust the shovel at him.

"If you're so goddamn sure it's here, you dig," he said.

There was dead silence. Bud stepped out of the hole. Everybody was watching Ted and the new guy. Ted looked down at the beefy hand on the shovel handle. Then he looked up into the new guy's face. He spoke slowly.

"I locates," he said. "Youse dig."

The new guy looked like he was going to haul off and punch Ted, but Sputum stepped in and grabbed the shovel. He didn't say anything, he just jumped down into the second hole and started digging furiously. The new guy and Ted were still standing there, glaring at each other.

Clink.

The shovel hit something. In an instant Sputum was down on his hands and knees scrabbling like a dog after a bone. A moment later the dirt stopped flying and he was working something out of the soil.

Ted had never taken his eyes away from the new guy's.

"You think I'm fake?" he said. "You think I'm puttin' it on? Just look."

A second later Queasy, Bud and the new guy were down on their knees, staring. Sputum was right. They'd found it.

Treasure.

AND NOW FOR MY BIG NEWS. Six weeks ago I was snowshoeing along the old Telegraph Trail. I'd been out about half an hour when I came across a clearing. Inside the clearing was a cabin! You could hardly see it for the snow, but there it was — a squared log cabin. I asked Alex about it and he told me a man named Quinn had lived there for years and years until he took sick. They flew him to Prince Rupert and he died three months later. I asked who lived there now and as soon as I asked it we both burst out laughing. Obviously no one! I asked him who owned it and he said whoever lives in it owns it. Every twenty miles or so when they were building the telegraph line, they built cabins for the crew. When the line was abandoned, so were these cabins. Most are still abandoned, but sixty miles up the line a trapper lives in one. Could I live in this one? I asked. Alex said it was a "good idee" and they'd help me move in. It's in remarkably good condition. Why not? It's been in continuous use for almost a hundred years. It's only the last four or five that it's gone empty. When Quinn got sick and they came and got him they pretty well left everything as it was. His oil lamps, an axe, his tools and dishes are all still here. There's a trap door in the middle of the floor and, to tell you the truth, the first time I was inside I was afraid to open it. But the next time Nancy and Nancy's Joe came along with me and Joe just said, Oh, that's the old root cellar. When we opened it there was a smell. There was still a lot of stuff down there and in pretty sad shape. We got rid of it. In a few weeks a whole bunch of people are going to come help me do a big clean-up. Alex, Ah Clem, Nancy, Nancy's Joe, Chili Charlie and Mrs Charlie. Alex says the chimney is dangerous — they'll rebuild it. The stove is amazing. It's cast iron with nickel plating and they say it's notorious for the heat it throws. Quinn had to damp it down even in the depths of winter or he couldn't get to sleep at night. Alex also told me that Quinn lived on what he called "continuous stew." It cost him, he used to say, one bullet a year to eat. He'd kill a moose, then cure the meat, start the stew and all year just keep adding to it: carrots, onions and swiss chard at the beginning of the year, down to barley by the end. On the day the salmon started to run, he'd empty the pot, scour it, and put it away until the Stikine started to freeze over in the fall.

I still find it kind of hard to believe — I found a house! Can you imagine just finding a house that you can live in? Whenever I go to look at it, I half expect the seven dwarfs to appear, or to find three bowls of porridge, but it really is going to be mine. In a few weeks I'll move in. I'll write you all about it.

THE FIRST "TREASURE" had turned out to be just a jar of silver dollars, odd change, but there wasn't a single coin from after 1927. It hadn't amounted to more than a couple of hundred bucks, but the Syndicate had been encouraged. Then Ted got a real clear impression and they all headed off with their shovels, only to find a construction crew at that exact spot, a bunch of Pollacks jumping around waving their arms. They'd found a stash of money.

It was after this that Sputum came up with the idea of a guide. He'd read about it in the books. What Ted was doing was called clairvoyant travelling and it worked best, the books said, when you had a guide. They'd tried for Al Capone, the Borgisi Brothers, even that kid — the go-fer — who'd led them to the silver dollars, but Ted kept coming up with a pirate.

After falling all over themselves when the pirate showed, now the Syndicate wanted specifics. They wanted the pirate to show Ted something that could be identified. But the pirate never would. He'd take Ted all over Florida, the Keys, some island in the Caribbean. Places they couldn't check out. The whole thing was getting more and more ridiculous. The new guy started implicating, implying sort of, never saying anything straight out, but sort of looking off to the side and speculating about certain con men he knew — he wasn't naming any names here or going into specifics — certain guys he knew or had heard of who'd suck guys in with a small bit of cash then gradually up the stakes until one day — whoosh — they were gone, hightailing it out of there; no one ever heard from them again. Sputum would take a drag of his cigarette and look the new guy in the eye, say, did he think him and Ted were trying to con them? The new guy would back right down, but Sputum knew him and Bud were getting suspicious. The Quease was different. The Quease kept whining if only they could come up with a real gangster. Ignorant goofs. They just didn't get how this stuff went — you got what you got. It's not like Sputum hadn't tried for gangsters — that was the whole idea — but they kept getting the goddamn pirate. Only he was different now, Ted said. Sort of transparent. Ted could see through him to the wall and the picture behind. He was getting more and more loosey goosey, talking about a place in Africa where maybe, just maybe, there might be something hidden. Some loot maybe. Africa, for godsakes!

Sputum couldn't even sell the Syndicate on the couple of grand to case Florida; how the hell were they supposed to go to Africa? They tried going right back to the beginning. Tried to get Ted to float around Chicago on his own. Ted could do this but he never came up with anything specific any more. He'd get feelings there was something buried here, there, somewhere, but when Sputum got him to describe the spot he became vaguer still. A big tree, a pond, an old brick wall. Nothing specific. Sputum wanted specifics. He needed something he could look at, identify, some X where he could stick a shovel in and dig.

He got it, of course. Oh, boy, did he get it. He got it, not in the way he figured, but oh, boy, what he got was more spectacular than anything anybody had ever got before. More spectacular than Mesmer, more spectacular than all them saints and charismatics, stigmatics and yogis he'd read about. Later, telling it to his cronies, Sputum would say it was just a hunch he'd had, a wild inspired guess. Some sort of crazy leap, he didn't know where it came from — but he'd never forget that day he'd gone over to Ted, told him to stop jerking them around and start getting something specific. Put it on film, why not? The day he'd handed Ted Serios a camera.

SHE SAW THEM EVERYWHERE. Beautiful thin young girls in short short skirts, their legs swinging along the sidewalks. She saw Them in the tube, some with legs so slender their thighs seemed concave. She'd see Them standing in little groups of threes and fours, giggling. She watched Them and she watched the whole world watching

Them. The men sweeping the station, the businessmen with their briefcases and brollies. She watched Them glide up the escalators, seemingly unconscious of their tiny derrières very nearly showing beneath their skirts.

They were everywhere. Beads and hair and eyelashes. And sometimes, invisible as she was, she'd stand close to Them and listen to their cockney accents.

"Ow, g'on, 'e isn't, is 'e?"

"Not my cuppa tea, anyroad."

She watched Them as they read their pulp novels on the tube. She knew they could barely read, they could hardly talk, they'd had none of her advantages. But everywhere she went, people were watching Them. They were shopgirls, ticket vendors, usherettes. They worked in the stores on Carnaby Sreet, selling underwear and ties to gentlemen with bowler hats. They weren't educated; they could hardly put a sentence together without sounding ridiculous. All they talked about were boys and clothes and hair and music, but she couldn't stop watching Them and wondering what it would be like to be one of Them. They had something she didn't. They were visible.

Shenute Morton was born in Cairo in 1945. In December of that year, forty miles south of Cairo, an event occurred that was to be inextricably intertwined with her life. A fellah was out searching for sabakh, a soft soil used for fertilizer. He was digging along the Jabal al-Tarif cliffs, an ancient burial ground honeycombed with caves, when he came upon a red earthen vessel about three feet tall. At first, Muhammad Ali al-Samman feared the vessel would contain a djinn or evil spirit and was too terrified to open it. But then, he thought, maybe the vessel was full of gold. Eventually, his lust overcoming his fear, he smashed the jar open with his mattock. Glittering dust billowed into the air, but it was not gold. It was the dust of ancient papyri. Inside the jar the fifty-two Nag Hammadi manuscripts had lain undisturbed for fifteen hundred years. A scholarly treasure of inestimable worth.

Shenute's day until now had always started with breakfast in her cold little flat, then a walk to the British Museum. She was the youngest member of the international team assembled to translate the Nag Hammadi library. Each morning at precisely nine a.m. she would take out the photographic facsimiles of the manuscript pages she was working on. From nine until noon she would transcribe the facsimiles onto specially made papyri. After lunch in the museum cafeteria, she would return to her desk, where she would work on her translation of the pages. In this way, she had come to virtually memorize many of the most important tractactes.

The day she began her descent, she had been working on the *Apocryphon of John*:

> | For the Perfect One | beholds | itself in the light surrounding it. | This is the spring of the water of life | that gives forth all | the worlds of every kind. The Perfect One gazes upon | its image, sees it in the spring of the spirit, and falls in | love with the luminous water. This is the | spring of pure, luminous water surrounding the Perfect One. |

At five p.m. that day she gathered up her books as always, making sure to seal her transcription into plastic envelopes, and headed out the door.

It was raining.

Shenute stood at the kerb. She'd worn her mac that morning but not her galoshes. It had only been foggy when she'd looked out the window, but now the rain was falling hard. She moved, intending to step closer to the kerb, and stepped off instead into a puddle, completely soaking her right foot. As the water seeped through to her stockings yet another cab went by. She turned up the collar of her mac and clutched it around her neck. She saw another cab coming through the lights at the corner. Empty. She let go of her collar and held up her hand but the cabby drove on by. He just drove right past her without even slowing down. This was ridiculous; she was soaking wet.

Just as she was about to give up, she saw one of Them come tripping out of a store and light upon the kerb for a few seconds, looking this way and that. She was dressed in one of the latest plastic raincoats that looked so stiff and shiny Shenute wondered how it could be at all comfortable. An instant later a cab pulled up and the girl hopped in. Shenute stood and watched in her comfortable mac and her comfortable, when dry, shoes, as the cab pulled away with the plastic-coated girl sitting perkily upright in the back seat.

Shenute was invisible. She couldn't bear the indignity of standing there any longer, so she sought refuge in the nearest bookstore. She stepped inside, one shoe now making an audible squelching sound. She would wait it out in the bookstore, wait out the shower, and then walk home. And if the rain lasted a couple of hours, so much the better. She felt safe in the bookstore. In a bookstore it was all right to be invisible.

There were rows and rows of books with ladders up to the top shelves and she immediately felt comforted. Bookstores had always done that for her, bookstores and libraries and museums. But this time, instead of making her way to the back of the store to the classics locked in their glass cases, she instead gravitated to the long brightly lit magazine rack beside the front desk. Newspapers and magazines from around the world. Magazines with glossy covers, some of them the size of atlases. She had stood in this bookstore before, reading poetry but surreptitiously eyeing this rack, this rack filled with triviality and silliness. This time, she walked right up and started thumbing through the magazines. Then she did it. She grabbed one of them off the rack and shoved it across the counter.

To her amazement, the clerk didn't even react, What, *you* buying one of these? He simply slipped it into a paper bag and handed it back to her. She opened her satchel and shoved it in. Then she stepped back out into the rain. Now she was looking forward to her flat. She would make a cup of tea. She would put some shillings in the heater and snuggle in under her eiderdown on the couch. She would open a tin of biscuits and then she would pull it out. The magazine that even now seemed to add such extra weight to her book-stuffed satchel. The glossiest and thickest of them all. *Vogue.*

When Shenute opened the magazine, the first thing she saw was a double-page ad for Revlon. A sophisticated brunette, stretched across a white rug, a pink feather boa draped about her shoulders, sipped champagne. Her nails were long and painted pink. Her lips were pink too. She looked warm. She looked loved. She looked adored. Beautiful.

Slowly, Shenute turned the page. Estée Lauder. An elegant blonde in a simple white dress looking out over the ocean. What was the woman thinking? She was just staring out over the ocean, looking beautiful. What would it be like, wondered Shenute, to be that woman?

She turned the page. The Contents. Shenute read every blurb, each one accompanied by a little boxed photo. Beauty News: The Sixties Face; The New Neutrals: How to Wear Them; Mary, Mary Quite Contrary: An Interview With Mary Quant. There was a section called "People Are Talking About." Shenute wanted to know what people were talking about so she turned to page 52. PEOPLE ARE TALKING ABOUT...Vanessa Redgrave...the words acidhead, psychedelic and LSD...The raga sound of some of the Beatle beat... Ulrika, the voluptuous American starring in Philip Shaw's *Cyrano*... Claude and Paloma Picasso, children of Picasso and Françoise Gilot ...Marshall McLuhan's book *The Medium Is the Message*, and his persistent fascination with Twiggy: "She is an X-ray, not a picture. A geometrical abstract."

She flipped through the magazine. There was a picture of a woman with her mouth open, her little finger lightly pressing on her lower lip. Shenute studied it. She couldn't imagine doing that. What on earth was the woman thinking while she did that? Her eyes were large and brown, like her own, and they stared straight out at Shenute. How could she be so apparently unselfconscious with her little finger almost in her mouth? She turned the page. A blonde dressed in a leopardskin bodysuit. She turned the page. A girl in a short coat and white boots, her legs spread so wide apart the toes of her boots touched the edges of the page. What was she thinking? Her mouth was open too, but in a laugh. Her hands were thrown wide. What was she thinking?

Shenute took the magazine and shoved it into the bottom of her chest of drawers.

Muhammad Ali al-Samman took the jar back to his village. There it lay unregarded in a corner of his house. His mother used some of the papyri to light the fire. Bahij Ali, a one-eyed bandit from al-Qasr, eventually purchased them from Muhammad Ali for a pittance. They started showing up in antiquities markets in Cairo and came to the attention of the authorities. No one knew what they were, but an immediate ban was put on their sale. Some had been bought by an Italian collector, who was forced to sell them to the Egyptian government for a nominal fee. Three years later, after much wrangling and litigation, they came into the possession of the Coptic Museum in Cairo.

Shenute translated more or less four pages a day contingent upon a given manuscript's intactness. That meant that by the end of December she would have the *Apocryphon* translated and transcribed. Then she would send it to the professor at Harvard who was co-ordinating the international committee. He would send it off to biblical scholars around the world. In July, she would present her translation to the First International Conference on Coptic Studies in Messina.

She was very lucky. Because of the extraordinary circumstances of her birth, she was in a position to be part of this prestigious international team. Her reputation as a scholar would be established by the time she was twenty-five. She was so lucky.

But her routine changed slightly. Instead of going down into the cafeteria at lunch, she went out onto the street. She would slip into a pub, or a fish-and-chip shop, and while she sat in her corner booth, she continued to watch Them. They were her age and younger. She'd never get used to the short skirts. They couldn't be comfortable. And the seamless stockings that went right up to their waists — pantihose — a silly word for a silly article of clothing.

They had fun. They were always laughing and giggling. They said things like "nuffing" and "bloody hell." They had no minds.

The Director of the Coptic Museum was Shenute's maternal uncle, Togo Mina. It was a part of Morton family mythology, the day that Togo Mina called Cyril Morton in and showed him the recently acquired manuscripts. The two men sat and studied them and Cyril Morton had never seen anything so marvellous. The black Coptic script, over fifteen hundred years old, on the golden-brown papyri, wrapped in their original leather. He knew immediately what the manuscripts were. They were the lost writings of the Gnostic heresy that had been so savagely suppressed by the early Christian Church. Sitting there with his friend, the brother of his Egyptian wife, Cyril Morton knew that his life's work was before him.

The next evening Shenute deliberately walked the other way so as not to pass by the bookstore. She went home and wrote up her application to The Foundation for the Study of Biblical Literature and Exegesis. The Foundation had a large endowment and its charter included studies in ancient scriptures. Her work qualified eminently and her father had written suggesting she apply. Perhaps she could get a little extra funding. He enclosed two letters of reference on her behalf from distinguished colleagues. She finished typing out her application and made herself a cup of tea. *Vogue* still lay untouched in her bottom drawer.

The day after Togo Mina had shown the Nag Hammadi manuscripts to Cyril Morton, Cyril had brought his young daughter into the Coptic Museum to see them. In the courtyard outside, Shenute's little friends were playing. She could hear their shouts and laughter as her father showed her one manuscript after another: *The Tripartite Tractate, The Apocryphon of John, The Gospel of Thomas, The Gospel of Philip, The Hypostasis of the Archons, On the Origin of the World, The Exegesis on the Soul, The Book of Thomas the Contender, The Gospel of the Egyptians, Eugnostos the Blessed, The Sophia of Jesus Christ, Thunder: Perfect Mind.*

"Shenute," her father said, "these manuscripts are the most precious scholarly discovery of the twentieth century. They are written in Coptic, the language of your ancestors. I am going to make sure that you can read these manuscripts, Shenute, and that you will grow up with them and know them better than any scholar on earth. This I promise you."

She was three-and-a-half years old.

Her father kept his promise. Summers in Cairo, she was tutored in Coptic by her uncle and his assistants. Back in England, she learned classical Greek and Hebrew. She studied demotic and hieratic ancient Egyptian. By age sixteen, she was an expert in five dead languages.

But now, sitting in the British Museum, Shenute was again aware of the girls her own age outside, swinging along the pavement. Aware of a life outside the museum. She bent over her translation.

> He sent, | by means of the holy decree, the five lights down upon the place of the angels of the chief archon. They advised him that they should | bring forth the power of the mother. And they said | to Ialdaboath, "Blow into his face | something of your spirit and his body will arise."

Her neck was stiff. She sat up from her translation, tilted her head back, then forward, and then did a neck roll. She'd noticed this lately. Something she'd never experienced before when translating. Pain. No, pain was too strong a word. Discomfort. She felt like getting up and walking around the library, but instead went back to her work.

> And he blew into Humanity's face the spirit which is the power | of his mother; he did not know [this], for he exists in ignorance.

The other problem was her fingers. They were starting to cramp. There was no reason for her to press so hard on her pen. She put her pen down and shook her hand.

> And in that moment the rest of the powers became jealous, because Humanity had come into being | through all of them and they [the archons] had given their power to Humanity, and its intelligence was greater | than theirs, and greater than that of the chief archon, Ialdaboath.

She'd done it again! She was holding the pen between her thumb and forefinger with all her strength. That's why she was getting that little ridge on her finger. She stopped and rubbed the ridge with her left thumb. She picked up her pen and went back to her translation.

> And when the archons recognized | that Humanity was luminous, and Humanity could think better than they, and that Humanity was free from wickedness, they took their creation and threw it into the lowest region of all matter.

That evening, after leaving the museum, Shenute walked straight to the bookstore and bought a magazine. That day and the next. The magazines started piling up beside her little couch. She learned the models' names: Twiggy, Verushka, Penelope Tree. She would stare in fascination at each of them. They were like strange animals, Bengal tigers, whooping cranes, sinuous boa constrictors, ibus with curving horns, fleet and svelte. They were from another world. They assumed bizarre poses, leaping in the air with their legs split, lying on their backs with their legs waving. They were beautiful contortionists. They stood in strange and exotic ways, hips jutting out, arms twisted around, necks high.

She got up off the couch and went into the bathroom. She stood before the medicine chest mirror. She stared at herself, trying to imagine what she would look like with makeup. She couldn't. She couldn't imagine herself putting that on her face. She knew that if she ever did she'd look ridiculous. And if people noticed her it would only be to laugh at her. She wished she'd never bought that magazine. She wished she could get those images out of her head.

Next day, while walking to the British Museum, Shenute spotted one of Them. One of those thin silly girls twirling and carrying on right out there in the open with her boyfriend. She was wearing a short bright orange dress and matching orange shoes. Shenute kept walking. The girl and her boyfriend were just off the kerb in the street and in moments she would be opposite them on the sidewalk. Would she stop then? Would the brazen little hussy stop her twirling and the batting of those ridiculous eyelashes once someone was that close?

No. Shenute stopped right there on the sidewalk and watched as the girl ran her hands all over the boy. Shenute glanced around, embarrassed. Her eyes came back to the couple embracing unabashedly. She shuddered and was about to move on when she heard a voice.

"Beautiful, beautiful, beautiful."

The speaker was a young man, shorter than Shenute, dressed entirely in black. A photographer. Only then did she notice the other people. A strangely dressed woman who frequently leapt towards the girl and dabbed at her face, a long-haired man holding three cameras and handing them over to the photographer so rapidly there was hardly a beat missed. It was then Shenute realized that the girl and boy weren't kissing at all; even from her short distance away they just appeared to be doing so.

"Up on the car, up on the car," the photographer said, and in seconds the girl was scrambling up onto the hood of a London taxi.

"Beautiful, beautiful," he said. "Keep going, up, up!" All the while he spoke, the man in black was snapping pictures.

The girl was on the roof of the taxi, giggling and dancing. One moment she would be standing, then lying on her stomach, leaning her face on her hands and waving her feet in the air behind her. Then she was sprawled sideways, then on her knees, her arms stretched into the sky, then back onto her feet, her hip jutting wildly to one side. Then she was laughing, then she was clutching at the buttons on her dress as if to tear them open, then she was standing on one leg and throwing an arm into the air. All the while, Shenute could hear the photographer: "Beautiful, beautiful, beautiful, on your side, give us some leg, more hair."

It struck her that these were exactly the kind of images she'd been furtively staring at lately. But the time sequence seemed all wrong. In a few seconds the photographer seemed to have taken dozens of shots, and yet Shenute knew that if any one of these shots appeared in a magazine, she herself would stare at it sometimes for minutes on end. It was all so strange. Here on the street it seemed to be happening so fast and furiously and yet when it appeared in a magazine it was so slow and still.

A crowd had gathered. Shenute was glad for that because she was fascinated; she wanted to stay and watch, but she felt so self-conscious. Now, with people on either side of her, she could do what she wanted to do — stare at the girl. She wore so much makeup she looked almost as orange as her dress. There was a glittery jewelled quality to her, like one of the four handmaidens on Tutankhamen's sarcophagus. She seemed unreal. She was there solely for one reason: to be looked at; to be photographed; to become one of those mesmerizing images that even Shenute found herself unable to resist. Other people in the crowd were laughing and talking and nodding to each other and making saucy suggestions to their friends, but Shenute just kept staring. The girl, at the photographer's urging, slid down off the roof and onto the hood again. She rolled and writhed and wiggled and Shenute tried to stop the action in her mind and imagine it in one of her magazines. It all happened too fast. She couldn't do it.

The boy didn't move so much. Often the photographer had him stand absolutely still in his striped bell bottoms and poet's shirt while the girl sidled up to him and played with his hair and nibbled at his ear. Of course she didn't really play with his hair or nibble at his ear any more than she had really kissed him. Her fingers, like her lips, grazed his body without actually lighting there.

How long could this go on? They must have taken hundreds of pictures just while she was watching. Some of the spectators, in fact, had already drifted away. The remaining crowd was now mostly composed of young women. They giggled and laughed and teased each other with phrases like, "You should go up there, Peg," and, "Ooh, what would me mum say?" or "Ned would be right pissed, wouldn't 'e?"

Shenute noticed that as the girls talked they were striking poses themselves. They would twist and preen and convolute themselves in strange ways. But none of them did it with the ease and quickness of the girl being photographed. That girl had something. She had a skill, a skill that was clearly not something every woman was born with. A skill that had been developed. Shenute turned her eyes from the girls and stared again at the model, who was now sprawled on the pavement while the photographer leaned over her, his camera nearly touching her face.

"Beautiful, beautiful, beautiful."

He was totally focused on the model. She was the most important thing in the world. She was a work of art. He seemed oblivious to the crowds and the noise and the traffic. Occasionally, his hand would fly out and the man with the long hair would thrust another camera into it; then he would go on, click, click, clicking furiously. How could anyone feel such intensity about photographing a woman? There was an energy between the two of them, a passion. Were they lovers? No. Because a few moments later another girl had stepped into the scene and he had the same passion with her, the same energy, the same focus. What would it be like to be observed so closely, so intently, so passionately? He seemed to be as involved with the model as Shenute was with one of her texts. He examined her in every detail. No nuance was too trivial.

Suddenly, it was over. All that intensity, all that passion, dissipated in a moment. The long-haired man was packing up an enormous black bag. The strangely dressed woman was drifting off with her arm around one of the models. It was like watching a play and having the actors walk off stage without taking a bow. There was no ending to it, and yet it was over. It felt unsatisfactory. She wanted more. Some sort of conclusion.

She leaned over, picked up her satchel, and started heading into the museum when she heard a voice behind her say, "Excuse me."

She turned around. It was the man with the long hair. He handed her a card.

"Breetz asked me to give you this," he said.

She looked down at a plain white card with the name Breetz Mestrovic printed on it and a phone number. She looked up and her eyes met the photographer's. He was staring right at her.

She turned quickly and left.

WESLEY SEEMS TO HAVE DISAPPEARED from this narrative, but in point of fact he, Mildred and I dined together every Thursday night. Wesley and I had produced a number of small papers together, starting with the one on Kirlian photography. That had led to other interests and lately we had become fascinated with the whole area of psychokinesis. J.R. Rhein had done a statistical study of telepathy at Duke University in the Thirties, getting vast numbers of subjects to guess at symbols on cards. One day a gambler stopped by Rhein's office and told him that he could influence the throw of a pair of dice. Rhein was naturally sceptical, but he ran some tests and found the gambler was indeed able to turn up certain combinations against statistically impossible odds. So began the study of psychokinesis, from *psycho*, the Greek word for mind, and *kinesis*, for movement. The ability to influence matter with mind.

The more we researched the phenomenon, the more we discovered that it was quite a familiar one. I think my favourite PK experiment was done by John Beloff in Belfast. Beloff reasoned that if large visible objects such as dice could be influenced by a gambler's mind, so also could small *invisible* objects. The smallest and most invisible object was, of course, the atom. In the nucleus of every atom there are two fundamental particles — neutrons and protons. Most combinations of these particles form stable alliances and make up almost all of the earth's matter. But there are about fifty combinations which aren't stable, and are therefore radioactive. These atoms give off particles in a totally random manner. So why not use the randomness of this radioactivity — "Natures's Own Dice" — to test the hypothesis that mind can influence matter? Beloff took a piece of uranium nitrate and used a Geiger counter to measure the rate of atomic disintegration. His subjects were two schoolboys and their task was to either accelerate or slow down the blips on the counter. They succeeded with scores of a billion to one against Chance.

Thus it was Wesley and I started compiling a bibliography of psychokinetic experiences, beginning with one of the strangest and best documented, that of the Italian psychic Eusapia Paladino, who, in the late nineteen hundreds, under strict controls, sculpted clay encased in jars. Wesley had also heard of a remarkable woman in Russia, one Nelya Mikailova, who under strict experimental conditions at the Utomski Institute in Leningrad was performing remarkable feats of PK. In one experiment, an egg had been broken into a saline solution and Nelya was able to separate the yolk from the white at a distance, a feat which clearly could not be explained in terms of any known forces such as magnetism. There was a little girl in Venice who was reported to be able to turn a tennis ball inside out with no discernible hole or break in the ball's surface. The list went on and on. A little boy who could point his toy gun at a plate on the wall, say, "bang bang," and have the plate drop to the floor.

It was an interesting diversion from departmental politics and the strains of trying to satisfy other peoples' criteria. Wesley and I spent Saturday morning poking around in obscure books and then returned for lunch with Mildred. The editor of the *Parapsychology Review* had expressed interest in our survey and we were hoping to have it completed by the end of the academic year.

"PLEASE BE SEATED."

Shenute was standing before an elegant woman dressed entirely in navy blue. A hand waved at the chair in front of the desk. Shenute closed the door behind her. A large part of her wanted to bolt through the door right then and there, but she turned around, approached the desk and took a seat.

"Toes out," the woman murmured as she ticked something off on a paper in front of her.

"I beg your pardon?"

"You toe out, dear, that's all."

"Is that good?" Shenute asked.

"No." Then, when she saw the look on Shenute's face, she continued. "But it's better, in my opinion, than toeing in. I seldom take on the pigeon toes."

Shenute felt panicky. She'd felt silly enough coming here, but if she'd thought for one second they'd turn anyone away, she'd never have come at all.

"Let's take your weight, then."

"My weight?"

"Yes."

Her weight was recorded on a chart.

"At almost ten stone you're a little hefty." She handed Shenute a folder. "There's a diet in here. Lose ten pounds as soon as possible. The course is fifteen weeks long, three hours a week, but we expect you to put in some effort on your own time. The girls who benefit most are the girls who think about their Look *all* the time, not just the three hours a week they're here. Needless to say. There's a session beginning next Wednesday, otherwise you'll have to wait three weeks."

Shenute felt giddy with excitement. It didn't matter that when she'd stammered that she didn't want to *be* a model, she only wanted to look like one, the woman had said, of course not. It didn't matter that she'd had to sign over two post-dated cheques for the full amount of the course. It didn't even matter that her toes had pointed in the wrong direction. They were going to teach her The Walk. That was one of the things they spent a lot of time on, The Walk.

The first day of The Diet was all liquids, and the sheet advised that the day be spent resting as much as possible. On rising she could have 8 ounces of grapefruit juice. At eleven a.m. she could have 8 ounces of vegetable juice. At two p.m. a cup of consommé, five p.m. 8 ounces of mixed fruit juices and at eight p.m. another cup of consommé. At eleven she was allowed some yogurt or a glass of buttermilk or, if she preferred, skim.

The liquid fast was followed by two weeks of The Diet proper. Breakfast each morning was a glass of skim milk, coffee and half a grapefruit, lunch was two boiled eggs OR a salad OR fresh fruit, and dinner was broiled meat, cooked vegetables (here's where the butter pat could be used!) and an apple, orange or two plums. As a bedtime treat she could have yogurt or skim milk. Every tummy growl, every biscuit or bit of trifle refused put you that much closer to goal weight. Goal Weight was always capitalized and sometimes referred to simply as Goal. In her case, Goal was nine stone.

Even before she opened the door, she heard their voices. That sound that had eluded her since her schooldays and haunted her still: the sound of girls. Giggling girls. Girls having fun. She stepped through the door into an enormous room with hardwood floors and a wall of mirrors. She tried not to look into the mirrors, but it was impossible to avoid them. Every now and then she'd catch a glimpse of someone with arms crossed tight, toes out, and she'd realize it was her.

All along the walls were blown up photographs of graduates she'd never heard of, but there was no denying they were beautiful. Shenute studied each one in turn, trying not to feel her isolation. Everyone seemed to be talking to someone else, as though they all knew each other, as though they were friends. As she studied a photo, she heard bits of conversation from one of the groups closest to her.

"I got all patches under me eyes."

"Nooo…"

"I feel awful."

"Yer look nice. 'Onest."

Shenute wondered if the woman in the photo had looked like any of these girls when she'd begun.

"'Alf a 'em, it ain' worth the bother, thass a fact."

"What about the other 'alf?"

There was a burst of giggles. This really was unbearable. She would leave. She would take advantage of the refund and put this nonsense behind her.

"'Ullo, me name's Pam, whass yourn?"

Shenute spun around. One of Them had come up behind her. A girl with the hugest blue eyes Shenute had ever seen. Blue eyes and an enormous blonde beehive.

"Shenute."

"Oo, 'at's lovely, whassat then, German?"

"No — " She stopped herself, well aware how "Coptic" would sound.

"Well, it's ever so lovely," she said. "I took the course last year, so anyfing yer wanna ask, ask me. 'Elps yer confidence ever so much. Found once I started taking the course I was able to talk to me boss — 'e gives me a 'ard time now, I give him a 'ard time right back. See that girl?" Shenute followed Pam's gaze to a tall brunette. "She took the course and got to be a personal secretary, can't even type. Working on 'er typing now she says, but first things first. 'Ang yer coat over 'ere.

Don' leave anythin' in the pockets, 'ad me fags copped one day. That's the little girl's room. Sheila doesn't like yer to come in 'ere when she's talking, so you have to learn to squeeze at bofe ends. When I began I was ever so shy like you. Girls took me under their wing, they did, so reckon I'll return the favour. We all stick together. That's me fren, Tina. She lost two stone takin' this course. Shoulda seen 'er, looked like a puddin'. Now you should see 'er wif the blokes. Bends right over, shows 'em 'er little tushy, accidentally on purpose, reduces 'em to jelly. 'Elps yer confidence ever so much. C'mon, then, I'll introduce you t'other girls."

And so Shenute found herself walking arm in arm across the hardwood floor towards a group of giggling girls. They were nervous too, only their nervousness took a different form. Whereas she wanted to shrink down into her shell like a turtle withdrawing its head, they fluttered and giggled and preened. Their hands moved to their hair, brushed down their skirts, picked fluff off their sweaters. They looked as if they might skitter away at any moment like the birds she saw as she walked through the park.

"Evvybody, this is Shenute," Pam said and in moments they had all greeted her and given their names. There was Tina, Steffie, Viv and Jackie, and they immediately truncated her own name to Shen. Jackie was a hairdresser, Stef worked in a frock shop, Viv and Tina were sisters who lived together and both worked in Marks & Spencer.

"An' I live with me mum," said Pam.

Just then someone came in. Sheila. Immediately, the girls stopped giggling and talking and Shenute realized what Pam meant by "squeezing at bofe ends." Sheila waited until there was absolute silence and then began to speak.

"Every year hundreds and hundreds of girls come to us. Most of them benefit enormously. They go away with more confidence and more poise. They are able to look the boss in the eye and tell him that they'll be taking Friday afternoon off. They are able to catch that man they have their eye on."

At this the girls giggled. Sheila paused until there was quiet again.

"You probably think that half of you will go on to be models. Perhaps a third. Some of you more realistic ones probably think a quarter. Let me tell you what I think. I know. Of the hundreds and hundreds of girls that take our course, only one or two will even attempt the world of professional modelling. And of the hundreds and hundreds of girls who attempt the world of modelling, only one or two will become recognizable names. Those few are our stars. But I want you to know that we are proud of all our graduates and all of our graduates do us proud. There are immense benefits to taking the course even if it doesn't lead to a career in modelling. So let's get to work, shall we?"

After Sheila's opening speech, the entire first evening was spent learning The Walk.

"Every modelling school has its own Walk," Sheila said, "And ours is this."

As she spoke, she demonstrated, walking up and down in front of the girls and turning. It looked effortless.

"Note, especially," she said, "that the heel and ball of the foot strike the floor at the same time."

It seemed so easy, but when it came time for them to try The Walk, every one of them had trouble. Jackie went first. She strutted across the floor.

"Worms wiggle, models glide," Sheila said.

Jackie tried again coming back the other way, but showed little sign of improvement. Sheila told her to imagine that she was holding a penny in her backside, which of course sent them all into fits of giggles — but it worked. This time when Jackie walked across the room, holding her penny, her backside didn't wiggle. Her feet, however, were hitting the floor heel-toe, heel-toe.

"'Ow can I concentrate on me feet an' 'old me penny?" she asked.

"Practice," came the answer. "Practice makes perfect. Practice, practice, practice."

Then Pam got up and walked across the room, then back, and across, then back again, all the while "holding her penny" and striking the floor with her heels and toes simultaneously.

"That's it, Pam, that's it. You walked the whole length of the floor that time like one of my girls." Then Sheila turned to the others. "See?" she said. "Pam's been practising and it shows."

Viv got up next. Viv toed out at first, like Shenute, but after a few times across the floor she improved somewhat.

Shenute went next. Pam had nudged her into the centre of the room.

"Toes are out," Sheila said.

Shenute froze. How could they be out? She felt like she was walking with her feet pigeon-toed, if anything, but when she looked down there they were, toes out. She pointed them straight ahead while she was looking at them. It didn't feel very good.

"Head up, up, up," Sheila said, and Shenute lifted her head and put her foot forward. She walked a few yards when the teacher spoke again.

"Toes out," she said.

Shenute looked down again. Yes, they were out.

"Head up," the teacher said.

It was horrible. It was embarrassing. She inched her way across the floor like that, stopping and looking down at her splayed feet. It was incredible. She knew that if she could just look down she could work on this toeing out problem, but there was no way Sheila would allow that.

"Head up, up, up," she kept saying.

Shenute finally made her way back to the side of the room, her turn over, and her cheeks burned as she watched the rest take their turns walking across the floor towards Sheila. By the end of the evening most of the girls had made progress, but each time Shenute attempted The Walk, she felt herself getting worse and worse. The harder she tried, the more paralysed she became.

"Juss do this, luv," Pam would say, and she'd walk a few paces, her feet hitting the ground evenly. "Juss do this, it's nuffin'."

But it was something, because Shenute couldn't do it. At one point Sheila came over to her.

"Practise at home," she whispered as she squeezed Shenute's shoulder. "Practice, practice, practice."

Next day, Shenute went out and bought a copy of *Anatomy for the Artist*, a big book of drawings of the musculo-skeletal structure. Shenute checked the table of contents and then turned to Plate XL: Bones of the Foot.

The foot consists of three parts: the tarsus, the metatarsus and the toes. Beneath a detailed side view of the bones of the foot there was a small sketch of a stone bridge with a river running under it. She looked at the sketch and then looked at the bones of the foot and could see what the author was getting at. They were both arches. If you excluded the toes, the bones of the foot were constructed like a bridge in which the tarsus was the keystone. The weight was distributed in both directions from that keystone/tarsus down through the metatarsus exactly as it was through the arch in the bridge.

She read the accompanying text. The upper part of the tarsus bone was called the talus. The talus was a socket into which the ball of the tibia (shinbone) fit. That meant that the weight of the body was going straight into the centre of the foot. Not into the heel. Not into the toe. Shenute placed her right hand on her right foot. Funny, she had always thought that this was her ankle, this bump, but it wasn't; it was just a protective protuberance of the tibia bone. Her ankle, the actual joint, was above this bump, where the bone fitted into the socket of the talus. She started to move her foot. Why did it always rotate out when she walked?

She sat down on a chair and held her lower leg with both hands, immobilizing it, in order to isolate the range of movement of her foot. She noticed it could move *in* quite a bit, but hardly *out* at all. Why then, when she had practiced The Walk in class, had her feet splayed out at least forty-five degrees? She checked and double checked, but each time it was impossible to make her foot turn outward the way it had in class. Where had that movement come from? She thought about it. Clearly, it wasn't her toes that caused her peculiar walk, so it must have something to do with another part of her body. The knee?

She turned the page. Plate XLI: Bone Structure of the Lower Limb. The knee consists of three bones: the femur and tibia and fibula. In front of these is a small little bone, the kneecap, called the patella. She put her hand on that bony protuberance. The patella was what Shenute had always thought of as her knee. But the knee — the actual joint — was where the femur (thigh bone) and tibia met. The patella had nothing to do with it. It was just a little bit of bony protection. The knee was a hinge. It could only move one way, forward or back. No twisting action could originate at the knee. So the problem with her feet had to originate somewhere else.

She turned the page. Plate XLV: The Hip Joint and Its Movements. She looked at the place where the femur joined the pelvis. It was L-shaped and it fit like a ball in a socket. The book had a number of quick sketches of the hip joint in action. The femur had a tremendous range of movement.

Here she had been living in her body for twenty years and she had never really thought about it once. She had fed it, cleaned it, dressed it, moved it about. Never had she tried to understand it. Or even think about it. That night, as she drifted to sleep, instead of going over the Coptic texts in her head, she found herself thinking about The Walk. She visualized herself looking like Sheila gliding across the hardwood floor.

If the splaying of her foot didn't originate in her ankle, and couldn't originate in her knee, then it had to have something to do with her hip joint. That much Shenute had figured out already. The next night, after lean chicken with broccoli and one pat of butter, she sat down with the anatomy book again. This time she opened it up to The Pelvic Girdle.

The sacrum is wedged between the two iliac bones. The body weight rests upon the sacrum. Under the weight of the pelvis it behaves like a two-armed lever. It is an elastic arch with the function of transferring body weight evenly through the hip joints.

Another arch. Here the keystone was the sacrum. Of course! The spine ended in the sacrum, so the entire weight of the torso came down onto this keystone where it was transferred out and down through the iliac bones to the hip joint. Shenute stood. She thought about her sacrum and then she slowly lifted one leg from her hip and looked at the toes — they were straight. Then she put her leg down. The toes remained straight. She picked up the other foot very slowly, brought it forward and looked at her toes — they were straight. Then she put her foot down. She did it again. Each time she lifted her leg from her hip joint, her toes would hit the floor pointing straight ahead. So why did they splay out when she walked?

She walked a few steps and realized it must have something to do with the fact that she was pushing her pelvis forward. That's where the problem originated — not in her toes at all, but in her sacrum. She concentrated on moving her spine up from her sacrum, and as she did she felt her upper body move forward and her knees start to lift. She let them. The knee lifted up and then the foot came down — straight! She could hardly believe it. She tried it again with the other foot. The knee floated up, the foot came down — straight. That was it! That was The Walk! That night she practised it again and again. Unlike at class, the more she practised, the better she got.

She practised all week. Every chance she got, she practised. She practised at home. She practised walking to and from work. She practised in the washroom at the museum. Practice, practice, practice.

"Squeeze the penny, squeeze the penny," Sheila was saying.

Shenute now knew exactly what "the penny" was. By getting Jackie to imagine holding a penny in her bottom, she was getting her to contract her gluteus maximus muscles. The gluteus maximus joined the ilia to the femur and by contracting it, the femur would be stabilized and the wiggle eliminated.

"Toes forward, toes forward," Sheila said as Jackie did The Walk.

But it wasn't toes, it had nothing to do with the toes. When it was Shenute's turn, instead of concentrating on her feet as she had in the first class, she concentrated on her keystone, the sacrum.

Sheila was amazed.

"Someone's been practising," she said. Then she turned to the other girls. "Do you see girls, the improvement Shenute has made? That's what comes of practice."

"Coo."

"Yeh."

"Nice, Shen."

But Shenute knew it was more than practice. She had thought about the problem. She had figured it out. This would set the pattern for the next fifteen weeks. She would listen to what the instructor wanted, usually perform dismally in class, then go home, study her anatomy texts and figure out how to achieve the desired effect on her own. For every hour spent in the class, she was spending ten at home. That night the group spent the first hour reviewing The Walk and the next two studying The Look.

At the end of the class, Shenute bought the school's Basic Makeup Kit: contour powder, highlighter, blusher, mascara, lipstick, foundation, eyebrow powder and an assortment of sable-hair brushes. But she didn't even open her makeup kit that night. Instead she took out her anatomy book and opened it to Bones of the Face.

Again, she found that there was more to it than Sheila had told them. Sheila had handed out a sheet of paper showing the four basic face shapes: Oval, Round, Square, Heart-shaped. But the face was so much more than that. The face consisted of frontal, parietal, occipital, temporal, nasal and mandible bones and within each of those categories there were hundreds of muscles and ligaments that produced a vast variety of facial expressions.

All weekend, she experimented with the kit. Because she had never used makeup Shenute looked at it with fresh eyes. It was so much more fascinating and complicated than simply dabbing on blusher or powdering your nose. The zygomatic arch was a symmetrical bone with three surfaces and three processes. It connected the frontal and temporal bone to the maxilla. Depending on which surface she highlighted, she could make her face look narrower or wider.

In the modelling school Shenute found a sanctuary. The more she worked on her walk, her turns and her makeup, the better she felt. Out on the streets of London, she was invisible, but inside, at the school, her every gesture, every move was observed and perfected. She could powder and cream and lipstick herself into existence.

The tap on the door was the landlady summoning Shenute to the hall phone. It was her father, "touching base." He'd finished his keynote address and had popped it in the post that afternoon. Merely a first draft, but he'd appreciate Shenute's observations. Of course, there would be eminent scholars there far more knowledgeable than he on every aspect of Gnosticism, but he was hoping his own humble effort would provide a general overview. Tie things together, so to speak.

Her father had been working to help organize this conference for over two years. It was to be held in Italy, in Messina, and scholars in all the various disciplines relating to the find were gathering together. The Gnostics had only been known through the writings of their enemies for the last fifteen hundred years. Now through the

Nag Hammadi texts, for the first time, they would be able to speak for themselves.

Of course the scholar he was most proud of was the one he himself had trained. His own daughter, his pride and joy. He had bestowed upon her his years and years of painful study, and she had been able to learn easily and effortlessly things that had taken him a lifetime to acquire. He was in awe of her, and he had always treated her as an equal. He had shared every bit of knowledge he had been able to glean with her, viewing her little person as merely a container for her fabulous mind. Her mind was what interested him. Her mind was what he could relate to. You have a fine mind, he would say to her, and it was the highest compliment he could give. Her person, her body, was the uninteresting cabinet that held this treasure. But now the cabinet itself was starting to interest Shenute and she couldn't share that with him. He wouldn't see it.

She had let go of the receiver, balancing it between her ear and shoulder, and held her hands out before her.

"How's everything at your end?"

"Mm? Fine," she answered.

Her hands were really quite pretty. The fingers were long and slender, the moons poked out above the cuticles the way the magazines said they should.

"Just think," he said, "all those years of work and in a few short months you'll be presenting it to the world."

The world? A few hundred old men was hardly the world. The world was all around her. London was teeming with life.

"Are you all right, Shenute?"

"Mm? Yes. Just busy."

For once her father's involvement with her life grated. He had always known every deadline, every professor, every journal. The beauty of Beauty was her father knew nothing about it. There was a secret part of her that he couldn't advise her on, wouldn't even approve of.

He had her mind, but her hands were her own.

"'Aven't any choice, do we? Gonna end up like our mums stuck wif a man, might as well get the best we can. Someone wif some prospects. Someone wif a future. Not some bloke slams yer up against th' wall in some back alley then finks 'es doin' yer a favour walkin' yer ter th' tube afterards. Ta."

The waitress had brought their drinks. Pam continued without missing a beat.

"Nooo...want some bloke, takes yer to dinner, buys yer some flowers, treats yer wif class. Teach yer class, that place does. 'Ain't nuffin' but a bunch of tricks, class ain't. Don' wiggle yer arse, stuff it wif a penny."

The girls giggled. Shenute along with them. She could hardly believe where she was and what she was doing. When they'd asked her after class if she'd like to come to Bob's with them, she'd said yes, but she'd been amazed at her own boldness — going to a boy's home she didn't even know. It wasn't until they were across the street from The Bucket of Blood that she got it: BOB, Bucket Of Blood. They did that with so many things. They spoke in acronyms, elisions and synecdoches. Everything was metaphor. Everything stood for something else. It usually took Shenute a few moments to figure it out.

As they raised their mugs, Pam was speaking.

"Roger the lodger 'ad a bad cough."

Stef picked up on it, "'E sneezed so 'ard, 'is doorknob fell off."

Then Viv, then Pam.

"'Is landlady said, we'll soon 'ave yer well."

"So she pulled off 'er drawers, 'an polished his bell!"

They all roared with laughter and clinked glasses.

Bell. Shenute, who had spent her whole life translating dead languages, was suddenly finding herself translating a living one. She was amazed at how much gesture informed the words — the lift of a shoulder, the flick of a tongue — and suddenly an incomprehensible phrase made sense.

"What's yer choice? Work in a bleedin' fish 'n chips shop yer whole bleedin' life? Come 'ome stinkin' a cod or 'addock. Noo...'ook yerself a good'un, 'at's what I say. Make 'im do the dirty work."

Shenute wondered how many of the phrases in the Nag Hammadi text she'd been having trouble with were something to do with this. She thought of all the sss and tssus that other scholars had deemed untranslatable. If she could sit among the living people, would those sounds make sense? Were they any stranger than Viv being Tina's Skin and Blister, or "oozy" meaning "who is he"?

"All we got's our looks, eh? Best get goin' on it early while we still got 'em. 'Ow old are yer then, twenny?"

Shenute came out of her thoughts. Pam was addressing her directly. She nodded in response.

"None too soon. Best get goin' on it early."

"Wait till she finishes the Course," Steffie giggled.

"Nooo, got to get to work on it early. Practice, practice, practice. See them blokes over there?" Pam nodded her head ever so slightly indicating a bunch of fellows playing darts. "Ain't one of 'em that really strikes me fancy, but what's the 'arm in a little practice? Show Shen some of the tricks?" She turned to Shenute. "Pick one out. Like a card, yeh, pick any one ya like."

Shenute glanced furtively at the boys. There was one who was taller than the rest wearing a leather jacket.

"The one with the leather jacket," she said.

"Juss watch," Pam said, then she winked at Shenute. "Dunno 'bout you girls, but I'm feelin' a bit pecky. 'Ow 'bout some chips, eh?"

"I'm for that," said Tina.

"Me too," said Steffie, signalling the waitress.

"Got to develop our skills. Most fellas ain't worth the bother, but they use us, why shouldn't we use them? Practise on ones ya don't like, so yer ready when one pops up ya do. Snag a goodun', then do what yer like — eat choclits, 'ave babies and chat wif the girls."

The waitress put an enormous plate of piping hot chips before them and they all tucked in. Shenute kept wondering when Pam would make her move. Would she stride over and talk to him? It was all very exciting. But Pam didn't do anything. She laughed, talked, ate her chips and sipped at her beer. Shenute wasn't thinking about the fellows at all when the one in the leather jacket came over to their table.

"'Evenin' ladies," he said, looking right at Pam. "C'n I join yer?"

"Suit yerself," Pam said, and the fellow dragged an empty chair from one of the other tables and sat astride it, beer in hand, while the girls giggled and Shenute watched.

"Wass yer name?" he asked.

"Yer ain't arf nosey," Pam said. The girls all laughed.

"Wass the joke?" he said, glancing at the girls.

"Why did the policewoman marry the 'angman?" Pam said.

"Eh?"

"They bofe liked neckin'."

The girls all laughed some more.

"Thass the joke," Pam said. "Now you tell one."

"Right then. What did the midwife say to the nun?"

"Dunno," Pam said.

The fellow leaned over to Pam and whispered into her ear. Pam's face went suddenly serious.

"Your mind wants boilin' in carbolic," she said. "Sod off."

"C'mon, I was juss jokin'…"

"Sod off. I mean it. I'm wif me girlfrens. Don' need your filth spoilin' our nice time t'gether, now sod off."

It took a minute or two for the fellow to get it through his head, his "thick" head as Pam kept saying, that the game was over. Over before it had begun. Finally, he left. When he was back at the dart-board, Pam turned to the girls.

"'Ad ever so much trouble keepin' me face straight," she said. Then she turned to Shenute. "Juss a game. If you don' like 'em, throw 'em back. See 'ow it's done?"

Shenute shook her head. She didn't have a clue how Pam had singled out one fellow from an entire pub and got him to come over to their table.

"Look," she said. "It's all in the eyes."

She faced Shenute, and for a fleeting moment opened her eyes wide. Shenute tried it.

"Nooo," Pam said. "Ya missed it. No eyebrows, see?"

She did it again and this time, Shenute saw. Pam had opened her eyes wide without raising her eyebrows, or altering her face in any other way. It was so subtle as to be almost unnoticeable.

"Go 'ome an' try it in front the mirror," Pam said. "Get it so slight they don' know ya done it to 'em. You'll see. Brings 'em in like flies to 'oney." She winked. "Practice, practice, practice."

Her body was taking over. It was making demands. It was so much more insistent than her work. By day, she continued translating at the museum, but by night she experimented with different Looks in her flat. She started going to work with her hair loose about her shoulders. She also wore a pale pink lipstick, one coat of mascara and clear lacquer on her nails, but that was it.

But even these subtle changes were making a difference. Her whole life she had been going up to librarians and requesting books. She had always been regarded as no more than a catalogue number, another call slip that needed to be processed. But now the man behind the counter would invariably look up, smile and make some comment such as, "Seems interesting" or "No one's taken this out for a while." Shenute would nod and then return to her cubicle. She was no longer invisible. It felt good.

Her bathroom shelves filled up with ungents and astringents. Foot creams, handcreams, undereye creams, neck creams. Lotions and potions for every particular body part! She began buying fresh lemons and cutting them in half and rubbing her knees and elbows with them, then following that with a rich cream made with cocoa butter. Lemons and cocoa butter each night before going to bed, an all-over lemon-scented lotion each morning to be lavished on after a tepid shower. In order to get her Morning Beauty Routine and exercises in and still be at the museum on time, Shenute was rising at six.

There was one morning when Shenute didn't rise at six. Her alarm didn't go off and when she awoke it was already eight o'clock. She threw back the covers and leapt out of bed cursing the fact that she had no time for her routine that morning. This would be the first time in five weeks that she'd missed it. She was hastily pulling a comb through her hair when it hit her. She didn't have to go. She could stay home. She was her own boss. A scholar. She could arrange her hours the way she pleased. And why not? Her whole life had been spent training her mind. Why not just one day for her body? "A Spa Day at Home." Tomorrow she would return to her texts.

"Nuffing I likes better'n spendin' uvver peoples' money," Pam said, poking through the racks.

It was Saturday and the girls were in the frock shop where Steffie worked. They were laughing and giggling, pulling outfits off racks and shoving them back, handing some to Shenute and some to each other with squeals of "Ain't that somefing, though?" and "Catch yer cold in this, eh?"

Shenute slipped into the changeroom. Slowly, she unbuttoned her blouse. It was one of ten such blouses made for her by the woman who kept her father's apartment. Her name was embroidered into the collar. She knew as she let it drop to the floor that she was going to leave it there. Likewise the grey skirt she let fall around her ankles then gently kicked into the corner.

This past Monday she had arrived home from the museum feeling tired and slightly depressed. She had been looking forward to running a bath, sinking into warm scented water and letting the soot and grime of London wash away. Before climbing the stairs, she had picked up her packet of mail from the hall table. It wasn't until the water was running that she opened the letter from The Foundation for the Study of Biblical Literature and Exegesis. She'd completely forgotten about her application.

A cheque dropped out. Retrieving it, she could hardly believe her eyes: five hundred pounds. A colossal sum. In the accompanying letter, the chairman of the Foundation congratulated her on her "invaluable contribution." The Nag Hammadi manuscripts were "one of the most important finds of the twentieth century" and her work on translating them was of "rare historical importance." It went on to say that the Foundation had been set up by many benefactors for the study of scriptures and texts relating to the scriptures and the committee was unanimous in its decision that her work eminently qualified. The chairman iterated that the cheque was to be in no way construed as payment for services, either past or future. Another cheque would follow in six months. It was a small acknowledgement of the important contribution she had already made to the field, and hopefully would encourage her in further pursuits of her own choosing. Shenute knew exactly what her further pursuits would be.

She slipped one of the dresses she had chosen over her head. It was a simple burgundy pinafore that came to just above her knee. She had chosen it because she could imagine herself wearing it to the conference in Messina. She would wear her hair up with simple gold hoops in her ears.

The second dress she tried on was black with a white collar and cuffs. She could wear this to the museum. It was elegant but not too fancy.

"Less 'ave a look, then," Pam said, "You don' 'alf take yer time."

Shenute stepped out into the store.

"Coo, very nice."

"Yeh, 'ave tea wif the Queen Mum in 'at."

"Very smart, Shen."

When Shenute was back in the changeroom she handed the Burgundy and the Black out to Steffie, who kept them for her behind the counter. She was about to try on a black skirt she'd selected when a dress came soaring over the top of the changeroom door. Pam's hand was attached to it.

"'Ere," she said. "Try this."

It was not what Shenute would have chosen. It was what they called a Jersey Knit. It was lime green with wide pink stripes travelling horizontally around it. It looked to Shenute like a sweater, not a dress at all. It looked like something she might wear with sensible black slacks if it came in navy and tan instead of green and pink. When she tried it on it seemed so short she was afraid to come out. She wouldn't have, if not for Pam reaching in and pulling her out.

"Less 'ave a look," Pam said, and before she knew it, Shenute was standing right out in the centre of the store where there was a big mirror and the girls stood watching.

"Oo, I like that, don' you, Stef?"

"Very nice," Steffie nodded. "Could do with a belt, though."

"Yeh, yeh," Tina said. "'And us a belt."

Steffie reached up to pluck a three-inch wide white belt from a rack behind the counter while Shenute stared at herself in the mirror.

Could she actually wear this anywhere? So much of her thigh was showing she was embarrassed. The dress clung to her body, even with the ten pounds lost. Stef was putting the belt around her, but not around her waist. She buckled the belt on the second to last notch so that it hung loosely about her hips.

"Nice legs, ain't she, Teen?"

"Yeh... we never knew." They burst into giggles again.

"Can you see my..." Shenute started to ask, then stopped.

"What, Shen, yer tush?"

She nodded as they giggled.

"No, ducks, we can't see yer tushy."

They watched as Shenute turned around and saw what seemed like the full length of the backs of her thighs exposed.

"Seriously, Shen," Tina said. "It looks great. Buy it."

"I'll think about — "

"Buy it," Pam interrupted. "'Ere, try this one."

When Shenute emerged wearing the yellow velvet mini-dress, the girls were even more enthusiastic.

"Oo, it's you, luv."

"Coo, what I wouldn' give — "

"Where would I wear it?" Shenute asked.

"Take yer anywhere...it's so simpow."

It was simple. It was just an A-line dress with gathered sleeves and neck, but it happened to be made out of saffron-coloured velvet and the hem was a foot above her knees. Shenute was amazed at how much such a small piece of cloth cost, but she bought it. She bought it, and the Jersey Knit, and the belt, and the orange and blue number that Tina picked out, and a flannel smock dress with thin vertical stripes that Stef said had just come in. And of course the black and white tea dress and the burgundy pinafore.

Steffie got off at three, and they had arranged to meet at Mumford's for high tea. They pulled things out of bags and oohed and aahed over each item all over again. Tina had bought a bubble blouse and Pam a kite-coat.

"An' this for me mum," Pam said, lifting some teal blue gloves out of one of her shopping bags. "Evvy paycheque," she said, "I buy somefing for meself and somefing for me mum."

"Coo, we ought to do this evvy Sattaday, oughtn't we, girls?" Steffie said.

As Shenute sipped her tea she thought that a few more Saturdays like this would soon take care of her windfall. But she didn't care. She'd had such fun.

As her Look changed, so did her personality. Now, when the man behind the desk at the museum made a comment, she smiled at him and met his gaze. She started lingering at the water cooler. She liked finishing her little paper cone of water, flipping it jauntily into the waste-basket, turning and feeling the men's eyes on her as she strode back to her cubicle. She was becoming a different person. She liked this new person. This new person had power, personal power. And she was beginning to think it was the only kind of power, because all the degrees and all the accolades and kudos had never, ever, made her feel this way.

Her father had always told her that with each degree she attained her confidence would grow, but it hadn't. She'd always felt inferior to the old men because she knew she wasn't an old man. And everywhere else in the world, each degree just made her more and more of a freak, a brain, an egghead, someone most people didn't want to have anything to do with. But this was different. With each new transformation she felt her personal power growing. Suddenly men weren't something to be in awe of, they were just jibbering idiots who smiled and stammered and stuttered when she appeared.

On the night of the last class Shenute left work early so as to have time to prepare. Sheila had told them they would spend the evening holding a mock fashion show followed by a party with wine and cheese. This would be the first time she'd worn the velvet mini outside her flat. She slipped it on and zipped it up and stood before the full-length mirror.

The mini came to about mid-thigh. Her long legs shimmered in glittery hose. Her hair hung loose about her shoulders and when she tossed her hair the little yellow and orange baubles dangling from her ears flashed and disappeared again. She looked like something out of a magazine. Her transformation was complete.

As she reached for her rings — one for the middle finger of each hand — there was a knock at the door. She opened it expecting to see the landlady.

It was her father.

"So sorry…" he was already turning to leave and mumbling an apology, when he swung around again. "Good Lord."

Shenute felt her body contract, her shoulders rise, her head pull down. She wanted nothing more in that moment than to disappear. To bolt. But she recovered. She remembered The Stance. Moving from her sacrum, she did it. She opened the door wide and Cyril Morton stepped in.

His face was ashen. His mouth set. There was a tiny pulse at the back of his jaw.

This was an encounter Shenute hadn't prepared herself for. Her father had never dropped by unexpectedly; his visits were always preceded by a note or a phone call.

"Dreadfully sorry...can't offer you tea...I have an appointment."

There was silence while her father looked around. He took in the full-length mirror, the shelves of ungents and potions, the stacks of magazines.

She maintained The Stance.

"An appointment?"

"Yes. I'm already late."

She knew exactly what he was thinking. She knew because he had thought his thoughts through her. When she had first arrived in London, she had looked at the Pams and Tinas on the street with his eyes. They were foolish, they were ignorant, they were flibbertigibbets. They were brainless and inconsequential. They were girls.

"You're not wearing *that* to the conference."

Of course she wouldn't wear a saffron velvet mini to a scholarly conference; she'd bought the burgundy pinafore for that, but her father just went on.

"I won't be made a laughing-stock in front of my colleagues."

His colleagues. His conference. His reputation.

Shenute didn't reply. Instead she shifted her weight onto her other foot and crooked her hand on her hip. She hardly heard his words.

"...not appropriate for a scholar..."

Why couldn't a beautiful young girl be a scholar? Why did scholars have to be old men with wrinkles and phlegm? Was a beautiful young body incompatible with a mind?

"...make me look ridiculous..."

She couldn't believe it. As long as she'd done exactly as her father wished, he was pleasant, benevolent and generous. But the moment she had done something on her own initiative, a different person was emerging. Rigid, authoritarian...

"...done up like a tart..."

...and abusive.

Was that all it took? A saffron mini and some pantihose to bring this creature out? Was she to spend her whole life chained to a desk like a medieval monk? Was she to have no life of her own outside of the texts? Was she to marry someone like him — dull and grey and dead?

But no! Not even he would marry her. He had married a beautiful Egyptian woman who treated him like a king, bringing his slippers and pipe, running his bath. Was Shenute to be another woman whose whole purpose in life was to reflect glory on him? Not domestic glory, but scholarly? A trained bear whose trainer gets all the accolades?

"Say something."

What was there to say? She had never talked to him. They'd discussed, compared and analysed together, but they'd never talked father to daughter. She looked at his tight mouth and throbbing jaw and realized that they never could.

"I have an appointment."

"It can wait."

Shenute picked up her bag, turned on her heel and walked out. A moment later she was flying down the stairs. She reached the bottom landing, opened the door and stepped out onto the street.

A cab screeched to a halt. She opened the door and stepped in.

"Bishop's Gate, please."

When the cab pulled up in front of the modelling school, Shenute's heart was still pounding. She paid her fare then climbed the stairs. Everyone had dressed to the nines, and the outfits were extraordinary — psychedelic colours and space-age materials, eyes made up to look like butterflies, epaulets of aluminum, gold braid over mock military jackets, fishnet stockings, go-go boots, a see-through blouse. Only a few months earlier, Shenute would have been terrified by this strange conglomeration of people, but she wasn't terrified, she was having fun. She was one of them. They loved her dress, they loved her pantihose, they loved her hair and her eyes and her nail polish.

Suddenly the sound of the Beatles' *A Hard Day's Night* blared forth. That was their cue. They lined up alphabetically in front of the coat hooks, as planned, and that put Shenute right in the middle.

They would do The Walk and Sheila would improvise a little patter. Shenute had chosen the velvet over the Jersey Knit because it was dressier, but also because it had a slight flare to it, which would give her something to do with her hands. When it was her turn, she walked to the centre of the room, letting her arms swing freely. After her first turn she adjusted her sleeves, then, standing in front of Sheila, displayed the flare with a sweep of one hand, turned and headed for the mirrors. She then made her way back to the centre of the room where, hands on hips, she executed a full turn and strode off back into the line-up.

Shenute knew she'd done well, but she was still surprised during the party afterwards when Sheila took her aside.

"Shenute," she said, "I've watched you. More than any other girl here, you've improved. For most of these girls, this is just one more evening out. It's a lark. A bit of fantasy. But it means more to you, doesn't it?"

Shenute nodded.

"I don't say this to everyone," Sheila continued, "because I don't believe in getting anyone's hopes up. It's a very difficult business. But you have the one quality that a model needs, Shenute."

What? Bone structure? Her figure? Hair? But when the answer came it was none of these.

"Desire."

"WHY DON'T YOU GO SEE BREETZ IN LONDON?" Elizabeth suggested. "My treat."

We were sitting in the former conservatory, now Action Central of the Toronto anti-war movement, and from the kitchen I could hear the sound of people talking over the music of The Mamas and the Papas.

"You'd have a fabulous time," she continued. "The theatre scene is the most vibrant it's been in years...and then there's The Tate."

Where so many of Blake's paintings and etchings were housed. My mother was clearly trying to entice me into taking her up on this offer. She was worried about Breetz, though why I couldn't fathom. Breetz had arrived in London at precisely the right moment. Suddenly photographers were becoming celebrities and their names as well known as the models they photographed. They were sought after all over London. No party was complete without one.

"He was drinking."

Something about the way she said it made me pause.

"Drinking?" I said. "Breetz has always been a drinker."

"Not like this," my mother said. "The afternoon he was here, he downed an entire bottle of scotch. I think it would be a good idea for you to go and see him. He's your oldest friend."

I sipped at my coffee. My mother's life had completely changed but she hadn't considered the possibility that mine had changed too. That I wasn't really interested in traipsing around after Breetz any more.

"He'd show you a great time."

"I'm sure he would," I said.

"Will you think about it?"

I got up and walked over to the far wall. What had begun with the photo of the Buddhist monk immolating himself had grown into a montage. There were photos of the war, soldiers interrogating blindfolded Vietnamese, bombs exploding over peasant huts. There were also photos of the anti-war movement. An aerial shot of a huge demonstration. A hippie defying a policeman.

"That's Xtro," my mother said.

I didn't reply. Instead I turned and said, "I think I'll go upstairs and lie down for a few minutes before dinner."

"You do that," she said. "I'll go help in the kitchen."

Everything in that house had changed. Elizabeth was sleeping in my old room, the master bedroom and study had been turned into dorms and the living and dining rooms were filled with tables and phones and mimeograph machines. I went upstairs. The door to the darkroom was still locked. I put my hand in my pocket and pulled out my keychain. I unlocked the door and turned on the light.

Everything was exactly the same. The shelves still contained the rows of chemicals. There was the interval timer, the scissors, the magnifying glass. The little clothesline where we hung the developed prints was still strung across the room with its drying clips attached. The four-drawer filing cabinet was still in the corner. I was about to step out when instead I stepped in.

What I stepped into was the Past. Ever since he was thirteen Breetz had been taking photographs, and every one of those photographs was in that cabinet. Negatives, contact sheets and developed prints. I went over to the filing cabinet and started thumbing through. There were photos of Anna, photos of me and Elizabeth, photos of all sorts of girls we'd known as kids. As I flipped through, the photos became more and more professional looking. I started to find photos of girls who were clearly aspiring models. There were dozens and dozens of a brunette I remembered Breetz photographing on and off for almost two years. There were hundreds of photos from the sessions he'd done over Halberstam's. I kept flipping until finally I found it.

Why had I not known? I *had* known. I'd known all along and yet something had stopped it from seeping into my consciousness. The photo of the girl with the hair was Kate.

I lifted the entire file out of its folder, took it over to the counter and opened it. Underneath the developed photo was a standard release form. There in her familiar hand was the signature: Katlyn Barnes.

Kate.

I picked up the magnifying glass and one by one went through the photos on the contact sheet. There she was, Kate, with long blonde hair. She was standing, looking at the camera. She looked awkward, pained, uncomfortable. The other girls were strutting and posing and she just stood there looking miserable, each shot more pained and awkward than the one before. Then I came to the point where I remembered Breetz starting his beautiful, beautiful, beautiful number. I remembered that he'd focused in on her hair. The next three photos showed Kate bent over, throwing her hair, as Breetz had insisted she do. There was some sort of distortion or blob over her head and the photo itself seemed out of focus. Then suddenly there it was: the photo of the hair. The one I'd insisted Breetz develop. The one that had turned out to be the most beautiful photograph of his youth. Even on the contact sheet it seemed much bigger than the square inch it in fact occupied. Then I looked again at the enlargement. So that's what Daniel Lloyd had meant...

Whatever it is she does on stage, she can also do on film.

She had done something. Kate had done something. Kate, or Katlyn, or Roxanne, or whoever it was. Whatever her magic, it had flashed forth for an instant there and Breetz had caught it on film.

I gathered up the entire contents of the file — negatives, contacts, release form and print — and put them back in the folder. I took the file, turned off the light and left the darkroom. I locked it but instead of putting the key back on my ring I placed it up on the moulding where it had been before. Then I went downstairs, stopping on the way into the kitchen to slip the file into my overnight case. Everyone was just sitting down to dinner.

SHENUTE'S NEW FLAT was the upper part of a bijou terrace house in Chelsea. It had been converted so that what was once a single family home now had three flats and an attic room. Daniela and Tamsin were on the second floor. They had been looking for a third flatmate when they'd met Shenute at the agency soon after she'd signed on.

Although the apartment was in one of the swishest districts of London, inside it was much like an anchorite cell. It was a place of ritual and devotion. Where Pam and Tina had been all chips and treats and noshing it with the blokes at Dirty Dick's, Daniela and Tamsin were all deprivation. They would go days without food in order to lose a single pound. There were strange cycles to their fasts, the way there was in the church calendar. When a shoot was coming up it was like Easter in that it was preceded by Lent, a period of fasting and mortification.

Daniela had done the most print work and a photo from every shoot she'd ever done was pinned to the walls of her bedroom. In real life she was thin and pale and very nervous, but her photographs showed a long-legged flaming-haired beauty with a haughty disposition.

Tamsin was arrogant and given to erratic bursts of temper but her peaches and cream complexion and her unnaturally pale blue eyes made her look fragile and delicate in her photos. She had done a lot of bridal work.

Shenute was amazed when she saw the first prints of her own photos at how sensual she appeared. There was probably no girl in London with less sexual experience than Shenute Morton, yet the face that gazed out from her portfolio suggested the sultry allure of a woman of the world. She photographed sexy. All three of them had what the agency called "flesh-impact."

While their bedroom walls held their own photos, the walls of the living room were reserved for photos from the glossies. All the top photographers were represented — Helmut Newton, David Bailey, Breetz Mestrovic, Richard Avedon — for it was the photographers who interested Tamsin and Daniela, not the competition.

Every time the name Breetz Mestrovic was mentioned Shenute suppressed a little shiver. She had never told anyone about that day in front of the British Museum. He had noticed her and this notice had started her on her strange quest. At times she thought she must have imagined it. But no, the embossed card still lay at the bottom of her jewellery box. Breetz Mestrovic.

Tamsin and Daniela knew everything about him, how he had been discovered by Diana Vreeland, how he had taken New York by storm, how he had launched Ulrika Wiklund. Now he was living in London.

Through all this Shenute kept quiet.

Yes, she had gone to Messina and given her paper and, yes, it had been a great success. Her father had been very pleased, but the conference had only served to strengthen Shenute's resolve. After all, when every last bit of dry papyrus had turned to dust, who was it people still remembered? The Great Beauties. Cleopatra, Nefertiti, Helen of Troy. They had achieved something no interpreter or translator of texts ever could. As long as men breathed, their images remained alive. She wanted that.

She'd gone from simply wanting to be noticed to wanting so much more. When she returned to London her mind was made up. She would pursue Beauty. She would strive to become one of those rare women who embodied an age.

"Modelling is hard work," the woman at the agency had said. "Modelling is getting up early and pounding the pavement with your portfolio in hand. Modelling is never being able to eat everything you want. Modelling is getting to bed early because you might have to spend ten hours on a photo shoot. Modelling is hurry up and wait. You have to remain professional and upbeat and, above all, beautiful through all this. You must not get a pimple, you must not gain a pound and a change in hairstyle could result in the loss of a year's bookings. Alternatively, it could result in three years' worth of bookings. It's a strange business. You still want to do it?"

Shenute nodded.

"Of course you do. Lose ten pounds and you'll be perfect."

The second ten was much harder to lose than the first but in less than six weeks Shenute had done it. The agency arranged a portfolio shoot. It was during these days that she had met Tamsin and Daniela. Shenute knew that if she was to become as beautiful as she desired to be, she would have to commit herself totally, immerse herself in that world. And so when the girls had sounded her out about moving in with them, she had readily accepted. She had been living with them now for three months.

Their days were long and hard and often yielded no work at all. Each morning began with a tepid shower, half an hour's exercise and then makeup. When doing the rounds you weren't to wear too much makeup because art directors wanted to see what you looked like. It took each of the girls two hours to achieve the look of not too much makeup. The people they saw were usually art directors, fashion consultants or layout editors who thought nothing of turning a girl away with a blunt "too busty," "too toothy" or "too short." Occasionally, you would get a call-back from a house that had turned you away only a few days before because so-and-so remembered you and thought you might be right for something. You never knew. You had to always be on because that boy you smiled at by the watercooler might just possibly have the ear of the art director and mention you as a possibility for the Yardley ad. You never knew.

Sometimes they would meet for lunch. All eyes were on them as they nibbled their lettuce and carrot sticks and toyed with their cottage cheese. If one of them developed a pimple, everything stopped and all three of them sympathised and waited out the onslaught. They would try every bizarre remedy for the offending spot from toothpaste to alcohol to hot compresses and Fuller's Earth. Only when they were beautiful again would they again venture out.

The shoots were long and gruelling. One day Daniela was modelling swimwear in a studio. For weeks she had been dieting strenuously in preparation. The shoot had started at eight o'clock in the morning and had lasted all day. The photographer was becoming increasingly irritated and demanding. He would get Daniela posed on the "sand" and no sooner was she down there than he would want her up on the swing, then back down on the sand again. As she was making the transition for the fiftieth time she keeled over in a dead faint. Ever afterwards this particular photographer would refer to Daniela as "difficult."

Tamsin was never difficult. She would spend whole days in a shoot smiling and being delicate and beautiful, then she would come home and tear up her clothes in a rage or throw a vase. Shenute and Daniela were often afraid of Tamsin, she was violent and unpredictable, but they understood it. Each of them had different ways of handling the tension. Shenute would sometimes disappear into a nineteenth-century novel and not emerge for days. Daniela would go on crying jags and weep on and off for as long as twenty-four hours. Just as they had different styles of coping with tension, so also they had different styles of dieting.

Daniela would pick a particular fruit or vegetable and eat nothing but that and water. This was her style — eat all you want of nothing. One day she was wolfing down a head of lettuce when Tamsin entered the kitchen.

"A whole head?" Tamsin sneered. Daniela burst into tears.

Tamsin was a calorie counter. She had a little book in which she would enter the caloric value of everything she put in her body, including black coffee.

They were like the Desert Fathers who wrote in Coptic. Marsius of Alexandria stood upright for an entire Lent, eating nothing but cabbage once a week. John of Egypt subsisted on seeds and water like a bird. A Gnostic sect called the Browsers subsisted on roots, leaves and grass, believing that if they followed the example of

Nebuchadnezzar in his madness they would recover their lost likeness to God.

Shenute would learn every trick, study every method, humble herself before her two mentors, then surpass them as she had surpassed Pam and Tina. She would diet more stringently. She would exercise longer. If it was good to cut yourself down to twelve hundred calories, then it was better to eat only a thousand. And if a thousand was good, then nine hundred or even eight hundred was better still. Simon of Stylites went without food for the full Lenten season. In 422 at Kalat Seman in Northern Syria, he lived on a six-foot column, then built taller ones until he made his permanent home on a pillar some sixty feet high. He lived on that column without interruption for thirty years. If Simon of Stylites could live on a sixty-foot pillar for thirty years Shenute could subsist on eight hundred calories a day for a couple of weeks. Or so she reasoned.

When they ventured out in the evening it was usually to one of the hotel bars in Chelsea or Knightsbridge where the young London set went to see and be seen. They never drank alcohol but stood in their little dresses and sipped at club sodas through straws so as not to muss their lipstick. The whole purpose of life was to become as visible as possible and to the right people. It was not enough to be beheld, one had to be beheld by the right eyes. Tamsin and Daniela would quickly brief Shenute on who was who in the bar. One was a filmmaker, another the stylist from Leonard's, and that, that was Peter Cook from "Beyond the Fringe."

And while they were immersed in the *Who's Who* of the bar they were to look as if nothing really interested them, as if there was nothing better for their eyes to light upon than a distant wall, the staircase, the terrazzo floor. Immersed in it all, they must appear above it all. They were Icons of Beauty. They were to be observed and admired, not fondled and held.

She was no longer a freak. The more shows she did, the more shoots she went out on, the more cold calls she made, the more Shenute met young women just like her. One had been in Mathematics at Cambridge when she was spotted by an agent. Another had been an Olympic-calibre swimmer. Another had come from a family that boasted three members of parliament. Still another was distantly in line for the throne. Whereas the male designers were mostly school drop-outs cashing in on a flair for colour and line, the girls who modelled their clothes were often ludicrously well educated. They came from highly ambitious families who highly disapproved of their ambitions. They were over-achieving mannequins.

One day Daniela came back to the apartment trembling with excitement. She had spotted him. He was standing in a local bar with a group of women, talking. She had thought it was him and then she had asked the waiter. Yes, he'd said. That was him. Breetz Mestrovic. Quite the bloke. Always surrounded by women. Daniela had stood at the end of the bar, trying to get noticed, but it had been impossible. He wasn't like other men. He wasn't looking, he was looked at. Daniela surveyed the group of women around him — not just models, civilians too, obviously — and thought that this was the most impenetrable barrier she'd ever seen. A wall of rapt women. How could she get near him? The usual tricks were useless.

"I'll do it," Tamsin said, and immediately started plotting. They would stake out the bar. If he went there once he'd go there again. If the usual tactics wouldn't work then Tamsin would try more direct methods. Worm her way into the group. Introduce herself. Hang around. Hell, she'd spill something if need be.

Through all this Shenute kept quiet.

The plan went into effect immediately. The following evening they took a table at Clancy's and ordered the first of many rounds of club sodas. He didn't show up that night or the next. But the following week he did. He came into the bar with five women, two of them models the girls recognized. The bartender set up drinks and within moments everyone was laughing.

The girls waited another twenty minutes then Tamsin made her move. She got up, walked over to the bar and, as she was passing Breetz, turned suddenly as if to wave at a friend and in doing so knocked his drink. An instant later she was all aflutter, apologizing for her clumsiness. Breetz put a hand on her shoulder and held two fingers up to the bartender, ordering another drink for him and one for Tamsin.

"I could never do that," Daniela turned to Shenute. Her hand was shaking. "I just know I could never do that."

Shenute said nothing.

By now Tamsin was part of the group. She was standing there looking at Breetz with rapt attention, listening to his stories. One more brick in the wall, Shenute thought.

"He's divorced, you know," Daniela said. "I read it in *The Tatler*. All terribly amiable. Flew down to Mexico with her husband-to-be, Philip Shaw. Shaw served as witness for his divorce, he acted as best man. Cool lot, aren't they?"

Shenute nodded.

"Not very good-looking, is he?" Daniela carried on. "Elegant, yes. Sexy, perhaps — if that's your type. But no one would call him handsome."

Shenute never looked at Breetz. She sipped quietly at her soda and listened to Daniela talk. At some point she became aware that he was looking in their direction. Slowly, she turned her head until she was looking right at him. This was the moment she had practised a thousand times in front of her mirror. Ever so subtly, she widened her eyes.

He returned her gaze. Then he did something astounding. Ever so subtly, he widened his eyes too.

Shenute burst out laughing.

A moment later he was standing in front of her.

"We've met," he said.

Shenute didn't reply.

"Outside the British Museum. You wore a grey skirt, grey cardigan and carried an enormous satchel. Your hair was combed straight back."

So he remembered. He remembered and he recognized her. She smiled. Then she introduced herself and Daniela. Breetz was friendly to Daniela but it was clear that his entire focus was on Shenute. He asked her to dinner. She accepted.

They taxied to an intimate French restaurant in Soho. He ordered for her. Breast of chicken in a white wine sauce, duchesse potatoes, salad, a robust soup. She had dessert and coffee. He told her she must eat. He told her that to be beautiful she needed her strength.

"This starving yourself is ridiculous," he said.

That night Shenute stayed with Breetz.

WE WERE MID-ATLANTIC, cruising at thirty thousand feet. The stewardess removed my tray and refilled my coffee cup. I reached into my breast pocket and took out Kate's letter. It was the fourth time I'd read it that day. All year Kate had been writing me. She wrote of the breakup of the Stikine — an explosive "bang" then massive chunks of ice heaving and hurtling down river. She wrote quite lyrically about the salmon running — the river black with their backs — and above, just as Ah Clem had said, hundreds upon hundreds of eagles circling. A few weeks later she had moved into her house. She wrote in great detail about getting it in shape, about cleaning the cabin and rebuilding the woodshed out back. She seemed to be forever cutting and stacking wood but no matter how much she stacked people who stopped by would say, Oh, you'll need more than that. Those letters had been long and rambling and rich in descriptive detail. But this one was short and to the point.

> Dear Richard,
>
> Your letter about the photographs has just reached me. I guess this is what you'd call a synchronistic (sp?) event. I can hardly believe that you were there and I don't remember you, but I do remember that through most of that shoot I was in a blind fury. Actually, that day is a lot like my whole life to that point. That photo session triggered something in me and I remember I left in a rage and cut off all my hair. The next day I left for Montreal. That all just seems so far away now. Richard, I don't think I want you to show those photos to anyone. The girl being photographed was Katlyn. Katlyn is as much a stranger to me as Roxanne. She was my mother's creation. A young beautiful girl with long strawberry-blonde hair whose only purpose in life was to be photographed. A Teen Tyme Barrette. The day I cut off my hair and threw it into the wind was the day I started to become me. I got sidetracked but I'm working on it again. At times I feel like I'm very very young, hardly formed. Then again, sometimes I feel like I've been around forever. Does that make sense? I think of you often.
>
> K

Extraordinary. I folded the letter and put it back in my pocket. A photo had been taken. That photo had changed Kate's life. Later I would learn it had changed Breetz's also. And still later, mine. But at the time I felt it had nothing really to do with me, that I was no more than a detached observer of the event. The scientist who observes the sub-atomic particles without affecting them. Something I now know is impossible.

Breetz met me at Heathrow. The moment I saw him I knew that while he would show me a great time I wouldn't necessarily have one. With him was his bride to be, Shenute Morton. To me she just seemed an exotic beauty — long black hair and almond eyes — I had no indication of what she would become. She was frivolous, vain and absolutely mad about Breetz.

They took me everywhere and I saw everything. Each place we went there was a Party, an Event or a Happening. There were so many people. Again and again I was introduced to someone who was described as a "genius." A hairdresser who was a genius with scissors. A makeup artist who was a genius with kohl. A designer who was a genius with buttons.

The wedding took place at the Arts Club Theatre. The impresario who ran the club was a friend of Breetz. Immediately after the evening show someone came out onstage and announced that the entire audience was invited to a wedding. Out of nowhere a band appeared. Chairs were cleared. Breetz beckoned me up onstage. The ceremony was brief. As soon as Breetz and Shenute exchanged vows the band played an improvised rock version of the Wedding March. My most vivid memory of the now-famous Shenute Morton is one of her dancing with wild abandon at her wedding.

Of all the events and happenings I experienced in those frenetic three days, the performance preceding the wedding is all I really remember in any detail. I was seated front row centre because of my subsequent duties as best man. The first act (if they could be called acts; they were really just separate pieces) was a re-enactment of Plato's *Republic*, in which the parts of Socrates, Glaucon and Polemarchos were played in turn by a fire-eater, a woman with a boa constrictor around her neck and a sumo wrestler. I have to admit it was very funny.

When we came back in after the interval there was an old woman sitting on the stage directly in front of my seat. She was talking and as we took our seats she would acknowledge one or another of us and make a pertinent comment. Her name was Miss Gentry. On a little table beside her chair was a pot of tea and a tea setting. She would sometimes pause to refill her cup and plop a sugar cube into it with a pair of silver tongs. She talked about her life. She'd been a designer of hats. She'd worked in a little store in Sloane Square. Her customers included among them some of the finest personages in England. Mostly, she talked of the war. And as she talked in this random but mesmerizing way, a young man came out onstage behind her. He was totally oblivious to her and she to him. She talked of the London Blitz. Her nights spent in the Underground. The children's Mickey Mouse gas masks. The interminable waits for the All Clear signal. As she talked, a young woman in a miniskirt sauntered onto the stage. She, too, was oblivious to Miss Gentry, who was now talking about the day a piano had crashed through her neighbour's sitting-room roof. The young woman was clearly aware of the young man's presence, though she pretended to ignore him.

As she talked, Miss Gentry seemed to be focusing more and more on me. To this day I don't know if this was an actor's trick or not. Using me and my central position as a way to relate to the whole audience. But I do know I felt that I was the person to whom she was talking. It was difficult to take my eyes off her. She talked of George the Sixth and how impeccably he'd behaved. The little princesses. Churchill's speeches on the Mall. She poured another cup of tea.

Behind her the couple was making eye contact. The woman tossed her hair; the man postured. At this point I could still take in all three of them. The couple started to move together. They brushed, touched. Miss Gentry was now talking about rationing. Powdered eggs and margarine — "marg," she called it. Soundlessly, behind her, the young couple were becoming more and more entangled. Soon they were embracing, kissing. The kissing became more passionate. They started to slip off their clothes. First the girl's blouse, then the fellow's shoes and socks. Off came her skirt. Down went his pants, kicked aside. They shifted their position on stage, no longer behind Miss Gentry but off to the side. The audience had to choose. Either we could look at Miss Gentry or at the young couple. This was especially true for me. She was talking right to me. An American soldier had given her a pound of fresh butter and, guiltily, she had used it all up in a single batch of shortbread cookies. In my peripheral vision I could see the naked couple, entangled down on the floor. They were simulating intercourse. Or at least I think they were simulating, as I found it impossible to avert my eyes from Miss Gentry. Then the stage went black.

SHE WAS DEVELOPING. Shenute was developing. Her face appeared before her, bit by bit, on the floating paper. Her almond-shaped eyes, her chin, her hairline. And then features filled in stronger — nose, lips, eyebrows and lashes. She was developing. Looking at the photo of herself in the tray, she realized this was the visibility she had been searching for. She stood, holding Breetz's hand and wondering how long the image would continue to get clearer and clearer, at what mysterious point it would be ready...

"It's magic," she whispered.

Magic. Whenever Breetz had asked Ulrika if she would help him develop her photos, she'd just said, Show me when they're done. But Shenute understood. Magic. Twenty years earlier, the young Norma Jean had used that same word as she watched an early photo of herself develop. In Shenute, Breetz had found a woman as fascinated by the process as Marilyn had been. As fascinated as he was. He squeezed her hand.

Standing beside Breetz, watching her image come into being, Shenute thought of the stauros. The X that joins the visible and invisible worlds. The stauros — the axis of a mighty spiral that reverses the order of the cosmos and takes Man from flux to changelessness, from becoming to being, from imperfection to perfection, from phenomena to noumena, from the world of illusion to the world of reality. The cross that joins two worlds.

"Shenute," Breetz said, "the camera is a mysterious tool that's able to see us in a way that we can't see ourselves. It can see into us, and it can see things that we can't see with the naked eye. It's one thing to be beautiful, but it's another thing to photograph beautifully. I think that if you learn how the process works, you can learn to affect the process."

Affect the process. Shenute felt a strange thrill hearing those words. Transformation, purification. A process by which gross matter was rid of its impurities.

"Most girls are afraid of the camera. They think it's going to show their imperfections. They think it's going to make them look too fat. They think it's going to show their pores. They fear the camera and so the camera captures that fear. Don't fear the camera, Shenute. If you fear the camera, it will photograph fear. If you hate the camera, it will photograph hate. If you love the camera, it will photograph love."

Shenute had heard this again and again. The model must "make love to the camera." And yet when Breetz said it she understood the words in a new way. They were not metaphorical — they were real. That was what she found so fascinating about everything Breetz said. He was not using words as images or metaphor. When he said you must love the camera he meant you must love the camera.

Breetz put down his drink, reached for the tongs and lifted the developed photo out and into the tray filled with stop bath. Shenute stared at the floating photo.

She would never be invisible again.

Breetz pointed the camera at Shenute. He stood very close, about four feet away.

"Shenute," he said. "Think about the Nag Hammadi."

Shenute started to laugh.

"I mean it," he said. "Think about it. Visualize it. See it."

Shenute visualized a page of *The Gospel of Thomas*. It appeared before her eyes with startling clarity.

"Good," he said, the shutter clicking. "Now read it to me. Read it to me in Coptic, just as you see it."

She did.

"Now," he said, "continue to visualize it in Coptic, but translate it for me, Shenute. Into English."

She did.

"Good, good," he said, still taking pictures. "Now think nothing."

She looked at him.

"You heard me," he said. "Think nothing." There was a pause. "What are you thinking, Shenute?"

"I'm thinking how hard it is to think nothing."

Her whole life she had been trained to think, think, think. Now she must do the opposite.

"Just try," Breetz said.

Shenute cleared her mind of the Coptic text. She cleared her mind of Breetz telling her to think nothing. She cleared her mind of all extraneous thoughts and as she did she could hear the shutter of Breetz's camera and his encouraging words.

"That's it," he said. "That's good, now you're getting it. *There*, Shenute, that was nothing."

Later that day, Breetz enlarged two of the photographs to almost twice life size. He pinned them up on the wall of their loft. Shenute could hardly believe the difference.

In the photo in which she had been "reading" her texts, her face was as tense and crabbed as the Coptic words she had visualized. She looked at that face and recognized it immediately. That was the face in embryo of her father and his colleagues. Her father's face was as dry and thin as papyrus and etched with tiny little lines. It was an unsettling experience.

In the second photo, her face was a blank. In those few moments during which she had been able to force herself to think nothing, her face had become more beautiful.

"Every woman can look like this, Shenute," Breetz said, tapping the first photo. "Of course they're not thinking about Coptic texts; they're thinking about gas bills or paying the rent or whether the old man's going to spend his paycheque at the pub. It's these thoughts that make an ordinary face." He turned to the other photo. "This is a beautiful face. This is the sort of face top models achieve. It doesn't matter what their features are; they make the features they've got beautiful."

But Breetz was looking to turn Shenute into more than just another top model. He wanted a woman who would be to the Seventies what Marilyn Monroe had been to the Fifties.

That evening Breetz took out a huge stack of photographs. They were all of Marilyn Monroe. No, not all. Many of the early ones were of Norma Jean and he spoke of them, always, as two different people. He would talk about how she started to find Marilyn. The seminal moment she learned the trick of her upper lip. They laughed over the Norma Jean photos. Denim and gingham. Plaid culottes and mohair sweaters. In many she had expressions on her face that were truly hilarious. A smirk, a toothy grin. These were pictures Shenute had never seen in any magazine. Photos of Norma Jean holding cats and dogs, photos of Norma Jean on beaches, in bathing suits and bathrobes. When they had finished laughing, Breetz reached into the carton and took out a photo of her taken twelve years later. She was holding a small bird near her face, her eyes nearly closed, her mouth smiling widely in delight. She was breathtakingly beautiful.

"She just got more and more beautiful," Breetz said. "She doesn't look younger, but she does look more beautiful. What was she doing?"

Breetz said many of her later photos *looked* like Marilyn but that they didn't always project Marilyn. Shenute was intrigued.

"If that's all there was to it," Breetz said. "The lowered lip, the half-lidded eyes, the mole, then someone else could do it, couldn't they?"

There were many more photos of Marilyn in that carton, but they didn't look at them all that night. A few days later, when Breetz left for Milan on assignment, he suggested Shenute look through the carton on her own. When she did, she found not only photos, but newspaper clippings, letters, articles from magazines and personal correspondence to Breetz from anyone he had ever met who had known Marilyn Monroe. Certain words were always circled — incandescent, radiant, luminous. Pinned to one picture of Norma Jean was a single-word note written in Breetz's compact hand. It said, Yipes!!

The photo was of Norma Jean in plaid shirt and cinched denim, beside a camera and tripod. The shot was from below so that the viewer looked up into her face. A round face. A pudgy face, squeezed into the strangest expression, creating a double chin in the teenaged Norma Jean. Shenute laughed out loud at the note and at the picture. She pulled it out and set it aside then proceeded through the rest of the pile. She found a series taken by Joseph Jasgur at Zuma beach in March 1946. Truly bizarre. There were three figures. A mustachioed man in a striped bathing costume, a woman in an outlandish polka-dotted dress and pantaloons, and Norma Jean. She wore a two-piece bathing suit, the halter stiff and pointy. A more stupid bunch of photos could scarcely be imagined. The woman pulls at the man's ear as he gapes at Norma Jean. Norma Jean primps and preens while standing on tiptoe. Then suddenly there is a photo that is completely different. The shoot was over, and someone had draped a man's suit jacket over Norma Jean's shoulders. Her back is to the camera, her legs entirely bare beneath the jacket, her head turned to look over her right shoulder, revealing only three quarters of her face. There was something different about this one. This one, taken at the same time as all the others, looked like a young Marilyn Monroe. Shenute set it aside too, glancing back at it occasionally as she sifted through photo after photo of Norma Jean smiling self-consciously for the camera, locking her knees, thrusting out her pelvis and chest.

Even once she'd shorn the unruly auburn hair and adopted the short bleached Marilyn hair, there were photos of her that just didn't have it. It was fascinating. Everything would be in place — the smile, the wiggle, the sleepy eyes, the mole, the hair — everything, in short, except that indefinable thing that made Marilyn Marilyn. Breetz had clipped an article from *Life* magazine and pinned it to one of the decidedly Marilyn photos. It was Marilyn's last interview:

> "Goethe said, 'Talent is developed in privacy,' you know? And it's really true. There is a need for aloneness which I don't think most people realize…It's almost having certain kinds of secrets for yourself that you'll let the whole world in on only for a moment…"

Secrets. Breetz had left her alone for three days with his Marilyn collection. She was alone with Marilyn and her secrets. What could they be? No one knew more secrets than Breetz Mestrovic. He was leaving her a message. It was all there. What is she doing, Shenute? he was asking her. What is she doing to become Marilyn? There is more to it than the sexy walk, the breathy talk, the lowered lids and signature smile. All those things can be imitated, but there's more, he was saying, and we will find it.

She sifted through the pile of Marilyn material twice again that first day. Over and over it became clear to her that Marilyn Monroe was a creation, a self-creation, and that the creation got stronger and better as she got older. This was why Breetz was impatient with diets and creams and holding back the ravages of Time — the obsession of every model she knew. Because he knew that that had nothing to do with the kind of beauty Marilyn projected in her photographs. At one point Shenute spread the Marilyn photos, chronologically, all over the loft. She read them like hieroglyphs — Norma Jean, Norma Jean, Norma Jean, Marilyn. Marilyn, Marilyn, Marilyn, not Marilyn. It was fascinating. In some photos, even some of the later ones, her face appeared a little too shiny, a little too round, a little too something, but in others she was positively radiant. Those words that Breetz kept circling: radiant, incandescent, luminous. She lingered over the one of Marilyn holding the tiny bird. There are fine lines around her eyes; her shoulders and the roundness of her cheeks show that she is not thin. But she is so touchingly beautiful.

When did it first appear? She went back and looked at the photo taken on the beach at Zuma. The photo in the man's jacket, looking at the camera over her shoulder. Definitely, in that photo there appeared the first seeds of Marilyn. She hadn't yet discovered the lip, the walk, the hair and yet the seeds of Marilyn were in that photo. Shenute examined it closely. In outer appearance it was still completely Norma Jean, and yet there was something there unmistakably Marilyn.

Velvet. The photo had a velvety quality that the later photos of Marilyn, the great ones, all had. A soft, velvety quality. Was it the light? No, because photos taken only moments before in the same light looked dense and harsh. There was something else. She had suddenly turned and looked at the camera and she'd got it. Of course, at the time, Marilyn wouldn't have known she'd got it. But Shenute knew that Marilyn studied her own photographs with all the fervour that Shenute was studying them now. If she had seen it, so obviously had Marilyn. She'd seen it and she'd learned to do it, whatever it was. She'd studied it. She'd studied it the way Shenute had studied old texts. She'd studied it and she'd learned how to do it. That was her secret. The secret she'd talked about in her last interview. Some sort of secret that Breetz wanted Shenute to learn. The old texts held secrets. The secret sayings of Jesus to Thomas. She was good at unravelling secrets. She would unravel this one.

When Breetz came back from Milan, the work resumed.

"Just think beautiful, Shenute."

Marilyn used to sit in front of the mirror by the hour, he said, once for eleven straight hours, imagining herself more beautiful. She would not see herself as she was, so much as how she wanted to be. She would stare into the mirror and imagine herself more beautiful. Once she could see herself more beautiful in the mirror, she would somehow alter her flesh to replicate the image. Not merely disguising imperfections, but imagining perfections. It was a subtle transformation, and it took time, but slowly, by imagining herself more beautiful, Marilyn had become more beautiful.

And so Shenute too would sit in front of her mirror imagining herself more beautiful. She imagined her neck as long and graceful as the carving of Nefertiti. She imagined her hair thicker, glossier and black as ebony. She imagined her almond-shaped eyes even larger. She stared at her eyelids and imagined the line of her upper lid firmer, more graceful in its sweep. She stared at her nose and imagined her nostrils even more defined. She stared at her lips and imagined them more full and sensuous. She imagined her skin flawless, golden and glowing.

The trick was to be beautiful, not to try to *appear* beautiful. Breetz said that too often models just tried to be beautiful for the shot. He said the camera doesn't work that way. The camera catches things, wispy things, as they appear on the surface. Like bubbles coming up through water. If you concentrate just on the moment when the bubble breaks through the surface, you can never catch it because it's too ephemeral, too momentary. He taught Shenute that she must imagine herself from the beginning of the shoot to the end of the shoot as one continuous action. Even with all the interruptions and distractions that a shoot involved. She must flow through the session like the bubbles rising up through the water and hope that the photographer had the intuition and skill to capture the moment they broke. That's why, Breetz said, even someone like himself had to take hundreds of photos, because the moment was so fleeting. It couldn't be forced and it couldn't be controlled. It was a kind of continuous awareness, a way of thinking.

He told her that he often saw models arrive at a shoot beautiful and get less and less so as the day went on. He said this was because they saw it as a kind of test or examination and that the moment the camera clicked they started to lose it.

He kept talking about incorporating images. Incorporation. The act of bringing into the body. If she could imagine herself more beautiful, she could bring it into the body. He told her that her body was made up of a thousand nerves and muscles that she had never thought about. If she thought about these muscles and nerves, they would become responsive. And if they became responsive, they would animate her. And if they animated her, she would become more beautiful. Beauty was awareness. It was not doing what she'd done all those years while studying ancient texts. During those years, she had been obliterating her body. But if she became aware of her body, her body would become more lively. And liveliness was beauty.

Mind. Shenute thought of the Serpent in the Garden. In the Gnostic version of the creation, light is enmeshed in flesh, but Mind, taking the form of the Serpent, came into the garden and revealed to Adam and Eve that the primal light could be recovered through Mind. She told Breetz this.

"That's why I knew the moment I saw you, that you were the girl," he said. "Flesh has nothing to do with Beauty. Beauty is manifested in flesh, but it's Mind that creates Beauty. Marilyn photographed more beautifully than any other woman, because she was able to think herself more beautiful."

Breetz was excited. More excited than he'd ever been with a woman. He'd never met anyone before who was able to follow him. He'd never met anyone before who understood what he was trying to get at. Light was enmeshed in flesh and the camera could catch it. That's what Marilyn had done, he told Shenute. She didn't reflect light, she released it. She released it from some inner source. She had discovered some way of becoming luminous, luminous to the eye of the camera. There was some process she had discovered; and they would discover it too, some process of Mind.

All her life, Shenute had studied these concepts in an abstract and intellectual way. But now she was going to involve herself in the search itself. Together she and Breetz would attempt the process by which the droplet of light enmeshed in flesh would reveal itself. Through film. It was the alchemy of the twentieth century. The secret process by which the alchemist purified himself and found the elixir of life.

"Think of the camera as a lover," Breetz said, holding it up to her face and snapping the shutter. "Look right at it. Look into it. Let it look into *you*, Shenute. It's friendly. It wants to love you. It wants to reveal your Inner Beauty. Don't hide from it, embrace it."

Openness. Breetz kept stressing that to photograph well you had to be open to the camera. Most people were closed, as she had been when "thinking Coptic." Openness was a quality that he wanted to encourage and he kept stressing that it was not the same as vulnerability. He had her do exercises to practise openness. She was to spread her arms and legs wide and imagine herself growing larger and larger. Just standing there, flinging her arms open felt wonderful. It was such a declaration of presence. It was like saying, "I'm here, I'm here."

In order to fully experience openness, he wanted her to experience its opposite.

"Curl into yourself," he said, "hide, get down on the floor, imagine yourself getting smaller and smaller."

And when she was curled upon her knees, arms clasped around herself, head bent almost to the floor, Shenute realized that this was how she had felt most of her life. Cramped, small, invisible.

"Yes," Breetz said. "The space around you is shrinking."

He showed her a picture of Marilyn on the beach in a white bathing suit. She was literally open, flinging her arms out and up, standing on one leg with the other flung higher than her waist. Behind her was the ocean and the sky and she seemed to be opening herself up to them. She was as big as the ocean, as open as the sky, as free as the sea air. It was a beautiful photograph.

He made her do the exercises over and over again, from open to closed, so that she could identify the feeling of them.

"Most people," he said, "find some spot on the scale that's

comfortable and spend their whole lives there. If you're too open in this society, you'll get overwhelmed, crushed. If you're too closed, you'll disappear. So people find some spot they're comfortable with and they stick there."

But Shenute was to practise going up and down the scale constantly, every day, so that she never got stuck. The camera hated stuck.

Breetz used words like "radiate." He said she must imagine herself radiating, her entire being emanating rays. She was to imagine these rays preceding her wherever she went. It didn't matter at all, Breetz said, if she thought she was only pretending to radiate, the point was that in thinking "radiation" something happened to the body; it was animated in yet another way.

So Shenute would spend hours standing and sitting and walking and picking up stray objects then putting them down again, all the while imagining herself radiating out, out, out. The sensation this seemingly simple exercise created in her body was remarkable. She felt at once light and yet expansive, as if she filled their loft with her presence. As she sat down she would send rays out to the chair from the backs of her thighs, her bottom, her elbows, her spine. Even as she stayed apparently static, legs crossed, sitting in a chair, if she imagined herself radiating outward from each body part, her whole body felt invigorated and alive.

She must make the camera come to her. She must create a psychic connection between her and the film. She must not think of the camera as a passive receptacle of her image; she must think of them as equal begetters of the photo. That's why the great beauties always talked about the camera in sexual terms — they would make love to the camera, the camera would come to them, they would open themselves up, surrender to the camera. The camera was not a passive tool picking up reflected light. It was not an appliance. There was a connection to be made and it was to be made through the mind.

Mind was the intermediary between Spirit and Body. She could use her mind to spiritualize her flesh. She could light herself up. Of course, the master of this had been Marilyn. Breetz always talked about Marilyn in Gnostic terms. She was like the first woman: a drop of light enmeshed in flesh. In her the primal light was entrapped. By

Mind she was able to release that light, to radiate, to be luminous. Marilyn was a mythic figure for Breetz. She stood for the divine spark within us all. The radiant luminous body that Ialdaboath in the garden had clothed in coats of skin. Marilyn had used Mind to return to the light. If Marilyn could do it, so could Shenute. She would go back to the mirror and practise.

TROUBLE WITH MY PhD THESIS PERSISTED. Twice I had worked out proposals that excited me and twice my adviser had tied me up into such knots with his questions and criticisms that I had abandoned them. I was now on my second adviser and working on a third proposal. Wesley felt that perhaps our published work in parapsychology journals was prejudicing the committee against me. He said that academic departments were very jealous of their disciplines and loathe to let any extraneous ideas pollute their streams. I was beginning to think he was right. My most recent adviser was even suggesting I consider Coleridge. Or Dryden. He believed Blake and I were a bad mix.

It was frustrating. All across the country new universities were springing up and I wanted to finish my PhD and start lecturing. I was especially fond of my exegesis of Blake's most famous poem, "The Tyger." Blake's original etching accompanying the poem showed a small tiger, in daylight, at the base of a tree. The etching was not at all in keeping with the poem. In the poem the tiger was terrifying, "burning bright." But I realized he was burning bright only because the speaker of the poem saw him "in the forests of the night." In daylight, as Blake had drawn him, standing beneath a tree, he looked downright cute and cuddly. Almost forlorn. Not a tiger, but a lamb. I saw the poem not as a debate about the existence of evil in a universe created by a benevolent God — "Did he who made the Lamb make thee?" — but a poem about perception. What appears terrifying in the forests of the night could be seen completely differently by day.

The doors of perception. If the doors of perception are cleansed, the tiger and the lamb are one.

But everything I came up with seemed to go against my adviser's traditional way of thinking and it soon became clear he would view anything I proposed as a thinly veiled excuse for my pursuits with Wesley Ames. Wesley, as he himself pointed out, had tenure and so no matter how annoyed people were by his unacademic and frivolous concerns, they could in no way affect his position. But I was at that vulnerable stage in an academic's life: the point where I had to prove to the Powers That Be that I was a serious scholar.

Wesley and I were discussing all this as we dealt with letters in response to our latest joint endeavour — our *Bibliography of Psychokinesis*. Among the letters was one from Chicago.

> Dear Doctors,
>   Ted Serios should have been in your article. Just because Ted is unedjucated and employed at present as a bellhop, doesn't mean he is not the most interesting phenomenan of the 20th century. If proffesors such as yourselfs won't investigate him and people such as myself aren't believed how is this phenomenan to come to light? I get mad when I think about it. When I think of the millions of dollars spent in this country on useless research.
>   Yours truly,
>   Jack Miller

Wesley and I debated whether we should even respond. This was the kind of correspondent who could take up an awful lot of time over nothing. But we finally wrote him a short note explaining that we were not investigators, and that in any case he hadn't told us what exactly it was his friend could do.

A couple of weeks later I noticed an envelope in our Saturday morning pile and immediately recognized Mr Miller's writing. "I cannot," he wrote, "send an example of Ted's extraordinary photos because I don't know who you are and twice before I have sent them to so-called distinguished scientists and they were never returned to me. These are, of course, irreplaceable documents of immense scientific importance and their loss represents a disaster that I will not risk repeating. But I enclose a testamonal of people who have witnessed Ted's photography."

There were five signatures at the bottom of the letter.

So whatever this Ted Serios did, it had something to do with photography. My curiosity was piqued, but it was Wesley who decided the matter.

"It has just occurred to me, Richard," he said, "that we are doing to this Jack Miller precisely what your thesis advisers have been doing to you. We are not listening to him, we're not taking him seriously and we're dismissing him out of hand without really hearing what he has to offer."

I thought about this for a moment and had to agree. That morning we wrote to Mr Miller saying we would be interested in seeing this Mr Serios but that he must understand we were not psychic investigators. We suggested a meeting in two weeks' time. We then received a very strange letter. Mr Miller said that these demonstrations were wreaking emotional havoc on Mr Serios. That Mr Serios was of an emotional nature, highly unstable, and Mr Miller wanted to make sure that before we came to see Mr Serios, we could guarantee him that we would do a proper investigation, that we were not idle curiosity-seekers.

We were flummoxed by this. We had already told Mr Miller that we weren't scientists, that there would be no "investigation," that we represented no institution, and that if we were to come it would be just as private individuals. Now he wanted a full-scale investigation, one we didn't have the means, money or expertise to carry out. We wrote him back explaining this again, and saying that perhaps in the best interests of all concerned we should call the whole thing off. He replied that he had talked to Ted about us and that Ted was willing to give us a demonstration. We wrote back thanking Mr Miller and confirming the appointment. He wrote back saying the appointment was no longer suitable as Mr Serios had left town. We wrote back informing Mr Miller that we had cancelled our flight.

THEY SAW HER EVERYWHERE. As they scooped sweets into paper bags for old ladies, as they sold umbrellas to men in bowler hats, as they walked about Piccadilly Circus or Leicester Square. She was everywhere. Her eyes, her lips, her hands. On billboards, in magazines. She had become so familiar to them it was a shock to actually see Her in person. She was coming down the escalator wearing a simple tan trench coat, her ebony hair swept back into a knot. One hand rested lightly on the railing, the other hung loose at her side.

"Oo, look..."

"Cor..."

"Shenute Morton..."

They all spotted her in the same moment. Later, one of them would say she'd felt her presence. Felt her presence even before she'd seen her. The others agreed. One of them knew someone who knew someone who'd known her once.

She seemed to float down towards them. She was taller than they thought from her photographs, her neck long and slender. By the time she stepped off the escalator the whole platform had gone silent. She stood alone, oblivious to the heads turning, the elbows nudging, the silence. Everyone was watching.

The girls had read all about her. Leonard did her hair. She had twice-weekly massages. She bathed in milk. She wore only original creations. Her husband was a famous photographer. He'd discovered her right here in London at the British Museum. She was clever. She spoke five languages. She could write in hieroglyphics. She was Egyptian, like Cleopatra. She had what the magazines called the most meltingly beautiful eyes in London.

She turned her head to watch for the incoming train. They could see those eyes. They were almond shaped and a deep chocolate brown. What would it be like to be Her? To be recognized wherever you went. To have all eyes upon you. What would it be like to be a woman like that?

Later they would tell their friends about this, embellish it. Tell about how she was so close they could smell her perfume. Tell how she wore hardly a trace of makeup, how she dressed so simply. How she had stood so still. How her presence had filled the entire platform.

The doors of the train slid open. People moved aside. She stepped in as if she were entering a private coach. She was so beautiful.

They hadn't followed her. They'd been so stunned they hadn't moved. They'd stood transfixed as the train pulled away, her classic profile passing in front of them, not three feet from their eyes.

Shenute Morton. What would it be like to be Her?

In London, Shenute's image was everywhere, but on the world stage, she was still largely unknown. There was an event in the making which Breetz said would be the perfect occasion for her entrance. Truman Capote was giving a party in Manhattan. "Just a party for the people I like." Breetz was among the select five hundred guests whom Truman had invited from all over the world — guests who included a maharajah, a Kansas detective, half a dozen presidential advisers, businessmen, editors, writers, artists, several heiresses, one country doctor and a sprinkling of royalty. It was to be held in the ballroom of the Plaza Hotel, the only truly great ballroom left in New York. A black-and-white ball. And, just like the fairy tale, the question already on everyone's lips was the one Breetz and Shenute intended to answer: Who would be the most beautiful of all?

"Picture the ballroom. It is the night of the ball. The room is filled with swirling couples, the men in black tuxedos, the women in white gowns. Picture yourself clothed in light, swirling among those couples. How big are you?"

"Life-size. My own size."

"Good. Now, imagine yourself gradually growing bigger than everyone else. Open yourself up so that your space bubble expands, like an invisible balloon, so that slowly, slowly it fills the whole space. What do you notice that's different?"

"The other couples are far away...they're on the periphery, watching me."

"Good, good," said Breetz. "Now hold that image in your mind."

They practised in restaurants, at theatre openings and at small parties. Six weeks before the grand ball they attended an opening at an art gallery. Before entering, Shenute imagined her rays preceding her through the double doors. Only when she saw her rays entering the doors did she then enter herself. As she did, she could feel herself rendering all the other women in the room invisible, as if they were candles and the sun had just risen. They were extinguished. Obliterated. This was to be the effect she must achieve at the ball. The ball would not be a Soho opening with twenty-five or thirty beautiful women. The ball would be an immense room filled with famous beauties. But if she concentrated, she could extinguish them all.

"Imagine you have a twin," Breetz said.

"A twin?"

"A twin. An invisible twin that accompanies you everywhere."

The Khaibit, Shenute thought. The etheric double of the Egyptians. The Gnostics had inherited the concept. In Gnostic cosmology, a curtain separates the Visible and Invisible realms. In the Invisible realm there exists a Being of Pure Light. Our bodies are merely a botched and clumsy reproduction of this image, copied from the reflection on the horus.

"As you walk across the room," Breetz said. "Your twin walks beside you. The twin can do anything you can imagine her doing. If you want her to walk six inches off the ground, she can do it. If you want her to float or fly or swim through the sea she can do it. Now, if someone's taking your photograph, you don't need to move. But that doesn't mean your twin can't. You can imagine your twin doing whatever you want and the camera will pick this up."

The twin was the concept into which Breetz now consolidated all his exercises. Instead of thinking beautiful, Shenute would think her twin beautiful. Instead of radiating, her twin would radiate. Instead of being open and expansive, her twin would be open and expansive. The twin was not constrained by the laws of this world. She was not subject to Time or Space or Gravity. She was a being of pure possibility. She could do anything Shenute could imagine her doing. She would accompany her to the ball.

Swirling sedately among the other dancers at the ball, to the corporeal eye Shenute would appear in the flesh. But above her, floating and soaring like a hawk on a thermal, would be her naked luminous twin. And this soaring floating twin would affect every nuance of gesture and expression of the fleshly Shenute below. It was her ultimate secret. Her ultimate secret that only a camera could share.

In her book, Shenute told what it was like to be Her. *Slave to Beauty* began with a description of her entrance to that mythic ball. The guests had dined with New York hostesses in groups of ten to twelve pre-arranged by Truman. They arrived at the Plaza by nine, already relaxed and chatting with their fellow dinner guests. Shenute wrote about how she had projected her invisible twin into the ballroom before she herself entered. Her twin soared and swooped above while she swirled on the dance floor below. Of all the photographs of all the beautiful women taken at that ball, hers was the one editors chose to print. In *Time*, in *Look*, in *Life*.

Shenute wrote about what it was like to be the beheld of all beholders. She wrote of what it was like to have a thousand eyes upon her and to know that every other woman in the room had been rendered invisible. It was the moment of her greatest triumph. It was the culminating moment she and Breetz had worked towards their entire marriage. It was also the moment of her greatest revelation. The moment she would later describe as the beginning of wisdom.

Was it on the stroke of midnight? It might as well have been — for in an instant the spell was broken. It was broken by a thought. An image. An image of a young woman standing alone, friendless and ill at ease. The young woman was her. Her that first night at the School. She saw the hardwood floors, the posters, the mirrors and her own form in those mirrors. And suddenly Pam's big blue eyes were looking right at her, "'Ullo, me name's Pam, whass yourn?"

He knew. In a moment Breetz was at her side. He looked into her eyes, then slowly raised his arms and taking her bare shoulders in his hands gently held her. He knew.

They left. They left quickly and unobtrusively.

When Pam had come across the room to her, Shenute had felt invisible. But Pam had seen her standing there. Standing there alone, ill at ease, friendless. Together they had walked arm in arm to meet the girls. Tina and Stef and Jackie and Viv. Where were they now? Was Tina still bending over accidentally on purpose? Was Pam still buying her old mum a present with every paycheque? Was Stef still working in the frock shop? She remembered the frock shop and the long-discarded Jersey Knit. She saw it flying over the top of the changeroom door. She remembered her own trepidation and the tug of Pam's hand as she reached in and pulled her out into the middle of the store. She heard them admiring her exposed legs. She heard the giggles, the laughter, always the laughter. Rodger the Lodger had a bad cough. Your mind wants boilin' in carbolic. The giggles, the laughter, the acceptance. For a few short months she had found what she wanted: visibility. But she had pushed on. What had begun as a desperate yearning to become visible, simply to be seen and noticed, had somehow turned into this.

Was there no way of increasing her visibility than by becoming more beautiful? She now knew she could become more beautiful. And she realized that if she concentrated and worked on it, perhaps she could become as beautiful as Marilyn Monroe. In the hagiology of Beauty Culture, Marilyn Monroe reigned supreme. But what was Marilyn Monroe but an abstract image which had destroyed the flesh that bore it? Marilyn ended up drugged, alcoholic, abused, suicidal. There was so much speculation as to how Marilyn had died — was she murdered or did she commit suicide? But Marilyn hadn't really died. Marilyn was still alive. She was alive in every photo that existed of her. For someone like Breetz she was more alive than all the women he had ever met. The person who had died was Norma Jean. Norma Jean had begun to die the moment she lowered that lip. It was murder. It was a long slow process of murder, but Marilyn had murdered Norma Jean until finally Norma Jean had ended up dead and all that existed was Marilyn. The face that launched a thousand photos. Is that what Shenute wanted for herself? To become a photo?

No. She wanted to become visible. She wanted to somehow affect the world. But she didn't want to affect the world as an icon. A mosaic on the wall that glowed with holy fire. She wanted to be somebody who could make all women visible. She no longer wanted to obliterate her fellow women, but to help them become visible in all their amazing diversity. Short and tall. Fat and thin. Black, yellow, white. Crooked teeth and straight. Big breasts and small. Short legs and fat arms.

Shenute's life until now had followed a pattern of perfect symmetry. As a child her father had trained her mind, ignoring her body. As a young woman she had trained her body, ignoring her mind. Then she'd met Breetz. She had returned to the world of the mind, but with a different purpose.

She no longer wanted to think about being beautiful. Nor did she want to translate Coptic texts. She wanted to think her own thoughts. She wanted to make sense of the strange pattern of her life. She wanted to understand her life in terms of a larger pattern. She wanted to think about the Gnostic texts, not in dry, scholarly terms — this version versus that version, Greek versus Coptic, Egyptian versus Demotic — she wanted to think about them in terms of what they actually meant. The world around her treated the masculine as spirit and the feminine as matter. But the Gnostic texts told a different story: a world in which the female principle was light and was enmeshed in the male principle of matter.

She thought about Pam and Tina and how, though they had never really considered any of these things, they lived their lives according to a mythology that saw them as mere flesh in the service of something higher. That was why their men could throw them up against walls in alleys for a quick bash. She thought of Tamsin and Daniela. That was why they mutilated and whipped and scourged their flesh. Because they saw themselves as flesh, not light. That was why Marilyn Monroe had destroyed herself, because she too hated her flesh.

She thought of Breetz. The most extraordinary man she'd ever met. He, unlike her father and his colleagues, understood Gnosticism. He, unlike them, understood in his guts what it was really all about. Light imprisoned in flesh. The desperate yearning to return to the primal source. The desperate search that so often led to drink. Alcoholism. A disease of the soul. A spiritual sickness. A search for something more to life. It dragged its victims down, down, further into matter. It enmeshed people in the lowest forms that life can take on earth. Its victims wretched and puked and stank. Its victims blacked out, stopped eating and committed the slowest form of suicide. They drank because there was some spiritual void in their lives. A void which only alcohol seemed to fill. A search for Spirit that took the form of spirits.

She couldn't do it. She wasn't Marilyn. She couldn't give herself over to the light. All she had ever wanted was to be visible, to be comfortable in this flesh and that had been accomplished. Painfully, and eventually with the help of Breetz, she had somehow united body and mind. She was now visible. She could return to the realm of the mind

— she would write a book. She would tell her story. She would use it as a way of exploring her thoughts about male and female relations. She would inform modern woman that although she was part of a tradition that regarded the female as chaotic flesh and the male as spirit, this was not the only tradition. Another had been suppressed. A tradition that saw the first creative principle as Light. A tradition that told of a stupid and jealous demiurge who had created matter in which this light had become imprisoned. She would encourage the Pams and Tinas not to hide their light under a bushel, or a miniskirt, or an apron.

And thus she ended up accomplishing after all, in her own way, what her father had wanted her to do through dry reasoning, what she had wanted to do through Beauty. She became one of those rare women who defines an age. The age of Feminism. The Seventies. An age when women became aware that they had minds as well as bodies and discovered a long tradition of feminine thought and mythology.

Shenute's apprenticeship with the Gnostic texts provided her a framework with which she was able to construct a new mythology for women. A mythology in which women were light. Droplets of light enmeshed in flesh. She wanted to make it clear that these droplets would shine brighter as the flesh withered and died. A Gnostic theory of the resurrection in which understanding — knowledge — spiritual insight — Gnosis — is the key to salvation, not simple belief. Certainly not blind belief in a male hierarchical structure. A theory in which the droplets of light the whole world over would unite to provide the light of clear understanding. Shenute's book was to eventually become one of the classics of Feminism. But it wasn't dedicated to a woman; it was dedicated to a man: Breetz Mestrovic. He had changed her life.

Beautiful, beautiful, beautiful, she thought. They were all beautiful. They came up to her, some so tentatively they were pushed or nudged by friends, daughters, sisters.

"G'on," they'd say, and the shy one, the nudged one, would step up and mumble something like, "getcher autograph?"

She would ask them their names, get the spelling right, and sign:

For Elsie, Shenute

and Elsie or Margaret or Jean or Lisa would nod and thank her and turn away clutching their copy of *Slave to Beauty*. Who knew what it cost them to step up and ask that? Who knew how they would be ridiculed by their men for even having such a book around — slave to beauty? Don' you wish, luv, don' you just wish.

Shenute knew. Shenute knew what it cost each and every one of them and she loved them for it. The Monicas in their minis with their makeup, the Hayleys in their jeans and baggy sweats. She knew and she loved them all.

They were all so beautiful.

I think of Alex. You know where to find us, he said. That's all. And he was really saying, I'm gonna let you alone, there, Kate, 'cause I don't want to interfere kind of thing an' I reckon the minute you set eyes on that cabin you saw yourself livin' there by yourself, you bet, but I'm here, Nancy's here, Ah Clem's here, we're all here. But "You know where to find us" was all he said. I never thought of Alex as a man of few words.

Three weeks and I'm getting into it now. There's a weird solemnity in being this alone. And when I think about it . . . I haven't walked into town, either. This is a two-way thing. A two-way kind of thing. I don't walk into town because there's nothing I need there. I don't have to visit Alex or Ah Clem because I know they're fine. It occurs to me that this is why they aren't visiting me. They know I'm fine too. They leave you alone because the assumption is you're fine.

⊚

Richard sends me books
& I build a little shelf
for them, over on the north
wall, taking care not to
cover — I don't know why — Quinn's
strange scratches. Counting scratches
they look like, though he
never crosses a fifth line
through the bundle like they
taught us in school | | | | | | | |.
I build a shelf
& try my body on it.
It holds.
And sometimes I lift a book to
smell it — especially
second-hand ones
the ones from Treasure Island
— but I do not read it.
Not yet.
I sleep & dream & eat
& dream & stoke & dream
& sleep
& dream.

⊚

"Stikine" is Tahltan for Great River. It is a great river. "Kitsu" is Tahltan for Northern Lights. I listen, and think it's how they sound. "Sidas" is Tahltan for cut, as in cut oneself with a knife. What says so much in so few words without missing any feeling? Tahltan. There are other languages too that do that. There must be.

⑥

I have passed through some sort of phase. I hope it isn't just temporary. I have stopped looking towards Telegraph Creek every five minutes. Now, when I go to the river to splash my face with water, I look at the river, into it. I used to scan. I used to look north to the Stikine Range, south to Telegraph Creek, east to the Spatsizi Plateau and west to the coastal range. It was as if I were trying to fix myself in space. Some sort of geographical pinpoint. Now — I'm just down by the river. The river is amazing. We all think so. Me, the salmon, the snow geese, the Canada geese, the whistling swans, the sandhill cranes and dabbling ducks. And the bald eagles. Ah Clem eagles, I call them. Stikine. Great River. In winter I'll have to wash my face with snow.

⑥

something small but
tenacious in me, like
the glacial meltwater
tumbling down the side
of an old old mountain
over rock and scrubby
trees & scree
en route
to the Stikine

◎

Richard writes, *Do you see a lot of animals?* Yes. I see a lot of
animals, yes. But not the way I expected. What did I expect?
From my National Geographic life I expected to see a bear,
glaring at me mouth wide, brownish-ivory teeth dripping saliva.
Just the scary head, no body. Just the bust of a bear. Before he
eats me alive. From my National Geographic life I expected to
see an eagle, glassy-eyed and angry, talons sharp, beak sharp.
A single eagle, alone and hungry, ready to rip out my eyes.
From my National Geographic life I expected to see a moose,
the big dopey mouth chewing, chewing, the soft fuzzy antlers
stretched out, close enough to hang candy canes on, like the
drawing I once saw on a Christmas card. And inside:
Merry Chrismoose.

But nothing is as I expected. There are no National Geographic
animals here. I have yet to see a bear, although I find evidence.
I see lots of eagles. Hundreds of them. Ah Clem eagles. They
arrive en masse for the salmon in the spring. They fly high and
stoop fast. I never see the colour of their eyes. And moose?
I've seen lots of moose. Extend your arm straight out in front
of you and look at the thumbnail. That is the size of the
moose I see. There are no National Geographic animals
here. And it occurs to me that the animals there are — those
tiny big animals — see me more than I see them. I wish
we were more equal that way.

◎

I saw a Tlingit totem. Part of it was a large head with a smaller
head jutting out perpendicular to it, as if sticking out of its right
ear. I have no idea what it is supposed to mean. I keep going back
to look at it. The big face is so ... normal. The big face isn't smiling,

isn't frowning, isn't anything. "Nothing going on here," it seems to say. But the little face stuck onto this face has a little downturned mouth.

⑥

The goat — how did he
get there? I know how I
got here. On all fours, using my
opposable thumbs to cling to this &
that, but he,
he stares at me
from an expanse of rock
a slab of cliff face
the nearest scrubby tree
to him is
half a mile away.
How's he do it?
I'll never tire of asking.

Stay there, goat.
The wolves and I
and even Johnny Carlick
will never get you there.

⑥

The canyon is a soundscape.
River, wind, and
shifting scree.
A rock plummets to the floor
and the sound
sounds, sounds,

sounds big
against the other
sounds.

⑥

I had a dream of a grizzly bear walking on the bottom of the
ocean. It was so vivid! I can still see it now. The grizzly, a National
Geographic grizzly, is lumbering along slowly and I'm terrified at
first, then I think, "It's okay, because I'm wearing flippers."

⑥

Startled out of deep sleep by the strangest noise. A ruckus, Alex
would say. A commotion. Has someone come to visit? At this hour?
And what on earth are they doing out there, anyway? I open my
door and peer out. It's a moosecalf! Not very old at all. A goofy
moosecalf and he's playing silly bugger in the river. I have to get
closer. How close can I get before it runs away? I start easing
myself out. He's bounding into the river. I'm off the porch —
good. He's bounding back out. Stand still when he's facing me
and move when he's not. Stop start, stop start. He's just playing.
He's kicking his knobby legs and flinging water into the air. Stop,
start. Stop start. Think I'll drop down now and pull myself
along on my belly. But it's too late. He senses something.
I freeze. This time I can see the colour of his eyes. And he
can see mine. Now I'm the goofy one, standing there — white
legs and plaid shirt against the browns and greens — and he
comes all over dignified, trotting across the river and into
the bush. It's over. It's thumbnail moose from now on but at
least I saw him.

Wishes do come true.

❀

So many nights alone, now.
Listening to the wind,
the animal sounds,
trying to decipher their
communications —
that's a mating call
that's danger danger
that's prey —
as if I'd know!
Citygirl.
But this is no different, really.
I've always been alone at night.
Nancy at the Diamond C Cafe
with pats, winks, nods, chat
"Good night, sleep tight
don't let the bedbugs bite"
that was the exception.
I've always been alone at night.
Listening.
Listening for, not to.
Listening for what?

❀

You can live in a man's house, use his stove, his pot, his skillet, his
one-holer, and not really know him. Today, cleaning up, I acciden-
tally hit a loose floorboard the wrong way and split it. Through the
split I saw what looked like paper. My first thought was that Quinn
had stuffed some newspaper in a spot where a draft was coming in,
or something. Then the idea of reading a newspaper from Quinn's
day got me quite interested and I ripped up the floorboard. There, in
pretty good condition, was a book on geology. It was a serious book,

not many pictures, lots of graphs and diagrams. Lots of definitions with words in them to send you looking through more definitions. Some of the pages were stuck together and a lot of them water-stained. I see Quinn sitting at the table, reading his geology book, smoking his pipe. Maybe he'd even memorize some of the definitions.

In the immediate vicinity of Telegraph Creek, the prevalent rock is a grey-green, speckled, altered volcanic material, which proves to be a fine-grained diabase tuff.

Whew. Quinn, hoarding geological information, hiding it. And making his odd scratches on the wall.

⑥

The only perennial in my mother's garden was grass
The only thing that came up year after year
Annuals were her thing
Skinny rows of bare earth along each side of the path to the gate
for Pansies
A semi-circle of bare earth on either side of the door
for Marigolds
And two cement pots, one on each end of the cement porch
for Petunias.

I hated petunias.

God forbid there should ever be anything with tendrils
that might creep over the edge of that trimmed grass
anything low and matted was out of the question.
Every year, May 24, flats of these annuals were bought
then poked into their various allotted patches of bare earth.

Cindy knew I hated petunias and sometimes she'd snap off their
heads before they were wilted.

What my mother didn't know was that beneath the single wooden step to the one-car garage there was a patch of moss. She couldn't have known about it or it wouldn't have been there, so different from the papery flowers stuck into the bare dry earth. I used to lie on my side with my head propped on my arm and stare at that patch of moss, reach out and touch it with my fingers, press them down and feel the moss give, let an ant crawl over my arm, forward and back, forward and back, taking its time finding a way back down to the moss and, sometimes, sometimes I remember going into that moss myself until it was no longer a tiny patch but an enormous encircling forest of green sponge, endless catacombs of green. I'd careen off green walls, I'd swoop through green tunnels, and no one could follow, not even Bobbin or Cindy. They were invisible, but they couldn't go into moss.

Only I could go into moss.

⑥

Diabase Tuff: A somewhat fine-grained clastic rock a good deal decomposed, made up of irregular-shaped grains of plagioclase, pyroxene and titanic iron ore, with a very little pyrite and some fragments of a fine-grained porphyritic rock.

Okay, this leaves me cold —
except for the pyrite
which Alex has shown me enough of
and which, anyway, I prefer to call
Fool's Gold —
but I do like Diabase Tuff.
Never mind what it is
I like the sound of it

and I like the fact that
it's all around here
all around me
I am surrounded by it
and it becomes my internal response
to imagined questions
How am I? Diabase Tuff
How's that? Diabase Tuff
You don't like it? Diabase Tuff
No one here to ask
No one to hear me answer
Tuff, Diabase Tuff

ya-za means sky in Tahltan
I just learned that

little Johnny Carlick came by
and each time he does
he teaches me a new word

ti-wuh, I say as he tries to
sneak in more than one word
no, and he grins
making me say for him the ones
I've already learned

klew-eh, salmon
kiw-igana, deer
gan-jeh, goose
klew-eh, I say again for fish
because the Tahltan word for
fish and salmon are the same
and he loves it when I say

it counts as learning two words
he laughs at me then

laugh, I say, and he laughs again
no, I say, ti-wuh — laugh, laugh!
oh, he says, getting it,
na-es-tlook
na-es-tlook means laugh in Tahltan

ⓖ

The Stikine Plateau is made up of old ocean floors thrust up by continental pressure, carved by glaciers and eroded by melting glaciers.

...a grizzly walking on the ocean floor.

ⓖ

Old habits die hard. Today, after a swim in the river, I found myself pushing back my cuticles with the towel. I was thinking about something else entirely. It was automatic.

What would happen if one never pushed one's cuticles back? Would the skin slowly creep up and grow over the tips of the nails? Would you go through winter like that and then, like a deer shedding his antler fuzz, would your nail skin peel and crack once you got back outside, back to rooting around in the garden? Would there be a time when your hands looked like they had stray pieces of sauerkraut dan-gling from the fingertips? The moon when the cuticles peel back.

ⓖ

No one was ever good enough
to bring home
I learned that over and over
and over again.

Thick ankles, sulky faces
Big noses, crooked teeth
Skinny legs, gormless faces
Pug noses, yellow teeth
Knock knees, common faces
Ugly noses, ugly teeth.
She'd actually call them
by these new names (to
me, not to their faces)
If Heather was over
"Gormless forgot her
sweater, again"
or if Susan phoned
"Thick Ankles called,
don't call back before
dinner."

If, by some chance,
I brought someone home
whose face and legs
were pretty, there was
always some flaw to be found
"Adenoids" "Clumsy"
"Loudmouth" "Mousey."

Not all mothers were like that
I know because, before I
stopped bringing anybody
home, I went to Susan's house.
Her mother had thick ankles
too and she didn't seem to
care. She didn't try to

slim them with dark stockings
or hide them in pants, or
tuck them under the chair
when she sat down. She
behaved as though
she didn't even know her
ankles were too thick.
I liked her.
She gave me cookies.
and called me sweetie
and made me feel welcome
by not paying much
attention to me.

Kids weren't made to feel
welcome at my house
They got the once-over,
a tight smile
and no cookies.
At dinner that night I'd sit
hands in lap
feet not swinging
shoulders not slumped
And wait for the pronouncement
"Katlyn had a visitor today"
(not a friend, never a friend)
"Common little thing."

For as long as I
could I ignored it
Then I tried to avoid
it — playing only with Cindy
or Bobbin —
but at some awful point
I absorbed it.
Probably puberty.

Boys. Danger time.
Duck Tail, Bow Legs,
Jughead and Adam's Apple
all inner names
for the poor brave
boys who tried.
The ones who didn't
got it worse.
Pea Brain, Grease Ball
Dumbcluck and Body Odour.
Cindy came up with that
last one. Cindy and
Bobbin were around a
lot in those days.

And now I remember.

The last time I saw Bobbin.
I was fourteen and in
modelling school.
I looked up and saw him
"Fussbudget," I thought
and, poof, he was gone.

He never came back.

⑥

Jump down a cliff
Light a fire in the grass
Scream like hell
Play dead.

All these are methods
of warding off a grizzly
attack and all of them
have worked, apparently,
at one time or another.

"Grizzly's like a person ...
different day to day"
This from Alex, who's
the exact same from day
to day, but never mind
I understand him to mean
that there's no surefire
way to escape a grizzly
I also understand that
I'm not likely to have to
I've yet to see one,
even thumbnail size
and that's fine by me

Johnny Carlick has so
many grizzly stories it
has only recently
dawned on me he might
be making them up
fed by my wide eyes
and open mouth

Still, Spatsizi Range is
grizzly country
there's no denying that
and the fact is I feel
safer exploring in
winter. In winter I
strap on snowshoes
and strike out for hours
getting into deep snow

and lifting my knees high
my thighs burning

Then Johnny tells me that
grizzlies often wake up
during a warm spell
That's just dandy
He says they might eat
an animal and finish
out their hibernation in
that animal's den

    I see a grizzly in front
    of my woodstove
    rocking in my rocking
    chair, reading my books

He says he might just
slash you up a bit
then bury you under leaves
and brush until he's hungry
"Don't come up on him,
then," Johnny says,
smiling and shaking his
finger at me
As if I would

    I see a grizzly gathering
    leaves over top of me
    like a big kid on the beach
    burying a friend in sand

I know enough to steer clear
of mama bears with cubs
Tiny cubs, at least,
apparently after a year,
when she's got toddlers,

she'll likely run from a
human even if she's never
been hunted before.

All this grizzly knowledge
and no grizzlies, I say
and Johnny Carlick grins
holding up his hands
fingers crossed.

☾

I trudge into town, my boots making sucking noises in the mud. The
Telegraph Trail leads me. At the sight of Ah Clem I feel my throat
clutch a bit. I only ever knew him to say hi to, really, but when he
sees me he gets up off his porch, which seems to neither have acquired
nor lost a single net or hide, and approaches.

"Still alive, then," he says as hello.

He knows darn well I'm alive. I've been getting my news of
him, of all of them, so I know they've been getting their news of me.
He walks with me to the Diamond C Cafe and everything's just like
it was when I first saw it that time with Richard almost — could it
be? — yes, two years ago. Nancy is pouring coffee; there are some
Americans over near the wall talking, no doubt, about the salmon
they're bound to catch; and Alex is sitting at the counter, spearing a
mound of Nancy's homefried potatoes. I never could get mine to
taste that good, try as I might. Must have something to do with the
varied mixture of fat she has to fry them in. Alex turns when Ah
Clem and I step through the door.

"Well, lookee there, Ah Clem an...some bush woman I don't
reckon I know."

I sit at the counter beside him and Ah Clem takes the other side
so I'm sandwiched between them and Nancy keeps leaning over,
big grin, and pinching my cheek. The two men give me softened,
though hard enough, slaps on the back and punches to the arm. It's

*warm in the café so I peel off my jacket and turtleneck down to
my t-shirt.*

*"Whooee, look a that," Alex says, feeling the muscle of my
right arm.*

*They're making fun of me but they're proud of me too, I can
tell. I can see it in their eyes, which they are in no hurry to take off
me. While the three of them take me in, I take myself in. I have
changed. For one thing, my hair is down to my shoulders now, tied
back with a piece of twine. They laugh when I suck back Nancy's
good strong coffee laced with real cream. I've been using powdered
milk so long this tastes too wonderful. As greasy as a butterpat
plunked in my mug.*

"Have to put some a that in with her rations," Alex says to Nancy.

*He always did call food "rations." Even when he was just pop-
ping over to the store he'd say he was going for rations.*

*I inquire about their lives — the dogs, the warehouse, the boats
— and occasionally there's a pause in the conversation and their eyes
hold still a minute, as if trying to figure out what I mean. Then they
brighten and begin speaking again, usually, but not always, answer-
ing my questions. Once I asked about the boat and Alex answered,
with that look in his eye, "Oh, she's still burnin', still burnin'."*

*It's only later, when I actually am shopping for rations, that I
realize I said "stove." I meant boat, but I said stove. In the hardware
store I ask for fish hooks but say "bullets" instead. There, because the
young Alaskan guy who runs the place doesn't really know me, he
doesn't try to figure it out. It's only after he's asked me a couple of
baffling questions about cartridges that I twig to what I've done.*

"I'm sorry, fish hooks," I say. "And sinkers too. Please."

*Some fish only bite if the bait lies on the bottom. It just depends.
I zip the hooks and sinkers into the pocket of my jacket. There is lots
of mail for me, all from Richard, and I stuff the letters in with my
rations, wanting to save them for when I get back. I'll light a fire
and make tea and sit and read them. In proper order. There's a package too, which I know will be books. Nancy says she'll come soon for
a visit. When the trail's drier.*

"It's the livin' alone, hon," she says, "makin' you lose words."

It's not until I'm a good fifteen minutes on the trail that I

*realize exactly what she was referring to. Losing words. She thinks
I'm losing words because I'm not talking much. This is both true and
not true. I'm not talking much. There was a time this winter I went
almost four weeks without speaking to anyone. And it's true that I
was calling boats stoves and fish hooks bullets back there, but I don't
think I'm losing words. I feel I have more words swirling around in
my head now than I've ever had. Words words words. I'm talking.
I'm just not talking out loud.*

⑥

*The Americans come for the fishing
        The lawyers and the doctors
From Vancouver and Victoria
        Come all the way up to sleep
On the hard ground in a tent
        And our nurse goes to Las Vegas.*

*I've never been on a holiday
        Unless you count ones as a kid
The ones you're taken on
        As opposed to going on
Do you count those?
        Let's not count those.*

*Holiday in that case means
        Throwing up before they stop the car
Frying on a beach while your
        Mother looks sad because
Your father's reading a book
        Instead of looking at her.*

*No, I've never been on holiday
        Not in Montreal nor here
I'm too bent on making for myself*

A life, a life, a life
A life I feel no tearing need
To get away from.

⑥

Soapberry brew
and hot moose stew
can warm those bones
all through and through

⑥

I'm gathering bits and pieces of woodsman lore as if planning to
make a trip. "Always kindling under a live spruce," "Always dry wood
on the inside of a dead tree," "Keep your matches in a bottle." This I
do anyway. I keep my matches in a pill bottle and zip it into my
jacket when I snowshoe in winter because I have no hope of starting
a fire Johnny Carlick's way. So far I've never been lost but I wonder,
am I pushing it? Am I heading further and further into woods, with
all the stories I've absorbed of lean-tos and spruce kindling, to see if I
could manage a night — or two — out there on my own? I don't
know. I do know that sleeping outside on my porch is a winter plea-
sure I would never have imagined. So toasty warm and so freezing
cold, both. The creaking cracking sounds of the trees like magnified
nighttime house sounds. But what a house.

⑥

"Taken by the country he dearly loved."
It's a white expression.

The Indians aren't "taken"
by their land.
They're already in it.

๖

smoked salmon salmon belly slimed salmon salmon sandwich
kippered salmon salmon steaks canned salmon salmon casserole
dried salmon

๖

In the smokehouse, blood.
It drips clear and red from
the mouths of salmon.
Why isn't this frightening?
Why don't I mind?
I welcome blood. I was
raised in a bloodless
house by bloodless people.
No ooze, no drip, no
colour.
Give me blood. I'll lick
blood. I'll watch it
drip.

๖

Of course, the guy before Quinn had the relay wires. If he got sick
or scared or lonely, he could communicate. We can't. I mean, I
can't. Say I fell and broke my leg, could I crawl the half-hour

walk into Telegraph Creek? Maybe. Say I swallowed wrong and
got a plug of moosemeat caught in my windpipe...what would
it be like, those last few moments, knowing this was it? Knowing
you'd done it now, lights out, curtains. What if the cabin caught
fire? What if the roof caved in? What if a grizzly slashed me to
pieces? What if? What if? So far, the biggest danger has been splin-
ters. It seems I can't reach up to my shelves without grazing my
knuckles along the wall and getting splinters. Most of them are so
close to the surface I just pick them out with my fingernails. This
upsets Richard and he sends a first-aid kit. So now I have, beside
my Dickens and Tolstoy, a little tin with a red cross on it contain-
ing gauze, adhesive tape, iodine, tweezers and an enormous
bandage with instructions on how to make a proper sling. I amuse
myself one evening making up slings and bandaging my head,
with no mirror to see how I'm doing. I'm reminded of the
nursery rhyme:

> Jack and Jill went up the hill
> to fetch a pail of water
> Jack fell down and broke his crown
> and Jill came tumbling after.

❦

The brush
lying on my
mirrored dresser
among the figurines
the porcelain animals
and the brush
tortoiseshell handle
boar's hair bristles
you were supposed
to care about
things like that
chintz, sterling, mahogany

boar's hair
how was I to know?
I thought it meant
a boring person's
hairbrush
but knew enough
by then
not to say it
not to ask

Living without mirrors
is the best thing
Not even a tiny one
over the enamel bowl
Why watch myself
brush my teeth?
Why watch myself
at all?
Strange things, mirrors.
We had them all over the
house in Toronto
A big one from counter
to ceiling in
the bathroom, an oval
one in the front hall for
hair smoothing,
a long one in every bedroom
for head to toe surveillance,
watching, watching, watching
ourselves.
Shoulders back, tummies tucked,
hair combed, hems straight,
smiles pasted on

eyes sad, sad, sad.
A dead giveaway, eyes.
Mirrors of the soul.

&

I understand the totem now. The big face is Katlyn. Nothing going
on here. Everything's fine here. No problems here. But sticking out
my right ear, nagging little Kate with sad, sad eyes and a down-
turned mouth. Something is going on here.

&

The brush
poised above my head
drawn slowly, slowly
through my long long hair
one-two-three-four
why does this upset me?
it's such a loving
thing to do
if I were to complain
to Heather or to Susan
would they roll
their eyes and say
"I wish" as though
their mothers were
exemplars of neglect
and mine of care?
Probably.

Always being told
how very lucky I am

my mother is beautiful
my father has a good job
and drives a big car
I have lots of
nice clothes
and my mother
brushes my hair

The brush
makes me uncomfortable
and yet I don't
know why
perhaps because
like the silver
and the damask
it's one more thing
that has to be
taken care of
it has to be washed
in warm sudsy water
and left to air
dry, you can't just
stand it in a jar
of hot ammonia-laced
bubbles, like Heather
does with her
Fuller Brush brush
then leave it on
the rad, no
you have to treat
it right
because it's beautiful

I was very young, she said

How young, Mummy?

Too young.

Was he handsome?

So handsome.

Tell me that part.

I've told you it before.

Tell me again.

> *He was so handsome. And so funny, kind of self-mocking —*

Dad?

> *Yes. He said he'd been in the army for months now and so far no action. But he was scared too. They all were, of course. Our job was to pretend not to notice.*

Us?

Women. Girls.

Why?

So they could do what they had to do.

Keep going. Do the dance.

> *My girlfriends and I went to a dance. Practically as soon we got there, he came right up to me and said if I danced with anyone but him that evening he'd jump off the boat in the middle of the Atlantic.*

Dad said that?

> *Yes. So I danced with him. He was a good dancer. He was leaving so soon. He knew someone who knew someone... who could marry us on short notice.*

So you married him.

Yes.

Because you loved him.

He was leaving so soon.

And you loved him so much.

> *He might never come back. A lot of them didn't. He wasn't supposed to. I thought he was —*

I don't like that part. Do the wedding.

My girlfriend made me a suit.

White.

Cream.
You were so beautiful.
Oh, yes.
And he was so handsome.
Yes.

⑥

I always thought it was nice of Jill to go tumbling after Jack,
just the sort of thing I'd do for Bobbin if he ever broke his crown,
but I could never figure out the next verse where they plastered
his head with vinegar and brown paper. White vinegar or malt?
And why brown paper? Wouldn't newspaper have done? And
what good did that plaster do, really? I seem to remember trying
it out, once, cutting a shopping bag into strips and soaking the
strips in a saucer of vinegar, then wrapping them around my fore-
head. No wait, did I do that or did I just think about doing it?
What I do remember, definitely, and more than once, is lying in
my darkened room, my mother dipping a facecloth into a
basin of cold water and — I can smell it now — vinegar!
I used to get dreadful headaches. I remember that now, though
I haven't had a headache in years. I remember lying in a dark-
ened room with a splitting headache while my mother dipped
the facecloth into the basin, rung it out, then folded it into a
narrow strip and laid it across my forehead. It felt so good. It
smelled of vinegar. The cloth would grow warm after a while
and she'd take it from my forehead, dip it, wring it and go
through the whole thing again. In the dark. It's funny how
memories bubble up when you live like this. I can't see my
mother's face, only her hands dipping and wringing and folding
and pressing. I can feel her palm on my forehead. I can feel
her hand slipping behind my head and lifting it up. She's holding
a little glass to my lips and the smell of it instantly overpowers
the smell of vinegar — rye. Sometimes, when I had my
headaches, I would get rye and warm water and sugar all

mixed up in a little glass. I don't remember them ever giving
that to Jack:

> Jack and Jill never took a pill
> The way they really ought-ter
> They'd simply fix a tasty mix
> Of sugar, rye and water.

⑥

It's as if I've woken up
but then
I keep waking up, thinking
this is it, this time
I really am awake.
Then, "poof"
I wake up again.
Woke up in that studio
twirling, tossing, spinning
on a sheet of paper
with two smiling idiots
beside me
their lips pout
their hair shines
their bodies sway
while mine stays rooted to one spot.
The photographer's a whirling dervish
full of noises
beautiful, beautiful, beautiful
as though we're pet kittens.
The others are loving it, though.
They're soaking it up
they actually get better at it
"it" being twirling and smiling and preening.

They are kittens
They're positively purring
beautiful, beautiful, beautiful
Is that what my parents paid all that money for?
One of those endless sacrifices I never wanted?
So I could stand on a sheet of paper with
a pair of giggling girls in too much makeup
while this dervish clicks away?
"More, hair, honey."

He's speaking to me.
More hair? I'm tempted to say
"This is all I have."
But I know what he means,
this is how he talks,
more hair, more leg, more oomph, more pizzazz
more je ne sais quoi
more more more more.

I'm bent over, humouring him
when he touches me.
A hand is in my hair.
I want to scream
but I don't scream
I'm back with mummy
beautiful, beautiful mummy
and she's brushing my hair
with the tortoiseshell brush
one, two, three...
Go faster, Mummy, please
Oh, I hate it when she takes so long
four, five, six...
but my pleading is silent
I mustn't say anything
or I'll hurt Mummy's feelings —
she has so many feelings, but I'm
the only one who knows that —

then she'll lose count
and have to start all over again
one, two, three, four
and it'll be like that to a hundred
only, I'll feel her hurt feelings
through the brush
through the boar's hair bristles
through my hair and scalp
and into my brain
bad Katlyn, five
bad Katlyn, six
bad Katlyn, seven.

⑥

Old-timer's lips are burnt
and swollen with the sun
sitting or standing he looks
half bent and creaky
but his eyes, those eyes
crackle

He carries papers for smokes
in his pocket and bug repellent
which he never bothers with any more
and not because the bugs
have lost their taste for his
blood

Like all old-timers he loves chat
if it should happen to come his way
but he warms to it slowly
like the thick dark liquid
he draws over those lips and calls
tea

Traders paid for his furs, sure
but truth is he and the wife
lived mostly on what they grew
and he rhymes off a list of things
you only half believe could grow
here

Ina passed some thirty years ago
and he's lived since on salmon, trout
and porridge, it's the tea laced with
lime juice that keeps those toothless
gums from turning, like the lips, to
black

When he's tired or simply had enough
there's no goodbye, he bends and
unbends and "gathering up his bones"
he disappears inside his house
the door closing on one last
cackle

⑥

Nine months inside someone
who wishes you dead
Nine months inside someone
who sees you as the ruin
of flat stomach
and slender thighs
Two years of having
your every need resented
Two years' apprenticeship
in pretending not to notice
Hungry?
Pretend not to notice

Wet?
Pretend not to notice
It worked for the boys in '42
didn't it?
Did it?
Then he came home
the man who was supposed
to have died
that dead man came home
and, suddenly, you were noticed
　　　"She's pretty, Eva, prettier'n you."
Oh, no, oh, please, it's wonderful
but it's the wrong thing to say
Pretty?
Pretend not to notice
pretty please

◌

The first time I went into moss
was after one of his "episodes"
I'd been eating lunch
quietly, always quietly
my mother and I had polished all
the silverware, and there
was the tablecloth on the table
as usual, the one with
the funny name — damask
everything was perfect
everything was orderly
but sometimes, she said,
that only made it worse
they'd come home and everything

was just the same
tablecloths, silverware,
roast beef and cookies
after all they'd been through
after all they'd seen

Everything was so quiet
I could hear us all chewing
chewing, chewing
then quietly, slowly
he transferred his fork
from his left hand
to his right
and he raised his right hand
and slammed it down
into the thick slice
of roast beef, well done
outside cut

I kept eating
pretending not to notice
though the food formed a
fibrous ball in my mouth
I knew I couldn't swallow
When he'd jabbed the meat
some peas jumped off the plate
and a little spatter of gravy
had touched my left cheek
but I didn't reach up to wipe it

I knew this was one of those times
those different times, when I could
leave the table without asking
so I put my knife and fork down
side by side, tines up
and slid off the chair
and I put one foot in front of the other

until the sound of the stabbing
was far far away
and I was out in the yard
lying on my belly
going into moss

⑥

When did the Ice Lady
turn to me?
When did she take
me on as a project?
From No One's Girl
to Daddy's Girl
to Mummy's Girl
by ten I was hers

Hers to dress
hers to coach
I should have been
reading Alice Through
the Looking Glass
not gliding around the
living room with it
on my head
"Stomach in, stand tall,
head up, smile
not too much."

Can you smile too much?
Apparently, and you
can smile too little
also, just right is

what we aim for
a little Mona Lisa
in mint-green dress
pink would be lovely
but clashes
with the hair
the hair, the hair
the strawberry-blonde
that Casey would waltz with

Part of me lived
in terror that someday,
somewhere — perhaps
shopping for green
hats and shoes —
I'd run into this
Casey and he'd
ask me to dance
then what would I do?
We hadn't practised
waltzing yet
just walking around
with books on our heads

And part of me, of course,
didn't care about Casey
not at all
part of me was outside
laughing, with Bobbin
and Cindy, picking
our noses and
farting, and
pretending not to notice
the one inside
in the mint-green dress
with a book on her head
and a smile

❧

She has so many feelings
but I'm the only one
who knows that
and part of why
she likes me now
is that I don't let on
I don't let on about her
she doesn't let on about him
that way, he can do what he has to do
whatever that thing is
that takes him away at six
and sends him back at six

Whatever it is, it buys her
some things she says she wants
chintz, sterling, mahogany
but I know what she really wants
she wants him to look at her
the way he sometimes looks at me

❧

It was Cindy who first told me about the beatings
I didn't believe her
"Why do you think you get headaches?" she asked
Because I'm over-sensitive over-imaginative and very delicate
She laughed, "Right, tell me another one..."
And she had a point, I mean, I could outspin her and Bobbin
And I could twirl longer and faster
And I could run farther and harder

But ... I was also sickly, a bit delicate and much too sensitive
Wasn't I?
She laughed again, a big gaping mouth laugh without putting her
*   hand over or anything*
It was beginning to get on my nerves
But I also wanted to hear more, this kind of talk made my skin
*   goose-bumpy*
"*With the brush — bam bam — shoulders, arms, tum tum, back-*
*   side, anywhere it doesn't show ... if you wear long sleeves*
*   anyways.*"
Anyway
"*What's the diff?*"
Okay, smartypants, if she hits all over, how come it's my head that
*   aches, huh? Answer that one*
"*From all the crying, stupid.*"
I never cry, I said, I was getting mad
"*Yeah, right, tell me another one.*"
Liar
"*I'm the one who never cries, you bawl your eyes out — wah wah.*"
Liar
"*Crybaby.*"
Liar, liar, liar!
"*Crybaby, Crybaby, Cry — *"

And that was the last I ever saw of Cindy. I missed her, though I
would never let on. And I never cried again, no matter what,
because you just never knew. She might come back. Cindy with
her big fat mouth and her dirty finger, pointing at me. You just
never knew.

✿

Most whites stay put. I'm
white. I stay put.
But sometimes I think about it.

Moving, following moose or caribou.
Camping on high mountains in fall
then down the frozen Stikine
in winter
as far as the mouth of the Iskut.

I would roll in the muck
I'd catch fish with my hands
I'd slit them open
with my sliver of obsidian
and eat the flesh raw.

⑥

Oh, so you've seen a lot, have you, Father?
Seen things, terrible things, things a
pretty little girl should never
have to know about?
Would you like to hear what I've seen?

> *I've seen ice-angry eyes*
> *in the face of someone I depended on for life*
> *I've seen a man whose sudden entry into my world*
> *filled me with so much hope it makes me cry*
> *I've seen hope evaporate with every episode*
> *as he shivered and shook and jabbered*
> *from his position at head of the table*
> *in the only chair with arms*

I've looked on hate
and longed for it to hold me

⑥

Lichens and mosses are the first plants to establish themselves following the retreat of ice. Their presence, together
with frost action and erosion, begins the long process of
creating soil.

I must have looked silly
lying there, stretched out on the rock
crying

I couldn't get in, you see.
Here I have moss that stretches
across miles
creeping into crevices
blanketing boulders
a veritable carpet of moss
a world of moss
to explore
to lose myself in
only I can't.

There was a time
when a fist-sized patch
of moss could be
my universe
and now
now I stand outside it
on it
but I can't get in.

Now I have to close
my eyes and dream
what I used to do
with eyes wide open.
Is that what it means to be an adult?
To only be fully awake
in sleep?

6

One-Eye Mike
likes caribou better'n moose
'n groundhog better'n beaver
but he's bats
too much a the home-brew
good shot, though
go through the year with two cartridges
one fer the first caribou
one fer the second
saw him wave "hi" once
'n the dumb beast
hung aroun', looked aroun'
caught it between the eyes
bang.

Oh, sure there's wolverine, marten
beaver, mink, fox
"When the rabbits are plenty
The salmon are not."
So. Salmon summer comin'
Kings any day now
Sockeye, then yer coho
crazy thing when ya
catch one so big
a knife won't do
to slit 'er throat
need a hatchet.

I never did mind
solid tude
never did mind
my own company
there's them

a course that do
they go nuts
"bushed" ya call it
lots a stories
men diggin' their
own graves then
sittin' on the edge
shootin' themselves
men walkin' on
thin ice
men juss layin'
down in the snow
so's to freeze
isn't that a
corker though?
to juss lie down
'n die.

The brush
was a threat
a tortoiseshell
threat
tell and you'll
catch it
tell and you'll
upset-the-applecart
be-the-death-of-me
get-what-you-deserve
what's-coming
your-comeuppance
every time I saw it

every time I held it
every time I felt it
drawn through my
long long hair
the brush
was a threat

I'm sorry, boar
I'm sorry, tortoise
to think that you died
for that

⑥

Nellie Cashman

Everyone talks about her with a glint
    in their eyes, even when calling her crazy
    like Alex calling me bush woman
    and meaning it as a compliment

It was 1876 that Nellie, a "murrican"
    up and passed through Wrangell
    without any fuss and bother
    on the winter trail on the Stikine

What must she have looked like
    that nineteenth-century woman
    and her dogs churning the fine white powder
    as they headed determinedly north?

When the gentlemanly commander
    of the U.S. troops heard about Nellie
    he couldn't abide it, it just wasn't right
    and he sent out a party to the rescue

It took the boys longer than they expected
    because Nellie and the dogs made good time
    but they caught up to her finally
    where she'd set up a most comfortable camp

Nellie thanked them kindly for their concern
    and all the trouble they'd put themselves to
    on her account, then she fed them some of
    her good hot grub and sent them back home

What must they have looked like
    those uniformed troops sent packing
    back to Wrangell with a good meal under
    their belts but no damsel in distress?

Anyway, Nellie pushed on and she made it
    and for years they talked about her in the
    mining camps with that mix of baffled pride:
    first fool white woman to reach the Cassiar

⑥

Lichens and mosses are the first plants to establish themselves following the retreat of ice. Their presence, together
with frost action and erosion, begins the long process of
creating soil.

I don't have to cry for the moss I can't enter
I am moss
The ice has retreated, I've retreated from ice
I like it here
I'm lichen here
I'm moss
And I've begun the long process of creating soil

BREETZ CALLED. He was back in New York and wanted to see me. He arrived the following day. He didn't look good. We went out for dinner and I thought the subject of conversation would be the breakup of his second marriage, but it wasn't. He was obsessing about something Diana Vreeland had told him over lunch. It wasn't she who had "discovered" Breetz, it was Marilyn Monroe.

"Her, Richard," he kept saying. "She herself. Her."

He drank a good deal that night and fell asleep on my couch soon after we returned to the coach-house. The next morning, after two strong cups of coffee and a shower, he looked more like the old Breetz but was still fixated on the same subject. He was amazed, he said, that he'd never questioned it before. Every year, thousands of portfolios were sent to *Vogue*. These went into the unsolicited pile — no one even looked at them. He knew this. Why in his years at *Vogue* had he never thought it peculiar that his photos had even been noticed? He'd never considered it, he said, because he was a young man utterly convinced of the extraordinariness of his talent. But as he said this, by the very fact that he said it, I sensed something in Breetz that I had never sensed before. He was starting to doubt his talent. He was starting to wonder if he was really the greatest photographer who had ever lived. He was starting to wonder if he would ever get the photos he had always dreamed of getting. He went on to tell the story again.

"She was in the office, Richard. Marilyn. Marilyn herself was in the office. She opened that envelope, pulled out that photo and told Diana that she would sit for *Vogue* if the guy who photographed that — "

I knew which photograph he meant. And I could tell by Breetz's intensity how much this photograph meant to him. Somehow, he had been chosen from the thousands of other photographers, all of whom would have given anything to photograph Marilyn, and it had been Marilyn herself who had done it. She, not Diana, not *Vogue*, had discovered Breetz. She had seen something in that photo that she wanted. She had singled him out. But as Breetz went on, I suddenly realized his attitude towards the photograph had changed. He had always acknowledged it was beautiful. He had always said that he had caught something quite extraordinary, but now he started talking about it in a different way. He asked me if I remembered it. Of course I remembered it, I said.

"Do you remember the velvety quality it had?"

I thought for a moment, or at least pretended to, then replied.

"Yes, yes, I remember it had a soft quality."

"Velvety," Breetz said. "Yet luminous. Velvety and luminous at the same time."

I kept quiet and let him speak.

"She did something. Whoever that girl was, she did something."

I was getting quite nervous. For the first time in all the years I had known Breetz, he talked as if it was the model who had done something, not him.

"What?" I asked.

"I don't know," Breetz said. "That's the whole point. I don't know what she did, but I do know that whatever it was, Marilyn did it too. And no one else can get it. I've searched the world. I've worked with the best in the business, the best on the planet. Shenute and I tried everything, but we never got it. Only Marilyn could get it. Marilyn and that girl, whoever she is."

"Excuse me," I said, and under the pretence of going to the washroom I escaped. I shut the door behind me and stood there for a few minutes, thinking. After I'd collected myself, I flushed the toilet and stepped back out into the living room.

Breetz sat at my desk, his head in his hands.

"Richard," he said. "I've got to see that photo again. That photo and the other ones from that session."

I'll always look back at that moment as the most decisive in my life. Breetz was my best friend. Granted, in the last few years we'd grown apart, but we'd had so many years together in which we'd shared everything. So should I tell him that the photo he was looking for, not just the photo, but also the contact prints of the entire session, were just six inches from his elbow? There they sat in the top drawer of my desk. I couldn't tell him, of course, because of what Kate had

written. Richard, don't ever show those photos to anyone. And Breetz
wasn't just anyone. Breetz was the most ambitious person I'd ever
met. And he was ambitious for the very thing Kate was fleeing from.
Obviously, Kate had something. And Breetz wanted it. I knew that if
he got it, he would destroy Kate in the process.

So I lied.

"Well, why don't you go to Toronto and get them?" I said.

"Yeah, yeah," he said. "We'll go, we'll go right now."

Another decision. Should I let him go alone or should I accompany him and play out the charade. I decided on the latter. So
that evening we took the train to Toronto. We ate in the dining
car. We had wine with dinner and Breetz followed that with a couple of cognacs. Then we drifted into the club car, where Breetz
continued drinking, mostly scotch. I didn't attempt to keep up. We
taxied from Union Station to Glen Road. The house was dark but I
knew that it was a place where someone was always awake, so I
rapped lightly on the door. A minute later, someone tentatively
peered out.

"I'm Richard," I said. "Elizabeth's son."

He looked relieved. "Sam," he said, offering his hand. "Elizabeth's
asleep."

Without acknowledging Sam, Breetz headed up the stairs. I followed. When we reached the door, Breetz automatically reached up
and felt along the ledge. Dust coated his fingertips. He put the key in
the lock, turned it and opened the door. I switched on the light. There
it was as it had always been — the darkroom. Breetz immediately
went over to the filing cabinet. Of course, I knew what he was going
to find. I had been preparing myself for this moment the whole trip.
He started working his way through the files. I could feel his excitement growing. Finally, he got to where he knew it should be. He
looked at me.

"It isn't here," he said.

"Of course it is," I assured him.

"It isn't here," he repeated. "You look."

So I walked over to the cabinet and thumbed my way through it.
As I got nearer to nineteen sixty I slowed down. I thumbed past where
I knew it had been. Then I turned to Breetz.

"Must have been misplaced."

Breetz looked at me and the glimmer of hope in his eyes made me feel sick.

"Misplaced?"

And as he watched, I made a show of checking the file in front and the file behind. Then Breetz stepped forward and gently nudged me aside. I could smell the scotch on his breath.

"They've got to be here, Richard. Somewhere in this filing cabinet is that photo."

"Best do it methodically," I said.

So Breetz started back at those first photos taken when we were thirteen. He would take a file out, flip through the photos and contact sheets and then put it back into its folder. I stood, watching him and feeling more and more nauseous. He was obsessed. He desperately wanted that photo. And just as desperately I knew he couldn't have it.

"Don't you have a copy?" I asked.

"No. No," he said. "I haven't seen that photo in years."

"What about Diana?"

"Marilyn took it."

"So there are no other copies?" I said, trying to sound as incredulous as I could.

"None," said Breetz.

And then he looked at me with what I can only describe as pure anguish.

"What's worse," he said, "is I don't even know her name. I have no idea who that girl was. She was someone sent to me by a modelling school. I figured I'd walk up here, open the file, find the photo, find the release form . . . find her."

"It must be here somewhere," I said pulling out the bottom drawer and beginning to look through each of the files once again.

"It's not here," said Breetz. "It's not here. Someone has stolen it."

"Breetz," I said. "No one has been in this room since you and I left it seven years ago. Look at the dust."

"Someone has stolen it."

"Be reasonable, Breetz. Why would anyone steal that photograph?"

"Someone knows."

"Knows what?" I said.

"That she can do it. That the girl in that photo can do it."

"Do what?" I said.

"Whatever it is," Breetz said.

"Whatever it is?" I repeated, half recognizing my father's technique.

"Whatever it is Marilyn could do."

"Breetz," I said. "You've been drinking."

"*You* haven't been drinking. Do *you* see the photo here?" As he said it, he thrust some files in my face.

"No," I said.

"Here?" he said, grabbing a handful of files from the lower drawer.

"No," I repeated.

He kept going. He stood and emptied file after file, crying, "here." He swept the empty trays off the counter — here? — he reached up and tore the clothesline from overhead — here? — the drying clips flying and ricocheting before clattering onto the floor — here?

"Breetz," I said, "stop. Stop!"

But he wouldn't. He wouldn't and he didn't.

The next thing I knew Sam was there. He assumed Breetz was having a bad trip and in a few minutes had restrained and settled him down. He sent me to the bathroom for a hot towel and when I came back Elizabeth was kneeling on the floor, cradling Breetz's head in her arms.

"Breetz," she was saying, "just tell me what the problem is, just tell me, I'll listen."

"I have to find that girl," he moaned. "I have to find that girl."

"Don't worry, Breetz," my mother said. "Don't worry, we'll find the girl."

And so there they were: Breetz, as if in a fever, rolling his head from side to side; Sam, alert and ready to restrain him again; Elizabeth, holding him in her arms, murmuring comforting words. Not one of them noticed me. Not one of them noticed me as I stood there, seemingly outside of it all. But I wasn't — I was more involved than any of them.

"Don't worry, don't worry," my mother kept saying, "we'll find her, we'll find that girl."

Over my dead body, I thought.

ELIZABETH POURED STRONG COFFEE into a couple of mugs. She'd hoped Richard would stay, but he hadn't. He had taken the morning train back to Montreal. She wondered if Breetz would come downstairs or whether she should take the coffee up to him. She decided to take it up. He was sitting on the edge of the bed, dressed, his hair still damp from the shower. She placed the tray on the side table. Breetz looked up at her and smiled.

"Thanks, Elizabeth," he said.

"Feeling better?" she asked.

"Much."

But she noticed his hands were trembling as he picked up one of the mugs.

"So who's this girl?"

Breetz smiled. There were fine lines in the corners of his eyes. He looked older than his twenty-eight years, and it occurred to Elizabeth that he might not have any memory of the night before.

"I behaved badly, Elizabeth. Sorry."

"Don't worry, Breetz," she said, pouring a little cream into her mug. "Now tell me about this girl."

"Oh, that. That's nothing."

"I think it's something,"

Breetz didn't say anything.

"So who is she, Breetz?"

"She's not anyone I know. I photographed her once. She walked out on me. In all the years I've taken photographs, she's the only girl who's ever walked out on me. I don't even know her name."

"But she's special."

"Special," said Breetz, nodding. "Only now do I realize how special she was. Like Marilyn." He took a sip of his coffee, then continued. "Milton Greene said it best — he said when you photograph Marilyn Monroe you don't get what you're expecting. Something happens between her and the film. Those aren't my words, Elizabeth, those are his. Something happens between her and the film that no other woman can manage. Something flashes forth; you don't see it until you develop it. I've photographed thousands and thousands of women and only once have I got what I didn't expect."

"The girl."

"The girl. Right at the beginning. Right when I'd just started, I went into that darkroom expecting one thing and got something else. I remembered the other girls, I remembered The Umbrella Sequence, but when we came to develop the photos, come to think of it, it wasn't me, it was Richard who first noticed it — Richard's photo — I was expecting nothing and I got this photo that was beautiful and became more beautiful every time I looked at it. I was expecting nothing. I don't even have that photo any more, but every time I think of it, it gets more beautiful. It gets more beautiful and it doesn't even exist; it's just in my mind. That's what a Marilyn photo does. You look at it once, you say, Gee that's a nice photo. You look at it again, you say, That's a fabulous photo. And every time you look at it, it seems to get better. There's some quality to those photos that I can't...she did something, Elizabeth, Marilyn did something. She didn't photograph how she was in reality, she photographed how she imagined herself to be. She didn't photograph what was there, she photographed what she wanted to be there. That was her secret."

They sat in silence for a while.

"I've got to find her, Elizabeth."

"That shouldn't be too difficult."

"I don't even know her name."

"People don't just disappear."

"I don't even know her name. How can I find her?"

"We'll find her, Breetz. I'll help you. We'll play detective."

SO MUCH TIME HAD PASSED since Wesley and I had cut off communication with Mr Miller that we were surprised when we received a letter from an Eileen Norris, a PhD candidate at the University of Chicago interested in the "Serios phenomenon." While she herself had never witnessed Ted taking a "hard" picture, she could supply a list of names of scientists who had.

This struck us as very peculiar. Mr Miller had initially contacted

us because no scientist had taken an interest. Now here was a letter saying that we should take this phenomenon seriously because it had been witnessed by scientists! If scientists were studying the phenomenon, why were they interested in us? It was all very curious. We replied to Mrs Norris that while we were not scientists, nor were we idle curiosity seekers and we would be interested in seeing what she and Mr Miller were talking about. She wrote back and said that Mr Serios would be glad to give us a demonstration, we could name our time and date...could we bring a Polaroid Land camera, model 95? So we wrote back and set a date in September.

We were prepared for everything from outright trickery to a no-show. The day before our flight we got a special delivery letter. Mrs Norris wanted to remind us that Ted had a problem with alcohol and, as with others suffering from this ailment, he sometimes failed to keep important appointments. However, she added, she would take it upon herself to remain in telephone contact with him on the day of our arrival. Then she added that if we wanted to bring along some sealed opaque envelopes containing pictures, Ted would try to reproduce these images for us. Ted preferred buildings, she wrote. She signed off wishing us a pleasant and successful trip.

Jack Miller met us at the airport. We immediately hailed a taxi and this was one of the few times in my life when I witnessed someone out-talk Wesley. Jack Miller never stopped. He smoked hand-rolled cigarettes and as he smoked one he would pack, roll and lick another. That and the Chicago accent made him a little hard to follow. But he was bright. He told us how he had begun reading about hypnotism and clairvoyant travelling, and during the ride to the hotel he supplied us with quite a bit of information about the man we were soon to meet. The amazing Ted Serios, as he referred to him. He told us about the Syndicate, which, he said, had long since lost interest in Ted as he had not led them to any treasure. As we rode along, our guide kept up a steady stream of chatter, occasionally pointing out significant buildings.

"Missin' the point," he kept saying. "They just kept missin' the point. That there's the Union Carbide building. Serios came up with a pirate, only the pirate kept screwin' around...wouldn't tell us where the treasure was hid and this pissed the boys off no end. The boys'd

pressure me, I'd pressure Ted and the more I pressured him...Ted not being the most stable guy...he's got a problem with alcohol, ya know, doesn't show sometimes. See that? That's the Montgomery Ward building. Anyway, after the pirate fizzled out I was getting real desperate. Didn't know what to do. That's when I came up with my inspiration — that's what I always call it, the Big Inspiration — and handed him a camera. Then he started getting these photos. At first, he thought he must be sleepwalking — though how you'd get a photo in the dead of night I didn't ask — anyway, I sealed his door up from the outside with masking tape and it never got broke. Never got broke and he still got photos. So now I know something weird, I mean, really weird, I mean something strange beyond belief is happening. That's when I write the guy at Kodak — there's the Wrigley Building, double your pleasure, double your fun — Kodak guy writes back saying that tampering with the film's impossible. Well, not impossible, but so difficult you'd have to have a lab and all sorts of guys working on it. I knew we were really onto something but the Syndicate was losing interest. Sure would be a pity if you professors come all the way from Montreal Canada and Ted doesn't show, but he's done it before. Gets drinking, meets a dame and that's it — poof — he's gone. Shows up a few weeks later all contrite. Kinda hard to keep people interested, ya know? But what could be more interesting than what Ted can do? Outta nothing. He creates them photos out of his head. I mean I'm no ignoramus, I done a lot of reading on this stuff. That's how I come across your article, professors, I come across this article — don't take this wrong — I ain't read nothing in that article half as interesting as what Ted can do. But them psychologists at University of Chicago, they just laugh. One guy even comes, sees Ted do it, signs the testamonal and then says he's not interested. He couldn't get no funding for it he says. So what crazy kind of world is this we live in? Ya need funding to do research, and ya only get funding if the research makes sense. Ted don't make no sense so he don't get no funding. That's the Palmer House up there — you brought a camera? Good. I don't see how Ted can fake anything when you bring the camera — you bring the camera, you supply the film — like the guy at Kodak said — impossible. Now I'm gonna leave you two once we get there, 'cause it's no good if I come. I seen this before, but that's not

the point. The point is everyone always thinks I'm in cahoots with Ted. Like somehow we're tryin' to put one over on people, though as far as scams go this one strikes me as pret-ty dumb, 'cause I don't see how anybody could make any money out of it. Ted, all he wants is recognition. He wants the world to say, 'Yeah, this happened, this little guy is amazing.' But of course no one but me and a few other people seem to think so. I don't get it. I just don't get it. Here we are... I'm gonna shake your hands and wish ya all the best. Sure hope he shows. Mrs Norris'll meetcha inside."

And, lifting his fedora straight up off his head then straight back down again, he left us. Wesley paid for the cab, I lifted our bags out of the trunk and a minute or two later we were standing at the reception desk. At this point a woman approached us.

Eileen Norris seemed quite nervous and kept smiling and nodding. She said she had been talking to Ted only an hour before and that he had assured her he was going to be here. With this she gave her crossed fingers a shake.

We had an hour to fill before Mr Serios was scheduled to arrive, so we decided to grab a quick bite. Mrs Norris was not nearly so voluble as Jack Miller, but over coffee and a sandwich we managed to get her story about the scientists, which more or less corroborated his.

"They came, they saw, they left," she said.

Just before eight we paid our bill and returned to the lobby.

There he stood. A strange little man. Black hair, fairly long on top but short at the sides, a large nose, bushy eyebrows and dark eyes. He looked to be about forty, neatly dressed in a trench coat, white shirt and tie. Wesley held out his hand.

"Mr Serios, I presume," he said.

"Call me Ted."

A clerk helped us with our bags, I retaining hold of the one with the camera, determined not to let it out of my possession. We stepped into the elevator.

"Bring a camera, doc?" Ted asked.

"Yes," Wesley replied.

"Polaroid?"

"Yes."

"Land 95?"

"Yes."

"Film?"

"Yes."

"How about some target photos. Bring those too?"

The elevator door slid open; the clerk led us to our room. How would we begin? Would we just turn to Mr Serios and say, Well, do your thing? Wesley clapped his hands together and suggested a round of drinks.

I watched Ted. He looked at Wesley, then at Mrs Norris, then at Wesley again and shrugged as if it were a matter of complete indifference to him.

"Perhaps a highball," Mrs Norris said.

I ordered orange juice as did Wesley (we had agreed on this beforehand so as to keep our powers of observation clear). Ted, still feigning indifference, supposed a scotch on the rocks would be all right. But when Wesley started talking to room service, he quickly added, "Make that a double, if ya don' mind."

While we waited for drinks, I did what I knew was the most important task of the evening. I unzipped the small bag that held the Polaroid Land camera and film. The Polaroid was new, still in its box. To further rule out tampering I had taped it up in Montreal. I ripped through the masking tape, opened the box and brought out the camera. I took out the film. Standing on the opposite side of the hotel room, twenty feet from Ted, I loaded the film. Ted was much more interested in the drinks that had now arrived and downed his immediately. He was also a chain-smoker, like his friend Jack Miller. After another round of drinks, at nine o'clock, Ted spoke.

"Ready to go?" he said.

I was certainly ready, but for what I wasn't quite sure. He stood up, walked over to one of the night tables and started emptying his pockets: keys, loose change, a rosary.

"Metal interferes with pitcher takin'," he explained.

He took his chair again and having not yet touched the camera, asked me to hand it to him.

"Gonna fog the first one," he said. "Mind if I take off my shoes?"

I stood before him, watching, as he unlaced his shoes and set them aside. Suddenly, he leaned forward.

"Small dot, big dot," he said.

He started concentrating, staring into the camera. This went on for a minute or so.

"Damn," he said. "Gettin' one of my headaches."

Then he tripped the shutter.

"That's it," he said, handing the camera back to me. "Tried for a plus sign. Print it an' see."

Fog, small-dot-big-dot, and then a plus sign, but the picture that developed was completely black. I didn't think much of this at the time, but in retrospect, because of the light in the room, I realize he should have got his own face.

"Black cat on a black night," Ted said, and as he did there was a tug at my memory. "Blackies," Breetz had called them.

I could sense Mrs Norris' disappointment, but Ted was completely unperturbed. He lit another cigarette and loosened his tie.

"You should see me when I'm hot, doc. When I'm hot, god what I can get. I got the Pentagon once. The Taj Mahal — that's dis temple in India — I got the Eiffel Tower. I got the White House — inside and outside."

At half past nine Ted was ready to give it another go. This time he wanted to work in his usual way, which was with what he referred to as his "gizmo." He produced it for us and I examined it closely. It was a half-inch section of plastic tube.

"Only if ya don' mind," he said.

He could work without it, but preferred not to. Wesley told him to work in whatever way was most comfortable.

"Mind if I take off my shirt?" he asked.

In a moment he sat before us shirtless and shoeless and again I handed him the camera. Ted held the gizmo between his thumb and second finger and pressed it over the lens. His legs were crossed and the camera rested on them. The lens was about a foot from his face.

"Doc, d'ya have a target photo?"

From his suitcase Wesley took out a photo of the Kremlin. He had sandwiched all the target photos between two pieces of cardboard and sealed them in manilla envelopes. He held the one of the Kremlin next to the camera.

"It's a driveway with two people on it," Ted said.

Wesley, no actor, tried to keep his face a blank. Ted started to concentrate. It was quite unnerving to watch him. His eyes were open, his lips compressed and his musculature started to strain and go rigid. His legs shook and once or twice his foot jerked convulsively. His face grew blotchy and red. The veins on his forehead stood out. His eyes grew visibly bloodshot. It was quite worrisome to watch. His breathing became deeper and faster and then suddenly he snapped the shutter. He thrust the camera at me. I counted the fifteen seconds that the photo required to develop and then, somewhat awkwardly, as I was still unfamiliar with these cameras, lifted it out and peeled off its backing. Another blackie.

"D'ya mind if we have a short rest?"

Wesley picked up the phone for room service and asked if anyone wanted anything.

"Double scotch. This broad at the *Chicago Tribune* — she comes to see me, she hardly even looks, then she writes this big article, the only article that ever got writ, about how I'm fakin' it. 'Course she doesn't say how I'm fakin' it, she just says I'm fakin' it. So everybody reads the article and that's that. Serios the fake. That bitch. We'll show her, eh, doc?"

Minutes later the drinks arrived and Ted immediately grabbed for his double. Lifting it to his lips he pointed at his throat.

"For my cold," he said.

The third try began at around ten to ten.

"An entrance," Ted said.

This time, at Ted's request, Wesley held the target envelope (another shot of the Kremlin with a couple of soldiers in the foreground) next to the top of the camera, just in front of Ted's knees. During this attempt I took his pulse. It rapidly reached one twenty. When the shutter clicked Ted gave a small gasp, then looked pleased with himself.

"A little somethin' this time I figger," he said.

But again he was wrong. Another black cat. Ted shrugged and lit a cigarette.

"I been constipated lately," he said. "Sometimes that affects pitcher takin'."

Mrs Norris got up to stretch her legs. Wesley kept the target envelope and I took the camera from Ted while he enjoyed a smoke and another drink. At ten-thirty he was ready to try again. I handed him the camera.

"White house, white boards, green roof," Ted said, changing from "entrance" without chagrin, his voice confident, and gearing up to try again.

One minute later Ted gasped and clicked the shutter. A blackie. Not quite so black as the others but as I knew nothing about Polaroid film perhaps this just had something to do with the development time.

We tried again. Same target, same procedure.

"Part of a building, white boards."

A complete blackie.

We'd now been at this an hour and a half with nothing really to show. Sensing the mood in the room, Wesley had a suggestion.

"I fear we're interfering with your spontaneity, Ted. Never mind the target photos, just go for whatever you can. See what turns up."

"Nah, nah," Ted disagreed. "I'll get somethin', sooner or later, you just watch." He downed his scotch. "I'm hot. My heart's startin' to pound. Feel 'at, doc," he said, thumping his chest, "go on, have a feel."

Wesley placed his hand on his chest and nodded.

"Always a good sign — poundin' heart — good sign, good sign. I'm gettin' hot, gettin' hot.

Then Ted grabbed the camera. This shot wasn't a blackie. There was something amorphous, some fogging and one or two lines and shadows.

"See 'at? See 'at? Somethin's happenin'. Gimme the camera."

I handed him the camera. He grabbed it and, without the usual preparation, tripped the shutter.

A blackie.

He didn't stop. He grabbed the camera again. By this time his entire body was shaking and his breath was coming fast and furious. He handed the camera back to me. I waited ten seconds, then lifted out the print. I waited another moment or two then slowly peeled off its cover.

He'd got something!

The four corners of the photo were black, but within the photo was a sort of illuminated egg shape, and within the egg shape was another amorphous shape going diagonally across the photo. A vague rectangular shape.

I showed it to the others. Wesley studied it intently, but it was Mrs Norris who recognized it. She began hopping up and down.

"The water tower!" she said. "The Chicago water tower!"

Now that I looked at it more closely I could see the indisputable emergence of a structure. At the base of the photo, a crescent shape which I had taken to be just a blotch, I now recognized as the curving arm of a street lamp.

As Wesley and Mrs Norris stared at the photo in amazement, I glanced over at Ted. He was sitting in his chair, staring into space, as if nothing extraordinary had happened. He didn't even ask to see the picture; he simply withdrew into himself, smoking his cigarette.

"A hard photo, my first hard photo," Mrs Norris kept saying, unable to contain her excitement. "The water tower — unmistakably — I can't believe it — the water tower!"

Ted sat there, his head sunk on his chest while I reloaded the camera. Wesley and Mrs Norris were chatting excitedly, when suddenly Ted seemed to come out of his stupor. He started snapping his fingers.

"I'm hot I'm hot I'm hot. Come on come on come on!"

I quickly snapped the camera shut and practically threw it at Ted. He grabbed it and without waiting to sit down, placed the gizmo over the lens and aimed the camera at his face. His face contorted. He was breathing hard. He tripped the shutter.

He *was* hot.

That photo, as it developed, was a partial blackie, but it did have an area of light fogging in the centre.

"Somethin's happenin'," Ted insisted. "Somethin's happenin'. I'm hot, I'm hot." Snapping his fingers, he again indicated for me to hand him the camera. I did.

He got something. The moment I stripped the backing off this next photo I could see that he'd got something. A bull's-eye. There, surrounded by murky darkness but absolutely distinguishable, glowing softly in the centre of the photo, were the illuminated letters of a sign: STEVENS. This photo required no explanation. Eileen Norris was beside herself.

"The Stevens Hotel, it's the Stevens Hotel!"

Another Chicago structure, but with a curious twist. The Stevens Hotel was apparently no longer in existence. It had burned down years before.

"He did it, he did it!" Mrs Norris kept saying.

Eileen wanted to push on immediately and try for more. Ted was game, but Wesley called a halt to the whole thing. Ted's pulse was now racing at a dangerously high one thirty-two. Wesley felt we had enough evidence that something very curious had indeed occurred.

Eileen Norris kept bobbing up and down.

"I'm so excited! I'm so excited! My first hard pictures — I've seen it now, actually seen it — a hard picture! A hard picture!" She turned to me. "Aren't you excited?" she asked. "How can you stand there so calm? Aren't you excited?"

I was calm. I calmly dated and signed the back as I'd done with the water tower shot. Calmly, I handed the photo to Wesley and Eileen for their signatures. Calmly, I watched them sign. But my calm was not complacency in the face of what I had just witnessed. If anything, I would describe my feeling in that moment as one of calm elation. A calm born of certainty. At last I knew what I wanted to do with my life. I wanted to write.

I wanted to write about this.

BREETZ WAS UNABLE TO REMEMBER even the first names of any of the girls from that session. All he could remember was that there had been three models and a sequence with an umbrella. He flew back to New York and the first thing Elizabeth did after he left was place a small personal ad in the *Toronto Star*, inquiring about models who had posed for Breetz Mestrovic in Toronto around nineteen sixty. She was inundated with calls, but was able to eliminate most of them over the phone. It was during a conversation with one of the women, an Amanda Hollis, that Amanda, unprompted, mentioned the umbrella sequence.

"Was there anyone else at that session?" Elizabeth asked.

"Oh, yes," Amanda said. "Linda Faulkner."

Elizabeth was encouraged. Maybe this Linda was the one. Did Amanda know where the other girl was? Certainly, she knew. Everyone knew. Linda Faulkner was the CBC weather girl. Elizabeth thanked Amanda and said she'd try to contact Linda. She was writing an article on spec for *Saturday Night* about the famous Canadian photographer and was particularly interested in talking to people who'd known him in his early years in Toronto. Amanda had a better idea. Why didn't the three of them meet for lunch? She would give Linda a call and arrange everything. So two days later, Elizabeth met the two women for lunch. She knew Amanda wasn't The Girl, but she had high hopes that this Linda Faulkner might be. A few minutes into the conversation, however, she realized this wasn't the case.

Both women remembered the session vividly. Amanda had even kept her copies of the photos and had them with her. Elizabeth tried to contain her excitement. She was about to see a picture of the mysterious girl. There was Amanda. There were four or five photos of her unfolding the umbrella. There were some more photos of Amanda and Linda together, laughing into the camera. And that was it. Not one of the photos showed a third girl.

Amanda said she'd heard that Breetz had sent these photos to *Vogue* and had been hired on their basis. They launched him and the son of a bitch never even acknowledged it. "You can print that!"

Elizabeth smiled and jotted down the quote. Elizabeth then listened, occasionally making notes as they laughed and talked about their lives. She picked up the photos again and studied them.

"There was another girl at that session, oh, what was her name... long blonde hair..."

Elizabeth waited. There was no flicker of recognition from either Linda or Amanda. They went back to talking about children and dogs. A couple of minutes later Elizabeth mentioned the girl again. Again, no recognition. Finally, she asked Amanda outright.

"Do you remember another girl at that session? A girl with long blonde hair?"

No, she didn't. In fact, they were both quite adamant about the fact that Breetz had been the only other person in the room. Puzzling. Elizabeth knew for a fact that Richard had been present at that session too. That night she called him.

Yes, he remembered sessions above Halberstam's. Yes, he thought he even recalled an umbrella sequence, but when she asked him if he remembered a girl with long blonde hair, there was a pause. Then he laughed.

"Elizabeth," Richard said, "do you realize how many girls that description fits? What's her name?"

But Elizabeth couldn't give her name. She and Richard chatted about other things, then they hung up.

She'd drawn another blank. This was proving to be tougher than she'd expected. Who was this girl that no one remembered, whose photo didn't exist, and who had no name?

THE MOMENT I SAW TED PRODUCE A BLACKIE in adequate light, I knew — this had something to do with Kate. I remembered that day seven years earlier, standing in the darkroom and looking at the contact sheet. What had struck me first were the two perfectly black photos in its centre. I had never seen this before. And until Ted I hadn't seen it since. A photo had been taken with more than adequate light and had turned out completely black. What had happened to the photons in that room? Why had they not affected the film?

I cleared my desk. I piled books, papers and file cards onto the couch, then went to the kitchen for a dishcloth to wipe the desk clean. Then I took out the photos that Ted had produced. I placed them in order down the lefthand side of the desk, starting with the first two blackies and ending with the photo of the Stevens Hotel. Then I slid open the righthand desk drawer and took out the file. I opened it and, thumbing through, found the first contact sheet of the session above Halberstam's. I removed it and replaced the file in the drawer. Then I took my magnifying glass and started to examine the images one by one.

The first five were of the three girls. The ash blonde and the brunette were looking at each other and laughing. Then they went through a number of quick poses — parting their lips, baring their shoulders, turning their heads. Off to the side stood Kate. She had long blonde hair almost to her waist. She was thin. She wore makeup. She stood, awkwardly, not posing at all. A less photogenic girl I have never seen. Contacts 6, 7 and 8 show the other two girls still involved with each other, but now Kate is staring into the camera. I examined these three for some time. It was so strange. Kate, with spiky false eyelashes, darkened lips and high heels. Staring straight out at me she seemed to have no expression at all, and yet even in that tiny contact print one got the impression she didn't like whoever was behind the camera. From that point on she is never seen looking into the camera again. Contacts 9, 10 and 11 show the other two girls bouncy and animated. Kate remains awkward and stiff-looking, but now her eyes are averted, in some they even seem to be closed. Contacts 12, 13 and 14 are strange. Kate's face is totally without expression, but her head is in very odd positions. I realized she must be doing something that Breetz was coaxing her to do. Mechanically following some instructions, without the least inner conviction. Breetz was telling her to toss her hair. I remembered how he'd stopped the session and gone forward and actually handled her physically. Contacts 15, 16 and 17 show this. They are of Kate, bent in two like the Tin Man, her hair falling forward like a curtain in front of her, her hands hanging lifeless at her sides. Contacts 18 and 19 were black. Blackies. Black cats on a dark night. I quickly glanced over at Ted's blackies — identical.

Contact 20 was fascinating. It was as if somewhere in the midst of total blackness, light was starting to emerge. That's all it was, just the faintest wisp of white. I examined it with the magnifying glass and then moved on to Contact 21. The wisp had become a blob, and I recalled how I'd first looked at this and couldn't figure it out. But now I had the experience of Ted. I looked over at the emerging photo of the water tower. I remembered how it had seemed nothing but blobs and striations, but once Eileen Norris had identified it as a structure, I was immediately able to see it. I remembered especially the crescent shape at the bottom of the photo that had looked to me like a defect in the film until we realized it was a street lamp. I now looked at what I had termed "the blob." The blob wasn't a blob. It was a hairbrush.

Once I knew it was a hairbrush, I could see it clearly as a hairbrush. Amorphous, yes. Vague, yes. Preternaturally bright. But unmistakably a hairbrush.

Contact 22 showed the hairbrush even clearer. It was hovering in the centre of the photograph, above — what? A foggy shape. I moved my magnifying glass down to Contact 23. At the bottom of the photo there was a circular effect. Bright, glowing, almost like a moon rising on the horizon. And above it floated the hairbrush. If I didn't know what that photo was, I would never have been able to identify it. But the next photo revealed clearly what it was.

Hair.

Contact 24 was *the* photo. The brush was gone and Kate's hair, nape and shoulders filled the entire frame of the contact. Again, I noticed how the photo seemed bigger than the square inch in which it was framed. I opened the file and took out the enlargement. I placed it down in the centre of the desk. I looked at it. Then I looked at Ted's photo of the Stevens Hotel. Two more different images you could not possibly imagine. One an illuminated sign of a demolished building, the other, the long blonde hair of a young girl. In content, utterly different. But they were the same. Both were velvety. Both were luminous. Both had been created by a light that didn't exist. The light of the mind.

Kate had conjured up a hairbrush and put it on film. In doing so she, like Ted, had provided a clue to no less than the mystery of the universe. If Ted and Kate could create images out of nothing and put them on film, then Sir James Jeans was right: The universe is looking less and less like a great machine and more and more like a great thought.

I got up and put on the coffee, then I sat down again and started to make notes.

ELIZABETH TRIED THE MODELLING SCHOOLS NEXT. There were only two up and running in nineteen sixty in Toronto and she visited both of them. She asked if they remembered a long-haired blonde from that year. As soon as she got the question out, she knew the reply.

"Do you realize how many girls that description fits? Can you tell us anything more?"

She told them she was working on an article about Breetz Mestrovic and that he'd said that a photo he'd taken of a young girl in Toronto had launched his career. This got everyone interested. They would sit up and try to remember the girls who had made it. There weren't many, and at any rate it wasn't necessarily one who'd made it that Elizabeth was looking for. Unfortunately, the modelling schools kept the barest statistics: name, address and phone number of graduates. No photos, no descriptions. She couldn't even narrow it down to just the blondes. So she copied their lists from fifty-nine to sixty-one and took them home.

Everyone at the house pitched in. One thing they knew how to do around that house was contact people, so instead of manning the phones trying to get people out for a demonstration, they manned the phones for this. They charmed, they sweet-talked, they spoke to hundreds and hundreds of girls and their families.

About twenty percent of the girls on the lists just couldn't be reached. They had disappeared. Families had moved, new tenants had taken apartments. Gone. But they persisted, methodically working through the lists. They would explain that they were researching an article on Breetz Mestrovic, had the girl ever been photographed by him? If she had, was she blonde? If photographed by him and blonde, could they talk to her? Of the twenty-five girls that Elizabeth actually interviewed, not one of them was The Girl. But they kept at it.

It was Philip who contacted Sarah Glass. It had taken some doing. She had married, changed her name and was living in Port Credit. No, she didn't have blonde hair and no, she hadn't ever been photographed by Breetz Mestrovic. Philip was just about to hang up when she said something that made him pause. No, she hadn't been photographed by Breetz Mestrovic, but she almost had...

"Almost?" Philip asked.

"Yes, it was *that* close."

"So what happened?"

"I was all set to go, I'd been looking forward to it for weeks and weeks, and then the night before I got terrible stomach pains. They got worse and worse…then I threw up and I *still* didn't feel any better, then they got so bad I started screaming with pain so they took me to hospital. It was my appendix. I had it out that morning. My mother called the school and they got someone else."

"Who?" Philip asked.

"When I tell you, you'll just laugh."

"Try me."

"Miss Teen Tyme."

"And who's Miss Teen Tyme?"

"Oh, I don't even remember her name, that's just what we all called her. She was in my class and she was the worst I ever saw. She hated it."

"If she hated it," Philip said, "why did she do it?"

"Her mother."

"Her mother?"

"Yes, her mother made her. She told me that once. She only did it because her mother made her. And her mother was the kind who used to call up the school and insist they send her daughter out, you know?"

"I get it…so when your appendix ruptured, Miss Teen Tyme took your place."

"Yes, but she won't be the girl you're looking for. Not her, anyone but her. She hated modelling."

By the time Philip hung up, the whole room had gone silent.

"Miss Teen Tyme…"

"Teen Tyme Barrettes," one of the girls said.

"What are they?" Philip asked.

"Barrettes, you know, barrettes to hold your hair. I used to have dozens."

"Teen Tyme Barrettes. What does it mean? Did she wear them?"

"Everyone wore them."

All eyes turned towards Elizabeth.

"Don't look at me," she said. "I just had sons."

ACCORDING TO JACK MILLER AND MRS NORRIS, Ted had been demonstrating his unbelievable gifts for over a year now. And yet no one seemed interested in doing further research. Was there something they were able to discern that we weren't? I knew I was not by any means an experienced investigator and I knew that both Wesley and I were credulous by nature. We often approached things with a more than open mind because, as Wesley kept saying, we were curious. But neither of us was stupid. And neither of us could figure out how in the hell Ted could have done what he did by fraudulent means. In fact, we both knew, and said to each other, that he couldn't have. What we saw, we saw.

We felt we should investigate further, but didn't know how to proceed. Then I thought of my landlords. Perhaps Alan Ross would have some advice. He and Wesley had met at my place a couple of times and had hit it off. I knew that at the very least we would have an enjoyable evening chewing it all over. I was just hoping for guidance, but we got much, much more.

"You're saying he somehow affects silver salts?"

"Precisely," Wesley said. "Just as light affects silver salts in the photographic process to produce an image, so Ted is able to affect them with images he sees in his mind."

"Extraordinary," said Dr Ross.

"Absolutely amazing," Hilary agreed.

Dr Ross looked at the photographs Jack Miller had given us. He flipped over the one of the Hilton. It was signed by a professor from the Psychology department at the University of Chicago. He shook his head.

"And this Professor Tosh witnesses this photo, but refuses to research it further?"

"That's right," I said.

"So nobody," Dr Ross said, sweeping his hand over the table, "nobody in Chicago is willing to take the next step."

"Precisely."

"Well, then, why don't we bring him here?"

"Bring him here?"

Wesley and I looked at each other.

"Yes. Yes, let's bring him here. Study him ourselves. I have a little discretionary funding...this, in my opinion, is an eminently worth-while project...I'll take responsibility for it as far as the Medical School is concerned. You two gentlemen can organize the protocols. As you say, Wesley, we need credible witnesses. Witnesses of stature."

"Witnesses of stature," I interrupted, "who are willing to go public."

"Yes, yes," agreed Dr Ross. "No one will be allowed to see the phenomenon who hasn't agreed beforehand to publicly witness what they see, whatever it is they see."

And thus it was that Ted came to Montreal.

I met Ted at Dorval International. Even as he came down the steps from the plane, I could tell he was three sheets to the wind. He scanned the waiting crowd and then started stumbling away from me. I went over and greeted him. Already I could see some of the difficulties we were going to have in studying this man. For a moment I almost sympathized with the Professor Toshes of this world who kept going back to rats and mice, which could at least be locked up in a cage, fed on schedule and would do more or less what was expected of them.

We had rented Ted a small furnished room on Sherbrooke Street. We taxied there and I left Ted sitting in a chair, groggily assuring me that he would be all right.

That night Wesley, Mildred and I had dinner at the Rosses. Also present was a golfing buddy of Alan's, Dr Ian Skillicorn. He was a physicist whose specialty was optics and he had not only agreed to sit in on the Ted session, but had brought along another interested party, Dr Anthony Posta, an electrical engineer. Dr Posta described himself as a benevolent sceptic and Skillicorn, Alan said, was a very shrewd observer.

"The sort of man who always notices which way the grass is bending on the green."

We planned our first session, which was to take place the following evening at the Medical School. While we were drinking coffee, Hilary and Mildred started flipping through one of Hilary's travel magazines.

"Here's a good one," Mildred said. "Isn't this the sort of thing Ted likes?"

She held up for all to see a black and white photo of Westminster Abbey.

"Why bother with target photos at all?" Dr Posta asked. "It seems to me it's not telepathy we're interested in; that's been amply demonstrated. What we're interested in is what is apparently unique to this Serios."

"Yes, yes," Wesley said, "Excellent point. But he seems to like them. Stimulates his unconscious. Who knows what his methods are, but the target photos — along with the gizmo and plenty of drink — seem to be part of it."

"I admit that gizmo interests me," Dr Skillicorn said. "I'll be examining it very carefully tomorrow, I assure you."

"I have it here," Wesley said and he reached into his pocket and handed the gizmo to Skillicorn. "Take it home if you like. Keep it with you till the session."

The next morning Wesley and I went for one of our long rambling walks. We had decided to let Ted sleep and would pick him up ourselves around four. We anticipated a relaxing lunch with Mildred when we got back, but instead she met us with the message that Ted was in jail.

"Serios?" the officer on the desk said. "Oh, yeah, Ted. What a card."

He looked around, pulled out a file and studied it for a moment.

"Under occupation he's got here — what's this — Thoughtographer."

"That's right," I said.

"So what's a Thoughtographer?"

"Someone who creates photographs out of his thoughts."

"What kind of photographs?"

"Buildings, mostly."

"Can you make money doin' that?"

"No," I said. "No, he doesn't make any money."

The policeman laughed and shook his head.

"He's a card that Ted, a real card."

He gestured to another officer.

"Go get Serios," he said.

In the meantime, we had to fill out some forms and vouch for Ted.

"No charges?" Wesley asked.

"Naw," the officer said. "Just get him outta here."

Ted emerged, his face bruised and bloodied, his coat ripped and torn, but he was clearly in high spirits. The more we got to know Ted, the more amazed we became at his powers of recuperation. On the walk back to Wesley's we got the whole story.

"These French broads — why didn' ya tell me? — I'd a been here in no time if ya told me about these French broads. Man, they're hot for me. They don' speak English, see, so they recognize what I got. I got this thing they really like, some sort a magnetism. It don' matter I don' speak no French, I just walked into one a them bars down on Sherbrooke Street there and right off the bat some dame's makin' eyes at me. Slides over. Had the hots so bad I couldn't keep 'er on 'er stool. One dame spots me, then another, then another — " he snapped his fingers three times. "Next thing I'm sittin' with three broads around me. You get three broads aroun' you, know what happens? Trouble. Some guy comes over wantin' to horn in. Figgers all these dames aroun' a little guy he'll get some action. Only, see, he ain' got what it takes. It ain' a square jaw an' straight teeth — no offense, Richie Rich — it's vibrations. Psychic force. Dames recognize it. They start vibratin' wit me and this other guy wants some a the action. Then one of the dames turns to the guy and tells 'im to buzz off. So he gets mad at me! It ain' me tellin' him, it's the dame. But next thing I know, he takes a poke at me. What am I 'sposed to do? I take a poke back. He has a buddy. Buddy gets in on it. Next thing I know, I'm takin' on both of 'em. They's throwin' punches left, right and centre, I'm duckin', the dames are squealin', the bouncer gets in on it…next thing I know the whole bar's fightin' — people smashin' chairs, dames screamin', busted bottles. It ain' easy, doc. It ain' easy bein' a psychic genius. Everywhere ya go there's trouble. Some days I wish I could just turn it off. Go into a bar, have a quiet drink, but no — everywhere I go some dame wants part a the action."

At eight o'clock we arrived at the medical school. Ted was delighted.

"This is more like it," he said. "A medical school, not some rinky-dink hotel. This is where I should be studied."

We walked upstairs to the seminar room.

"Yeah, this is more like it. My own room. I wanna thank you gentlemen. I'm gonna come up with somethin' tonight, gonna do ya proud."

Difficult as Ted was, you kind of had to like the guy.

Hilary and Alan Ross were already there and Drs Posta and Skillicorn arrived shortly thereafter. Mildred volunteered to take notes.

Dr Skillicorn passed around the cylinder, Ted's gizmo. "There is," he said "no discernible way this object could be used to create a pinhole camera effect. I could find nothing about it that could produce a photographic appearance. For one thing, there simply isn't enough light getting through when it's held even loosely over the lens to allow the normal reproduction of any image source that might be concealed in it."

Suspicious as the gizmo was, no one could find anything remarkable about it. Eventually Dr Posta handed it over to Ted who, during the whole discussion and inspection, had sat chain-smoking and staring at the floor.

Next Dr Ross opened four factory-sealed film packages and loaded the cameras. Ted began by trying for the usual things, a plus sign, a dot, fogging. He kept missing, not even producing blackies. He also kept asking Wesley for more scotch.

Ted's next few attempts were clear misses.

After an hour people began to get restless. Some went into the kitchenette to get Cokes (only Ted was allowed to drink any alcohol).

Two more misses.

"This is really pissin' me off. You gentlemen bring me to Montreal, get me this nice room, lay on all this stuff and now I'm not gettin' anythin'. Maybe I'm bunged. This is pissin' me off, dammit, gimme that camera." He grabbed the camera, clicked the shutter.

Another miss.

"Shit. Shit! I ain' gettin' anythin'. I ain' gettin' anythin' — but I will. Bound to get hot sooner or later. Maybe we should take a break, or somethin'. I could take a leak — any volunteers to watch me take a leak?"

Dr Posta volunteered for this honour.

Ted came out of the bathroom swaying and talking volubly. He was on his *Chicago Tribune* rant, one we were becoming increasingly familiar with.

"Goddamn bitch, she says I'm fakin' — doesn't say how I'm fakin', no one ever does, says I'm fakin' an everyone believes *her*, they don' even see me, but they believe her — goddamn bitch. Someday I'm gonna show 'er."

Dr Posta listened to all this, but you could tell he wasn't letting it distract him from his main objective: scrutinizing Ted's every move.

Ted sat down, asked for a camera and announced that he would try again for a plus sign. This time, unlike earlier, I noticed his concentration becoming more intense. He started to shake and his face grew a little blotchy. His knees began to jerk. Then he clicked the shutter.

This time when we peeled off the paper, there was some sort of amorphous form, nothing definite.

Ted slammed his fist on the arm of his chair.

"Damn," he said. "I can get somethin'. Feel my chest. See, doc? I'm gettin' hot. Need a target."

At this point Dr Ross stepped forward. He had a sealed manilla envelope containing one of the target photos Hilary and Mildred had selected the evening before.

"Try for this one, Ted," he said.

"Gimme that." Ted grabbed the camera.

A black cat. Followed soon after by another. And another. All in all, five black cats in rapid succession. But a sixth photo showed fogging.

By this time, as the evening was wearing on and Ted didn't seem to be getting anything, the group examined this last photo, taken with Dr Posta's Graflex, only cursorily. Then Dr Skillicorn placed it on the counter in the kitchenette along with the others. Ted himself made no comment about this photo, but he did ask — d'ya mind? — if he could change chairs.

"Sometimes," Ted said. "Changin' position helps. Sometimes it does, I dunno why. Sometimes I gets up, stretches, moves aroun', I dunno but it helps."

He sat in the more comfortable chair.

"Ya," he said. "Feel somethin' happenin' now. Feel I'm hot, hotter than them pitchers show. I don' get it."

Ted made two more tries, after which I went into the kitchenette for a Coke. What I saw still amazes me. There, on the counter, now completely dry, was the photo taken with the Graflex.

"Oh my god," I said out loud.

A moment later Dr Skillicorn was at my side. There, in front of our eyes, was a discernible photo. In the fifteen minutes since the signing and numbering, it had mysteriously developed further. Not just lines and shadows, it was now clearly a structure. In a moment everyone was surrounding me. There were cries of astonishment and excitement. Dr Ross went back into the seminar room, picked up the sealed target envelope, brought it back into the kitchenette and opened it in front of the rest of us. Westminster Abbey. Dr Ross held it next to the photo. Shot from a different angle — above and to the side — amorphous and velvety, with a large luminous blob in the upper lefthand corner — the photo was nonetheless a perfect match for the clock tower of Westminster Abbey.

"KATLYN BARNES. Don't even ask me how I got it. Slogging. Pure slogging. Anyway it's not much but at least it's something. She was photographed by you. The family moved to Florida."

"Where?"

"Miami. The neighbour gave us an address."

Breetz thanked Elizabeth and was on a flight to Miami the next morning. He didn't call ahead, but instead taxied from the airport to the address Elizabeth had given him, stopping twice on the way, once for a bottle of scotch and once for some flowers. He knocked at the door.

It was too much to hope that the girl he'd photographed seven years earlier would open the door, but that's exactly what Breetz was hoping. Instead, when the door slowly opened, there stood in front of him a striking woman. Her figure was trim and she wore precisely fitted pants and shirt. Breetz quickly noted the French manicure, the skilfully applied makeup, the lush red hair. She was beautiful.

"Hello, my name is Breetz Mestrovic — "

Her eyes indicated instant recognition. Just stepping out of the bathroom was a man putting on his tie. Mr Barnes, obviously.

"So, who's this?" he asked, addressing his wife, "and what's he selling?"

"This is Breetz Mestrovic," the woman said, "Mestrovic...the photographer..."

As she said it, Breetz was taking in the pile of glamour magazines on the coffee table. The man looked at Breetz blankly.

"I'm looking for a girl by the name of Katlyn Barnes," Breetz said. Dead silence.

"Katlyn Barnes," Breetz repeated. "She lived in Toronto seven years ago. Do you know her?"

The husband and wife exchanged glances. Then the woman spoke.

"Yes...yes...we know her. She was our daughter."

"Was?"

"Is," said the man.

"We never hear from her."

"Why are you looking for her?"

"I photographed your daughter once..."

"Yes, I know," the mother said. Then, turning to her husband, she added, "that was the day."

"Mind if I take a seat?" Breetz asked, sitting in the nearest chintz-covered chair. He put the bottle of scotch down on the coffee table. Neither the man nor the woman made a move.

"She cut off her hair," the woman said.

"Cut off her hair?"

"Yes. She literally shaved her head."

Breetz wanted a drink but no one offered him a glass and he wasn't about to open the bottle and take a swig, though he felt like it.

"She shaved her head. We had words. The next morning she left."

"Broke her mother's heart."

"After all we'd done for her," the woman said. "The lessons...the money we spent — "

"Where did she go?"

"We don't know," she said. "She's never written. She's never made any attempt to contact us."

"But when you tried to contact her..."

"Couldn't. We had no idea where she was."

Breetz felt very strange sitting so low on the chair, looking up at these two people who had not moved an inch since the conversation had begun. The man was totally impassive with the same dull expression on his face, but the woman was reacting. She was fighting tears. Breetz lay the flowers down on the table, stood and offered her his handkerchief. The man still made no move. Breetz squeezed her arm.

"What about her friends?"

"She had no friends."

"What about the police?"

Silence. More silence.

"The police," Breetz repeated. "What about the police?"

"One day, two days, a week, a month. She never called. She just disappeared." The mother stopped, sniffed and blew her nose into Breetz's handkerchief. "We gave her everything. We gave her every opportunity. It was that acting teacher — "

"Eva."

The woman pulled herself together. Then the man turned to Breetz.

"You've upset my wife," he said. "We don't know where our daughter is. We haven't heard from her in years. Now, please go."

Breetz looked at the woman. She had stopped sniffling. He wondered if there was anything more he could get out of her. But then he looked at the man and knew that there wasn't. They were a unit, these two. Without saying another word, he left.

"She shaved her head...what else?" Elizabeth asked. "There must be something. Go over the conversation in your head."

"Nothing, Elizabeth. I gave them a bottle of single malt and they gave me nothing."

"Nothing, Breetz?" Elizabeth said. "She shaved her head, she ran away, they didn't contact the police, that's all interesting…anything else?"

"Oh, yeah…she had an acting teacher. That's when he cut her off."

"An acting teacher? Well, that's something," Elizabeth said. "I'll get to work on it."

Two days later, Elizabeth was on the phone to Breetz again.

"I've found the acting teacher. Her name is Ruby Nielson and she remembers Katlyn vividly."

"I'll be on the six o'clock."

Ruby Nielson walked along Bloor Street. She was very curious about the woman who was coming to visit her today. Something about Katie Barnes. She stopped at the fruit market and picked up some vegetables and a loaf of bread, then walked up Madison to Number 78.

For years she'd lived here. It was a stately brick Victorian house, divided into rooms. Hers was at the top of the stairs on the lefthand side, overlooking the back garden. She loved it. She opened the door and Maggie the cat rubbed up against her ankles then disappeared downstairs. The room, though small, had a little sitting area over by the bay windows, complete with a love-seat, a blanket box that served as a coffee table, and a favourite rocker.

There was a knock at the door. Ruby opened it expecting one person and saw two: a handsome woman with a lovely long grey braid and a short, dark-eyed young man dressed all in black.

"You must be Elizabeth Hathaway," Ruby said.

"Yes, and this is Breetz Mestrovic — "

"Oh! How interesting, come in…for me?" she said as Breetz held out the flowers. "Thank you."

Breetz and Elizabeth stepped inside.

"I have just the thing," Ruby said, walking over to the bookcase and taking down a blue vase. "My students gave me this last year. Blue's my favourite colour. Please, have a seat."

Breetz sat down on the love-seat and Elizabeth beside him. Ruby poured a little water into the vase, arranged the flowers in it, then placed it in the window.

"There," she said. "Perfect. And as the evening sun comes through the trees it'll catch the blue of the vase."

When she turned back to them, she noticed the bottle of scotch on the blanket box.

"Is that for me too?"

Breetz nodded.

"Single malt. So this is a party, is it? I'll get us some glasses."

From a tiny cabinet at the base of the bookcase, Ruby extracted three crystal glasses.

"No ice, I'm afraid; straight up okay?"

"A little water, please," Elizabeth said.

Ruby ran a little water into Elizabeth's glass, then placed the three of them in front of Breetz.

"You can do the honours." Ruby sat in her rocker, tucking one leg under her. "So this is the subject of your article," she said, smiling as Breetz handed her a glass. "I'm sorry, I'm unfamiliar with your work. Elizabeth said you're a photographer?"

"That's right," Breetz said. "A fashion photographer."

"A fashion photographer. And why do you want to know about Katie?"

"I photographed her once."

"You photographed Katie? Of course, she did some modelling, didn't she?"

Breetz and Elizabeth exchanged glances.

"Miss Nielson — "

"Ruby, please."

"Ruby, I think we should come clean. I'm not doing an article on Breetz. Breetz and I are old friends and we're trying to find this girl."

"Ooh," she said. "Time for some scotch." Ruby sipped a few moments. "Okay, you said you're trying to find her, which means she's still disappeared...I'd hoped you might have news...so you photographed her?"

"Yes."

"But I suppose you've photographed lots of girls in your time."

"Yes," said Breetz. "Hundreds."

Here Elizabeth interjected.

"Thousands."

"I see, I see," said Ruby. "Thousands of girls and yet — how many photographs did you say you took of Katie?"

"One," Breetz said. "Or at least, just one that worked."

"So she did it to you, didn't she?"

Breetz looked up quickly from his drink.

"Yes," he said. "Yes. She did it to me."

"Then we can talk. Pour me another."

"Talk, please," said Breetz, pouring. "Talk."

"See that wall?" Ruby indicated a gallery of photographs. "I've taught hundreds and hundreds of kids. Lots of them have gone on to be well known. A few of them, famous — I won't name names — but I've never had anyone like Katie."

"So what did she do?" Breetz asked.

"What did she do? What did she do? What do any of them do? Actors." She sipped at her drink again, then turned and looked out the window. "I've spent my whole life working with actors. Beginning actors, maturing actors, actors in trouble, actors who've found it, actors who've lost it. Actors who have something, actors who don't. I never tire of it. It's a mysterious mysterious gift this becoming someone else. This playing, this bringing into the world other personalities, other things. Does the actor get into himself or get out of himself?" Here she turned back to Breetz and Elizabeth. "You know, they say there are two different types of actors — roughly speaking, of course; in reality there are as many different types of actors as there are actors — but roughly two. Those who become the part and those who make the part become them. Olivier and Gielgud. Olivier disappears into the part. He becomes whatever he's acting. He becomes Lear, he becomes Archie Rice, he becomes Oedipus. Olivier disappears and the character emerges." Ruby shifted in the rocker. "Now, Gielgud, Gielgud doesn't become the part, he brings Gielgud to the part. Is he playing Hamlet or is Hamlet playing him? No one quite knows. Both personalities are there. Katie, if I had to choose, is more the Olivier type. She disappears into the part. She vanishes. But what makes her so incredible is — she really does vanish into the part." Ruby looked at Breetz. "Totally. She vanishes, and whatever it is she's playing emerges. I remember the very first time. I had them doing inanimate objects — probably just to keep them still for a while

— anyway, easy, non-threatening stuff. But when I looked at the class I saw a bunch of awkward kids and . . . a fire hydrant. I repeat, a fire hydrant . . ."

"Suspension of disbelief," Elizabeth said.

"My disbelief was suspended all right, so suspended I practically had to pinch myself to get it back. I didn't of course, I mean, you saw the girl and the hydrant, but you did see the hydrant. You did see the hydrant. Uncanny. Scary. She took classes with me for only a year, but you know . . . she never played anything that I can't remember to this day. To this day. In fact, maybe it's the scotch, but I can close my eyes now," she did, "and I see her. I see her — or, more accurately, whatever it was she was playing." She opened her eyes. "How, how, how did she do that?"

Breetz had been staring at Ruby with total concentration throughout her whole reverie.

"What became of her?" he asked.

Ruby turned and looked at Breetz.

"What became of her?" she repeated.

"Yes," he said. "What became of her? Where is she?"

"Oh, no one knows where she is. She disappears. She disappeared out of my class. She disappears, but then . . . just as mysteriously, she appears again. She appeared to me in Montreal at precisely the right moment."

"She did?"

"Yes. I was sitting with Brian Reed in a restaurant and we were discussing who could play Nina — Nina in *The Seagull*. We'd been looking for days and hadn't found anyone we thought was right. Then Katie appeared. Out of nowhere. With short short hair. She disappears. She appears. I hadn't seen her for years and there she was."

"And did she play Nina?" Elizabeth asked.

"No, no she didn't play Nina. Nina didn't even play her." Ruby leaned forward. "She *was* the seagull."

"I'm afraid I don't understand."

"When the curtain went up, I don't know what I was expecting. I knew it was Katie's first professional production. I knew she wasn't an actress — not in any professional way. She had no professional skills, no training. I just knew that she was Katie and I'd never looked forward to a performance so much. Of course, I know the play, I've done it myself many times. So I was sitting there, waiting for her cue. Her cue came — I'm wildly happy — and I looked. I looked and there was no one onstage. And then I saw it."

"Saw what?" Breetz asked.

"The seagull. The seagull soaring out over the lake. I didn't see Katie. I didn't even see Nina. I saw the seagull. Of course, Katie came back, or at least Nina did. Then I'd look up again and there would be the seagull. Uncanny. It was uncanny."

This time it was Elizabeth who reached out and poured them all another round.

"Did anyone else see the seagull?" Elizabeth asked.

"I don't know. I don't know. I never talked to anyone about it. There are some productions that affect you that way, affect you so strongly you don't even want to see anyone after — that's why I never go to opening parties. If the show's bad all that kiss kiss stuff drives me crazy, and if it's good I'm too overwhelmed. Of course, the reviews were wonderful . . . everyone loved it. But did anyone else see the seagull? I don't know." She took another sip of scotch, then suddenly sat up. "Of course, *he* must have. Yes, *he* must have."

"He? Who?" asked Breetz.

"Daniel Lloyd! Yes, of course he saw it. That's why he cast her. I'd never thought of it till this moment."

"Cast?" Elizabeth prompted. "Cast her as what?"

"Roxanne."

"Roxanne?" Breetz said.

"Yes, that unbelievable Roxanne at Stratford. That was her."

"Roxanne at Stratford?"

"Yes, yes, Roxanne."

Breetz and Ruby inhabited two very different worlds, and it took a few minutes to sort this one out. For Breetz, the stage production had been an unimportant preliminary to the film. For Ruby, the film was an unimportant spin-off of the play. But both agreed the coincidence that Breetz's first wife and Katie had played the same part was astonishing. Elizabeth remembered hearing talk of an amazing production at Stratford. A show that had taken the country by storm and ended in chaos.

"Chaos, exactly," Ruby nodded. "Katie jumped ship. Created havoc. But I understood — Katie appears and Katie disappears — and clearly someone else understood too."

"Who?"

"Daniel Lloyd. He was very protective of her. He never said a word to the press. He never disparaged her professionalism. He took responsibility for the fiasco himself. He simply resigned with great dignity and left the country."

Then Ruby looked at Breetz.

"Daniel Lloyd, she said. "Daniel Lloyd. She did it to him too."

WHEN I READ THROUGH MILDRED'S NOTES from that session with Ted at McGill, my heart sank. A few days' distance on the whole thing allowed me to see what in my excitement I had missed. There was a way that fraud could conceivably have been perpetrated. The photo that came out of the Graflex was unusual. There clearly was something on the film — lines, blotches, shadows and blurs. But then the photo had lain on the table in the kitchenette, unobserved, for almost fifteen minutes, before I saw it again. When I had gone in to get a drink I was alone. So someone *could* have switched the photo. Me. The fact that I didn't doesn't negate the theoretical possibility and when dealing with something this extraordinary, every possibility of fraud has to be eliminated. I discussed this with Wesley and we agreed that henceforth everyone would sign the photos as soon as they came out of the camera and that they would thereafter be kept in full view of everyone.

Meanwhile, there was the problem of keeping Ted entertained. As long as he was the centre of attention he was happy. But if he wasn't, he would retreat into himself and stare vacantly at the floor. Even when the centre of attention was one of his photographs, I noticed Ted going into this other state. There seemed to be no middle ground with him. Either he was talking a mile a minute about his various exploits or he was staring morosely at the floor. Either he had our total attention or he had none. He couldn't be part of a group, only the centre. He was impossible.

A week after the session, Alan Ross phoned with some good news. Ron McCall, the dean of medicine, wanted to witness this phenomenon himself. Ted was delighted.

He had five days to get into shape.

"Five days to the Big Day. I gotta get in trainin', doc. I'm constipated. Haven't had a crap fer days. See constipation's serious, doc. When I get bunged up the photos don't come out right. They get blurry. Gotta get my bowels movin' right or the Big Day might fizzle. Get them bowels movin' and then, two days to go, I cut out the broads. Big day like this I cut out broads, 'cause broads they suck out my energy. And booze. Gotta cut back. Four or five a day, that's all. Gotta be good stuff though, the best. Some a that Johnnie Walker, that's what I need. I'm gettin' in trainin' cause this is gonna be the day I do it for a dean a medicine. Once the dean sees this, he'll phone all his buddy scientists. All his buddy scientists they'll come an' see me, they'll vouch for what I done, they'll announce it to the world. Headlines all over the world — Serios Produces Photos — Eyewitness Account — Amazing Ted Serios. All them newspapers, they gonna come rushin'. You're gonna have to line up the interviews. But don' worry, doc, Richie, I know who my friends are. You guys, Sputum, I'm gonna tell the world you guys, you guys stuck by me when that stupid broad at the *Trib* was sayin' I was fake. When all them two-bit jerkoff scientists in Chicago couldn' be bothered. I'm gonna tell them how you guys discovered me. Showed me off to the dean. The dean, once he sees me, he's gonna know I'm a nuclear reactor. I'm the most important discovery since Einstein. I'm the man who can produce photos out of his head."

Two days before the Big Day, Ted was in the best shape ever. He couldn't stop talking about how he was going to dazzle the dean. He was going to get photos so clear they'd put him on the cover of *Life*. He was going to pluck them out of outer space. He was going to go back in Time, maybe get some Greek temples. He'd knock the dean's socks off. He felt like a dame but, dammit, he'd stay clear of dames, cut back on booze. He'd been eating the "mush" Mildred had given him and his bowels were working better than ever. He could feel his vibrations building.

"Once a dean sees me," he kept saying, "then things'll start movin'. Things'll really take off. This is the moment I been waitin' for. This is the Big Day my whole life's been buildin' to. They'll make me king of some new institute, gimme one of them PhDs. I'll be head prof and everybody can study me."

While it was unlikely anyone would ever make Ted head prof, it was true that interest in the Serios phenomenon was growing. Drs Ross, Posta and Skillicorn had told a number of friends what they had witnessed. There was now no shortage of people wanting to see Ted at work themselves. Because confusion always prompts suspicion of fraud, Ian Skillicorn and Hilary Ross volunteered to sit out this next session. We limited it to two new parties along with the dean. Dr Denis La Casse, who taught anatomy at the medical school, and Dr Colin Dewitt, a psychiatrist in private practice. Altogether we were nine.

Again, the room had been cleared of the regular conference table and two comfortable chairs had been added. Dean McCall parked himself in one of those chairs, took out his pipe and tobacco pouch and went through the ritual of filling, tamping and lighting his pipe as Wesley explained the protocol to the newcomers.

This time Wesley took even greater precautions with the gizmo. He produced a long string which he threaded through it and put around Dr Posta's neck. When Ted wanted his gizmo he would have to reach out and grab for it. It was a little awkward to say the least, but as the gizmo was always under great suspicion it was well worth the inconvenience. Ted was asked to remove his shirt, and was quickly examined by Alan Ross. Ted then donned a fresh shirt. He looked alert and comfortable.

I was very nervous. This truly was the Big Day. If Ted didn't produce a photo tonight, I wasn't sure what we would do. But Ted didn't seem concerned — he sat there casually chatting and talking and drinking his scotch.

"Say, Dean," he said, taking a healthy swig, "what you oughta do, see, is set me up in your hospital, get me a nice lab, bring all them medical students in to look at me."

By the time the dean had removed his pipe to reply, Ted had already turned to Wesley.

"This is the chance I been waitin' for, doc. I got the dean a medicine, I'll show him what I can do. I'll get somethin', don' you worry, I always get somethin'." He turned back to Dr McCall. "One time I was so hot they thought I'd swallowed uranium. No bull, Dean, I was doin' it for these guys in Chicago? These scientists? Kept gettin' foggin', no real beauties that session, but I was gettin' blobs and blurs, lines — know what they figgered? They figgered I'd swallowed uranium. Now, you're a dean a medicine, you tell me. Tell me how a guy could swallow uranium and light up a photo. Think I'm stupid? Think I'm gonna swallow uranium? An' even if I was stupid enough to swallow uranium, what the hell good would that do? I'm here, the photo's there, what the hell's swallowin' uranium gonna do? 'Course that day I was only gettin' blobs an' blurs. When I'm really hot, ain' nothin' can explain it. I could swallow an atom bomb, it don' explain how I get the Taj Mahal."

Ted was leaning in close to the dean, breathing scotch into his face, and I was suffering from an old problem. Here I'd used my connections with the Rosses and they'd used theirs, to get one of the most influential men in the whole medical establishment to witness Ted, and what was he witnessing? A drunk. A slobbering, boasting, all but incoherent drunk. And, of course, we were getting nothing. Every now and then Ted would say belligerently to somebody, Hand me that thing, and he'd stare into the camera, trip the flash, and all we'd get was a Polaroid of Ted's increasingly drunken face.

"I need another, make it a double, doc. Ooh, I can feel it, I'm gonna be hot tonight. A fella don' get many chances to perform in front of a medical dean. I tell ya, Dean, this is the chance I been waitin' for. You're a good man. Not many of your high falutin' deans'll take the time . . . most a your high falutin' deans . . . they read somethin' like the *Chicago Trib*, they figger I'm fake. They figger I'm fake cause there ain' no textbook on Serios. Ain' no theory on how he can do it, so it must be he can't. But a man such as yourself . . . man such as yourself has stature. People gonna believe you. You tell 'em whatcha see tonight, they'll make a textbook outta me. They'll be studyin' me in all them medical schools — Ted Serios — The Amazing Ted Serios."

Not surprisingly, Ted had to go to the bathroom. He asked for volunteers to go with him. He swung around to face Dr McCall.

"How 'bout you, Dean?"

Dr McCall reluctantly stood up. Ted was delighted.

"Ya see that, Mil? You get that down. Whassa time?"

Wesley looked at his watch.

"Eight thirty-five," he said.

"Get that down. Eight-thirty-five the dean a medicine observed Ted Serios takin' a leak."

A couple of minutes later, they returned. Ted had his arm around Dr McCall's shoulder, still talking.

"Oh, I prepared for this session. I stayed away from the dames. 'Course, juss 'cause I stay away from dames, Dean, that don't mean dames stay away from me. I been in trainin' for this session. I know this is the Big One. If I impress you, Dean, then you get fundin'. Then I'll really do some beauties. Dames can wait. Always lots a dames."

Initially Ted's boasting was somewhat amusing for the dean and his colleagues, but I could see it was wearing thin. Amusement gave way to impatience, then boredom. Nine. Nine-thirty. Ten. Ted was getting more and more drunk and more and more obnoxious.

By ten-thirty he was almost incoherent, could scarcely stand upright and was lunging around the room accosting people. Finally, when Ted spilled scotch all over the floor trying to pour himself another drink, Wesley intervened. He picked up the bottle, firmly replaced the cap and started to walk with it into the kitchen. Ted stumbled after him.

"Whassa madder, doc? Don't cha think I'm gonna perform fer yer frens? Think ya go to all this trouble, get all these bigwigs, high falutin' deans and scientists and ol' Ted, he's too drunk to perform? Well, I ain'. I may be drunk, but I can still do it. I can feel it comin' now. I'm startin' to get hot. Gettin' hotter and hotter like a pistol."

I covered my eyes with my hand, and the next thing I knew Ted was lashing out at me.

"Whassa madder, Richie Rich? Boring you?"

This was the most impossible session yet. Wesley and I quickly consulted. It was time to end it. Wesley went over to Ted.

"Okay, Ted, you've given it a very good try, but I think we must declare the session over."

"Ya mean yer callin' it quits?"

"Yes," Wesley said. "We're calling it quits."

"Like hell…gimme 'at goddamn camera…I'll show you what I can do."

With this he grabbed the camera from Dr Ross and yanked at the gizmo still tied around Dr Posta's neck, glared into the camera and tripped the shutter.

Then he turned savagely on the dean.

"There," he said. "Put that in yer pipe 'n smoke it."

No one stood as Dr Ross lifted the print out of the camera. We were tired. We were fed up. We'd been abused and harangued for two and a half hours. We were expecting the umpteenth blurred photo of Ted's face. Instead, the image that emerged seconds later, once again oriented diagonally across the print, was unmistakably an English double-decker bus.

IN A MOMENT OR TWO Breetz and Elizabeth would see The Girl. Since talking with Ruby Nielson things had moved fast. The next day they'd gone to Stratford, a very different place in winter. There were almost no actors around and The Festival organization was reduced to a minimum. But people didn't need a lot of prompting to talk about Daniel Lloyd's *Cyrano*. Again and again Breetz and Elizabeth heard what an astounding production it had been. They'd never seen anything like it. Unique. The work of a genius. But when questioned about the girl who had played Roxanne, people's answers became more confused. They remembered the part but not the girl. It was an ensemble, it was amazing, no one wore costumes, no one wore makeup, people played all sorts of different parts, and one thing would metamorphose into another. At one point the whole cast played Cyrano, at another someone played his nose. Everything was fluid. Everything changed. It was astounding.

They got a clearer idea of the production as a whole, but not of the girl. Kate had been invisible, but Roxanne was remembered by everyone. Kate had made no friends in the company, but no one spoke ill of her. There was no boyfriend, only hints of an affair with Daniel Lloyd. When Elizabeth and Breetz pressed anyone on this point the speaker always backed off, unable to quote a source, unable to give any specifics. It was just a vague rumour that had circulated after she'd disappeared.

It was Sofi Lamereau who sought out Breetz. She'd always been an admirer of his work, would he like to look at her sketches? He would, and he did. Over drinks, Sofi made it clear that not everyone had been entranced by the stage production. She herself much preferred the movie. Ulrika had been so gorgeous in the film. The stage production had been just some sort of avant-garde rubbish.

"What about the girl who played Roxanne?" Elizabeth asked.

"Dreadful," Sofi said. "Totally unprofessional. She even burst in on the costume parade and screamed at Daniel Lloyd. She was in a fury at him, you see, for not giving her the part in the movie — "

"Costume parade?" Breetz said. "Were the cameras running?"

"Yes, she threw a fit. They had to grab her and restrain her. She was hauled out of the studio hysterical."

Within the week Breetz had organized a viewing of the outtakes.

Circled black numbers flickered up on the screen: 5, 4, 3, 2. A girl held up a slate, then a man appeared in costume, faced the camera for a moment, turned and left the frame. Another took his place, then another. Sofi had told them that she thought the girl had thrown her fit near the beginning, but memories could be faulty. They sat through costume after costume after costume — nothing. It went on and on, endless shots of men and women stepping into the frame, turning and stepping out again. Finally, they were staring at a white screen as the film flapped in the projector.

"Maybe it wasn't the costume parade," Breetz said. "Maybe she interrupted some other scene."

So they got the technician to bring the canisters with all the early outtakes from *Cyrano* to the screening room. The technician threaded the first one in for them, but said they could do the rest themselves.

And so they sat, all that afternoon, watching take after take. By four-thirty, they were exhausted. They were just packing the last reel into its canister when Elizabeth said, "Let's look at the first reel again. The costume parade."

"Why?" Breetz said.

"Because things are always in the first place you look, the last time you look there."

Breetz dug down to the bottom of the canisters and took out the first one. As they watched it again, Breetz noticed something.

"See that?"

"What?"

Breetz jumped up and headed for the projection booth. Elizabeth followed. Breetz rewound the film and lifted the reel off the spool. He then began pulling the film off the reel. There were yards of it coiled on the table when he stopped.

"What is it, Breetz?"

Breetz was stretching a section of film towards an overhead light.

"You were right, Elizabeth," he said. "The first place you look, the last time you look there."

WE HAD SUCCEEDED. We had succeeded beyond all reasonable expectation. In front of the dean, in fact not three feet from the dean, Ted had produced a remarkable photo. One of his most remarkable yet. Three days later we all met in the dean's office. The purpose of the meeting was to decide what to do next.

Having witnessed what he'd witnessed, Dr McCall admitted he'd be remiss as a scientist not to investigate further. However, he said, the Serios Phenomenon would always be suspect. Suspect by its very nature. Unless the whole world could witness it as he had done, there would always be somebody who would come up with some theory as to how it could've been fraudulent. So he, for his part, was prepared to make the facilities of the medical school available to our study. He would also throw the prestige of the institution behind it. But in return we had to start doing more controlled experiments.

"The gizmo has to go," he said. "And Ted has to be separated from the camera."

Dr McCall felt that if the phenomenon were truly genuine — if Ted was imprinting the film with his thoughts — then he shouldn't even need a lens. He shouldn't even need a camera. He should be able to just do it on film placed, say, in a box.

The problem was that Ted was, in his curious way, as Wesley put it, an artist. The gizmo, the camera, all the drinking and carrying on were part of the act. They weren't essential, but they were a psychological mechanism by which Ted pumped himself up to perform. If they were going to remove the gizmo, take away the camera and ultimately — as someone suggested — have Ted affect film he wasn't even in the same room with, then they would have to start slowly and eliminate variables one by one. So after tossing a few ideas around, someone — I think it was Dr Ross — suggested that we begin by placing a single piece of masking tape over the lens. This would allow light to penetrate the camera, but no image. Then we could add successive layers of masking tape until no light could get in. If Ted could still produce photos, we would be well on our way to demonstrating that the phenomenon had nothing to do with the normal photographic process.

When we told Ted, he became enraged.

"What do I gotta do? What do I gotta do? What in hell am I knockin' myself out with them scientists for? What do I gotta do, huh? I produce a double-decker right there in front of the goddamn dean's eyes and he still ain' convinced. What the hell am I doin' this for — every time I do it somebody wants more. Now I gotta get rid a the gizmo. Goddammit, didn' that Posta have the goddamn gizmo tied around his goddamn neck? What's a dean think, I got a little photo lab stuffed in there? The gizmo's tied around Posta's neck, the camera belongs to somebody else, the film's bought god knows where, everybody sittin' around two feet from my mug, I produce a photo and they want me to prove I ain' fakin' it — what do I gotta do? What do I gotta do? Goddamn scientists, they don' believe what they see with their own eyes. Bunch a goddamn narrow-minded bigots if ya ask me. They should try producin' photographs, see what it feels like — your pulse racin' your heart thumpin' your head splittin' your goddamn bowels turnin' over. They should try it then see how they feel if somebody says, He must be fakin' it. Goddamn buncha idiots. Okay, doc, Rich, we'll show those bastards. We'll produce a goddamn photo without a gizmo. I'll produce one without a camera — lock me up in a lead room and put the film in a lead box in China. Goddamn it, I'll produce a photo. Hey, I'll produce a photo without film, that'll show 'em. I'll produce a photo in mid-air — then see if they can explain it, buncha goddamn idiots. I'll show them stethoscopes what I can do."

A few days later we began. One of the concerns repeatedly expressed was the old chestnut that Ted had something up his sleeve, that somehow he was concealing something on his person that would explain these extraordinary photographs. So we came up with a one-piece suit made of lightweight cotton with no buttons, no zippers, no pockets, nothing in which anything could be concealed, and we literally had to sew Ted into it prior to each session. His monkey suit, as Ted called it. But he wouldn't give up the scotch.

"Goddamn it," he said, "if you can tell me how scotch can have anythin' to do with fakin' it…if I don' get my scotch, I ain' doin' it."

We quickly relented.

Despite the constraints, Ted produced. But what he produced was singularly unimpressive. Unimpressive if you didn't think about it. With a single piece of masking tape placed over the lens, time and time again Ted produced what we called a "whitie." The photo was simply white, as white as a piece of bond paper, without a trace of shadow. These results would have been unremarkable if Ted were pointing the camera at a lightbulb a foot away, or at any source of strong illumination for that matter. But he wasn't. He was pointing the camera at himself. Several times, one or the other of us tried pointing the camera at something else, with the masking tape over the lens, and triggering the shutter. Again and again these control shots showed the same thing: a blurred, grainy mess. Nothing like the pure white photos Ted was getting.

Ted could even produce whities with his hand held over the lens thus preventing *all* light from entering. Somehow he could reduce the silver salts in the same way a strong light source could. But how? The assembled company was always duly impressed by the whities, but Ted grew more and more despondent.

"I keep floodin' 'em, Rich," he'd say. "Why do I keep floodin' 'em? I don' get it."

The more depressed Ted became, the more obsessed he was with the idea of showing the world. He felt restricting himself to only a few witnesses was messing up his powers.

"This showin' one scientist, then another, then another...it's gettin' me down. I convince one, then I convince another, but nothin' ever seems to happen. Why don' we get all the top scientists of the world together in a big room and then I'll show 'em my stuff."

As the whities continued Ted got more and more dejected, drank more, became irritable and surly. Then one afternoon I went down to fetch him at his room and he wasn't there. Both Wesley and I knew what had happened. Jack Miller had warned us of this. Ted had gone back to Chicago for one of his on-the-bum periods. So after giving him a few weeks, we called Chicago. Ted was fed up. He was through with scientists. We argued, we cajoled. When finally he relented, his conditions for returning were outrageous.

With some trepidation we arranged another meeting with the dean. We decided to just inform him of Ted's demands, outrageous as they were. Ted wanted to put on a performance; he wanted a big auditorium filled with scientists; he wanted to show the whole world what he could do. We expected a polite rebuff. But instead the dean leaned back in his chair, took a puff of his pipe and nodded. He said perhaps Ted had a point. Perhaps, in this case, instead of trying to slowly compile a mass of irrefutable evidence, perhaps if he could demonstrate what he did in front of a large number of people, that would generate the interest we needed. Then, perhaps, we could get some funding. He took out a calendar, flipped through it and noted that the small auditorium was free two Fridays from now. Then he picked up the phone, verified its availability and booked it. He leaned back in his chair again and puffed at his pipe. The whole matter, which Wesley and I had dreaded and geared ourselves up for, was dispatched in mere minutes.

On the night of the performance, Ted was in high spirits. When we arrived at the auditorium everything was already set up. We had agreed earlier that Wesley and I would have no contact with Ted throughout the evening, so at the door we handed him over to Drs Ross and McCall. They immediately escorted him backstage.

Ted wanted a big performance in front of scientists and that evening he got it. Physiologists, psychologists, physicists, chemists, engineers and biologists were among the many crowded in the auditorium. There were even people standing at the back. The place was packed.

At precisely eight o'clock, Dr McCall stepped up to the lectern and briefly introduced Wesley. Wesley walked up to the podium, adjusted his tie and began to speak.

"Ladies and gentlemen, I am delighted to see so many of you here tonight. But before we see the star of the show, I think it would be appropriate if I spoke a few words on the curious phenomenon we are hoping to witness.

"The term 'thoughtography' was coined in nineteen ten by a Japanese physicist by the name of Tomo Fukarai, whose sad story is a lesson to all of us in academia about the importance of keeping an open mind when faced with that for which we have no known explanation. In coming up against phenomena of this sort, it seems that one — and here I include myself, I do include myself, unsceptical by nature as I am — I, too, have a great deal of difficulty accepting the possibility of what I have witnessed lately and all too often try to persuade myself of a fraudulent explanation which, ironically, would demand more credulity, actually, than the hypothesis that Fukarai first proposed in nineteen ten, namely, that film can be imprinted by thought. An unlikely hypothesis to be sure, but I feel confident that none of us here would try to rig a demonstration simply because our department wouldn't want to be associated with such outlandish work, which, sadly, is what happened to Dr Fukarai. The department head at the University of Tokyo deliberately rigged — and later admitted to rigging — a demonstration so that Dr Fukarai's experiment would appear to be fraudulent. In that society so great was the shame, the loss of face, that one of Fukarai's psychics committed suicide and Dr Fukarai himself immediately abandoned his experiment — in my opinion, one of the most interesting and elegant experiments of the twentieth century. But I have forgotten to tell you what that experiment was, haven't I?

"Dr Fukarai, a physicist working with psychics, one day, in an extraordinary leap — the same leap a Mr Miller took in Chicago not too long ago and to whom we can be thankful for today's demonstration...but I digress — Dr Fukarai suggested to one of his psychics that she try to imprint on a photographic plate an image of a calligraphic character. To his astonishment, she was able to do so. Dr Fukarai then took three photographic plates and placed them in a lead box. The same woman was able to imprint upon the middle plate and only the middle plate, thereby disposing of, in one elegant move, all conceivable radiation hypotheses. Those of us who stumble in Dr Fukarai's footsteps have yet to come up with any explanation of thoughtography that is considered acceptable to science. Oh yes, there is ample evidence, but this evidence has been presented under the unfortunate nomenclature 'spirit photography.'

"Let me give you a couple of examples. In nineteen sixteen, in Denver, Colorado, a commercial photographer started noticing faint images appearing on his photographic plates. He naturally assumed that somehow he'd messed up the processing and so invited his clients back for another session. But the faint images kept appearing and then, remarkably, the sitters identified the images as people they had known. This, as you might imagine, created quite a stir and 'spirit photography' became all the rage. As always when there is a demand, all sorts of chicanery, fakery and fraud began emerging, and so we have a number of dubious photos from that period in which favourite Pekingese hover above solemn-faced dupes, clearly shot through cheesecloth with double exposures. But amidst these blatant fakes there seems to exist a number of photographs that remain inexplicable. A Mrs Marguerite Dupont Lee — one of *the* Duponts, a wealthy philanthropic woman — was in correspondence with an episcopalian minister. They corresponded in the usual way, through automatic writing...did I mention that the reverend had been dead ten years? At any rate, Reverend Bocock made the extraordinary suggestion that Mrs Lee try to photograph him. She proceeded to do so under conditions that make fraud seem most unlikely. Sitting for a Dr James Hyslop, a professor of Philosophy at Columbia University, Mrs Lee produced a number of curious photographs, over a hundred in all, actually, that according to Dr Hyslop, were impossible to reproduce from double exposure or any other normal photographic means. The photographs included a number of images of the late Reverend Bocock in a variety of poses quite unbecoming to a minister.

"There is also a body of work out there consisting of photographs of things, or entities, that apparently *don't* exist, or never did, or exist in realms unfamiliar to many of us — "

Oh no, I thought, Wesley is actually going to talk about the fairies.

" — in the summer of nineteen seventeen, two little English girls — Elsie Wright and her friend Frances Griffiths — spent their days playing in a wooded dell, among fairies they described as having little green coats, pointy boots, long-stemmed clay pipes and gossamer wings. Now, so far, this story is not at all extraordinary — many children have what we term imaginary friends, and some of these imaginary friends have a reality for the children that even the most sceptical of adults acknowledge as quite remarkable. But Elsie and Frances persisted in talking endlessly about their fairies, and when their parents, good custodians of reality that they were, tried to gently persuade them of the imaginary nature of their little companions, the girls resisted, and one day Elsie came up with the extraordinary suggestion that she borrow her father's camera so that she might take some photos of her little friends. Her father, seizing this opportunity to put the whole thing to rest, gave her his camera; whereupon the two little girls disappeared into their dell. They re-emerged an hour later with some delightful photos of little men with gossamer wings sitting on leaves, wearing tiny pointy boots and smoking clay pipes. In examining these photos, one is struck by their total unreality — these photos are exactly a child's depiction of the fairy folk. But as blatantly concocted as these photographs of the fairy folk seemed, it still was hard for the custodians of reality to explain how they came to be. The photographs were subsequently published in the *Strand* magazine and no less a figure than Sir Arthur Conan Doyle became interested in the case. He did what all of us who are first introduced to this curious phenomenon do — he turned up with his own camera and his own photographic plates, marked in a way that couldn't be duplicated, and gave them to Elsie and Frances. They, of course, returned with some superb photos of the little fairy folk. Well, Sir Arthur, like his fictional creation, given the evidence, could only deduce one thing: that the world must be inhabited by a plentiful race of Little Fairy Folk that hitherto had remained invisible to the majority of mankind. Those of us who now look at these still extant and charming photos taken by Elsie and Frances, especially in light of Dr Fukarai's experiment, can perhaps hypothesize a different explanation: namely that the wee folk were thought *creations* of the two children that they somehow managed to imprint on film. This brings me to the main event of the evening — the star of the show — and so, ladies and gentlemen, it is now my pleasure to welcome to McGill — for one performance only — the stupendous — the incredible — the amazing — Ted Serios."

Ted walked onto the stage. I'm not sure what the audience was expecting, but by the sound of the applause it was something stupendous — incredible — amazing. He sat down. Then he coughed. Dr Ross was conferring with Dr La Casse. Ted coughed again. This time Dr Ross got the message. He opened the bottle of scotch, poured a generous amount into a glass, walked across the stage and handed it to Ted. Ted downed it, then turned to the audience, pointed to his throat and said, "For my cough."

This protocol now established, Ted was handed the first camera. Dr La Casse picked up one of the sealed opaque envelopes and held it just above the camera. Ted started to concentrate. His musculature began to grow rigid; the cords on his neck discernible from my seventh-row seat. His face went red and blotchy. He started to shake. He tripped the shutter, then shook his head: no. He coughed. He coughed again. Dr Ross poured another scotch. Ted tossed it back. Meanwhile the photo — a blurred image of Ted's face — was removed, developed, numbered and initialled, then relegated to a table.

While all this was being carried out, Ted turned to Dr Ross.

"D'ya mind if I have a cigarette?" he said. "Could do with a smoke."

Dr Ross lit a cigarette and handed it to Ted. His head down, staring at the floor, Ted took a few deep drags, shook his head, then dropped the cigarette to the floor, putting it out with his slippered foot. He was ready to try again.

Same procedure, same target photo, different camera. This time Ted crossed his legs in the opposite direction but everything else was the same. He strained, he shook, he grew red and blotchy, then he tripped the shutter and immediately shook his head again.

This time Dr Ross didn't even wait for the cough. He poured Ted a stiff one. Ted downed it, then leaned over, picked up the cigarette he had ground out and put it to his lips.

"Gotta light?"

Dr Ross took a cigarette out of the package, lit it himself, took the old cigarette from Ted's lips and handed him the new one. Ted, his head sunk onto his chest, sat smoking until the cigarette was almost finished, then he flipped it onto the floor and ground it out with his foot. He was ready to try again.

Same procedure, same target photo, a third camera.

Ted shook. His face went blotchy. He concentrated a lot longer this time. You could feel the tension in the audience. He finally triggered the shutter, shook his head and swore.

"Shit!"

There was some nervous laughter.

Ted coughed. Dr Ross poured him another. He quickly downed it. I noticed that the bottle of scotch, a twenty-sixer, was already a third finished. He'd had almost nine ounces of hard liquor in half an hour, enough to put me under the table.

He tried again. And again.

By nine-fifteen he had made twenty-seven attempts, all misses, and the bottle was almost empty.

He tried again. And again.

The audience, which for the first half hour had been electric with tension, was starting to get restless. Between attempts, I could hear people starting to shuffle, turning to their neighbours, whispering and talking. I was becoming embarrassed. Clearly this wasn't working and everyone was beginning to wonder why they'd wasted a precious evening watching a witless drunk do god knows what.

Ted tried again. And again.

I don't know if the others noticed it, but I did. Ted was no longer concentrating the way he had been in the first few photos. He was still going through the motions but he knew he wasn't hot. He was starting to fake it.

He called for another drink. Dr Ross, with a flourish, upended the bottle. I heard two people behind me.

"If nothing else, I've witnessed a champion drinker," said one.

"He should be unconscious by now," said the other.

Ted tried again. Another blurred image of his face. I was aware of people slipping out of the back of the auditorium. I was reminded of that lecture Wesley had given on Kirlian photography. It had that same feeling. People realizing that this wasn't what they had been led to expect.

Drs La Casse and Ross must have noticed the defectors in the audience too, because at this point they began to encourage audience participation. They enlisted someone to choose and hold the target photo.

Nothing.

They enlisted an audience member to remove the developed photo.

Nothing.

They enlisted an audience member to hold the gizmo.

Nothing.

Ted had now made forty attempts, all misses. Drs Ross and McCall conferred with Wesley. I knew they were about to bring a halt to the proceedings, to declare the session over. Suddenly, I heard a moan from the stage. It was eerie. Like a wolf's howl, only low and plaintive.

It was Ted.

"I'm a failure!" he cried. "I'm a failure!"

The "ure" transformed into a sickening moan of hopeless disgust.

"I'm a failyuuure!"

He dropped to his knees.

"I'm a failyuuure, a failyuuure!"

He began pounding his head against the stage floor.

"I'm a failyuuure!" he sobbed. "The whole world's here an' I'm a failure, I'm a failyuuure!"

Then he pushed himself up and started staggering around the stage. What happened next certainly recaptured the audience's attention. He kicked off one slipper, then grabbed the other and hurled it at the table, sending target photos flying. Then he grabbed at the neck of his monkey suit. He ripped it right off his body. He tore, he ripped, he grabbed, he shredded, all the while screaming,

"I can't do it! I'm a failure, I'm a failyuuure!"

Standing only in his underwear now, he grabbed this too and ripped it off. The issued undershorts fell to his knees, then to the floor, whereupon he stamped on them, shrieking.

"Failure, failure, failyuuure!"

And there he stood, in front of one hundred and sixty of Montreal's most important physicians and scientists, in all his naked glory, stamping and screaming,

"I can't do it! The whole world is watching and I can't, I can't, I can't do it! I'm a failure! I'm a failyuuure! Failure, failure, failyuuure!"

And then, with one last dying ululation, he collapsed...and there he lay, a heap of limp white hairy flesh stretched out unconscious on the stage floor.

PARIS. MAY 1968.

Medieval Paris had been a jumble of tangled narrow streets. But tangled narrow streets hide people and people can be dangerous. People can rise up in spontaneous revolt and overthrow their masters. So Napoleon III tore apart the jumble of houses and streets and created the famous boulevards. Straight lines radiating out of L'Etoile. Wide straight boulevards that troops could easily march along. But now these same boulevards were not filled with troops of marching soldiers, they were filled with people.

People dancing and shouting. Old distinctions breaking down. Worker, intellectual. Student, teacher. Young, old. Bureaucrat, citizen. Suddenly, people were just people and they were talking and exchanging ideas. There was an atmosphere of party — not party politics, but party fun. Painted slogans appeared everywhere:

BE REALISTIC, DEMAND THE IMPOSSIBLE.

UNDER THE PAVING STONES, THE BEACH.

NEVER WORK.

Was this revolution? It was certainly different from any other revolution that had happened in modern times. DON'T SEIZE POWER, DISSOLVE IT. There were no leaders. People gathered in what could be called assemblies, but the assemblies had a festive atmosphere. Everyone was dancing and talking. There was a huge outbreak of erotic energy. I TAKE MY DESIRES FOR REALITY, BECAUSE I BELIEVE IN THE REALITY OF MY DESIRES. People would talk politics and then disappear into the parks to make love. Strange ideas were circulating. In Holland, thousands of bicycles were painted white and left on the streets of Amsterdam. People would ride them then leave them for the next person. PROPERTY IS THEFT. In London, people were moving into abandoned buildings and creating communes. In San Francisco, tens of thousands of people were gathering in parks to make love not war. IT IS FORBIDDEN TO FORBID. Everywhere, all over the world, people were demanding the impossible. NEVER WORK. The parties on the streets of Paris kept growing. No one was excluded. One class was not set against the other. Everyone was realizing that their freedom involved everyone else's. PERSONAL FREEDOM *IS* PERSONAL RESPONSIBILITY. An end to hierarchy. An end to centralization. ALL POWER TO THE IMAGINATION. Out of this developed the great General Strike of France. One of the greatest general strikes in history. A general strike unforeseen by any leftist theoretician. A general strike not against masters and capitalists so much as against the very concept of work itself. A general strike against the industrial system. A strike for play. THE MORE YOU CONSUME THE LESS YOU LIVE. A strike to take time for oneself. To nurture one's own imagination. Not to rush through the streets in order to get to work on time, but to stop and talk, argue and dance. A strike against hierarchy. A strike against oppression. A strike against masters, even if one's master was oneself. FREEDOM IS THE CONSCIOUSNESS OF OUR DESIRES. A strike for human liberty. On the Place de Concorde, a beautiful young girl, features firm as chiselled marble, is carried on the shoulders of virile youth. In her hand she holds a black flag. Onto the streets they swarm, but not to storm the Bastille. DON'T SEIZE POWER, DISSOLVE IT. It was understood that the more blood shed in a revolution, the less things changed. That play was more important than work. That masters are given their power by people wanting to obey. It was one of those rare outbreaks of history where people desired liberty and didn't flee from it. Who could be there and not be involved? LIBERTY IS THE MOTHER OF ORDER, NOT THE DAUGHTER. Who could be there and not get swept up in the heady, intoxicating freedom?

Breetz Mestrovic.

Breetz made his way towards his predetermined destination — a warehouse on the Left Bank of the Seine where he mistakenly believed The Girl was working with Daniel Lloyd. While all around him people were breaking the chains of their mind-forged manacles, Breetz Mestrovic was in the process of forging his. He was hypnotized by the flickering light of his own monomania. He could see The Photo. He could see The Girl. He could see the magic he was going to create with her. But he couldn't see what was occurring before his eyes: the transformation of everyday life. He was stuck in the future. He was blinded by his own vision. He made his way through one of the great outbreaks of human freedom of this century and saw it as an inconvenience. The crowds made it difficult to travel. He had a destination and they were in the way. C'EST POUR TOI QUE TU FAIT LA REVOLUTION.

THE POST-MORTEM TOOK PLACE NEXT DAY over a pitcher of beer in the Rosses' living room. Present were Alan and Hilary, Drs McCall, Posta and Skillicorn, Wesley, Mildred, myself and a much-chastened Ted. He was inconsolable, still dribbling.

Dr McCall was prepared to give it another go. He wondered if perhaps next time we should go a little easier on the scotch. Maybe if people weren't expecting anything, he hypothesized, something might happen; much like the end of his first evening with Ted. Dr Ross agreed. It was Mildred who next spoke. She said that she felt that the controls were stifling Ted. Here she turned to me.

"Richard," she said, "it's like your frog. You pith him, slit him and pin him down. Then what you learn about is a dead frog. But we're not interested in the dead frog, we're interested in the living frog. And if we're interested in the living frog, then we've got to allow it to hop, to be free, to do whatever it wants."

At this point Ted suddenly perked up.

"Yeah," he said. "I can do it, dammit, I know I can do it. I done it before I can do it again. I can do it, but I can't do it in a huge auditorium filled with all those important people. The pressure's too much, the fluence bungs up, the images won't come."

Of course, none of us mentioned that the auditorium and all the important scientists had been Ted's idea, not ours.

"I can't do it if I'm tied up in some goddamn monkey suit, somebody holdin' the gizmo, somebody else peerin' over my shoulder, everybody suspectin' me of bein' a fraud. I'm not a fake, but people gotta believe that. They gotta trust me an' then we can get on with this stuff." Here he turned to me and Wesley. "An' I gotta do it my way. I gotta be in control, otherwise I won't be inspired, otherwise the images just won't come."

And so — we decided that night — henceforth we would do it his way. Of course, this meant that we lost the official backing of the medical school. Dr McCall said we would have to understand that without strict experimental procedure the medical school couldn't partake. He himself, he said, was still interested and agreed that we would probably fare better with Ted in control.

And from that moment on he was. Ted became the maestro of his own show — playwright, producer, director and star. And, suddenly, things started to happen. In fact, they began that very night in the Rosses' house. We decided to just have an informal go at it right then and there. We used cameras and film left over from previous sessions. Mildred took notes, minimal notes — who shot what, where and with which camera. Needless to say there were no random number lists — if we took a control shot, it was simply on the spur of the moment. Dr Ross had a gizmo handy and Dr Posta produced one of the sealed target envelopes from the night before.

Ted began with one or two normals of his face. They quickly faded out and he started producing blackies of increasing darkness. In that well-lit room he produced two perfect blackies.

Then, slowly, in the next three prints, light started to emerge. Of course, it wasn't the light of the room any more, it was Ted's light. Light with that ghostly velvety quality to it that we could never produce in any control shots. At this point, the Ross grandchildren wandered in from outside. Bobby was now ten and Judy eight. Dr Ross gently suggested to Hilary that this wasn't the time, etcetera, but Ted intervened.

"Let 'em stay," he said.

Ted's intuition to include the children was dead on. It was Bobby who first noticed that a form was emerging.

"Look, look, Grampa, lines! Those are lines!"

He and Judy were jumping up and down now, shouting with glee as the next two photos emerged from the camera.

"A picture! A picture! Look, Grampa, a picture!"

"Lemme see! Lemme see!"

Ted was delighted and we could see him getting hotter by the moment. This was what he clearly needed: childlike faith, delight and amazement in his prowess, not scientific scepticism and detachment.

Ted started snapping his fingers rapidly.

"I'm hot, I'm hot! A camera, a camera, gimme a camera!"

Dr Posta handed him a camera and Ted, pointing it at his own face, clicked the shutter. Then he started chanting.

"Go baby, go!"

The children joined in, "Go baby, go baby, go baby, go!"

"A windmill!" Hilary Ross exclaimed when the photo emerged. "It's a big windmill! Those are the blades."

"They don't look like blades to me," Bobby said. "They look like toothbrushes."

Ted was still on his feet, snapping his fingers.

"Richie Rich, gimme a camera, gimme a camera, come on, come on, quick, I'm hot!"

I handed Ted a camera. He immediately triggered the shutter, then again started snapping his fingers furiously.

"Go baby, go baby, go, go, go!"

The kids joined in.

"Go baby, go baby, go, go, go!"

All three of them were jumping up and down when the next photo emerged. It was a beauty. Once you knew what to look for, you could see the tubular structure of the windmill, its windows and the blades.

Ted didn't stop. He hollered for another camera and Dr McCall handed him one. Without bothering to concentrate, he simply tripped the shutter.

"Go baby, go! Go, go, go!"

But this time, when the photo was revealed, the windmill was starting to fade. Both Bobby and Judy groaned.

"Oh, no! No! Come on, Ted, you can do it, you can do it!"

But when the next photo emerged it was greeted by groans of disappointment from the kids. Two more photos and the structure was gone completely.

We'd forgotten about the target photo until Dr Posta removed it from its sealed envelope. What Ted had produced in no way resembled the photo Dr Posta now showed us. The Piazza San Marco in Venice. In the background was St Mark's church, in front of that, the famous Campanile tower, and in the right foreground of the photo, at right angles to the church, was a striated triple-tiered structure.

"Toothbrushes," Bobby said.

We all looked. Sure enough, Bobby was right. The tiered structures resembled his toothbrushes. This got everyone looking a little closer at Ted's photos.

"Say," Dr Posta said, "look here."

He was pointing to the tiny windows that lined the lefthand side of the tower in the target photo.

"These are the same windows," he said.

Sure enough, as soon as he pointed it out, we all saw what he was getting at. On the windmill in Ted's photo there were also windows and they were identical to those on the tower in the target photo. And the blades of the windmill — Bobby's toothbrushes — were composed of the striated triple-tiered structure.

Strictly speaking, Ted had missed, but he had created an entirely new picture made up of components and elements in the target photo.

"I'm hot, I'm hot," Ted said. He quickly swung around to Dr Posta. "Got another a them target photos?"

Dr Posta quickly produced one. It was still in its opaque envelope. None of us knew what it was.

"I wanna hold the camera, I wanna hold the camera."

It was Judy. Her grandmother attempted to distract her, but she was adamant.

"Can I hold the camera, Gram? Can I hold the camera?"

Ted wasn't at all annoyed, nor did he ignore Judy as the rest of us were trying to do. Instead, with a magnanimous gesture, as if he were royalty conferring a special honour upon a privileged subject, Ted handed her the camera.

"Stand there, point at my mug, and when I yell, 'shoot,' click that there."

Then he bent over, hands on thighs, and stared straight into the camera lens.

"Shoot!"

Judy's little finger triggered the shutter.

"It's a clock, it's a clock!" Ted shouted. "Develop it, develop it, you'll see!"

As the others chanted the countdown, I turned and looked at Wesley. The same thought had obviously hit him. For weeks, we had been trying to move slowly and delicately towards the moment when we could get the camera out of Ted's hands. It was a condition that every scientist demanded: physical separation of subject and object. Yet here, on a generous impulse, at a small child's request, he had simply handed it over. I don't think I've ever been so anxious for the arrival of a print. It *was* a clock. A clock on a tower.

"We did it, Gram! We did it! We got a photo!"

Mildred immediately identified Ted's photo. It was Big Ben. Again, blurry and oriented diagonally across the print, but unmistakably Big Ben. Dr Posta opened the target photo. It, too, was a clock tower, but one from a church in an Austrian village that in no way resembled Ted's photo. Ted had got "clock tower" and come up with Big Ben.

Dr Posta had another target photo in his briefcase. He went to get it, but Ted was so hot he couldn't stop. He spotted a book lying on the coffee table.

"This is the sorta thing I could get somethin' out of."

The book was *The Rome I Love*. He picked it up and, riffling through the pages, said to Bobby,

"Pick a card, any card."

Bobby thrust his finger into the book and Ted glanced at the photo. Then he shut the book firmly and placed it back on the coffee table.

"All set, Judy?"

Judy nodded vigorously.

At this point, Dr Posta reappeared with the the new target photo in hand. He looked a bit bewildered that we had proceeded without him.

"Gotta go, gotta go, gotta go, go, go. Bobby!"

Ted tossed the gizmo to Bobby.

"Hold this over the lens," he said. "An' when I yell, 'shoot,' squeeze."

"Squeeze?"

"Yeah, yeah, squeeze the gizmo when Judy triggers the camera."

Bobby held the gizmo over the lens. Ted was standing with his arm in the air, bouncing on his feet, his right hand poised to snap.

"Shoot!" he shouted, snapping his fingers.

Judy triggered the shutter. Bobby squeezed the gizmo. A moment later Ted started snapping his fingers and chanting.

"Be there, baby, be there, baby, be there!" As he did this, the kids joined in.

"Be there, baby, be there, baby, be there!"

Dr Ross counted off the seconds while Ted and the kids kept chanting,

"Be there, baby, be there, baby, be there!"

Ted was improvising wildly. He was doing strange things for no apparent reason, but no one could argue with the results. The photo that emerged was incredible. One of the best he'd ever produced. It was clearly a statue on top of a column. But we had no time to admire the photo. Ted wouldn't stop.

"Gotta go, gotta go, I'm hot, I'm hot!"

Dr McCall was holding a loaded camera in his hand. Ted swung around to him and yelled, "Shoot!" He almost dropped his pipe, but he did manage to click the shutter. Fifteen seconds later, another amazing photo appeared. A domed structure.

"It's here, it's here!" Bobby shouted.

In the short time that the second photo had taken to develop, Bobby had flipped through *The Rome I Love*. There, in one of the photos, was a figure on a column — Trajan's Column — and behind it stood the church of Santa Maria de Loretto. The column and the dome of the church were exact matches for Ted's last two photos, but, of course, as soon as we examined them closely the match was not so exact after all. In Ted's photo, Trajan was facing the viewer, while in the original he was in profile. I never will get over this. It was as if Ted were somehow floating around somewhere inside the target photograph and able to take it from a different angle. And of course, once again, the more we looked at the photograph, the curiouser and curiouser it became.

"Good god!" Dr Posta exclaimed. "Look here."

He had removed from its envelope the target photo he had gone out to get and placed it on the table. We all looked. It was a photo of the Great Pyramid of Giza. I looked at the photo of the pyramid and then at Dr Posta. I couldn't understand what had excited him.

"The clouds," he said.

Then the rest of us saw it:

In the target photo of the Pyramid of Giza, the clouds were cumulus.

In the target photo of Trajan's column, there were no clouds.

In Ted's photo of Trajan's column, the clouds were cumulus.

Ted had combined the two photos. Not only had he changed the angle of Trajan himself, he'd put clouds from the Giza photo into his photo. But there was no time to marvel at these compilations.

"Gotta go, gotta go, I'm hot, I'm hot."

Too much was happening all at once. The kids were beside themselves with excitement. But Ted wouldn't stop.

"Someday it's gonna be curtains, doc, we gotta go when I'm hot. If I learned anythin' doin this it's to keep goin' when the fluence is comin', otherwise kerboom."

So we kept going. Our heads were spinning, our pulses racing. Ted stood there as calm as I had ever seen him. Gone were the blotches, the rapid breathing, the shakes and the drinking. He was like a top performing artist in full control of the situation. He looked terrific.

"Come on, baby, come on, come on, keep 'em comin, keep 'em comin! Bobby — you hold the camera. You — you there! — get a gizmo, back a foot, okay, shoot, shoot!"

We were tossing cameras back and forth to each other. There was no procedure, no protocol. Suddenly one of us would be designated to shoot and there was no time to think, we just had to do it. I looked at the camera I was holding in my hands and saw it was out of film. I was desperately looking around to see if I could find some, when maestro Ted yelled at me.

"It's out of film," I said.

"Gimme the camera, gimme the camera!"

"But it's out of film."

"I don't care, just give it to me!"

Ted grabbed it.

"You," he said, turning to Dr Ross. "Stand there!"

He pointed to a spot about four feet in front of him.

"Bobby, Judy, go in the den."

The den was separated from the living room by a small vestibule. Bobby and Judy started to do as he asked.

"Take a camera, take a camera," Ted shouted and Wesley handed Bobby one of the loaded Polaroids.

As the children left the living room, Ted turned to Hilary Ross.

"Hilary, Hilary, you go with the kids — quick!"

Hilary immediately joined the children in the den.

"Hilary, can you hear me?"

"Yes," she shouted back.

"Put your hand over the lens...Bobby?"

"Yeah?"

"Point the camera at the outside wall."

Ted stared into the lens of the empty camera he was holding and shouted to the next room.

"Ready?"

"Ready!" they shouted back.

"Shoot!"

Bobby triggered the camera. At the same time, Ted triggered his dummy shot. I remained standing in the corner, watching Ted, dumbfounded. This time there was no chanting, no snapping of fingers.

There was an unnatural silence in the whole house. Fifteen seconds later we heard a scream from the next room.

"A photo! A photo! We got a photo!"

Hilary and the children rushed back into the living room, the children still squealing, "We got a photo! We got a photo!"

Hilary's face was white. We soon saw why. The developed print was a photograph of Dr Ross. Not Dr Ross where he had been standing, four feet in front of Ted, but Dr Ross where I had been standing!

"It's Grampa! It's Grampa!"

I turned and looked at the corner. There was the valance, the drapes, the picture. The same ones that were in Ted's photo. Then Wesley and Dr McCall saw it too. Then everyone saw it.

"The valance!"

"The picture!"

"The drapes!"

"Take a control shot," someone said.

We did.

Dr Posta walked over and stood in the corner. "It's as if there were a spotlight right here." He pointed at a spot on the wall. "Which there certainly isn't."

We looked at Ted's photo again. Sure enough, Dr Ross was backlit, as if there were a powerful light in the corner of the room. He was backlit. In the control shots, he wasn't. The control shots consistently showed the lighting as it actually was in the room.

So to recapitulate: Ted held an empty camera pointed at his own face. Dr Ross stood directly in front of him. I stood in the corner of the room. The photo, produced by a camera with a hand held over its lens in another room, separated by a vestibule and two solid walls, showed Dr Ross standing where I had been standing, lit by a completely different light source.

That evening we shot fifty-six photos — twenty-three inexplicable, ten hard — with five different cameras held two to thirty feet from Ted.

It was amazing, but it was just the beginning of Ted's phenomenal hot streak.

DANIEL LLOYD AND HIS GROUP OF ACTORS had locked the doors to the Paris warehouse and worked for two years unobserved. But when the time came to unlock the doors and show the world what they had been working on, Lloyd realized the fatal flaw in his conception. The audience. Lloyd and his actors had worked at destroying all expectations about the theatre. But as soon as they opened those doors, the expectations would come flooding back. And so Daniel Lloyd didn't unlock the doors. Instead, he left Paris to find an audience that had never seen western theatre. He left Paris and took his group of international actors into the Sahara desert — the emptiest space on earth.

Desert Crossings was an English firm that handled trips across the desert into equatorial Africa for tourists who liked to camp or play Big White Hunter. The fellow in black had signed on late. The expedition leader told him to go get outfitted. When the guy came back he looked completely different. He still had the camera, but the shop had outfitted him with the works: boots, pants, shirt, hat, jacket and kitbag. He looked like something out of a catalogue. A couple of days, Charlie Visser thought, and he'll look like the rest of us.

"Hop in," he said.

At the same time Breetz was climbing into the passenger seat of the Land Rover, five hundred miles to the south, at an oasis called In Salah, Ray Galdikas was stepping onto a carpet. The carpet was all that remained of western theatre. The carpet defined a space. An empty space under an empty sky surrounded by empty desert. On the carpet was a pair of empty boots.

Galdikas walks onto the carpet. He is in his stocking feet. He looks at the boots. Then he looks around to see if anyone is looking. Quickly, he grabs the boots and puts them on. Then he stands up. He is pleased. He starts to strut around, proud of his boots. But as he heads in one direction, the boots want to go in another. He struggles against the boots. The boots start to do strange things. The boots start to dance. He struggles against the dancing boots but the more he struggles the more exuberant they become. They fly up in the air, they kick their heels, they spin and jump. He is helpless against them. The crowd of veiled Tuareg men and children sit watching this in stony silence. They do not smile. They do not laugh. They show no flicker of emotion. Daniel Lloyd cannot believe what he is seeing.

The other passengers rode with the camp master, but Charlie had taken on this Breetz character himself because he seemed a little more interesting than your typical tourist. He'd called it right. Charlie had seen them all. The guys looking for oil, the guys looking for Yahweh, the guys looking for reptiles, or lost gold, but this guy took the cake. This guy was a photographer and he was looking for a model.

"If I was looking to photograph a woman, I'd go to Paris, London, New York," Charlie said.

"I've been there."

"So where is she?"

"Somewhere in the Sahara."

Somewhere in the Sahara. The guy was bats.

"The Sahara? The Sahara's the size of Australia, my friend."

But the guy didn't care. There was a girl out there and he was going to find her. And if he had five crisp American bills, why not?

"What's this girl doing in the Sahara?"

"She's an actress."

"Oh, so she's on location. Shouldn't be too hard to find then."

But she wasn't a film actress, she was a theatre actress.

"Theatre? In the Sahara?"

"Yes."

Some character even loonier than this bird had dragged a bunch of actors over from France. Either that, or this guy had been chasing mirages even before they'd left Algiers.

What could be simpler than a pair of empty boots on a carpet? An actor comes on, he puts on the boots, to his amazement and consternation the boots have a life of their own. The boots strut, they dance. The actor struggles against the boots. The more he struggles, the more they kick themselves up in the air with joy. But the audience of Tuareg had not cracked a smile. They had not moved a muscle. Lloyd was astounded. And then he realized that a pair of boots that transforms someone is a convention. What we in the West call make-believe. But the Tuareg didn't have to make believe. There was no distinction for them between real and imaginary. The visible and invisible worlds were equally present and equally true. There was no split. They were not primitive, as we westerners like to think, but super-sophisticated. They understood that the boots only danced because the actor wanted them to dance, and they couldn't understand why he would behave as though the boots and not he himself were making his feet move.

Even when Daniel Lloyd reduced theatre to its minimum, or what he had thought was its minimum, there were still assumptions. He would have to strip it down further.

Once out of Algiers, they seemed to come to a small town every few miles. When they entered these towns the Land Rovers would almost come to a halt, because of the children chasing after them. Charlie would shoo them away but always gently and with good humour.

"Yo, yo," the children were yelling.

"Sounds like yo-yo," Breetz said.

"It is," Charlie said.

Apparently, someone had brought a box of glow-in-the-dark yo-yos over from France, and the people had become so crazy about them there were now bidding wars going on in kasbahs all over North Africa.

When they stopped in a small square, a camel poked its head right through the open window of the Land Rover. Breetz pressed back against his seat. The camel slowly withdrew its head, then stood there looking at him and chewing its cud.

"Know why he looks like that?" Charlie said. "The Koran has ninety-nine names for Allah, but when Muhammad died he whispered another to his camel. So that's why they look so damn superior, 'cause only they know the hundredth name of Allah. That's what the Arabs say, anyway."

They passed through Aïn-Oussera, Chellala and Djelfa, cubistic mazes of square stucco buildings. On the flat roofs people dried laundry or grew vegetables. There were goats and sheep everywhere. The expedition frequently had to stop while men herded animals across the road. Women, standing around a well, would look at them as they passed by. They wore traditional robes but on their sandalled feet, fluorescent-green socks. Young men zoomed in and around every-body and everything on motor scooters.

They passed groves of olive trees and saw an olive-oil factory where a huge stone was being turned by four mules.

"They spend their lives like that," Charlie said, "just going around in circles. Like lots of people, I guess."

Charlie found it odd that Breetz never took a photograph. He knew Breetz had never seen anything like this before, but the guy seemed utterly uninterested in recording it.

They climbed higher into the Atlas mountains and the villages grew further apart. They passed people leading camels loaded with bundles of firewood. The road was no longer paved, still a road but merely packed gravel and clay. Men they met on this road would look up and gesture for cigarettes. Whenever this happened Charlie would pull one out of his pack and hand it to them.

As night fell so did the temperature. They camped outside the village of Aflou high in the mountains. Charlie told Breetz to sleep nude in his sleeping bag as it would distribute the heat more evenly. He warned him it would get very cold, probably around fourteen degrees.

All next day the convoy bumped over rocks — small round rocks, oval rocks, smooth flat rocks. The heat was incredible. Where only the night before Breetz had never felt so cold, now it was as if he were sitting in a blast furnace. It came wave after wave and it seemed to have weight to it, so strong that it pressed against his flesh and sucked the water out of his body. He was allowed only half a canteen about once an hour. It was like drinking from a hot tap.

"When do we get to the desert?" Breetz asked.

"You've been in the desert all day, my friend."

"I thought the desert was sand."

"Some of it. Some of it's sand, some of it's pebbles and cram cram, and some of it's just plain rock."

When Allah made the world, Charlie told Breetz, first he divided the land from the water. He planted date palms and fragrant flow-ers in oases and arranged everything so there would be lots of space.

But when he was finished he found he had a whole bunch of rocks left over.

"So he dumped them here. That's what the Arabs say, anyway."

The convoy moved slowly. The stony landscape dotted with the odd scrubby bush stretched off in all directions, always the same, as far as the eye could see. They camped that night in a valley of boulders. The members of the group were each given half a bowl of water each night to wash up. Breetz dipped his fingers in his bowl and patted a little water over his face and neck. It was the first time in his twenty-nine years that he hadn't showered twice a day. He hadn't showered. He hadn't shaved. He hadn't changed his clothes.

On the third day the landscape finally started to change, but as they entered this changing landscape, *erg* Charlie called it, they encountered a new problem. Sand. The prevailing wind, the *alizé*, blew steadily from morning to dusk and the sand with it. The Land Rovers stopped travelling in single file and formed themselves into a diagonal procession with Charlie leading the way.

Around dusk they came to a village made of mud blocks. But the desert was encroaching. Two houses were partly buried, only the tops of their roofs showing. Other houses were completely buried. They acted as wind breaks protecting the houses that remained, but the sand would sweep over them, around them, through them. If the people closed their doors, the sand would come in through cracks and crannies. The wind would stop and the women would sweep out the sand. Then the wind would come again. The village was slowly being buried alive. It was an unequal battle. The village so small and the desert so huge. They camped there for the night.

Two days later they reached In Salah. It was mid-afternoon and the market square was almost deserted. A few old men sat on their haunches beside a battered kettle, drinking tea and gossiping, apparently untroubled by the flies.

By late afternoon the sun was somewhat less high in the sky and people started to emerge from the shadows. Quiet veiled men in indigo robes moved calmly through the streets, hardly acknowledging Breetz and Charlie as they walked. Breetz still had his camera slung around his neck.

"Don't use that thing," Charlie warned him.

There were no women. Once or twice Breetz saw a veiled face peek out from behind a wall or through the slit in an almost closed door. Breetz and Charlie searched the whole town looking for evidence of Daniel Lloyd's presence. They soon found it. A group of boys were playing in a shady part of the square. In French, Charlie asked them about a troop of actors. They went back and forth in French and then finally the children understood. Charlie translated: a group of crazy people. They rolled out a carpet. They put a pair of empty boots on the carpet, then they did strange things for no reason. One of them danced even though he wasn't happy. He danced for no reason.

Was there a tall man with silver hair? Breetz asked. Charlie translated and the children nodded. Such a man had sat cross-legged in the sand and watched, but he hadn't been watching the people on the carpet. He had been watching them. The next day the crazy people headed south.

"That's a bit of luck," Charlie said. "They're on their way to Niger, same as us."

It was an hour or two before anything actually happened. Life on the desert took its time. The people were used to that. There was no feeling of expectation, no feeling that something was about to begin. The atmosphere was totally different from that of an opening night in western theatre. There was no curtain time, indeed, no curtain. No seats to fill, no lights to dim, no music to swell. Only the camels were in anything resembling a formation, sitting as they did in a semi-circle. Everything moved along in a leisurely and unhurried fashion, until the distinction between audience and actor blurred.

Toshi Miyake wandered onto the carpet. In his hands he held a bamboo stick. He stood quietly holding it. Jikele Bisacca joined him. She also held a stick. A few minutes later Lise Dupin and Paul Kinch stepped onto the carpet with their sticks. They all stood quietly holding their sticks gently in both hands. The sun dipped lower in the sky. Life in the oasis continued. Men rolled date flour into balls and popped them in their mouths, camels were fed and watered, old men blinked and looked on. Women, beating washed clothes on stone, stopped and stared. Children wriggled their way onto the edges of the carpet.

And then slowly, slowly, almost imperceptibly, the bamboo sticks began to move.

"The Garden of Allah," Charlie said. He gestured to the endless vista of shifting sand. "Allah wanted to have one place in the world where he could walk in peace, so he removed all unnecessary life. That's what the Arabs say, anyway."

"Some garden."

Desert Crossings had been travelling for days over sand, endless sand. Sometimes the dunes were six hundred feet high. Sometimes they rolled like small hills. They were always covered with their undulating ribbed patterns. They shifted constantly. Always the same. Always different.

Breetz and Charlie would drive by the hour saying nothing. Then Charlie would talk. His father had been a G.I. in the Second World War and had married a French girl. They'd moved to Algeria before the revolution. His father had seen trouble coming and so he'd left. But Charlie had come back. "Got sand in my blood."

"I've got sand everywhere," said Breetz.

The Land Rover was an oven. A moving oven pushing its way through hell. The next oasis was almost two days away.

When they stopped for the night and people were drifting off to sleep, Breetz lay in his sleeping bag enveloped by silence. He had always moved in a world of noise. In a world where people were talking and making deals. A world of passing cars, clattering typewriters, shouted demands and blaring music. But this was silence. Much more than the absence of sound it was the presence of silence. Silence palpable. Silence like a force that sucked all sound into its bottomless void. A shout disappeared. The honk of a horn was swallowed whole. Evening chat disappeared into the silence like a stone dropped in mud.

They'd awake early, five o'clock, and be on their way by six. They would drive and drive over the endless dunes. Sometimes to break the monotony, Charlie would question Breetz. It turned out he was quite famous. He'd photographed top models for all the big fashion magazines. Charlie couldn't quite understand it. What did this one particular girl have the others didn't?

But Breetz wasn't able to tell him. He just kept saying she had something. Some connection to the camera the others didn't. She had something and he had to find her.

The guy was bats. But then the desert was famous for drawing madmen. It drew madmen to it the way water drew camels. They would come thinking they were looking for one thing, but really looking for something else. A burning bush, a voice from the sky, an angel's embrace. All the great western religions — Judaism, Christianity, Islam — had come out of the desert. Out of this nothingness. Out of this void. Charlie knew: something about the desert put you face to face with yourself. He'd left the desert when his family had moved from Algiers, but he couldn't stay away. He'd had to come back. Back to the silence. Back to the void. So he knew there was more to this guy. This guy was looking for something. He thought it was a girl, and maybe it was and maybe it wasn't, but whatever it was, the desert would put him face to face with it.

The stick play had worked. Again and again in Paris when all else had failed, Daniel Lloyd had gone back to the sticks. The sticks were basic. The sticks were basic because they didn't present an image or an idea; they were just sticks. And Daniel Lloyd realized that in the oasis he had found the perfect audience. An audience who was willing to sit quietly and wait until the sticks led the way. There was no pressure on his actors to "do" something with the sticks, to make the sticks move, but there was an immediate awareness when the sticks moved them. The sticks were a device that joined the visible and invisible worlds. A simple device. As simple the pole down which the spirits in a voodoo ceremony descended. The nomads had sat quietly, but Lloyd in his long years in theatre had never experienced a more attentive audience. They had become part of the play. Their energy had contributed to the movement of the sticks. The sticks were moving but they were moving out of an energy that had been created by everyone. The separation between performer and audience had ended. There was no split. Theatre and life were the same. Both were simple, natural, spontaneous events. Daniel Lloyd was finding the bedrock experience out of which words grew.

Desert Crossings reached the oasis two days after Daniel Lloyd and his actors had left. Once again, it was the children in town who told them about Daniel Lloyd. They had gained a day. That night, after the others had turned in, Charlie and Breetz got quietly drunk. Charlie told Breetz he was a crazy son of a bitch. Breetz told Charlie he was going to get some photos the world would never forget.

Next morning, Charlie instructed Breetz to drink as much water as he could hold.

"Piss that stuff out before the sun hits its zenith," he said.

They were just heading out of the oasis when one of the Land Rovers behind honked its horn. Charlie looked in the wing mirror and saw a bunch of kids chasing after them. He stopped. The same kids he and Breetz had talked to the night before. No, no, not that way, they were gesturing. The man with the silver hair didn't head south, he headed west.

West.

Charlie looked at Breetz. Breetz looked back. Then Charlie spoke.

"Listen, my friend, I contracted to take these people to Niger. You were the afterthought. If you're not coming to Niger…"

Breetz looked at Charlie, then he slowly opened the door to the Land Rover and got out. He walked around to the back and pulled out his kitbag and jerrycan. He nodded at Charlie and turned towards the oasis. Charlie just shook his head, then put the Land Rover into first and slowly let out the clutch. "The crazy son of a bitch," he muttered. "Crazy son of a bitch."

As Charlie drove into the desert his irritation subsided. He realized this guy Breetz was on what the Arabs called the "Journey." A long journey undertaken only to discover that what you're searching for can be found on your doorstep — Mecca is where you are. It's the paradox of Islam. Without the journey, you'll never understand that you needn't have taken it in the first place.

And so he swung the Land Rover around and led the convoy back to the oasis. He found Breetz in the market square, sitting on his jerrycan.

"I'll lose two hours because of you."

"I'm going to find the girl."

"Listen, know what's between here and Timbuktu?"

Breetz shook his head.

"Nothing."

"I'm going to find the girl."

Charlie looked at him.

"I thought that's what you'd say. All right then. Got another one of those shiny bills?"

Breetz nodded.

"Give it to me."

Breetz reached into his pocket, pulled out his wallet and handed Charlie a hundred-dollar bill. A small crowd surrounded the two men. Charlie took Breetz's hundred and ripped it cleanly in half. Then he turned to the crowd and said something in French. There was a commotion, a lot of talking among the men, until one of them stepped forward, said something to Charlie and plucked the half bill from his hand. Charlie turned back to Breetz.

"This is Rahoued. Do what he says."

Rahoued gestured for them to follow. They did, and so did the crowd. Half an hour later, Rahoued had loaded two camels with water-filled guerbas and food. He made the camels kneel, then said something to Charlie.

"Time to get on your camel," Charlie said.

Breetz stepped on a foreleg and swung his right foot over the camel's back. The beast rose suddenly on its hind knees and Breetz was pitched over its head onto the sand. The crowd laughed. Rahoued made the camel kneel once more. This time, Breetz was ready when the beast rose to its hind knees. But when it rose to its foreknees, Breetz almost went over backwards.

Rahoued bent down to the jerrycan. He twisted off the cap, sniffed and said something to Charlie in French. Charlie spoke back. Rahoued spoke again and Charlie turned to Breetz.

"He won't take you into the desert with this and he's right. The camels can only carry so much and it's got to be water. Change your mind?"

Breetz looked at his jerrycan, then at Charlie.

"It's yours," he said.

Charlie handed him the other half of the hundred.

"I've told him you're an important ambassador and that if you disappear, people will come looking. Don't give him the other half until he finds Daniel Lloyd."

Ray Galdikas was an actor. He had been an actor since the day of the Christmas pageant in kindergarten. He had always performed. On stage and off, he performed. He was larger than life. He was a character. He inhabited different personalities. He was sometimes boastful, sometimes charming, sometimes vicious and witty, but he was always acting. He looked at the audience of nomads watching him. They weren't expecting to be dazzled by the great Ray Galdikas. They had no idea who Ray Galdikas was.

And who was Ray Galdikas? Separate from the roles he'd played, who was he? Reflected in the eyes of these Tuareg men he was no one at all. He experienced a powerful desire to haul out a trick, to show *them*, to make them laugh or weep, but it wouldn't work. Here, none of the old tricks worked. The boots play hadn't worked. Only the sticks had worked, and the sticks weren't anything. They weren't a performance, they were simply a means by which something happened. And now Lloyd had even taken away the sticks.

As Ray Galdikas sat out his desire to perform, he noticed that the audience wasn't fidgeting, coughing, or growing restless. He didn't have to grab them; they sat calmly watching him. And this gave rise to another feeling, a very unfamiliar feeling. Trust. He trusted these people. He trusted them precisely because they were expecting nothing. They weren't expecting to laugh or cry or be dazzled. They were just there. Attending. It was new for him. His whole life he had been protecting himself from the audience. Lise said they had a phrase for it at the Comédie Français: se défendre. The actor defends himself. He defends himself by putting on a role. He learns lines, puts on makeup, wears a costume, affects certain mannerisms, employs time-tested techniques for evoking laughter and tears, and all as a defence against the audience, against their judgement and hostility. But here there was no hostility. Looking into the eyes of the Tuareg men, he saw that they would wait, that there was no need to defend himself because no one was attacking. They would wait and so he could wait. He could wait and new possibilities could emerge.

Two camels moved forward into the heat. Rahoued, wrapped from head to toe in his blue robes, perched against the hump of his camel, his feet resting lightly on its neck. Behind him, Breetz clung to his own camel. The heat drove into him. Everything seemed in slow motion. There was no way to orient himself in time or space. Had he been travelling a minute or an hour? He tried to count. He would get to about twenty-five and drift off. He would return to the counting. The heat was unbearable. Up ahead Rahoued floated in a haze, a blue cloud drifting in a sea of golden sand.

It took only three days for Rahoued to track Daniel Lloyd. But for Breetz, they were all one. On the first day he fell off his camel twice, crushing into the sand. After the second fall, Rahoued switched the water and food from his own camel to Breetz's and strapped Breetz on behind him. As Breetz would grow faint, he felt a sharp elbow in his ribs and the command to wake up. The whole trip was this: jabbed, strapped onto a camel, jerked awake with a blow to his ribs. Réveillez! His head pulled back. Water on his lips. Strapped on again. A blow to the ribs. Dizziness. Heat. Unendurable heat. Réveillez!

Behind them, the red ball would move higher in the sky, slowly heating up like metal in a blast furnace, turning from red to white. As the sun reached its zenith, Rahoued would stop. He would pitch a small tent and together they would crawl in under it. There they would wait. Breetz could feel the heat of the sun coming through the cloth. He closed his eyes and still the light would penetrate. He put his arms across them and still, somehow, the light would seep through.

By mid-afternoon Rahoued would get them back on the camel again. As they moved west the shimmering disk hung above them, a hole punched in the sky. A hole punched in the sky through which the heat of the universe flowed. Breetz squeezed his eyes shut. If he opened them even for an instant, the light of the sun would blind him. He couldn't see. He couldn't see for light.

A commotion. Daniel Lloyd looked up. A figure in blue on a camel was emerging out of the yellow haze. It wasn't until the figure entered the camp that Daniel Lloyd noticed another figure on the same camel. A westerner. The Tuareg tapped the camel behind its ear and the camel kneeled. He untied the man behind him who slumped off the camel. Then he lightly slapped the man's face until he revived. He took the man's head in his hands and turned it until he was facing Daniel Lloyd. The man looked at Daniel Lloyd and Lloyd looked back. The man nodded. The Tuareg put his hand into the man's breast pocket and pulled out something that looked like a scrap of paper. He held it next to another scrap of paper retrieved from his own robes and nodded. There had been some sort of deal, obviously, and now the deal was done. Having got his payment, the Tuareg left his charge in the sand. Lloyd and his expedition leader took the man and got him into one of the tents. He must have travelled over four hundred miles in the open desert. It was absolutely extraordinary. Who was he? And why was he here?

The company medic took a look at him. He was suffering from heat exhaustion, he was suffering from over-exposure, he was suffering from dehydration. The medic set up an intravenous tube with a solution of glucose and water. The man slept. Through the night Daniel Lloyd sat by him. He wasn't still or quiet in sleep. He kept murmuring words and sentence fragments — the girl...photograph ...luminous...velvety, somewhere in the desert, doesn't matter...I'll find her...

It was very odd for Daniel Lloyd to hear, bit by incoherent bit, the central experience of his life recapitulated in this way. He, too, had been spellbound by the girl. The girl was Kate Barnes. The girl who had created magic for him on stage.

When Breetz awoke next day, Daniel Lloyd was sitting by his side.

"You have gone to rather a lot of trouble," Daniel Lloyd said. "And all for nothing, I'm afraid. Kate's not with us."

"She's not here?"

"No," Daniel Lloyd shook his head. "She's not here."

"Where did she go?"

"I don't know. She was never here."

"Never here? I followed her here. I've tracked you across the desert. She's got to be here."

"She's not. She never was."

"She is. I know she is. She's here. You're hiding her from me."

Daniel Lloyd simply shook his head.

"I give you my word. She's not here."

For the third time in his life Breetz went berserk. He kicked, he thrashed. In a moment he had knocked the intravenous over and ripped the tube out of his arm. Daniel Lloyd didn't react. He simply sat and watched as Breetz wailed and thrashed. A face appeared at the tent flap. Daniel Lloyd merely held up his hand to indicate no interference was necessary. He sat for many minutes, until Breetz's fury was finally spent.

"Now shall we talk?" he said.

Breetz said nothing.

"So you're a glamour photographer."

Breetz opened his eyes.

"We went through your wallet. One of the actors recognized your name. That's fame, isn't it? Name recognition in the middle of the Sahara."

"I need a drink."

Daniel Lloyd poured a glass of water and held it out to him.

"No. A drink, drink."

"Sorry," Daniel Lloyd shrugged.

"Anything. Scotch, rum, vodka, tequila... anything."

"I know the feeling. Sorry."

And he did. He, Galdikas, and so many of them knew the feeling. It seemed anyone involved in theatre did. They were searching for something, all of them, and too often they tried to find it in a bottle.

"An interesting word, 'glamour.' Do you know what it means?"

Breetz lay back down on the cot.

"It's a term from witchcraft, actually. It's a sort of charm, or spell. But it's a very particular kind of spell. It's a spell cast on a person or an object so that it appears beautiful to the beholder. Kate had glamour."

At the word "Kate," Breetz opened his eyes and looked at Daniel Lloyd.

"You're under her spell. How did you meet her?"

"I didn't, really. I photographed her once."

Lloyd nodded — he understood perfectly.

"Unbelievable, isn't it? Something came over her. A spell. And the camera caught it. On film, her face filled the screen. She was pure light. I've never seen anything like it."

"Where is it?"

"Where's what?"

"The film. It was spliced."

Daniel Lloyd took a deep breath. This young man was amazing. He'd tracked down the film of the costume shoot and discovered that Kate had been spliced out. He was truly obsessed. He was a mono-maniac.

"Yes," Daniel Lloyd said. "I did that."

"So where is it? You have it?"

"Oh, no, no. She was under a spell. It was witchcraft. I got rid of it."

Breetz groaned.

"Her performance of Roxanne was the most exciting I've ever witnessed in theatre. But there was also something very disturbing about it. She didn't play Roxanne; she became Roxanne. She vacated the house and Roxanne entered."

"She what?"

"She vacated the house. The person and the loa cannot occupy the same body at the same time. She left and Roxanne entered. But that's not theatre, that's possession."

It was clear to Daniel Lloyd that Breetz didn't understand what he was talking about, and didn't care to understand. But as Daniel Lloyd talked, the issue was becoming clearer in his own mind. He had stripped theatre down to nothing so that magic could happen. But out here in the desert he was learning that magic was nothing extraordinary. Out here what we call magic, they called life. It was merely a certain receptivity to the spirits. A certain openness. Here, his actors were able to invite the spirit in and yet not be pushed out themselves. And so at last he was starting to get all the qualities he was looking for in theatre: a performance that was spontaneous, nat-ural, open, true, and which united the visible and invisible worlds.

"Spirit," he said aloud. "Our western world has shut spirit out. We've built walls around it. We forced it out of our everyday life. The spiritual is something we don't acknowledge. And so it finds its way in. So many of us who are involved in theatre, in make-believe, also have a drinking problem. Why is that? Because we're searching for spirit."

"I don't have a drinking problem," Breetz said. Then he rolled over on his side facing away from Daniel Lloyd.

Demon Rum. Those old melodramas knew what they were talking about. The drunkard can't pay his mortgage and the landlord forecloses. He vacates the house. That's what this young man had done. He'd let alcohol in and it had pushed him out of his house. But there was no point saying any of this to him, Lloyd knew that. Alcoholism was a spiritual illness and it required a spiritual cure, but this young man was not ready. He was young, he was ambitious, he felt that this girl was the answer. She wasn't, of course. Any more than alcohol was, but he would have to find that out for himself.

"You're not home, Breetz," Daniel Lloyd said to his back. "You're not home."

But Breetz wasn't listening.

THE SESSION AT THE ROSSES' WAS THE BEGINNING of Ted's phenomenal hot streak. A hot streak that lasted many weeks. Night after night he would produce photos. We tried to get him to take a break — I sometimes even longed for him to take off for Chicago again — but Ted wouldn't stop. He was hot, he kept saying, he was hot. He had to keep going.

"Gotta go, doc, gotta go, Richie Rich, gotta go go go, keep goin' while I'm hot, cause one a these days — Kerboom — it's gonna be curtains."

Each night I would go back to the coach-house and reconstruct the evening's session on paper, trying to remember every detail. I would draw diagrams of the rooms, showing who was sitting in what chair, where they moved. But of course I couldn't limit myself to mere recording of Ted's astonishing work. To me, thoughtography represented a way into a whole other world which, as a student of literature,

I had studied but never experienced directly. The doors of perception. Ben Jonson grumbled that Shakespeare never blotted a line. When Shakespeare was "hot" did the doors just open up and the images come pouring forth the way they did for Ted? Certainly, when you analysed a photograph of Ted's, it started to have the complexity and depth of a great poem. It had allusions, puns, visual tricks, its own time and space.

We are all so used to cameras, we grow up with them, we know that if we point them at a tree and click the shutter, if there's adequate light and the camera is properly loaded, an image of that tree will appear on film. But a camera around Ted didn't behave like a camera. It might as well have been a dummy prop. It was a talisman for evoking the interaction between his mind and the film. It didn't matter where it was pointed or whether any light was entering the aperture or even if it was in the same room with Ted. It didn't work like a camera, it worked like a charm.

Night after night the photographs kept tumbling out: a mechanical clock in Munich, a Neanderthal Man, a house in Thailand, an Olmec stelae, Queen Elizabeth, a Staggerwing airplane, a Caindain mounted police outpost with the word Canadian, characteristically for Ted, misspelled. On and on it went until, in those few weeks, Ted had produced over a hundred hard paranormal photographs.

There was one photograph of Ted's that couldn't be called "hard" though, and couldn't really even be called a photograph. But it was certainly paranormal. It happened at the end of one of Ted's hot sessions. Inexcusably, we had run out of film.

"I'm gettin' somethin', I'm gettin' somethin'," Ted kept saying, swinging from one to the other of us. "Somethin's pressin' in."

But all the cameras at that session were empty.

"It's pressin' in...people, they're walkin'...people...looks like the corner a State 'n Jackson."

We felt terrible.

"Ted," I said. "There's no film; we've run out of film!"

"Gimme that camera!"

He grabbed it, swung around and faced the blank white wall. Then he tripped the shutter and the winklight flashed. There, witnessed by myself, Wesley and eight others, for the briefest of instants, was a square about fourteen inches, in black and white, of what appeared to be men and women walking, caught frozen for a mere second. We could see their shapes and even some of their features. Then it was gone.

So Ted had done what he had claimed he someday would: he created images out of nothing. As it turned out, Ted always did what he said he would do.

More and more people wanted to come to our sessions. We tried to get an even mix between regulars and initiates and, whenever possible, included children. As the witnesses grew in number we were forced occasionally to hold sessions back in the medical school. There were just too many interested people to try to fit into, say, the Rosses' living room.

On July 15, 1968, we held a session in the seminar room at McGill medical school. Besides the five regulars there were six new people. Ted was having a tough time, the first tough time he'd had in many weeks. He kept getting blackies. Of course, only the regulars knew he was having a tough time; the newcomers had been told again and again that blackies signalled the beginning of activity. So expectations were high.

"Damn!" he shouted when yet another blackie emerged.

"Damn! Damn! Damn!"

For the first time since his performance in the auditorium, I could see Ted was becoming enraged. His face was turning red, he was blotchy. The thought crossed my mind that maybe we should intervene, call a break, but Ted had been master of his own show for so long by this time that I blocked the impulse.

"Damn! I should be gettin' somethin'! Damn! I feel I should be gettin' somethin', damn! damn! damn!"

Wesley was holding a camera when Ted shouted, Shoot! As soon as he triggered the shutter, Ted yelled at him.

"Gimme that thing, gimme that goddamn thing!"

Wesley thrust the camera at Ted, who grabbed it, slammed it down on the table (Kerboom!) and smashed his fist onto the back of it.

"Develop that, goddammit!" he said, then turned away in disgust.

Fifteen seconds later, to cries of delight from almost everyone in the room, a photo emerged. It was a perfect photo. Velvety and luminous. Filling the entire print. No embryonic forms, no blobs, no blotches. No need for interpretation, it was immediately recognizable to every participant in the room. It was as good a photo as Ted had ever produced. Plush — fluted — theatrical: curtains.

I felt sick.

What Ted had always said would happen, *had* happened. Kerboom. Curtains. That's all, brother.

Ted would never again get another paranormal photo.

MY MOTHER HADN'T GIVEN ME MUCH WARNING: she'd been down to see Breetz in New York and she'd stopped off in Montreal on the way home. I got a call from the airport that she was on her way. Quickly, I looked around the coach-house. Many of Ted's best photos were pinned to the wall where I could study them. There were books that Ted had used as sources for his thoughtographic sessions, a pile of monographs on psychokinesis. I started cleaning madly. It took me almost fifteen minutes to carefully remove the photos from the wall and put them in the same drawer as the photos of Kate. I shoved the books under the couch. I grabbed my Blake and a few other English texts and threw them on my desk. I scanned the room. As far as I could see all evidence of my real interests was gone. I quickly straightened up the kitchen and had things looking fairly good when the taxi pulled up.

My mother looked tired and drawn. I offered her a drink but she declined. She asked if I had coffee. I brewed her a fresh pot. She didn't waste any time.

"He looks awful," she said. "He's dressed just in old pants and a grubby sweater. He hasn't shaved. He's drinking. He tried to be the old Breetz for me but he couldn't pull it off. He's not getting any work. All his friends are abandoning him. He's still obsessed with The Girl."

"The girl?" I said.

"Yes, yes, that girl he photographed back in nineteen sixty. The girl with the strawberry-blonde hair."

"I don't understand."

"He thinks she's the new Marilyn Monroe."

"The new Marilyn Monroe?" I said, sounding just like my father. Picking up on this, Elizabeth tightened.

"Yes," she said. "Breetz feels Marilyn Monroe had some special quality that she brought to photography that no one else has."

"Except this girl."

"Except this girl," my mother said. "That's right."

I sat, quietly, trying to listen while my mother told her story. She told me how after the episode in the darkroom she'd promised Breetz she'd help him find this girl. Then she told me about her lunch with the two models from The Umbrella Sequence. I was becoming very uneasy. Breetz and my mother were apparently determined to intrude on Kate's life. Then she told me about the weeks of phoning and how they'd turned up Teen Tyme Barrettes. I excused myself and got another coffee. When I returned, she told me about Breetz's trip to Florida. I felt sick. She told me about Ruby Nielson, and Stratford and the costume parade, and the spliced film. At that point, I braced myself. I expected her to look at me and say, And that's when we connected her to you. But she didn't. Instead she said that Breetz had gone to Paris.

"Paris?"

Even I was stumped by this one. I couldn't understand why he would look for Kate in Paris. Then my mother explained. He'd assumed she was with Daniel Lloyd. She then told the story, as best she could, of Breetz tracking Daniel Lloyd across the desert. It was madness. It was insanity. I had to stop him. I had to stop *them*.

I got up and walked over to the window. I was so upset I hardly heard what my mother was saying. This gift — this gift that Kate had — this gift was a gift that destroyed people. I thought of Ted. Ted was a wreck. Now that the curtain had come down on him, would he end up like Marilyn? Dead of an overdose? Had we made such a fuss over Ted's gift that he couldn't live without the acclaim it brought him? Was the gift worth the price? Marilyn thought yes. Kate thought no. She had decided to nourish other gifts. And so she'd gone to a place where the world didn't intrude. And now my mother and Breetz wanted to hunt her down. She was an exotic animal they wanted to track through the jungle, so they could shoot it and put its head on their wall.

Behind me I could hear my mother still talking.

"If you saw him, it would break your heart. He's not Breetz, he's shabby, he's dishevelled. He needs your help."

I was still looking out the window when she said this. And I remember that I didn't snap at her, or shout, or get angry. But I said something that I'd never said to my mother before. I said no.

"No?" she repeated, and suddenly she was up on her feet behind me. She grabbed me and spun me around.

I'll never forget what happened next. It was involuntary and explosive. I shoved her. I shoved her so violently that she was propelled across the room. And then, all my calmness gone, I was yelling at her. I screamed at her that she and Breetz had no business interfering in this girl's life. That if she'd wanted to be a model, she'd have been a model. That if she'd wanted to move in Breetz's corrupt world, she'd have chosen to. That not every young woman wanted to be dressed up like a Barbie doll and photographed by an egomaniac. That Breetz was shallow, exploitive, that he cared nothing about women, and that he was simply ending up the way people like him always ended up.

Then I came to. I looked at my mother. She was down on the floor, looking up at me with pure terror. I moved to help her. She recoiled. I suddenly realized what I had done and put my head in my hands and started to weep. I wept and I wept until I was sobbing convulsively.

When I next looked up, my mother was gone.

JUST WHO WAS RAMONA, ANYWAY?

Not Ramona, certainly, that much got settled early. But in each succeeding interview her story changed slightly. To one interviewer she came from lowly origins. To another, she revealed her secret: in point of fact, she was the illegitimate daughter of a prominent businessman who had made an arrangement with her adoptive family and who had paid for her training in dance, singing and elocution. To another, her real father was highly placed in government; to another he was an ambassador to the U.N.; to yet another he had royal blood.

It wasn't that she had to keep all these stories straight; it was that each time she told a story, she told it afresh and with utter conviction. Only after her fame started to grow did reporters begin checking the details. She was Theresa Marie DiGaetano, one of three daughters of a prosperous Illinois dentist. She had always been at the top of her class. She was chosen to give the valedictory address at her high school. She wore a tasteful pink gown with side buttons and her mother's pearls. Her speech was entitled *A Time of Transformation*. She spoke of the time when one ceased to be a child and became an adult. The time when one passed from the protective world of the home and school into the greater world beyond. As she spoke, she nervously fiddled with her buttons. She was an attractive girl, and much of the audience was more attentive to her nervous fingers than to her spoken words. Another distraction was the loudspeaker. It started to splutter and whine. An instant later, at top volume, the Rolling Stones belted out "Satisfaction." At this point, the valedictorian spun away from the lectern and her pink gown fell to the floor. All that remained were her white bra and panties, nylons and a crinoline. By the time His Worship the Mayor, trustees, teachers, principal, ladies and gentlemen, and fellow students, could fully react, the crinoline was off and she was into a full-scale striptease.

Theresa Marie DiGaetano wanted attention. Throughout her young life she had got attention in the accepted ways. She had excelled at school; she had been president of the debating society; she had starred in dance and drama recitals. She was admired by all. But it wasn't enough. And so, on that memorable day, she had transformed herself from the highly admired but conventional Theresa Marie into the outrageous, scandalous, Ramona. Theresa Marie was destined for Radcliffe, but Ramona went to Hollywood.

Hollywood. Ramona felt that in Hollywood she would get the attention she craved — and yet Hollywood was more immune to attention-seekers than anywhere else. In Hollywood, the more outrageous you were, the more studiously you were ignored.

She had a dreadful year. She'd try this, she'd try that. She cut her hair short. Then she grew it long again. She bleached it. She died it red. She decided that was all wrong and started to let it grow out again. But whatever style she chose, as soon as she chose it, she noticed hundreds of beautiful girls had got there first. The harder she tried the worse it got. She couldn't get an interview with a producer or director. She got only the worst of agents. At parties, she found that even when people did talk to her they were always looking over her shoulder. She couldn't bear it. She just couldn't bear it. She was living week to week, miserable job to miserable job. She started wondering whether she'd made a mistake. Whether she should simply transform herself back into Theresa Marie DiGaetano and go to Radcliffe.

In retrospect, it seems obvious that a girl with no sense of identity would adopt the identity of someone else. It had started off so small. Fooling around in the ladies' room with a girlfriend, she had lisped like Marilyn. The girlfriend had turned from putting on her own lipstick to stare at her. She didn't try it again that night, but a few days later, after some practice in the mirror, she did it again. This time in front of some men. The reaction was immediate and gratifying. Standing there, checking coats, suddenly she was the centre of attention once again. At last she had a strategy. She began studying Marilyn. Photographs, films, interviews. She didn't look like Marilyn, but she felt maybe she could.

Ramona had discovered something that many young women would discover in the future. That Norma Jean had created a tulpa and that the tulpa had an existence that was independent of Norma Jean. Marilyn Monroe was a creation. She was created by Norma Jean in collaboration with millions of men across North America. Marilyn Monroe was a male fantasy. Innocent, yet sexually experienced. Dumb, yet devastatingly witty. Infinitely vulnerable, yet able to withstand any brutality. A mass of contradictions which Norma Jean had been able to combine in a single image. The gorgeous blonde who always got the fuzzy end of the lollipop. Norma Jean had embodied these contradictions and a phantom had been created. Once the phantom was created, others could step into it too.

Others did. But Ramona was the first.

She got better at it. She started practising in front of the mirror. One day, she took a big step. She went to one of the best hairdressers in Los Angeles and had her hair bleached platinum blonde. The effect was amazing. She could walk down the street just as herself, and people wouldn't turn and stare. But as soon as she threw in the asymmetrical wiggle and the parted lips, the effect was remarkable. Heads would turn. Traffic would stop. She'd show up at parties with her hair in a ponytail, wearing a baggy sweater. As the evening wore on, she'd have half a bottle of champagne, then she'd go into the bathroom and emerge as Marilyn. Everyone loved it. She started getting invited to more parties, better parties, parties attended by some of the big stars.

Ramona had started out doing a gross caricature of Marilyn. All the obvious signatures. The little girl voice. The inhalation of breath before she spoke. The lowering of the upper lip. But as she imitated Marilyn, she became obsessed. Ramona no longer interested her. Ramona was merely an aspiring starlet, like a thousand other girls in Los Angeles. But Marilyn was a star, a superstar. Why waste her on parties? Even big parties. Marilyn was too valuable for that. Instead, she would get good at Marilyn. So good her Marilyn would be virtually indistinguishable from Norma Jean's. So good that Marilyn could make a comeback. She'd go to Vegas, play the big hotels. Marilyn Monroe: Alive and in Person. She was determined to learn Marilyn's every trick. And it was this that led her to Breetz.

She had of course heard of Breetz Mestrovic, but it was a photographer who tipped her off about his obsession with Marilyn Monroe. She read about him in old movie magazines. In an article on Ulrika, she read about how Breetz had discovered her in a pastry shop in New York. In another article, she read about how he had got her into weight-training, given her the now-famous centre part, taught her how to dress and walk. She read about how he had launched her into stardom. And then, when Ulrika had landed her first major part, the marriage broke up and Breetz went to London. In *Slave to Beauty*, she read about the countless hours Breetz and Shenute had spent developing the discipline of beauty. Then he had disappeared. And the trail went cold. He'd dropped off the face of the earth. Was he developing someone else? Did he have some new girl he was about to launch? She was determined to find out.

She found him in New York, lying in his own vomit in the Chelsea Hotel. She could hardly believe it was the same Breetz Mestrovic she'd read about. He was filthy. He smelled. His eyes were bloodshot, his breath foul. He was incoherent and obnoxious. She took him in hand.

It was easy to remake Breetz because the Breetz persona was so well documented. She knew about the signature black pants and silk shirt. She'd seen photos of him before the beard. She knew that he had been meticulous about his nails, that he'd showered twice a day. She had a blueprint she could follow. She wasn't designing a new product, just reintroducing the old.

The first step was to get him out of the Chelsea. She made him shower and change his clothes. She knew she couldn't get him off the booze immediately, but she began that first day to take control of his drinking. He didn't protest. She allowed him a shot of scotch and then she shaved him. She brushed and combed his hair. She cleaned and clipped his fingernails and toenails. She got him halfway presentable and then they went shopping. They bought only black. New pants, shirts, shoes, underwear, socks. Then she took him to a barber where he had another shave and a haircut. A manicure. He now looked like a weary version of his former self. She took him to dinner. He drank, but not excessively. They checked into a new hotel. She told him her plan. She said that she was going to be the next Marilyn Monroe. He liked her chutzpah. She said she would learn anything he could teach her. He said he would teach her everything he knew.

"You should marry me," she said.

"Of course," he said.

They began work that night.

IT WAS IN MAY 1969 that Marilyn Monroe appeared on my doorstep. Later, the appearance of Marilyn here, there and everywhere would not be that remarkable an occurrence, but imagine my surprise when one morning I opened the door, a champagne cork exploded, and there she stood. Wearing tight-fitting white slacks, white high heels, a loose fitting white-and-black shirt with the sleeves rolled up to the elbows and dark sunglasses. She produced three champagne glasses from behind her back and kissed me with some fervour. Breetz laughed — a little too long and a little too loud. I was reminded vividly of that evening years earlier when Breetz had arrived on my doorstep with another blonde and another bottle of champagne. This was clearly meant to be a re-enactment of that occasion.

"We're going to get married, Richard. And you're going to be my best man."

"Fine," I stammered. "Where?"

"In L.A., handsome. Gosh, where else?"

Where else, indeed.

And so began my strange sojourn across the continent with "Marilyn Monroe" and Breetz. We taxied to Dorval, then boarded a jet. I had no bags, Breetz had only the Leica slung over his shoulder, and Ramona carried something that somewhat resembled a hatbox. Ascending the stair ramp to the plane, Breetz and I following, Ramona paused on the third step from the top, turned to look at us over her left shoulder and smiled. There was no ostensible reason for doing this. She held the pose for a moment, then turned and continued up the ramp. Once inside the plane she stopped to greet the stewardess. Another pose. She stood with her hands at her sides, pelvis thrust slightly forward, left foot angled out so that only the toe was actually touching the floor. As she walked down the aisle, Ramona turned and whispered loudly to us, "Golly, businessmen!" Needless to say, everyone in that plane was watching her. I took the seat by the window, expecting Ramona to slide in after me, but it wasn't Ramona, it was Breetz. Ramona took the aisle seat. A long flight would normally provide ample opportunity for two people who'd just met to get to know each other, but Ramona clearly wasn't interested in getting to know me. She was interested in creating a sensation.

As the plane taxied up the runway, she said,

"Hang on, fellas, we're taking off. I love to take off."

She gripped each armrest and stretched her legs taut so that her high heels were well underneath the seat in front of her and her shoulder blades pressed up against the backrest. Her head was turned towards the aisle, but I could just imagine the parted lips and the closed eyes. Her timing was exquisite. As the plane lifted off the ground she started to coo softly, and then her breath came faster and deeper.

"Oh, golly, fellas," she said, still turned away from us, "we're heading into the strat-oh-sphere."

As we did head into the strat-oh-sphere, she continued this performance punctuated by a few delicate Marilynesque "ohs."

As the plane levelled out, so did Ramona and the rigidity she displayed during takeoff softened. She sighed and relaxed back into her seat.

"I just adore supersonic jets," she said.

She'd get up occasionally and go to the "powder" room. She made her way down the aisle, her swaying hips gently bumping every other backrest. When she returned, the scent of Chanel No. 5 was even stronger. Taking her seat again was quite a production. She had to, as she said, squeeze into such a teeny weeny space. Feet first, shoulders angled, she didn't sit down so much as shimmy into position.

When Ramona wasn't holding a pose, she was in motion, even seated. The movements were small and slow but they were continuous and they drew the eye. As her hips and pelvis slowly undulated, a hand would drift from the top of her thigh, up the buttons of her shirt, to trace along her cheek. Her face would turn, her shoulder lift, her chin rub lightly against it. She was constantly shifting her awareness to different body parts. By the time the observer arrived where she had been, she'd already subtly moved on.

Breetz and I tried to talk but it was forced. As the flight wore on I realized that Breetz was playing himself just as surely as this girl was playing Marilyn Monroe. The old fire was gone. I noticed something else. He wasn't controlling the girl, she was controlling him. She moderated his liquor consumption with the delicacy of a physician administering medication: a scotch after takeoff, a glass of wine with lunch, an ounce of cognac after. Enough to keep him functioning, but not enough to put him over the edge. She dabbed at his shirt when he spilled wine on it. She smoothed his hair. Leaning over to say something to me, she brushed some food away from the side of his mouth. And she did it all using the sweet, kittenish non-threatening persona of Marilyn Monroe.

At customs, in Los Angeles, Ramona held her case straight out in front of her for inspection.

"All I brought is this itty bitty box."

The customs man took her itty bitty box and flipped it open. It was empty.

"Oh. I ought to have something in that," she said, and as she did, she stared wide-eyed into the case with her right forefinger pressed against her lower lip.

The man laughed and nodded her through. As he questioned Breetz and me more thoroughly, Ramona stood off to the side. Undulating.

As we made our way through the airport Ramona created a bubble of excitement around us. The bubble would hover in the air, shimmer in the sunlight and then, "poof," it would disappear. Passing businessmen would give her a double or even triple take, but as the distance between Ramona and them increased, they would turn and continue on their way. Construction workers stopped working and stared at her as she wiggled by, but after a few low whistles they returned to laying tiles. She was the centre of attention, but the attention was brief, fleeting and harmless. I couldn't help but compare it with the trip I had taken with Kate. The excitement Roxanne had created had not been effervescent and fleeting. It didn't dissipate like bubbles in air. It was more like the moon governing the tides. It was that invisible and that irresistible.

And it was scary. I'd been frightened at the diner. There, the situation had been clearly out of control; here, it wasn't. Nothing was remotely scary about this attention. It was fun. It was frivolous. There was never that sense of incipient violence.

We taxied from the airport to a "chapel" where everything had been pre-arranged. Ramona's dress had arrived and she was whisked off in one direction while Breetz and I were taken into a room of suits and tuxedos of every imaginable size and style. Ramona had forwarded

from New York a new set of slacks and shirt for Breetz. He changed
into these while I was fitted into yet another charcoal-grey suit. With
some temporary adjustments to the waist and hem of the pants, I
looked the part. Someone pinned a boutonnière to my lapel. Someone else handed me a ring. Through most of this, Breetz remained
slumped in a gilt chair just outside the changeroom. He looked tired
and defeated. All the old energy was gone. But when the ceremony
began, he pumped himself up and went through the motions.

So once again I found myself standing beside Breetz, holding a
ring. This time there was no bride's side or groom's side. No turning
of heads. Handel's "Wedding March" began. I turned and there was
Ramona. She wore a white halter dress with a full pleated skirt. It was
instantly recognizable as the dress Marilyn Monroe had worn fourteen years earlier in *The Seven-Year Itch*, the dress that had blown up
and over her head as she stood over the New York City subway grate.
She held a bouquet of white roses. She minced down the short aisle
and when she reached us Breetz put out his hand. She took it and he
folded her arm into his and there they stood. The solemn sacrament
of matrimony had descended into this vile parody. Here, not only
the love was fake but everything symbolizing it. Fake plastic flowers.
Fake stained glass. Fake crepuscular light. A fake choir and fake
organ. The fake grain of the fake plastic pews. The faked enunciation
of the fake magistrate.

I went through the fake ritual, faking my part as best I could. The
fake vows were exchanged. A fake ring was placed on a fake finger
and the fake groom faked a kiss with the fake bride. Then we all faked
our way out of the fake chapel to an antechamber where a photographer was waiting for us.

With Breetz by her side, Ramona went through five or six famous
Marilyn poses. Marilyn leaning on Yves Montand. Marilyn looking
up into the face of Clark Gable. Marilyn laughing at Joe DiMaggio.
Marilyn worshipping Arthur Miller. Breetz just played Breetz, but
Ramona went through three marriages in as many minutes.

Once the photographer had finished with us, and the suit was
back on the rack, my part was over. I was only there so that when
the articles were written it could be stated that his childhood friend
had flown to L.A. to be best man. I was only there to legitimize the

succession: Ulrika, Shenute, Ramona. I was not a person, but part of a performance and the performance was over. I felt nothing but relief as I stood waving stupidly at the white limousine that would take them to the Ambassador Hotel. Without lowering my hand, I hailed the first available taxi.

"BEAUTIFUL, BEAUTIFUL, BEAUTIFUL."

Ramona caught the white shirt as he tossed it to her. She turned and with a backward glance entered the bathroom, giggling.

Who knew? When Breetz looked at Ramona he saw a scrappy, attention-getting little girl imitating Marilyn Monroe, but who knew? She wanted it so much. He'd never met anyone with her drive. Hadn't Norma Jean begun as a scrappy attention-getting little girl?

When she emerged from the bathroom, Ramona turned and twirled but the shirt didn't caress her body. It didn't even move with her.

"Beautiful, beautiful, beautiful."

Norma Jean had worshipped Jean Harlow. She had incorporated Jean Harlow into her very being. Out of Jean Harlow grew Marilyn Monroe. It hadn't been easy. There had been many false starts. Often she'd appeared ridiculous, but a stunningly original beauty had grown out of that initial impersonation. Maybe Ramona could develop something out of Marilyn.

"Beautiful, beautiful, beautiful."

Ramona was lounging on the chair now, her leg dangling over the arm, her head thrown back. She looked brassy, uncomfortable. But Milton Greene said she doesn't photograph like she looks. She doesn't photograph like she looks. Just point the camera and shoot.

"Beautiful."

Ramona posed in the chair. She raised one leg, then the other, pointed her toes; she curled up and stretched out and Breetz just kept the camera clicking. She got up to move toward the bed and as she did so, her foot caught on the rug and she lurched forward.

Marilyn used to stumble around, miss her lines, and yet when they developed the film, she was incredible. Marilyn used to stumble around, everyone said it.

"Beautiful."

Ramona flopped on the bed, then turned and looked at the camera through half-lidded eyes.

She flickers up for a second, the camera gets it, catches it, locks it away, then it disappears again and we're left with god-knows-what. A mess.

Ramona's foundation was caking. She'd applied and reapplied the powder on top of it so often that now when she smiled tiny fissures appeared across its surface.

Just keep the goddamn camera clicking and hope for the best.

She pursed her lips and blew him a kiss.

"Beautiful, beautiful, beautiful."

But she wasn't beautiful. Something had happened to her mouth. The teeth were no longer perfectly aligned. They had moved. It was as though the soft exhalation of the blown kiss had forced them out slightly, making her appear buck-toothed. It was amazing how much that altered her face.

"Beautiful."

Was this the magic? He'd said again and again that she didn't photograph the way she looked. Through the lens Breetz saw a woman with a huge smile on her face. A smile that seemed almost bigger than her face. Her teeth were gleaming, but there was something wrong with them. They were too big. All out of proportion. They seemed to be longer than they should be. Maybe this was it. He was getting excited.

"Beautiful, beautiful, beautiful."

She pulled her upper lip down over the protruding teeth, but the effect was the opposite of what she'd intended. The teeth protruded even more so that her face had a hideous quality to it.

"Beautiful."

She crossed her hands above her breasts and he saw that her fingernails had thickened. Faint liver spots had appeared on the backs of her hands. Deep purple veins protruded there.

"Beautiful, beautiful, beautiful."

The blonde hair was growing coarse and wiry. She was aging, aging before his very eyes. Her skin was drying out. Her nose was starting to lose its shape. She smiled again and as she did he saw inflamed gums. Her chin protruded. The bones and flesh of her face were not adhering properly.

"Beautiful, beautiful, beautiful."

He kept furiously clicking his camera, but with each click the process accelerated. She was horrible. She was ugly. Her flesh was decomposing before his eyes. The overpowering scent of perfume had turned into a stench.

"Beautiful...beautiful..."

It was sickening. He thought he might vomit. But he couldn't stop. He was caught in a compulsion he couldn't resist. He kept clicking the shutter, though with every click the disintegration worsened. She was no longer a woman, she was part skeleton, part flesh.

When hotel security burst through the door, Breetz was huddled in a corner screaming, one hand covering his eyes the other clawing at the air in front of him. What had begun with a protrusion of teeth and thickening of nails had ended in full-scale delirium tremens. The poses he had dreamed a thousand times had become reality and the reality had become a nightmare. Her flesh had sagged and then disintegrated. Her bones had protruded, her hair had gone from glossy platinum blonde to wiry grey and then had fallen out in clumps. Her perfume had turned into the stench of rotting flesh. Then the flesh had fallen from her face into her mouth so that the skull had emerged. Her eyes, enormous without surrounding skin and lashes and brows, had stared out at him, fine blood vessels branching over the whites. Her nose first drooped, then disappeared into her gaping mouth with the rest of her flesh. Finally, only empty sockets and the twin elongated holes of a nasal cavity remained. And it all happened as though in time-lapse photography. He had watched her disintegrate through the lens of his camera. Beautiful, beautiful, beautiful. When the ambulance arrived, Breetz was sedated, strapped onto a stretcher and taken to the psychiatric unit of the Los Angeles County Hospital. The following morning, the hotel manager got in touch with Ulrika. She and Philip Shaw took responsibility for Breetz and arranged his transfer to a private clinic where he remained for several months.

Beautiful, beautiful, beautiful.

THE DECISION TO THE SELL THE HOUSE on Glen Road hadn't come quickly. Elizabeth and the others had talked about it for almost a year. They'd flown to Vancouver and bought an old school bus, then started travelling around through the interior of B.C. — Kelowna, Sicamous, Salmon Arm, Kamloops — ending up smack in the middle of the province at Topley Landing. It was a town with little more than a post office, a sawmill and a general store, but they'd found a fellow who sometimes acted as a real estate agent. The agent showed them a farm. He'd expected them to examine the house, the barn, the windmill, but as soon as they'd arrived, everyone had just scattered, gone exploring.

In the last year it had become increasingly apparent to Elizabeth that the house on Glen Road couldn't contain the energy that had been flowing into it. While she could give the young men a bed and a meal, she couldn't help them realize their tremendous idealism. That desire they had to change the world. All they could really do was change themselves, and a very small part of the world they lived in. And so the idea started to grow not to try to change society, but to go somewhere where they could live the way they wanted. Where they could build things with their own hands and eat food they'd grown themselves and make their own music whenever they felt like it.

The farm was huge, over six hundred acres if you included woods, and it had so many different types of terrain. Meadows, cultivated fields, streams, a small pond. It was perfect. To the south lay tiny communities: Burns Lake, Endako, Notalee. Further south, towns: Vanderhoof, Prince George, Williams Lake. Then cities: Vancouver, Seattle, San Francisco, Los Angeles. But to the north lay nothing.

Nothing but one of the last untamed wildernesses left on earth. The farm was on The Edge. Here they would start their commune.

By late August they had divided the tasks at the farm into Pressing and Not Pressing. Everyone agreed that the most pressing job of all was insulating the house. Elizabeth was thinking that if someone had tapped her on the shoulder ten years ago, or even five, and told her that some day she would be working at hard physical labour and loving it, she wouldn't have believed them. She thought of how for most of her life she had avoided it altogether. She had gone off to her meetings and her conferences while professionals had done any work that needed to be done. But now she was finding out how totally absorbing this kind of work could be. At each stage in the project, Sam would point out to them how carefully the old house had been made. Dovetail joints, wood planed and chiselled to fit perfectly. The windows, all made by hand, were a work of art, he said. He took out each one, scraped it down, replaced broken panes, stripped and painted it, then each was replaced and caulked. They couldn't get him to stop working and Elizabeth was reminded of how her Glen Road neighbours snarled about the lazy good-for-nothings staying at her house. In point of fact, they were industrious good-for-everythings. When she teased the fellows about this, they just laughed.

"This isn't work."

"Why not?"

"Because this stuff has to be done. Work is what you don't have to do."

It was a perspective she'd never thought of. One day the bus rolled in absolutely full of insulation and clear plastic. In a matter of a week the boys put a vapour barrier up inside and filled it with the bright pink fibreglass. Then they lovingly replaced the old walls, board by board. Of course, they were always complaining that there were never enough C-clamps. One day Elizabeth went into town intending to buy every clamp in Topley Landing. She returned with three. The cedar boards went back on, the windows were replaced, the woodpile was straightened up and replenished, the two wood-stoves were cleaned and blackened. The women worked into the late hours putting down preserves and storing food. They'd cleaned the attic of bat guano, which they spread on the garden. They'd cleaned out the root cellar. Elizabeth noticed how, despite all the talk of women's liberation, the tasks had been divided primarily according to gender. The fellows just never tired of working on the house. The women were more concerned about food.

Elizabeth tired more easily than the rest. She was almost sixty now. She would sit on the porch and watch the children playing in and around the barn. This was something she'd never done as a young mother: sat and watched her child play. She'd always been too busy. Always off to this meeting or that, always trying to raise money for some organization. She had never realized before what she'd missed. They were so delightful to watch. Their little limbs always in motion. They moved with such natural grace and ease. She marvelled at how they could play for hours on end with nothing, no toys, no expensive gadgets, just sticks and mud. How little taking care of they really needed. They just needed people around. Everyone kept an eye out for them. She noticed the young mothers had an instinctive alarm system. When a toddler waddled off, it was only a moment before someone said, Where's Kaya? Where's Taliesin?

On Glen Road she'd been alone. Isolated. There had been no one else to keep an eye out for the child. No other children for him to play with. That's why she'd latched onto Breetz and Anna. It was Anna who had picked Richard up like Karen was picking up Kaya now. Anna who had hugged him and given him that physical affection. Anna who had simply been there day after day, year after year, ostensibly cleaning the house. Anna had mothered her son, not her.

I HAD JUST GOTTEN USED TO THE IDEA of my childhood home being filled with draft-resisters, their girlfriends and god-knows-who, when my mother called to tell me that she was thinking of selling the house. The next thing I knew, I got a postcard from Kamloops, B.C., in which she mentioned that she and the people who lived with her were looking at property. The next thing I knew, they had bought six hundred acres near the small town of Topley Landing.

It's difficult for a young man to grow up. I still thought that, if things went wrong in my life, I could always return to Glen Road and my mother would take care of me. But now Glen Road was gone. And in some respects so was my mother. We never talked about the incident at the coach-house in which I'd exploded and thrown her across the room, but I often wondered if this had anything to do with her decision. She seemed to be moving away from me, and at a very crucial time in my own life. I had dropped out of the PhD programme at McGill and work on the Serios book was not going as well as I had anticipated. I had envisioned a short and rather factual account of our thoughtography sessions, but trying to be factual about thoughtography was impossible. Every sentence I wrote seemed to generate a footnote almost a page long, and before I knew it I had this strange manuscript in which for every paragraph of text there were four or five pages of notes. I also had another problem. Money. Money had never been something I'd concerned myself about. I was the only son of wealthy parents. I had always been encouraged by my mother to pursue my own interests. If I needed money, it would appear. But my contact with my father now was reduced to a couple of lunches a year and my mother, whom I had always relied on to help me financially, had disappeared into the interior of B.C. with a bunch of hippies. It was a disorienting time in my life. Eventually, I started working at Treasure Island evenings and weekends. This allowed me to live the simple life I was used to and gave me ample time to work on my book.

One day I was showing an early draft of the manuscript to Wesley when Mildred spoke up.

"Richard," she said. "There's only one problem with this manuscript as far as I can see. There's not enough you in it."

"Me?"

"Yes, you, dear boy. Whenever you talk, whatever you talk about, I sit here mesmerized. But when you start to write it's as if another voice takes over and all we get are convoluted proofs, references and indecipherable words with latin roots."

Wesley was more diplomatic.

"Perhaps, Richard," he said, "you should just go off somewhere by yourself, go off somewhere where you're just by yourself, and you can think your own thoughts and not be oppressed by the need for footnotes and documentation."

"Perhaps Telegraph Creek," Mildred said.

"Telegraph Creek?" I looked at her in amazement.

"Why don't you go visit your friend?"

The way she said "friend" gave me pause.

"I can't think of a better place to write than Telegraph Creek, Richard."

As Mildred spoke, images flooded into my mind. Kate and I reading by the woodstove. Kate and I writing. Kate and I snowshoeing across the Stikine. Kate and I picking berries in the summer. Kate and I walking through the woods. Kate and I talking and laughing and talking and talking and talking. Why should I remain here in Montreal? Originally, it had been to do my PhD, but academia no longer interested me. I used to think I couldn't be away from bookstores and libraries, but now bookstores and libraries were oppressing me. There was no reason why I should stay in Montreal. There was no reason why I shouldn't do what I had been longing in my heart to do for years. There was no reason why I shouldn't go and see Kate. There was no reason why I shouldn't stay with her. There was no reason why I shouldn't live with her. I had been repressing this possibility so long that when the dam broke, the feeling was overwhelming. Mildred was looking at me very intently.

"Go, Richard. And go soon. Don't put this off any more."

I nodded. At last I would go see Kate. And I would go soon.

Once I had decided to go, I could think of nothing else. She had always said, Come, just come whenever you feel like it. And now at last I would. I wouldn't plan or write or give schedules; I would just arrive one day. I would knock on the door and she would be expecting one of her visitors, little Johnny Carlick or Nancy, or one of the Tahltan who sometimes stopped by with a salmon. Instead it would be me. I could see the look of surprise on her face. And joy. She had described the cabin so well for me I was easily able to see the two of us sitting there in front of her stove, drinking tea and talking. Suddenly, I couldn't get out of Montreal fast enough.

I gave the Rosses notice on the coach-house. I crated my books and moved them to Wesley and Mildred's. I sold most of my things to students and gave the rest to the Salvation Army. I was down to what I could put into two suitcases when the phone rang.

"Richard," the voice said, "it's Cam Bienenstock...you might not remember me."

Of course I remembered him.

"Richard, I have some bad news. Your father has had a stroke. He's in bad shape, but he spoke your name. Do you think you could come?"

Of course I would come. I grabbed the two bags I had already packed. I called a taxi. I blurted out something to the driver about my father and a stroke and he skilfully wove his way through a maze of dark streets, racing to the airport. As we sped along I thought, If only I can make it in time, if only I can make it. Because I knew that if I made it in time, that long silence that had existed between us would be broken. He had asked for me. With all the effort it must have taken to form words after the stroke, he had formed my name. My father wanted to talk to me. I burst out of the taxi, thrusting money at the driver, and lunged into the airport.

People must have seen the desperation in my eyes because there were no murmurs of protest as I pushed my way to the front of the line. There, the man told me that the Air Canada flight for Toronto had just left and no, no, there wouldn't be another flight that night. But then, compassionately, he said the airline three counters down still had a plane on the tarmac.

I stumbled and lurched, excusing myself as I cut across line-ups until I reached the other counter. The woman, moving slowly, deliberately, glancing back and forth, back and forth, accepted my scrawled cheque.

"Gate Twelve," she said. "Run."

And I ran. I ran down the escalator, I ran along the narrow corridor: 6 — 8 — 10 — 12. I ran through the gate and across the tarmac just as they were getting ready to roll the ramp away from the plane. I cried out, "Wait!" and they stopped. I took the ramp two steps at a time, lifting my bags up above my waist, and, a moment after slipping through the opening, I heard the mechanical sound of the door being slotted into place behind me.

I stood. Everyone was looking at me. My chest was heaving. I made my way to my seat at the back, placed my bags in the overhead compartment, and as the plane taxied down the runway I knew I would make it. And my father and I would talk. And the long silence would be broken.

In less than two hours I was at the hospital. And I looked at my father. And he looked at me. In his eyes I did see recognition. But as to my notion that we would speak to each other, it was no more than what it had always been: a fantasy. I spoke little, he not at all. I sat all night listening to the muffled sounds of the hospital going about its business, and the metallic silence in my father's room. He died the following morning.

The funeral was held at one of Toronto's most prestigious churches. It was filled with flowers. In the few minutes before I was seated, I glanced at some of the cards. They were from firms around the world. And as I took my seat at the front of the church I could sense the pews filling up behind me. Glancing around I saw that there were a few women, wives I suspect, my father's long-time secretary, but mostly the church was filled with men. Men in blue suits, men in grey suits, men in dark pin-striped suits. Men who looked a great deal like my father. The service was short and tasteful. The young minister, who obviously didn't know my father, spoke briefly about his contribution to society. Then he stepped aside and Cam Bienenstock took the pulpit to deliver the eulogy. Cam said he'd had a long association with my father. They had been yearmates and when he'd been called to the bar, John Hathaway had been his first client. He then told a story.

"John was up on Baffin Island... fifty below zero, when the generator shut down. Entire camp without power. No one was too worried, after all there was the back-up generator. No one, that is, except John and the operations manager. They knew this *was* the back-up. The main generator had blown two days before..."

He told the story well. As I sat there, numb, Mildred's words were running again and again through my mind. "Go, Richard. And go soon. Don't put this off any more." Today I would bury my father, tomorrow I would leave for Telegraph Creek.

The reception was held at my father's club. I stood in the line and shook hands with men whose names I recognized, but whose faces I didn't. They all murmured very similar phrases: Man of his word, your father...Known him all my life...Someone you could rely on ...With each phrase I nodded agreement and thanks.

Two days and two sleepless nights later I was finally on a plane to Edmonton. Kate. I was going to Kate.

In Edmonton I caught another plane going five hundred miles north to Fort Nelson. At Fort Nelson I hired a bush pilot to fly me into Telegraph Creek. I remembered the Stikine river that we followed all along the northern edge of the Spatsizi Range. Once again I realized how utterly isolated Kate was. The pilot pointed out Iskut and Forty Mile Flats and, finally, we spiralled down into Telegraph Creek in the same manner I had spiralled out of it five years earlier. The dock where Kate had stood, waving, grew more and more distinct until I could see each individual board. We landed in the choppy water.

I couldn't wait. I had put it off so long that now I was here I scrambled off the plane and onto the dock. I remembered everything vividly, but somehow Kate's letters, which I had read and reread so many times, made the town seem even more familiar to me than it was. I looked at buildings that on my first visit to Telegraph Creek had been just buildings and now they spoke to me of their inhabitants and their life stories and the people that Kate had met and knew. I even thought I recognized some of the dogs. I was a little surprised when I passed Ah Clem and he didn't acknowledge me. Of course he wouldn't.

Kate had described so perfectly where she lived that I knew I would have no trouble finding it. I picked up the Telegraph Trail at the edge of town. There was a small path but it was clearly not that frequented and I wondered if it was mainly Kate who used it. Kate. Kate. All I could think of was Kate. I had so much to tell her. I imagined her sitting there while I told her about Ted Serios, and Breetz, and my father's death, and my mother's moving away. I thought of how I had put off this visit for too long.

The ground looked like it was grass and moss, but occasionally I'd step forward and my foot would sink into mud. Kate had told me that she was about a forty-minute walk from town, but after forty minutes I knew I was nowhere near her cabin. There were brambles, small rivulets that cut across the trail, logs that had fallen. Still, it didn't matter. All that mattered was that I was going to see Kate and see her soon.

I saw the look of joy on her face. I saw us hugging in her doorway, a big warm rocking back and forth hug. I saw us sitting, laughing, drinking tea. I pushed on. Twice I fell, once quite badly. I was walking down a slight incline and my feet just went right out from underneath me. I landed flat on my back, my two bags flying in opposite directions. Increasingly, I was growing short of breath, I who walked miles around Montreal. But none of this mattered. I was going to Kate. I kept to the trail and the further I got from town the more overgrown it became. I was now starting to wonder if anybody walked beyond this point. I knew Kate did, but there was no longer a sign of a path on the trail. After a while, I began to worry that I would lose the trail, wander unknowingly from it. Kate had written me that if you rooted around you could find the cable, still lying where it had been abandoned a hundred years before. I had to do this at one point when the trail became particularly overgrown. Sure enough there the line was below the weeds and grass. A hundred years ago the cable had been strung on poles, but the poles had rotted and fallen, trees had overgrown and pushed it down, tentacles of grass and weeds had pulled it into the earth. Now it had vanished into the undergrowth and would soon completely disappear. I looked at this inch-thick cable — once the only link to civilization, now my clew to Kate — and I followed it. Minutes later I saw her cabin. I walked up onto the porch. I knocked at the door. Kate's door. No answer. I knocked again. Still no answer. This wasn't how I had imagined it. Instead of knocking again I tried the latch. It was well oiled and I pushed it down and as I did so the door swung open on its hinges. I stepped inside, automatically pausing to wipe my feet, but there was no mat, just the plain planks of the cabin floor.

The cabin was just as she'd described. I looked around. The fire in the woodstove was damped down. She was obviously there but not there. She'd gone out. Well, okay, I thought. I'll sit here, dry off, she can't be too far as the fire's still burning. She'll open the door and she'll see me. I put down my bags and sat in the chair. Her chair. The chair where she sat in the evenings writing her poetry.

I tried to imagine what she would be doing right now, right at this very moment. Probably fishing. I imagined myself on the bank alongside her as she cast her line into the river. I was sitting on the dappled bank, and it was not until I saw myself reaching for the bottle of Beaujolais from the wicker basket that I realized this was all wrong. She wasn't fishing in a painting by Monet, she was fishing on the Stikine. I would have to rethink this. I tried to imagine myself fishing on the Stikine, up to my hips in the icy water. I couldn't. Nor could I imagine myself reeling in a fish, whacking its head against a rock, gutting and cleaning it. Recalling my total inability to pith a frog, I couldn't see myself so much as baiting a hook. And yet, you couldn't get through a winter in this place unless you were prepared to fish. Fish? More than fish. Fish and hunt and skin and disembowel.

As I mulled that word, disembowel, over again in my mind, I noticed several dark stains on the floorboards just by the door. I lifted my eyes to a hook sticking out of the wall about six feet above the stains and I realized that would be where Kate hung her fish. She would hang them there and the blood would drip and dry and age and those were the stains I was looking at now. Dried bloodstains.

The merest ache began to throb behind my browbone. I rubbed there with my thumb. I knew I shouldn't think about the fish and the blood and the skinning and the disembowelling, but how could I sit in this cabin and not think about these things? That cabin was permeated with blood and scale and skin and bone. This was how you lived in a cabin like this. Kate and Quinn before her, and the men who had been building the Telegraph Trail. Years and years and years of blood saturating into its floorboards. My head felt heavy.

As I rubbed my temples, an old familiar feeling crept up on me. Embarrassment. Here I was, sitting in this wilderness cabin in my city shoes and my grey flannel pants — the same pants I'd worn to my father's funeral — while Kate was out hunting or fishing. Whatever had I been thinking? I'd been thinking Henry David Thoreau at Walden Pond. But Telegraph Creek wasn't Walden Pond. Walden Pond was only four miles from town. Emerson used to visit regularly. Thoreau could hear the train whistle from his front porch. Kate heard wolves. This was true wilderness. Raw, untamed wilderness for a thousand miles in every direction. I felt myself growing panicky. I had imagined us picking berries and drinking tea, writing poetry and talking philosophy. But she was out hunting. Artemis creeping through the woods, staying downwind, her feet avoiding twigs, silently stalking.

While these thoughts were going through my head I had moved from Kate's chair to the bookshelf to the pine chair to the edge of the single bed. The cabin was suddenly small and I felt constricted and I realized that it hadn't been built for two. And I looked again at the bloodstains and the bed and the books and I realized that I wasn't ready for this life yet. I needed to become tougher. I needed to think things through more. I needed to understand what I was really going to do with my life. Until I understood where I was going and what I was doing, I would just be an intrusion in this cabin. I wouldn't fit. Here, I would be like a piece of nineteenth-century overstuffed furniture taking up space and not contributing anything. I, who had once been Kate's saviour, would be nothing but a burden. Her dearest friend would appear as an incompetent idiot. I couldn't hunt, I couldn't fish, I'd never chopped wood, I had no skills. I was good for nothing. I would be useless here. All I could do was think and what good was thinking in a place like this? Suddenly, I was dreading Kate's return. Suddenly, I was enormously relieved that I hadn't written to say I was coming. I picked up my bags and fled.

MY FIRST MONTH after leaving Kate's cabin was wretched. My only social contact was Cam Bienenstock. My father, it turned out, had left me a good deal of money and Cam helped me to organize it. This just added to my wretchedness. All I had of my father was money. No good memories, no deathbed communication, no breach of the metallic silence: just money. I wrote my mother and she wrote back quite a moving letter, ending with a suggestion that I come stay with her. Of course I didn't. I wrote Wesley and Mildred too, telling them of my father's death and never mentioning my botched attempt to see Kate. As for Kate, I couldn't bear to write to her. I started several letters, but they either remained on the desk unfinished or were thrown away. And so, for the first time since she'd gone to Telegraph Creek, Kate and I were out of touch. My depression deepened.

When I'd returned to Toronto I'd booked into a hotel, thinking I would only be there for a short time. But I just kept living in the hotel, eating breakfast and dinner there and signing for bills I would never see. My father's money enabled me to live a life similar to his own in his last few years — going down to dinner, meeting Cam Bienenstock for lunch — it depressed me, and yet I compulsively re-enacted it. I was behaving like a younger version of my father but without my father's self-imposed discipline for work. The manuscript on Serios lay untouched.

One day I was browsing in a bookstore when I saw a small notice on the bulletin board. Group Meditation. It was for that night and as I had nothing else to do, around seven o'clock I wandered down to Harbord Street. There was a sign on the door: Come In. So I opened it and did just that. About a dozen people were inside, some sitting on the floor on cushions. There were also straight-backed chairs around the room — I took one of these.

The room was simple and uncluttered. At one end, beneath a scroll of the Buddha, there was a cushion and beside the cushion a bowl of sand with two sticks of incense burning. I was feeling a little apprehensive when a young Asian monk, about my age, walked in. He was wearing a garnet-coloured robe and running shoes. He was completely at ease, unassuming, and smiled and nodded at faces he recognized. My apprehension soon melted away. This wasn't a wild-eyed guru, this was an honoured guest from a different culture. He sat down on the cushion, adjusted his robe, gently swayed back and forth a couple of times as if finding his centre. Then he started to hum. I knew of course that he wasn't humming; he was chanting a mantra, the most well-known mantra of all: OM MANI PADME HUM. Hail, Jewel at the Heart of the Lotus. The others joined in softly. As I sat on my chair I watched the shadows playing on the wall, the slow swirl of the incense smoke as it spiralled up to the ceiling. I listened to the quiet hum of the other participants and, to my surprise, the mantra started to work. I started to feel a little better, a little more connected to my fellow human beings. The humming, or chanting, went on for fifteen or twenty minutes and then, just as quietly and unobtrusively as it had begun, it ended. The young man at the front of the room adjusted his robes and then started to talk.

He had a round face, perfect teeth, rosy cheeks, but his accent was as incongruous as the running shoes. He rolled his "r"s, producing a somewhat comical effect, but his English was perfect. He spoke of non-attachment to things *and* ideas and of being free of opinions, ridding oneself of the treacherous this or that. He went on to talk about fear. Fearrr, he said, derived its power from misunderstanding. Fearrr, he maintained, caused more commotion than the feared event itself.

Kate's cabin. What was it I had felt there? I'd called it embarrassment, but had it been fear?

Fearrr of death, fearrr of suffering, arose from the desire to have it otherwise — whereas acceptance of pain, of the fact of death, relieves fearrr of it.

Whatever it was, clearly the emotion had caused more commotion than the event. If Kate had walked in, we probably would have been reunited and I would be there now. But instead my mind had become agitated. I'd sat there in the grip of an illusion, an illusion that was clearly more powerful than the situation.

I had never heard anyone talk quite like this or about these sorts of things. It appealed to me, this detachment and the insistence on the importance of understanding.

After the monk left, I chatted with a couple of people. I asked them how often they met and they laughed. They said that it was completely unpredictable. Two years before, Tsering, as they referred to the monk, had been through Toronto and had stayed for about six weeks. Then he had moved on. No one had been expecting him to arrive this time and no one knew how long he would stay. But I was certainly welcome to hang around as long as he remained. They would be meeting again the following night. I said I would be there.

I was only to learn Tsering's story in bits and pieces over the next eight months, mostly from other people. He was Tibetan, born in the northeastern province of Amdo in the town of Siling. One day he was playing outside the village with some friends when his youngest brother ran up with the chilling news that Chinese officials had arrived in the village and had arrested some of the more prominent towns-people — Tsering's father among them. His brother and he grabbed what money they could from neighbours and friends and started out on an impossible journey across the Tibetan wastes. Here they were adopted by Khampa warriors in slow retreat. One moonless night the brothers found themselves near the arbitrary new border of the so-called autonomous Tibetan region. They slipped across. A few days after that, they met up with a caravan of Tibetan pilgrims who took the two young boys with them to Lhasa. The year was nineteen fifty-six. Here, Tsering, only fourteen years old, started on a path that would never have been possible had he grown up peacefully in Siling. As the firstborn son he was destined to take over his father's business and raise a family. Instead, Tsering was taken in by a monastery in Lhasa. If this second chance had gone its course, Tsering would have lived out his days meditating and studying. But fate intervened once again.

Though all was quiet in the capital, in the northeast, Khampa warriors were heroicly resisting the Chinese invasion. Their resistance increased the belligerence of Peking and the Chinese government started pressuring central Tibet to send troops against its own people. This the Dalai Lama politely refused to do. As Tsering studied his Buddhist scriptures, day by day the sound of guns grew closer to Lhasa, and Khampa warriors started to arrive in the capital. For hundreds of years the Khampas — bandits and independent warlords — had resisted the authority of Lhasa, but now they came to the Holy City's defence. As the capital filled up with Khampas and refugees, tension mounted. Rumours started to fly that the Chinese were planning to abduct the Dalai Lama, the earthly manifestation of Chenrezi, the Bodhisattva of Compassion. Virtually the entire population of Lhasa surrounded the Dalai Lama's summer residence in an effort to protect him. On March 17, 1959, under cover of a dust storm, the Dalai Lama secretly left the capital. He and his retinue made their way south through mountain passes and across the Himalayas, somehow undetected by Chinese aircraft. On March 31, to the amazement of the world, the Dalai Lama arrived safely in India.

Tsering remained in Lhasa during the full fury of the Chinese retaliation. Monks were mowed down outside their monasteries; the streets were filled with the dead. When it became clear that all was lost, Tsering escaped once again into the countryside. Like thousands of refugees, Tsering made his way slowly to the western border of Tibet and escaped into Nepal. There, his skill with language brought him to the attention of Tibetan scholars who arranged for Tsering to go to a monastery in Scotland, where he spent the next five years helping to translate Tibetan texts.

I went back the next night to the little house on Harbord Street, and the next, and the next. I found it gave a sort of focus to my days and there was no question that the chanting of the mantra calmed me. I liked listening to Tsering talk — this was what I'd been looking for in my professors when I'd been struggling with Blake. Here was someone who seemed to understand Blakian concepts and talked about them with an ease and flexibility that I myself had never been able to achieve. Blake wrote,

> Mental things are alone Real; what is call'd Corporeal,
> Nobody knows of its Dwelling Place: it is in Fallacy, &
> its Existence an Imposture.

Tsering said everyday physical reality is illusory, empty, and that which we commonly perceive is purely the product of Mind.

Blake wrote,

> The wanton Boy who kills the Fly
> Shall feel the Spider's enmity.

Tsering spoke of Buddhist compassion and the interrelatedness of all things.

In fact, like Blake, the Buddhists, with their complex pantheon of deities and demons, have constructed an alternative realm which Tsering insisted is every bit as devoid of inherent existence as the world of tables and chairs, but which, nevertheless, corresponds far more closely to the deepest levels of the human psyche.

I found myself drawn to this teaching and was therefore disappointed when one night I showed up at the house and Tsering wasn't there. We did the chanting as always and then afterwards sat around and drank tea. It was one woman's comment, if it wasn't for the mortgage she'd have followed him, that prompted me to ask where he'd gone.

"Niagara Falls, I think," someone said. "He said he's always wanted to see Niagara Falls."

I returned to my hotel that night, packed up my few belongings and the next morning hopped on a bus to Niagara Falls. I was standing at that point along the railing where one feels one can almost reach out and touch the mass of water rushing hypnotically downward, when I heard someone call my name. I looked up and there was Tsering together with five other people.

"What are you doing here, Richard?" he asked.

It was a good question and I didn't quite know how to answer.

"Well," he said, looking towards the falls, "they certainly are magnificent."

Then he turned and started walking. I followed.

I followed him across the Peace Bridge to the American side. I followed him to Buffalo. I followed him to Rochester and Syracuse and Watertown. I followed him through Lake Placid and the Adirondacks down into Vermont and the Green Mountains, and finally into Boston.

In Boston he resumed the life that he'd had in Toronto. There was a group of people there who knew him and at night in one of their homes we would chant, meditate, and then he would give one of his wonderful talks. During the day it was a little unclear what he did, though someone told me he loved the Harvard libraries. Eventually, Tsering booked passage on a freighter, or at least someone booked it for him. Tsering carried no money. In fact, his only "possession" was a small stone he held in his palm while meditating, so all arrangements were made for him by someone else. This booking caused some consternation in the group and all but two of us who had followed him since Toronto had to drop out. But we were joined by four Bostonians.

I had no idea of the freighter's destination, no one did. That first day, walking across the Peace Bridge, I had asked Tsering where we were going. He had just smiled and said, We're not going anywhere, Richard, that's why there's no rush to get there.

On the freighter our days were more structured. In the mornings we would sit on the deck and Tsering would give us a short talk. Then we would meditate. Our afternoons were our own, and they were very long. I had anticipated this and bought a number of books in Boston for the trip, one of which was a Tibetan grammar. One morning I greeted Tsering with toshi dili and he was delighted. After that he gave me quite a bit of help. He would point to things and pronounce their names in Tibetan. He himself was wonderful with languages and when I teased him about the rolling of his "r"s, he pointed out to me that he was one of the few Tibetans who could pronounce "f" as "f" instead of "p" and I should be content with that.

Each day was very much like the day before. The freighter stopped in Miami, Nassau, the Dominican Republic, and then sailed down to Columbia. Tsering always gave his talks and they were always different, yet always the same. I was becoming familiar with the names of some of the Buddhist tantric deities: Padmasambhava — the lotus-born; Maitreya — the Buddha of the future; Vajrapani — thunderbolt in hand.

But as for meditation, I seemed to get worse and worse at it. In the first few weeks I was quite pleased with my ability to sit quietly and attend to my breath, but now the moment I sat down my mind seemed just a jumble. It would jump from what I had for breakfast to eating with Mildred and Wesley to wondering how Ted was doing to sitting in the cabin waiting for Kate to that horrible fiasco in Los Angeles. Back and forth, around and about, here, there and everywhere. And then slowly, painfully, I would become aware of what was happening, and I would pull my awareness back to the simple act of breathing. When I mentioned to Tsering that the longer I meditated the worse I seemed to become, he laughed and said, The longer you meditate the more *humble* you become. There's a difference.

We sailed to Panama and I'll always remember the strangeness of slicing the continent in half. Out we went into the vast Pacific.

In Hawaii a warm wind constantly blew so that our clothes rippled over us, making our bodies appear to be always in motion.

Tsering enjoyed this optical illusion, saying it was, in fact, much closer to reality. Our bodies were, he said, constantly changing, shifting, moving, just as our thoughts were, and that by the time we had registered an image of each other, it was really an "after-image", no longer what was actually there.

We stayed six weeks. One night Tsering mentioned to me that it was time to book passage on another freighter. People were so hungry for his teachings that wherever Tsering went, he gathered a crowd. But he believed so strongly in non-attachment that he didn't want people to become attached to *him* and lose sight of what he was teaching. And so while he gathered people to him, he also kept moving, and peoples' money would run out, or their time, or their commitment. He reassured them by telling them that they would see him again sometime and that in the year or two that they didn't see him, they would have a chance to ponder what he'd said, or study on their own. He kept repeating the Buddha's words, that a teacher is only a guide, a help along the way. Everything he said, or anyone said, must be tested by one's own experience.

I spent a lot of time at the stern of the boat watching the seagulls following us. In fact, it almost became a pastime, watching as one soared up into the sky and hovered there, and then trying to predict that precise moment when it would release itself into the wind and swoop in a long graceful arc down, down, down, and then up, up, up, until the resistance of the wind seemed to bring it to a halt, and the process would repeat itself. I was doing this one day when Tsering came up beside me. I was by now the person who had been with him the longest, and we were on quite friendly, if not intimate, terms. This particular day he asked me about something we'd never talked about before. He asked me about my book. So I told him about Ted Serios and that extraordinary period in my life when Wesley and I had conducted our thoughtographic experiments. He just listened. I was so used to western scepticism and disputation that this response jarred me.

A few days later I raised the subject again. Tsering said that what Ted was doing was unusual but not unheard of. He told of a high lama who had been photographed and when the photograph was developed, instead of the lama's image, a mandala had appeared on the print. He said it was unfortunate that Ted was using alcohol and tension to suppress his grosser levels of consciousness. He also said that this was a gift that Ted clearly didn't understand and couldn't use for the benefit of other sentient beings, or even himself. He said that if these psychic gifts are not used for the benefit of sentient beings, they often harmed their possessor. I asked Tsering if he himself possessed any psychic gifts. He laughed and said no. He said that he hadn't had time. With escaping from the Chinese, studying Buddhist texts, learning English and travelling about, it was all he could do to get a few hours of meditation in each day. These special skills take years and years to develop, he said, and should be of some use. He then gave the example of tummo, the practice whereby hermits high in the Himalaya are able to raise their body temperatures sometimes by as much as eighteen degrees.

"But what's the point of you or I learning this skill, Richard? We're in no danger of freezing to death while meditating, are we? If we get cold, we can simply put on a sweater."

In New Zealand I received my first letter from my mother. She wrote me with the astonishing news that Breetz was now living on the commune. Evidently his marriage to Ramona had been the shortest in history. The very day I had left him in Los Angeles after that ghastly wedding, he had suffered some sort of breakdown. He'd been hospitalized. At Breetz's request, Ulrika got in touch with my mother, who flew down to Los Angeles to visit Breetz at the clinic. They had a long talk. My mother asked him if he would like to live on the commune. He accepted.

That night, I dreamt of Breetz. It was a particularly vivid dream and I saw him in the farm kitchen, chopping onions the way he used to when he was making meals with Anna and me. In the same dream, and I'm not sure if it was connected, I saw Kate moving through the woods, silently, as if stalking an animal. Kate's hair was longer now and she wore it loose. As she moved silently through the woods she seemed to have some destination in mind. And then I saw it: a high thin trickle of glacial water dropping into a beautiful clear cold pool.

That morning Tsering spoke about seeds. The seed of an oak produces an oak. That of a dog, a dog. A whale, a whale. Each seed produces its own kind, but in order to do so, it must find the proper soil or receptacle. The Sanskrit word for receptacle is *alaya*, as in Himalaya, which literally means Receptacle of the Snows. Just as there are so-called material seeds, there are also psychic seeds. Each thought that we have is a psychic seed, each emotion. Even those thoughts and emotions that are beneath the level of consciousness. These seeds flow out into the universe and only come to fruition when they find the proper soil, the proper receptacle. This gave me some understanding of the theory of reincarnation. Not that our ego passes from one body to another, our personality moving through the ages in a long succession of different bodies, but that each of us is formed by, and forms, psychic seeds that find their receptacles in the so-called material world. Nor must we think of the receptacle as something solid. We should rather think of it as a river that flows ceaselessly, psychic seeds being born and dying continually. The whole universe *is* movement and we are part of this movement. All aggregates are impermanent.

In Singapore we lost three people, reducing our party to seven. There we caught yet another freighter that headed through the Strait of Malacca and then slowly up the Burmese coast, finally slipping into Thakuran, one of the many mouths of the Ganges river.

India.

To speak of my first impressions of India is to speak the obvious. Poverty. For days, for weeks even, it was all I could see. Children gathered around us, their hands softly touching, imploring. We would brush them away like cluster flies and they would form again. In Calcutta a young boy lay sleeping on a mat, oblivious to the endless throng of people passing by; a family huddled under a blanket; a baby with enormous eyes clung to its mother's bony chest: and each instance of poverty was repeated again and again, over and over and over, like an image posed between two mirrors, multiplying itself into infinity. It was here that I came the closest I had ever come to just getting on a plane and flying home. I didn't, but others did. Suffice to say that this time as our group dwindled, it wasn't replenished as it always had been. We were now down to four, including Tsering.

Tsering simply walked. He walked through the heart of Calcutta, through its industrial area, through its suburbs, until finally even this huge metropolis ravelled out and we were in the Indian countryside. We followed the Ganges north. Of course there were always villages. India is a country of villages, over five hundred thousand, but to me, each one looked much the same as the last. Each day we got up early and walked until shortly before noon, then we would find some shade where we could rest. We never knew where we would spend the night, but each evening someone approached us with a place to stay and for a pittance our group was fed and housed. We walked and walked, day after day, along the sacred Ganges, but unlike the thousands of other pilgrims I couldn't see its sacredness. All I could see were the babies black with flies, the green slime, the excrement, the pus and filth and disease. Was it all illusion?

On the boat it had been easy to entertain thoughts about the illusory nature of reality, staring out over the Pacific and contemplating the emptiness of all that we see. But was what I saw now illusory? a baseless fabric? The bloated baby covered with flies, was she merely a mental construct? The beggar child defecating on the curb while a mangy dog scrambled to lick up his shit. Was that a mental construct? The sightless eyes, the amputated limbs, the three-legged dogs, were these just products of Mind? What mind? What mind would construct this?

I hated Tsering. I hated the sight of his robe as it seemed to just float along before me, the sight of his head turning to gaze at the fields. I hated what he was making me see. He talked of the illusory nature of everyday physical reality and yet he was walking through mile after mile of degradation, filth and squalor. I hated him.

And I envied him. I envied him his detachment. I envied him that he had nothing to give. He knew who I was. He knew I had money. He knew that all these outstretched hands I had to ignore or brush away could be filled with something. He knew that one day's interest on my father's money could feed those children, those bony children I saw by the roadway. Why was he doing this to me?

And yet I walked on with Tsering as one after another of my western companions slipped away. He wasn't doing it to me; I was doing it to myself. I was free to leave as all the others had. But I didn't. And with each mile I walked into India I hated it more and more.

Everywhere there was human excrement. Beside railway tracks, in gutters, on the banks of the Ganges, behind every bush, in every corner, beside stalls of food, near meat that lay on the cobblestones covered with iridescent flies. At every turn and step there were mounds of excrement. He didn't seem to see it. I did. I saw it, and smelled it, and stepped in it. It seemed at times that the whole country was just one huge pile of excrement. I was nauseated, I was repulsed.

Tsering and I had been walking three weeks when it happened: Ground and Background reversed. The Obvious no longer claimed all my attention. Suddenly I saw, as Blake wrote, not *with* but *through* the eye. Looking *with* the eye I'd seen nothing but squalor, excrement and poverty. But looking *through* the eye I was able to see something else. Those ragged children playing in the mud, a light shone in their faces. That family of beggars huddled on the street looked at each other with love. The peoples' bodies, thin and wretched as they were, moved with an erect grace that I'd never seen on the streets of North America. The faces here were open. They smiled. They looked directly at me. Their brown eyes had depth and feeling. I started to wonder if this was why all the other westerners had left. They'd said it was the stench, the poverty, the incessant begging they couldn't bear, but maybe it was this. What greater affront to all that we believe in the West than that one could be happy under such circumstances? It made the great experiment of the last three hundred years pointless. It made everything that we believed in, and worked for, pointless. It made our whole desire to accumulate and rise above this, pointless.

And I looked at Tsering, who had hardly spoken to me in weeks, and I realized that the teaching was still going on. The teaching was still going on and so I continued to follow him.

We left the main Ganges and began following a tributary northwards; the ground started to slowly rise. A hundred and fifty miles ahead lay the Himalayas.

I found myself thinking of Breetz. In my mind's eye I could see him at my mother's commune. She had written that he was no longer wearing his trademark black. He wore jeans, t-shirts and sweaters. He did a lot of the cooking. The women loved him. They teased him remorselessly about his life as a fashion photographer. He never defended himself. He spent a lot of time in the fields at the edge of the woods gathering herbs and greens out of which he made fantastic salads.

As Tsering and I crossed the border of India into Sikkim I recalled his saying that as we weren't going anywhere, there was no rush to get there. But in the last few weeks I felt that beginning to change. It seemed to me that Tsering was moving towards his beloved Himalayas in a more purposeful manner. And when we got to Gangtok he asked me to buy two white silk scarves — katas — and then he added a phrase that he had never in all our months of travel used before. Spare no expense. So I spared no expense and bought us two scarves of the finest white silk.

Two days later we had an audience with His Holiness the Sixteenth Karmapa, head of the Kagyu School of Tibetan Buddhism. We went through a courtyard into the monastery and were shown to a room where the Karmapa was seated on an elevated chair. He looked magnificent in his ceremonial garb and red hat. As we entered, one by one, each of us presented him with an offering. When it was my turn I walked up and handed the Karmapa my kata. The translator asked me, in English, where I was from and what the purpose of my visit was. Not trusting my Tibetan, I told him I was from Canada and that I'd followed my friend and teacher, Tsering. The Karmapa nodded and smiled. He took my white scarf, placed it around his own neck and then touched my bowed head in blessing. I took a cushion on the floor.

When it was Tsering's time to present his offering, he spoke in Tibetan. Whereas with the rest of us he had just nodded and given his blessing, the Karmapa asked Tsering a question each time he finished speaking. Rudimentary as my Tibetan was, I was able to gather that Tsering was telling him, briefly, about his escape from the Chinese, his time in Scotland, and that he was now a wandering monk. The Karmapa nodded and kept looking at Tsering with a particular intensity that I found quite unsettling. When everyone had presented their offerings, the Karmapa gave a short talk on the importance of generosity and compassion. The translator briefly repeated the talk in fair English, acceptable French and halting German. Then the audience was over. I wasn't the first to leave, nor was I the last, but as in everything I was waiting for Tsering to show the way. But Tsering simply remained seated on his cushion in his meditative posture. I started to feel embarrassed about being there so I slipped out the door with the others and waited for him outside. I waited fifteen minutes. Half an hour. An hour. Two hours. When the door finally opened, standing there was His Holiness the Sixteenth Karmapa and his translator. Looking straight at me, His Holiness started to speak in Tibetan. It was still more music than meaning to me, but I was able to make out a few words and phrases: Tsering's name, the word Rinpoche — Precious Jewel — and then my heart almost stopped. Tulku. Before the translator had begun I knew what had happened. My friend, henceforth to be known as Tsering Rinpoche, had been recognized as a tulku. An Incarnation. He was now to go into an intensive three-year retreat. The Karmapa blessed me again and stepped back inside. But the translator remained.

"Tsering Rinpoche asked me to give you this."

He stretched forth his hand and in it was the small stone Tsering always held while meditating. I took it and looked at it. It was inscribed with Tibetan characters. Om mani padme hum. A miniature mani stone.

I thanked the translator and he smiled, closing the door behind him.

I stood there looking at that closed door for the longest time. Then I stepped back a few yards and looked up at the monastery. There were some windows, and in one of them stood Tsering. He looked at me and I looked at him. Then he waved goodbye: not pompously or ceremoniously, but in a way so characteristic of him — childlike and playfully, he fluttered his hand. I stared a moment, then raised my own hand and waved back. Then he was gone.

NOW WHAT?

The mist that had been closing in all afternoon slowly changed to rain. I walked through Gangtok looking for a place to eat and sleep. For months I'd just followed Tsering and now suddenly I had to start making decisions for myself again. I spent a few days in Gangtok before making my way down to the border of Nepal. There I got on a bus bound for Kathmandu. It might have been easier to walk.

The seat beside me was taken by a mother and three children. Soon there were women wearing anklets and bracelets, men in baggy white jodhpurs, people pushing down the aisle and taking up positions on the floor. Even the stairwell leading down to the rear door was jammed with bodies. There were bundles and packs. Somebody held a goat. Children were squeezed everywhere, even under the seats.

With a blast of the horn we lurched forward. Twenty minutes later we hit our first obstacle: a river. To my amazement the driver just headed across it and I could feel the water sloshing against the underbody. Having made it to the far side, with a grinding of gears, we lumbered onto a gravel road, which wove and wound its way through the countryside. Half a mile later we came to a washed-out bridge. The driver put the bus in reverse and we inched our way back. We took what I suppose was a detour, but looked to me like a cattle path. The bus heaved and swayed. Someone wretched in the seat ahead of me. It was still raining. I could feel the bus's wheels sinking into the soft clay. We slogged to a halt. The bus driver got out of his seat and started talking. Everyone piled out of the bus and stood there in the rain. Some of the men reluctantly walked around to the rear of the bus and I realized that the bus driver had asked them to push and as a male I would be expected to help. We heaved and shoved and leaned and pushed. Finally the wheel spun loose, plastering us with mud, and the bus, once rolling, didn't stop. For the next couple of miles we all trudged along behind it. When the road bed improved, we reloaded. We continued on and on. I dozed off.

Finally we reached a small town where we got out and relieved ourselves. Then we climbed back on the bus and waited. We waited and waited. I eventually gathered from someone who spoke a little English what was happening: we were refuelling. I wiped the window with my sleeve and saw a young boy emptying a beer bottle into the gas tank. Beer? Then I saw him spin around and run over to a huge oil drum, where he refilled the bottle and ran back to our bus. We were refuelling, all right. One beer bottle at a time.

In this way we inched our way up into the Kathmandu valley. By the time we arrived, I was so desperate for western comforts I checked into the Royal Hotel, sparing no expense. I wired Cam Bienenstock, then had a bath. It took only one bath and room service for me to quickly slip back into my western ways. I slept and slept.

When I finally emerged from the hotel the fog had lifted, and I set out to explore Kathmandu. There was so much to see: the gorgeous palaces, the solemn temples. It was a relief when I finally stepped into a small bookstore tucked up a narrow alley. My old habits reasserted themselves with familiar force. I started picking up books written in languages I couldn't possibly understand and thumbing through them. There were two people minding the store, one old, one young. The young man's face was full of laughter and he had apple cheeks much like Tsering's. I tried my Tibetan out on him. He smiled and replied. Then he tried his English out on me. I smiled and replied. Unbeknownst to either of us, Norbu and I had struck a bargain.

When I left the bookstore, it was cooler. I was unable to find a store which sold western clothing, but back at the hotel a houseboy, after I'd explained my problem, came up with a solution. He led me to a rack of second-hand suits abandoned by former guests. I picked out two, tried them on, and his mother, a seamstress, pinned them for me. Just a few hours later there was a rap on my door and I was presented with the two suits and a couple of silk shirts that the boy's mother had run up for a few extra rupees. I put them on. They fit perfectly, though I looked like a character out of a Forties movie. No matter, I knew it was important to be appropriately attired for dinner in the Royal Hotel.

The grand dining room at the Royal was just starting to fill up. The *maitre d'* bowed slightly and asked if sahib was alone. I said that I was and he gestured to a waiter. The waiter, dressed in a white tunic cinched at the waist with a wide cloth belt much like a cummerbund, led me to a table for two. It was right in the middle of the dining room beneath a magnificent crystal chandelier. As I felt it was a little too central, I motioned to a table off to the side, but it was reserved, apparently; the waiter then asked if I would like a cocktail. I ordered a drink, which was brought to me by still another waiter, who disappeared as quickly as he had arrived.

As I sat in splendid isolation the room began filling up around me with parties of four, six, eight, on either side. Just as I was on the point of picking up my drink and moving to a less conspicuous spot, a large balding European in a Tyrolean jacket entered. He was alone. He surveyed the vast room and then his eyes lit on me. He immediately strode over and held out his hand, introducing himself as Anderl Huber, and then asked if he could join me. I was delighted to have some company. The moment he took his seat a bottle of Austrian Riesling and two glasses appeared at our table. He talked in a loud voice, his words punctuated with operatic gestures.

In the next half hour, as our glasses emptied and were refilled, I learned that he'd been born in Kitzbühel and was a contemporary of the great Austrian ski team of the Fifties. He told wild stories of racing down the Hanenkampf in a blizzard; of childhood exploits in the mountains; of skiing glaciers; of unofficial jumps done in high winds. He told of climbing in his youth and how he had first read about Heinrich Harrer as a child. He'd wanted to do what he'd done. He wanted adventure, he wanted to go to places no one had ever been before, he wanted to discover lost lands. But by the time he had got to the Himalayas, they were covered with invisible barriers. The ice curtain had dropped between Tibet and the rest of the world. An impenetrable barrier that not even a Harrer could get through. Bandits and nomads could be bribed and cajoled but the political implacability of the Chinese was unshakable. He ranted and raved about the "old days" and how he had been born fifty years too late. He had the courage, he had the strength, he was a man of Harrer's mettle, he knew he was, but there was no chance for discovery. Everest had now been climbed so often it was getting to be like a picnic site at the top, he said, with abandoned oxygen cans and the detritus of civilization. Harrer never went to the top out of respect, but all respect was lost now. He longed for the days when men lived by their wits. He hated governments and boundaries and regulations designed to protect him from the very things he longed for: entering forbidden kingdoms, discovering forgotten civilizations.

"Why do you smile?"

"I'm smiling," I said, "because as a child I had those same dreams myself."

"Then you understand, then you under*stand*."

He said it with such incredible fervour, as though he'd found a soulmate, a man like himself capable of dreaming the impossible. Then, abruptly, his fervour changed to dejection.

"But the lost lands have been found," he said. "The undiscovered kingdoms discovered. The forbidden lands entered and destroyed." He shook his head. "For years and years it seemed nothing was left. Nothing, nothing, nothing." He leaned forward and lowered his powerful voice to a whisper. "But there is still one. One undiscovered kingdom left untouched."

By now I was totally intrigued. But as abruptly as he had changed moods and subjects before, Anderl jumped to his feet and thrust out both arms.

"Janar!"

Across the dining room, standing by the door, was a Nepalese couple. The woman was beautiful in her apricot silk and sparkling jewels. Anderl leaned over to me and said, "My dear, dear friends... do you mind if they join us?"

Of course I didn't mind and in moments he was striding across the floor to greet them. My attention was still on Anderl's receding back when two waiters, with deft celerity, appeared with another single table, which they added to our own. By the time the Nepalese couple had accompanied Anderl back to our table, it had doubled: four magenta-patterned plates with gold trim; four wine glasses; four sets of silver cutlery.

I was introduced to the couple.

"I present Mahabir Jung Bahadur Janar and his lovely wife Bahi."

Then Anderl turned to me and in a serious voice said that Mr Janar was a senior official in the Nepalese Ministry of Tourism and had the ear of King Mahendra. Mr Janar began to shake his head in protest but Anderl brushed this aside and introduced me as Professor Richard Hathaway. Now it was my turn to explain that I was not yet a professor, but Anderl fixed Mr Janar with one of his intent looks and said, "Professor Hathaway is from the snowbound land of Canada, where the inhabitants live in houses made of ice."

The Nepalese official was clearly impressed and eagerly took a seat beside me. I found myself trying to explain to a man with very little English that, yes, there were houses of ice, but I myself had never seen one, much less lived in one. He looked across the table and spoke to his wife in rapid Nepalese. Her dark eyes went wide and she looked at me in astonishment. I knew that from that moment on I was a professor who lived in an ice house and that no amount of explaining on my part would ever change the story.

Mr Janar and Anderl immediately started talking and I was impressed by the fluency of Anderl's Nepalese. He took pains to include me and often translated. They were talking about trekking and tourism and the difficulties of finding a balance between those who wanted to exploit this incredible country and those who wanted to protect it.

Bahi knew the words "please" and "thank you" and used them inappropriately but delightfully. Since arriving in Kathmandu, I had been struck by the beauty of Nepalese women. The word "lovely" best describes them. With Bahi across the table I was able to appreciate this loveliness in detail: a tiny diamond in her nostril, a series of gold rings all along the outer rim of her ear, glittering eyelids, dark hair parted in the middle and adorned with gold chains.

Anderl continued to translate back and forth. I kept hearing the same words: Khampas, politically unstable, border area, Mustang, impossible. When a waiter appeared, Anderl consulted me. I suggested a bottle of champagne. He heartily concurred and said something to the Nepalese official, who turned and thanked me. I felt it was time to order dinner but Anderl was on his feet again looking at the door, where the *maitre d'* was greeting a party of four. He turned to me and said, "Do you mind?"

"Not at all," I replied and as he went to meet them, the waiters added a table for four, threw on another cloth, and we had once again doubled: eight plates; eight wine glasses; eight sets of cutlery.

Again there was a flurry of introductions with much nodding and smiling and shaking of hands. Mr Singh was a merchant and his wife, though older than Bahi, exhibited that same Nepalese grace and loveliness. They were dining with an Italian, the front man for the proposed Italian attempt on Everest. He was delighted to meet Mr Janar as Mr Janar was conversant with the progress of his permit. The fourth member of their party was a Sherpa, the guide of the Italian expedition, and I was able to gather that the Sherpa and Mr Singh had some sort of business relationship that was as yet unclear to me.

By the time our meals arrived I had consumed a good deal of wine and champagne on an empty stomach and was feeling somewhat light-headed. The women in their colourful dresses were jewels in that great mahogany box of a dining room: saffron, apricot, scarlet, vermilion; all reflected in the many-mirrored high-ceilinged room. The serving of the food was a performance in itself. Swift waiters, flourished napkins, silver trays, carved bowls, intricately woven baskets.

We ate and drank and talked and laughed. A *mélange* of languages so that each story told was told and retold in different tongues. The conversation tumbled like a stream running downhill, branching off at times into eddies where it seemed to swirl into silence, only to reappear flowing somewhere else in yet another language and another translation. The party went on and on — dessert, coffee, liqueur — and I began to wonder how we were going to divide the bill, as it had been such a jumble of this person ordering that, and that person ordering this. Then it hit me.

When Anderl had first entered he had asked if he could join me. When Mr Janar and his wife had entered he had asked if they could join us. When the party of four had entered, he had again requested my permission . . . and I realized, somewhat belatedly I suppose, that we weren't going to divide the bill, that it was assumed I would pay it. To refuse would have caused an embarrassing scene and I was in no mood for that. And so when next I was referred to as "our charming host," instead of protesting, I got to my feet and announced to the assembled company that it had been a great pleasure and I was honoured by their presence at my small party.

Anderl turned to me and smiled as if to say he, of course, had been conning me all along and now I knew it. And now he knew that I knew and he appreciated that I had accepted it with such grace and good humour. I smiled back.

That night I stumbled into my room and after kicking off my shoes fell onto the bed. I slept badly. Twice I had to get up to relieve myself and drink some water. When I fell back into my fitful sleep, I dreamt of Breetz. This time he was cooking, stirring, tasting, adding salt and pepper. Now he was peeling and washing something. They were root vegetables. Things I didn't recognize. Obviously wild. Now he was in the meadow. He was looking intently at the ground and every so often he would squat down and pick something, some sort of wild flower or herb. He would gather it up and put it in a bag, then keep looking and walking, walking and looking. He was alone. Breetz was alone in my dreams now, and yet in real life he had always been surrounded by people.

I avoided the grand dining room at the Royal for the next few days. Sometimes I ate at small cafés in Kathmandu or ordered from room service. But about a week after my splurge, I dressed myself up again and went down. When I looked through the big doors I saw an older American couple sitting at the single table in the middle of the room. They looked a little lost and forlorn, just as I must have that first night. I turned and went back upstairs. When I returned three quarters of an hour later, Anderl was sitting at their table and they were all roaring with laughter. I ambled into the dining room and looked around. Anderl stood, held out his arms to me, then turned and said something to the couple. That evening, I was not the professor in the ice house, I was simply Anderl's dear friend, Richard. We were joined by four others — yet another official from the Ministry of Tourism and his wife, an Indian doctor and a Jesuit priest who was writing a book on the mix of cultures in Kathmandu. We had a great time and early on in the evening the American, a retired neurosurgeon from New York, ordered a magnum of champagne and announced with a flourish that this was his party and there were to be no arguments. We all drank his health.

About every fourth night Anderl would do his routine, and I noticed that he picked his mark so astutely that they were almost always so happy to have the company and to be included that they insisted on picking up the tab. Only once did somebody seem to figure out what was happening and on that occasion I announced that this was my party. A moment or two later Anderl turned to me with a twinkle in his eye and mimed wiping his forehead in relief.

It was Norbu who was able to explain to me some of the negotiations that were going on below my level of awareness at these meals.

Take, for example, that first night. As part of their payment, Sherpas were outfitted for each climb and inherited their equipment when the climb was over. Mr Singh owned a shop that sold used trekking equipment to tourists. The Italian was the front man who negotiated the delicate procedure of getting a permit, a procedure which Mr Janar could delay or expedite. So everyone at the meal was getting something out of it. The merchant got the used equipment from the Sherpa, the Sherpa got the equipment from the Italian, the Italian got his permit through Mr Janar... and Mr Janar got to be seen in the Royal Hotel with his beautiful wife. Nothing illegal or even immoral, but everyone benefited from Anderl's little parties — always thrown at someone else's expense.

But what was Anderl getting out of it? After four or five of these dinners I noticed there was always one constant. No matter who later strolled into the dining room, Anderl had always invited one guest — an official of the Ministry of Tourism. In this way Anderl cultivated the friendship of everyone in the Ministry, from senior officials to the most lowly of clerks. For even a clerk could shift a piece of paper to the top of the pile.

At one of these parties, I met an imposing official who actually did have the king's ear. He spoke impeccable English and so I used this opportunity to ask him about Anderl's obsession. Yes, there was such a kingdom, he said. When King Mahendra passed the Raja Abolition Act in 1962, the Kingdom of Mustang, or Lo as the inhabitants call it, was excepted. The only exception.

"It is utterly unique, you see. The last feudal kingdom on earth. Yes, a tiny independent kingdom high in the Himalaya."

The King of Lo gave King Mahendra nine hundred Nepalese rupees a year and two horses. But this was accepted as the gift of a monarch, not the tribute of a subject.

When I inquired further about Anderl and his permits, the Nepalese official merely chuckled. He said Lo had remained independent for some very good reasons. Historically, it had always been difficult to reach, hidden behind the Annapurna Range, and now its inaccessibility was even greater. Khampa warriors were making their last stand against the Chinese in that area, and the Nepalese government couldn't possibly guarantee trekkers any protection. The official sipped his wine, then smiled and said, "Part of the costliness of permits is that the Nepalese government guarantees protection, you see. If no protection can be provided, it would be unconscionable to take a foreigner's money."

When I later told Anderl what the minister had said, he just laughed.

"They keep telling me it's impossible. If it weren't impossible, someone would have done it by now! But I intend to be the first man to get to Mustang, Richard, you mark my words."

He was a mesermizing talker, Anderl. And the more he talked the more fascinated I became. That same night he went on at great length about the City of Manthang in the Kingdom of Lo. Lo Manthang, he said, was the last place on earth where one could see the mysterious Tibetan culture unviolated. Untouched.

"But what about the Khampas?" I asked.

"Khampas, Khampas, Khampas, god! As if there haven't always been bandits, thieves, outlaws — goes with the territory. In the nineteenth century a man strode out into the wilderness and took his chances. If he ended up at the bottom of a gorge with his throat slit, so be it. At least he died a glorious death in the attempt, not like one of these fat bureaucrats who sit in their plush chairs saying, no, no, no, can't be done, impossible."

Sometimes Anderl reminded me of Breetz, who would go on like this while the adults in our lives smiled indulgently. But he'd pulled it off — he had gone to New York, he had photographed the world's most beautiful women — so I didn't dismiss Anderl's obsession lightly.

Those eight weeks I spent in Kathmandu were a strange mixture of quiet afternoons spent with Norbu in the bookstore practising Tibetan and extravagant dinner parties with Anderl. One day, after I'd come to know Norbu quite well, his uncle beckoned me into the small room adjacent to the shop. This was the library where the old man kept not only his own precious books he had escaped with, but those of his friends. The walls were lined with wooden shelves and on these shelves lay books wrapped in red and yellow silk. It was here in a little store in Kathmandu that I learned the proper ritual for opening and reading a sacred text. Touching it to your head, unwrapping the silk, removing the carved wooden cover, and lifting leaf by leaf the elongated pages. The old man's fingers moved slowly across the page while he read to me aloud in Tibetan. This was a great compliment he was paying me, Norbu explained. Books, of all the sacred artifacts in Tibetan culture, were held in the highest esteem. They were believed to have magical properties, and all sorts of legends surrounded their existence: books that mysteriously wrote themselves; books that spoke out loud; and books that appeared and disappeared at will.

In my culture, medieval monks had created books like these — the Cologne Bible, the Book of Kells — but the tradition had been long since abandoned, and Blake's heroic attempt to revive it had met with failure. Nowadays books have become just one more disposable item: shoddily bound, hastily read, soon forgotten. I hardly knew how to thank Norbu's uncle, who spoke no English, for the honour he had bestowed upon me, but when I tried he smiled and said something back, slowly, so that I was able to understand.

"I think, Richard, you are a little bit Tibetan."

Around my fifth week in Kathmandu letters started to arrive. Other guests at the hotel were desperate to open their mail but I did so with a certain reluctance. Somehow I was part of another world here and becoming more so all the time. Wesley and Mildred wrote, the Rosses, even Cam Bienenstock, but the longest letter I received was from my mother. The first two pages were devoted to stuff about the farm — the garden, the bees, the well — but the last two were about Breetz:

> Well, last year the excitement around here was
> Galen, the first baby born on the farm. This year it's
> puppies. I can't remember if I mentioned to you that a
> dog followed us in from town one day and adopted us.
> Over the fall we noticed her getting fatter and fatter
> and attributed it to all the good food and care she was
> getting with us until someone said, That dog's not fat,
> she's pregnant. Anyway, Dawg gave birth to five pups.
> She's some sort of Labrador cross but whoever the
> scoundrel father was, he must have had a lot of
> hunting dog in him too. So the puppies are a bit of

everything, but they're certainly healthy and they're certainly energetic. Dawg doesn't seem too interested in motherhood and that's just as well because her babies have bonded to Breetz! They go everywhere with him. Now that spring has arrived he's spending a good part of his day with the dogs, wandering in the woods. He even takes his camera. The Breetz you and I knew was always obsessed with photographing beautiful girls, and although our commune has lots of those, he never photographs people any more. He just wanders with the dogs and photographs whatever he comes upon that interests him. He lets the dogs lead him into the woods and never worries about finding his way out, he says, just follows the dogs back home. Strange... but then who would have guessed that *you'd* be the one to tramp halfway round the world? We think of you always and talk of you often,

Love,
Elizabeth

In August 1966, Mao Tse Tung had stood up in Tiananmen Square and announced the beginning of a second revolution. The first revolution had destroyed the political apparatus of the old society. This second revolution would be aimed at destroying the cultural basis on which this apparatus had rested. He addressed himself to the youth of China and urged them to destroy the Four Olds: old culture, old ideology, old customs and old habits. All over China, Red Guards formed. Quasi-military brigades made up of young people whose task, as they saw it, was to destroy and eradicate. The Cultural Revolution grew in force and fury until it almost obliterated three thousand years of history.

China suffered terribly from this second revolution, but it was nothing in comparison to Tibet. Precious books were being pillaged and destroyed. Sacred texts shredded and used for toilet paper. Thangkas cut up for clothing. Huge buddhas melted down for their metals. Temples turned into movie theatres. As Norbu related these stories, I could see the pain he suffered. He himself could barely remember Tibet and Tibet was now being systematically destroyed. Norbu knew that this destruction could never be undone. That he would never again see the old Tibet.

And so I knew that day, as I slipped the piece of paper across the table, that Norbu would be unable to refuse. Unable to refuse a chance to see the last unviolated vestige of his culture left on earth. Just as I had been unable to refuse Anderl when, the night before, he'd shown me Permit #0002 and offered me first refusal to be his companion on the trek to the mysterious Kingdom of Lo Manthang.

That night I sat down in my hotel room and for the first time in over a year wrote to Kate. I told her that from the moment I had seen her a seed had been planted and that I was the receptacle in which that seed had been growing. Now I finally understood where next I had to go. I wanted her to understand that in the last year she had seldom been out of my thoughts and that somehow this strange journey to Lo Manthang involved her in a way that I didn't quite understand.

I started my letter by telling her about my attempt to visit her in Telegraph Creek. I told her about Tsering and my wanderings. And not just my physical wanderings, but my emotional and intellectual wanderings too. In a way I had been wandering my whole life but now, at last, I had direction. As I wrote to her about Lo Manthang, the ancient walled city high in the Himalayas, I realized that my journey to Lo Manthang was really a journey towards her. Towards an understanding of her. A journey that had begun that day ten years earlier in Halberstam's. I told her everything. And I told her that when this journey was over, I would return to where it had begun. I would return to her.

ON APRIL 23, 1970, Anderl, Norbu and I flew to Pokhara, a community of brick houses with thatched roofs amid fields of rice at the foot of the Himalayas.

Anderl didn't waste any time. The moment our gear hit the tarmac he began negotiating. He had insisted that we buy the best equipment and he had packed it into stainless-steel cases. I couldn't possibly imagine how anyone could carry these steel cases up and down across the huge ravines that lay between Pokhara and the Kali Gandaki river, but within minutes there were four groups vying for our custom. I still hadn't got used to the idea of bargaining, so central to commerce in the East, but Anderl was an absolute master. He was able to play one set of porters off against another and the price kept getting lower and lower. I didn't see how anybody would carry such a load for such a piddling price, but by mid-afternoon everything was settled. Six porters would meet us next morning outside the checkpost. That night we slept at a small inn.

At the checkpost I watched the Nepalese officer's face closely as he scrutinized our permits. Permits for Dolpo, Manang, Mustang. I tried to read the officer's face as his eyes took in that last word, Mustang, but it revealed nothing.

"Himal Jhane," he said, stamping the permits and handing them back.

Yes, we nodded, we are going to the Land of the Snows. We then walked out of the small hut and joined our porters.

For the next few days we would trek west across the base of the massive Annapurna Range. Huge ridges swept down from this range and so our trek would be a continuous winding and wriggling to the top of a ridge and then over and down, down, down sometimes as much as five or six thousand feet to the river below, where we would cross the waters on swinging bridges only to start an ascent again. In the morning the cloud would hang above us. By mid-morning we would climb through the mist and by afternoon what had been our ceiling would be our floor. Up and down. Up and down.

We weren't two hours out of Pokhara when a problem started to arise that only got worse. The porters, struggling under far too much weight, were falling behind, and the indefatigable Anderl kept urging them on. Walking along with Norbu, I felt embarrassed that this large European, who carried nothing, kept pestering these small barefoot porters struggling under huge loads. But Anderl wouldn't let up. He had contracted them to carry the baggage and he insisted that they keep to his pace.

As the morning went on the mist started to lighten, and the sun didn't break through so much as make the mist brighter. We had left the terraced hills of Pokhara and were now climbing through a jungle. As I climbed through this incredible landscape Anderl's voice berating the porters jarred me. He was now going on about not falling behind, reaching Nodara by nightfall. I stopped with Norbu and we waited and in a few minutes the porters caught up to us. One of them, a young man of about eighteen, was having trouble with his ankle. I looked at it. It was slightly swollen. I offered to take his basket, but Anderl, in English, insisted that I mustn't. They were hired to do the task, he said, and I must walk unencumbered. So on I walked but at my back, always, I heard the insistent harangue of Anderl's voice. I longed to get away from him and for a time Norbu and I did, but then I felt guilty that we were setting an even faster pace, and so I determined that we should reverse our positions and let Anderl lead the way. This he did with a manic energy, climbing up one side of a ravined hill, waiting at the top till we arrived, sometimes coming part way down again to urge the porters on. The porter with the swollen ankle was falling farther and farther behind but Anderl had no sympathy and kept calling him lazy and yelling at him to quicken his pace.

Of course we were not alone on the trail. This was not a wilderness, but a well-travelled route. Every so often we would meet a group of porters, women as well as men, clad in loose cotton clothing. Like our porters they carried enormous loads, hauling the country's livelihood on their backs in woven baskets. Up and down, back and forth they travelled, their splayed toes grasping hold on the myriad trails linking the tiny isolated villages in this roadless land.

At the end of the first day I examined the porter's ankle. It was badly swollen now and showing some discoloration. I knew it would be impossible for him to make another day's march carrying such a load. I felt that the compassionate thing to do would be to jettison some of our gear and pay him off, but Anderl violently disagreed. We argued about this and at one point the argument became quite acrimonious. Anderl finally won out. He said that we must wait for the porter to say he couldn't carry the load and in that way a new contract could be negotiated which would come from them, not us. In terms of bargaining it made sense, but the next day I could barely watch as the young porter heaved his load onto his shoulders and we began our first ascent of the morning.

That morning the mist was especially thick. Even before we started to climb I could feel my clothes becoming wet. The mist was so thick we could hardly see each other, though at times only a few feet apart. Other senses were heightened. I could smell the clay underfoot, I could hear birds and the purling of streams, but always Anderl's voice. Soon Anderl's chiding irritated me on my own behalf not just the porters'. We were moving into a world where time was measured by paces not clocks, and unless we accepted its slow and steady rhythm we would be constantly at odds with it. He kept insisting on keeping to schedule, getting to such and such by such and such, as if an hour or two "lost" mattered. But what was the point of venturing into this world if you tried to change it instead of letting it change you? Behind me, I could hear the soft hum of Norbu's mantra. The mantra beat in time with one's heart and pulse and it kept one moving at a pace in rhythm with the landscape.

We stopped for our mid-day meal and ate rice cooked the night before. I was sitting across from Anderl when the head porter tentatively approached us. He spoke in Nepalese but I gathered that he was admitting to Anderl that the young porter could no longer proceed. This was the moment Anderl had been waiting for. Because he had outwaited the porter, he was able to make him stick to the original terms of the deal. And so we repacked, dividing the injured man's load among the other five, so that each one of them now carried close to one hundred pounds. I was glad the young porter could return to the nearest village and give his ankle the rest it needed, but sickened that the others had to carry his share for the same measly price. Anderl had proved his point, though to what advantage I couldn't fathom.

About half an hour after we reloaded we reached the top of the ridge and started down into the next ravine. After a few miles we emerged into a spectacular world of rhododendron thickets. A shimmering torrent of blossoms flooded the valley in waves of purple, red and white. Below, I could see the porters' heads emerging otter-like from the sea of flowers that surrounded them. Down and down we went through these waves of colour until we reached the river below. We camped that night amid orchids, azaleas and rhododendrons.

Day three began with yet another arduous ascent. Up terraced fields, along airy walkways and precipices. That day we climbed out of spring and into winter, then back into spring again. To my surprise Anderl was not displaying his usual energy. At lunch, I noticed him kneading his right hip with his hand, but when he noticed me noticing, he made a pretence of reaching into his pocket for a handkerchief. That afternoon he fell behind.

When Norbu and I got to the top of a ridge we would give the porters a rest and sit and wait for Anderl. I, of course, couldn't help but think that only twenty-four hours earlier an hour lost had been something to yell about. Now we were waiting for him. I knew Anderl; I knew he was an experienced climber. That he had trekked all over the Himalayas. So I knew that whatever was slowing him down must be something serious. That night I asked him about his hip and he brusquely dismissed my inquiries, saying it was nothing. But the next morning he was limping. Not limping so much as slightly dragging his right foot. I'd seen that movement before, my adviser at McGill, so I wasn't surprised when that afternoon Anderl fell farther and farther behind.

The next day he couldn't get up. He lay in his tent and when I went in with morning tea, he had a look of such pain in his eyes I couldn't sit with him, but simply put the tea down and withdrew. It wasn't until mid-morning that I was able to talk to him. He said that when he was a boy in Austria he'd injured his back skiing. It had briefly flared up a couple of times in his twenties, but he hadn't had any trouble in years. He assured me that it was a temporary spasm, that it would go as quickly as it came, and that we would make up for lost time. But the next morning he was still unable to move. So we sat around for a second day. That evening, the head porter came to me and, using Norbu as a translator, explained that they had been contracted to carry our luggage to Tukutcha, which normally took six days. This was day six, so I immediately renegotiated the deal and paid them extra.

On day seven Anderl was even worse. He couldn't lift his heel off the mat and he had excruciating pain, he said, running down his right leg. I knew he could never make it to Mustang. Of course he knew that too. When I bent low to enter his tent with a mug of tea on that day, we both knew what I was really coming to say. Soon the rains would start and we had to get above the monsoon line before that happened. He knew that as well as I. I felt terrible. This trek to the forbidden land was a lifelong dream of Anderl's and only a very recent dream of mine, and now I was planning to go on without him. We said things to each other like, I'll come along in a few days and, Yes, we'll see you there. But we both knew that while he had led me to Lo Manthang, he would never enter it himself. I wanted to thank him, to say something profound, to do anything to ease the heavy silence that fell between us, but Anderl simply rolled over onto his side away from me.

As a child I had always followed Breetz. In Montreal, Wesley had led me in directions I never would have ventured on alone. I had followed Tsering to Gangtok. Anderl had led me to where I was now. But that night it was me the porters looked to. It was a turning point in my life. I was now in charge. I was leading. And so great was the lure of the Kingdom of Lo that it overrode all feelings of inadequacy and apprehension that I would normally have felt. I made a decision. Two of the porters would accompany Norbu and me to Tukutcha, the rest would remain with Anderl.

We left camp the next morning before dawn. Even though my doko was much lighter than the porters', and somewhat lighter than Norbu's, I still felt a sense of equality as I put it on. My load was heavier, but I felt lighter. We climbed in the dark while behind us the sky grew pale. As we reached the top of the last transverse ridge the sun's rays strode before us. With steady steps they moved up the blue-black backdrop of the Dhaulagiri Range, illuminating one granite tier after another, and igniting them with a golden pink light. Up and up the light travelled as ridge after ridge burst into flame, until finally it reached the eternal snows of the peaks, transmuting them into a blinding luminescence.

As I watched, I thought how out of character this was. This couldn't be Richard Hathaway — Richard Hathaway who never played sports, who never camped or took canoe trips like other boys, whose greatest pleasure was a book in a quiet corner. This couldn't be that Richard Hathaway. How did I get here? Each step of the way had seemed so small. Yet here I was. I stood and looked at the range, not solely in awe of it, but also of the changes that I myself had undergone. I wondered what changes lay ahead.

None of us moved until the sun had risen high behind us. Then solemnly, following Norbu's example, I circumambulated, left to right, the cairn that marked the top of the pass and, like him, placed a stone on that cairn as a token of recognition to all those who had preceded me here, and those who would follow after.

As we left the ridge and headed down into yet another ravine, I broke the awed silence.

"Which do you prefer?" I asked Norbu. "Going up or going down?"

Norbu laughed and said, "Going up when I'm going down and down when I'm going up."

As for myself, on the whole, I preferred going up, but down it was that day, down and down we went, zigzagging and winding down, until finally, just after lunch, we heard a distinct hum. The muffled roar of the Kali Gandaki river.

On one side of the Kali Gandaki stands Mount Dhaulagiri, elevation 26,810 feet. On the other, Annapurna, 26,504 feet. Between these two mountains the Kali Gandaki cuts a canyon that is the greatest on earth. We would now follow this river north, up, up and up, until we reached the plateau above, truly the roof of the world. That night we stayed in the tiny village of Tatopani.

Next morning I got up early and took my permit to the police checkpost. At the other three checkposts we'd passed through since Pokhara, Anderl, with his fluent Nepalese, had done the talking. So it was with some trepidation that I placed permit #0002 before the officer. Was it my imagination, or did he examine it more carefully than those of the Nepalese traders preceding me? But after taking it, turning it over and looking at it again, he stamped it, and I came out of the checkpost exhilarated.

When I returned to our campsite Norbu was just finishing his morning prayers, and the porters were in good moods. With luck, in two days we would reach their native village of Tukutcha where they would be reunited with their families. But the days ahead of us would prove to be the most amazing yet.

The walk from Tatopani to Gasa was at once the most treacherous and the most spectacular I'd ever experienced. I was torn between examining every footstep to make sure I had a secure hold and stopping to gaze. In many places we were walking along impossibly narrow ledges above the river and a moment's inattention would have meant instant death. We walked for half a mile along a ledge no wider than three feet that had somehow been scooped out of the cliff. As we inched towards the massive peaks ahead, the canyon grew narrower and tighter and the trail, hugging the cliff, would sometimes meet a landslide. At this point small hand-dug tunnels would be the only access to the other side. We would emerge from these short dark tunnels to another hair-raising walk along the etched-out cliff, which seemed to get narrower and more precipitous with every step we took. At times the trail would simply run out of cliff, and here was the most terrifying thing of all. Rickety bridges spanning huge gorges over hurtling waters. We crossed, one at a time, as the bridge swayed in the southerly winds. Once on the other side we would scramble up the next cliff to walk along another perilous path that would end in yet another bridge, this time two tree trunks lashed together and resting precariously on either side of the gorge. As I clung to a rock face or made my way painstakingly across one of these bridges, raptors circled above me.

By late afternoon we reached the hamlet of Gasa and the first intimations of another world, a world I had been hankering for since I first met Tsering. The world of Tibet. The houses in Gasa were all of stone, with flat roofs, upon which women were beating newly reaped barley. As we walked into the village the chaff snowed down upon us. Exhausted and shaken by the day's ordeals, we made early camp. As always, we slept well and woke the next morning to clear skies. By now the change in vegetation that had been occurring over the last part of the trek was complete. We had passed from subtropical shrubs and bushes to the more alpine vegetation of birch and pine.

On the other side of Gasa, the river bed grew wider and we were able to walk along it. As it was pre-monsoon the waters lay low in individual strands — sometimes braiding together, sometimes moving separately amid the polished boulders. I was watching my foot placement when Norbu drew my attention to what looked like a grey rope far in the distance. It took me a moment to realize it was a mule caravan moving down the gorge towards us. As it drew nearer we could hear the clang of the copper bells.

The muleteer himself had a thick tassel of red wool woven into his lanky black hair, identifying him as a Khampa. He was taller than our Nepalese porters and bigger, and his creased leathery face bespoke the toughness of this much-feared tribe. On and on came the mules. Ten, twenty, thirty, fifty, until finally I stopped counting. I saw three other Khampas as fierce looking as the first, but none seemed to notice our presence as we watched them pass.

So this was one of the mysterious Khampa muletrains that travelled down from the plateau around Mustang into Nepal to pick up supplies. Ostensibly grains, but everyone knew the bags of grain concealed guns and ammunition. This was my first experience of Khampas, but I knew it would not be my last.

All morning we progressed up river, passing a series of villages built on the alluvial plains. The women in Gasa had been threshing the barley, but in the next village they were reaping it. In the one after that, it was barely ripe, and finally they were just sowing it. In those few hours the agricultural calendar had moved back almost an entire season. It was a miniature version of what had been happening since we'd left Pokhara. As we moved up in space we moved back in Time, and the villages became more isolated, more remote, more medieval. Now they were Tibetan in appearance. Chortens started to appear, and prayer flags, and I noticed more and more apple-cheeked round faces. I saw my first yak, a huge horned creature grazing by the river.

Annapurna and Dhaulagiri were now only six miles apart and we were nearly in line with their highest peaks. They towered over eighteen thousand feet above us, and as we drew closer to Tukutcha, the gorge narrowed again until we were in the deepest cleft of all. Waterfalls careened for hundreds and hundreds of feet, falling as if from heaven as we made our way up this tremendous canyon. During monsoon season, three hundred inches of rain would fall, filling the gorge and cutting Tukutcha off from the rest of Nepal.

We reached Tukutcha and paid off our Nepalese porters in paper rupees and Norbu found two yak-men, Lobsang and Pemba, boisterous Tibetans from the village of Samar. They had brought down salt on their yaks to Tukutcha and were now returning with grain to their families. They were delighted at the prospect of carrying our gear up to their village. When I asked them if they could take us further, they apologized and said that beyond Samar the territory was Khampa-controlled and they couldn't proceed. When I heard this my heart sank, and yet the thought of turning back never entered my head. I was determined to go as far as I could and see what happened next.

Our Nepalese porters had been hardworking and cheerful, but with Lobsang and Pemba and their six yaks, the journey took on a completely different tone. It became riotous. Everything was a source of merriment and laughter for them. They roared with laughter as Lobsang held one yak by its nose ring and Pemba strapped our two steel cases onto the animal's rearing, bucking back amidst the flailing of hoofs. As we crossed on foot a treacherous bridge, they hooted and yelled and threw rocks, somehow coaxing their yaks to ford the river below. As they dragged their yaks along precipitous ledges they shouted and joked with each other and with us. Every challenge seemed to be a source of merriment and delight. It was infectious and joyous and it took Norbu to point out to me, mid-morning, that we were now beyond the peaks of the Annapurna and Dhaulagiri ranges. Without noticing, I had passed to the other side of the Himalayas, the greatest geographical barrier on earth. No wonder I felt giddy with excitement. No wonder my spirits soared.

Part of my giddiness must have been due to sheer height. I was running out of breath more easily. Tukutcha was over seven thousand feet and Jomosom, towards which we were headed, was ten. So we were climbing steadily, and while I was feeling none of the symptoms of the dreaded altitude sickness, I did find the going tough. Fortunately, I didn't have to carry anything through this stiff part of the climb, and the strong winds were behind us. As always, Norbu recited his mantra and I followed his example. Om mani padme hum.

As we moved slowly up the gorge, the vegetation didn't so much change as disappear. We were now above the monsoon limit. Ahead lay Jomosom and the last checkpost of the Nepalese government. Beyond there all travel, except by local people, was forbidden. Slowly and steadily we were moving out of Nepal into no-man's land. A politically undefined area nominally Nepalese, but in actual fact controlled by Khampas. I knew I had a duly signed and authorized permit, and yet as the town of Jomosom appeared ahead of us, I felt a growing apprehension.

I suppose there were things to see in Jomosom, but all I could see was the small stone building on the outskirts of town. The check-post. The yak-men found some pasture to graze their yaks as Norbu and I headed up to the stone building. Standing outside the door were three soldiers in dusty uniforms with scarves wrapped around their heads. As they led us inside, we saw three more. To my aston-ishment, they knew exactly who I was, and the purpose of my appear-ance. Word had preceded me up the gorge, one trader after another passing on the rumour of the fair-skinned westerner arriving with a yak train.

Norbu stood beside me and translated as one of the soldiers talked. The captain wasn't in at the moment but was expected shortly. We would have to wait. He then asked to see my permit. I took it out of my pocket and handed it to him. He took the precious permit out of the envelope and looked at it. He seemed bewildered and confused, as if he'd never seen such a thing. He then handed it to the soldier beside him who also examined it and then handed it to the next sol-dier. They all looked at it as if it were some sort of strange document, when I knew it to be simply a standard permit like all others, the only extraordinary thing about it being that last word: Mustang.

Behind me I heard a voice. "So this is our traveller from another world," it said. I turned around. Standing behind me was a Nepalese officer in full uniform. I was astonished to hear English spoken. He introduced himself as Captain Poudyal and asked me to step into his office. The "office" consisted of a table and a couple of chairs on a cobblestone floor. He sat down and asked me for the permit, which he took and spread in front of him, smoothing it open. Then he took out of his pocket a pair of reading glasses. He looked at the front of the permit and then the back. Then he said to me in his excellent English, "This is very rare, Mr Hathaway. I have been the officer in this godforsaken cantonment for four years now, and never have I seen such a permit. Dolpo, yes, many times. Manang often. But Mustang, never. You must have excellent relations with King Mahendra. I can see no other reason for such an extraordinary privilege."

He then looked back down at the piece of paper. Not a precious parchment in handwritten calligraphy, or even a booklet with photographs, but a cheap piece of brown Nepalese paper with a few stamps on it and a couple of signatures. Remarkably cheap, when I thought how much it had cost. Then it struck me...

How did I know this scrap of paper was genuine? I had only Anderl's word. And as the officer picked it up once again, turning it carefully in his hand, I realized that I had fallen for the oldest trick in the book. I had, without thinking, paid a small fortune for this permit *and* I had allowed Anderl to handle the entire transaction. I had simply put my faith in him, as I had by that time complete confidence in his abilities. Confidence. That's what he was, of course. He was a Confidence Man. He created confidence and then used this confidence to suck people in. I had seen him do it time and again at the Royal Hotel and had rather enjoyed my smug superiority. That I, unlike his marks, was aware of what he was doing. And all along, of course, I had been the biggest mark of all. By drawing me into his game he had created a sort of bond between us. A confidence. It was superb. Everything now suddenly fell into place. In Kathmandu, Anderl had been one of the most charming men I'd ever met. On the trail, he had become increasingly obnoxious until I was subconsciously wanting to be rid of him. Having created this climate, he played his trump card. Of course. Of course. And like a master he had told me beforehand what he was going to do and then gone ahead and, with perfect aplomb, done it. Time and again, sitting long into the night, he had told me about the influence of Heinrich Harrer's book. His favourite book. His hero, his model. Heinrich Harrer had escaped from a British prison camp; crossed undetected through India; climbed the Himalayas without proper supplies or equipment in winter; crossed the Tibetan Plateau, and — just outside his destination, the forbidden city of Lhasa — had finally been stopped. By what? Not cold, not hunger, not bandits or officials or terrain, but by sciatica. Sciatica. Pain running down his leg. An inability to bear weight. I stared at the Nepalese officer as he turned the permit over once again and flattened it on the desk. How could I have been so stupid? I had put myself in Anderl's hands and he had picked his mark with perfect acuity. I was new to Nepal, unaccustomed to its ways, well off, and had reverberated to his story of the mysterious Land of Lo as if he were one tuning-fork and I, in perfect resonance, another. He probably tossed out his Land of Lo story to lots of people, and most ignored it and switched to something else. But I had resonated, and from the moment I had resonated, he had sucked me in deeper and deeper, until I'd handed over my traveller's cheques and wired Cam Bienenstock for the balance — completely blinded by the lure of a trip to a forbidden land. And now I was standing before this clearly worldly officer still fingering my permit, the stamp on the corner of his desk untouched, and I looked across the table to where his eyes were resting. A radio transmitter. Of course. Even though this was the last cantonment of soldiers in this remote and inaccessible area, he still had radio contact with Kathmandu. All he had to do was stand up, walk over and put a call through to the ministry, and the whole thing would be exploded in a moment. Worse than exploded. I would be seen as someone who had tried to dupe the Nepalese government. A foreigner who, through trickery and forgery, was trying to enter a forbidden area. I felt sick as the officer reached over, picked up his stamp and pressed it onto my permit.

I stood there stunned, dazed, as he folded the permit, put it back in its envelope and handed it to me. Then he stood.

"You are a brave man, Mr Hathaway. I have nothing but admiration for you. Why anyone would want to do such a thing I do not know, but I would ask you now to join me and my men in some chang. We will drink your health and wish you success."

We spent that night entertained by Captain Poudyal and his men. They told us about the miseries of being the last bastion between Nepal and six hundred million Chinese. A hundred million each, as the captain kept saying. We laughed, and the captain told his stories of his days with the Gurkhas and the parts of the world he had seen, translating as he went along for the benefit of his men. He was clearly well liked and admired by his men and only once or twice did he make reference to the loneliness of such a post. He made me promise to stop in on the way back from Mustang, and even winked as he said perhaps I would come to my senses and not go beyond Samar.

"Some fool has given you permission, but permission for what? Permission to walk off a gangplank into a shark-infested sea."

That night we slept in the cantonment with the soldiers, the yaks grazing in the tiny pasture just outside town.

We awoke the next morning to the hoots and hollers of Lobsang and Pemba as they attempted to load their grain and our gear. They roared with laughter as the yaks fought and twisted and careened about. Each tussle was a fresh source of amusement. How many times had they done this, yet still they approached it as a completely new experience, turning what others would see as a dangerous and tiresome job into an endless game. Taking our leave of the gracious Captain Poudyal, we made our way down to the river bed.

The day was cloudless. Looking to the north the sky was blue, a deep velvet blue. There was almost no vegetation now and the rocks and cliffs were outlined with perfect clarity in the thin air. We were moving from a world of moisture and vegetation into a harder more distinct wiry world. A world that had been swept clean of all paltry blots and blurs. Looking up the great barren canyon of the Kali Gandaki, our route beckoned us north towards that velvet sky.

The Kali Gandaki was just a stream now and we followed the river bed throughout the day. Around noon we entered the town of Kag, very Tibetan in appearance: square stone houses, prayer flags, prayer wheels and chortens.

It was a long and gradual climb from Kag. The sun was sinking in the west when the golden stone walls of Tayen, where we would stay the night, appeared high above us. We made our way up a gravelly slope to where the town crystallized out of the cliff. Tayen, like the other towns we had been passing through, was built out of the very material it rested on, and it seemed to be a part of the landscape, the way modern towns and villages never are. We walked through a high gate into this cubistic wonder and made our way through narrow streets to a central square. That night, amidst the howling of Tibetan mastiffs, we slept at a small inn.

The following morning we left under another cloudless sky. As we progressed up the valley the high fluted cliffs almost imperceptibly moved in on us, and the river bed, which the day before had been at times a mile wide, was squeezed into a tighter and tighter canyon. I was watching my foot placement along the boulder-strewn bed when I looked up to see the door of this canyon closed shut.

A huge reddish rock slab, hundreds of feet high, had somehow split off from one side of the canyon and fallen against the vertical face of the other. The Kali Gandaki was able to flow under the narrow opening, but all further progress along its bed was halted. Lobsang and Pemba led us across a bridge that took advantage of the constricted river.

We started up a small dry tributary. On either side of us the walls of the gorge went almost straight up so that all we could see above us was a ribbon of blue sky. We slowly climbed up through this gorge, clambering over the bone-dry boulders. Up and up we went, almost a thousand feet, and though my breath came in short pants and I had to pace myself, my heart was not only beating with exertion but with anticipation. Finally we emerged out of the gorge onto the plateau above, and I knew that we had reached the very roof of the world. Pemba and Lobsang shouted, La so, so, so, La so, so, so. I turned around to gaze back in wonder at the journey I had made. In the distance was a sight never seen by a westerner. The cloud-capped towers of Annapurna's north face. Following Norbu's example I placed a stone on the cairn that marked this colossal achievement.

Ahead lay the Land of Lo. Five hundred square miles of territory that projected thumblike into Chinese-occupied Tibet. I looked over at the small range of mountains spreading in a large inverted U in front of us, and I thought with some trepidation that on the other side, Chinese border patrols guarded the passes.

Singing Tibetan songs, we headed down a gentle slope towards Lobsang and Pemba's home village of Samar.

That evening in Samar I finally understood what bargaining in the East is all about. It is not about beating the other guy down, or getting the better of him, or making a profit. It is about forming a relationship in which two people get to know each other by means of a process where both emerge satisfied. By the time I had spent the night bargaining with Lobsang and Pemba's friends and relatives, I felt I knew them better than almost anyone I had met since leaving home. They offered me things they thought would be helpful; I offered them things in return. While doing this we drank chang and talked, and the evening stretched out beneath the stars while the two steel cases that I always considered excessive were traded for a mule.

If Norbu and I were to continue on alone, as I was determined we would, then we were going to have to carry everything ourselves.

The next morning we loaded two sleeping bags, one kerosene stove with fuel, extra shoes and other necessities onto the back of our mule. The whole village of Samar came out to watch our departure. We were about to take our leave — I looked around for Lobsang and Pemba. Somebody called for them and they came out of their father's house, each carrying a large piece of khaki material in his arms. As soon as I saw them, I knew what it meant. How could they have known? For days I had been watching them as they moved so gracefully in their chubas, secretly wishing I had one. Was I that obvious or had they known with that mysterious intuition all Tibetans seem to have that this was a gift I could never ask for myself. Pemba slipped a chuba over my head and Lobsang over Norbu's. It was like a huge dressing gown and it seemed to envelop me in a hundred folds. But as soon as it was on I realized why people in this region had been wearing these robes for thousands of years. It hung loosely, and the many folds acted as layers of insulation. It was heavy, but no heavier than the duffle coat I'd worn in Montreal, and yet it covered my entire body. The sleeves, unless rolled up, hung well below the tips of the fingers, eliminating the need for gloves. I could pull the collar up and be covered head to toe.

Again, amidst promises to visit on our way back, we left the village of Samar and headed out into the bare and windswept plateau. When we reached the first ridge past Samar I pulled the collar of my chuba close around my neck. Spring was just beginning here and in the early morning hours it was bitterly cold. We walked in silence. After a couple of hours I broke the silence and asked Norbu how he was feeling.

"Bjeeginduk," he said. "I'm scared."

He had reason to be. Since leaving Jomosom we had both been thinking about the same thing: Khampas. Again and again we had been warned about the dangers that lay ahead. Now that we were on this lonely path together — no boisterous yak-men, no mule caravans, no smiling Tibetans, nothing but our own thoughts and the howling wind — it was hard not to be scared.

On and on the trail wound past eroded cliffs and pinnacles of rock buffeted by wind and blowing sands.

I thought of the Nepalese official in Kathmandu. Of course they wouldn't grant a permit, that would be "unconscionable." And yet here I was deep into this "politically unstable territory," that euphemism for "a shark-infested sea."

We were high, almost eleven thousand feet. Vultures circled above us in the spotless sky. The day grew warm, then hot. I loosened my chuba.

Why couldn't I just turn back? Hadn't I reached the Tibetan plateau? Hadn't I already seen more than any other westerner of this almost vanished world? Was the lure of Lo so great that I felt compelled to continue on and on?

Apparently. We entered a valley of juniper trees where we let our mule drink from a muddy pool, then climbed again towards yet another pass, skirting yet another gorge. As I looked down I thought of Anderl's line, So you end up at the bottom of a gorge with your throat slit, but at least you die a glorious death. It was all bombast. Rhetoric. Meant to entice me into a land that he never for an instant thought I would reach. But here I was. And against all reason here I continued.

No, I couldn't blame Anderl for this. If I continued, I was continuing on my own responsibility. If I continued, I was putting not only my own life in jeopardy, but also Norbu's. These were my thoughts when, on the horizon of the plain that stretched before us, I saw a swirling cloud of dust.

As the dust cloud moved closer we began to discern three horsemen in it. On and on they came. One of them looked different than the others and I soon realized why. He was riding without holding his horse's reins, a rifle raised to his right shoulder and trained on us. Instinctively, I threw up my arms and Norbu did too. In an explosion of dust the horsemen reined up in front of us, all three rifles now pointed at our chests. In that moment, which I thought was my last, my mind was wonderfully concentrated. I took in every detail. Fierce crevassed faces, red yarn wound through lanky hair, big-boned men in Chinese jackets taken from dead soldiers, long daggers, army boots. Khampa warriors who lived on what they scavenged. In my mind's eye I saw Norbu and me stripped of all our valuables and gear, left dead on the plateau, our bodies picked clean by the vultures.

And who would care? We'd entered this territory illegally. I had only myself to blame.

But no trigger was pulled. One of them looked at us long and hard then wheeled around and headed back the way he'd come. His two companions pulled in behind us. There was nothing to do but walk.

We walked and walked. Past eroded cliffs, over boulder-strewn hills, along dry stream beds. The sun beat down on us, the wind whipped at our backs. All afternoon we walked until finally we crested a hill and saw below us hundreds of black tents scattered over the plain. In Kathmandu no one had known just how extensive the Khampa presence south of Mustang was, but now I knew. Thousands.

Half an hour later we reached the camp and entered it. Hundreds of eyes watched as we followed the horsemen past smoky fires, patties of yak dung drying on rocks, boiling kettles. Black Tibetan mastiffs barked, snarled and lunged in our direction. These were the fiercest people I'd ever seen. Men who had begun fighting the Chinese fifteen years before and a thousand miles away. Men who wouldn't give up. On and on we went past one black tent after another, till finally we came to one larger than the rest. Here the three men dismounted, led us into the tent and told us to sit. We sat. Then the three soldiers left. We were alone and I turned and looked at Norbu. What was there to say? In a moment I shall never forget, he smiled at me before closing his eyes and reciting his mantra.

We waited. Outside we could sense people gathering. I could make out the word Inchi. Round-eyed foreigner. The word travelled around the outside of the tent in different voices as it was passed from one person to the next. The voices grew louder and louder. So many were talking at once that I couldn't make out any words any more. Then they fell silent. Norbu and I waited.

The flap of the tent was held open and a huge man strode through it. He barely looked at us, then sat down, cross-legged. As soon as he did so, others entered the tent, including the three who had brought us here. They threw our gear down. More and more men entered the tent. I sat motionless. The leader, or pombo, stared at me. His eyes were cold and hard. They were all big men, but he was bigger than the rest. He nodded and one of his men stepped forward. Undoing our gear, he spread it out on the carpet. There lay our sleeping bags, a stove, sunglasses, katas, a compass, shoes and, finally, at the bottom of my bedroll, the thing I most dreaded: the money pouch. In the week prior to leaving Kathmandu, knowing paper currency would be useless here, I had purchased every silver coin I could get my hands on. There was a flurry of talk among the men. The warrior who had met us on the plateau picked up the money pouch, opened it and dumped it out on the carpet in front of the pombo. There was a jingle of coins as they hit each other and spread out in a heap at his feet. His men exploded. They started shouting and slapping each other. But the pombo remained silent. He remained silent until the rest of the tent quieted down too. Then he reached forward and put his hand into the midst of the coins, pulling one out. But it wasn't a coin. It was the small mani stone Tsering had given me. All those silver dollars, all those piastres and shillings, coins that represented precious medical supplies, arms, absolute necessities in his struggle against the Chinese, and he had picked out a simple mani stone, the sort of thing that could be found anywhere in Tibet.

Suddenly, I knew why. I looked at this man and said, "The young boy you helped in the province of Amdo is now a Rinpoche."

He said nothing, but something had changed. I could sense it and I could sense his men sensing it too. I told him then, as best I could in my Tibetan, how I had met Tsering in my own country, a distant land, and had followed him across the great ocean to India and then to Sikkim. There, at the monastery, His Holiness the Sixteenth Karmapa had recognized Tsering as a tulku. Before going into seclusion Tsering had given me his only possession. The mani stone carved by the man now seated before me. Bowing my head and cupping my hands in a gesture of respect I said, "I now return it to you."

The tent was completely still. There was a long silence while the pombo looked down at the stone in his hand and composed himself. Then he spoke.

"If it has been held by a Rinpoche through all these years, then truly it is a precious jewel."

"Yes," I said. "Truly. It has saved my life."

The pombo looked at me and smiled.

"Yes," he said. "It has."

Then he scooped up the money, put it back in the pouch and handed it to me. He stood and addressed his men.

"Ya dong tang lu chang," he said. "Let there be arrow shooting and song with beer."

With his words, the silence broke around us and the men roared their approval. The pombo's voice rose above the clamour.

"Do the donkeys stop and rest and make merry? Do the animals in the field drink beer? No!" he cried, turning now and striding towards the opening in the tent. "I say to you, you are not animals. You must drink and sing and be merry, for you are not animals!" The men followed him, laughing. "We are not animals!"

"You must drink and sing for you are not animals, and having toiled you must make merry, for such is the wish of the three holies!"

Outside it was moonless. A fire of precious juniper wood crackled and snapped. The men surrounded the fire and the chang started to flow. The faces that on entering the camp had seemed so hard and fierce now twinkled with laughter and glowed with human warmth. My whole life, at gatherings, I'd always felt slightly out of place, slightly outside, but here, amidst these wild warring men, I felt completely at ease. If I wasn't an enemy, then I must be a friend.

A flaming arrow shot into the sky and the men shouted, "Let there be arrow shooting and song with beer!"

Then another arrow. And another.

Norbu and I cheered and drank from the bowls that were thrust into our hands. More and more men gathered round the fire.

"Let us drink, sing and be merry for we are not animals!"

It was like one of those movies that Breetz and I used to watch at the Roxy when we were boys. The leathery faces, the strange costumes, the crackling fire, the star-studded sky.

"Let us drink, sing and be merry for we are not animals!"

Only now I wasn't outside the film, I was in it. I was part of this strange adventure that only a child could dream up. I was no longer an observer but a participant.

"Let us drink, sing and be merry for we are not animals!"

We drank some more and the men sang songs. Songs that told of their struggles. Songs of sorrow at the death of loved ones. Songs of rage at the theft of their land. They sang of battles, of hardship and death, and small triumphs amidst many defeats. Songs of an ancient culture pitted against a modern foe. They sang of their way of life, a way of life they all knew would die with them. They wept and they laughed and they sang and the chang flowed.

The chang, the thin air, the day's exertion, adrenalin, relief, all combined to remove my inhibitions. I drank and sang and even danced. I don't know how long our revels went on nor when they ended. I only know that eventually I must have slept because I dreamt of Breetz. He was in the meadow with his dogs, but the dogs were well ahead of him. They ran and they ran until they entered a wood. Breetz followed. He could no longer see them but he could hear their barking. He was carrying the Leica and every now and then he would stop and take a photo. Tiny bell-shaped mushrooms by a lichen-covered rock. *Click*. A towering Douglas fir shot from its base. *Click*. A stream. *Click*. Then, with uncertain steps, Breetz moved on, following his dogs deeper and deeper into the virgin forest.

I awoke suddenly. Strange faces and shapes were moving above me in the tent. Outside I could hear the howling of mastiffs. The smell of rancid yak-butter tea permeated the air. The dream of Breetz taking photos seemed so real, so ordinary, compared to the world I was waking up to.

We are such stuff as dreams are made on.

The pombo had left camp before we awoke but not without a parting gift. The three men who had escorted us into the camp the day before arrived with two extra horses to escort us out. That morning, as Norbu and I ambled out of camp we were greeted by shouts, waves and gestures of good will. There we were with the same three horsemen, the same mule, the same vultures circling above the same harsh landscape. But how different! We were to be escorted through Khampa territory to the very border of the Land of Lo.

We rode all morning under a spotless blue sky, climbing up and down over small ridges. Finally we came to a hill no different from any other, but in ancient times a boulder had been rolled down it to the valley below, its impartial path marking the border to the Kingdom of Lo. At the top of the hill we dismounted and handed the reins to our Khampa escorts. Then, in a cloud of hoof-churned dust, they took their leave. We stood and watched them until they had disappeared. We turned north and looked across the barren hills.

It was a new world. Pink and red cliffs veined with blue shadows. And beyond these cliffs ranges of mountains fading into the distance in delicate shades of purple, beige and yellow. And above it all the deep blue velvet of the sky.

Up ahead we could see the dark clew of track as it wound its way over hills and along ridges, down into gorges and back up onto the dusty plain dotted with scrubby juniper bushes. On and on we followed it over rounded hills, along rock-strewn valleys, past fluted cliffs...on and on and on.

Ever since Anderl had first talked to me of Lo Manthang, it had existed as a place in my imagination. The highest kingdom on earth, hidden in the Himalayas, mysterious, lost, forgotten. A forbidden city which no living westerner had ever seen. Could such a place exist? Somehow, in Kathmandu and during my entire journey, I had never doubted the possibility of its existence. But as we drew closer and closer to Lo Manthang's supposed physical location, its material manifestation in this visible world, I was overcome with feelings of doubt. Everyone had assured me of its existence, but no one knew of it except by hearsay. A passage in a book. A story told by a friend who'd heard it from a friend who'd heard it from yet someone else. Everything had seemed so dreamlike these last few days, I wondered if this dream too would vanish upon waking. Could anything exist in such a barren wasteland, where nothing moved but the biting wind? We climbed yet another hill and as we reached the top I looked down and there, in a miraculously green plain, stood a four-walled city. The city of Lo Manthang. In the very moment that I had doubted its existence, it had appeared like magic in the plain before me, more beautiful than anything I could possibly have conceived of.

The highest kingdom on earth. A walled city, four sided. And a fourfold vision now I see and a fourfold vision is given to me. And I knew that my search was coming to an end, that I had found the fabled city. A walled city which represented a lost world where phantoms and demons and spirits were still realities. And I knew that my entrance into the city would be a return to some vision that I had lost in childhood. A vision of lost innocence that could only be rediscovered through the almost inhuman toil of a journey through misty forests, along rivers and gorges, up over the highest mountains on earth. It was all I had journeyed towards, and all I had lost. And I looked down at the city of Lo Manthang, the city to which I'd been struggling my whole life, at its walls of barren rock, and I thought of Kate.

I thought of the first time I'd seen her. And then fate had intervened and I'd met her again and got to know her. I had thought of her and approached her and run away and now I was looking at Lo Manthang. A city that was more than a city. A city that existed not only without but within. Mere possibility to everyone else, but to me, now, a reality. A city and a bride. An emanation of all that I loved. Kate.

This time I would enter her realm.

I AM THE CITY OF LO MANTHANG. I stand on the Plain of Prayer, high in the thin cold air. Behind me rises the mountain Ketcher Dzong. I am very old. I have seen the rule of twenty-six human kings. I was founded by the great Ame Pal, who asked in a dream where I should be. In the morning, a herd of sacred goats led him to a plain where bubbled many springs. There, he gathered his people together and built my walls.

The peoples' lives grew up within my walls and the patterns that they walked became my streets and the places where they gathered became my squares and the places where they dwelt became my houses. Out of their need to pray and study arose my monasteries. My stones took solid form out of the patterns of their lives. In the beginning they shaped me, but now I shape them. In the morning, I listen to the tinkle of copper bells as my communal herdsmen gather my animals together and take them out onto the plain to graze. In my sunny nooks and crannies women sit gossiping and spinning while my prayer flags flutter in the wind. By my great gate the old men sit, resting their backs against my sun-drenched stones, and tell the stories of their passing lives. Young women gather in my doorways and they talk and laugh and eye my young men. I have watched while they court and marry and give birth to other young men and women who court and marry and give birth.

Yes, I am more than well-fitted stones. I am a city of relationships, of people, of ideas and customs that stretch back unbroken for seven hundred years. I am a city of beautiful women with fine teeth, clear skin and laughing eyes. I am a city of strong men who make their way in caravans between the Plateau of Tibet and the lower lands of the Kali Gandaki gorge. I am a city of traders, scholars and saints. I have a king, Jigme Dorje Trandul, who has the same bones as my founder, Ame Pal.

I am very old, but I am not a mountain. Built by man, I can be destroyed by man. I stand here, the highest kingdom on earth, hidden. But daily, another world grows nearer. In the Song of Milarepa my people were told that the wheel harms the earth and so they will not use it. But beyond the mountains that surround me I hear the rumble of many wheels. My great sister, Lhasa, is now filled with wheels, soldiers with guns, lightning that runs through wires. The hum of mantras has been replaced by the hum of commerce and the chanting of monks by metal speakers that sing the praises of a foreign king. I have protected my people for twenty-six generations against bandits and warlords and the incessant wind that howls from the south, but can I protect them from new ideas?

It is summer now and my people are moving from my interior rooms to the sunny terraces of my rooftops. Above me, the cranes are flying to their northern nesting grounds. On the Plain of Prayer the green barley is sprouting. A stranger enters my gate.

IN LO MANTHANG, everyday ordinary life was extraordinary. Norbu and I would wake up in the morning to the sound of drums announcing morning prayers, not knowing what we would do with our day, only knowing it would be different. And fun. There was a day when the demons were chased out of town, amidst the wail of trumpets and the clash of cymbals, by lamas dressed in blue and gold brocade. There was a day spent helping Nyima in her kitchen, piping a thin paste into boiling butter and spinning it into delicate lotus-flower shapes. There were evenings spent with Wangdu, examining his library of precious books. There was a day spent talking to the old men twisting strands of yak wool as they leaned against the sun-drenched walls of the city. There were the days spent simply exploring the narrow alleys of Lo Manthang that would twist and wind, sometimes disappearing under houses to emerge in little secret squares of sunlight abutting the massive walls. There was a day spent playing games with a bunch of children in their tiny chubas. And there was the day Norbu first met Khandro.

She was a classic Loba beauty: small, with high cheekbones and black braids falling almost to her waist. A girl we had seen each morning among many other girls, carrying brass pots out of the city walls to fetch water. She would look at us and smile as she went by and Norbu said to me the first time we saw her that she was the most beautiful girl he had ever seen. Soon he was waiting by the gate for her and would walk with her while I sat on the terrace with Nyima drinking my third cup of butter tea. Half an hour later we would see them return, laughing, and Norbu looking so happy. Khandro would disappear among the whitewashed houses and Norbu would join Nyima and me on the terrace. By afternoon Khandro would be out on the street again singing with her friends and glancing up to Norbu. He would excuse himself and disappear down the notched log ladder. In Lo Manthang, relationships were as open as the terraces where the people lived. The whole community somehow partook in the flirtation and courtship. Things were arranged, visits happened, women showed up on neighbouring terraces. Norbu met Khandro's brothers, she left a basket of greens at Nyima's door. In the evening, Norbu would sit on her doorstep, talking. There was nothing coy about Khandro, or elusive. It was not a flirtation in the western sense — teasing or mocking — there was just a simple openness and it was obvious to Norbu that she was as attracted to him as he was to her.

Ever since we had entered Wangdu and Nyima's house, Norbu and I had been treated as more than guests. Like so many Lobas, they had lost several children in childbirth, and the one son who had survived had died in an accident five years before. Nyima said our arrival in her house was part of our mutual karma. I had thought this merely part of the hospitality of Lobas, but it turned out that Wangdu and Nyima had made a decision that Norbu's falling in love only hastened. One evening, Wangdu and Nyima asked Norbu and me if we would do them the honour of partaking in tro. Tro is a ceremony by which Tibetans adopt children. It was a public profession of what had taken place over the last four weeks in this house. We were indeed sons. Nyima's beautiful beautiful boys. In Tibetan, the word for happiness and the word for beautiful are the same. Norbu and I agreed we had never been more beautiful.

The ceremony of tro took place in the small courtyard just outside Wangdu and Nyima's house. All the people in our quarter of town arrived dressed in their finest clothes. Wangdu was in a blue chuba with gold brocade trim and Nyima wore a black sleeveless chuba over a fine silk blouse and her finest jewellery. Norbu and I wore handsome black velvet chubas with a heavy ornate silver medallion that hung on chains from our waists. We also wore ceremonial caps trimmed in gold brocade. A lama presided as Wangdu and Nyima adopted us as their sons, and we promised to honour them as parents. A radong, a twelve-foot-long trumpet, blasted out confirmation over the city. There was a feast that included plenty of chang, barley cakes and salad. Then we were introduced to everyone — from that moment on, I would be known in the city of Lo Manthang as Richard, son of Wangdu and Nyima.

Now that Norbu had a lineage and property, the courtship with Khandro began in earnest. One night, I heard Norbu slip out of the house. Wangdu and Nyima and I sat around drinking tea and talking. Of course, we all knew where Norbu had gone, but that first night we didn't talk about it very much. He had gone to Khandro's house, climbed to her window and whispered, "Let me in, let me in." She, as was the custom with Loba girls, had rushed to the door shouting, "Go away, go away, never never will I let you in!" This, Wangdu explained to me, was customary. The reason she shouted so loudly was to alert her father. If her father had objected to Norbu, he would have got up and that would have been that. But he didn't, and as Khandro also liked Norbu very much, although she continued to yell, "Never never will I let you in!" she opened the door. Thus father and daughter agreed that Norbu was acceptable. So Norbu and Khandro spent their first night together and both enjoyed it very much. Next morning, Norbu told his adoptive parents what a good time he and Khandro had together. Wangdu and Nyima seemed pleased. That afternoon Khandro's father came to visit Wangdu and they disappeared into the library. When they emerged they were laughing and talking and I was introduced as Norbu's elder brother. Now began an intensive four-day exchange of compliments and gifts. Wangdu, Nyima, Norbu and I all went to visit Khandro's family. Wangdu placed a little butter on her forehead and Norbu gave her brothers katas. The day after that, Khandro and her father arrived at our house and her father gave Norbu a little talk about cherishing his daughter. The next day Norbu more or less moved into Khandro's household. They would live like this until the lamas announced an auspicious date for the wedding.

One day I was seated inside the great gate of Lo Manthang, talking, when I saw an old lama shamble past. He was through the gate before his face registered. He was someone I had met a few weeks before in Nyima's kitchen. In Lo Manthang, there is a long tradition of feeding wandering monks, but this old fellow wasn't exactly a wandering monk. He was the gatekeeper of a monastery, or gompa, called Nyphu, that lay a few miles north of the city. Nyphu was abandoned, but the old lama stayed on out of devotion. Every few weeks he came into town for food, which various families provided. On impulse, I got up and followed him. It was my intention to walk along with him a bit and find out about the history of Nyphu. He had only a minute, or even less, head start on me, and it never occurred to me that I wouldn't catch up to him immediately. But as he shambled across the Plain of Prayer I fell farther and farther behind. For an old man he was moving at quite a pace. Still, as I crossed the plain, the barley now almost ripe, I felt confident that I could catch him. But he kept moving farther and farther ahead. Once beyond the Plain of Prayer there was no vegetation to anchor the soil and protect it from erosion. Twisters moved across the landscape picking up sand and grit which they hurled against the hills, grinding them into a fantastic array of shapes. Ahead, I could just see a black dot almost out of sight. The fierce sun of the Tibetan plateau played on the strange shapes around me, giving rise to innumerable forms. It was as if demons and fantastic creatures were rising out of the cliffs and hills. The old lama entered a large canyon. I followed, but by the time I got into the canyon, he was nowhere to be seen. I knew he had to be ahead, as there was no way out, so I pressed on. When I emerged from the canyon I saw a massive cliff with horizontal striations, in the middle of which was a gigantic red square slab. This had to be Nyphu. But where was the old man? Suddenly I heard a terrifying sound. Dogs. They wheeled out from behind some rocks, churning dust as they charged in my direction. Five huge black Tibetan mastiffs. I had always found these snarling mastiffs that guarded gompas and temples unnerving, but they were usually tethered. Here, in this desolate valley, I was petrified. They were almost upon me before I instinctively knelt down and picked up some rocks. The moment I did so, they stopped and backed up slightly, though they continued to snarl and growl and eye me with menace. Desperately, I looked around for the old monk, but he was nowhere to be seen. The wall of the cliff was only a few hundred feet ahead of me and so, warily, I made my way towards it, thinking I would find the old gatekeeper somewhere nearby. Behind me, the dogs followed, snarling and growling. There was no one around. Where was he? Then I saw it. A half-opened wooden door riveted into the side of the cliff. I inched towards it as the dogs became bolder and started to lunge at me and snap. I backed through the open door and stepped inside, closing it in front of me. Though the space was tight, I felt so much safer than I had outside with the dogs. It wasn't dark. Turning, I saw twelve lit butter lamps resting on a ledge of rock.

I was in a small man-made cave. I saw a passageway and, taking one of the lamps, stepped into it. There were stairs leading up, and so, moving slowly and carefully, I started up through the passageway and as I mounted higher and higher I felt strangely safer. Here I was all alone in an abandoned monastery and yet I felt only relief at escaping the dogs. There were more ladders and more stairs, but eventually I felt a slight breeze on my face and moments later emerged from a passageway into a massive rectangular room. There was some natural light coming from a perforation on the far wall. As my eyes adjusted to the light, I walked toward this wall and looked out the window. Down below — a hundred feet at least — I could see the floor of the canyon and hear the dogs still howling.

This whole cliff was filled with small domed caves where the monks would have meditated before coming together in this vast room for the reading of scriptures and group chanting. But I wasn't thinking about chanting monks. I was thinking of home.

Not home. Breetz. I had an image of him much like the one that I had dreamt of last, only this time he was deeper into the woods. So deep that there was hardly any sunlight. He was following his dogs. He still had his camera but he wasn't taking any pictures. All his attention was on the dogs, first following the barking of one dog, then stopping, looking around, hearing the barking of another dog, and starting off in yet another direction. It was clear that he was lost and that he had only his dogs to lead him home. But they weren't leading him home. They were on the scent of something and going deeper and deeper into the woods. With uncertain steps, he followed.

Breetz. How had he intruded himself into this sacred space? I shook myself and decided that I would explore the room completely before leaving. That's how I found the steps. They were on the wall opposite the perforation and led up to yet another passageway. This passageway was quite large and regular. I walked along it until I came to what I thought was the end. But it wasn't the end, it was a door. Beside the door there was a ledge with eleven snuffed butter lamps. I placed my lit lamp beside them and tried the door. With the slightest touch it swung instantly open and as I stepped out into the blinding light the door clicked shut behind me. I stood there, my eyes adjusting slowly to the brilliance, and my lungs to the thin cold air. I was very high. Higher than I'd ever been in my life. When my eyes did adjust, I saw in front of me a small smooth oval of glass. But it wasn't glass, it was a lake. A frozen lake. It lay there, the eye of Nyphu, gazing into the velvet blue of the sky. I turned and looked to the south. What I thought I would see was the back of the same rugged striated cliff that I had seen from the canyon below. Instead, I saw something totally unexpected. A hundred yards in front of me there stretched a curtain of rock. I had seen formations like this on my way to Lo Manthang, but none on this scale. It was astonishing. The top of the cliff was absolutely flat and the rock face seemed to hang from it in enormous folds, giving the impression of a pleated cinema curtain pulled across the landscape. I felt so fortunate to be here. The sky, the curtain of rock, the oval eye of the sacred lake. All of a sudden I felt a chill and saw a dense white cloud tumbling over the curtain. There was some sort of temperature inversion, and this billowy white cloud tumbled and dropped to the plain. It was so dense it was like water flowing over falls and it rolled along the plain with astonishing speed. I stood there, staring at it; into it. A beautiful sight. So white and billowy as it rolled majestically and effortlessly across the flat plain towards me. I knew I should get back into the monastery, but it was so beautiful. I watched the cloud flow towards — then over me. I was immersed in cloud. The temperature plummeted. I waited for it to pass beyond me, but it didn't. It just kept coming and coming. I pulled my chuba up over my head and dropped the sleeves to below my hands, but it wasn't much help. The temperature must have fallen twenty degrees in the few moments I'd been standing there. I now realized I had to find my way back to the passageway and find it fast. I started retracing my steps, but there were no steps to retrace. I couldn't see the ground. Then it started to snow. Rather than falling from above, the snow seemed to be forming in crystals all around me. I did my best to stay calm. I knew that the entrance back into the monastery had to be within twenty yards. I decided I would pace twenty yards forward, then twenty back, then forward again, and in this methodical fashion I would find the door. This would serve the dual purpose of finding the entrance and keeping me warm. I paced and paced but the entrance eluded me. It was so cold. I tried walking in a circle. A mistake. I became even more disoriented. It was so cold. Snow was forming all around me. It was so cold. I had to keep moving. My feet and hands were numb. The chuba that had always provided ample protection felt like a thin cloth. The cold soaked right through it. I had to keep moving. But moving where? Back and forth, around and about I went, stumbling now, because my feet, like my eyes, were no longer giving me the right signals. I couldn't see, I couldn't feel, I was suspended in space. Then I fell. My whole body was numb. What was the point of getting up? I would just stumble around some more, looking for a passageway that had vanished. So I decided to rest there, just for a minute, and gather my strength. I watched as the snow, one flake at a time, fell onto my chuba. One flake became two; two, four; four, eight...It all seemed to be happening in slow motion and I started to wonder if it was really happening at all. Was I dreaming? Maybe this was just a continuation of my dreams of Breetz...It all seemed so unreal...We are such stuff as dreams are made on...It seemed that the flakes were falling even slower now, and I watched as each one fell gently, softly, onto the light-brown surface. Each single flake seemed so insubstantial, neither water nor air, but a combination of both — each flake nothing in itself, yet as they slowly accumulated, one after another, they formed a thin silvery surface. I lay there as the silvery layer grew in substance, thicker and thicker, and I thought what a beautiful thing snow is, how it surrounds us and envelopes us, and, paradoxically, keeps us warm. I felt no urge to get up. It was so warm under the snow. The snow was forming a thick blanket over me, a white quilt. I was disappearing into the snow. Everything seemed so unreal, so dreamlike...We are such stuff as dreams are made on...

And our little life is rounded with a sleep.

IN THE MOMENT OF DEATH our senses dissolve and with them the objects of these senses. And with our senses and sense-objects, our ordinary mind dissolves, and with it all the prejudices, desires and obscurations that have kept us from seeing our true nature. And so with the death of our ordinary mind, there dawns the Clear Primary Light, which is our true nature and the ground of our being. This is not light as we know it, but the natural radiance of the Void. Wisdom. Emptiness. Without centre or circumference. Limitless. Unbegotten. Unending. Immutable. Some people, after countless lifetimes of practice, are able to recognize this luminosity for what it is, and thereby achieve liberation. But, of course, Richard Hathaway couldn't.

Because he couldn't, next dawned the Clear Light of his own intellect. After many lifetimes of meditation and practice, some people are able to recognize the nature of their own mind and, so to speak, dissolve the obscurations between their own Light and the primary Clear Light, and thereby achieve liberation. But, of course, Richard Hathaway couldn't.

Nor could he experience the next stage in which he took on a body of light, and a shimmering landscape appeared of brilliant, radiant, transparent colours, dimensionless, endless and dazzling. This landscape of light passed Richard Hathaway by like a bolt of lightning in a summer sky, and instead he found himself in the Bardo of the Wrathful and Peaceful Deities, where luminosity manifests itself in form. Spears of light hurtled towards him, and from out of these spears a vision coalesced of a lamb: soft, woolly, bright. This lasted but a moment, and then the sky went dark, and in the distant deeps two orbs of fire appeared. At the same time Richard heard a deafening pounding, like an immense hammer being swung down onto a gigantic anvil. And as this pounding increased in volume, the two orbs rushed towards him with fantastic speed, and these orbs became the eyes of a gigantic tiger burning bright in the midnight sky. Had he been able to recognize this tiger as merely a thoughtform of his own making and no more fearful than a child's stuffed toy, Richard Hathaway would have achieved liberation. But he didn't. Instead, overcome with fear, he swooned and fainted.

When Richard next awoke two lights simultaneously appeared before him. A bright yellow light, flaming with luminous intensity, and a dull bluish light comforting to the eyes. The intense yellow light was the light of infinite compassionate wisdom. The dull bluish light was the light of the human realm. If Richard had been able to recognize the yellow light as the radiance of his own natural wisdom, he would have achieved liberation. But to his untrained eyes the intensity of the yellow light was so overwhelming that he was overcome by fear and instead of moving towards it he withdrew, resting his eyes on the dull bluish light of the human realm.

In this way he was drawn towards rebirth in a human body.

O nobly born, Richard Hathaway
O nobly born, Richard Hathaway

When I awoke everything was dim, so dim I could hardly see. It wasn't night, it wasn't day. There seemed to be a lot of people around but I didn't recognize them. I was in the house. I could smell Nyima's cooking. I could hear somebody reading something.

> *O nobly born, Richard Hathaway*
> *Now that thou hath recovered from thy swoon, know*
> *that thou exist in thy Mental body, which resembles*
> *thy former body.*
> *Being unable to recognize the Chönyid Bardo, thou hast*
> *strayed down this far. Be not distracted.*

There were so many people. I felt agitated, claustrophobic, I wanted to get off by myself. And as soon as I had the desire, I found myself sitting at my typewriter. I took a fresh sheet of white bond paper and rolled it into the machine. Then I started to type.

PHOTOGRAPHY. IN THE TWENTIETH CENTURY WE ARE SUR-ROUNDED AND ENVELOPED BY PHOTOGRAPHS. PHOTOGRAPHS IN MAGAZINES, ON BILLBOARDS, IN NEWSPAPERS.

The words just came without thinking. I found myself writing about Halberstam's that first day with Katlyn and Breetz. Then Breetz and I were in the darkroom. I typed and typed. As I finished one page, another appeared in my machine. The words came effortlessly. No revisions, no discarding of drafts, no feeling of desperation and hopelessness. The words flowed out of me into sentences, then paragraphs, then pages. And the strange thing was, every now and then another voice took over, and I'd find myself writing about people I hardly knew, or just knew of. People who had touched my life in a way that only became apparent to me after I'd written it.

> *O nobly born, Richard Hathaway*
> *Now, if thou art to hold fast to the real Truth, thou must*

allow thy mind to rest undistractedly in the nothing-to-do,
nothing-to-hold condition of the unobscured, primordial,
bright, void state of thine intellect.

"BRIAN," KATE SAID.

"YES?"

"I WAS WONDERING IF AT THIS POINT NINA MIGHT JUST TURN FOR A MOMENT AND GLANCE TOWARDS THE FRONT YARD. I KNOW IT'S A CHANGE AND I KNOW IT'S LATE."

O nobly born, listen.
Know that thou art endowed with all sense faculties and
that thou art able to travel at will as easily as stretching
forth thy hand. These various powers of illusion and
shape-shifting desire not, desire not.

SHE SAW THEM EVERYWHERE. BEAUTIFUL THIN YOUNG GIRLS IN SHORT SHORT SKIRTS, THEIR LEGS SWINGING ALONG THE SIDEWALKS.

I was figuring things out as I went along. Things I could never understand before, I understood now. I understood Breetz's obsession with Marilyn Monroe, Ted's origins, Daniel Lloyd's theory of theatre. It was all coming together. I typed furiously. I could hear Wangdu's voice trying to get through to me, trying to say something —

O nobly born, Richard Hathaway

— but I didn't want to listen, I wanted to work on my book. And so I ignored him and wrote. I wrote and wrote.

BY LATE AUGUST THEY HAD DIVIDED THE TASKS AT THE FARM INTO PRESSING AND NOT PRESSING.

My fingers were flying. They were typing faster than I could think. First thought best thought, it just kept pouring out. I was writing about Tsering now and the trip and Kathmandu. But Wangdu's voice

kept getting louder, more insistent. Try as I might he kept intruding
— but I didn't want to listen, I wanted to get my book done. I wanted
to finish my book. I knew I could finish it if I just ignored Wangdu.
And so I ignored him and wrote. I wrote about Anderl and getting the
permit and the trip to Lo Manthang. I wrote and wrote and then suddenly I couldn't write any more. I couldn't think of anything more to
say. There was nothing more to say, and it was only then that I realized what Wangdu was reading: The Bardo Thödol, The Book of
Liberation Upon Hearing. He was reading it to me. He was reading
it to me because I was dead.

> *O nobly born, Richard Hathaway*
> *Till the moment which has just passed, all this Bardo hath*
> *been dawning upon thee and yet thou hath not recognized,*
> *because of being distracted. Shouldst thou become*
> *distracted now, the cords of divine compassion will break,*
> *and thou wilt go into the place from which there is no*
> *immediate liberation. Therefore, be careful.*

I was dead. Where was my body? I wanted my body. The second
I thought it, I was in a wood. A dark wood. Huge trees stretched up
into the sky. I was lost, I knew I was lost, but I could hear my dogs.
They seemed to be all around me but out of my sight. I would follow
them. I followed them as they led me deeper and deeper into the
woods. Ahead of me, I saw some sort of clearing. I stumbled through
the dark woods towards it.

She was standing in a small pool, facing away. A shaft of sunlight
penetrated from above. She was naked, bathing. The water glistened
on her luminescent skin. Her strawberry-blonde hair, falling almost
to her waist, shone, not just with the light from above, but also from
within. She was unaware of my presence and so I stood and stared.
She was more beautiful than I'd remembered. She was more than
beautiful, she was unearthly, celestial. I stood and stared and then
slowly she turned and looked at me. She looked straight into my eyes.
She bent down and, with her hand, angrily slapped the water. In slow
motion the crystal clear droplets came up and stung me in the face. I
felt a searing pain in my head.

When I came to, I was high, floating high, I was floating over the city of Lo Manthang. Down below I could see a procession climbing the hill behind the city. There was a lama leading it. I knew what the procession was; it was a funeral procession. Nyima, Wangdu, Norbu, Khandro, the people of the quarter, the people of Lo Manthang whom I'd got to know so well. *My* funeral. They were laying my body out on a flat rock. My body, my body. I knew I only had to think "body" and I would be back in an instant. I rushed down, down towards the rock, then I saw a glint of sunlight on swords lifted high in the air; with a whir they sliced into my body, severing limbs from trunk. In a moment my body was hacked to pieces and strewn over the rock. Blood, bone and guts. And in that moment, I realized I was not alone. The sky around me was filled with circling birds. Vultures. Waiting for my body. Again, I fainted.

> *O nobly born, since thou was unable to achieve liberation and hast strayed down this far, henceforth the body of the past life will become more and more dim and the body of the future life will become more and more clear.*

The theatre was dark. An old woman was onstage drinking tea and talking. I wasn't interested in her, I was interested in the two shadowy figures in the background. They stood, eyeing each other. Then they started moving towards each other. The old woman was looking right at me but I wasn't going to let propriety stop me from seeing what I wanted to see. I moved through the old woman to the couple behind her on stage. They were beautiful. They were both wearing robes, beautiful robes that shimmered and revealed their bodies beneath. The longer I looked at the robes, the thinner, the more evanescent they became, and I noticed that if I focused on a particular spot — her breasts, his groin — the robe thinned out and disappeared and I could see whatever I wanted to see. They were naked now, clothed only in light, and they were two of the most beautiful people I had ever seen. The man reached out a hand and the woman took it. Slowly he pulled her towards him and they began lightly brushing, touching. I wanted to know what he felt like against her body. I wanted to experience that, and so I mingled with the woman.

I didn't want to be inside her so much as to *be* her, to experience what she was experiencing. An overwhelming longing for union. I wanted him inside me. I felt I was smaller now, that I was somehow enveloped inside the woman, down in the depths of her being. I could see the man's penis, erect and glowing. I was calling him towards me. I wanted him to come. I could feel him slipping in. It felt so wonderful, as if he was surrounding me and yet I was surrounding him. He started to move with a slow and steady rhythm. With each movement I became more and more excited. I could feel this tremendous urge towards Becoming growing within me. He moved and he moved and it seemed that I was moving with him both inside and out. Then suddenly there was a tremendous wave, a shudder, and I felt a thousand points of light rushing towards me and

The truck was so crowded that the side ropes were bulging, but Breetz was too determined for even the tough-looking Tibetan driver to resist.

"Okay, okay," he said, and Breetz leapt on, then held out a hand to me. When he pulled me up beside him and managed, somehow, to find a spot for us amid water jugs and cookpots, I could hardly believe it. This truck, and all these people, were destined for Mount Kailas in western Tibet. So were we.

It was on another assignment that Breetz and I had met. I was sitting in The Diamond C Cafe when a bearded stranger walked in. We hit it off immediately. He spent that summer photographing on the Stikine and the next summer he came back again. He showed me his photographs. I showed him my poems. That fall, he stayed. It was only after we'd become lovers that we realized how very much we had in common.

With a wrenching jolt the truck shifted into gear. Years ago, Tibetans walked for months and months to reach their sacred Mount Kailas. Now they travelled on Chinese-built roads. On this route we would meet more pilgrims in Chinese trucks, decked with prayer flags and as crammed and precarious as our own. We spent four twelve-hour days in that bone-rattling truck until finally, ahead of us, out of the plain, rose the four-sided sacred mountain. Unlike the Spatsizi, Mount Kailas is not part of a range but stands on its own. It is amazingly symmetrical, a conglomerate dome of snow-covered rock. This, and the valleys around it, are what make it possible to circumambulate it, which pilgrims such as the ones we were travelling with had been doing for thousands of years. Breetz took his first photographs.

But this trip was much more than an assignment. We too were on a pilgrimage. Twelve years earlier, our friend Richard Hathaway had disappeared somewhere on a journey to the Land of Lo. Though we couldn't get anywhere near Lo, we wanted to visit the land that had so captivated our friend. It was a way to honour his memory, which was still very much alive for both of us.

Our closest companions on this journey were a nomad family — Dorje, his wife Mingmar and Dorje's sixty-eight-year-old mother. The weather was perfect and Breetz got a series of photographs that would turn out to be among the best he'd ever taken. He was able to catch Kailas in all her many moods. The sun-streaked west face at dusk. The sheer north face against the solid blue of the sky. The east peak at midnight, gleaming beneath the moon. And, unobtrusively, he caught the spirit of the pilgrims. Mingmar and her mother-in-law in their jewel-coloured capes trudging over jagged stones. Dorje kneeling in prayer atop an enormous boulder. A Nepalese woman lifting her small son so that his head could touch the Dolma stone. Mingmar anointing it with butter. A Bon Po shaman shaking a drum and invoking the spirits. An old bent woman leaning on a staff. A close-up of a prayer flag, the sacred mountain appearing in the distance through its gauzy filament.

To make a pilgrimage around Kailas with someone is to form a special bond. By the end of the four days, Breetz, I, Dorje, Mingmar and Dorje's mother had a relationship that went beyond words. To them, we were the foreign pilgrims with whom they had circumambulated the sacred mountain. To us, they were our connection to a way of life and a spiritual vision that we were trying to somehow reforge in our own land. This family considered every rock, every stone, every plant sacred. And it is this connection with the earth that Breetz and I are trying to remake in our own lives. So it wasn't really a surprise when, at the end of our pilgrimage, Dorje's mother invited us to come and stay with her family. This was a rare privilege and for the next twelve days we travelled with a group of nomads, sharing their fire and their tents, but mostly sharing their vision of a world in which we are visitors only. And brief ones at that.

It was on our last morning together, as Dorje was loading our belongings onto the mules, that I felt a tug on the hem of my sweater.

I turned and standing under me was a young girl. Standing under me. Standing under. Richard's favourite word reversed. She held a carved wooden box in her arms and gestured for me and Breetz to take it. Inside the box, on white bond paper, was a manuscript.

But that wasn't all. At the bottom of the box, there was a photograph. It was a photograph of a man in a chuba. It was in perfect focus and yet also soft and velvety. It was a remarkable photograph in every way, but what was most remarkable about it was its luminosity.

PERMISSIONS